A SONG OF AWAKENING

Roby James

Cover Image Details: "Pass at Glencoe, Scotland," by Thomas Moran (1882); "Harp," Museum of châlons-en-Champagne (51) France. Harpe, Hurtz, 1791. Photo by Vassil (5-03-2007); "Sheath of a celtic copper sword," Middle La Tène (300 -100 B. C.), La Tène (Neuchâtel).N° inv. MAR-LT-540. Picture by Y. André / Laténium; "Celtic sword and scabbard circa 60 BCE," Metropolitan Museum of Art. Photo by PHGCOM (2007); "A Celtic design," by Tacosunday (2009); "Star of David," Leningrad Codex cover page E (Folio 474a). c. 1010 C. E.

Cover Design Copyright © 2011 by Vera Nazarian

ISBN-13: 978-1-60762-086-0
ISBN-10: 1-60762-086-3

Trade Paperback Edition

March 15, 2011

A Publication of
Norilana Books
P. O. Box 2188
Winnetka, CA 91396
www.norilana.com

Printed in the United States of America

A Song of Awakening

Norilana Books

www.norilana.com

Acknowledgements

My heartfelt gratitude to everyone who believed in this book during the long evolution into its present state—ten years and innumerable changes and rewritings. From as long ago as the Spinners, where the first version was workshopped, to the nuns and the Vovniks, and others along the way, I thank you all for making the journey with me. Five versions later, here we are. Especially, I want to thank Vera Nazarian, for having enough faith to agree to publish it. Of course, any errors are my own.

For Keith forever and ever

"The English fight for power, the Welsh for liberty."
—Giraldus Cambrensis

A SONG of AWAKENING

Roby James

Chapter 1

The breeze from the sea ruffled his hair. Ine, Bard of Dubhain, paused on the crest of the hill to admire the sweeping flatlands between him and the estuary of the Dee, below. He glanced behind him to see how far ahead of the other two bards he was, picked them out of the trees more than half a mile back, and observed that they were moving well, if slowly. He slid from his shoulder the bag that held his harp, set it down beside the track, and sat cross-legged in the gently waving grass to wait for them.

He would not enter Flint proper without them.

Ine was twenty-two years old and had been Bard of Dubhain for less than a month. Prior to that, he had been the apprentice of the two old men with whom he was making this journey and to whom he had great difficulty in considering himself equal. *In title perhaps*, he thought wryly, *but surely not in talent.* In the years he had been apprenticed, first to one, then the other, and finally to both, the habit of respect for their gifts had become deeply ingrained in him. The love of music all three of them shared formed a bond among them breakable only by death. "And perhaps not even then," Myrrdin, Bard of Bangor, had said just the night before, by their small fire, for there were no monastery guesthouses or estates this far to the north until Flint itself. "The dead constantly reach out to us. Why should we not, when death is our portion, reach out to you?"

Bertran, Bard of Poitou, nodded in agreement, but did not speak.

"All you've taught me is part of me," Ine said to them. "And you've said none of us truly dies while our songs live." Such sentiments worked best, Ine thought, in firelight, with the mysteries of night hovering about them.

Now, in the bright sunlight of a clear, crisp day in early summer, he looked down at the quiet seaward plain, the village, and the unobtrusive manor house beyond it. Unlike many men of his time, Ine's talent was not weapons, it was wonder. Now he wondered about the babe they had traveled here to see. That the other two bards, his former masters, had made this journey was not a surprise to him. They had spoken many times for the past several months of the necessity to be at Flint at this particular moment. So, despite their age, they had taken to the roads again—a place bards and minstrels, music-makers, spent much of their lives. These two were the best of their time. Ine was different. He was, he knew, a small, commonplace, unprepossessing man in an age that valued warriors or mystics, where if the masculine ideal was not to be large-muscled and wielding a sword, then it would be magicked. He had neither magic nor muscles. All he had was the wonder.

Myrrdin seemed to think that was enough, though Ine was never sure why. "If you have great wonder in you at the world," Myrrdin had said a dozen years before to the ten-year-old child he was training, "why, then, you may make a bard. If you can see small wonder in the things about you and still want to play and sing, then you may make a minstrel. If you have none of wonder about you at all—" He had paused.

"Then what, master?" the boy Ine had asked. "A farmer? A soldier?"

Myrrdin shook his head. "Nay, there is some wonder in the souls of even the simplest of men. If you have none of wonder about you, then you can be an English king."

Seabirds wheeled inland from the estuary, crying mournfully. Ine shaded his eyes and looked up at them. He loved the natural music of their calls, but then that was the Celt in him.

For more than fifteen years, Ine had studied to become a bard, learning the mystery and the mastery of the twenty-stringed harp first, and then the more difficult thirty-two-stringed harp without which he now felt incomplete. All nascent bards, minstrels, troubadours, and poets began with the same studies, but in one way Ine was unlike any other bard of his generation—and perhaps of all the generations before his own. He had been apprenticed to two masters.

His work had begun when he was six and Myrrdin had come to Dubhain, in Ireland, to find him and bring him to Bangor, in Northwest Wales. By the time he was twelve, Ine had completed the preliminary studies and mastered both the English and Ogham alphabets, the rules of grammar, the rudimentary philosophy of singing, and fifty of the stories of his people. In the ordinary course of events, he would have continued learning stories of the Celts, but instead, Myrrdin had sent him to Poitiers, in France, to Bertran.

Bertran, Bard of Poitou, was the fourth of that name, descended directly from the first, most famous, Bertran, who had learned and practiced his craft in the Courts of Love created by Eleanor of Acquitaine when she was Queen of France more than a hundred years earlier.

Ine did not at first understand why he had to leave Bangor for France. There were so many more Celtic stories to learn, and he was starting to feel the increasing tug of inspiration that would spur him to begin creating songs of his own, though he regarded himself as less capable than most other bards because, unlike Myrrdin, Ine had never touched the will of the gods. Myrrdin seemed to be able to commune with the old Celtic gods daily, to understand their will, to learn from them what it was that he was supposed to do. So Ine did not question that he was supposed to travel to France, but he did question why Myrrdin had directed him to go. Myrrdin's reply was no help, only part of the general mystery. "I have seen the path your study must take you next," he said firmly, discouraging further probing. "It leads to Poitou."

For the first year of his apprenticeship with Bertran, Ine still did not understand. True, the jongleur tradition was not one of stories of gods, heroes, and magic; he had not expected that. The Courts of Love celebrated the much more human aspects of life, and the ways in which those humans aspired to be more, by loving one another, than their ordinary human limitations would customarily allow. Their stories were romances, filled with allegory, but always celebrating above all else the love between man and woman. Ine absorbed them quickly, curious about the importance of songs which did not arise from the gods or from the very bones of the land itself.

Then, in Ine's fifteenth year, Bertran set out from Poitou to travel the roads of France, and Ine rapidly discovered two things. First, that the songs of love were by far the ones the people wanted to hear, and second, that there was a great deal to be learned by playing in ensemble with other musicians.

The Celtic way was to play and sing the important songs alone. If more than one musician was present, they played in turn, sometimes even competing for praise and purses. If they played together, it was so that everyone could sing, and the songs were the easy ones, those which would not be insulted by many voices of dubious skill. In France, they played the important songs together—a lute, a viele, and an oliphant might combine to lay a foundation for the singing. More than one player often meant more than one talented singer, and Ine learned to appreciate the intricacies of polyphony, how melody could simultaneously separate and combine, soar and sink, support as well as shine.

Clouds scudded over the sun and moved on eastward, momentarily dimming the afternoon. Ine glanced behind him again. The two old men had closed about half the distance toward him, still moving slowly, but without noticeable hesitation. The roads were hard when youth withdrew even the memory of its tendrils from a man's body. Bertran was more than sixty now, and Myrrdin older, perhaps by twenty years or more. It was as if his regular communing with the old powers of Wales's own youth—of Arthur and Merlin before the church coopted their legend—kept him young, but not young enough for him to bring his harp with him. Nor had Bertran brought his viele. Ine was the only one who carried an instrument on this journey; the old men walked burdened solely by their individual infirmities.

Yet Ine never questioned their insistence on making the trip to Clwydd. "Forces gather at this place at this time," Myrrdin had said. "We will be in Flint when they touch it."

Ine looked at the quiet village again, the lazy flocks in the fields, the calm that the past four years of peace had brought to Northern Wales. Before that, there had been only the destruction that accompanied war, but since Prince Llewelyn had coaxed King Henry of England to sign the Treaty of Montgomery, serenity had laid its gentle hand on the land, which had healed quickly and welcomed the quiet with its own hard-edged beauty.

Ine let his mind drift again to the long journey of his training. He remembered his five years in France with affection, for he had learned there some of the music of the human body, as well as the music of the songs. Love was highly regarded in France, and there were artists of the flesh to rival the artistry of words and melody wrought by the poets. When Myrrdin sent word that Ine was to return to Bangor, Ine prepared to leave Bertran with real regret. He was astonished when Bertran said, "Please tell my friend that I will join you by Michaelmas, so I will see you again, young harper."

Ine was fully as surprised that Bertran would come to

Wales as he had been that Myrrdin would send him to France. He accepted that there was a reason for it, and whatever the reason—and for the two years the three of them were to spend together in Bangor, he never came near to discerning what the reason was—he was certain it was a good one.

The years were personally rich for him. He was surrounded by, immersed in, the best music of his age. Slowly, the last year or so, he began composing. He did not think he was particularly good at it yet, but he did enjoy it. And at odd moments, sitting quietly like this in the sun and sea breeze, he felt that someday he might be better at it than he was now. He did not feel he could ever create the magic that Myrrdin did, or work the enchantment of the ensemble that Bertran knew so intimately, but he might find a niche into which he could fit the songs he would create. Sometimes, idly, he wondered what it might be. He wondered if it could have something to do with the present life of Wales itself.

To a Celtic bard, Wales was the dream of an earthly beauty that the Courts of Love found in the joining of man and woman. Neither as green as Ireland, across the water, nor as tamed as the England which abutted it on the east, Wales was a land that the old gods had cherished; it entered the souls of its people and filled them with mystical longing, even as the world struggled to free itself from the mysteries of the old powers. The Welsh people lived in partnership with their land, loving it, traveling over and through it, only recently settling into small towns in places like Flint village. The people were a part of its weather, its misty mornings and rare long, sunny summer afternoons, accepting the hardships it often visited upon them as the price for its richness.

In the West, the Isle of Anglesey rose like a fortress from the seas, rocky-edged and isolated, yet a part of the mainland itself in a way no unimaginative person could have understood. In the Northeast, in places like Flint, the tidal flats gave views across land and water which drew the eye into infinity. The

cultivated lands of the East and South, where the settlements
were older, larger, and more prosperous, rolled gently westward,
pocked by vales and woodland, rivers and moorland, until the
land ran up against something obstructive and rose into the sky,
creating the peaks around the hard place, the central height
called Snowdon. The mountain reared high above the others,
watchful, often cloud-shrouded, gathering into itself and its
surrounds of forest, cliff, and narrow valley the guardianship of
the Welsh dream.

The older Celtic bards said the root of Snowdon was the
taproot of the world's rocks, sunk down into the heart of the
world itself. The songs of Snowdon were the most ancient songs,
speaking of the guardian spirit, the wellspring of hope, the
generator of courage, the sentinel of freedom. It was the center,
the first child of the gods. No matter where he lived, in Wales or
in exile—and anywhere in the world other than Wales was
considered exile—a Welshman drew his strength from the
heights of the mountain. A bard of the Celts, of which Myrrdin
was the greatest and Ine currently the newest and least, knew
that all the old powers, the great mysteries, drew together in the
land where Snowdon lay.

The European bards sang of love and longing, Myrrdin had
taught his apprentice, because they were too far from the skirts
of the mountain, a region called Snowdonia, to breathe in the
spirit. Even the Irish singers performed the newer tales with
more truth than they did the older ones. The old tales belonged
to Wales.

Ine was humbled by having been taken from Dubhain and
made a part of the Welsh tradition. He was honored to learn the
songs and stories and even more honored to sing them. While
once he had thought he would never find anywhere to love as
much as the warm green of the childhood home he had known in
his earliest memories, he knew now that Wales had invaded his
being as he became caretaker of her stories. Now there was
nowhere else in the world he could imagine being, nothing else

he could imagine doing.

Except that he could not, somehow, touch the currents of prophecy that Myrrdin bathed in whenever he chose. It was as if Ine had learned all the forms of the task but could not use them to encounter their foundations. Ine never understood why his own lack of this ability did not seem to disconcert Myrrdin in the slightest, why the older bard did not find Ine's limitations a disqualification from the work.

"There is seeing and seeing," Myrrdin said, unpreturbed, when Ine reluctantly raised the question one day just before Bertran arrived in Wales.

"Will I eventually be able to see?" Ine half-wanted to let the subject drop, but the answer was too important to him.

"Of course," Myrrdin said casually, as if the question were too inconsequential to merit much attention. "But what you come to see may be very different from what I have seen. Be patient."

Ine had waited two years longer now, and the need to continue being patient was growing heavier within him. Still, while he waited, he sang and played and composed, and grew more confident in his craft. And all the while he wondered what nexus of forces Myrrdin could see, but Ine could not, especially now, especially here, at this particular time.

The older bards caught up with him. Ine got to his feet and picked up his harp. The three of them stood for a few minutes in companionable silence, broken only by the far-off cries of the seabirds. Then they started down the hill toward Flint.

Heavily pregnant, but not yet in such hard labor that she had to return to her chamber and the birthing stool, Lady Nonne of Flint walked lazily among the trees in the orchard, waving a long twigged and leafy branch to keep the insects away. The blossoms had fallen some weeks before, and the carpet of whiteness they'd formed on the ground, through which she had strolled every day, kicking up swirls of petals, had browned and become part of the earth beneath the thickly leaved trees. She hummed under her breath, stopping briefly when a cramp struck at her, resuming the simple melody when the pain eased.

Nonne had lost little of her youthful loveliness at twenty-seven, had lived through the birth of a healthy son, now three, and was about to, she hoped, provide a second son so that her husband, Bryn ap Emrys, the lord of Flint, would have a more secure hold on his posterity. Children were chancy creatures; there was so much that could carry them off. Having more than one was necessary, even though the birth might be dangerous to the woman attempting it. Nonne had had some trouble giving birth to Griffith ap Bryn, but it was little compared to that which many other women endured, and she was not a timid woman.

Hearty male laughter drifted out of the manor house on the freshening sea breeze, and Nonne looked up, smiling. Prince Llewelyn had come to Flint to meet with his friend Bryn, and because the birth of Bryn's child was imminent, he had chosen to linger. Nonne felt honored by his presence, and she knew that all the inhabitants of the manor, fiercely loyal to their prince, felt the same.

The sound of footfalls coming across the kitchenyard toward the orchard made her turn, and she saw the familiar figure of the local midwife, a woman whose husband was one of the Flint cattlemen. The midwife was fleshy, in contrast to Nonne's normal slenderness, but Nonne thought to herself that her belly now put the other woman's to shame. She smiled at the midwife, grateful for her presence, because childbirth was perilous enough without having a skilled woman to help if something untoward happened. Even with a midwife, the process could go irreparably wrong.

The midwife's stoutness made her progress over the low stile in the kitchenyard wall somewhat laborious, and she was puffing when she reached Nonne. Her motherly air was unaffected by her breathlessness, and she smiled, the expression marred by the gaps where several teeth were missing. Nonne started to smile back, but at that moment was caught by another cramp, this one more urgent than those before. Despite her attempt to appear composed, she must have grimaced.

"Are you well, my lady?" the midwife asked, laying a hand on Nonne's distended belly.

The cramp began to pass, and Nonne at last managed her smile. "The babe grows impatient," she said. "I believe 'tis time to pay heed."

The midwife linked her arm with Nonne's and firmly led her away from the stile. "We will go around to the road, my lady," she said in a voice that made no allowance for argument. "The front steps of the manor be broader and kinder than those ones."

Nonne let herself be led. The ground was flat to the narrow track, and the track was not rutted, since carts rarely needed to come to the manor itself. The two women could enter the house with little difficulty, for the gate stood wide, and the three steps to the front hall were long and flat. The stairs to the second floor, where the master chamber had been prepared for the lying-in, were steeper, but they could be negotiated very slowly. The women arrived at the track of hard-packed earth just a few moments before the three men, one of them bearing a bulky satchel across his shoulder, reached the corner of the wall.

Nonne looked up and recognized the eldest of the travelers. She was surprised enough to momentarily ignore her condition. "Myrrdin!" She spoke with real delight and held out the hand the midwife was not restraining. "You are most welcome here!"

The old bard cast one fast glance at the swell of her belly, not so long as to appear rude. "I see we come in good time," he said with a smile. He presented the other two bards. Bertran bent over her extended hand and brushed it lightly with his lips, a gesture that startled Nonne. Ine, noticing her unfamiliarity with courtly manners, bowed to her slightly but sincerely. The midwife was frowning, and Ine thought it was because her authority over the lady of the manor had just been undermined.

Nonne looked at Myrrdin. "In good time?" she repeated.

"For the birth of the babe," said Myrrdin.

Nonne's free hand brushed the distended front of her gown. "I had no notion my condition was known as far away as Bangor," she said. "I have hopes of gifting my lord husband with a second son."

"Ah," said Myrrdin, "I have not seen such. I believe 'twill be a daughter."

Nonne was momentarily very still, but Ine noticed she did not seem disappointed. Nor did she seem to be doubtful. Slowly she smiled. "I'd not seem disloyal to my lord husband," she said, "but your words do not distress me, for God's choices are not to be questioned." Her face clouded slightly. "Yet you come here for the birth of a mere girl? Or do you seek Prince Llewelyn?"

Ine wasn't certain he understood the question, but Myrrdin seemed instantly to apprehend the situation. "'Twill be an honor to play for the prince again," he said firmly. "I saw him last when I was on the roads near Ruthin, well before the treaty."

The midwife shifted her feet, obviously feeling a need to reassert her own authority, and more firmly grasped Nonne's arm. "Enough converse, my lady," she said. "Come. We have steps to climb yet, and the music will keep."

The bards smiled at her, then waited respectfully on the road as the midwife led Nonne inside.

"We should have brought your harp," Ine said regretfully to Myrrdin. "Mine is not as strong an instrument."

Myrrdin shook his head once, emphatically. "'Twill serve well. Strength oftimes resides not in age, but in newness. And—" His voice slowed, deepened a little. "—when times change, that which is fresher slides along more readily."

Ine frowned. "How is it that the presence of Prince Llewelyn means that times change?"

Bertran laughed. He had the hearty, carefree laugh of a young man, and Ine never thought he was the object of his teacher's mirth. Myrrdin smiled. "'Tis not the prince. Had we wanted the prince, we would have gone to Ruthin. 'Tis Flint we must attend." He glanced at the front of the manor house. "The Lady Nonne will have reached her birthing chamber by now. We may enter."

Ine let the two old bards go first, and followed them up the three broad steps to the manor door, which was unguarded. Peacetime had its laxities, and the Welsh did not fear each other. There was, Ine reflected, a brotherhood of Welshmen which far exceeded any kind of unity he had seen in France or any he had heard of in England. Of the Scots, he had no real idea, though he knew their society was clan-based, and clans usually meant rivalry of a kind that often led to battles. "Brothers fight each other more fiercely than other combatants," Myrrdin had said once. "But we Welsh have a different kind of brotherhood."

Ine had often had occasion to wonder at Myrrdin's pronouncements, but he never questioned their truth. His love for the old bard gave a powerful weight to opinions which indifference might have been willing to doubt.

The manor house at Flint was simple and compact, as were all buildings of any presumed permanence on Welsh soil. It was less than a hundred years since the Welsh began to settle on lands previously wandered over. Flint manor was built of the soft gray-blue stone which could be seen scoured from under the local earth by wind and rain. The roof was a thick thatch, recently replaced and made fast against the coming winter's cold, for Nonne and Bryn were good stewards, who believed taking care of their possessions was a better use of them than taking all they could from them. The front wall of the manor was of the same stone as the house, mossy, with stray wisps of meadow grass sticking out from between the stones. The dooryard garden was thick with summer wildflowers, in which a lazy dog rolled. It cast an eye on them as they crossed the space to the double doors, which stood wide and inviting. Ine wondered if it would bark, to alert someone inside at their arrival, but it seemed to think them harmless and went back to its rolling.

I suppose we are harmless, thought Ine, *or at the very least, I suppose I am.*

Just inside the open door was a large archway leading into the hall, which took up almost all the building on this floor. The stairway to the upper floor was at the far end, and it was vacant, which meant that Nonne and her companion had had sufficient time to reach the master chamber, above.

The hall itself was filled with men, jostling each other genially, drinking cups of what was probably ale. The three bards paused in the archway and waited for the shifting crowd to expose the high table. Then Myrrdin, using a voice accustomed to carrying despite its slight, age-caused quaver, said, "Glad tidings, Bryn ap Emrys!"

The men in the room quieted in a wave of discovery. At the high table, four men looked toward the archway. One of them rose, a smile breaking across his even-featured face. "Myrrdin! You are most welcome here," he said warmly. He held out his hands in greeting and started around the table. The men in the rest of the room, some in the center, some at the trestle tables on either side, were completely silent now. Those around the unlit firepit in the floor parted to allow the master of Flint a clear view of the newcomers.

Ine looked at Lord Bryn's open, pleasant face, then moved his gaze beyond Bryn to the men remaining at the high table. The one in the center, he guessed, was Prince Llewelyn. No one would ever have called Prince Llewelyn handsome, but when he occupied a room, everyone in it was aware that he was present. At thirty-nine, he was a formidable man who, two years earlier, had won from King Henry of England the treaty which gave the prince the rule of all of Wales, something which had never before been achieved. The English king had been distracted by a revolt among his own barons and unwilling to split his armies in order to face a Welsh threat as well. Llewelyn took advantage of that reluctance and persuaded Henry to recognize a local sovereign for Wales, giving the land its first true peace in memory.

Yet Llewelyn never asked anyone to swear fealty to him, believing it an English custom based in an inability to trust one's retainers or make friends of them. And he never used the title "Prince of Wales," rightfully his, preferring to base his principality in the lands around Snowdon, where he was born.

Usually, he traveled with ten men whose service he had the use of, but Bryn ap Emrys was an old and treasured friend, and the absence of war gave him ease, so he had brought only a single guard, and his younger brother, with him.

Bryn ap Emrys had all the looks that had passed Prince Llewelyn by. He laughed now, sitting at the high table in his small but comfortable hall, and the prince laughed softly with him. The prince's laugh was edged in melancholy, which Bryn did not appear to notice, though it was clear to Ine.

Llewelyn's guard also seemed aware of it. Anian Glyn was taking advantage of the peace to travel with his son, as well as with his prince. He was recently widowed, another reason he did not want to let the seven-year-old boy out of his company. He was not a particularly perceptive man, and thus he did not attribute any part of Llewelyn's melancholy to the presence of the boy, who sat quietly on the front of the dais, playing with one of the manor dogs.

Prince Llewelyn had accomplished everything he wanted in terms of the nation, but he had no children of his own, and he was aware of his increasing age. He had not married, because he had fallen unpredictably, desperately in love with the wrong woman. Love was not only unfashionable; in Llewelyn's case, it was inconvenient. Unfortunately, he was helpless to escape it.

Had Bryn noticed the prince's sadness, he would have put its cause to pining for the woman and dismissed it as a momentary weakness on the part of the man the ancient prophecies implied would rule all of the Isles, a new Arthur.

Llewelyn could have told him that was not all. Eleanor de Montfort, called by everyone the Demoiselle for her breathtaking Plantagenet beauty, had captured his heart well before her father, Simon, took the leadership of the baronial revolt against the king, who happened to be her mother's father and therefore Simon de Montfort's father-in-law. The child of the revolutionary and the granddaughter of the king, the Demoiselle was a rare, glowingly alive child when Llewelyn first saw her. He'd felt as strongly bound to her in the first hour of their acquaintance as he was to Wales, and she instantly returned the devotion. The prince had thought that once the treaty was signed, he would be able to wrest permission from the king to wed her, but then Simon de Montfort openly tried to usurp the throne, and King Henry decided he could not ally the blatant English rebel to the presently quiescent Welsh one through marriage.

Now, even though de Montfort had been dead these four years and the barons' revolt crushed, Henry was unwilling to consent to the match, though the Demoiselle was undeniably nubile. *'Tis the only firm decision King Henry has made in years*, Llewelyn thought with a rush of anger, *and it keeps me from making sons.*

He enjoyed being at Flint with Anian and Bryn, but he could not help but be affected by the presence of Anian's fearless son, and by three-year-old Griffith, Bryn's boy. He looked up from his mug of mead as one of the manor maids came in and whispered to Bryn that Nonne's labor had begun. Bryn called for brandywine. Llewelyn's keen hearing let him hear the whisper, and he felt another pang.

The prince wanted sons before he was too old to sire them. Sons could continue to rule this land when he himself was gone. To distract himself, he greeted Myrrdin directly. "Pray, who are your companions, bard?"

Myrrdin bowed his head deeply. Bertran bowed at almost the same moment, and Ine bowed very low indeed in the presence of the prince, hindered slightly by the bulk of the harp sack on his shoulder.

Llewelyn smiled and said, "Rise. I am not a monarch to demand obeisance." To the prince there was a world of difference between being a ruler and being a leader. He far preferred the latter, even at the risk of the former. "In truth, fealty is an English custom," he'd said to Bryn when the lord of Flint had asked about it after the treaty had been signed and the Englishmen had re-crossed the border to Chester. "We Welsh are family. I ask not for submission, though I shall always be grateful for loyalty."

"You know you have mine," Bryn said, thinking it a weak word for love.

"Aye, that I do," Llewelyn said easily.

The crowd of men in the center of the room had parted, some to the wall which held a fireplace, currently standing cold in the summer, others to the wall with two tall windows, shutters wide to the warm air. They murmured a little, quietly, as Myrrdin introduced the other two bards. Ine saw Prince Llewelyn show open surprise, as Bryn said, "Three bards! Myrrdin, I'd no idea you traveled in company."

"Customarily we do not," Myrrdin said cheerfully, as the bards moved up the impromptu aisle to the high table. "This is an occasion demanding our presence."

Bryn frowned, confused. He glanced at Llewelyn, who shook his head. "Mean you the presence of my friends, the princes of Gwynedd?"

Ine looked at the man who sat beside on the other side of Bryn, realizing that it was Llewelyn's younger brother, David, since it was common knowledge in Northern Wales that Llewelyn had fallen out with his older brother, Owain, and sent him home to Lleyn, a distant peninsula near Anglesey. It was also common knowledge that the prince was not greatly happy with his younger brother, either, but it was said that Llewelyn believed he could not do away with both brothers simultaneously.

"Nay, my friend," Myrrdin was saying. "The presence of the princes is indeed a joy, but 'tis not the cause of our coming. We are come hither for the birth of the babe." He nodded to the men on both sides as they walked across the hall, yet it was not the greeting a king might have made, Ine thought. Rather, it was as if they were all old friends. Ine could not help smiling.

"The babe?" Bryn repeated.

"Aye," said Myrrdin firmly. "We are come to sing her into the world."

Ine saw Llewelyn react subtly to the word "her," but Bryn seemed not to have noticed. "I am honored by your presence, whatever its cause," Bryn said. He waved to some of the men at the sides of the room, standing or at the tables. "Someone bring a bench here for the bards," he ordered.

Men pushed several benches forward from the trestle tables, and after a bit of good-natured rivalry, they selected one bench to set in the space in front of the high table. Myrrdin and Bertran sat with grateful sighs, but Ine remained standing to better free his harp from its satchel.

Prince Llewelyn waited until Bryn had reseated himself at the high table before saying, "I had not heard tell that you sang Bryn's first son into our nation, Bard of Bangor. What draws you to this one?"

Myrrdin smiled across the rough surface of the table at the Prince of Wales. "Time and aplenty for that when the babe is here among us," he said. "If we could have drink to keep our throats wet, we will begin."

Bryn gestured to the men near the fireplace, and one of them ran out of the hall.

Ine felt Myrrdin's gaze on him. He cradled his harp and tuned it to itself. The clear staccato notes climbed into the air, and the men all fell silent. Music was too rare and too deeply beloved to let even a few random notes go to waste. Ine tested the harp with several chords, adjusted one more string, and then was satisfied. He looked up to see Myrrdin smiling at him.

Servingmaids came into the room with pitchers of ale and flagons of brandywine. A tall, solidly built woman directed the handing out of the drinks. When she asked the bards which they would prefer, Myrrdin addressed her as "Lady Maud," and Ine knew she was Bryn's sister, probably come from her own home in Oswestry to help Nonne during her confinement and care for the manor until Nonne was churched. He studied her briefly and realized she was as even-featured as her brother, without any vestige of delicate beauty like Nonne's.

"Will you have brandywine?" she asked Ine, gesturing at a flagon like those chosen by the other two bards.

Ine was tempted, for he had never tasted brandywine, but he wanted to play well, and he was much more familiar with ale, so he declined the headier drink.

The bards looked at the high table for permission to begin the performance. As was proper, Bryn offered them food, shelter, and a small purse, with assurances that he would give Myrrdin more before the bard left Flint, but he did not overpromise, which Ine was pleased to see. Some people, overcome by a bardic performance, chose to shower the bard with gifts, not realizing they insulted both the bard and themselves by the implication that the musician would not have chosen to play for them without the elaborate payment. True bards believed music should not be sold.

And this performance—by two of the greatest bards alive, and by Ine—was clearly of great importance to the bards, as well as to the listeners.

Myrrdin nodded, and said, "The Lay of Cuchulainn." Ine stuck the first chords. The notes bounced back off the stone walls of the hall with sharp clarity over the heads of the listening men.

For the next sixteen hours, while Nonne labored upstairs to give birth to Bryn ap Emrys's second child, Ine accompanied his two masters as they sang songs from both Europe and the Isles, taking turns. As the night drew on, the men of Flint filtered from the hall, despite their reluctance to go away from the music. By dawn, only Bryn, the two princes, and Anian Glyn, whose identity Ine had not discovered, remained, though Anian's son had fallen asleep on a bench beside one of the trestle tables. The two old bards paused in their singing only long enough to eat and drink a little, and when they did, Ine sang by himself. He was in awe of the other bards, honored to be singing with them, and, still wondering what it was that he was a part of here, he tried to acquit himself well.

He let the older bards choose the songs. He had no doubts that what they were singing was as important as the fact that they were doing this, but since he did not know why they were singing, he would not presume to select an inappropriate song.

After singing of Cuchulainn, Cadbath and Fionn, they moved on to the early legends of the Isles; the blessing/curse tales; the stories of ancient magic battling with the inroads of Christianity, which brought its own god-stories and sought to vanquish the old ones. Then they sang of other heroes and the women beloved of the heroes, of passion and longing, of misunderstanding and betrayal, of sacrifice and loss, of joy and immortality. They sang of Tristan and Iseult, of Roland, of Alamanda, of the Breton knight. They sang songs composed by the great women troubadours, many of whose compositions were rarely performed, songs by Almus and Iseut, by Maria de Ventadorn, by Lombarda and Isabella, by Guillelma de Rosers, and the mysterious Bieiris de Romans, whose poems had never been heard in Wales before. They sang lays which lasted a few minutes and saga-tales lasting an hour.

When he could pause briefly between songs, Ine studied the men at the high table. He was always fascinated by people—their reactions, their choices, the similarities and differences in their lives. Prince David had drunk quite a lot and had fallen asleep in the middle of Capellanus's "Rules of Love." Bryn, who must have been caught between delighted awe at the performance and concern for his wife, exposed to the dangers of childbed above their heads, was alert and attentive throughout the night. Ine saw his head turn toward the archway whenever anyone appeared, as if he was expecting a report from the master chamber.

Prince Llewelyn moved only briefly throughout the night, and usually only at times when the bards rested and everyone visited the privies. Otherwise he sat, hands at rest on the table before him, eyes half-closed, glittering between his slitted lids. His body never appeared to relax, its power muted, but undeniable.

The last man, whom Bryn and Llewelyn called "Anian" during one of the privy trips, excused himself just before dawn to take his son to one of the crofters' huts, where he could leave him with some other children in the care of the smith's wife. Before he left, he bowed deeply to all three of the bards, and he returned before the performance was over.

The sunlight, revealed by the burning off of the low clouds of morning, had crept up and made long bars of pale gold on the wooden slats on the floor and between the lower tables before Maud came to the archway and gestured for Bryn. The lord of Flint got to his feet and hurried from the hall. The bards fell silent at last. Ine set his harp on the rush-strewn floor beside the bench with hands that trembled from weariness, and put the fingers of his right hand into his mouth, unobtrusively sucking on his sore fingertips. The dozen years he had spent building calluses did not seem nearly enough; both hands ached, fingertips burning.

The silence and the daylight roused David as the music had not, and he stumbled to his feet, shaking his head, and shambled out toward the privy. Ine reflected that he had slept through most of the night and morning.

Prince Llewelyn rose to his feet, arched his back, stretched his arms, and rubbed his neck. As Ine watched, he picked up a large flagon of the brandywine and brought it from the high table to the bards, refilling their own, smaller vessels. To Ine, he said, "Ale will not be enough," and gave him the rest of the large flagon. As Ine gratefully drank, Llewelyn leaned back against one of the lower tables and crossed his arms.

"Master Myrrdin," he said, "I marvel at your feat this night. Tell me, pray, what about the babe occasions such tribute."

Myrrdin finished drinking his brandywine, looked at Bertran, and asked, "Do you do well?"

The Bard of Poitou nodded. "'Tis a fine thing to know I have the strength for such as this," he said. His voice grated and cracked, but he smiled broadly when it did, as if proud of his accomplishment.

Llewelyn waited calmly, not disconcerted to be put off. Ine was impressed by patience in a man of easy power, for it did not accord with his idea of rulers.

Myrrdin set his flagon down and rose stiffly to his feet. "The child who drew us here," he began, and then his voice, rather than weakening, deepened into sepulchral tones which might have seemed out of place in the increading brightness of the calm summer morning, "is a child of the changing world, a child the powers give a legend to. I have seen that she will rise from fetters and bring freedom with her."

Ine felt the hair on the nape of his neck rise as he was chilled by the undeniable truth that engulfed the room in Myrrdin's prophecy, despite its unknowable meaning.

Llewelyn frowned, but it seemed more in bewilderment than in disapproval. "A babe is a chancy thing," he said, "for such a large mission, bard. And Wales, I remind you, *is* free."

David plodded back into the hall, but Myrrdin and Llewelyn ignored him, their gazes fixed on one another.

"I freed Wales with the treaty," Llewelyn continued. "This land needs not a babe—nor a girl babe at that—to bring freedom."

"Freedom is not a permanent state unless accepted as such by all," Myrrdin said calmly, his voice in its normal, quiet tones again, the current of prophecy gone. "Wales will remain free, as you describe it, until the English decide to take it back." He spoke confidently and fearlessly to the single man in the world who had the most to lose by that statement. "Your treaty with England is only as good as the king who signed it."

Ine half-expected Llewelyn to grow angry at that, but he did not appear to do so. Llewelyn was not angered by the impertinence of a subject. Just as he demanded no fealty, he demanded no one tell him what they thought he wanted to hear, even if they were right that he wanted to hear it. He believed himself a strong enough overlord to give those who followed him great license. Instead, he thought about Evesham. It was not merely the battle at which Simon de Montfort had lost his bid for the throne and his life; it was the battle in which Prince Edward Plantagenet, King Henry's son and heir, learned how to kill.

Of his own accord, Prince David had sent Welsh regiments of foot soldiers to aid Simon de Montfort, believing that anything which confounded King Henry could only be good for Wales. Llewelyn was furious that the treaty was put at risk, but he did not call them back, because de Montfort was, after all, his beloved's father. de Montfort's army had steadily been defeating the army of his wife's brother, the king, for months. de Montfort recognized that England had a weak king and believed it needed a strong one, so he determined to become that monarch. Llewelyn would have been glad of de Montfort's accession, not least because he expected to wed the Demoiselle, but he would not have openly aided it himself. David had removed that choice.

King Henry was not a military leader, and de Montfort had learned tactics on Crusade. The king did only one thing right as the civil war swept over Worcester and to the River Avon; he gave the leadership of the army he had managed so ineffectually to his son.

Prince Edward was just twenty-five, and had been defeated by de Montfort at Lewes a year earlier, then captured and held in

:rience which convinced him he would never

rcy of anyone else. He spent that year thinking

:es between defeat and victory.

>uld well imagine the English prince in

ould equally well imagine his ultimate escape.

d became a weapon. Llewelyn had been told

rd took his place at the head of Henry's army

as only a golden Plantagenet could. But in

inspirational, he was inspired. He divided his

arts, sending one down the west arm of the

y possible retreat in that direction. The second

east arm, to prevent the rebels from escaping

Then, commanding the bulk of the army

a frontal assault on de Montfort across a field

Chroniclers did not call it a battle, though Edward's own historians did. The chroniclers called it the murder at Green Hill, and later, the murder at Evesham. Prince Edward was so thorough that, of the 168 knights loyal to de Montfort, only a dozen survived the fight. de Montfort himself was decapitated and hacked to pieces on the Green Hill field.

Llewelyn believed what the chroniclers wrote of Prince Edward, that, as he watched his soldiers carry de Montfort's head on a pike, his own sword streaming with the blood of his enemies, he was heard to say, "Thus will perish all who rebel against the crown." It would, Llewelyn reflected, probably become his motto.

So, when Myrrdin declared baldly, fearlessly, that the treaty could fail, Llewelyn nodded slowly. "Aye, and kings do not live forever," he said. "Prince Edward would not be the same sort of king as his father."

David had obviously been overhearing the conversation. Now he spat out, "Edward is a snake!"

Myrrdin turned to face the younger prince. "Seek not to die of snakebite, David," he said strongly. "The venom may well spread beyond you."

Ine saw David start to reply hotly, but swallow what he might have said in response to Llewelyn's raised, forestalling hand.

Llewelyn said, "I agree Prince Edward has not the honor his father bears. He proved that at Evesham when he butchered de Montfort. But he is not king yet."

Before Myrrdin could reply, Bryn came into the hall, smiling, and saying, "Is there drink remaining? We'll drink to the babe's head."

"Son or daughter?" Llewelyn asked, as if Myrrdin had not already declared her and a prophecy with her.

"'Tis a fair girl," Bryn answered. "Nonne wants to christen her Briana, after me." He sounded embarrassed, and Llewelyn laughed.

Word of the birth had spread through Flint, and the villagers came into the hall even as more wine was being brought from the kitchen. Anian's son, Owen, slipped in among them and made his way to his father's side.

Myrrdin drew himself up, a gesture which quieted everyone, even those still crowding into both sides of the hall. "Have the babe brought here before she is taken to be christened," he said. "We must see her." The imperiousness of the command was completely unlike him, and the command itself was unexpected. The Roman church did not permit anyone or anything to interfere with the baptism of a new soul, even if it were merely a female. But Myrrdin's command had the weight of law, and despite its novelty, despite the fact that everyone but Bertran stared at him, momentarily nonplussed, it would be obeyed. A true Celt—and Bertran was the only person in the hall who was not a true Celt—would never question the actions of a great bard. Myrrdin was the greatest they knew. Bryn seemed to be the first who realized that there was something to be done, and he sent one of the servingwomen up to the master chamber to tell Maud to bring the child down.

Ine picked up his harp and slid it back into the satchel. He was pleased that it had held its tune well throughout the hours of singing. Even in the pauses, he had not had to do much adjustment of any of its strings, and that was truly extraordinary. He wondered that he did not feel tired, though he owned to a lightheadedness which seemed to put all these uncommon events in the realm of the possible.

Llewelyn went back to the high table, taking David with him by a curt gesture. Myrrdin and Bertran stretched their legs a little, and Bertran murmured something too softly for Ine's sharp ears to hear it.

Myrrdin said, more audibly, "We will know when we see them."

"You will know," said Bertran. "My gift is a different one."

"But no less important," the Bard of Bangor said.

Maud came down the steps with a small, swaddled bundle in her arms. She looked around the room—the villagers holding simple cups of ale, the bards and Bryn in the center of the hall, the princes, Anian and his son at the high table.

Bryn waved a hand at Maud to bring the child.

Maud carried the baby to her brother and the bards, a little puzzled, but in no way reluctant.

Myrrdin stepped forward and moved the wrappings away from the infant's head, still misshapen from the birth, the eyes tightly closed. The bard stared at the little pink face, closed his eyes briefly, then studied the child again. He said softly, "A true Celtic soul, filled to its edges with the music we gave her as she struggled into this world. A soul that can make the journey from the old world to the new." He raised his voice. "She will rise from fetters and bring freedom with her," he said again, this time in the hearing of all. He gestured to Bertran.

The Gallic bard took several steps closer to them and also studied the child, who yawned in his direction now, as if worn out from her birth journey. Bertran looked at Myrrdin, rather than at any others in the hall. "Aye, she has full capacity for the spirit of Poitou," he said, "but I cannot know if she will grow to it. My wish is that she knows it as she walks the path you see for her."

Myrrdin nodded, and then to Ine's astonishment, both bards turned their heads and looked at him. As they did, he felt all the others in the hall do likewise. Maud's eyes, small and sharp, seemed especially to bore into him. He had no idea what was expected of him. He held onto his harp in its satchel and moved the few feet which would put him nearer to the babe. He was thinking as fast as he could, trying to discern what he was supposed to notice, what he was expected to say. The baby, surprising him, opened her eyes, still the milky blue of the newborn, without focus, and yet she seemed to see him.

Ine felt a jolt, whose source he could not have identified, whose meaning he could not judge. The baby closed her eyes.

"So be it," said Myrrdin. "That was well done. Let us all drink to the new lady of Flint. May she grow to her legend's worth."

Bryn seemed to sense that whatever the bards wanted, it was over. "Come," he said to Maud. "We'll take her to St. Maedoc's." He and his sister left the hall with the baby, accompanied by the good wishes of the people of Flint.

Prince Llewelyn rose to catch the bards' attention, and when he gestured them to the high table, the three of them obeyed the summons. David was drinking again, but Anian and the boy were watchful.

Llewelyn waved a hand toward the center of the room, where the bards and the babe had met. "Tell me, what means all that?" he asked. Ine realized he might have asked it himself had he had the opportunity to do it.

Myrrdin answered obliquely. "The legends were once immense, prince, for the gods were closer and easier for all men to hear. As the times change, their greatness grows distant, and we more intimate in their absence."

"Freedom is not bought with legends nor won by gods,"

Llewelyn said. "'Tis bought by blood and won by unyielding resolution."

Ine looked past the prince to the boy, whose eyes were glittering as if he hung on Llewelyn's every word. *There will always be more men to fight for this land,* Ine thought, *but what does the child of Flint have to do with it all?*

As if he had spoken the words aloud, Myrrdin said to him, "The time will come that you understand."

Ine shook his head, but did not contradict his former master.

They would rest here at Flint throughout the day and night and then make the journey back to Bangor. Not for the first time—and certainly not for the last—Ine wondered what the future would bring him.

Chapter 2

Bertran, Bard of Poitou, knew that he was coming to the end of his time on the roads. He had taught all the apprentices he was likely to teach, had seen the Isles in the company of his old friend Myrrdin, had sung the songs of his youth throughout Gascony, Toulouse, Auverge, Guyenne, Anjou, Chartres, Champagne, Vermandois, and now Brittany. His next stop—his last—would take him home to Poitou. He had sung and played for three French kings, and he would entertain royalty no more. He was quite content to think that soon the world would go on without him.

The late year rains caught him on the road near the estate of Count John de Bretagne, and he sought shelter there without a hint of premonition. The count was away, on some sort of mission whose full nature the staff of the house had never troubled to understand. But Bertran was told the lady of the house would be happy to offer him food and shelter for some songs. He was shown to a place in the hall where he would be able to sleep.

Gratefully, he settled his aching bones onto the battered straw pallet and leaned back against the stone wall, closing his eyes and listening to the rhythm of the rain pounding down on the vaulted roof overhead. At this time of day, the hall was empty, and the staccato sound seemed to fill the space, dropping down around the tables, benches, and firepit almost musically.

Bertran opened his eyes. He *was* hearing music within the natural rain patter, high-pitched, hesitant, but tuneful all the same. Tired as he was, the melody drew him, and he sighed, laid aside the cloak he had been too tired to remove when he entered the hall, and got to his feet to follow the sound.

The corridor outside the hall was deserted. In fact, had he thought carefully about it, he might have reflected that there were far fewer servants and retainers than a house of this size might warrant. The stillness helped him identify the source of the music.

It originated in a small alcove at the end of the corridor, an embrasure formed by a pair of pillars near the top of a downward-leading stair. A young man sat on a leather chest in the alcove, playing slowly but determinedly on a recorder. He was clearly picking out the tune by ear; it was a very well-known ballade. Bertran stood still and listened long enough to gauge skill; then he cleared his throat. "Do I disturb you, young player?"

The young man lowered the recorder, but did not appear either startled or discomfited. "Nay. I suspect I disturb you," he said. His voice cracked in the middle of the word "suspect," deepening momentarily and unexpectedly.

"You'll be a baritone, troubador," Bertran said.

"I'll be a knight," the young man said. He gestured toward the instrument. "This is just—" He paused.

"—play?" Bertran finished, amused. "Why think you they call it 'playing'?"

"Being a knight is a serious thing," said the young man, but he did not put the recorder aside.

The sound of the rain seemed to grow in volume, and Bertran suddenly felt a wave of dizziness pass over him, something that affected his senses without affecting his equilibrium, except in internal ways. He had never experienced such a feeling before, and yet he recognized it. Myrrdin had described it to him. Here, in a strange place, at a point close to the end of his life, without his viele in his hands or a song in his mouth, Bertran knew he had just touched a mystery. Or, rather, he had been touched by a mystery. He had no notion of what it might be trying to tell him, but he knew it had to be vitally important for the Celtic ancients to seek him out. He knew they had certainly had endless opportunities to do so before, and thus their contacting him now, in this place, had to have something to do with the young man with the recorder, looking at him so curiously.

He tried to reason it out, was not at all certain he was getting it right. *Mayhap had I more practice over the years*, he thought with a flash of unusual petulance directed at whatever force had decided to contact him now.

"Is aught amiss?" the young man asked.

Bertran shook his head. "You should not abandon your playing, young knight," he said. "'Tis important."

"Who are you?" asked the young man.

"I am a bard, the Bard of Poitou," Bertran answered. "And I believe I have been brought here at this time to give you that message."

The young man laughed, his voice splitting again. "I have no illusions about my ability. Surely my amusement can hold no great interest for the Bard of Poitou."

"Think you that bards care only about music?" Bertran drew himself up, forgetting the stiffness in his body in purposefulness and the astonishment of having been touched by something intangible and great. "Bards carry the truth of the world's spirit, and bards seek to ensure that certain people understand the rareness of that spirit, no matter who they are and what they dream. People who will be at certain places at certain times, and who must then do certain things."

"I am not a bard," insisted the young man.

Bertran smiled. "But you are one of the certain people. Keep playing your recorder, young knight. 'Twill be as necessary as your sword."

"I have been taught to respect the words of bards," said the young man, "even when they speak—" He paused. "—unlikely things." He had clearly been about to say "nonsense," and thought better of it.

"You will remember what you need when your need is present, and if you do not, 'twill not matter." The strength of the mystery drained out of him, and he shrank back on himself. "What name do you bear?"

The young man said, "Rees de Bretagne." He frowned, perhaps wondering at the phrasing of the question, that it had not been a simple, "What is your name?"

Bertran lowered his head. It had been the correct question for the only answer the young man knew. The bard was not aware of how he knew that, but he was aware that he had done what was needful. He turned and went back into the hall.

Though he had hardly troubled at the thought of dying before the twin encounters, with the mystery and the man, he felt joyful now, as if the last thing he had to accomplish had been done at last, and had elevated all else he had achieved in his time on earth. He wondered if, somehow, Myrrdin would know.

Flint—August 1273 A.D.

Briana liked to play in the flowers that framed the edges of her mother's grave. She never picked the blossoms, because she'd learned that only made them fade more quickly, and she liked the bright colors. Sometimes she sat on the little mound of the grave itself and wound the grasses around her chubby fingers, but she was careful not to uproot those, either. Her aunt Maud had explained that grass which grew in the gardens was bad grass and should have known better. That grass could be pulled up and laid on the compost pile by the garden wall. Grass that grew in the churchyard, where the grave lay, however, was good grass. It made a warm blanket over the woman who slept there and who otherwise might be cold.

Once, in her clumsiness, Briana had pulled some of the churchyard grass out of the ground. She had immediately begun to apologize to it, to the yard, and to the mother she no longer remembered. She tried to push the little roots back into the earth and patted them down, hoping that they would grow again. She prayed very hard for that, and now she was always aware that she could pet these grasses, but not pull them.

The new priest, named Father Ciaran, a Celt in his mid-thirties originally from Ireland, found the four-year-old kneeling beside Nonne's grave several days after he arrived, her eyes closed, small lips moving. He waited quietly until the little girl seemed to be done, then crouched down beside the only headstone in the walled yard. "Do you pray for your mother, Lady Briana?" he asked gently.

Briana opened bright green eyes and piped, "Aye, I do, Father, but not now. Now I pray for the good grass, so that it will live and keep her warm when the days grow cold." She scrambled to her feet, smiling at him, failing to notice his surprise, and ran out to the road that led through the village to home.

She loved knowing and being fussed over by everyone she was likely to meet. The only one who didn't make much of her was her older brother, Griffith, who, at seven, was already trying to be as good a swordsman as their father. Briana forgave him for his failure to cherish her, but still devoted all her brother-directed energy to her younger brother, Meredith, who had appeared in the family just as their mother was called to God's side and had to leave them.

As she danced along the road in the last warmth of summer, her dark curls bouncing because she always took off her barbette the moment she was out of the house, she decided she would stop by the smithy to see if the smith's cat had had her kittens yet. Everyone in the village was interested in the smithy cat because kitten season was usually early in the spring. Briana had overheard Maud saying to some of the village women that she had never known a litter to come so late in the year. There had been much laughter which Briana did not join and whose cause she did not understand, though she enjoyed the sound.

Before she could cover the distance to the smithy, however, her legs being too short to allow her to move as quickly as she would have liked, she heard the sound of hooves approaching from behind her. She darted from the road and turned to look.

Three male riders, one only a boy, were cantering down into the valley of Flint. They drew to a walk as they neared her, and Briana shaded her eyes to look up at them.

The first to reach her pulled his horse to a stop and leaned down toward her. "Am I greeting the Lady Briana?" he asked.

"Aye, sir," she said, bobbing a small curtsey. "Who might you be?"

The man smiled. "I am Prince Llewelyn," he said, "come to visit your father."

"I am going to see the smithy cat," she announced, unimpressed by either his title or his mission and deciding that her destination was at least as important as his.

The men laughed; the boy, watching her, did not. She noticed it, but ignored him. Griffith was often solemn, too, and she disliked it. She expected such behavior from boys, was hopeful that her own influence could keep Meredith from falling into such unattractive sobriety.

"It must be a very interesting cat," said Prince Llewelyn.

"Do you want to see it, too?" she asked, certain that Flint village could provide nothing better in the way of fun for visitors.

Llewelyn shook his head. "We shall ride on to the manor, little lady."

"Well, then," she said, dismissed them with a small wave, and waited for them to ride past so she could continue to the smithy.

The boy looked back at her, frowning, as the horses moved, so she made a face at him, then turned away before she could see whether he returned the expression.

L lewelyn had liked the baby prettiness of the little girl. She seemed to have gotten the best of her parents' looks and their brightness of spirit. In some strange way, she reminded him of things he had loved in the Demoiselle—a sort of fearlessness, as if there was nothing in the world that could hurt her. He wondered if the child yet had any knowledge of the legend Myrrdin had pronounced at her birth. If there was anything calculated to give her a sense of her own immortality—not to say importance—it would be the portentousness of being a child of legend.

Anian Glyn was also very pleased that Bryn's daughter was healthy. He had asked Llewelyn to make this trip to Flint for a specific purpose, and the prince had agreed, though Anian suspected he had his own reasons, as well.

They rode into the front yard of the manor through the always-open gate which would have provided scant protection against an enemy even had it been shut. They were greeted by a thin, plain, but practical and competent woman in her late twenties. Bryn's sister, Lady Maud ap Emrys, had found no husband because the first Welsh war had cost the land so many of the men of her own age and older. She had been managing the manor and raising the children since Nonne died of milk fever after Meredith was born.

"We are honored by your visit, Prince Llewelyn," she said by way of greeting, gesturing to one of the household men to catch the reins of the horses.

"Lady Maud." Llewelyn swung easily off his horse and raised her from her curtsey. "May we impose on your hospitality for a night or two? We travel to Chester to arrange some trade with the visiting Norsemen."

"You are always welcome here," Maud said warmly. "My brother will be delighted to see you." She glanced past him, acknowledging his companion. There could have been no stronger indication of Wales's current peace than that the prince still traveled only with Anian Glyn.

Anian Glyn did not appear to have aged recently, but his son, Owen, now eleven, was half again as tall as he had been when Briana was born. He still had the thinness of youth, though he was wiry with the promise of muscles to come. He often laughed easily, but just now he was serious because his father had made it clear to him that this visit was an important one. And it concerned the little girl.

"You are welcome, and your son is welcome here as well," Maud said, greeting Anian's mounted half-bow.

Owen made a small bow of his own, but he was not very good at courtly manners. Llewelyn had no court, only companions.

Bryn was in the armory helping Griffith hone a dagger when news of the guests' arrival reached him. He put the dagger on the shelf, put his hand on his son's shoulder, and walked back around the house to add his welcome to the others.

Briana usually did not take meals in the hall. She and Meredith ate in the solar, cared for by Maud or one of the household women. But with interesting guests in the manor, curiosity took hold of her, and she sneaked downstairs into the hall while servants bustled back and forth from the kitchen with trenchers, dishes of meat and vegetables, loaves of bread, flagons of mead or beer, and a special platter of spiced eels. This was the sort of dinner her father only served to the most cherished of his guests.

She wrinkled her nose at the smells and crawled under the high table, where the drape of linen, in honor of the visitors, would hide her from sight. If the dogs went prowling for dropped food and discarded bones, they would go hungry until the next meal, forestalled this time by the linen that made a perfect container for a little girl to hide in.

She knew the men had come in when several pairs of legs pushed in one side of the linen fastness, and she heard her father's hearty laughter. For a while there were thumpings and clinkings, then a short silence, and the voice of the man who had spoken to her on the road said, "We've had news from France."

Unaware of his daughter secreted beneath the table, Bryn stopped laughing and took a tight hold on his tankard. "Is the English king coming home from Crusade, then?"

"He has to come sometime now that he's succeeded to the crown," Llewelyn said. "But this news concerns him not."

"I am relieved to hear it," said Bryn. "We prosper without him."

"Aye," said the prince.

"What, should King Edward return?" Bryn asked.

"I'm told he lingers in France," Llewelyn said, "for whatever reason," and dismissed the subject with a wave of his hand. "The news concerns Eleanor de Montfort."

"Simon's widow?" Bryn was surprised. "I'd a notion she was living in Brittany with a few retainers and the Demoiselle."

"Was living," Llewelyn repeated deliberately, "and is very near to living no longer."

Bryn absorbed that, then asked slowly, "What of the Demoiselle?"

"What, indeed," said the prince. "I am sending friends across the channel to bring her back. I will go on to Chester, and they leave for the south on the morrow."

"And you've stopped at Flint?" Bryn was openly surprised.

"I was of a mind to take you with me," said Prince Llewelyn. "I understand from my sources that Eleanor will decline for a month or more before she is actually carried off. And Anian asked me to raise a question with you before he departed. I've agreed." Llewelyn allowed Bryn to serve him a scoop of the eels, for all the servants had left the hall, and the men at the lower tables were occupied with their own meal. "How say you to a betrothal between Anian's son and your daughter?"

Under the table, Briana had been trying to listen attentively, though she was dozing a little, but she woke to full alertness when she heard herself referred to. "Betrothal" was a long word, but it happened that she knew very well what it meant. Maud had been discussing a betrothal just this week past with Father Ciaran and some of the village women, and Briana had been interested in the idea of matching a man to a woman for purposes of marriage.

"Do you endorse the suit?" Bryn asked Llewelyn.

"Oh, aye," said the prince easily. "Anian hasn't the old ties to the land the people of Flint do, but the boy is strong and will be a good match for her. Had you other plans?"

"Nay, I had not," said Bryn. "Had you a son—"

Llewelyn sighed, cutting him off. "Mayhap soon," he said, "but mayhap not. And we might be daughtered as well, so you and I can speak again about matches should that occur."

"As God wills," Bryn said.

"If God were the only one doing the willing, I'd have less concern," Llewelyn said softly. "I am troubled by the assumption that God has made his will known only to the English kings."

Maud came into the hall to direct the placement of a flagon of brandywine and some cups.

Bryn bade her linger when the serving people left the hall. "My friend here has proposed a match between Briana and Owen Glyn, and I have agreed."

"I think it a wise decision," Maud said. "He looks fair to be able to protect her. What holding has he? Or will he have?"

"I intend to see him settled near Radnor, in Powys," Llewelyn said. "'Tis where his family has some lands. I'll gift them with more, and he can build Briana a house there."

Briana sat upright. Some of the conversation had gone over her head, though it was interesting to conjecture on being a betrothed person. She understood immediately, however, that the three people outside her linen-walled hideaway were discussing sending her away from Flint, and she knew that that was wrong.

Incautious, she scrambled out from under the table, nearly falling headlong off the dais before she got her head free of the linen and found firm footing. "You'll not send me away!" she cried at the people on the other side of the high table.

Maud was shocked by the sudden appearance of a child she thought upstairs and obedient. Bryn's brow creased, and he looked as if he were about to yell at her, something Briana never sought, but certainly did not fear, when Llewelyn gave a bark of laughter.

"Do you not wish to leave Flint, then, Lady Briana?" the prince asked, amused.

"This is my place!" she insisted, hands fisted on her hips, looking up at him fearlessly. "This is where my mother is!"

Bryn's reprimand died unspoken. He said only, "Maud, take her upstairs."

Maud scooped up the wriggling little girl and carried her out of the hall. Briana did not make it easy for her.

"I apologize," Bryn said once he and Llewelyn could speak privately again, and the men at the side tables had stopped laughing enough to allow soft conversation. He reached for the brandywine and lifted a cup to fill.

"No need," said the prince easily. "She's high-spirited. I'd not take her to task for that."

"When the time comes, she'll be obedient," said Bryn.

Llewelyn accepted the cup. "Women usually are," he said. "Now, how long will it take you to ready yourself to accompany me to Chester on the morrow?"

Bangor, Gwynedd—May 1274 A.D.

Myrrdin was dying. He was not nearly as bothered by that notion as was Ine, who could not accept that the man who had been his master, teacher, father, and guide would soon be no more.

In their small cottage at the edge of the tumbled wall that surrounded the ancient monastery of Bangor, long abandoned when what was good enough for the Celts was deemed beneath the Roman church, Ine hung a small pot of herbs to boil over the fire. He returned to the pallet on which the old man lay to put a hand gently on the wrinkled forehead.

Myrrdin opened his dark eyes, filmy now with age, and smiled. "No use to make too great a fuss, my boy," he said, his voice mossy. "You'll not hold me here, no matter what you try to do."

"I'd not hold you," Ine said quietly, "but I'd ease your last time so that you might teach me more before you set off on your journey."

Myrrdin chuckled, a liquid sound brought up from great depths. "I've done with teaching."

"But I've not done with learning." It was a protest.

"Of a surety not." Myrrdin closed his eyes. "I've not done with it either. But I must look to a new teacher, and so must you." He drew several breaths, working at it, then opened his eyes again. "'Twill not be your first new teacher. You grew accustomed to Bertran. Now learn from all around you. Make your songs from what you learn."

Ine knelt by the side of the pallet. "Master, you never taught me to see. What will happen to the visions when you are gone?"

Myrrdin sighed. "Ages come and ages go. You carry some of the last age, but it is—quieter in you. I think your sight is not of the old kind, but of a new. You will know it when it is formed in you. It depends not on my presence."

Ine felt the beginnings of grief. When Bertran had left, to return to France after the birth of Briana of Flint, Ine had been sad to see him depart, but he had not been wracked by it. He believed it to have something to do with the quality of the songs, with the breadth of their reach. Songs of love did not have the depths of the songs of the Celts.

He would miss Myrrdin with all his being. "I cannot believe I can be without you what I would have been with you," he said.

Myrrdin's voice was suddenly surprisingly strong, as if a power inhabited him briefly which had not been present before. "Aye, you cannot," he agreed. "With me, you would always be less. Others would see you so, and you would ever see yourself so. When I am gone, you will be the bard. And so you should be."

Ine recognized the voice of prophecy and had to accept it, but self-doubt still gnawed at him. "You would leave and entrust only me with the stories of Wales?"

Myrrdin's withered hands trembled a little. "An age is passing," he whispered. The breath sighed out of him with the last word. Ine bent his head, unable to pray, wondering how much of the world was changing because Myrrdin was no longer in it.

After a few moments, he heard a hissing, realized the now unneeded herbs were boiling over and got to his feet to remove them from the fire.

Brittany, France—July 1274 A.D.

The golden-haired young man spun lightly on his toes, dancing in a semicircle in the sun-dappled courtyard in order to keep his instructor slightly off balance. The clang of blade against blade resounded from the courtyard walls. The instructor was a veteran of the last Crusade, but age had lessened only his speed, not his timing or his skill. The young man was only just fourteen, and already outstripping his teacher in swordsmanship. They exchanged blows for several more minutes. Then the young man gave a casual twist of his wrist and sent the older man's sword flying across the courtyard. He immediately lowered the point of his own sword to the ground.

"Excellent, Master Rees," said the older man. He went to retrieve his weapon, hefted it, and then stood still as a dozen riders poured into the courtyard.

Rees stepped back out of the way of the horses, sheathing his sword and wiping sweat from his face with the back of his hand.

Servants came running out of the house to greet the newcomers with the kind of bowing and smiling reserved for visitors of the highest prestige. Rees knew instantly that the first rider, a tall man with an air of ownership about him, was his Uncle Edward, the King of England.

Before any of the riders could dismount, a wagon turned into the courtyard as well, its driver drawing it to a halt before the team of horses neared any of the destriers of the knights.

Curious though he was about his uncle and the party he brought with him, Rees realized he was in no fit condition to be presented to a king, even one who was part of the family. He turned and slipped quietly into the kitchens.

Edward had not seen his sister Beatrice since her marriage to John, Count de Bretagne, fifteen years earlier. He had decided, upon gaining the throne while he was in the Holy Land, to make this household his last stop before crossing the channel to England. When he learned of his father's death, he had chosen to make his return a progression to visit European allies instead of travelling directly to a realm which instinct told him might turn troublesome once he arrived, but which was now calm, in the strange interstitial period between the death of one king and the ascension of the next.

Instead of sailing for Gibraltar, he and his party had left the ship in Calabria and begun a slow progress northward through Italy, slowly enough, in fact, for him to send for his wife and now queen, Eleanor, to join him from Cyprus, where he had installed her. Eleanor also brought her younger daughter, Joanna, still a baby. She had lost too many babies to risk the very young out of her sight, even though she had left her older daughter and namesake, and the two surviving boys, John and Henry, behind in Westminster. Together, the new king and queen made a leisurely journey, getting to know and make pacts and trade agreements with noble households and the Pope before sailing to Southern France to resume their northward travel. They went up through the rolling hills of Gascony to Paris, where Eleanor was brought to bed of another son—her third, though this new babe was only son living and therefore heir to the throne.

When Edward congratulated her and praised the ease of the birth, she said, "'Tis fortunate we are already transporting the nurses for Joanna. We needn't trouble to find more," and he laughed heartily, proud of her. He had never doubted her ability to give him a son, but when the first died, he refused to let time pass before sowing his seed on her again. He visited her often enough, leaving the Holy Land for sojourns on Cyprus, to ensure his own posterity. Joanna was the early fruit of that campaign— this boy was its second blossom.

They lingered for a month in Paris, and then word reached them that Edward's Aunt Eleanor, Simon de Montfort's widow, was dying in Brittany. Edward wanted to be there before the Demoiselle slipped away, and then he could take her into his protection. After that, he would visit his sister, her husband, and her two sons.

Rees de Bretagne was interested in women; he could hardly have grown up in Brittany without that interest. Because he had not yet had a real sexual experience—though he had seen several and found them even more intriguing than he had previously imagined—he had become a keen observer of the habits of women.

By the time the first after-Mass meal of King Edward's visit was over, Rees knew several indisputable things: First, that the young woman everyone called the Demoiselle (who was his aunt, as Edward was his uncle) looked very much like Rees's own mother, Beatrice; and second, that the newcomer was just as unhappy as his mother was.

Rees had grown up listening secretly to his mother weeping. She never wept in his presence, nor in the presence of any guests, or even any of the household staff except the taciturn child who served as her maid and who did not interact with any of the rest of the household.

Once Rees overheard Beatrice say to the child, between sobs, "I cannot hold much longer," and the child reply, "Only a few more years, my lady. Then you can rest." He did not understand it, and he could not ask.

The banqueting hall was the largest room in the house, occupying as it did the entire length of the building between the northwest and southwest towers. Its outer wall was plentifully pocked with slit windows, and its inner wall contained several doors to the balcony over the bailey. The doors stood ajar, allowing light to come in and illuminate the King of England's party.

John, Count de Bretagne, the overlord of these acres and brother-in-law to the king, sat at one end of the high table, having insisted on giving the central place to his honored guests. His wife, Beatrice, sat at the other end, beside the Demoiselle, giving Rees an excellent opportunity to observe them together.

Though he knew quite well that these strangers were his family, he was having some trouble accepting it. The king and queen were, though as yet uncrowned, a different breed of people from those he was accustomed to. They had, it seemed, a confident ease at their place in the world unlike any he had yet seen. And more than that, they were solicitous of one another, attentive to each other's needs. He thought of them as affectionate.

He did not perceive such caring between his own parents and had thought the distance, the silence, normal. Now, observing closely if covertly, he wondered at it.

Edward laughed easily at something Eleanor said, then turned to lean past the Demoiselle and ask Beatrice a question. Rees could guess, from the way they both looked over at Rees, that it concerned him.

Beatrice answered with a genuine smile in Rees's direction, a look filled with the powerful pride she took in him. He carefully did not glance at his father, still as stone at the table's other end.

Edward gestured at Rees to come up from the side table where he was sitting, and the boy rose and went between the side and high tables to stand in front of the king.

"So, nephew," said Edward, "I hear you are a fair hand with a sword."

"I am told I learn well, my lord uncle," Rees said.

"And when do you plan to compete for your spurs?"

Rees was surprised. "I have just fourteen years, my lord," he said. "I need train a while yet, I think."

"And once you have won them, will you seek to enter the service of the King of France, my good ally?" Edward pursued.

"I had not thought it," said Rees, glancing at his mother.

Edward followed his gaze, then studied the boy again. "Why not?" he asked bluntly. "Knights exist to serve kings, do they not?"

Rees didn't have time to think of a diplomatic answer. "The French court is very mannerly," he said. "Knights have not the feats of arms they did before the last king died and took the will to fight for the Holy Land with him." He did not say, "I seek to serve my father." He could not be sure his father would accept his service.

"Do you seek to fight?" the king asked.

"Does not every knight? Is that not what the training is for?" Rees still did not look down the table at his father, who should have been involved in any conversation about his son's military prowess and possible future, but who had, for reasons unfathomable to Rees, never taken an interest. "I would seek one day to rule a manor, as my father does. 'Twould be a fine way to make a life in the world, and 'twould needfully be away from the court."

Eleanor leaned forward, smiling. "But the French court is well noted for its chivalry. Do you not wish to be a chivalrous knight, as well as a powerful one?"

Rees smiled back at her. "'Tis the power that makes the chivalry possible, my lady aunt. A knight without power cannot support generosity, and this court values power less for its use than for its own sake."

Eleanor was startled, but not nearly as startled as her husband. "I would watch you practice later this day," the king said.

Rees bowed to him, acquiescing.

"I might enjoy teaching you what I think of the uses of power," Edward said.

The Demoiselle raised a hand to her mouth, rose, and hurried from the room. Beatrice and Eleanor both looked after her in some distress.

"She is my guest," Beatrice said softly. "I should go to her."

"We will both go," Eleanor said after a quick look at Edward. To John de Bretagne, she added, "Please excuse us."

He waved a hand in her direction.

Rees went back to his own place for a moment, as his father began to speak to his uncle about Arthur, Rees's younger brother. Rees did not want to be present to hear Arthur praised by a man who never praised him, Rees. He slid quietly out of the hall to follow the three women. He was curious about the Demoiselle, especially since he had a notion that if he knew why she was so unhappy, he might have an insight into his mother's own unhappiness, which troubled him greatly.

But he had no opportunity to observe unnoticed, so he sought out the armorer to ensure his sword had not lost its edge during the afternoon's practice.

Chapter 3

Ine had made a wide circle through Wales in the months since Myrrdin's death, leaving Bangor for Powys, then Dyffed as far as Llandovery, back north through Powys again to the east of the Radnor forest, through Oswestry into Clwydd. He had intended to stop at Ruthin to see Prince Llewelyn, but something drew him instead past the forest-edged tranquility of the meadows at Fearndon and on to Flint.

He had not been to Flint since the birth of the babe Briana, and he was curious to see the child the baby had grown to be. As soon as he reached the manor, his curiosity was satisfied, for two of Bryn's three children met him at the gate.

At six years old, Briana was endearingly pretty, her face a perfect oval, plump with health, despite a number of smudges on every visible skin surface. Her black hair was tangled and escaping in all directions from her askew barbette, and her simple gown was hemmed in mud. She looked, Ine thought, remarkably happy. The boy she held by the hand was a little shorter than she, and just as dirty, with a wide, welcoming grin.

"Who seek you?" the girl asked.

"The lady of Flint," said Ine.

"Someday 'twill be me," Briana assured him confidently. "But just now 'tis my Aunt Maud. She'll be seeing to the chickens in the dooryard at the back."

"Will you take me there?" Ine asked.

She sized him up quickly, her gaze lingering a moment on the misshapen sack he carried slung over one shoulder. Then she nodded acquiescence and took a firmer grip on the little boy's hand. "Come, Meredith," she said.

Ine matched his pace to the children's shorter steps, enjoying the tang of sea air that came in on the breeze from the estuary.

Maud was gathering eggs as one of the other women scattered dried grains for the hens. She looked up as the children rounded the corner, started to click her tongue at how disheveled Briana was, then saw the man who followed them. She frowned, not recognizing him, though there was something familiar about him. She picked up the straw-lined basket in which she had carefully lain her harvest of eggs and walked toward them.

Ine bowed and introduced himself. He saw her plain face illuminate with both recognition and pleasure. "You are most welcome," she said warmly. "I should've known you on sight, and my brother has oft spoke of you. He will be very pleased that you've come, as am I." She turned to speak with Briana, and Ine was surprised to see the little girl raise a forestalling hand.

"I will bathe before I sup," Briana said calmly.

"You must needs be more ladylike," Maud said in a tone which led Ine to believe she had said it countless times before.

Briana smiled. "When I grow to be a lady, I will practice more of the ladylike arts," she said. "For the nonce, I would prefer to play with Meredith."

"Thank you, Brinna," piped the little boy.

"Hush," Maud said to him.

The boy grinned at her and with his free hand casually lobbed a clod of dirt generally in her direction. Briana shook the hand she was holding and said, "Nay, Meredith. Remember Griffith said throw hard if you seek to throw at all."

"Briana!" said Maud indignantly.

Utterly unpreturbed, the little girl insisted, "'Tis only good sense. Come, we'll try again, with a more proper target." She and the boy turned and scampered off.

"I beg pardon for their ill manners," Maud said to Ine. "My brother indulges them far too much." She walked with him to the manor entrance, gave the basket to a servant, and took the bard into the house and upstairs to the solar. "I hope you will be able to stay with us some few days."

"'Twould be pleasant," Ine said. He opened his sack and drew out his harp, checking its tune.

"One of the local minstrels has come on some occasions to play here," Maud said, seating herself on a cushioned bench and picking up one of Griffith's shirts, which she was currently mending. "His complement of songs is somewhat limited, and I well recall the glorious music I heard from Myrrdin and Bertran." She deftly threaded a needle. "And I have heard tell of the music that happened the night Briana was born."

"I shall try to surprise you with a few new songs," Ine said, plucking the melody for a marching song he had learned in Bala. "Is the manor well?"

"Oh, aye," she said. "We'd nineteen new lambs in the spring, and full sixteen of them ewe lambs. Next year should see our flock the largest in Clwydd. And we traded two of our bull calves for a fine heifer."

Ine set his harp down and walked to the window overlooking the front yard. "I've heard no recent word of Lord Bryn," he said. "Is he well?"

"Aye," said Maud, paused, then went on. "We heard noise of the passing of Myrrdin. Has it fallen to you to take his place?"

"There is no one to take his place," Ine said, "least of all, me. I am not Welsh."

"But Celt, like us, all the same," Maud said.

He shook his head, not turning back to face her. "Celts are not all alike."

"Not even the bards?" Maud asked.

Ine wanted to laugh, but he did not, worried that she would think he was laughing at her. "Most especially not the bards," he said.

Maud decided not to pursue it; she did not understand such subtlety. Instead, she turned to a subject she might have some success broaching. "Father Ciaran gave Briana the most beautiful little psaltery. I believe he also feels it may be time for her to develop some ladylike pursuits. Would you be able to take time to instruct her while you are here?"

At that, he did turn around. "Has she shown any desire to learn? Any aptitude?"

Maud nodded. "When a minstrel came from Chester these two months past, he showed her how to pluck the strings, and she made quite a noise after he left. She has a pretty voice."

"I am encouraged," Ine said, wondering what relation "quite a noise" had to actual music. "Six years of age is a bit early for mastery."

Maud smiled. "We had not set our hearts on mastery," she assured him. "We will be pleased to ask you to provide that. And mayhap get from Briana a little less noise."

The bard smiled back at her.

Evening fell gently on the manor at Flint, with quiet mist stealing in from the sea. Briana and Meredith had finished their soup in the solar, and Maud was just getting ready to take them to the small upper room they shared when Ine, who had played softly, but had not sung as they ate, asked, "Know you any lullaby songs, little Lady Briana?"

"Oh, aye," said Briana proudly.

Meredith tugged at a curl of her hair, saying, "Brinna! Sing to me!"

Briana took his hand, at least partly to disengage him from her hair, and went on seriously to the bard, "Our father taught us the lullaby our mother sang to us."

"Sing it me!" Meredith insisted.

"Do," Ine said, smiling in encouragement, swinging his harp off his shoulder.

"Will you know it?" Briana asked curiously.

"Perchance I might," said Ine.

"Brinna!" Meredith bounced a little from foot to foot.

Briana sang the first line in a piping voice, but despite her youth, she was tuneful. "*Hotl am rantir sekhu weedont,*" she began, the words liquid and the melody true.

Ine began playing to accompany her on the fourth word, for the lullaby was an ancient and familiar one. Meredith joined in, sure of neither words nor melody. Maud, who had watched the interchange from the doorway, came forward and stood between the children, laying a hand on the shoulder of each. She added her untrained voice to the singing. Though Ine knew the melody well, he didn't sing along. He recognized that this was a family activity; it might even, he thought, be a ritual. Even as he played, he wondered about family rituals. He had no family that he remembered now, except for Myrrdin and, to a lesser extent, Bertran, and they were both gone. He had seen families everywhere he traveled, had sung for them, had watched them, and he had seen all kinds of families—some, not unlike his own experience, were individuals without blood ties who cared deeply for one another, but were still essentially strangers; others were formed by duty and property; still others, by habit. He wondered how strongly he was affected by the legend in seeing in this family something rare.

He was not sure why he felt this so strongly. With the exception of the legend, he had seen nothing he considered remarkable, nothing he could describe as responsible for the feeling. If anyone had asked him to defend his supposition, he could not have done it; he could not even have answered his own questions. And then the lullaby was over.

Briana sighed. "If Father was here, we would all embrace now," she said.

Meredith pulled away from Maud's gentle hand. "No," he said firmly and marched toward the door.

Maud leaned down and embraced her niece. "Mind it not, Briana. He's just a boy."

"Boys are silly," Briana agreed with a wise nod.

Ine hid a smile and watched the woman take the child's hand to lead her after her brother. Briana started out with Maud, then stopped and looked back at Ine. "I give you my thanks," she said. "You play well."

Ine smothered a nearly irresistible laugh. "Would you seek to play your psaltery for the lullaby?" he asked.

The idea had obviously never occurred to her. He saw her bright green eyes widen a little with surprise, and then she nodded.

"I shall teach you," he said.

Maud smiled approvingly.

Windsor—September 1275 A.D.

The servants had removed the bright decorations they had hung in the solar when Queen Eleanor gave birth to her third daughter, named Margaret. At six months of age now the baby was very healthy, cried lustily, and generally made her mother and her six-year-old sister, Princess Eleanor, laugh a great deal.

But as if the new life had to be balanced somehow against one already in the world, as the girl grew healthier, Edward and Elizabeth's son and heir, Alfonso, sickened and became weaker.

Edward seemed to accept his son's illness as part of the uncertainty of children, just as he had earlier accepted the deaths of his sons, John at five and Henry at six. He had three healthy daughters, and his wife was still birthing children without any ill effects. He would have more children—and Alfonso was hanging onto life.

Eleanor would have liked to stay at her son's side, too aware that she had been half the world away when John departed life, but she had duties to perform, not only as queen, but as the estate manager for Windsor itself. Edward rode out with his knights to several cities in the realm to study the individual censuses, laws, and judgments, for he had an ambition to unite the disparate parts of England into one power, under a single law. And he needed to know what part of England's riches were held by the Jews, a troublesome people he had first encountered on Crusade and whom he regarded as much the enemies of Christendom as the Saracens, whom he had come to the Holy Land specifically to kill.

The queen stayed at Windsor and administered to the household, fearful in her quiet way that this third son would slip away from her before she had an opportunity to know him. It was part of her secret sorrow that her husband did not understand why she could become attached to a child before it proved itself valuable.

Because Eleanor was at Windsor and Edward was not, it was Eleanor who received Rees de Bretagne, newly knighted and in mourning for his mother. Eleanor had gotten word that very morning of Beatrice's death. The courier sent to Edward from John de Bretagne's estates, who had ridden into the courtyard after a rough channel crossing to tell the King of England that his younger sister was dead, was a very young woman, carrying messages for both the king and the queen. Eleanor accepted the news with equanimity, expressing sympathy, read her own message, and dismissed the messenger with several quiet words and before anyone else in the castle could speak with her. Then she went to the kitchens to deal with one of the local merchants.

She had just finished when Rees was announced.

Eleanor remembered him well. She also remembered Beatrice's pride in her older son, so open-hearted that Eleanor could not even feel envious of a mother's joy in a tall, handsome, healthy boy. And Beatrice had a second son who also lived, the boy named Arthur, but by far the greater part of her love seemed to have been centered on Rees.

The queen did not keep him waiting. In a year, he had grown several inches and begun developing the muscles that any knight needed in order to wield steel weapons, support the weight of chain mail, and control a powerful warhorse. She saw also that he had a good share of the Plantagenet height and beauty. There was about him, however, an air of bewilderment. As he knelt to her, one hand on his sword hilt, his clear blue eyes darted around the room, searching.

Eleanor said gently, "Rise, Sir Rees. The king is not in residence."

"My mother, his sister, is dead," he said shortly.

"I know," said Eleanor. "Your father sent a messenger who delivered that news. You chose not to remain in France?"

Rees seemed to debate what to reply to that, started and rejected several things, and finally said, "Before she died, my mother asked a boon of me. She wanted me to enter into the service of her brother, the King of England. I've come to offer him fealty."

"We are honored," Eleanor said carefully. "I am certain your mother would have excellent reasons for wishing you to be part of her family. Come, let me show you quarters you may occupy until such time as my husband returns to accept your pledge." In her secret heart, Eleanor knew exactly what those reasons were, but there was no way she would reveal them to the handsome, still somewhat bewildered young man who followed her at her behest. She had not even revealed them to her husband, the king.

Beatrice was a fragile beauty and seemed to be weakening when Rees won his spurs. Immediately after his knighting, she sent for him, forestalling his intention to seek out his father and offer him fealty.

Rees was shown to her solar, where Beatrice lay, white-faced, on the large bed. She was unexpectedly alone, for her servant had withdrawn from the room before her son arrived. Beatrice smiled at Rees and held out one thin hand, which he grasped gently. Then she stunned him by saying, "I am dying, Rees." And before he could gainsay her, she went on, "I require you to swear to me that you will leave this day for England and offer fealty to my brother, the king."

"But—why?" Rees asked. "I sought to be a de Bretagne knight. I wanted—"

She overrode him, which was very unlike her. "Nay, you must not. Go not near John de Bretagne from this moment. Leave at once."

"I would stay with you, especially now." His protest sounded weak; she shook her head to negate it.

"Swear it to me. 'Tis the last thing I shall ask of you. Swear!"

He heard her voice weaken, even as she tried to make it stronger, and, helpless in the face of her intensity, he swore. She pushed the hand holding her own away from her. "Leave at once," she repeated.

He walked obediently to the door of the solar, looked back, saw the tears rolling from her eyes into the soft yellow of her hair. He paused, and she waved her arm to send him away. So he had gone down to the courtyard, mounted his horse, and ridden for the coast.

Now Queen Eleanor walked with him through the corridors of the great castle, and down across the inner bailey to the long dorter that housed Edward's unmarried knights, most of whom were traveling with their leige lord.

Only one man was actually in the dorter, and he looked up as the queen came in, then hastily rose from the bed on which he'd been lounging and dropped to one knee.

"Sir Galen Knauter," Eleanor said to Rees. "Sir Galen, this is Sir Rees de Bretagne, newly knighted in France." She did not mention that Rees was her nephew. Her instinct was that he would himself tell what he wanted told. She laid a hand on Rees's arm. "You will take supper with us in the solar this even. I shall send to you."

Both men bowed their heads as she turned and left the dorter in a swirl of skirts.

"Where's your bundle?" Galen asked, rising from his knee and strolling over to size up the new knight. "With your squire?" He was several years older than Rees and more fully developed across the chest and shoulders, but he was not as tall as the younger man.

Rees looked around for a bed that bore no signs of occupation. "I have no squire," he said. "I care for my own things. And I've only my clothes and mail. I left France somewhat precipitately."

Galen frowned. His education was limited—and, hence, his vocabulary—though he was good at guessing what unfamiliar words meant. He was unbothered by the fact that his misapprehensions sometimes created a howler or two. "Outlaw?" he asked. "You steal that sword?"

Rees glanced down at the sword that hung at his side. The hilt was wrapped with leather, but the ball at its end gleamed with good steel. "Nay," he said mildly, unoffended. "Just— precipitate." He identified a vacant bed, went to it, dropped his cloak across its foot, unbuckled his swordbelt, and laid the scabbarded weapon on the cloak.

Galen had followed him down the row of beds. Now he watched as Rees took a cloth-wrapped object from his tunic and set it beside the sword. "How is it you have no bundle? You've come to court without court clothing. 'Tis not usual."

"I'd not discuss it," Rees said. "How long have you been in my—in the king's service?"

"This year past, since His Majesty was coronated," Galen answered. "Won my spurs in the first tourney he put on. I minded not the fighting, but the night on my knees came near to flattening me."

Rees pulled off his chain mail shirt and laid it on the chair beside the head of the bed.

"No squire, either," Galen commented, having absorbed that part of Rees's earlier statement. "Pretty poor showing for a knight."

Rees bent toward the bed and suddenly—Galen could not have said how—the leather-wrapped sword hilt was firmly in his grasp, the shining blade clear of the scabbard, and the point just an inch from Galen's throat. "You think so?" Rees asked softly.

Galen was startled, but not stupid. "I'd be happy to spar with you," he said, "but weapon-play is forbidden in the dorter." He raised his voice. "Ralf!"

A curtain at the far end of the room swung aside, and a boy of about twelve came in and summed up the scene in one glance, his eyes widening at the sight of the stranger with the naked blade.

"Meet us on the practice field and bring my sword," Galen ordered.

The boy vanished behind the curtain.

"Unless you are weary from your travels," Galen added to Rees.

Wordlessly, Rees gestured with the sword in imitation of a bow.

Galen grinned and led the younger man back to the inner bailey and out of the castle grounds to a stamped-out packed-earth expanse pocked with hoofprints.

Rees had had no expectations of a sparring match when he arrived in England, but he had never turned aside from a challenge, and he had no other pressing business until King Edward returned. In addition, he had always been taught that the only way to maintain his skills was to practice them regularly.

Ralf, obviously Galen's squire, came out of the castle carrying a scabbarded sword and battered wooden shield. Galen unsheathed the sword, waved the shield away, took his stance, and waited.

Rees held his hilt lightly, his own sword raised, but did not attack.

Galen feinted; Rees's sword blocked the feint and twisted in what looked as if it were an awkward move, though Rees did not make it seem awkward. Galen's sword flew toward Ralf, who jumped backwards out of the way.

Rees stepped back from his unarmed opponent.

Galen looked at the younger knight, standing so still, sword in hand, then gestured to Ralf to bring him back his sword. The boy did so, casting a wary but respectful glance at Rees, then retreating beyond the distance Galen's sword had traveled a few moments before.

Galen took a firm grip on his own sword hilt, warier now, tried a frontal attack, using his strength to carry him at Rees, slashing downward as he did. Rees blocked the blow, danced sideways, countered a second, lateral slash, then twisted his wrist again, used his swordpoint to catch Galen's handguard, and sent the weapon sailing in the other direction.

"My thanks," called Ralf.

Galen glared at him, then at Rees. "'Twould be easier to spar if you let me hold onto my sword," he said.

"'Tis quicker and safer if I do not," said Rees.

Galen thought about that for a moment or two, then decided it was not unflattering. He waited while Ralf trotted around the edge of the practice field and retrieved the sword. Hefting it, Galen looked at Rees. "I'd be pleased to hold it a time longer," he said.

Rees grinned.

By the fourth day of practice, Galen had admitted to himself that the younger knight was the more strongly skilled of the two, and had begun—without acknowledging what he was doing—to seek instruction from Rees. They were in the midst of a match, in which Rees gave quiet suggestions to Galen about his footwork—and Ralf drank it all in—when Edward and his other knights returned.

The stables were on the opposite side of Windsor from the practice field, and it was to the stables that the party of knights went first. The king left them to care for the horses and made his way into the outer bailey. Ralf had just run out of the dorter with a dagger in one hand and a pair of gauntlets in the other. His face was shining with sweat, and he was so preoccupied with his errand that he didn't notice the king.

Edward was drawn to the urgency in the squire's manner and, curious, he followed. Nothing of great importance should have happened in his absence, Edward knew, and to see the squire of the only knight left at the castle racing out to the practice field was provocative. He paused in the shadow of the walls, momentarily surprised to see Galen sparring with another knight, not one of his own. It wasn't until Rees removed his helmet that Edward recognized his sister's son.

The king knew in less than two minutes what Galen had taken four days to admit to himself. Rees was very skilled. Edward did not need to watch any longer to confirm what he had discovered; he went back into the castle.

Eleanor joined Edward in his rooms as he was dressing to receive the fealty of his nephew, Rees. She read the deep thoughtfulness on his face and dismissed his attendants, assuming the role of helping him with his hose and tunic herself. "What worries you?" she asked.

"The boy is a fine fighter," he said. "I've seen his skill myself. Why comes he to me, not to his father's king or his father's own company?"

Eleanor lifted the red wool tunic, and he bent his bright head so she could reach high enough to drop it onto his shoulders. "Beatrice begged him to seek your service as she lay on her deathbed," she said. "He told me 'twas his last promise to her."

He ran his long fingers back through his hair and then slid his arms through the armholes so that she could pull the tunic down along his body. "Despite that," he said, "were he my son, I would fight to hold onto him. I fail to understand John de Bretagne."

Eleanor closed her eyes briefly at those words, partly because she was feeling a criticism he might not have implied. His own son was sickly, and Edward sometimes did not truly appear to care whether he lived or died so long as she could make others. But that was not the total cause of her sadness, and Edward sensed that there was something important causing her to be melancholy. She tried to ignore it, picked up his soft shoes, and knelt to help him put them on. "Mayhap John de Bretagne places more faith in a man's sacred vow to his dying mother than you might under like circumstances," she said. "Or mayhap he believes you will use Rees in his youth and then release him to Brittany."

She rose as he said, "If I accept him, I shall keep him. I do not release what is mine."

She lifted his swordbelt from the chest on which it lay and deftly drew his attention from Beatrice and her son. "Is the Demoiselle yours then? Or will you render her up to Prince Llewelyn, who desires her greatly? He still requests to wed her with great steadiness, and he has kept peace in Wales these years."

He took the belt from her hands to buckle it on himself. "That stiff-necked bastard Welshman must submit to me before I hand him de Montfort's daughter. She holds sway over him between her legs, and I shall not let him get there until he has acknowledged my rule. He must understand that I shall only trade him the Demoiselle for Wales. And soon I shall have to venture there and see it for myself."

She handed him the gold circlet he would set on his brow and smiled up at him. "I see not how any man could long resist your rule, my lord husband."

He offered her his arm, but was thinking about Rees again. "What was de Bretagne thinking in releasing him?"

Eleanor answered, "de Bretagne favors Arthur."

"I wonder why," he said, watching her closely.

She tried to show nothing, but he guessed that she knew more than she was telling him. He determined to have it out of her another time.

He took her hand to escort her from the room, but they were forestalled in the corridor by one of her ladies, who knelt before them as they approached, eyes downcast.

Eleanor felt a familiar cold climbing over her.

"Your grace, the prince is very poorly," the woman said, not looking up.

Eleanor feared she would once again be a sonless queen. Her hand tightened momentarily on Edward's, drawing his gaze to her.

He felt her tremble, said tonelessly, "I'd have you with me for the ceremonials."

"Of course," she said as steadily as she could. She would not yet be able to go to her son, worthless to his father in not being likely to live.

He led her downstairs, where much of his household had gathered to watch the golden young knight place his hands between those of the equally golden king and swear to serve him faithfully.

They took their separate seats in the hall. Edward sat in the large chair on the raised platform and leaned back to study the young man who came to kneel before him. Seated at his side, but on the floor rather than the dais, Eleanor also looked at her handsome nephew, waiting now with an unnatural stillness for words from the king to whom he would pledge. Edward's knights and their squires, along with a number of Eleanor's ladies and the Demoiselle, putatively still a guest of the royal family, ranged around the sides of the hall, watching.

Edward leaned forward and held out his hands, palms facing each other. Rees put his hands between them and said the oath in a clear voice that belied the tremble Edward could feel. Then Rees sat back on his heels as Edward rose, drew his sword, and set it point down in front of the knight. Rees raised his face and kissed the sword where hilt met crosspiece. Edward resheathed the sword and said, "Rise."

Eleanor kept her face carefully serene, though inside she ached with a sorrow she could not express. She would miss her little boy when God took him from her. She was the mother only of healthy daughters, and she had lost four of those for the three who lived. Her husband the king never shared her grief.

"I accept your service, Sir Rees," Edward was saying now. "My earl, Gilbert de Clare, leaves within the week to lay siege to Antioch. And as I believe all young knights should—as did I— spend at least a season in the Holy Land battling for the Cross, I detach you to his service." He raised his voice. "If there are others among you who harbor a yearning for the sands, you may join Earl de Clare as well."

Among the watchers, Galen Knauter decided he would join de Clare's company. He had learned more sparring with the younger knight than the last two years among the other knights at Windsor or Westminster had taught him, and he preferred not to lose its source before he believed he had gotten all he could.

Eleanor had long ago perfected the art of speaking to Edward in public in a voice only he could hear. Now she said, "He is so fine. A liege—could take much pride in such a youth. And he is only just sixteen."

Edward turned his face directly toward her. "He will be older if he returns. Then I can decide how best to wield him."

Not for the first time—and she was certain not for the last—Eleanor wished her husband were a more loving man. She had observed Rees with his cousins, Eleanor and Joanna, at the family meals they had shared before Edward's return. She had seen that he, while young, had an ability to combine power with gentleness. She envied it. His mother had told her it would be so.

And now Edward had sent it away. She hoped it would come back again. At the same time, she prayed that she might someday have a son like Beatrice's. Though she was infinitely grateful that she would not have to get him in the way that was still nearly destroying his mother.

Chapter 4

Ruthin, Clwydd—April 1277 A.D.

There had been two dozen men at the table for the meal, but now only four were left, one of them a boy of fourteen, one a boy of eleven. The two older men sat grimly, cradling their mugs in work-hardened hands.

"His heart is not in this war," Anian Glyn said after a lengthy silence.

Bryn and the two boys knew that Anian spoke of Prince Llewelyn, who had left the table before any of the other men.

"'Tisn't his war," said Bryn. "He's just the better man to fight it. He should have locked David up when he locked up Owain. David is a hothead."

"David is a spendthrift," Anian corrected. "He is profligate with the lives of Welshmen, and many of them know it."

"'Tis why they cleave to Prince Llewelyn," said Bryn. "He gives the best chance for continued life and freedom."

Owen Glyn, fourteen and solemn, said, "Suppose they can have one, but not the other. What will they do then? Which will they choose?"

The men stared at him, and Griffith ap Bryn, younger but no more inhibited, said, "Freedom is everything to a Welshman. That's why Prince David attacked the English troops."

"David attacked the English because he lost his temper with the Marcher lords," Anian said.

"And the English strike back not because of the attack, but because Llewelyn has refused to pay homage to King Edward," Bryn said.

They were silent about that, uncertain whose side to take, wanting to be loyal to Llewelyn at all costs, but unclear on why it was so difficult for him to say a few words which he would in no way mean and for which God would surely forgive him.

"He did not have to yield to Henry and still won the peace," Anian said. "Mayhap he feels he need not bow to Henry's son."

No one said what the men were thinking. Henry's son was nothing like Henry, and there were no barons in rebellion against Edward. The same rules did not apply.

Anian went on, "I suspect it has to do with the Demoiselle. He does not want to appear to be trading his nation for a woman."

"How long will the war last?" Griffith asked, as if such things were predictable, and these men would know what those predictions were.

When no one else answered immediately, Owen said, "'Twill last as long as it needs to."

They all looked up as Llewelyn entered the doorway and beckoned to Bryn. Then, as the two men left the hall, Anian raised his mug and reflected on a future which held as much of peril as it did of promise.

Bryn paced along with his silent prince as they left the building and then the yard. Llewelyn was silent, and Bryn was reluctant to break into his thoughts. The curfew bell rang out across the valley as they walked along the road between fields and forest, the sound of their footfalls muffled by a layer of drying mud on the surface of the road.

It was not until they reached the hilltop across the valley from the manor house that Llewelyn lessened his long strides to more of an amble. Bryn matched the pace and waited to see what the prince would say.

There was a stone cairn at the northern edge of the hilltop. It could have been built anytime by anyone, but the local legends held that it marked the spot where King Arthur defeated his enemies and stood to survey all his lands around Ruthin. Llewelyn stopped walking at the cairn and laid his hand on it. "The stones here are always warm," he said to Bryn. "Even in winter, there is warmth in this place." He straightened. "Edward is hiring unpledged knights, buying their service with gold. I have heard he will pay them a bounty for dead Welshmen."

"'Tis dishonorable!" said Bryn hotly. "To buy loyalty he cannot command shows a failure of leadership!"

"Edward writes his own definitions of leadership and honor and expects the rest of the world to abide by them." Llewelyn looked at the light fading over the valley. "'Twill not be peaceful here much longer."

Bryn hesitated, then ventured, "You could submit." He wasn't certain if the prince would be angry, but the thought was hardly an unfamiliar one to Llewelyn.

"Aye," said Llewelyn, "but I fear he will have to force me to it."

Flint—June 1277 A.D.

K ing Edward stood by the estuary of the Dee and looked long and hard at the promontory of land on which he had decided to build a castle. He had been at Chester with his army, ready to join the armies he had sent to the Marcher lords months before, when one of the men to whom he had confided his line of march into Wales told him of the legend attendant on the lady of Flint. While his first instinct was to scoff, he kept it to himself, because he could see instantly that the men who spoke of it were somewhat in awe of it.

He consulted some of his advisers and learned how much the people of Northeast Wales thought of the prophecy. Then he sent for his architect, Master James of St. George, with whom he had been considering a castle at Rhuddlan. The man was neither a warrior nor a scholar, but he could design a stronghold better than any other in Europe, and he had a knack for speeding the construction of his designs. Edward was going to use him to place castles in strategic locations across the land as he conquered it, and now he believed he should start here, on this windswept expanse of land over which the seabirds wheeled and cried.

In Chester, Edward had taken over one of the best inns, a house pressed closely to other houses along a narrow lane, but whose common room held sufficient tables to seat many of the king's men. When the architect came in, Edward waved him over to his own table, near the fireplace. "We have cause to alter our plan," the king said at once.

"In what respect, Sire?" Master James asked, bowing, though it would never have occurred to him to argue.

"Instead of journeying straight to Rhuddlan, we will make for Flint to survey the land there," Edward said.

Master James may have conjectured privately, but, on seeing the site for the castle, he concluded that Edward was worried about the protection of the mouth of the Dee, and Edward was content to let him think it. While the architect and his men tested soil, located nearby sources of stone, and altered existing physical designs to better fit into the actualities of the site, Edward took the Marcher lord for the Northern March, Roger Mortimer of Montgomery, Earl Wigmore, along with Roger's son Edmund, who might reasonably expect to succeed to the title upon his father's death, and several other knights with him to call on the manor house at Flint. At twenty-five, Edmund Mortimer was already one of the most efficient commanders in Edward's service, for he had proved unwilling to refrain from practices some other commanders might have considered less than honorable and to be quiet about it afterward. Edward appreciated that in a soldier.

The lord of Flint manor was not at home, having left earlier in the year to follow Prince Llewelyn to Ruthin, and then from Clwydd, as the English captured it, to Gwynedd and the fastness of Snowdonia.

Maud and some of the household women received the King of England, but neither welcomed nor greeted him. Maud was wary, uncertain whether either he or Wigmore—whom she personally disliked for the evil she sensed about him and his son, unrestrained by the sense of responsibility Edward projected— would seek to take her from the manor.

Edward had no interest in her or in the manor. "Bring me the Lady Briana," he commanded her.

Maud was tempted to lie, to tell him the child was in Anglesey or Radnor or Swansea, but her information was outdated enough so that she had no idea what parts of Wales were now in English hands. And while Snowdonia harbored both Prince David, who had retreated to it the moment the war began to go badly, and Prince Llewelyn, who had followed his brother reluctantly, and only to save as many of his troops as possible from the encroaching English troops, no one would send a child there, and Edward would probably know that.

Edmund Mortimer laughed at her discomfiture. "We can send our men to search the house," he offered.

"No need," said Maud quickly. There were several caches of weapons, forged in the smithy in the last few weeks, which would not bear discovery. She sent one of the other women to fetch Briana.

The girl had been in one of the rooms under the eaves, practicing the dulcimer Ine had given her to replace Father Ciaran's gift of the psaltery two years before. She was aware there was tumult in the village and that some of it had spread to the manor itself, but she had made herself ignore it. With Bryn and Griffith gone from Flint, she was missing them very much. Only two things helped alleviate that particular loneliness—one was to go to the seaside, to some of the coves and bays that were part of the great estuary beside which Flint stood; the other was her growing prowess with her music. Ine had visited four times before the war drew too close, each time teaching her a little more. She did appear to have an aptitude for melody and a good memory for notes and the poetry that they accompanied. Ine had even told her once that, had she not been Celtic nobility, he could have turned her into a fair minstrel.

She brought the dulcimer with her, cradled in her arms, when she came downstairs to the front yard to see and be seen by the King of England, whom she knew to be the sworn enemy of her father's friend and prince. Even at eight years of age, Briana knew to be careful around an enemy. She bobbed a curtsey and waited, wary.

Edward was not easy with children, though he was the father of three daughters, one living son, and Eleanor was pregnant again. He looked at the pretty little girl holding the instrument and the two small hammers, saw nothing about her to credit the legend, but remained unwilling to discount it because it was, the Mortimers were able to assure him, widely accepted. "Mayhap you should simply kill her," Edmund Mortimer had suggested. "That would put an end to any talk of legends."

The king had looked coldly at his normally welcome servant. "She may be useful as a tool," he said. "You have certain good qualities, Edmund, but you will never be a master manipulator if you cannot tell the difference between a weapon and a tool."

Roger Mortimer, angry at his son's impertinence and poor judgment, in that the suggestion had not been met favorably, berated the young man at some length later, but his son took no offense at it. "The king has his methods and I have mine," he said to his father.

Now all of them studied the girl who stood so still at Maud's side.

Briana was thinking that the king was very tall and radiated power in ways no other man she had ever known. She could not have said how she knew it or how he was showing it to her. She wondered what she could possibly say to him.

Edward had wanted to see her and, having seen her, thought himself right to have chosen to put a castle here. But, having seen her, he could not converse with a child. "Send her away again," he said to Maud.

Briana bobbed another curtsey and gratefully escaped back into the manor. She hoped she would never have to see any of those men again, most especially the tall golden one whose regard had filled her with such apprehension. She set her dulcimer down in the window seat of the solar and went to find Meredith, who was somewhere in the orchard.

Worcester, England—June 1278 A.D.

Briana had never journeyed from Flint before. The trip to Worcester had taken only two days, but she felt as if they had entered another world. Worcester was not remotely as vibrant and busy as Chester, but she had barely noticed Chester as they rode through. Worcester was sturdier than most villages in Wales, though not nearly as sturdy as the castle that now dominated the valley of Flint. She tried not to think about that. She was to be attendant to the Demoiselle, for Prince Llewelyn was to be married at last.

According to the reasoning of the English, the Welsh war was over. According to the Welsh, who did not trouble the English with their own thoughts in the matter, the war was in abeyance. There had been a number of battles in several parts of the country, testing the strength of the English resolution, and the Marcher lords had prevailed by superior numbers and Edward's unyielding determination to bend the Welsh to his will either by winning them over or by force of arms. His army had steadily pushed the prince back to Snowdonia, where, Llewelyn thought, David should have stayed in the first place.

At that point, reluctant to sacrifice more men when a good portion of Wales had already fallen and was trying to make surface accommodation to the English, Llewelyn sent word to Edward that he would swear fealty. All Edward had to do was name the time and place.

Edward was disposed to be generous in victory. He had proved his point at small cost to himself or his kingdom, and he was sure the Welsh had learned it was his divine right to rule them. His reply to Llewelyn read, "Do it at your wedding."

Eleanor was delighted for the Demoiselle. She arranged to sponsor the bride herself, with her two oldest daughters in attendance. She now had four daughters, but Mary was only three months old, and Margaret was not yet three years. Princess Eleanor, at nine, and Princess Joanna, at six, would be lovely complements to the Demoiselle's fragile beauty. When the queen saw Briana, just Eleanor's age and Joanna's height and dark-haired like her second daughter, she was completely enchanted.

Llewelyn watched her admire the girl and was touched by a hint of worry, a nudge of Celtic premonition. Sometimes he could sense the beyond, when he was preternaturally alert, as now, having just come into the hands of his enemy. He glanced at Bryn to see if his friend had also sensed anything unnatural, but Bryn was sizing up the defenses of the small castle at Worcester and oblivious to undercurrents.

Prince Llewelyn had been invited to Worcester for the fealty and the long-delayed marriage. Edward had concluded the invitation with a request that the Welsh leader bring "as many companions as may be needed for ceremony, and no more." The request suited Llewelyn's purpose admirably. The fewer Welshmen who saw him bow to Edward, the better. So, once again, he had chosen two companions, but not the ones who had accompanied him around Wales in past years. This time he chose Bryn, since he very much wanted Briana to attend the Demoiselle, and in place of Anian Glyn, who had been killed in the last battle Llewelyn agreed to fight before his retreat to Snowdonia, Llewelyn brought Anian's now sixteen-year-old son, Owen.

Owen had mourned his father with equal shares of acceptance and anger. The acceptance was born of the attitude of a man of the sword toward another who has met a not unlikely fate. The anger was slower, hotter, longer-lasting, directed at the men who would not let Wales keep her liberty. He hid it well. He was more curious to see King Edward than he was to attend the wedding, and he was also interested in watching Briana, who had grown a little since last he saw her. No one had recently mentioned the betrothal, but he was certain that everyone remembered it, as Llewelyn would be keen to carry out the wish of a faithful companion, and Bryn had also agreed.

Edward did not come to meet the party when Eleanor did, so it was the queen herself, honoring either a noble enemy or the Demoiselle's soon-to-be husband, who escorted them to the room prepared for them. "I'd take the Lady Briana to bide with my own daughters," Eleanor said as the three men entered the part of the castle designated to them. "This chamber is masculine in nature."

Bryn waited to see if Llewelyn would speak, but the prince did not. "That would be kindly done, Your Grace," said Bryn.

Briana dropped a quick curtsy to the prince and her father and accompanied the Queen of England down the long corridor that divided the residence areas from the larger gathering halls. She was surprised by the fine quality of the gown Eleanor was wearing; clothing at Flint was much more functional than decorative, and Briana had reached an age where the way people dressed, the way women wore their hair, what different fabrics felt like, what jewelry they wore, were of growing interest to her.

The Princesses Eleanor and Joanna were braiding ribbons into headbands. They looked up as Queen Eleanor brought Briana in and presented them to one another.

Princess Eleanor was blooming with a full measure of the Plantagenet beauty. She was already much taller than most girls her age, for she took after her father, who was known as "Longshanks" because of his unusual height. She inherited her lovely smile and sweet nature directly from her mother, and her considerable charm, even in one so young, was characteristically her own.

Princess Joanna was olive-skinned and raven-haired like the Castillian forebears of her mother. Still too young to be growing as tall as her older sister, she was nevertheless of a height to be able to look directly across at the Welsh lady, who was three years her senior, because Briana was small for her age and still sturdy with the solidity of childhood. Joanna's flashing dark eyes were already filled with more mischief than would ever have occurred to either Eleanor or even to the lady of Flint, known for her near reckless defiance at home.

Princess Eleanor laid aside her ribbons and rose politely to greet the younger girl, saying, "How pretty you are, Lady Briana."

Briana was uncertain whether to curtsy or not, but bobbed a little just in case.

Queen Eleanor said, "I shall leave you to make acquaintance. Eleanor, you will need to attend the Demoiselle within the hour."

"We shall be there, Mother," said the princess.

The queen left, firmly closing the door to the small solar.

Princess Joanna curiously studied the newcomer. "Are you one of the rebels?" she asked.

"Joanna!" Eleanor's voice was sharp. "There are no more rebels. The Welsh are our father's loyal subjects, just as any others, excepting only the Scots."

"Father says the Welsh are stiff-necked and hot-headed," Joanna persisted, making Briana flush. With satisfaction at the redness in Briana's cheeks, Joanna added, "See there? Her head is hot."

Briana was piqued enough to be incautious. "*My* father says the English have no sense about controlling their tongues," she snapped. "I can see that he was at least correct about the children."

Eleanor took Briana's hand and drew her aside before Joanna could spring to her feet, insulted. "Joanna, finish braiding your ribbons," she said quickly, forestalling a probable lunge for the Welsh girl. "Briana, would you care to join us? We have need of help to get all these braids finished in time."

In truth, Briana was a little embarrassed over her outburst. For one thing, she had heard Prince Llewelyn describe his brother David as a "hot-headed fool" just a few days earlier, at Flint. For another, she was older than Joanna, and both Maud and Father Ciaran had tried to instill in her charity for and kindness toward those younger than herself. And for still another—"We interpret 'stiff-necked' as a compliment to our strength and stubbornness," she said conversationally in Eleanor's direction.

Joanna opened her mouth, but Eleanor started speaking instantly, and the younger princess subsided. "Briana, come and sit here with me. We only have a few minutes before we need to take these braids to the bride." And as Briana seated herself next to Eleanor, the princess continued, "What part of Wales come you from?"

Briana picked up some of the as yet unbraided ribbons and told them about her wonderful home at Flint, leaving out any mention of the monstrosity that their father had inflicted upon it by building his castle on the sweep of sands beside the estuary.

E dward undertook the full expense of the wedding, from the cost of the banquet to the cost of the ribbons which, braided by her attendants, hung over the Demoiselle's bright, free-flowing hair, and across the brows of the three young women who stood beside her on the steps of the chapel. The contingent from Wales might have been more grateful for the king's openhandedness had he not made the swearing of fealty such a conspicuous part of the ceremony.

"I suppose we might have imagined it," Bryn said under his breath to the stern-faced Owen Glyn. "He cannot be generous in victory unless he noises the victory particularly loudly."

Owen, narrow-eyed, nodded, but said nothing.

Prince Llewelyn behaved with considerable grace, as if the paying of homage to a man he hated were nothing more than a mild annoyance, a pebble in his path on the way to a goal for which he had striven for years, as, indeed, it was.

Briana, dressed in the finest light-blue fustian, a gown made hastily to match those of the princesses, watched with fascination as the prince was wed at last to the Demoiselle. She had never seen a wedding at which so much fuss was made over the ceremony. In Flint, the marriages of villagers were quick things in front of the tiny church, with just enough ritual to forestall sin. The man representing the church here at Worcester, unlike Father Ciaran, for whom simplicity was considered only proper, wore richly decorated robes, embroidered in metallic threads that glistened as he walked. He gave a long speech about the rewards of peace before pronouncing the couple wed, and though Briana did not try to understand much of it, she liked his thin, ascetic features and the even tenor voice. She had heard the queen refer to him as "my lord archbishop," and found out from Princess Eleanor that his name was John Peckham, and he ruled the see of Canterbury.

He had taken her aside before the wedding ceremony, after she had been dressed in her attendant gown, drawing her into one of the window alcoves. She studied him curiously, unafraid. He seemed a very gentle man, not unlike Father Ciaran in that respect, and she trusted the priest at St. Maedoc's unreservedly. She wondered what this churchman wanted with her.

Peckham squatted down in front of her to bring his narrow-featured face to a level near her own. "What church do you attend, Lady Briana? Or do you hear Mass in a private chapel at home?" he asked her.

Unlike great English houses, Welsh homes did not contain chapels, because the Welsh rather scorned private worship. It divided the community, and the Welsh had never held with classes of society, with saying that one person's ties to God were better than any other's.

"Our church is St. Maedoc, in Flint," Briana answered.

"Who is your priest?"

"Father Ciaran."

Peckham nodded, making a note of the name. Since the war, the Welsh church had come under his jurisdiction, and he was slowly learning the names of the clergy serving the new group of souls now entrusted to his care. "And has Father Ciaran ever given you Holy Communion?"

"Me?" Briana was surprised. "No one in Flint—except Prince Llewelyn when he visits—shares Communion with Father Ciaran."

"'Tis for that reason I wish to speak with you," the archbishop said. "As part of the wedding party today you will receive Communion with everyone else. I want to be certain you understand what it means."

"Me?" Briana repeated.

The archbishop smiled. "Tell me what you understand about Communion."

"I thought I understood 'twas only for priests and sovereigns," said Briana.

"Not who 'tis for, but what 'tis."

She didn't need to think about that for very long. "Communion is the body and blood of our Lord Jesus Christ, given to the world by God as a blessing."

"And do you know why God gave the world this blessing?" he pursued.

Briana had an answer for that. "God gives us gifts because He loves us," she said, obedient to Father Ciaran's teachings.

"Excellent," said Peckham. "And so to show God that you love Him as well, you will accept Communion as a moment in which you and God touch each other in a way that honors you, honors your body and your soul."

She absorbed the words slowly, because she sensed that they were important, and she wanted to be certain she understood them. Fascinated, Peckham watched her think about what he had just said to her. He didn't rush her, or cut off the process of reflection. It was rare to find it in anyone, but to find it in a young girl was remarkable.

When she thought she understood well enough, her startlingly clear green eyes refocused on him, and she said, "I think I know what you mean, my lord archbishop. Communion is a moment that gives each person's immortal soul an early taste of heaven."

For a second or two, he did not know how to respond, other than to admire the leap of her logic. Then he swallowed and said, "Very good, my daughter. I believe we can proceed with the ceremony without any hesitation."

She had brought her dulcimer, because her father and Prince Llewelyn liked to hear her play, but Edward provided six full-grown musicians for the banquet, and Briana was not yet skilled enough to accompany their singing or join in the ensemble. She thought none of them as talented as Ine, and she soon was barely paying attention to them. Instead, she watched Llewelyn and the Demoiselle, who were also hardly cognizant of the music, rejoice in each other's company. She could not imagine what created the wellspring of such joy, but then she had never before seen a man and a woman so much in love. The Demoiselle was radiant, laughing easily, frequently touching the husband she had despaired of ever obtaining.

The songs grew bawdier as the banquet drew to a close, and Queen Eleanor sent her daughters and Briana to their room before the newlywed couple was escorted to the bridal chamber, stripped, and seen into bed. Then the wedding guests went back to the hall to drink more and wait for morning.

Bryn and Owen were sitting at one of the side tables, preferring their own company to that of the king or any of his knights. They were both uncomfortable at being on English soil, in an English castle, albeit a minor one, with the English king. They would be happy to leave for home the next day, with Llewelyn and his new wife. They would not feel easy until they were back across the border.

Someone approached them, crossing the distance between the rowdy group of English knights and the two silent Welshmen, who looked up in surprise. "May I join you?" the man asked politely, gesturing to a seat on the bench beside Owen. He was tall, thin, and wearing a plain black and pale brown serge robe.

Bryn recognized him as the clergyman who had solemnized the marriage. The Welshman nodded. Owen shifted his position minutely, just a hint of a gesture, enough to recognize the difference between them and the man who was joining them.

"Bryn ap Emrys, Lord of Flint," Bryn said, "and this is Owen Glyn."

"I am John Peckham," said the priest. He did not use any titles, but when they heard the name, they knew they were in the company of the most powerful churchman in England, and they were surprised that no one had made much of him hitherto.

Bryn and Owen exchanged a glance, and Bryn asked, "Why seek you our company?"

"As you heard me say at the wedding, I believe in peace," said Peckham.

Bryn bit back the comment which sprang instantly to his lips. "You have chosen the wrong king, then." Instead, he said, "'Tis a noble belief."

"And you welcome peace in your nation?" Peckham asked in a steady voice. "I have thought you would wish it, or I would not have mediated this peace for Wales' sake."

"*You* did?" Owen asked.

"Aye," said the archbishop without any overt pride in the word. "I did not wish to see King Edward lay waste to any part of his kingdom. That is not good stewardship. And in order to keep him from being provoked illy into action, you Welsh need to feel that you will be able to still be yourselves, even as you become part of England."

Bryn didn't react at all, but Owen was unable to avoid a wince.

Peckham pretended not to see it. "The king does truly wish all his subjects to be happy," he went on steadily. "'Tis why he permitted this marriage."

Bryn found he could no longer merely remain silent. "Is it the king's notion that making Prince Llewelyn happy will make Wales happy?"

"Will it not?" the archbishop asked. "Is not Wales truly part of Prince Llewelyn?"

"English thinking," said Owen softly. "Wales is Wales."

Peckham sighed. "'Twould be a fell thing should Wales not permit the peace to continue."

"I've the notion that 'twill not be Wales which makes that choice," said Bryn.

"I ask you to believe that Canterbury is your friend," said Peckham.

Neither Welshman spoke a word in reply to that, and after a few minutes, the archbishop rose and left them, crossing back to the Englishmen gathered on the other side of the room.

"Think you he means it?" Owen asked when they were alone.

Bryn snorted. "Think you it matters?" he asked in return.

Chapter 5

Windsor Castle—December 1281 A.D.

All the knights agreed that a visit to a nearby tavern the night before Galen's wedding to Ermentrude Hythe, a pretty, landless young Saxon woman, would be an excellent idea. It was generally accepted that a man's sexual appetites should not be imposed too quickly upon a tremulous virgin and would therefore benefit by a good deal of blunting beforehand. Most of the town taverns were willing to supply a complement of whores for any number of purposes, many far less noble than the sparing of a new bride's sensibilities.

Galen, Ralf, and Rees chose a tavern called the Griffin, about a mile upriver from the castle precincts. Ralf had been knighted several months before de Clare's troops sailed home to England, and, his status now equal to that of the other two men, fought beside them in the last battles, including the one in which the Mamelukes tried to cut off their final retreat to the ships. de Clare, who was wounded in the shoulder by an arrow that skimmed past his shield, maintained his seat on his horse, and most of his nearest knights fought to his side to guard him from further harm. Rees, Ralf, and Galen were at the far left of the progress, and therefore exposed when the bulk of the knights swarmed rightward to defend de Clare.

Rees took the brunt of the attack that fell upon them, with the other two knights at his shoulders. At some point as they fought like a single person, as if they had practiced this kind of battling all their lives, Rees's helm was knocked from his head, revealing his face to the Mamelukes. Something they saw in it as he cleared his way through them with neither hesitation nor mercy, seemingly unstoppable, made one of the men he was facing cry out something. The other attacking Mamelukes took up the cry, and suddenly they broke and fell away. Several of the knights around de Clare had also sustained wounds, but no one had been killed, and they reached the ship with no further incidents.

"What were they shouting?" Ralf asked as they loaded horses and equipment on board the ships.

One of the interpreters drew Rees aside and spoke with him in a low voice. Rees frowned and waved him away.

Ralf repeated his question, but Rees refused to answer. Galen later, after the ship had sailed, intimidated the interpreter, then returned to Ralf and said, "They were calling him the angel of death."

There might have been a time when Galen and Ralf would have teased Rees about such a sobriquet, but not now. He had been wounded in the second battle they fought in the Holy Land, had nearly died, and something had happened to him. He had come back more strongly than ever, so it was not that; his fighting skills seemed to have increased to the level of art, as though that single instance of horrible injury had somehow made him resolve that he would never experience its like again. He had then, they conjectured to themselves, made some sort of bargain with God—it never occurred to them it could have been the devil; he was too gentle a man when he was not fighting—to keep him from ever being injured again. And they were both aware of the numerous times his very recklessness had saved their lives.

"What in God's name did his face look like?" they asked each other.

They continued to seek out his company. They did it not only because fighting beside him lifted their own martial efforts beyond their expectations, but because they genuinely liked him.

They had left de Clare's service and returned to the king's upon their return to England. The genuine liking they felt extended itself to their lives between the battles they fought on English soil: a brief foray into Wales at the very end of the Welsh wars, and border skirmishes with the Scots.

Because they liked being in each other's company, they formed the habit of sharing women among them. Rees had realized as early as their first experiences together in the Holy Land that he would learn nothing about this set of skills from Galen, who was brusque, or from Ralf, who was shy. He had been inducted into the world of the senses before he left Brittany, and while he had enjoyed it, the French were far more sophisticated than he was then ready to be. He filed those lessons away for future use, when he might want to investigate them again. In the meantime, he chose to learn from the women themselves, a process of observation, exploration, and experimentation which entertained and sometimes pleased him.

At the Griffin, which they had patronized on several previous occasions, they chose from among the available women and retired with them to the upstairs loft. Galen worked vigorously to ensure he would not overly trouble his new wife. Even Rees admired his dedication.

Rees also admired Galen's choice of wife.

Ermentrude, called Menty, was just fifteen, with good, sturdy Saxon features, wide hips, a deep bosom, and thick brown braids. She also had an education, rare among Saxon women, but she was the only child of Edgar Hythe, one of the founding scholars of Merton College, Oxford. She had been born two years after the college, and she liked to say, "He raised us together." Her mother had made sure she mastered the womanly arts, and her father had taught her scholarly pursuits. She liked the former better than the latter, but she never wanted to disappoint her father. Her ability to read, write, and engage in some level of abstract reasoning made her interesting to Rees, but because she was promised to Galen, he was careful not to spend any time alone with her.

"Remember," Galen's worn-out whore said as the men prepared to depart for the castle, "you mustn't expect your wife to develop any of the skills we have."

The men grinned at her, paid her generously, and hoped she was wrong. Women were believed to have the capacity for great passion; it merely had to be awakened by the right lover. Many young men wondered if they were right for their wives. Even Galen was among them.

As one of King Edward's knights, Galen had been given the privilege of being married on the steps of the royal chapel, and John Peckham came up from Canterbury to perform both the ceremony and the Christmas rituals.

The king and queen were both in attendance at the wedding, along with the parents of the bride, come in from Oxford to see their daughter secure a good husband; the congregation also included one of the Marcher Lords, come to court to see the king, and some of the king's landed nobles, as well.

The archbishop entered the chapel after the spectators and the bridal couple. Menty was lovely in a gown of murrey fustian, and Galen looked substantial and proud in a fine wool supertunic, his skin shiny from a bath both Rees and Ralf had alternately supervised and lent a hand to.

Watching the brief ceremony, Ralf said in a whisper to Rees, "He looks well for a man who's had no sleep."

"I was more worried about the bath," said Rees in return. "He knows how to go sleepless."

In less than two minutes, Galen was married, and the company went into the hall for the wedding feast. Queen Eleanor, pregnant again, sat with three of her four daughters beside the bride, and the king sat beside the groom. Rees had stayed with Ralf and those other knights present, instead of joining the family of which he had never really felt a part. He had flirted with the idea of bringing his recorder to accompany the minstrel who had been engaged to play at the banquet, but thought better of it. While Galen and Ralf knew he played, his uncle did not, and Rees saw no reason to make him aware of it. The minstrel played a love song or two in honor of the wedding, then switched to carols to honor the season. The absence of bawdy songs delayed the bedding until Rees and Ralf—neither of whom had slept the night before either—were hiding yawns behind their hands.

Eleanor finally got Edward's attention and signalled that they should get on with the evening, and the king rose, silencing the minstrel and the banqueters at the same time. "'Tis customary to gift the couple with more than blessings, though most usually that occurs in the morning after the consummation," he said. "However, I would like to make Sir Galen's future known now, for reasons best revealed in a few moments." He beckoned to one of his retainers, who brought him a scroll. Then, unexpectedly, he said, "Sir Rees de Bretagne, rise."

Startled, Rees rose, glancing at Galen and Menty, then, banishing his sleepiness, he fastened his attention on the king.

Edward held out the scroll. "We appoint you, in your own honors, Earl Connarc, and give into your service my knights Sir Galen Knauter and Sir Ralf FitzHugh. Your income will be decided by your duties to me, and your fief I will place in your hands later. Now we'd see this couple bedded. Then I'd have you join me for some talk while we await the morrow."

Rees was so surprised he was speechless. He was gratified by the wide smiles on the faces of the two men who had just been seconded to his service, by the gentle approval on Queen Eleanor's. He realized abruptly that he had not moved, left his place to approach the high table, bow to his liege lord, and accept the scroll.

The king signalled to the minstrel, who at last began the bawdy songs that preceded a bedding.

Rees was trying to absorb the fact that he was now an English earl, his rank identical to that of Gilbert de Clare, whom he would never have to serve again. He only hoped Galen wouldn't mind that Edward had chosen to make the announcement at this particular time.

Roger Mortimer, Earl Wigmore and castellan of Montgomery, in his capacity as Lord for the Northern March, also happened to be cousin to Prince Llewelyn. Mortimer was a small, lean man with restless eyes and a habit of never looking at anyone directly. He had come to Windsor to speak with King Edward, had found himself swept along to the wedding, and now that the couple had been put to bed, he was finally to have his chance to meet with Edward.

Edward had a table and chairs set up in his closet, and Mortimer was already there when the king came in with John Peckham and Rees de Bretagne, who had been an earl for about an hour.

Mortimer rose, and then they all sat, leaning forward on the table in the light of a single torch in a sconce on the wall.

"What have you to report?" the king asked.

Roger Mortimer looked at Rees. "How much loyalty do you bear Gilbert de Clare, my lord?" he asked.

Rees frowned.

John Peckham said, "Allow me to explain that there is a past of bad feeling between the man you previously served and Earl Wigmore."

Rees accepted that; there were often power struggles among the nobles. He realized with a start that he was now numbered firmly in that company. He answered Mortimer, "When de Clare was wounded in the Holy Land, my lord, I was not among those who went to his defense. Will that suffice?"

Mortimer gave a curt nod, then turned his attention to the king. "I have done as you asked, sire. I went to Ruthin and met with my cousin, the prince. He has no strength of arms. He and his lady wife live as if their realm can hold no dangers for them."

Edward's voice went low and hard. "*My* realm, earl. See that you forget that not."

Peckham made a soothing motion with one hand across the wood of the tabletop. Rees consciously kept his own eyes from narrowing. It was the first time he had seen his uncle show a flash of naked power; the menace it conveyed was chilling.

"I beg your pardon," Roger Mortimer said in a muted voice. "My thoughts were directed to Llewelyn's point of view."

"Cease that and direct them to your duty to me as a Marcher Lord," said the king. "I take it, then, that despite his obeisance to me, he still believes Wales is his."

Mortimer nodded. "Much of Wales believes it as well. 'Tis as if the fealty blew past them in the wind."

Peckham clasped his hands in front of him and made a small sound of distress.

The king ignored him. "How did Llewelyn respond to your offer of a pact?" he asked Wigmore.

"He was quite pleased," Mortimer answered. "He believes I will support him should any trouble resume."

Edward leaned forward, tensing. "And has he plans for any such trouble?"

"None," said Mortimer flatly. "I am in place to hear if he chooses to begin anything. You will hear noise of it if ever the intelligence reaches me."

The king nodded with a grunt of approval. "Return to Montgomery and be watchful," he said.

Mortimer rose, bowed, and left the closet.

The archbishop said quickly, "You see, sire, there is no treachery."

Rees bit back the urge to say, "Other than Wigmore's." He knew his uncle would not appreciate it, and he was uncertain why he was here.

"Not yet," Edward said. "My instinct is that we are not done with Wales." He looked at Rees. "And what think you, my lord earl?"

For a moment, Rees wasn't sure the king was speaking to him, and then he adjusted to the title. His next thought was that he was being mocked, but he put it aside. To Edward, he appeared to hesitate only momentarily. "I've fought only one battle with the Welsh," he said. "I think them brave men."

"I ask not for an assessment of their character," Edward said sharply. "Think you that we will be fighting them again ere long?"

Rees was about to say he had no notion, nor was he given to prophecy, but he changed his mind. "Shall we be giving them cause to seek to rebel?" he asked instead. He had hesitated minutely before the "we."

Edward noticed it, sat back in his chair, and studied his nephew. "My lord archbishop, leave us, if you will," he said.

Peckham rose at once and went out, closing the door quietly behind him.

For the space of a minute, the two men regarded one another steadily. At last, Edward said, "If there is aught I should know about your loyalties, best you tell it me now."

Rees was genuinely astonished. "You are my liege lord," he said. "You can have no doubts about my absolute obedience."

"Obedience is not the same as loyalty," said Edward. "Lacking the latter, I will accept the former." His voice went lower. "Do I lack the latter?"

Rees decided to be honest. "Not yet," he said, repeating Edward's earlier comment referring to Wales. "But I bestow not my trust blindly."

"de Clare said you were his finest knight," Edward said. "He argued with passion when I withdrew your service from him."

Rees said nothing.

"'Tis for that reason I have elevated you to the rank of earl," Edward went on. "I trust you will fight for me as you fought for him. What meant you that you defended him not?"

"I was not strategically placed to do so," said Rees. "I will do for you what I am charged to do. My oath holds my honor."

Edward nodded. "I shall see that I strategically place you where I require you, then. Keep yourself and your knights at the ready."

"Must we remain here?"

The question took the king, caught in the act of rising, by surprise, and he settled back into his chair. "You have no desire to remain at court?"

"Truly, none, Sire," Rees said, an infinitesimal pause before the title. "I'd see more of England. I'd no time to do so before leaving for the Holy Land." If there was any implied criticism in either the phrase or the request, it was so well disguised that Edward missed it. And the king could not bring himself to believe that Rees would openly challenge him. Even had the young man seemed inclined to do so, Edward thought he was more intelligent than that. In fact, Edward thought, Rees's mind might be one of the strongest things about him. The king wondered how his nephew had attained that particular strength and how he would use it.

"Stay in the South," ordered Edward. "And let your locations be known. I've a notion I may need you."

As he was returning to the dorter to pick up his belongings—an earl could not be expected to share accommodations with his knights—Rees turned the corner of a corridor and nearly collided with Princess Eleanor. At seventeen, she was lovely, with a robust health that at times seemed rugged and at other times fragile. She smiled at him and said, "My felicitations on your new title, Cousin Rees."

He was burdened with belongings whose bulk limited his ability to bow. "'Twas a surprise," he said. "I've not sought honors."

"Doubtless you shall grow accustomed to them," she said. "'Tis part of being a Plantagenet."

"But I am a de Bretagne," he protested.

Eleanor showed him a pair of dimples that appeared when she was being mischievous. "I think you'll find that any Plantagenet blood becomes all soon enough." Someone called to her and she spun, skirt whirling with the motion, and ran off.

He wondered if she were right. He did not feel like a Plantagenet, but neither did he feel overly much like a de Bretagne. In the quarters he had been given, a small room in one of the lesser towers, he looked out the slit window over the fields leading southeast from the castle, eager to be off. Then he pulled his recorder from the bundle of his belongings and set his fingers on its sound holes. He was a little amused to see that he was trembling. He had thought he had escaped unscathed from the interview with his uncle.

Chapter 6

Frowning, Briana dipped a cloth in the basin of herb-scented water, lightly wrung it out, folded it into a compress, and laid it on the Demoiselle's sweat-drenched forehead. Llewelyn's wife was in her thirteenth hour of hard labor.

Briana was not supposed to be attending her; Maud had forbidden it in the name of Bryn, and Briana had ignored the order just as she would have ignored Bryn's had it come directly from him.

It was the third month of the new war. Bryn and Griffith were gone to Prince Llewelyn's side again, and Meredith chafed that he had not been allowed to accompany them. Most of the able-bodied men of Flint had picked up axes, scythes, even wagon staves, and followed their lord to join up with the prince's forces. And, of course, once again Prince David had started it all.

David had gathered as many men as were willing to follow him, the hotheads, the angry, those who cared not if their homes were laid waste under the hooves of the English troops. His camp had about it the air of permanence that settles upon places under long occupation. He had emerged only briefly since the beginning of the Welsh resistance in King Henry's time, his movements governed by what Llewelyn contemptuously called "his strike and run away" view of the world. David's greatest skill was provocation; he failed utterly at responding to the provocation, and Llewelyn believed his younger brother recognized his inadequacy enough so that he was perfectly willing to let Llewelyn fight the battles he, David, had begun and then sidled away from.

So Llewelyn and the others had joined him. Llewelyn had hoped he could be with his wife when her time came, but it was a futile hope.

Llewelyn's babe was coming now, at Flint, where he had bade the Demoiselle go for friendship's sake, in the sweetness of a June day and in the shadow of a castle recently manned by a number of knights and soldiers sent by Edward to meet the increasing hostilities. There had been some battles, but they had been mostly to the south, so the Welsh could withdraw to Snowdonia if the opposition grew too heated. That seemed to suit the English, who could use the south to test and assess and learn. Edward was not in a hurry this time.

Briana went to soak another compress. Maud came into the chamber, her face drawn with anxiety. While she was angry that Briana had disobeyed the order to stay away, she was also grateful for the girl's presence. "The midwife we sent for will not be coming from Chester," she said.

"Why not?" Briana asked, distressed.

"The English have closed the border."

"Who best in the village can safely deliver a babe?" Briana changed the compress on the Demoiselle's brow.

The Demoiselle moaned, but bit her lips. Despite the length of the labor before it turned hard, despite the pain, she was still conscious, still listening. "No others than you," she said, her voice raspy and breaking. "The babe will come soon. I know it."

Maud shook her head. "Your grace, we must have women more skilled than I," she said. "Forgive me for denying you this. Briana will stay with you."

Briana looked at her, surprised, but certainly willing.

Maud turned and ran from the room again.

Briana sat down on a stool next to the bed and took the Demoiselle's hands, which immediately bit down on her own.

"No others," said the Demoiselle again. "Where is my lord husband? Why does he not come?"

"'Tis too great a risk," Briana said. "The English are too close. They lie in wait for him." Even as she said it, she had no idea how close they were.

Queen Eleanor had just risen from childbed of her fifth healthy daughter when word reached Westminster that the Welsh were once again in revolt against King Edward. The queen left the infant, christened Elizabeth, with the nurses and hurried to the hall, where her husband was sitting, hands fisted on the arms of his chair, listening to Edmund Mortimer. She arrived just as Mortimer was saying, "There appears to be no single Welsh army, Sire. There are a hundred Welsh armies, in a hundred different places. Men do not so much flock to Llewelyn's banner as to Llewelyn's cause. Every village is a hotbed of resistance."

Edward sat back in his chair, thinking, one of his hands unconsciously opening and refisting itself. He had put the rage aside and was trying to find a way to a strategy he might like to follow. Unlike many of his predecessors, Edward neither depended on nor consulted advisers. He had watched his father's advisers bring King Henry to the point of losing his kingdom; indeed, Simon de Montfort had been one of Henry's most valued advisers until the moment he rebelled against him. Edward kept his own counsel, made his own decisions, and he intended to continue doing it as long as he sat on the throne.

His gaze went distant as he thought about the problem of a nonconcentrated enemy, of a many-headed creature he could not slay with a single blow. Instinct told him that, no matter what Mortimer thought, if he could neutralize—or destroy— Llewelyn, victory would be easier. He tried to assess how much of that instinct was grounded in solid military strategy and how much was based in his rage at Llewelyn for breaking fealty.

After several minutes, he refocused his gaze on Edmund Mortimer. "Have you any intelligence as to Llewelyn's location? Is he in Snowdonia?"

"He is thought to be in Snowdonia, but he is said to be everywhere," Mortimer answered. "We know not where he truly is." He paused.

Edward knew that he was not finished. "Well?"

"We do know where he is likely to be come June," Mortimer said. "Llewelyn's wife is due to deliver their babe at that time. He wishes to be with her."

"Is she at Ruthin?" Edward asked.

Mortimer shook his head. "He feared she would be alone at Ruthin. We know he took her to Flint, to the manor."

Edward was momentarily startled at the audacity of the man, to place the Demoiselle in the sway of the only castle Master James had as yet completed for England on Welsh soil. He almost admired the gesture, but he did not think it was deliberate. Llewelyn might be defiant, but Edward did not believe he would use the Demoiselle in his tactics. Llewelyn was not nearly as calculating as Edward himself.

"What steps has your father taken to subdue the part of the Welsh army he finds around Montgomery?" the king asked.

Mortimer gave an answer involving preparations and the securing of property.

The king cut the answer off. "Fine. Return to Montgomery and increase the secure area outward from there. Accept into service any Welshmen who express loyalty to the crown, but give them no tasks that the war depends on. Above all, trust them not." He waved his hand to indicate dismissal, and when Mortimer had gone, turned to Eleanor. "Has Rees informed you of his travels, as I requested?" he asked.

"Aye," answered Eleanor. "I can get a messenger to him in two days."

"Get him here," said Edward. "I can use him in Wales."

He watched her leave the room, then rose and walked to the slit window that overlooked the garden outside the walls. The flowers were still in bud, but beginning to show colors in slits as the green pods opened. They would be in their second, magnificent bloom by June, but he did not intend to be here to see them. In June he would be at Flint Castle, waiting for Llewelyn.

Briana looked up from the Demoiselle's tormented face as Maud came into the room with Ethel, one of the older village women. She was relieved to see Ethel's plump, practical face and tried to disengage her hands from the Demoiselle's to step away from the bed. The Demoiselle did not release her, so Briana could not move.

"Where is he?" the Demoiselle asked anxiously. "He said he would be with me. Where is he?"

Briana knew she meant Prince Llewelyn, but did not know what to reply.

"Saints, my lady," Ethel said, "you're surely not waiting for him." She bent at the foot of the bed to turn back the covers and examine the princess.

Maud pried Briana's hands out of the Demoiselle's. "Briana, go to the herbary and get the thyme, the orris root, and the onion. Go on."

Briana hurried from the solar and down the steps, along the corridor to the kitchens, and through them to the herbary. It was a small room almost entirely taken up by a table and lined with pigeonholes, each containing a different set of dried leaves, seeds, flowers, or roots. She took some of the small cloth sacks that lay on the table, located each of the substances her aunt had requested, filled a sack with it and pulled the drawstrings taut. She had never been permitted to attend a birth before, but she was thirteen now, and she would have to learn. She picked up the three sacks and went back through the kitchens in the direction of the solar.

There were men just entering the corridor from the front door. For one moment, she thought it would be her father, Griffith, and Prince Llewelyn, and she started forward, smiling broadly. Then her step faltered, for she saw the tallest man had bright golden hair and, as he turned to face her, cold blue eyes. Four years had passed since last she saw him, but she knew him. She stopped walking; she did not curtsey.

King Edward remembered the child of legend. Her previous prettiness was trembling on the edge of true beauty. As a man who appreciated beauty, he admired what she would shortly become, but he refused to be distracted by it. "Where is Prince Llewelyn?" he asked.

Briana shook her head. "I've no knowledge of that," she said. "He has not come here, nor will he." She prayed silently that she was right.

Edward signaled the men with him to spread out through the lower floor of the manor. "The Demoiselle?" he asked Briana.

"Upstairs, in childbed," she said, inclining her head toward the steps. She was about to ask if he expected to call upon her, but he fixed her with a piercing stare, and the words sank back into her throat. This wasn't a man she could speak freely to or defy, as she did her father; this man would stand for none of that. She had no idea what penalties might be involved, what anger might be invoked, should she behave as she normally did, and she was quite unwilling to find out.

The king took a step backwards and waved her past him toward the stairs.

She might not have gone, but she knew Maud and Ethel needed the herbs, so she edged past the king and darted up the steps.

The men returned and reported that the manor contained only women servants, and one boy, and all of them denied any knowledge of where the Lord Bryn was, let alone Prince Llewelyn. "We will wait," said King Edward. "He may yet present himself." They found seats in the hall and settled down, sending one of the servingwomen for beer.

Briana let herself back into the solar which was now the Demoiselle's birthing chamber.

"We heard men's voices," Maud said.

"Has he come?" asked the Demoiselle, overlapping.

"'Tis the English king," said Briana. "Here are the herbs."

Maud and Ethel were astounded by the announcement, but the Demoiselle was crushed. "He will never come to me now," she said, her voice a low moan tightened with pain. "He must not. He must not."

Maud wanted to tell Briana to leave, but the presence of the king vastly complicated matters. She hoped that he would leave before the actual birth, but she feared he would not. She was right.

The Demoiselle gave birth to a daughter during the second day of her hard labor. Maud washed the tiny girl, wrapped her in linen, and gave her into Briana's arms as Ethel mixed a restorative draught for the exhausted new mother. The Demoiselle raised herself onto an elbow, tried to focus her eyes on the bundle Briana was holding and said, "Call—her—Gwenllian. For Wales' sake."

"Lie back," said Maud, taking her gently by the shoulders to push her back down. "Briana, take the babe to the church so Father Ciaran can baptize her."

"I'll go at once," said Briana. She cradled the new baby against her, overwhelmed by the strength of the protective impulse that rose over her. She had never held a newborn before. She had been only a year old when Meredith was born. This child, so small, so perfectly beautiful, even with her head still misshapen from birth, touched her heart in a completely unexpected way. "I shall protect you, Gwenllian," she whispered to the baby. She stepped very carefully on the stairs, conscious of the precious burden she was carrying. One of the king's men stopped her when she got to the front door of the manor house. She was not afraid of the soldier the way she had been afraid of Edward. "You dare not stop me," she said hotly to the soldier. "The child must be christened. If she should die unsaved and unshriven, you will burn for it."

The threat was a real one. The church had declared that those who were present when a new soul entered the world were responsible for seeing it brought into the church as well. The man stepped aside, and Briana held the child closer to her and hurried to St. Maedoc's.

Father Ciaran had been praying fervently for peace since the war began, three months earlier. He had had news from other areas of the country that indicated the Welsh clergy were being replaced by English priests, leaving the people without their singularly Celtic brand of religion. He had not had any word as to the fate of non-Welsh clergy, like himself, but he was fearful that he might be relieved of his place here, should the attention of Canterbury be drawn to him by the Marcher lords.

He was on his knees in the church when Briana came in, holding a small bundle that began to make mewling sounds as she brought it nearer. The priest rose and walked to meet her.

"'Tis a girl, Father," Briana said. "She is to be christened Gwenllian."

"Are you godmother, then?" Father Ciaran asked, going to the altar for the chrism and the water.

That had not occurred to Briana, but she felt a frisson of delight. "I know not," she said honestly, "but the Demoiselle gave her into my hands to bring her here."

"That will suffice," said the priest. "Come here, child, close to the altar."

Briana took several steps in his direction, looking down and placing her feet carefully in order to give the newborn as smooth a ride as possible. She glanced up at the altar to see how close she was and stopped walking, halted by the expression on Father Ciaran's open face. The priest was staring past her, over her shoulder, at the doorway of the church. His hands, holding the vial of chrism, had stopped moving, caught in the act of beginning to draw out the stopper.

Briana turned slowly, uncertain what she would see.

The opening was blocked by the shoulders of a tall man, silhouetted against the exterior light. The man bent his head to pass through the doorway. He was, Briana knew, too tall to be Prince Llewelyn, and, having seen him lately in the hall, she recognized him immediately.

The King of England stepped into St. Maedoc's, unescorted, the sword at his side sheathed, but his hand resting on the hilt.

Fear rushed over Briana. She immediately thought he had come to kill the baby. She could not have said what force radiated from him that prompted that thought. She would not have imputed such a horrible thing to any other man she had ever met. It seemed absurd to think that a man might kill a baby, and yet somehow she believed this man capable of it.

Father Ciaran made a late, awkward half-bow.

Briana could not move.

King Edward walked up to her, bent and used one long finger to move aside the blanket in which the baby was swaddled, exposing a bright red-pink cheek. "Boy or girl?" he asked.

When no answer was immediately forthcoming, his blue eyes swung from the baby's face to Briana's, compelling a reply.

"Girl," she whispered.

The eyes darkened. "Show me," Edward commanded.

Briana could not open the blanket without setting the child down, so she had to force herself to take another several steps to the altar itself and carefully deposit the baby on the altar, trying not to think that altars were sacrificial as well as sacramental. She unswaddled the tiny body, wondering if he would only kill a boy, if he would let the girl live. Her hands shook.

The king grunted approval at the baby's sex, or perhaps that she had told him the truth, and looked at Father Ciaran as Briana wrapped the child again. "Proceed with the christening," he said.

The priest opened the chrism, added two drops to the bowl of water already on the altar, and began the ritual. Briana had to remind him of the baby's name, for Edward's presence had unnerved him as well.

The king stood silently, watching as the baby was named Gwenllian and received into the body of the church, but when Father Ciaran asked if Briana were willing to care for the child's physical and spiritual health in absence of her parents, he spoke before she could. "I shall undertake the responsibility for this child, Father. Lay the charge upon me, not upon the girl."

Briana felt as if he'd slapped her, but she couldn't, somehow, open her mouth to dispute with him. Instead, she heard her mind crying, "Nay, this was to be *my* duty," but she stood still and wordless, holding the baby tightly as Father Ciaran obediently gave her body and soul into the guardianship of a man who could in no way wish her well. She felt as if she were failing the Demoiselle, but she seemed unable to do anything about it. This man's power was a different kind from any she had encountered before—naked, self-sustaining, impervious to any other will or concerns.

She fought with her fear; she had an obligation to Prince Llewelyn, whom her father and older brother fought beside and for. What would they think of her if she disappointed everyone now? How could she face them if she were a coward in the light of their bravery? She gathered every bit of courage she could muster while still in the aura of this man's singular hardness, and while he stood so close beside her, and said, "The Demoiselle wants me to care for her daughter."

"The Demoiselle," said Edward expressionlessly, "is dead."

Father Ciaran gasped audibly.

Briana clutched convulsively at the bundle which was the child in her arms, and Gwenllian began to cry. Briana could neither speak nor weep. He had killed Prince Llewelyn's wife, rather than the prince's child. She did not dare to accuse him of it, but she was certain beyond doubt that he must have done it.

"I must go to her, poor lady," the priest said, restoppering the vial of chrism. "She must be blessed on her way."

Still expressionless, Edward stepped aside to let Father Ciaran get past, his even stare unwaveringly fastened on Briana's face. She hushed and gently rocked the crying child, her heartbeat racing, wishing there were someone—anyone—else in the church besides her and the king. Gwenllian fussed a moment or two longer, then quieted.

Edward said, "Give me the babe, lady."

Briana had not believed she could be more horrified than she already was, but the toneless, unarguable command made her shake with fear for the baby. Unconsciously, she took a step backward and whispered, "Don't kill her."

The words were barely audible, but he heard them and frowned thunderously. "Lady, you have lessons to learn. Had I wanted her dead, I should have dispatched her before I took responsibility for her life." He paused and waited, while she stared at him, wide-eyed. When she did not speak, his voice dropped to a growl. "You may beg my pardon for the accusation."

Briana felt a flush rise in her face and made herself say, "I—am sorry for—" She was stuttering, and her voice fell away. She knew he would think her a coward, but she didn't desire his good opinion, only that he go away and leave her alone. "—having thought—" She was fighting for words that would not make him angrier. "—you ignoble," she finished.

Had she failed to struggle so strenuously against her obvious fear of him—an attitude he prized greatly—and perhaps had she not been so pretty, he might have tormented her further. Instead, he inclined his head briefly to acknowledge what she had said, then took a step forward, bent, and took Gwenllian out of her hands.

Briana kept herself from either backing away from him again or clutching at the infant to keep hold of her. "What—what will you do with her?" she asked.

He ignored the question. "Come," he said. He turned and went out the church door. Briana, simultaneously relieved at not having to lose sight of the child and apprehensive over why he should want her with him, obediently followed him out the door. He had stopped short on the church steps; so did she. For a moment she thought that everyone in the world was waiting outside St. Maedoc.

A group of English soldiers circled the steps at a small distance away, creating a clear area. The inhabitants of the village of Flint—everyone who had not gone to war, the elderly men and women, the women whose men had gone to fight, the children—were crowed behind them.

Briefly, the king thought they were there because of him, that they had come to observe his progress, a tradition which had existed since Henry II created it to add spice to the process of moving from palace to palace as the residences grew dirty from occupancy. Then his sharp ears heard the low murmuring. They were saying Briana's name, very softly, with a note of inquiry, of apprehension.

He remembered the legend.

He raised his voice so that the soldiers could hear him without difficulty. "We return to the manor. Clear the path."

The soldiers took several steps in the direction of Flint Manor, but the people parted before them, melting off the road as if they were grain, bowing in the wind.

"They are an obedient lot," Edward said to Briana.

In front of the people who loved and honored her, Briana felt strength flowing back into her. "My people are not stupid, Sire," she said firmly.

He noticed that she used an honorific of address for him for the first time, as if the presence of others had buoyed her up. He was also keenly aware that she had called them *her* people. They were nearing the manor steps, where Maud waited, her eyes red from weeping, so he did not press Briana on the question of whose people they were.

Maud dropped a rigid-backed curtsey to the king, her eyes sliding to the child in his arms.

"This girl is in your charge?" Edward asked her, nodding toward Briana.

"Aye, Sire," Maud said steadily. "I am her aunt, the Lady Maud, and I care for her well-being until her father returns."

Father Ciaran chose that moment to emerge from the manor, realized he had interrupted a conversation between the king and Maud, and stumbled to the side to get out of the doorway.

Edward did not need to ask where Briana's father might be returning from. He looked at Father Ciaran. "Priest," he said.

Father Ciaran, still grasping the vial of chrism, answered, "Aye, Sire?"

"I charge you a duty," said the king. "Should the lord of Flint fail to return from this beknighted rebellion, I wish to be informed of it. In return, I will instruct Archbishop Peckham to not relieve you of your post here, as he has so many others of the Welsh clergy. Should you fail in your duty to me, you will be considered a traitor to the crown and unfit to minister to my people." He might have emphasized the "my" a bit more than was strictly necessary.

"Aye, Sire," said the priest, confused, but pleased at the reassurance that he would be able to remain at Flint.

Edward looked back at Maud. "I'd speak with you and the Lady of Flint private." He called to one of his soldiers and handed the surprised man the baby. "Take her to the castle," he ordered.

Briana wanted to reach out and take Gwenllian back, but she did not dare. "She'll need a wet-nurse," she said to the soldier as he turned away. He did not look in her direction, and she did not know if he had heard her.

Maud had already turned to reenter the house, and Briana took a handful of skirt and darted up the steps past the king. The servants had been outside on the road, so the hall was deserted. Maud took several steps into the empty room, then turned and stood still, wary. Briana took a stand beside her aunt, also apprehensive, unable to think of anything except that Gwenllian was gone—and so was the Demoiselle.

Edward stood at the doorway of the hall, thumbs hooked into his swordbelt and looked at the plain woman, the lovely girl. He studied them, unreadable, until Briana took one defensive step nearer to her aunt, and then he addressed himself to Maud. "Lady, I have a war to pursue and a country to rule. I can wait at Flint no longer for Llewelyn to arrive. When you see the traitor, or send him a message about his wife, be kind enough to see that he also receives *this* information: that I have assumed custody of his daughter, and I intend to keep her. And also that I intend to ensure he does not live through this war he started."

"Prince Llewelyn did not start this war!" Briana cried, unnerved by the flatness of Edward's condemnation of the prince her family served.

Edward didn't realize he'd grasped his sword hilt as he snapped, "I'll have no defiance, lady! Do you dare to accuse me again?"

She gasped at the sudden threat and shied back from him as Maud said, "Nay, Sire, please!" and put her arm across Briana's shoulders. "She is distraught at the death of the Demoiselle!" She did not add, "And the abduction of the babe."

Edward realized that he had almost drawn sword on two women. His hand dropped away from the weapon, and he forced himself to calm. "Then tell me, Lady Maud, if Llewelyn did not begin this war, and if I did not begin it, who began it? The King of France, perchance?"

Briana looked up at Maud. The older woman did not know how to respond. Briana saw her confusion and hesitation, looked squarely at the king who so frightened her, and said, "Prince David begins the wars. Prince Llewelyn only ends them."

Edward believed her instantly. It was a bit of intelligence that his Marcher lords had never supplied him, and yet it made a great deal of sense. It also changed nothing. His voice gentled. "Tell Llewelyn that this time I shall end the war," he said. He turned and left the manor.

Out of sheer relief, Briana felt tears welling up. At that very moment, an unfamiliar ache blossomed in Briana's middle, striking hard enough to cause her to gasp. She thought at once that she might be being punished for her failure to protect Gwenllian. She tried to ignore the ache, but it grew into a hard cramp, and she had to sit down on one of the benches.

Maud was startled. "Briana? What does?" she demanded.

Bewildered, her eyes still tear-dewed, Briana looked up. "Something—hurts. I don't understand."

Maud knelt beside Briana, gently touching her sides and belly. "Of all times," she said. "Your flux has arrived. This is normal, child. You are becoming a woman."

Briana swallowed hard.

"Perhaps it is the Demoiselle's gift to you," Maud said briskly. "Come up. Help me wash her. Then I'll undertake to explain what you need to know."

They climbed to the solar in silence, and there the two of them gently washed the Demoiselle clean of the lingering stains of life. Then Maud took a fresh smock from a chest at the foot of the bed. They dressed her, and Briana, still wincing when she moved, brushed the tangled golden hair until it lay neatly around the Demoiselle's face.

Once the English had departed, Briana fled the manor for an inlet by the estuary, where she could not be seen from the castle, and where she sometimes ran when she was sad. The nearness of the king and his soldiers was too much for her, coupled with the death of the Demoiselle and the loss of Gwenllian. She had no idea how long she'd been by the shore, seeking to be soothed by the soft rhythm of the small waves when she was abruptly aware of the feeling of being watched. She looked around, but saw no one else on the pebbly beach. She raised her gaze up the steep embankment and encountered the silhouette of a man against the brightness of the sky. She feared it was King Edward, and something in her rebelled at the thought that he would see how much despair he had caused her. She got to her feet, slowed by the weight of her sodden dress. The man started down the cliffpath toward her, moving quickly. She stood where she was and braced for his approach, but as he neared, she recognized him. It was Owen Glyn.

As soon as she knew who he was, she hurried to meet him. When she was within speaking distance, she asked, "Is Prince Llewelyn here, too?"

"Nay," said Owen. "He sent me to try to organize another troop in this area. He is hopeful to provoke resistance in the counties the English think they have subdued. I've hid these two days since I arrived here so as not to encounter the English. What does the king at Flint?"

Her efforts to detach from her feelings vanished instantly. "'Twas a horror!" she cried. "He took the babe, and the Demoiselle is dead!"

Owen frowned. "Took the babe?" he repeated. "Mean you he cut it from her?"

Briana was so horrified by the question that for several breaths she could not respond. Then she asked, "Do people *do* such things?"

"I'd not doubt it of this king," Owen said grimly. "I take it he did not, then?"

Briana shook her head. "He took her with him. I know not where."

"Why did Edward come here?"

"He was waiting for Prince Llewelyn to come to the princess. But the prince stayed away." Briana's voice rang with regret for the failure of the two to meet, but it was colored by relief that the prince was still free.

"Are you well?" Owen asked her.

She knew he asked cautiously; they did not know each other very well, and he had found her sprawled on the beach. "Well enough," she said. She did not want him to think her uncontrolled or uncontrollable. "How came you to find me here?"

"I followed you from the manor. Come. I'll see you safe home." He held out his hand to her.

Briana put her hand in his without thinking about it, because she was so shaken by the words "safe home" that she nearly stopped breathing. The King of England had proved to her that home was not safe, and she feared it might never be safe again. She made herself move with him toward the cliff. She was surprised that her surroundings did not look any different. The world had changed, and she sensed it was not yet done with changing.

Westminster—August 1282 A.D.

Because the war was briefly in abeyance, Rees took Galen and Ralf and returned to Westminster to seek permission to marry. He was twenty-two, and he wanted a fief of his own, a place to build the kind of home he remembered from Brittany— with the exception that he would be a more loving father than John de Bretagne had ever been to him. Menty was well and robustly pregnant, a state over which Galen showed the kind of pride he had previously applied regularly only to his swordplay.

"'Tis swordplay of a sort," Ralf pointed out as the three of them rode toward the stables at Westminster, making the first of what would be numerous connections between swords of metal and swords of flesh. Galen had ridden on ahead to alert the grooms of their unexpected arrival, so the comment was for Rees's ears alone.

"A bit gentler, mayhap," Rees said with a grin.

"Not the way Galen does it," said Ralf. "When first he wed, I feared for Menty."

"You've too tender a heart," Rees said. "Wives are given strength to withstand the strength of their husbands."

"Think you they might enjoy it, the wives?"

"Doubtless some do," Rees acknowledged, "because husbands often boast of it. And of course, men never exaggerate their prowess."

Galen came out of the stables carrying the saddlebags containing his bundle, and he and Ralf, who lifted his own saddlebags from his gelding, headed for the small dorter in one of the outbuildings. Rees watched them go with regret that he could not join them. He gathered his own saddlebags before the groom could take them from the saddle, and walked quickly from the stableyard to the palace itself.

The guards did not challenge him, making him wonder whether he had been recognized or whether Edward was so confident that no one would ever try to assassinate him that his security was lax. The latter reason did not sound at all like Edward, but Rees was somehow uncomfortable at the thought of the former reason. Yet if he had not been an earl, he could never have sued for Margaret of Norwich's hand.

Earls of England did not want for funds, since they all received stipends from the treasury. All but Rees had been given fiefs to rule in the king's name and as his steward; Rees had been given only the service of ten knights. Ten more, who knew of his prowess in the Holy Land, swore to him in the weeks following his elevation. The king had laid no lands upon him, no manor, not even a forest. So Rees decided that, if he wanted a home of his own, people whose quiet daily lives he could affect, even make better, he would have to marry it.

He found his potential bride by, one night, speaking seriously to the Earl of Norwich in the hills around Swansea, after a very small skirmish that took place in an ill-chosen, heavily wooded dale. The earl was one of the land-richest men in England. Rees guessed he was a good overlord, for Edward liked his peaceful lands administered well.

His daughter Margaret was scarcely fourteen years old. Her age did not matter, nor were her looks or personal attributes relevant. The germane issue was her marriage portion. She brought two substantial manors and a town, along with their income from the crown treasury, and as the earl's only heir, she would, at his death—provided the king approved—also be given the care of Norwich and its allied lands.

Rees felt the hunger for lands and peoples to care for sweep over him, so he waited for a lull in the war and then he sought out the king at Westminster to ask for approval of the betrothal.

Galen and Ralf were pleased that Rees seemed to have found a path for his future. When Rees went to his meeting with the king, his two knights ventured out to the practice field near the stables to do a little sparring.

Sparring was a slow dance of the movements which in combat were much quickened. "Speed is crucial," Rees told them over and over again. "And speed is destroyed by thought. Instinct is your only guide on the battlefield, so the movements must be part of you before an enemy confronts you. Repetition is the key to training your instinct."

"Only do it," Galen paraphrased. "Then do it again. And after that, do it more." Rees's knights trained constantly, as did Rees. Practicing the dance of defense and death was something they all anticipated with relish. It was generally accepted that one of the fastest ways to improve was to fight against a superior opponent, and Rees was an adept.

His knights had determined not to speak of the changes wrought in the Holy Land after his wound. They simply followed him.

They had gotten only a third of the way through the hour-long pattern when Rees came to find them, his face dark and rage radiating out of him with enough power to startle them, though they knew instinctively that it was not directed at them. They stopped sparring instantly, and Ralf ventured, "What's amiss?"

"We are leaving this place to return to Wales," Rees said, biting off the words. "I care not if ever I return here. Galen, get the saddlebags. Ralf, come with me. We need the horses."

Galen asked no questions, only turned and ran. He'd have to go to Westminster Palace for Rees's things, as well as to the knights' dorter for his own and Ralf's, and he knew from Rees's tone and expression that delay of any kind would be insupportable.

Ralf hurried to match Rees's stride toward the stables. In the shade of one of the huge elms which lined the drive between the stable complex and the palace, Rees stopped so suddenly that Ralf nearly crashed into him. Ralf was stunned to hear Rees let loose a string of oaths, clenching his fists as if to smash or crush something, then even more astonished as the anger seemed to drain out of the older man's body, his shoulders slumped.

Ralf laid a hand on his arm, hoping it was not an intrusion. "Did the king disapprove the match?"

Rees laughed humorlessly. "Oh, aye, he did that."

Ralf sensed the question and answer were tangential to the issue which had caused Rees such rage, and he knew he dared not ask further.

Rees straightened, drawing in a deep breath and letting it back out slowly, a ritual of calming Ralf had seen him use on other occasions. "I'll not speak of it," he said. "You may tell Galen and the others they are never to ask me. My uncle has given me charge of his army in North Wales and charged me with the elimination of Prince Llewelyn's force. We get our troop in Swansea and ride north to Conway."

"Surely," said Ralf hesitantly, "that is grounds for pride."

Rees shot him a look which made him wish he had not spoken. "And Ralf," Rees added, "pass this word also. I have ceased from this day to call myself de Bretagne. I am to be known as Plantagenet. Rees of Plantagenet, Earl Connarc."

Ralf couldn't stop the sigh that hissed out of him. "He's taken your name," he said. He expected Rees to turn on him for that impertinence, though he had not meant it to be such.

Rees surprised him yet again. "'Twas not his to take," he said, "nor was it mine to surrender. Come." He strode out again toward the stables, not with any of the anger of his previous strides, but with something akin to a determined resignation.

Ralf followed, more slowly this time, wondering even more curiously what had happened between Rees and the king.

By the time the horses were saddled, Galen had appeared juggling all three sets of saddlebags. His inquiring gaze at Ralf received no more than a shake of the head. He took it to mean that Rees was angry at the breaking of the match, and he did not ask further.

Rees's anger was, however, far less at the destroyed hope of lands and wife than at the information Edward had revealed to him with what Rees could only regard as an unholy relish.

Rees had dressed impeccably for the interview in a deep gray supertunic. He was shown to the king's closet, where Edward awaited him, seated, crownless, but hard-faced. The petition Rees had sent asking for Margaret's hand lay on the table in front of the king. A quick glance from Rees revealed that Edward had not added his seal to it, nor was there a seal in evidence on the wooden planks. Rees tensed.

"I have received your petition," Edward said unnecessarily.

Rees said nothing and concentrated on not clenching his fists.

"The match with Norwich pleases me not," the king went on. He paused to see if Rees would ask why, but when the question was not immediately forthcoming, he did not wait for it. "The line of Norwich is an ancient one. I choose not to have it polluted."

Stunned at those words, Rees fought hard not to react. All he could think was that Edward had somehow learned of his time in Antioch with Abraham ben Zeniuta, because Norwich gave place to one of the largest Jewish communities in England, and Edward's hatred for Jews was well-known. But, on high alert, his reason told him that, had that been the case, Edward would likely have said "*further* polluted," and he had not.

The king rose to his feet. "I had great hopes that you might grow to exhibit some of your father's more admirable qualities, but 'tis a regret that you have not done so."

Rees frowned. "'Twas not my thought that you admired my father overmuch."

Edward smiled unpleasantly and blew Rees's world to pieces. "I admire not John de Bretagne," he said, "but I do not refer to him. John de Bretagne was not your father. You were sown on my unfortunate sister by a Norseman from the embassy of King Hakon."

Anger swept over Rees. "My mother would never have whored—" he began.

Edward cut him off. "Nor did she. You are a child of rape, nephew, by a brute of a man, some of whose qualities I would hope you might have inherited."

He might have said more, but Rees did not hear him. The disaffection John de Bretagne had shown toward him made some sense now, as did his mother's deathbed demand. The gaze he turned on Edward made the king stop speaking, startled.

"The name," he said. "What was the man's name?"

Edward brought back his equanimity. "Your father's name was Bjorn Magnussen," he said.

"What did you to him?" Rees asked. "How did he pay for his crime?"

Edward laughed once, shortly. "We sent him back to his king," he said. "He was an ambassador and, royal or not, she was only a woman."

Before he realized he was going to do it, Rees took one stride toward his liege lord. Edward, though taken by surprise, fisted his hand and struck his nephew a blow that knocked the younger man to the stone floor.

Rees realized what he had done, shook his head to clear it, and got to his feet, but he did not apologize. Instead, he asked coldly, "Have you aught more to tell me?"

Edward was furious at having been threatened, but not so furious that he would destroy someone who could be valuable to him. "Nay," he said. "Get you gone to Conway, in North Wales. Find Llewelyn precipitate and dispatch him. Then I will let you know how I intend to use you in future!"

Rees spun and left the closet.

Conway, North Wales—September 1282

The castle at Conway was older than Edward, though Master James had plans to build it larger, improve on its gatehouse, make the living quarters more livable, and heighten the walls to make it more nearly impregnable. Like Flint, it stood near the estuary of a river, in this case the one which had given the castle and one of the nearby towns their name. Master James had surveyed it, found its location a fine one, and had only begun drawing up his plans when Edward sent Rees into the field of the North with orders to find Llewelyn "precipitate." So Rees brought his troops to the rundown castle, which was the only place in North Wales big enough to shelter them all in semi-security, in reluctant obedience to the king's command.

Rees's troop—knights, foot soldiers, and the small army of support personnel and camp followers—followed him into the baileys and behind the walls. Cooks, grooms, armorers, physicians, wagonmasters, smiths, the men afoot, and the inevitable whores soon had the baileys alive with humanity as Rees and his knights took over the towers and used the sheds to stable their horses.

As twilight fell, Rees decided to walk the walls, looking for vulnerable areas, seeing if pickets were placed correctly, simply circumnavigating the fortress from which Edward had directed him to seek to engage the enemy. He strode up the steps of the tower he'd dropped his bedding in, without a torch to draw fire, should the Welsh have arrows, then slowed on the uneven paving of the walkway behind the merlons.

Conway had eight major towers, set into a formation that curved along the hilltop on which it had been built, and the tower from which Rees began his circuit was highest on the hill and furthest inland from the sea. The dark water stretched northward from the hills which grew gradually lower as they neared the beach.

Rees's instincts told him the quiet night was likely to remain so. The Welsh would not strike at the walls, especially as they no longer had access to any forges to make arrowheads and spearpoints. They would wait until he brought his men out.

He had made half the circuit and was near the center of the seaward rampart when he paused. He wondered what he might have been able to do as castellan of the manors which would have come to him as part of Margaret of Norwich's dower portion, then carved those tempting tendrils out of himself. That door was closed with the revelation Edward had given him of his heritage. His bastardy had come as quite an unpleasant surprise, for he had been confident of his identity, his forebears, his place in the world, his probable destiny should he survive to his thirties.

He leaned on the battlements, gazing out over the shore to the swells of the calm water on which faint reflections of distant starlight appeared and disappeared with sporadic regularity. It was strangely disconcerting to have reached the age of twenty-two only to discover that he did not know whose son he was. As it was a dilemma the like of which he had not encountered before, he fell back on the processes of thought that he had learned from Abraham ben Zeniuta and began to analyze what difference it made. That Rees had been taught the art of reasoning by a Jew in Antioch would have come as a shock to all who knew him. His uncle would, of course, have been outraged. For that reason alone, Rees treasured the secret.

John de Bretagne had not been a loving or concerned husband or father; it used to bewilder and hurt him. Now he understood it. The understanding did not reduce the pain, but it banished the confusion. He wondered if he would behave in the same way should a wife give him a child he knew not to be his own, and then he laughed wryly. Edward would not let him wed until Edward had use for it. Just now, his uncle needed a fighter, not a lord of the manor. So Rees would have to put aside his hopes until the war was won.

And his being a bastard made no difference at all to his ability to fight. It didn't matter whose seed had joined his mother's to create him; that was done. He was a separate being, and whatever he was, he had been it before he knew, and he was the same now. He found that comforting.

He stood in the darkness a few minutes longer, then went down into the tower to find Thomas Newby, his provisioner.

They rode out for two days without drawing Llewelyn out of Snowdonia. The first day they went west, where the town of Conway lay in a valley between some rolling hills characteristic of the area, ringed with woods which led southward toward the fastness of Snowdon.

The woods had been cleared from a number of fields for grazing, and Rees led his troops through these fields, even if they had to disturb herds of cattle or flocks of sheep to make their progress. He was giving the Welsh every opportunity to come at him, and his intelligence told him they had spies in the area. But they did not attack.

After the second foray, Rees sat with Galen and Ralf at dinner in a lower room of one of Conway's towers. Without a table, they sat on the floor as if at camp and passed around a flagon of wine, drinking from it without troubling themselves for the utility of mugs.

"How think you it goes with Llewelyn that he will not come and meet us?" Galen asked, ripping at a lightly cooked haunch of beef and wiping grease from his beard with his fingers.

Rees ate some of his own beef with quiet fastidiousness, not wanting to appear to be correcting Galen's lack of manners. He wondered offhandedly if Menty would have any effect on the way Galen attacked food, then dismissed the speculation. "I fancy he does not want to fight us on the ground to the west," he said. "We have other directions to try."

"If he knows the ground 'round here well," Ralf said after a swallow of wine, "mayhap we should let him choose his place."

"Unwise," began Galen, but he inhaled as he said it, choked on a stray piece of meat, and began to cough. Rees took the flagon out of Ralf's hands so that Ralf was free to pound Galen on the back until he could breathe again.

Rees didn't want to wait for Galen to regain the capacity for speech, just handed him the flagon and said, "Were we in the Holy Land, I'd not let an enemy choose the ground, but I am confident we will prevail here. With the Marcher armies, we have the numbers on the Welsh. We have need of the battles—Llewelyn must be conquered quick, or Wales will be destroyed. If his choosing where we meet him will begin it, then I'd have him choose."

"You are eager to fight?" Ralf asked.

Rees shook his head, one short, decisive gesture. "I am eager to be done with fighting," he said, "but the only way to be done is to begin."

Chapter 7

Flint—November 1282 A.D.

Briana was wrapped in a cloak against the cold that crept into even the most protected rooms of the manor. She sat now on a bench in front of the hearth in the solar, practicing her dulcimer. Had she been further from the fire, her hands might have been too cold to grasp the hammers. In the last several months, ever since her father and elder brother marched off to join Llewelyn, she had spent a great deal of time practicing her music. She used the songs Ine had taught her to keep at bay the fear that she might never see them again.

Meredith, who at twelve was turning into a fair hand with a sword and who was frustrated that he had to remain in Flint with the women and old men, was sitting across the solar, in the chill of the window seat. He'd long since dropped the slate on which he was supposed to be practicing his letters and was staring moodily out into the gray afternoon, one leg drawn up, bouncing restlessly.

Briana looked over at him several times, but said nothing. When he got into these moods, he would reject any suggestions she might make. She sighed and concentrated on a complex passage in her melody. She was only a year older than he was, but sometimes she felt like his mother.

She had reached a particularly fast part of the song when Meredith leaped up, staring out the window, then turned, almost tripping over the slate, and ran from the room, ignoring Briana's startled, "Meredith?" He was gone from the solar before he heard her.

Briana set the dulcimer on the bench and, carrying the hammers, went to the window to see if she could tell what had made him bolt out. The solar overlooked the road from the church, and there were some townspeople moving along it. For a moment she frowned, wondering what Meredith had seen, and then she realized that the people from the village were all hurrying toward the churchyard. Three men emerged from that low-walled area, one of them Father Ciaran.

She recognized the other two, drew in a sharp breath, and was momentarily unable to move. Then she breathed out in a whoosh, threw down the hammers, gathered handfuls of skirt, and ran out of the solar in Meredith's wake.

Unwilling to take horses the army might need, Bryn and Griffith had walked from Snowdonia in thirteen days, slowed by Griffith's recovery from a wound sustained at Dinas Bran, and the need to carefully avoid any English patrols. They ate food purloined at night from the storehouses at farms and small holdings they passed. They were footsore and weary by the time they reached Flint, but they were so pleased to be home they ignored their aches. Griffith's wound was paining him as well, though he had been careful not to complain of it.

Bryn saw Meredith running down the road toward him and had barely time to call Griffith's attention to his younger brother's arrival when he realized that Briana and Maud—whom she had alerted on her way out—were just a few paces behind him.

The people of Flint, who had recognized and come to greet their lord, stood back, either smiling broadly or fighting back happy tears, as the family was reunited.

Briana was laughing and crying at the same time. She squeezed Griffith's hand tightly, waiting impatiently for Meredith to step away from her father so she could throw her arms around him. Once she did, she was aware that Maud was close behind her, but she could not let him go. "I feared you'd not be returning!" she cried at him.

Bryn held her tightly for a long moment, then set her back from him. "I've not been gone so long as all that," he said. "Your brother's been wounded. Help him to the house."

"Is the war over?" Maud asked hopefully. The villagers all silenced, waiting for the answer.

"Nay," Bryn said seriously. "Prince Llewelyn still harries the English, and they hunt him yet."

"Then—" Maud began, but stifled the question instantly, afraid it would sound censorious.

Bryn guessed. "Come," he said. "We need food and drink and to sit still under a roof for a time. Then we'll speak of it."

Briana had offered Griffith her arm, reluctant to slide her hand around his back lest she be seen to emphasize his weakness. Meredith fell in on Griffith's other side. Briana kept glancing around to reassure herself that Bryn was actually there, just behind them, walking with Maud. As a result, she lost her footing on a loose rock in the road, turned quickly to avoid falling or twisting her ankle, and would have pulled Griffith off balance had he not grabbed at her and leaned back toward Meredith.

"I'd rather 'twas you helping me," Griffith said to his brother.

Meredith laughed out loud, and Briana found herself laughing along with him. She realized how much she'd missed laughing while Bryn and Griffith were gone, how much her happiness depended on having them near her.

Despite the cold, which had turned a drizzle into ice, the solar seemed warmer than possible that night. Maud had insisted on preparing and serving an elaborate meal of meat, bread, vegetables dried to last the winter, and a hearty turnip soup, thick enough to be filling by itself. Though it was extravagance, no one spoke of its sumptuousness; Bryn and Griffith had not had this fine a supper since they left home.

Briana listened quietly as one or the other of them answered Meredith's eager questions about the battles, the weaponry, the prowess of the Welsh, the cursed skill of Earl Connarc, and the valor of Prince Llewelyn. She was not very interested in war, and so she concentrated more on their familiar and beloved faces, their welcome voices, than she did on what they were saying. Maud asked some questions about campsites and provisions, answered a few about relations with the men who had occupied the castle before most of them left to join Edward's force at Rhuddlan, and then asked, "What of the enemy? We are told that the king does not take to the field himself, and Earl Connarc is only in the North. How is it with the other men who serve their cause?"

Bryn finished the bread he'd been eating as Griffith said, "Prince Llewelyn called them a fearsome lot."

"We know not all," Bryn continued. "One Marcher lord is new to us. We know only the treachery of the other two, Audley and Granville."

"Surely Edward would not choose a new lord of the March were he a normal man," Griffith said. "Therefore he must not be normal, just as Connarc is not."

"How, not normal?" Meredith asked.

Bryn held out his mug to Maud, who refilled it with ale. "The enemy is the enemy," he said.

Griffith was not satisfied by that. "Earl Connarc is a madman," he said. "He'll not wear a helmet, and he fears not that he will be killed. Mayhap he's made some pact with the devil."

"As does any who serve with the English pigs," Maud said hotly. "Why can they not leave us and our lands alone?"

Bryn had drunk just enough ale to edge him into an unaccustomed thoughtfulness. "'Tis the value of the lands, I think. The lands are good, and our roots are in them. Theirs are not. They are all greedy for what we have. And some of us want peace so much that those Welsh are helping them."

Briana set the spoon down carefully and studied the worn boards of the table, hearing overtones of condemnation in her father's voice.

Maud wanted to speak out to deny that any Welshman would aid the English, but even in the relative quiet of Flint, they had heard rumors that some of the Welsh in the South and even the middle March were tired of war and were cooperating with the invaders. She shook her head, but she kept silent.

Briana could not. Since the conversation had begun, she grew increasingly ashamed, and now, at the mention of collaborators, she whispered, "I was not able to stop him. I did want to, but—" Tears gathered in her eyes and her throat closed.

Bryn frowned. "What say you?"

Briana swallowed hard to clear the lump out of her throat. "I gave the Demo—the Demoiselle my word to care for—and he—he took her." She bit down on her lip, reading Bryn's frown as condemnation.

Actually, Bryn was confused. "Someone took the Demoiselle?" he asked.

Maud, who was seated beside him, laid a hand on his arm to draw his attention. "The king came to take the child," she clarified.

Things fell into place for Bryn. "You'd not have been able to stop him without an army behind you," he said to his daughter. "And perhaps not then. He understands naught but force."

Griffith slammed his fist into the table. "We've an army behind us," he said hotly. "We've shown him force. Will he bend to it at last and go?"

Bryn was silent for long enough to take a long drink of ale. "If the English can be driven from our valleys," he said at last, "Llewelyn will see to it that they are."

Briana looked down at her dish. She could not shake off the feeling of guilt or the despondency it engendered. She could not make herself believe there was nothing she could have done.

Then Bryn said, "Come. It grows late. I'd have a bath and my bed. Gather 'round. It's been too long since we prayed together and sang the lullaby."

Briana looked up, blinking back tears, swallowing the hardness that had returned to her throat. Since Bryn and Griffith had left for war, she and Meredith had faithfully stood in the corridor outside the solar and sung the lullaby-prayer at bedtime, but Meredith had not wanted his sister to embrace him. Now, with his father home and directing the prayers, with his older brother participating, she knew that he would have to acquiesce.

All five of them surrounded each other with their arms, and Bryn commended them to Jesus for the night. Then they sang the lullaby, their voices all blending for the first time in months.

Briana let the tears go and relaxed into the fragile safety of being with the people she most loved in the world.

Aber, Wales—December 1282 A.D.

There was nothing that could be described as a field of battle, but a battle was occurring nonetheless. The ground was carved as deeply as many of the defiles in Snowdonia, but, unlike them, these defiles went nowhere. The land was so severely gouged, so irregular, that no one was on horseback. Even the ponies would have found the footing so uncertain that they were simply safer kept away.

Of course, the men would have been safer elsewhere as well, but that was never an option, not in war. And the battle of Aber would ultimately turn out to be a draw, but the larger, stronger English army had to work twice as hard as the Welsh to ensure that it stayed that way.

Rees had gathered them together in camp the night before and spoken to them in tones a man might use with his friends or his family. "'Tis my desire that the men under my command be the most skilled fighters in King Edward's forces," he said, speaking clearly enough to be heard by the bulk of his silent troops. He had mounted his huge gray stallion so that he could be seen more clearly, and the destrier tossed his head now and then, snorting, restless to be moving once his rider was on his back.

"'Tis one thing to drill against each other," Rees went on, holding the reins firmly to keep the animal from dancing sideways and perhaps stomping on someone. "In practice, you know your opponent intends you no real harm. Tomorrow on the battlefield you will know that you are not safe; yet I do not wish you to fear the enemy's power—only to explore the limits of your own. If we can win the day, hold the field, and yet refuse to kill those we fight against, we will have tested and magnified our own skill beyond anything other of the king's troops can do." He paused to let the murmurs of surprise ripple through them and then die away.

"I tell you not to leave yourselves defenseless," Rees said strongly when they had quieted again. "I tell you if you must kill, you are to kill quickly. But I tell you that we will have the numbers and the strength, and 'twill still be our victory should we kill no one, nor let one of them kill us. We will have pride in true victory in this devilish war."

The stallion trumpeted, pulled hard against the reins, and tossed his head again. Rees waited for him to calm, then said, "I am aware I ask a great thing of you, and that 'tis a rare thing as well. I believe that you are able to give it me."

Someone shouted, "Aye!" and other voices took it up. Rees nodded at them, satisfied, and swung down off the horse, who turned and shoved at Rees with his head, as if asking why they had not galloped off.

Ralf and Galen emerged from the dispersing troops and walked up to Rees. They exchanged a glance, but neither of them spoke.

Rees suppressed a grin. "What think you of this exercise?"

Galen snorted. "'Tis a new notion, that. Battling without killing."

Ralf said quickly, "I doubt you'd recognize any kind of notion, Galen, much less a new one."

Galen swung at him good-naturedly, and Ralf evaded the swing.

"'Tis an interesting test of my men's prowess," said Rees firmly. "Defensive fighting is more difficult than offensive."

Ralf seemed to consider that, while Galen stepped aside as the balked warhorse tried to bite his arm. "I've a notion the king would not be pleased at the tactic."

Rees smiled, but there was no humor in it. "I took an oath to obey the king, my uncle," he said. "I promised not that I would please him." He glanced out over the camp. "Go among the men and make stronger what I've said."

"I doubt 'twill be needed," said Ralf.

"Nevertheless," said Rees. "I go to see to the guards."

"Think you they'll attack this night?" Galen asked.

"Nay," said Rees. "Llewelyn is a day fighter, and he does not meet us on ground of our choosing." He swung up on his horse again and let the destrier walk the short distance to the edge of camp, which spread across the plain between Aber and the sea. To the south the land was treacherous, broken, and he knew instinctively that Llewelyn would choose to meet him there. Rees would oblige.

The battle of Aber was more like a dance with edged weapons causing some inevitable injuries than it was a full-fledged battle. It continued until Llewelyn called his men back out of the drainage channels and defiles into the sheltering skirts of Snowdon. The English neither tried to stop them nor chased them.

During the actual battle, on the uncertain ground Rees had correctly identified, Ralf nearly fell.

The English soldiers had some problems with the concept of restraint, but fortunately there were enough of them so that if one withheld too much power, seeking that elusive balance between self-protection and vulnerability, another could help block a blow or turn a thrust.

Rees tried to watch everything, but he was not mounted, and the ground forced small pockets of fighting in a hundred different places. He knew he was asking a great deal of his men, to fight in ways so different from their training, but he thought he was doing something Abraham would have been proud of. On this terrain, however, the gullies fragmented normal formations, and any strategic plans he might have created would have been thrown into chaos. Indeed, the land between the gullies, though higher, was not rocky and thus unstable. Several men who attempted to climb up and gain the advantage of height lost their footing when damp earth was unable to support their weight.

It was sheer luck that Rees saw Ralf slip from the sleek side of one of those sloped walls, dislodging pebbles when he tried to dig in his heels. His sword shot from his hand, and he stumbled to his knees as he hit the ground.

Rees leaped around a group of soldiers to cut off the Welsh spearman who was charging toward Ralf, managing to catch the thrust with his outstretched sword and turn it toward himself. Ralf realized he was under direct attack and threw himself forward past Rees's legs, grabbing his sword with a handful of mud-covered hilt. He rolled to his back and raised the sword in time to meet and deflect a blow from a Welsh swordsman. The slickness of the hilt made it impossible for him to grip it securely enough, and the sword twisted in his hand. The Welshman leaned in to strike again. Ralf jerked himself sideways with just enough speed and distance so that the Welshman's sword bit into the ground beside his shoulder. By the time the point buried itself in the earth, Ralf was spinning toward the sword again to take hold of the man's arm before he could draw it back to thrust again.

Rees had avoided two spear thrusts after the blocked one aimed at Ralf, and then he was able to move inside spear range. He used his left fist to strike the man's midsection with enough strength to leave him winded and unable to catch a new breath. In the luxury of seconds that gave him, he turned his sword quickly and reached behind the spearman to cut a slice across the back of his leg.

When he turned his attention to Ralf again, the younger man had dragged the Welsh swordsman down to the ground and wrestled the sword away from him. As Rees watched, Ralf used the hilt to knock his assailant on the head. The swordsman collapsed. Rees held out a hand; Ralf reached up and clasped his wrist. Rees hauled him to his feet.

Ralf had time only to say, "My thanks," before they were plunged once more into the fragmented melee.

Later, Ralf and Galen would sit together, after Rees had congratulated his army on their conduct of the battle, and reminisce about other times when Rees had saved their lives and the lives of others. Despite the strangeness of his thinking, they admired him and would be endlessly loyal to him. It was inconceivable to them that anyone could feel otherwise.

Nursing their wounds, the Welsh sat in their temporary camp hidden in the folds of the mountain. Llewelyn could not stop wondering what orders the English had been under and wished he had Bryn and Owen here to speak with.

He had deliberately sent away the men he loved best. It had been an instinct to remove them from peril, a desire to see them safe no matter what befell the army now.

He walked through the makeshift camp, speaking to the men who had been wounded, discussing the few who had died with those who had known them. For once there was enough to eat; before they left the main camp, Owen Glyn had been successful at getting a supply train through, and they had been able to load their packs and saddlebags.

Llewelyn sat down near his tent, his back against the flattest part of a stunted mountain oak, lowered his head to rest his forehead on arms laid across his raised knees. He felt alone, even surrounded by the men whose loyalty should have gratified him.

A twig snapped, and the prince looked up.

"I'd not disturb you should you seek solitude," Ine said softly.

Llewelyn gestured the bard to join him. "Have you yet written your song of Aber?" he asked.

Ine laid his harp on a reasonably flat spur of rock whose roots probably sank down under Snowdon. "I know not what to sing of Aber," he said, sitting down beside the prince.

Llewelyn frowned slightly. "*You* know not? But you were in good view of it. We did well."

"Aye," agreed the bard, unwilling to let as much doubt as he felt creep into his voice, "and yet 'twas a victory for no one."

Llewelyn rubbed his eyes wearily. "Must you have a victory to sing of it?"

"Nay," said Ine readily, "but I needs must understand that of which I sing, and I do not yet comprehend Aber."

Llewelyn was too tired to pursue the question. "I often have cause to wonder," he said, as much to himself as to Ine, "whether I would have had cause to spend so much time in battle had David been older than I am. He might have desired peace more."

Ine said softly, unsure if he wanted Llewelyn to hear him or not, "Fifty is a good age. Many fail to reach that length of days."

Llewelyn laid his head on his arms again. He had heard, but he would pretend he had not. He was accustomed to bards knowing and speaking truth, and he thought, but would not say, "I wish that I had seen my child."

Ine took up his harp and began quietly to play.

Queen Eleanor and her two eldest daughters were decorating the solar at Rhuddlan Castle when Edward came in. His wife saw the expression on his face, put down the sprigs of holly she'd been adding to a bowl of wild rose branches, and said calmly, "Eleanor, take Joanna to the courtyard and see if we have any snowberries."

Princess Eleanor, who had been stitching the wrappings closed on one of the presents for their father, heard the nearly inaudible tones of stress, recognized the tension in the king's posture, and rose. "Come, Joanna," she said. "Saw you any snowberries in the foliage they sent us from York?" The two girls left the solar, though Joanna, always curious, looked as if she would far rather have lingered. They gathered cloaks against the cold from the chests by the door.

Once they were gone, Edward paced between the table, on which Queen Eleanor was calmly continuing to guard her fingertips from the sharp ends of the holly leaves, and the brazier in the center of the room. She let him stride back and forth, and though she glanced at him occasionally, she did not ask him what was amiss. At last he planted himself near the brazier, legs apart, fists on his hips, and stared at her.

Eleanor laid aside the holly twig whose leaves she'd been carefully polishing and folded her hands on the table. "Well?" she asked.

"He has defied me," Edward said instantly.

"Who has?"

"Rees." Edward was unable to remain still. "I've received intelligence that he is deliberately slowing the pace of this war, that he has given away battles which he might have won. That tends to treason."

"Surely not," Eleanor said, remaining calm, but startled nonetheless. "No one can say with certainty who will win or lose a particular battle excepting perchance the Lord. Are we not winning Wales day by day? Archbishop Peckham says 'tis all but certain."

He fixed her with a stare of barely hidden rage. "Winning is good had we no opportunity to have already won," he said.

Eleanor had lived with him long enough to know that the fury he was so tightly controlling was not directed at her. "You cannot know that," she said. "You engage in wishful thinking and seek someone to blame that God has not seen fit to act according to your plan."

Edward ignored the statement. "I will need to respond," he said more to himself than to her. "A fitting response." He grew thoughtful.

Eleanor slowly reached out and picked up the sprig of holly again. She was certain that nothing she could say or do at this point would convince Edward of Rees's loyalty; the men were too different, and they would never be alike. She cared for Rees. In the few encounters she had had with him, she had found him to be an appealing and interesting man and a very unusual knight.

But she also knew that Edward would never recognize aims different from his own. She wondered what would happen, how Rees would react to it, what it would change. Not for the first time and, she was certain, not for the last, she wished she had more influence with her husband. But he was the king, and he would allow no one to influence him now.

Briana could not remember ever having been happier. Happiness made her more willing to take physical risks, as if the world could not harm her now that she had her family around her again. As a result, she sprained an ankle slipping on ice at the edge of the estuary, fell from the rocks she was climbing on the far side of the rime-covered pasture and scraped an arm, and was thrown from the new horse Bryn had found wandering, and which he had forbidden her to try to ride.

Griffith snorted at her with derision when she limped home from that escapade with a sore shoulder and hip. "You've no need to take an injury as I heal," he said to her.

"I do it so Father has not the heart to beat me," she said airily, knowing herself to be safe from Bryn's wrath. At worst, he would express deep sorrow at her disobedient and unladylike misbehavior and send her to bed without any supper. She never minded that punishment, because one of the kitchenmaids always snuck her food when Maud wasn't paying heed.

Her favorite time of day was evening prayers. Even if she had been sent to her bed in disgrace, Bryn called her out again so that all five of them were together. Maud's face lost the hardness that had begun to settle into it when Bryn and Griffith went off to war, giving her an unusual prettiness in the torchlight. As they stood in the compass of each other's arms, accepting Bryn's blessings and then singing the lullaby that sent them to sleep each night with soft music in their ears and their thoughts, Briana could feel her heart swell with joy. She could believe that it would never change, that she would always feel so protected, so cherished as she did at those moments before she and Meredith went to sleep and the other three went back into the solar.

It was the kind of joy, childlike in its simplicity, that she had felt as a baby, sitting in the midst of the riotously colorful flowers on her mother's grave, which she saw as much an embrace as this one, involving her entire family. She would lie in the darkness of her tiny chamber, no longer shared with Meredith since her flux began, rolled into blankets, and feel the safety of being at home. Sometimes she would even hug herself and giggle, glad she was able to forget the war, the king, the Demoiselle's death, the abduction of the babe. She told herself that if she thought of none of those things, then she could be free of them. Her sleep was untroubled by painful dreams, and her waking hours were untroubled by reality.

It could not last.

Builith Wells was a small village, normally sleepy and undistinguished until market days drew everyone in from the outlying farms, crofts, and even smaller hamlets. Since the arrival of a mounted English force, however, the village had lost its serenity in a flurry of activity involving men, arms, shouting, a little casual looting, a few rapes, and some wholesale slaughter and consumption of the herds and flocks.

Those few English soldiers who had nonviolent dealings with the village folk informed anyone who might have inquired that all the armies in Wales were actually under the direct command of Earl Connarc, who had been battling Prince Llewelyn to a standstill in the more northerly climes.

Stories of Earl Connarc—the large, cold knight on the steel gray warhorse—had already begun circulating throughout the towns and shires of Wales. It was said that he had made a pact with Satan, since he clearly had no fear of the battlefield, and therefore knew he would not die. It was said that his powers were such that his control over his men was instantaneous and absolute, that they were all but an extension of himself. In some quarters, it was even believed that the only way Prince Llewelyn could be defeated was by magic, since Merlin himself had chosen the prince to rule Wales, and it must take strong magic to defeat strong magic. Everyone agreed that there was a way Connarc could disprove the tales, and that would be to die, but he showed no inclination to oblige them. The belief was common, if unuttered, that good magic could not defeat evil magic on its own, not once its creator was gone. Merlin was long gone.

So Builith Wells was not at all pleased to have Connarc's forces so close, but like many other loyal Welsh villages—as opposed to the larger towns, which seemed to be bending to the inevitable notion of English rule—they lowered their heads, nursed their hatred, and tried not to be noticed, lest they provoke the thoughtless cruelties of which the English were so very capable.

Llewelyn's party gave the village and the encampment a wide berth, but the villagers somehow knew that he was nearby. Some arcane fiber in their truly Celtic souls reverberated like a plucked string to his presence. They said nothing to one another, for fear the English would hear of it and Connarc would swoop down upon their prince with all the power he wielded. Their hidden smiles told each of them that the others knew.

Ine, following behind as he had for two days, had no way of knowing the effect Llewelyn had on Builith Wells, but when Llewelyn and his men turned south to circle the village, Ine went directly in to play for those gathered at its single inn and earn himself a meal. The English tossed coins; the Welsh gave what food they could spare and refrained from asking for the songs they truly wanted to hear. Ine didn't linger. He didn't want Llewelyn to get too far ahead of him.

He picked up the trace of the party's passage where he expected it to be and hurried his own pace to catch up, to see where they had gotten to. He overtook them, still at enough of a distance not to be noticed, at a rocky field leading to the wooden bridge over the Orwein River.

Llewelyn had been surprised by the message sent to him under flag of truce, but its sources were impeccable. The parchment itself was under the seal of John Peckham, Archbishop of Canterbury, whom the prince knew to be one of Wales's staunchest friends among the English, and the message concerned Earl Connarc. It seemed, according to Peckham, that Connarc wished to see Llewelyn privately for the second time during this war—though the message did not actually allude to the earlier meeting. That first meeting Llewelyn kept entirely secret, but nurtured to himself. This time it was a proposal for peace to be tendered. Peckham asked Llewelyn to bring a small guard, as King Edward refused to let his nephew arrive without one of his own, and they should be of equivalent strength.

For the sake of a peace he still hoped for, despite the odds, Llewelyn decided to trust once more. So far he had had no cause to regret that first meeting.

"The meeting cannot be in the North," Peckham had written. "The king does not wish it to be too near to him at Rhuddlan, so that he may, should things go poorly, repudiate the knowledge of it and lay it all on the earl." That part rang solidly true, and it was that, coupled with what Llewelyn knew of Connarc, which impelled him to agree.

Besides, he reveled in once again riding through his realm. He had not actually been to the middle March since David broke the peace in April, and yet he knew that men were dying for Wales here just as they were in the area around Snowdonia. He thought he might like to visit the South as well, even though he knew most of it was firmly in English control now.

He and the small troop of knights skirted Builith Wells on that crisp, clear day in mid-December and rode on to Orwein Bridge.

They fell upon him there.

Ine arrived in more than enough time to witness the ambush.

The bridge lay in a part of the river where turbulence made passage uncertain at best. Hills clustered thickly on the upstream side, more gradual than the cliffs downstream, but nonetheless still enough so that the river had carved through. Other than the bridge, there was no reasonable crossing point for miles in either direction. The approach seemed quiet, and the possible areas of concealment were some distance away. For whatever reason, the

Welsh party did not appear to anticipate anything amiss as they approached the bridge.

Ine had paused far enough back on the track to once again escape detection; a lone rider would be unlikely to be considered a risk, and if he were challenged, his being a bard would let him escape. He was just estimating when he should start the pony out of the meager foliage he was using for cover—the approach to the bridge was open enough that he thought he should wait until Llewelyn was well beyond the river into the hills on the far side before he left cover—when suddenly there were men all over the hills.

The English troops came from three directions at once— from the steep hills and hidden folds upriver to the left, from the gentler rolls downriver to the right, and from the other side of the bridge itself. They were mounted, swords already drawn, and Ine quickly counted: among the three groups, there were at least a hundred men bearing down on the twenty in the Welsh party. The attacking force was so great that Ine feared their aim was to capture Llewelyn, in which case the prince would be subjected to humiliation, torture, and a most unpleasant death on alien soil.

For the first and only time in his life, Ine wished he had a sword.

The Welshmen drew swords and pulled their horses into a tight, if misshapen, knot, ready to take the assault by presenting as small a target as possible. The attackers were forced to keep half their numbers back, because they could not all crowd into the small space around the Welsh.

Ine scrambled off his pony and up the slope beside the track, trying to get as high as possible to better see the fighting which, despite the iron-hard ground, was beginning to cause dust as the horses' hooves damaged the earth. By the time the bard reached a good vantage point, several of the Welshmen were already down, and the weight of the English opposition was falling on Llewelyn.

The prince fought with inspired grace, as if age had not slowed or stiffened him. Constantly at the very edge of disaster, he felled four or five of the English soldiers before so many of his own men had fallen that his enemy was able to surround him, and then a dozen swords cut him down at once. He disappeared under the onslaught.

Ine clutched at his arms, breathing hard, but fighting to calm himself. It was the death Llewelyn would have wanted, quick and spilling his blood into Welsh soil, where he belonged, where he would rather have been than the heaven to which he was surely being taken.

The Welsh were dead. The English soldiers pulled back from the scene of the carnage. One of them dismounted and bent over the bodies, then used his sword to hack at something.

Ine turned away, not wanting to see the man lift Llewelyn's head from the destroyed body. He was not a man who often prayed with the prayers of nonmusical men, but he prayed now for the soul of the greatest prince Wales had known, the only true Prince of Wales. Ine remounted the pony and turned its head back toward Snowdonia. Wales's freedom was now delayed for even longer; he wondered briefly if it would somehow depend on Briana, that child of legend. He did not understand how that might be possible, but then, he told himself, there were many things he did not understand about the world.

As he rode, he thought about Llewelyn, admiring the man more than he admired the prince. Llewelyn, Ine believed, had lived in the wrong time. Against Henry, Llewelyn would have been successful in freeing his nation from the rule of an overlord. Against Edward, who was entirely ruthless and unforgiving, he had had no chance. Ine mourned him, nursing his memories, already beginning to compose his song.

Owen Glyn accompanied the next train of supplies back to the camp, arriving shortly before Ine rode in on the pony with the news that Prince Llewelyn was dead. Most of the men in camp cried out, denied it even though they knew the bard would never lie; some began to weep. Owen went pale and quiet, holding tightly to the reins of his horse.

Ine walked up to him and stood at the side of his saddle, watching him react to the abrupt change in the world. Ine judged that Owen was taking the loss much harder than the men who were reacting openly.

Owen tried to speak, but his throat closed, and he had to cough to clear it. "How?" he asked.

Ine took hold of the reins just under the horse's chin and waited for Owen to dismount. "Ambush," he said softly.

"Treachery," Owen hissed. "Why was he not here? Or why was the army not with him?"

"Treachery it seems to be," Ine confirmed. "I suspect he would not have ridden off with so few had he not thought he'd be safe."

Owen pressed his lips together as color rose in his face. "May God damn them all to everlasting hell," he said tightly. "We will never give up the fight. Have they taken his body?"

Ine answered reluctantly, "I saw only that they took his head."

Owen clenched his fists, took in a lungful of air, and bit down on the shout he wanted to give. It would serve no useful purpose. Llewelyn was gone; they would have to cope with it.

"What shall you do?" Ine asked him.

Owen looked at the bard, seeing the concern, the smaller man's quiet sharing of the pain of loss. "We must ensure that the word is passed. David is our leader now. He should know. And so should Bryn."

"I can carry word to Prince David," Ine said.

"I will go to Flint," said Owen. He took the reins of the horse back from the bard, glad beyond words to have a task, especially one which would allow him to escape for a time from the company of other men. It would afford him the opportunity to mourn without showing his feelings to anyone else. "Then I shall return to Snowdonia to resume the struggle."

Ine saw the hard determination come over Owen at that moment, so he kept silent instead of saying that he feared the struggle, as such, was over. All he said was, "Journey safe to Flint."

Owen clasped Ine's arm in a sudden, abortive gesture encompassing gratitude, the need the share one more moment with the man who had seen Llewelyn die, and an urge—partially stifled—to seek comfort.

The tide of vengeance was running strong among the Welsh, but even so, a full third chose to lay down their arms and return to their homes, many of these in the northern March near Ruthin or Rhuddlan, Conway or Flint. Those from the South or the middle Marches knew that returning meant bowing to subjugators already ensconced in the lands. The North, for all that it contained, just now, both Earl Connarc and the king, had somehow not bowed to them.

Ine left before the last of the farewells. David needed to know before the men arrived that he was now in charge of the war, that the legacy of Llewelyn had fallen to him.

Chapter 8

Briana was deeply asleep, dreaming of making wonderful music which she could never quite hear, nor did she remember it in the morning. Despite an inability to actually hear the music, she was always made happy by the dreams. When Bryn and Griffith had been gone, the dreams were comforting; now that they were safely home again, the dreams were unremittingly joyous.

So she was annoyed to be called awake in the middle of one such dream by Maud shaking her and calling her name. "What?" she asked, her voice and head still thick with sleep.

Maud was bending over her holding a candle, her hair still touseled, a robe hastily thrown over her shift. "Briana, wake up," she repeated. "You must come down to the solar."

Briana shook the vestiges of sleep our of her eyes as the soundless music finally faded and was gone. "What's amiss?" she asked.

"Owen Glyn is here with news," Maud answered. "Don your robe and come with me."

Briana pulled herself from the warm hollow into the icy room, snatched up her robe from the top of the chest at her bed's foot, thrust her stockinged feet into her shoes. "I'm ready," she said, but Maud was already turning to the door.

The solar was lighted by the brazier that burned in the center of the room and by the candles on the walls. Owen stood near the table, rubbing his hands together, for very little heat escaped the brazier into the rest of the room. As Briana came in, he put his hands so close to the brazier he might have burned his fingers, but he seemed not to feel the heat.

Bryn and Griffith were already in the solar, and Bryn was saying, "—have ridden long and hard to get here so quickly."

"From Snowdonia two nights past," Owen said. "His teeth chattered a little. He bit down to stop them.

"Where's Meredith?" Briana asked Maud in a whisper.

Owen heard her. "Let him sleep," he said. "We can tell him in the morning."

"Tell him what?" Bryn asked, frowning apprehensive about what was to come.

"Prince Llewelyn is dead," said Owen flatly.

No one moved or spoke. Briana looked from her father, whose face was immobile, to Griffith, who was fighting the sudden tears that Maud silently shed without any change of expression. She waited to see if anyone would say anything, but the time stretched away and the only movement in the darkened room was Owen flexing his fingers, rubbing his hands together again in the glow of the brazier. She felt sorrow squeezing her heart, but there was something else as well, something warmer. Finally, into the silence, she said, "Then he is with the Demoiselle, and no one can ever part them again."

Owen opened his mouth to say something, seemed to think better of it, and closed it again.

Maud said, "Hush, child."

Bryn lifted a hand to forestall her. "Nay," he said. "Let her be. 'Tis the fate Llewelyn would have wanted in any case." He looked at Owen, his eyes terrible in his still expressionless face. "How did he die?"

"Ine saw it; I did not," Owen answered honestly. "Ine said a messenger came under pledge of truce to ask him to parley, and they sprang upon him on the way. I would guess they have taken his head to the king."

Griffith made an involuntary noise as Bryn spat at the floor. Maud covered her mouth with one hand, tears continuing to flow across her cheeks.

Briana did not at first realize what all of Owen's words meant. As the image of the prince's head separate from his body penetrated, she felt nausea strike her. She wasn't certain if she felt more pain for Llewelyn or for the baby, Gwenllian, who would have to learn someday the horror that had been her father's death. Briana was seized with an impulse to throw her arms around Bryn and hold him as tightly as her strength would permit, but she suppressed it. She was not a baby any longer.

"I shall grieve for him," Bryn said, a vein jumping in his cheek. "And tomorrow we shall ask Father Ciaran to say a Mass for his soul. But tonight—at whose door do we lay this treachery?"

"The king put all the armies of Northern Wales in the sway of Earl Connarc," said Owen.

"Then we must see that the prince does not pass away unavenged," said Bryn.

"I have sworn to continue on until Wales has what Wales is entitled to," Owen said hotly. "I will go to Snowdonia to join Prince David on the morrow."

Bryn shook his head. "David is a fool," he said. "I was present when Llewelyn named him that. Go fight as you choose, but I beg you, go not to David. I do not believe he will be able to win anything."

Owen lifted his hands away from the brazier and sighed. "'Tis possible you have the right of it," he said slowly.

"Indeed," said Bryn. "'Tis why he made Llewelyn—" He stumbled briefly on the name. "—Llewelyn fight his battles for him."

"Mayhap I shall have to find a way of my own, then," said Owen.

Rhuddlan—December 1282 A.D.

"He's sent for me again," Rees growled. Galen and Ralf looked up from the daggers they were sharping, surprised.

They were in one of the tower rooms at Conway Castle, to which Rees had returned with his arms after Aber. He had sent some spies out to find Llewelyn, but the men could not venture far into the region around Snowdon without being discovered. When they returned to report that an army had descended upon Builith Wells, and that they believed it to be composed of mercenaries, Rees decided to leave the field to them. If Llewelyn returned to his northern battlefields, Rees would confront him again. Aber had been difficult, and he was reluctant to restrain his men again—certainly not so soon.

When the summons to Rhuddlan arrived, Rees guessed it was because Edward had learned he had returned to Conway and was angry at him.

"Mayhap he merely wants you to join him for Christmas," Ralf suggested.

Rees gave a short laugh. "I much doubt he misses me. I'd have you accompany me."

"When do we depart?" Galen asked, sliding his dagger into its sheath and dropping the whetstone into his scrip.

"Misfortunately hastily," said Rees. "Meet me at the horses in a quarter-hour."

They left promptly, but rode slowly. The roads were icy and snow lay like a cover over the hills, spotted here and there by the black blotches that meant copses, hedgerows, or denuded trees. They talked little, though Galen could be counted on to swear volubly anytime his horse stumbled on the hard, ridged earth. The weather was growing even more bitterly cold, but Rees was happier in the frigid air than he would have been in the presence of his hot-tempered uncle. Even after the snow began to fall again, they did not quicken their pace.

Nor had Edward's temper undergone any discernible improvement since Rees had last seen him. As soon as Rees and his companions entered the outer ward at Rhuddlan, a page ran out from the shelter of the walls and said, "My lord earl, the king wishes you to attend him immediately you've arrived."

Rees tossed his mount's reins to Ralf and gestured to the page to lead the way. Within ten minutes, he was back in the antechamber where Ralf and Galen waited for him. They leaped up from the bench on which they were sitting when they saw his face.

Rees tried to gentle his expression at least enough so that they would not think they were the object of his all too apparent anger. "Go back to Conway," he said to them. "I shall follow in some days."

Galen and Ralf exchanged a glance, and Ralf opened his mouth.

Rees overrode him. "Ask me no questions, either of you. Just go. I shall see you in no more than a fortnight." Then he added, with a heavy irony he knew they would not understand, "Of a certainty before year's end."

They understood none of it, but, obedient, they went. Rees watched them ride away and then went to Edward's barracks, built outside the walls of Rhuddlan, to speak to the mercenaries.

The challenge to battle at Fearndon was cried about in every town, village, hamlet, and croft in the Northern March. And the men answered it. As Edward had guessed, they could hardly have done otherwise.

The battle of Fearndon began around eleven of the clock on the icy, steel-cold morning of December 22. It was over by 3:00 pm, and the English did all they could to ensure that not one Welshman remained alive. It consumed all the men who had chosen not to join Prince David but, rather, had yearned after and sought their homes. In addition it consumed Bryn, Griffith, and even Meredith, who had been ecstatic about getting to fight at last. Just as Llewelyn's blood had watered the soil of Wales, so the blood of fully a thousand of her men sank down, removing the cold with their body heat, then cooling, and drawing the warmth of life with it.

Later, it was said that the freedom of Wales died that day, crushed by the dark magic of Earl Connarc and his knights.

One man Fearndon failed to consume. Owen Glyn had returned to Snowdonia two days before the challenge was issued.

Galen and Ralf got word of the massacre in Conway the day before Christmas.

"Why did he not take us with him?" Galen asked, bewildered.

Ralf had a greater concern. "Why has he not returned to us?" he asked in turn.

For neither question did they have an answer.

Flint—December 1282 A.D.

Briana had exhausted herself with weeping. She had defied her father and Maud and secreted herself in the scratchy, bare copses on a hill above the field at Fearndon. The price for her defiance was that she had been forced to watch Wales die. She was too much in shock, too entirely held together by refusal to believe what she had seen, to cry on the ride back to Flint, but as soon as Maud, frantic with worry, nearly dropping her candle as she ran into the yard, cried, "Where have you kept yourself?" then Briana began to sob.

She fell from the pony she'd purloined to carry her to a horror she had never expected. She would have to say the words, and even considering doing so made it too real. She doubled over, holding herself to try to keep the pain at bay, but it crashed down upon her.

"Are you hurt?" Maud persisted.

"F—fe—fearndon." The word seemed to burn her tongue. She thought for a moment that Maud would shriek, but before her aunt could gather her wits, Briana made herself say, "They're dead, all of them."

Some of the housemaids had come out into the yard after word went around that Briana had returned, and they gave out a simultaneous moan that echoed around the courtyard in the frigid air.

"What mean you, all?" Maud demanded.

"They—died," said Briana, her voice sinking to a whisper, strained by the fact that she would have to keep saying it. "The English—they killed everyone. Everyone." She could not personalize it, could not draw it closer to Flint. She wanted the truth of her family's destruction to remain unspoken.

Maud had absorbed that Bryn was dead. She was trying not to accept the other deaths. After the grief over Llewelyn, this felt like no new grief, just a continuation of the mourning, a deepening. She let her tears flow without actually recognizing they were there, just as she had at the news about the prince. She was unable even to reach out and put her arm around the girl, who was now blinded by her own tears, moisture that threatened to begin freezing on her face.

"Come inside," said Maud, and to the maids, "Build up the fire in the solar hearth." Only then, with something to do, a recognizable task, could she slide an arm across Briana's shoulders.

Briana was trembling so hard that shivering had turned directly into shock. She was now incapable of independent thought, partly from cold, partly from flight to a place where thought was unnecessary. The sobs were choking her. She was barely aware that the women bundled her into blankets and put her directly in front of the now leaping flames. She had no idea how much time had passed.

Briana hoped that she would die. It would be the only way that she could again be in the company of the people she loved best. Her mind began to warm, despite the fight she was waging against the return of an ability to think coherently. She thought about Llewelyn being reunited with the Demoiselle; she thought that now Bryn would be reunited with his prince; she thought she might want to join them. The warmth seeped back into her limbs as well, and as the hurt reached her core, it freed even more tears.

She wept the entire night and into the next day. Maud, grieving deeply, too, worried over her and brought her soup Briana could not force down. Finally, Briana fell into a fitful sleep, still curled in blankets in front of the solar fire.

Maud thought that the worst was horrible, but perhaps at least, it was over.

Then, at six in the evening, King Edward came to Flint.

When the king rode into the dooryard at Flint with an escort of a dozen guards, Maud was once again coaxing Briana to drink some soup. The girl had passed from shock into the first stages of grieving, where terrible pain slipped away for a time into dull emptiness. The pain would return, was only briefly in abeyance, but for the moment, the emptiness held sway.

One of the maids was building up the solar fire again when another came in to stutter out the news that the king had come.

Maud was sitting on the hearth floor holding the bowl and a spoonful of soup she had been propelling toward Briana's mouth. It spilled abruptly as her hand trembled.

The maid's anxious words penetrated Briana's consciousness, and the girl, still swathed in the blankets, struggled to free her arms, as if she would be better able to defend herself from the threat. The dull ache of unrestorable loss faded into the anxiety of being in the presence of the king.

Maud put the spoon back into the bowl and got to her feet. She had barely straightened before Edward appeared in the solar doorway, took in the room with one sweeping glance, then fastened his gaze on Briana. His question, however, was directed sideways to Maud. "Is she ill?"

Maud bobbed her head in a counterfeit of a curtsey she would not fully perform. "She is grieving, Sire."

Edward took three steps and towered over Briana. "I have been told that the men of Flint went to Fearndon."

"Aye," said Maud. It was unnecessary for her to add, "—and did not return."

The king reached down and held out his hand.

Briana hesitated, not wanting to touch him, but he waited, unmoving, until she finally had to put her hand in his. He pulled her to her feet. The blankets dropped, tangling her legs, and she would have fallen, but the king's other hand shot out and caught her around the waist. She pulled violently backward and tripped again on the piled cloth, but Edward did not relinquish his hold on her.

"Calm, lady," he said. "I come not to do you harm."

She couldn't speak, and she refused to weep in front of him. She looked aside as long as he was still holding her. Without effort, he lifted her clear of the blankets, set her down on the solar floor, then released her and took a step backwards.

Briana's balance was unsteady, but she caught herself before she could wobble severely. For a moment or two she fought herself out of the mists of lingering dullness and rising fear. Then she raised her chin, met his gaze as squarely as she could, and asked, "What seek you, Sire?" She was exhausted enough so that, although she intended venom, she could inject none into the words.

Edward looked at her for a breath longer, then turned his head toward Maud, noticing in passing that several of the maids now clustered in the doorway. "I would speak with Lady Briana alone," he said. "Go pack her things and deliver them to my men."

Both women were electrified by that statement. Maud opened and closed her mouth, uncertain what to say or ask, for the order had been clear. Briana felt any vestiges of the torpor vanish in a flood of fear. She found her voice before Maud could speak.

"Pack?" she repeated.

Edward gestured, one strong movement of his arm, for Maud to leave them, and Maud had no choice but to obey, casting one more look at Briana before she went reluctantly from the room.

Edward returned his regard to Briana's now openly stricken face. "Aye," he said. "You are a prize, lady. I cannot leave you unprotected, and I do not wish you to fall into the hands of men who might wish me ill." He bent a little so that his face was closer to hers. "You see how I honor you with what I have no need to provide. You will obey me in this. My queen and I will care for you."

She was too distraught and too tired to be cautious. "As you cared for the Demoiselle?" she burst out. "As you are doubtless caring for the Princess Gwenllian?"

His color rose, as it had when she had challenged him before, but he did not move, and after a moment or two, his voice even and steady, he said, "The Demoiselle was a hostage. Llewelyn's daughter is going to be a nun, as is one of my own daughters. You will be a member of my family."

The word raked over her nerves as if she had been physically abraded. Edward cocked his head to one side and subjected her to an icy glare that recognized her reaction and forbade her to bow to it. As tired, fearful, and angry as she was, she could not bring herself to defy that look.

"Please—" she whispered. "Please take me not from Flint."

"I must," he said. "Ask not again."

She was to lose everything, then, except her life: Bryn, Griffith, Meredith, and Flint. She felt the dullness return, and it blocked the despair which threatened to overwhelm her. Without moving, she seemed to be about to fold in on herself.

Edward saw it, not just because her face was mobile, but because he was studying her so intensely that he could almost sense what she was feeling. He said softly, "Fight it, lady. This is your destiny."

She shot him a look of hatred, but it stiffened her spine.

"My soldiers will escort you to Rhuddlan," the king said, straightening. "We pass Christmas there and then return to Westminster. Prepare yourself." He turned and left the solar.

Briana's legs threatened to collapse under her, but she refused to allow them to do so. She would have to be strong from now on, until they let her come home again.

Maud hurried in, and Briana told her what had happened.

Rhuddlan—December 1282 A.D.

Edward reached Rhuddlan several hours ahead of the soldiers bringing Briana and the trunk with her belongings. He had a duty to perform before he took the girl upstairs to meet Queen Eleanor and their daughters.

In the courtyard Edmund Mortimer waited, sheltered from the wind by the slope of a thatched roof originally built to cover a woodpile. He walked out into the ward and bowed as the king rode in and dismounted.

Edward wasted no time in preliminaries. "You have served me well," he said. "I will be willing to appoint you Lord of the Northern March." Mortimer bowed at once, but Edward could not tell if it was abject gratitude or an inability to disguise the triumph. "Before I do, I require another favor of you."

They would not speak of the first favor, the one that involved borrowing John Peckham's seal and Earl Connarc's name. In a bizarre way, it suited Edward's sense of justice that since Rees could not speak the truth of it, neither should he and Mortimer, his instrument.

Mortimer had straightened again, his face wiped clean of whatever expression it bore when he bowed. "What additional service may I do Your Grace?" he asked blandly.

"I want Prince David," said Edward. "Llewelyn may have been the greater threat, but David is the hothead. This time I want him not to die in Wales. Capture him live, and bring him to me. There are more than sufficient legends abroad in Wales now. We need not create another."

Mortimer was shrewd. "The lady of Flint?" he asked.

"She comes with me to England," the king said. "The legend will be less powerful if I control it."

Mortimer bowed again. "I shall try to serve you well, Sire," he said.

Edward didn't respond, but he was certain that Mortimer was telling the truth. The man would do all he could to become a Lord of March. It was only a question of time before Northeast Wales would be completely beneath his heel. Edward was satisfied.

He dismissed the man and went into the castle to find Eleanor.

The queen was piling the wrapped gifts on the table in the solar. She loved Christmas. It was, to her, another story of the strength of woman, for she deeply admired the Virgin for her faith and her boldness in being willing to risk the censure of her entire community.

Edward came in, and she greeted him with a smile. "I am most pleased you've returned in time for Christmas," she said. "What of the lady of Flint?"

"She is an hour or thereabouts behind me."

"How does she?" Eleanor left the packages and came to her husband's side.

"She will bend," he said.

Eleanor knew that was what Edward considered important. She nearly asked again, but she thought better of it. When Briana arrived, she would speak with her directly. She wet her lips. "What of Rees?" she asked.

Edward frowned. "I've heard naught of him since the battle. He dismissed my mercenaries, but neither accompanied them nor sent word."

"What shall you do?" Eleanor asked. She feared that he would make a choice she regarded as unwise, and she wondered how she could say it without angering him.

Edward drew out a chair and sat down, stretching his legs out before him and crossing his ankles. "I think," he said slowly, "that I shall hold him in reserve. He has proved his worth, but I have used him hard. 'Twill be a time before I use him again."

The queen smiled, relieved, bent and kissed his cheek. "You are wise, my lord husband," she said contentedly.

He reached up half-absently and stroked her arm. "God grant that I am wise enough," he said.

Chapter 9

The Roads—April 1284 A.D.

Briana knew that she could not take her palfrey. If they thought she was going to ride out, several of the knights would go with her; it was only within the precincts of Westminster or the walls of Windsor that she was permitted to go about alone. So, then, she would have to leave on foot. The prospect did not distress her, nor would it deter her. The queen and her daughters were in Wales, and the king was in Chester. Her counterfeit family obligations were temporarily in abeyance, and she had learned several months earlier that Gwenllian of Wales was far to the north, in Sempringham Abbey.

Since the palaces were guarded much more diligently at night, she left during the day, her hood raised, a basket over her arm as if she were merely one of the maids on her way to the market. Once on her way, she lowered the hood to feel the sun on her face and walked briskly through the crowded, lively streets, making her way toward the village of Charing, which would be her first stop on the road to Sempringham. When she was well away, she pulled her knapsack from the basket and slung it over her shoulder, leaving the basket in a ditch by the roadside.

She did not believe she was running away; for herself, alone, she would have remained in captivity, miserable as it made her. She did not believe that she was doing this for herself. She had promised the Demoiselle that she would care for Gwenllian, and she was now in possession of a rough map that told her the path she would need to take to reach the Gilbertine abbey where the little princess of Wales was being raised.

And she was not a fool. Having neither coin nor an acknowledgeable station in life, she would have to find something to barter. Since she was adamant about not bartering her body, something about which she knew in a detached, objective way as the currency many women used, she had decided to imitate Ine. She could not be a bard, but she could feign an identity as a minstrel, and while women troubadors were very rare in England, they were not unknown. The role carried a somewhat greater risk of discovery because of its rarity than she would have incurred had she simply vanished into the countryside, but the physical safety was greater. It was considered nearly as unfortunate an act to molest a minstrel as it was a bard; only a truly stupid person would risk damaging someone who was considered the property of the nobility. She had no public performance in her background, but she was a Celt, soul-tied to music. She thought she could do it, and to get to Gwenllian, she was willing to try.

She reached Charing before dusk on her first day, and with relative ease, for it was only a mile or two from Westminster. With good fortune, she would not be missed until morning, for her maid, Enlis, often left her supper on a tray outside her door now that none of the family was present. The inn at Charing was already full of men, roistering and shouting, so she hesitated, and then finally decided against going in. Some of them could have recognized her from Westminster, and she would be questioned and perhaps stopped. She was standing in the shadow of a nearby shop, closed now, when a fistfight broke out and the combatants were shoved out of the inn's common room into the road. Most of the inn's occupants poured out with them, cheering and laying wages.

The casual violence, combined with the risk of discovery, confirmed her decision to move on, and she slipped deeper into the shadows. She wondered if she should perhaps return after all; she might be able to get back in without even being missed. She quelled the thought as entirely unworthy. It was her duty to continue on. She owed it to the Demoiselle and, even more, to Prince Llewelyn. She slipped around behind the shop and stayed in the darkness as she passed several other buildings, making for the woodland at the northern edge of the village.

It was not so much that she was reveling in the freedom; she did not have the same understanding of freedom as the men of Wales might have, for as a woman she could have no real expectation of the kind of free choice that would have come to her as a boy. It was more that she did truly enjoy being out of the hands of the English. She found an isolated copse near a stream in the sparse edge of woodland just to the north of the village, ate some bread she'd brought with her, drank her fill of stream water, curled up under the shrubbery with her head on the knapsack containing her dulcimer, and slept far more soundly than she had a right to expect.

The order in which King Edward received the messages had a material effect on his response to word that Briana was missing. The messengers from Wales and Westminster had come to Windsor, where the king was meeting with his councillors and some of the representatives from Oxford. They were developing the wording of a new code of laws which Edward wanted to use to unify jurisprudence, especially with regard to the usury practiced by the Jews. The outlines were firmly in place; the arguments over large things had been mostly resolved, and now the discussions were over smaller specifics. Edward was beginning to feel he could absent himself from the meetings for some short periods. He had made clear what he wanted, had ensured that his imprint was on every line of the proposed code, and he would let nothing be cried abroad until he was certain it was correct. He might, therefore, be able to take some few days away to travel to Wales and be with Eleanor when she gave birth.

He had just made that determination when the first messenger arrived, bearing a dispatch from Caernarfon Castle, near Anglesey. It was one of the places scheduled for the queen and the princesses to stop on their progress to show how confident the English now were about their hold over Wales.

King Edward took the sealed dispatch from the messenger in the corridor outside the council chamber. The seal was Eleanor's, and the message was in her own hand, rather than a secretary's. He read it, and he could not resist smiling. "Our son was born this even, in full health and with great ease. Anticipating your approval, I have asked to have him christened Edward after you, my beloved lord."

He knew it was her plan to keep death or illness from claiming another of their sons. She would give him his powerful father's name, rather than giving him a name he might share only with the dead or dying. Alphonso looked fairly likely to join John and Henry, while only the king's daughters continued to thrive. He thought his wife superstitious, but he humored her because he had great affection for her. Still holding the message, he returned to the council room to announce the birth of his son and to request that a banner be flown from the walls in celebration.

He was still receiving the congratulations of the council members and the academicians when the second messenger arrived with the news that Briana of Flint had vanished from Westminster.

Edward's first reaction was amused annoyance, rather than fury. He made an immediate assumption that she could not be far from the palace, that she was probably upset that he had forbidden her to reenter Wales by accompanying Eleanor and the princesses on their tour, and that, therefore, she would be on her way toward the Welsh border. He was more concerned for her safety than he was at the thought of losing her. He set a company of his knights on the roads westward, confident she would soon be recaptured, then turned his attention to composing a warm letter to Queen Eleanor.

On the fourth day of her flight from Westminster, footsore, hungry, aching from sleeping on the ground, Briana walked up to the gate of the Augustinian abbey at Waltham and rang the bell. One of the brothers opened the wicket panel, summed up the pilgrim with a quick glance, then closed the panel again and opened the whole wicket door, gesturing her in.

"My thanks, Brother," she said softly, aware of the depth of prayerful silence that hung over this place within the walls. "I'd impose on your hospitality for a night's shelter."

He reclosed the door, thrust his hands into the rough, grayish-white sleeves of his robe, and inclined his head to indicate she should follow him. Limping a little, she walked behind him across the courtyard. The guesthouse for men was large and close to the chapel and the cloister, but the guesthouse for women was very small and a long distance away, hard up against the sturdy walls, and within its own gate. The monk opened the gate and gestured her in, but did not enter himself. As she walked haltingly toward the opening, he stepped back and tucked his hands into the folds of his sleeves again. "Will you wish to speak with a priest?" he asked.

"Nay, though it is kindly asked," Briana said. "Would the brothers wish to hear any songs? I am a travelling minstrel and can gift them with music, should they so wish."

"I shall ask," said the monk. "The church may be visited at any time." He turned silently and vanished toward the cloister.

Briana let her breath out in a long sigh and went into the house, which contained only a dark fireplace, four string beds with rolled ticking of straw at their feet, and a tiny table with two bench seats. The candle sconces were empty; no guests had been expected. She was as relieved to be under a roof and safe even for a single night, as she was simply to be holding still. She unrolled one of the straw mattresses and sat on the low, narrow bed. After a moment, she slid her shoes off to examine the sores, bruises, and blisters on her feet.

The church bell tolled the introductory notes, and then the hour of four. Briana sat, looking at nothing, luxuriating in stillness and in not carrying the weight of her knapsack. A light tapping forced her to get up and hobble, barefoot, to the door. No one was there, but a pitcher of water, a blanket, and some candles waited on the doorstep. She gathered them all up and carried them in, wondering how she was going to light the candles, but then spying a flintstone on the hearth by the fireplace.

She wasted some of the precious water to bathe her feet, which caused her to shed a tear or two from the stinging. She was not used to such long walking, though she thought she would become more accustomed to it as the trip wore on. And the pain was unimportant to her, a mere inconvenience, because she could not go back now even if she wanted to. Sometimes she regretted leaving, not because captivity had become more bearable to her, but because it was at least familiar, and on the journey of her life, it was closer to where she wanted to be— home—than where she was now. She wanted to go back to Wales again, and yet she could only go forward, for Sempringham was in another direction from home. What she would do when she got there, when she secured Gwenllian, she had no notion. She had never thought beyond getting to the Gilbertine abbey; it was a long way off. Just now, the walk was absorbing all of her energy.

July 1284 A.D.

Ine was travelling south of York on a return from his yearlong journey through the borderlands of Scotland when he heard from some other musicians of the woman minstrel who had appeared in Peterborough several weeks before and was making quite a sensation there. Women troubadors were a much more common phenomenon on the continent, in France and Italy, than they were in England, where their presence might occasion remarks among ordinary folk. Those who played and sang, however, were sure to comment on anyone new in their numbers, male or female, and this female had been completely unheard of until now.

Scotland had depressed Ine utterly, because he saw in its environment and among its people that same inevitable leaning toward war which had destroyed much of what he loved about Wales. The Scots were a rougher, angrier nation than the Welsh. Their Celtic roots ran as deep, but it was more firmly intermingled with the Pictish strain, a harsher bloodline than that of the spiritual Celts. Ine felt, on Scottish soil, as if he were reliving Wales before the storm of King Edward had struck. He never stayed long in any one place; he found no solace in men laying a course into war with the heedlessness of Prince David at his densest.

When he heard of the woman minstrel from the viele player entertaining in the household of the Archbishop of York, Ine knew instantly—without the slightest notion of how he knew, and despite the fact that reason told him he must be mistaken—that it was Briana. He finished his evening's performance, collected the coin the archbishop generously proffered, begged off performing another night, took his horse from the stable, and rode south without even pausing to sleep. He'd become adept at dozing on horseback or catching short naps when he was on the roads, but now he hardly even paused for that. Some instinct told him that the Lady Briana was in danger, doing something so entirely reckless that he feared for her.

He didn't stop to think that he was acting inexplicably. He knew he was doing a right, even a necessary, thing, and he did it without second thoughts. His only fear was that she would move on from Peterborough before he reached it.

August 1284 A.D.

With each day that passed, Briana grew more confident as a musician. Her walk to Peterborough had seen her finding shelter where she could, playing for small crofters and their families, for farmers or herdsmen, and she grew easier at both playing and singing. Being appreciated increased her ability to perform in front of others. By the time she reached Peterborough, where the companies were greater, as were the rewards, she was polished and skilled enough to hold her own.

As she traveled, she discovered, to her complete astonishment, that she liked both the English people and the English countryside. The people, outside the royal circle, were very much like the Welsh, yeoman stock, with Angle or Saxon roots, rather than Norman, and with concerns of home and hearth and a hunger for good crops and good stories. The land they lived on did not draw her as Wales had, but it drew her in different ways. England was not as wild as Wales. It had extremes, but it moderated them; its greens were brighter, its aspects somehow softer. It was, she decided, very pretty, while "pretty" was not a word she would ever have applied to the land from which she had come, where the beauty came from its drama, from its demand that it be met on its own terms.

By the time she reached Peterborough, the summer was in full flower, and she was enchanted by the bright colors and delicate petals. Briana had loved flowers since she sat among the posies on her mother's grave. England's flowers seduced her.

She began, slowly, to forget that she was an escaped prisoner, and to believe that this life, of music and admiration, was one she could continue to live.

She lingered long in Peterborough, where there were many people who wanted to hire her services and who could pay with enough coin so that by the beginning of August she was able to buy her own horse. She had been under roofs for most of the spring and summer showers, and there were no strong storms that year, so she had come to regard even the weather as milder here than on the other side of the Welsh border. When she rode out of Peterborough on her own palfrey, the dulcimer in her saddlebags, she was as nearly happy as she could remember being since before the Demoiselle died.

After Peterborough, she would find no real towns again she reached Botolph's Town, perhaps three days away. But she had some coin, and she could pay for hospitality as well as play for it. She wondered what it would be like to travel comfortably, quickly. She smiled, thinking of it, as she rode.

She was only a day ahead of him, Ine discovered, when he reached Peterborough. He paused only long enough to buy some ale to drink on the journey, and then, knowing where she'd gone as surely as if she'd left word for him, he followed behind her. Some sense of foreboding made him think about following after Llewelyn those months—years, now—ago, as Wales's gallant prince rode into treachery. He still did not pause to wonder how he knew these things, why he seemed able to sense her; he only knew with confidence that he did, and that she was, somehow in danger. He rode faster in his effort to close the distance between them.

The sense of peril that Ine felt in no way affected Briana, who grew more certain each day that danger was what she had left behind in Westminster, and freedom was where she could be most fully safe. She rode slowly on toward Botolph's Town, letting the horse set an easy pace of its own, dreaming distractedly of taking Gwenllian from Sempringham and vanishing with the little girl into someplace the reach of the Plantagenets did not extend. Where that might be, she could not guess, but she did not try, seeking to believe that the Lord would guide her when guidance was needful. She could not conceive that God, having recently harmed her so completely, would not now gift her with something for which she wished so devoutly. She did not perceive her own hubris in thinking, in effect, that, having incurred her enmity, God would now want to regain her good graces.

God, it seemed, had other plans.

Somewhere along the narrow track, a nameless spot in stretching woodland between Peterborough and Botolph's Town, Briana encountered a knight on foot. He was built like many knights were—huge, muscled, ham-fisted. He had not recently bathed, nor trimmed his hair, and his surcoat was badly ragged. That, combined with his lack of a mount, indicated either a poor master or none at all.

Briana touched her heels to the palfrey's sides to pass him quickly, but he reached out as she neared with the speed of a man trained to fight and caught first the reins of the palfrey, before it could attain a full trot, and then with his free hand grabbed for Briana's skirt.

She knew she was in trouble at once, thought he might be satisfied with the animal, and threw herself off the farther side of the horse, jerking her skirt loose from his fumbling hand.

She had spent enough time around the knights at Windsor in the past year to know better than to try to reason with this one. Flight was her best option. Perhaps he would take the horse and go. In her panic, it did not occur to her that he could take the horse and use it to try to pursue her. It did not occur to her yet that his object could be other than theft.

As she hit the ground, she stumbled on her skirts, but with the horse between her and the knight, she had time to recover her balance. She fled back down the track in the direction she'd come, while the knight, after shouting, "Come back, Mistress!" struggled to mount the now spooked and bucking palfrey.

Briana had reached a bend in the track some distance away when she heard hoofbeats behind her. Reacting completely by instinct, she dashed from the track into the downhill tangle of brush and close thickets, where there would not be room for a horse to maneuver. If chasing her was his object, then she could at least make it more difficult for him.

The knight tried to drive the palfrey off the track in her wake, but the horse did not like either the downward angle or the tightness of the foliage and spun around on her back feet, then balked. He clapped her sides cruelly with his heels, but she refused to yield, screaming out her anger, and then trying to crush his leg against a tree. The knight wavered momentarily between continuing to fight the animal or leaving it to pursue the woman. Lust won. He swung off the palfrey and plunged into the bushes.

She was smaller and quicker, and despite occasional snags and scratches, she was able to gain considerable downhill distance before the undergrowth thinned out at the bottom of the slope. She ran to the left, where the treeline at the far edge of the expanse of meadow was closest. The weeks of walking had toughened her feet and strengthened the muscles of her legs, making her resilient enough to be as fleet as fear dictated.

The knight crashed his way through the tangles of thicket, plowing a path as he did so, and once on the flats, his greater power closed the distance between them in several minutes. Had he thought, he might have wondered why she was not tiring as quickly as he would have expected, but like most knights, he wasted little time in thought.

Briana did not dare to look back, for it would have slowed her, and she could not afford to slow. She could hear the heavy steps behind her drawing closer and closer; her breathing turned into quick gasps that made it seem harder to get enough air. Then something struck her heavily from behind and knocked her off her feet, slamming her into the ground. She cried out as she fell. Yet when she felt rough hands on her, smelled hot, rank breath that warmed the side of her face, she disregarded breathlessness and weakness and twisted around so that she could see her attacker. She regretted it, for he was a brutish, ugly man, with gapped and rotting teeth. She tried to kick at him, but her legs tangled in her skirts. She flailed at him with her hands, unaware of whether she was fisting them or not.

He pulled at her skirts enough to rip them down one side, which gave her more leverage for her kicks. She tried to use them to connect with something, but was hindered when he leaned his considerable weight on her body, knocking the breath out of her again and making it harder for her to inhale. She pushed at him to try to raise him enough to let her fill her lungs, but it was like pushing at a wall. She lashed at his head with her hands.

He tried to catch her frantically thrashing arms, and more by fortune than by design, one of her blows connected solidly with his eye. He roared at her and backhanded her, snapping her head back and bouncing it off the ground. She saw bright flashes in front of her, fought to stay conscious, her efforts to get him away from her continuing under the driving force of even greater terror. He removed one of his hands from the fight in order to reach downward, whether for a dagger or simply to begin opening his clothing, she could not tell. She used the opening to sink her nails into the side of his cheek.

He stopped whatever it was he was trying to do, put both his hands on her throat, and squeezed.

Briana fought for consciousness, tearing at his face with her hands, feeling the pain of being throttled combined with the growing darkness. Her hands began to feel heavy; her right hand fell to her side, the knuckles landing on something hard. Her barely functioning mind identified it as a rock. She grasped at it, made a superhuman effort, and slammed it into the side of his head. The blow was a glancing one, but it jarred him enough to momentarily break his grip on her neck and slide sideways off her chest, crushing her hip into the pebbly earth. She got one swift, icy, lung-filling breath before he threw himself at her again, snarling, "Bitch!" He wrenched the rock out of her hand, dropped it, and began to choke her again.

She couldn't seem to break his grip this time, and after a few seconds, the world began to fade to gray.

Ine saw her flee from the track in her desperate downhill flight, saw the huge knight follow her. He reined in quickly, left his horse on the track not far from where the palfrey now stood. He started to take a step or two toward the slope, but some instinct pulled him back, a feeling that if he moved after the pair now— despite Briana's obvious danger—he would not succeed in saving her. Against all reason, he stood on the track waiting. He didn't know what he was waiting for until he heard hoofbeats.

In the past few weeks, when he had sent his knights to the south, east, and north, King Edward increased the reward for finding Briana and returning her safely to Westminster. In addition to the amount he had promised in coin, the king decreed a barony to any knight who returned Briana of Flint to his care. The opportunity for a mercenary knight to become landed was great enough to spur all the king's knights who heard of it to even greater effort. Singly, or in small groups, they left off the futile hunt on the roads to Wales and spread across the length and breadth of the kingdom in other directions.

A pair of these searcher-knights had ridden south from Botolph's Town just an hour ago. Ine waved them down the moment they came into view. He knew if he told them it was just any damsel in distress, they might well have helped the knight who was hurting Briana rather than rescue her. But he, too, knew of the king's reward, and so when the knights reached him, Ine bowed, pointed downhill, and said, "I am Ine, Bard of Dubhain. I have been following the Lady Briana of Flint, and she is in danger, there."

The two knights exchanged one quick glance, swung off their mounts, drew swords, and with Ine following, started downslope. Ine shouted at them to bear to the left, knowing which way Briana had gone with absolute certainty.

They emerged from the underbrush near the rogue knight and his now still prey, having closed the distance in a diagonal descent down the hill.

Ine felt one moment of panic that the girl was dead, but then calmed as he realized that he would have known if she were gone.

The rogue knight had just taken his hands from her bruised throat and was raising her skirts above her waist when one of the pair from Botolph's Town shouted at him. He glanced over his shoulder, saw drawn swords, and thought that he would have to fight to keep his prize, since the weaponry implied that these men would not let him share what he thought was his even if he had offered to share her with them. To ensure that she did not waken and try to run while he was fighting for her, the knight punched Briana's already reddened face, nearly breaking her jaw, as he scrambled to his feet and drew his own sword.

Ine darted around the armed men, who were now largely concerned with one another, and knelt beside the unconscious young woman, whose face was already swelling darkly. He cradled her against his chest, holding her limp body with a protective tenderness that he hadn't realized had been growing in him since she'd opened her baby eyes the day Myrrdin and Bertran took him to be present when she was born. Though he had not held her that day, he felt as if this were a repetition. He recognized that, beyond any further doubt, he was somehow tied to her.

As the two knights with dreams of baronies dispatched the one knight whose dreams extended no further into the world than his belly or his loins, Ine watched the labored breathing of the lady of legend, wondering how he, who had never touched the mysteries, had managed to do this.

The rogue knight was good, so the fight went on for long enough for Briana to stir, to become cognizant of pain in a dozen places, to try to draw a full breath and fail, and then to recognize the face that bent above her. When she tried to say his name, her voice grated and failed to emerge, and then she fell out of consciousness again. She did not see her attacker die, nor did she see Ine give her to one of the searcher-knights to carry up the hill.

Riding hard, changing horses three times, they reached Westminster in only three days. She was nearly dead by the time they got her there, but the king had decreed that she should not die, and so she did not.

Westminster—September 1284 A.D.

She had almost completely healed before King Edward sent for her. It was a summons she had been expecting since she began to recover, after the knights brought her back to Westminster. Once her body grew stronger, it was only Queen Eleanor's intervention that kept the king from sending her to prison in the White Tower, but Eleanor had taken one look at the battered face, and the contused, bruised, abraded body and simply countermanded her husband's command. Briana reflected that it was the single thing for which she might have to thank her would-be rapist. Without such extensive damage, she could be languishing in that grim fortress from which Prince David had emerged in five separate pieces.

Instead, she was kept comfortably confined in the royal quarters in Windsor, ministered to by the queen's physician and her own servants, visited by the queen and Princess Eleanor, spared much of Joanna's thoughtlessly malicious company, and encouraged to rest and regain her strength. Yet she knew that punishment must be forthcoming at some point, since King Edward had to have been wrathful.

She knew how fortunate she had been that Ine was in time to save her from the rape, though she was very hazy on the details of how, and she regretted that she could tell no one it was the bard to whom she owed her honor, and perhaps her life as well, rather than the two knights who had claimed the reward. Yet she knew that he had left as soon as she reached Westminster and was in the hands of the physicians, leaving only her dulcimer, retrieved from the palfrey's saddlebags, and she would not betray him. She wondered when she would see him again every time she played the instrument. She did not sing. The physicians said her voice would return, but very slowly, and she was unwilling to try.

Usually Princess Eleanor, unfailingly kind, accompanied Briana back to her room with her after-Mass meal, for Briana was not allowed to join the family for meals in the solar or hall. The princess sat on the windowsill while Briana ate, telling her the gossip of the court, Joanna's latest foibles, and the new stories about young Prince Edward, who was thriving. Briana looked forward to the visits, and to Mass, which constituted the sum of her entertainment. She never prayed at Mass, but she enjoyed the chanting, the spectacle, the companionship of other people besides Enlis and Hulde, her housekeeper, who were more often silent than not. At first she was frightened at having to be in the same chapel with the king, but he stolidly ignored her, and Queen Eleanor always gave her a small smile, tinged with regret. Soon she was no more hesitant to venture into the chapel than she was to return to her room again.

And then, with the autumn leaves falling all around the castleyard, when she had just begun to think perhaps things would never change, the king commanded her to attend him.

She went calmly with the messenger, her serenity an overlay, the placidity of the condemned. She was unaware that her calm smoothed her newly healed face, that it imparted to her a very adult elegance, a noble loveliness.

King Edward had put on his crown, an unmistakable gesture of power, even though his closet, to which Briana was shown, was small and close. He occupied the only chair, drawn forward so that the table was not a barrier between them. Candles banished some of the darkness, but cast shadows that lent ominous lines to his face.

Briana curtsied, and then stood, waiting to hear her fate.

Edward was thinking that he had not realized she had become so exquisite. He had always thought of her as a child—a perception his wife encouraged, he realized now. In the months she had been out of his hands, Briana had matured. She was no longer a child, and the womanhood she was approaching showed the promise of extraordinary beauty. The king was far from immune to the attractions of a beautiful woman; his growing number of bastards proved that in a tangible way. He recognized that her nascent comeliness could weaken him, and he hardened his resolve against it. "Well, lady?"

She was unsure what reaction he wanted from her. "You sent for me, Your Grace," she said cautiously.

"Aye." His voice was little more than a growl. "You led me a merry chase. I await your apology."

Briana wondered if he wanted her to kneel, but she did not. She clasped her hands in front of her, held them tensely against the soft wachet of her gown. Her serenity was leaking away under the need to be a participant in this meeting. She had expected to listen to either a long tirade or a short sentence. Neither, it seemed, was forthcoming. She drew a breath, wet her lips. "I—I apologize for offending you," she said in a low voice.

"Offending?"

Her hands began, irresistibly, to tremble.

"You defied me, lady," said the king tightly, "and you shall not do it again."

She swallowed hard. "I ran not so much from you," she said as steadily as she could. "I had taken a vow, Your Grace, and my honor—"

He rose suddenly, the motion silencing her. "Honor!" he repeated. "Have you your honor still, lady, or was it taken from you somewhere on the way?"

She guessed his meaning at once, and her face flamed. She could only whisper, "I am as I was."

He chose to believe her, because it would not be important until or unless he decided to wed her to someone. "I'll have your obedience now, lady. Should you fail in it again, you will know my wrath." He watched her closely. "Shall I tell you what I will decree should you disobey me?"

She couldn't nod. She raised her chin, but the trembling had been slowly increasing, until it threatened to become visible.

When he saw that she would not speak, that—finally—she was recognizing his limitless power, he said, "The price for any further disobedience will be paid not by you, for I may have need of you. Your debts will be paid by Flint."

The trembling ceased entirely in the shock of what she had just heard. "Flint?" she repeated, distressed.

"Aye." He was enjoying her discomfiture. He felt that once she feared him properly, he would have no further trouble with her. "I shall extract that price from land and people both. The manor house will be torn down stone by stone, the village burned, the livestock slain in the fields, and the people either driven away or put to the sword. Run from us again, and Flint dies. Harm yourself, and Flint dies. Behave other than we expect of you, and Flint dies. What say you to that?"

It was as though he had struck her. The blood drained from her face, leaving even her lips ashen, and she swayed but did not faint. She had no doubt he would do exactly as he said. She felt her vow to the Demoiselle slipping away from her. The nameless place on the track outside Peterborough was as close to Gwenllian as she was going to get. The unbreakable chains of her captivity settled themselves upon her again, locked this time by her love for Flint. "I shall obey you, Your Grace," she said, each word a pain worse than the feel of the rogue knight's hands around her throat.

"Be sure that you do," he said. And now, having extracted the promise he wished to obtain, having witnessed her capitulation, he was prepared to be magnanimous. He never imagined any response to his magnanimity other than gratitude. He told her she could leave her confinement in the small upper room and rejoin his wife and daughters.

She barely heard him. She was thinking only that she would have to bury her hatred deep within her, where it would not be found by anyone who might betray her to the king.

Chapter 10

Windsor—February 1289 A.D.

The arrow struck the target exactly in its center, with a most satisfying thwack. Briana smiled as she lowered the bow and stepped back to give Princess Eleanor the next shot.

"Excellent," the princess said approvingly. "You are a far better shot than I."

Briana did not reply. It would not have been politic to say to the princess what her reply would have been. "I have so little control over anything in my life, 'tis a pleasure to control precisely where an arrow strikes." The breeze freshened, pulling some strands of hair out of her caul and whipping them across her barbette and into her face. She tucked her bow under her arm as Eleanor lowered her own bow and nocked arrow to wait for a lull in the wind.

Briana pushed the hair back into her caul. "Let not moving air be a deterrent, Highness. A soldier must shoot no matter the wind."

Eleanor grinned impishly, but did not raise her bow. "I am not much of a soldier," she said, "and I remind you for the countless time to call me by my name when we are solitary."

"For the countless time, I fail to remember." Briana said it lightly, and if Eleanor disbelieved her, she made no mention of it. "Be not discouraged by the wind. Shoot."

The princess was saved from having to reply by the appearance of a messenger, who bowed to her and said, "Highness, your mother the queen requests you join her in the solar."

"I attend," said Eleanor. She set her bow down, raised her eyebrow in Briana's direction, and followed the messenger across the wide swath of turf toward the castle.

Briana bent, picked up another arrow, nocked it, drew it, felt the wind against her hand and cheek, compensated for it with a skill born of long practice, aimed, and let it fly. The arrow thudded into the target barely left of Briana's first arrow. She set her bow down beside Eleanor's, walked to one of the hay bales which lined the archery butts, and sat down. The day was a cold one, which the wind edged with frost, but there was no snow. She preferred waiting outdoors in case the princess should return; an intention to do so was how she interpreted Eleanor's raised eyebrow.

Briana often sought solitude, and the otherwise deserted archery field was more pleasant than the quiet of her tiny chamber above the solar. She knew she was unlikely to be approached, even if one of the king's knights saw her here. She was as much crown property as any of the princesses, though she was not, nor would she ever be, royal. Nor, truth to tell, would she have wanted to be. She had been King Edward's prisoner for seven years now, and that had given her an intimate understanding of the Plantagenet rulers of England. She had often thought to herself that her soul would wither should she have to be one of them.

When King Edward first took her from Flint, she had thought she was likely to die of misery, not merely because she was being stolen from her lands and her people, but because the abduction occurred at the worst moment of her life, immediately after Fearndon. She refused to think about Fearndon. She had resolutely refused to think about it all these years, because it still had the power to destroy her. After her unsuccessful flight, she had determined not to be destroyed. She wanted to go back to Flint again, chose to believe that was possible, and she had to be ready when the opportunity presented itself. Until that time, being with Princess Eleanor was one of the least objectionable ways to exist.

The King of England had never acknowledged that she was his prisoner; he called her his ward, and—to her complete astonishment—he seemed to sincerely want her to consider herself his seventh daughter, just the age of his eldest, the gentle Eleanor. How he could ever have expected such a thing of her after the threats to ensure her good behavior was a mystery to her. Even more mysterious was that he always acted as if he had succeeded, mistaking her compliance for obedience, her forbearance for affection, and her surface cheerfulness for genuine happiness or even gaiety. He did not seem to notice that she rarely smiled broadly—something which certainly never happened in his presence—and he would have no way of knowing that she could not remember the last time she had laughed aloud.

She felt chilled sitting still, so she rose and walked down to the target to retrieve her arrows. She nourished a secret pride in her ability to shoot and to ride, two activities which drew her out of the court, where she often felt Edward's knights staring at her. She thought that they must still have seen her as a curiosity; it did not occur to her that they stared because of her beauty. She considered Princess Eleanor to be the ideal of feminine beauty, and she did not resemble Eleanor.

Plantagenet beauty was golden, and Briana was dark. She was certain that the only reason Princess Joanna did not insult her over her looks was because Joanna's coloring more matched Briana's than it did any of her sisters'. Briana did not share Joanna's wish to be fair, but she did admit to herself that in general, Plantagenets were as stunning as they were powerful, their bodies tall and strong, their hair sunlight, their skin cream, their eyes clear sky blue. Briana was small, though not frail, her hair deep black, her skin a rich beige, her eyes the bright green of spring grass, her cheeks normally flushed with rose. She thought little of her looks, for they had never been a part of her legend. At nearly twenty, she had not seen her home or her nation for more than a third of her life, but she had not forgotten it. It was because of the legend that she was here at Windsor or at Westminster with the court, and not in Wales. It was because of the legend that she lived a life torn from her land. King Edward was, she told herself, afraid to let her return to Wales, because it had been prophesied at her birth that she would bring freedom.

The King of England could not allow a free Wales. Because of the legend, he had built the first of his massive castles at Flint. Overall, he had given Wales a ring of fortifications to ensure its continuing submission during and after the conquest, tangible signs of his power and that of the Marcher Lords. She had seen none of these castles, but she knew their names as she knew the names of her own family. Besides the one at Flint, there were Rhuddlan, Builth—near where Prince Llewelyn had been slain—Aberystwyth, Cricieth, Caernarfon, Harlech, Beaumaris, and Conway. She could imagine the huge piles of stone, scarring landscapes she remembered, though in her mind the castles tended to all look rather like Windsor, with whose keep and courtyards she was too familiar.

She shivered a little as the wind freshened, clicking the bare branches of the trees across the field with enough vigor for the sound to carry to where the Welsh woman waited to see if Eleanor would return. Briana picked up the cloak she had dropped to allow her to draw the bowstring unhindered. She wondered if she should go back to her chamber and collect her dulcimer. Playing it was the other thing which lifted her spirits, and she played very well. None of the Plantagenets had musical gifts. Briana treasured anything which made it clear she was made of different stuff from the Norman rulers, but she thought she might have treasured her music even had every princess played something with more skill than she herself possessed.

Had any of them played, Briana thought, Princess Eleanor would probably have been the musician, and Princess Eleanor was the Plantagenet whom Briana thought least badly of, though her mother, the queen, also called Eleanor, had won a place in Briana's tolerance as well. The two Eleanors had always tried to be kind to her, and though Briana could not forget that the English rulers were Wales's enemies and therefore her own, she understood that there were gradations of inhumanity. And she never spoke her mind in captivity, so she was certain they would have no idea how she really felt.

Princess Eleanor had been born the same month and year as Briana, was exquisitely beautiful, and doted on by her parents not only because she was their first-born and their favorite among the daughters, but because she was loveable. She was much more proper and kinder than the willful Joanna, now seventeen, much brighter than Margaret, three years Joanna's junior, much more accessible than eleven-year-old Mary, who had already been a nun for six years, and much better company than either nine-year-old Alice or seven-year-old Elizabeth.

Princess Eleanor was unmarried, and at her age, that was an extremely rare thing, caused by the fact that Eleanor had been heir presumptive to the throne of England until she was fifteen. The queen had borne three boys to inherit the crown, but two had died young, and the third had never been strong until he was finally carried off as well. So the then Prince Edward— subsequently and presently king—had been notably reluctant to marry off his eldest daughter, since by doing so, he would likely be choosing his own successor. He had no desire to do that until and unless he died sonless. By the time the long-awaited, vitally healthy fourth boy was born, Eleanor had become so accustomed to independence that she was unwilling to be rushed into a now presumably harmless marriage. She began a reasoned and ultimately successful campaign, under cover of her father's joy at a male heir who seemed likely to survive, to secure his promise that he would not wed her to any man without her consent.

Briana envied her that promise. She herself would be a prize in the marriage market, bearing as she did title to such a strategic section of Northern Wales. Indeed, sometimes she wondered why King Edward had not handed her to someone before now—one of his trusted barons was the likeliest, and she knew she would hate them all equally. There wasn't a single knight loyal to Edward without Welsh blood on his hands. Some had less than others, but none was clean. They ranked from young Fulk de Lacey, elevated to Baron Andevin very recently, through the three Marcher Lords, who regarded the killing of Welshmen either as no more than their duty or as great sport, to the Earl Connarc, who, as Baron Connarc prior to his own elevation, had commanded the force that devastated Fearndon. It was also said of him that he had been responsible for the betrayal and murder of Prince Llewelyn. Briana could not have decided whether Llewelyn's death or Fearndon had had greater consequences for Wales, but for her, personally, there was no doubt. Earl Connarc would have to answer before God for hundreds of Welsh lives besides the prince's, and among those were Briana's father and her two brothers.

The sound of hoofbeats broke into thoughts she would rather have let pass anyway, and Briana looked up to see a group of horsemen approaching Windsor. She recognized King Edward in the lead and had to overcome an impulse to duck behind the hay bales in case he should notice her. Briana had always found it difficult to be confronted by the King of England. The mere thought of it brought bile into her throat and a truly dangerous hatred into her heart. The priests would have told her that hatred was dangerous to her soul, but she knew that people who hated Edward Plantagenet incurred grave danger to their bodies as well. Yet, she was aware that the king was a very handsome man. The priests—who seemed to profess care of the soul at the expense of the body, though they themselves were usually quite comfortable—had also said that the devil had a pleasing aspect. Briana believed it, for Edward Plantagenet, called "Longshanks" for his imposing height, was graceful, strong, and magnetic. She thought that he was simultaneously fair to look at and foul to upset, disappoint, or disobey.

Her body still trembled when she remembered her encounters with him. She fought the shaking as she fought the urge to crouch down so that he might not see her. The three times in her life when she had been confronted by the King of England had not resulted in a bettering of her situation. She could live best day to day by burying those memories, and she did so now, watching the king and his knights canter through the park toward the stables. The wind drew more strands of hair from her caul, and this time Briana did not reach up to tuck them away.

She was still standing, hands hidden in her cloak, trembling either from the increasing late winter cold or from the recollection of Edward's hawk-like gaze pinning her to earth stripped of her illusions and dreams, or both, when she spied a messenger on his way to the archery butts from the castle. She guessed that Eleanor would not be coming back and bent to recover all the arrows they had stuck into one of the hay bales, ready to be plucked for shooting.

Despite the fiction that she was part of the royal family, the messenger did not bow to her, nor did she expect him to. He was one of the younger pages, fostered to Windsor from a manor in the East, but he had quickly learned the precedence required. "Lady, the Princess Eleanor regrets duties call her away."

"My thanks," Briana said absently.

He made a gesture to tell her he was not done. "She sends word that you have received a letter, and she knows you would wish to be informed of its arrival."

Briana repeated her thanks, this time with genuine feeling.

"Please be so kind as to return the bows and arrows to the armorer," she said. She gathered her skirts and ran lightly across the lawns toward the west bailey.

Whether here or at the palace of Westminster, she was given her own small chamber in the royal apartments. She knew she had Queen Eleanor to be grateful to for that small mercy. She reached the shelter of the curtain wall around the bailey just as the wind began to carry snowflakes with it.

Letters were very rare and very precious, because they brought news of home. Sometimes months in transit, going from monastery to monastery with travelers, eventually they would find her. Her last letter from Flint had been over a year ago.

She passed through the open gate in the thick curtain wall and crossed the bailey to the buildings housing living quarters for the king and his family. Windsor had a number of halls; the one in the royal apartments was only slightly larger than the solar, and it was quiet as she entered it. She could hear voices in the solar, however, as she crossed the empty room to stairs built into the narrower inner wall.

Her chamber was large enough for a bed and a trunk, but little else. She was glad to reach it and shut the door behind her. The door had no lock, so it was more a symbolic than an actual barrier. She treasured the symbolism anyway. With the door closed, the only light was from a narrow slit window, too thin to give her a seat on its sill.

The letter lay on her trunk, next to her dulcimer. She had no doubt that it had already been opened and read by Edward's spies. The letters she sent were also subjected to such scrutiny, so she and her Aunt Maud, who was caring for Flint in the absence of every other member of Bryn's family, used a circuitous language of harmlessness through which they could sense some of the realities of each other's lives, but not all.

Briana dropped her cloak on the bed and carried the letter the two steps to the slit window. The wax seal looked whole, but when she slid her forefinger against it, the wax popped easily away. She was not surprised. The careful ecclesiastical writing told her that Father Ciaran, priest at St. Maedoc's church, was still in residence, still serving as Maud's scribe, since she was an unlettered woman, as most Welshwomen were. Briana had learned to read and write as she learned to play her dulcimer.

"My niece Briana," the letter began, "I send you greetings for the Nativity of Our Lord." That meant the letter had probably been scribed at the beginning of Advent, and it was now mid-February. The letter had arrived quickly, in less than three months. "The harvest has been as expected. The comfort of the Mass brings every day rewards to all. We one and all welcome the season chastened by snow. The hens are all in egg at this time. We must let some of the eggs hatch for the new seasons, with some lack of eggs to eat thereby. Flint is still in the care of the Marcher Lord of the North, the honorable Baron Wigmore. We are reminded that his father was our castellan these years hence. All hope that you are well and that you will by God's grace return to us. Your dutiful aunt."

Briana read it through three times and then laid it back on the trunk. They were hungry this winter at Flint. She could only hope they were not very hungry. There had been hard winters before, especially in the year of the Welsh war, but in times of peace Flint had usually been prosperous. She wondered what peace looked like in Wales this year.

She sat down on her bed and picked up the dulcimer, sliding the two little hammers from under the strings. She played quietly, songs she'd learned as a child, songs with Welsh words she would not sing here, in the hands of her enemies, no matter how pleasant those enemies tried to be to her.

The main meal of the day was normally an ordeal for Briana, whether in the large hall with the king's knights and any palace guests in attendance, or in the small hall involving just the family. The latter was the case after Mass the day following the arrival of Briana's letter.

She left the chapel—a much larger and colder place than the small wood-lined chapel at Westminster Palace—with Princesses Eleanor and Joanna. The princesses' ladies left them to go into the kitchens, and Briana dismissed her only two attendants, Enlis and Hulde. She thought they were as much in the service of the Plantagenets as in her own, and sometimes she wondered if they spied on her, but since she truly had nothing to hide which would be found by anyone who could not guess her thoughts, she never fretted herself about it.

As always, Mass provided entertainment and prompted thought. She had a vague feeling that it should have given her comfort, but it did not. The priest always seemed disinterested in some parts and too proud of his role in others. She was, however, fascinated by the Eucharist, taken by the priest and offered routinely to the king and queen as well when the king was in residence. Only on Easter or on truly special occasions were the wine and wafer given to all the attendees, visible evidence of things invisible and guideline to the Resurrection. Briana had welcomed it the few times she had received it at court, but each time was bittersweet, a reminder of the joy she had felt with her first Eucharist, attendant to the bride at Prince Llewelyn's wedding. Her beloved father and brothers had been alive then; her future had seemed safe and secure. Whenever the memory came of the time when she was a person, not a pawn, she would have to fight tears. And fight them she did. It was a point of pride with her that the Plantagenets had never seen her weep. And, she swore to herself, they never would.

After Mass, at the meal in the small hall, the king and queen seated themselves at the high table and signalled their daughters to sit at one of the two trestle tables. Briana perfunctorily smiled at Queen Eleanor as she took her place. The hall was lighted by the large fireplace, which took up one of the end walls, by sconces with heavy wax candles, and by the smokeholes under the eaves on the south side. The queen smiled back, her face alight, her eyes twinkling. Briana wondered why.

Princess Eleanor, at the high end of the lower table, to Briana's left, leaned over as the servants laid their bread trencher in front of them. "Pray join me in my mother's rooms when the meal is done," she said. Her voice bubbled a little with a gentle anticipation. "She and my father will be in the council chamber much of the day, and she's granted us the use of her rooms."

"As you like," said Briana. She wondered what sort of project the two Eleanors were hatching. Previous such invitations had resulted in new shoes or headdresses, in learning a new board game from France, in practicing some new embroidery stitches, and such like. It meant she would not be able to ride today, but any diversion was worthwhile.

To Briana's right, Joanna chattered with Alice and Margaret, twitting the younger girls about yesterday's Latin lesson. Briana assumed the younger princesses were not included in the invitation to the queen's rooms. If they had been, Joanna would have been telling Briana what the project was going to be, since Joanna had ways of finding out everything and was entirely incapable of keeping secrets.

The cold meats and cheeses were brought and set in front of the family. As Briana moved a piece of cheese onto the bread, she sensed that the king was studying her. She risked a quick, sideways glance past Eleanor toward the princess's parents, and it was as she imagined. King Edward sat, his fingers on the stem of a goblet, his other hand lightly stroking his short yellow beard, his gaze fixed on her face. Queen Eleanor was speaking to him, and he nodded in response, but he never looked away from Briana.

She took a bite of the suddenly tasteless cheese. It being Lent, she would not have to juggle a soupspoon with hands that might tremble and betray her. Being the object of Edward's scrutiny could in no way be good. She was relieved, though not comforted, when he looked at last at his wife.

Chapter 11

After she washed her face and hands at the basin the servants filled from the water shaft and set in the solar every morning, Briana went through the gallery to the private chamber everyone called "the queen's rooms." Anything that would keep her from conjecturing about Edward's possible plans for her was to be welcomed. Knowing she was expected, Briana did not scratch at the door, only opened it and stepped in.

The queen's rooms had a door and two high windows looking into the courtyard between the keep and the chapel. A soft carpet covered the stones of the floor, and cushioned benches stood in most of the available space. The back of the room was decorated with several unexpected columns, as if at one time it was thought it might give onto a gallery, but then the builders changed their minds. Draperies hung over parts of the wall between the columns, and their vibrant colors brought the room a brightness few other areas in the castle attained.

Briana glanced at the four people in the room and halted, one hand still on the doorlatch. In addition to Princess Eleanor, sitting on one of the benches in front of her embroidery frame, and two of the ladies who served and companioned her, the room held someone Briana had not seen for more than three years. It was a slender, still youthful-looking man in a dark gray supertunic. He looked up, smiling broadly as she came in.

Her pleasure at seeing him was so great and so genuine that she entirely forgot her concern about the king. "Ine!" Then she remembered her manners, closed the door behind herself, and dropped a perfunctory curtsey toward Eleanor. They maintained court manners in front of any members of the court who could spread stories about the Welsh woman's conduct.

Eleanor accorded her a gentle nod in return. "I thought you'd be pleased to know Ine was back, Lady Briana," the princess said formally. "Come, sit and join us. He's going to sing for us."

Ine watched the small pageant of politeness without the slightest doubt as to its duplicity. In the three years since he had seen them last, both women had matured in very different ways. Princess Eleanor had grown into a true Plantagenet, her face even-featured and fine, her hair a rich sun yellow. She moved and spoke as if she were utterly secure about her place in the world, and the confidence increased her beauty in a specific way that he recognized, but was not drawn to. She had been only seventeen when he last saw her, so the changes in her were a deepening, a refining, undramatic, expected.

Briana, on the other hand, was breathtaking. She had none of Eleanor's confidence, but rather a nervous energy she strongly controlled, giving her a hint of mysterious power beneath a surface of barely effective placidity. She had grown, in the years between seventeen and twenty, more beautiful than he would have imagined. She had taken all of Nonne's delicate loveliness and all of Bryn's handsome robustness and combined them into something instantly arresting, arriving a little short of perfection, but he could not imagine what she lacked.

Briana smiled at him, openly, fully, and he realized with a start that what elevated her beauty beyond the norm was that moment of joy at seeing him again. He wanted to tell her to be careful—bards were not immune from suspicion, and the ward of King Edward needed to be beyond accusation. He cast her a quick, cautioning look, which she read instantly. She lowered her gaze modestly to the floor and went to sit beside the princess.

Ine was in all likelihood the best bard alive now that Myrrdin—and probably Bertran as well—had passed from this life to the heaven reserved for the makers of music. He removed his harp from the satchel in which he always carried it, sat down on a low footstool, and struck the first chord of a solemn hymn he had not composed, but one suitable for a performance during Lent.

Both he and Briana were unaware that a shadow stirred in a hidden recess at the back of the room, concealed from view by one of the columns and one of the draperies. For all the times Briana had been in this chamber before, she had never seen that there was a couvert there. When she smiled at Ine, an utterly genuine smile, the beauty of her face and the sudden warmth of her expression broke upon the couvert like a wave of unexpected feeling.

The man in the tiny recess had wrapped himself in a hooded cloak of dark gray when Eleanor told him he should conceal himself in order to see the Welsh woman without having to make his presence known. "You've not heard the bard before, either, I believe," Eleanor had said to him, smiling up at her tall cousin. "And the lady in question very much likes the bard."

"Enough to have favored him?" The question, in the deep, even voice, took Eleanor by surprise. He saw it, and his lips twitched, marring the clean, strong lines of his face. "'Twould give me a reason to try to break the match."

"I had not guessed you were reluctant," Eleanor said slowly. "Rees, you have near thirty years, and lands. Have you never wanted a wife to administer them? Sons to inherit them?"

Rees, Earl Connarc, intensely disliked feeling uneasy or out of control. He had been permitted to serve as overlord of Conway in Northwest Wales since the end of the Welsh war, and he believed he had acquitted himself well. He had stayed away from Westminster and Windsor until the summons he had received two weeks earlier. "I had a wish to wed once," he said to Eleanor. "The king refused it. Now I have no wish to marry, especially not to suit my uncle, and Edward knows it. To order this—" He swore under his breath.

"'Twill increase your lands and your revenues." Eleanor tried to use reasons which would have swayed any of the numerous other knights she had known in her life, but the argument had a different effect on Rees. His face darkened more, and his blue eyes seemed to lose color as he battled rising anger. Eleanor was startled at the change in him.

"Any lands but these," he said through gritted teeth. "And if I do not wed, I believe I'll not have to take the lands."

Eleanor had great affection for Briana, whom she had just left at the archery butts. She had lived with the Welsh woman for all the years since her father had brought Briana from Wales. In truth, the princess had more affection for Briana than she bore for the tall, distant cousin she'd met only rarely before. Rees was reluctant to spend any time around courts or politics, and that was where Eleanor spent her life. She knew—because she'd heard her father speak of it—that he had been a good overlord for Conway, Edward's largest castle west of Flint, larger, but of less strategic importance than many of the others. She had thought, when her mother first told her of the match her father contemplated between Rees and Briana, that it would be a fine thing for Briana. Now she wondered if she had been quite wrong, and instantly wondered as well if there were some way she could help ease the road.

"My father is not a flexible man, as well you know," she said, convinced that none of them would ultimately escape the king's ambitions. "Have you seen Briana of Flint?"

They stood in one corner of the solar, speaking quietly enough not to be overheard by any of the other conversants in the room—the queen and little Prince Edward with his nurse by the fireplace; the Princesses Margaret, Alice, and Elizabeth in

another corner being instructed in embroidery by one of the
queen's ladies; and Joanna in the center of the room, looking at
some skeins of yarn brought to Windsor by one of the town
purveyors and probably trying to listen in on everything around
her.

Rees looked around the room as if trying how to decide to
answer what Eleanor regarded as a perfectly straightforward
question. She knew he was thinking hard, and she had once
heard her father say reluctantly that he believed Rees possessed
a better mind than three-quarters of the kingdom. The princess
could see evidence of the intelligence, but knew her cousin was
still a man of suppressed violence, of potential mayhem, of
accomplishments in the field. She tried to see him objectively
and felt a sudden stab of compassion, with a real component of
envy, for the younger woman who did not yet know that she was
to be compelled to marry any man, let alone this one. She
repeated, "Have ever you seen Briana of Flint?"

"Nay, I've not seen her," he answered at last. He was still
distracted, and his deep voice held no tones of curiosity.

Eleanor wondered if she might awaken some in him. "Why
not come on the morrow after the meal and secrete yourself in
the couvert in the queen's rooms?" she suggested. "I'll invite her
to hear the bard, and you can see if she pleases you."

Rees was about to say that she would not please him, but
then he reflected that if the woman seemed overfond of the
singer, he might have a weapon to use when Edward actually
chose to speak to him about the match. Thus far, he had not seen
the king. When he had arrived at Windsor in answer to the
summons, he was met only by John Peckham, sent to welcome
him and convey news of the match the king was planning. Now,
paying his duty to the queen in the solar, his cousin Eleanor
confirmed the information the archbishop had given him. Rees
thought his uncle would likely not wait much longer before
confronting him himself, not if Eleanor already knew what was
planned for him.

So Rees agreed to her suggestion, and a day later, wedged his wide shoulders into the narrow, shadowed recess, his bright golden hair covered with the dark wool hood.

Rees was Plantagenet, but he was not only Plantagenet. The vitriol with which King Edward had informed him of his Norse ancestry was still fresh in his mind. After that, Rees had decided that Edward did not intend him to wed. Now, after all this time, for reasons of his own, Edward had chosen a bride for Rees, and the huge man was not at all pleased.

Then he saw the woman. She was no longer a mere child, as many brides were at this time, as Margaret of Norwich would have been, and just as Eleanor was considered the beauty of England, this woman had to be the beauty of Wales. She was dark-haired, like Joanna, but her flawless complexion was not Joanna's olive. Her catlike green eyes were framed with heavy lashes. Every feature he studied seemed more attractive than the one he had just studied, and her face was an oval that would have seemed angelic, except for the fires that blazed, dampened, in her emerald regard. This was a woman, he realized, who kept her feelings under a veneer so hard that she appeared to be trying to make herself from the flint she bore as part of her name.

The moment she smiled at the bard, however, the banked fires softened to a glow that warmed Rees so unexpectedly he had to catch himself to stop from stepping out of the couvert into the room. That action stirred the drape, but no one seemed to notice. He realized that Briana of Flint was exquisite, graceful, and more elegant than he had imagined. A wry smile pulled at the corners of his usually stern mouth, for he understood well what Eleanor was doing, understood why she had thought that seeing Briana might be enough to reconcile him to the match. He even laughed at himself silently for a quick thought that he was sorry he had not come to court sooner. He might have seen her had he paid his duty to newborn Prince Edward in Westminster, instead of hurrying to do it in Caernaefon, before Queen Eleanor left Wales with her long prayed-for son. He knew if he said such a thing to his knights—that he should have considered coming to court earlier—they would laugh heartily at him, especially his friends Galen and Ralf, who had known him longest and were closest to him. They would be surprised to learn that he, who had been for years proof against the entanglements of any softer emotion, found himself stirred by the woman he would soon be commanded to marry. Rees admitted to himself, grudgingly, that Edward knew his tools very well.

In the queen's rooms, Ine strummed the harp in a soft minor key and began to sing "The Three Ravens," a tale of unrequited love said to have originated with the troubadours at Eleanor of Acquitaine's Courts of Love. The chorus at the end of each line was "Derry down, ah hey, derry down," and Briana joined in to sing it. Her clear, soaring soprano voice blended well with Ine's fine tenor, and she and the bard smiled at one another as they sang.

Briana was delighted to have a chance to sing. There had been a time in her life when she had feared she might never sing again, because her throat had been so badly injured, but that had been long ago, and she had chosen not to recall it for many years now. The return of her voice was a great relief to her at a time when little else gave her pleasure. She loved singing, for it helped her to pretend that she lived in a better world than she really did.

When the song ended, Eleanor sighed with pleasure and said, "You always choose the best songs, Ine, but 'Ravens' is an old song. Have you learnt any new ones on your travels? Or perchance made any?"

"Aye, I've learned one," the bard said in a low voice, "but I knew not if you'd wish me to sing it."

"Why would I not?" the princess asked, puzzled.

"'Tis in Welsh," Ine answered, carefully looking only at Eleanor.

Rees saw the fires spring up in Briana's eyes and be instantly quenched as she slid a mask of genteel interest over her face. He fancied he could hear her heartbeat accelerate.

Briana was indeed fighting against the excitement. If the song was in Welsh, then Ine was telling her he had been to Wales on his travels. He could tell her—she could not guess what, but certainly more than had been contained in the few, circumspect lines of her aunt's letter. She wanted to ask at once if he would tell her what was happening in her homeland and if he had gone to Flint, but it would not be wise to seek that information in the presence of the princess and her ladies. She would have to wait and hope to have an opportunity to speak with him later. Her heart raced ahead at the thought.

"Is it a love song?" Eleanor asked.

Ine nodded. "Songs of love are the only kind being imagined in Wales now, Highness," he said. "Any new songs of heroism or of gathering have been outlawed, as I would guess you know."

Briana looked down at her hands. Eleanor saw the motion, but did not call attention to it. Instead, she leaned an inch closer to the rose she was currently stitching at the center of the embroidery frame. "Pray, sing it, Master Ine. I'd hear a new song."

He plucked a series of chords on the harp and then added his voice to the rhythmic, plaintive melody. The words were innocuous enough, the tale familiar, but Briana resonated to the sound of her native tongue, and even as she smiled at Ine, her throat thickened and tears pricked at her eyes. She blinked them back and did not shed a single one, though she knew that, unshed, they made her eyes sparkle.

Ine noticed the effect the song had on her and ended it after the second verse, though there were actually three more. Without waiting for permission, he swung directly into the bawdy, "Happy Tinker," whose English words would have been highly improper had his female audience been younger than it was.

Eleanor laughed heartily, and Briana smiled, shaking off the melancholy which the previous song had engendered in her, thinking instead of how she might get to meet with Ine alone. Perhaps a music lesson, because it was known that it had been Ine who taught her to play when she was just a child—first the tiny psaltery that Father Ciaran had given her and then, when the plucking of the strings would have begun to callus her fingertips, her hammer dulcimer. The instrument was among those which had been brought back to the Isles from the Holy Land by the first crusaders, and Ine had carried it to Flint and given it to his young student. Memories of those days threatened to make her sad again, so she determinedly banished her homesickness and resolved to ask Eleanor if she might receive her old teacher's instruction again. She was certain Eleanor would not refuse it.

Rees was feeling extremely cramped in the couvert and beginning to believe that Eleanor had suggested he stuff his big frame inside because she knew he would be unable to remain there for very long. He wondered idly what kind of penalty Edward would mete out to Rees if he chastised Eleanor for this trick. While he enjoyed the thought, he knew he would not act on it. Say what you would about King Edward, you could not deny one unarguable thing about him: The man knew how to punish, and punish memorably, mercilessly. Rees had incurred the king's wrath once and been punished for it with the act that darkened his life and stained his soul. He feared he would never be free of it, and he would not take such a risk again.

Ine began a pastoral song—one that spoke of the natural things so highly valued by the Celts: the fire which represented God's presence; the trees denoting fertility and life, most especially the beech, the holly, and the oak; the water which meant healing and rebirth; the special, sacred animals and birds. The bard sang of the boar, the otter, and the dove. Briana found that the evocation of Celtic values made her nearly as homesick as the sound of the Welsh words had. She wondered how the people of Flint truly were faring. She would never have written Maud asking about specific people, and Maud would never have answered, because either case involved the use of names, and names would bring their bearers to the attention of the crown, a prominent, perilous place no Welshman could afford to be.

Ine finished singing, played one last chord, and looked up. Briana cleared her throat to say something to the bard, but then her gaze slid past him, and her eyes widened. Eleanor hid a smile behind her sleeve.

Rees had stepped into the chamber from the tiny recess, a sudden presence that loomed over all of them. He shot Eleanor a glance that told the irrepressible princess he knew quite well what she had done, then knocked back his hood and stared penetratingly at Briana.

Accustomed though she was to scrutiny, Briana felt a tremor go through her at the intensity of his gaze. Unconsciously, she returned it. There was a great deal of the Plantagenet about him, she thought, for he was immensely tall and handsome, his golden hair falling to the collar of his cloak, his presence commanding. And yet there were differences between this man and the standard for a Plantagenet set by the king. This man was half a head taller than the king and broader through the chest and shoulders. Rather than the sun-yellow hair of the fair Plantagenets, his hair was a richer, brighter gold. Instead of the clear sky blue eyes of Edward and most of his children, this man's eyes were blue-gray and seemed to darken as he looked at her. His smooth cheeks and strong chin complemented the nose that was a little more hooked than a straight Plantagenet nose. His lips seemed fuller, but they were pulled into a line as he studied her. He took two steps forward, bent, cupped her chin in his hand, and turned her face left and right, his eyes blazing at her.

Briana felt her chest tighten, as if it had suddenly become painful to draw a breath. Something unknown prompted her to stand up, her hands clasped together before her. The top of her head came just short of his shoulder, but her eyes remained locked in his.

Eleanor cleared her throat. Rees wrenched his eyes away

from the Welsh woman to whom King Edward had decided to wed him, let go of her face, made a fast, somewhat insolent bow to his cousin the princess, and said, "My thanks for your hospitality, Eleanor." He looked briefly at Ine, then whirled and went out of the chamber, leaving an emptiness behind him.

Briana sat down again as her knees weakened. She looked first at Ine's startled face, then at Princess Eleanor, who was seemingly occupied with tying off a thread. "What happened?" she asked. "Who—where did—" The questions were fragmentary; she seemed unable to get hold of her leaping thoughts. She glanced at the place the stranger had emerged from, at what she had thought was a solid wall, squinting slightly to make out the slit of the dim couvert, revealed by a disordered drape.

Eleanor answered promptly, as if she had been expecting questions from the beginning. "'Twas a sort of cousin of mine. He's only come to court a few times before this visit, so his manners are rougher than might be hoped had he been schooled in the graces."

Briana frowned slightly, understanding that that was not a satisfactory answer, but before she could ask anything else, Eleanor looked at Ine, smiling. "Pray, play something more, Master Ine," she commanded, using his title to add strength to her words.

"As you wish, Highness," the bard said easily, and swung into a lilting ballad that had its origins in his native Ireland.

Briana was drawn to the rhythm of the song and resigned herself to the fact that Eleanor would say only what Eleanor wished to say. Sometimes, at odd moments when she felt very comfortable, surrounded by music, practicing their archery together, embroidering or weaving, Briana could almost forget she was essentially a prisoner here and make herself believe that she and Eleanor were not merely friends, but actually equals. When, years ago, she had finally accepted that Edward was not going to send her back to Wales, when she understood that the king could, on a whim, destroy Flint if she did not behave, she had sternly cautioned herself that relaxation was a trap. She should have no friends among the Plantagenets, for she was not and never would be one of them. More recently, such cautions were rare. At times like this, however, when Eleanor gently reminded the Welsh lady of her lack of rights, Briana remembered those early hesitations with rueful acceptance. She tried to be grateful to the princess for the reminder.

At the conclusion of that song, Eleanor sent her two ladies on an errand, and when she, Briana, and Ine were alone in the queen's rooms, she turned back to her embroidery frame, picking up the needle she had tunneled into the fabric when Rees emerged from the couvert. She said casually, "I should like to hear the lullaby."

Briana's dark head came up suddenly, a glint already in her eyes, trying to understand whether Eleanor was somehow testing her or thinking to compensate her for things the princess could not, or would not, say. There were many lullabies, but both Ine and Briana knew instantly which one Eleanor meant. The very first time Ine had come to the court, then at Westminster, Briana, only a captive for a year's time, had chanced revealing that she really cared for something and requested the lullaby. Ine had played it, but had not sung the words, and Eleanor always remembered that. In the years since, Eleanor had become aware that the song did indeed have a lyric, in Welsh.

Ine immediately guessed that the princess had sent her ladies away because she felt too many Welsh songs would occasion comment. He did not look at Briana as he lowered his sandy head close to the harpstrings. His voice caressed the Welsh words, and Briana could not clear the lump in her throat enough to sing with him.

> "*Hotl ahm rantir seku weedont;*
> *Ahr heed uh nochs.*
> *Dum ahr forthir vrawn gaw gawnyunt;*
> *Ahr heed uh nochs.*"

As the beloved song continued, Briana closed her eyes, once again battling against tears. Her father, her brothers Griffith and Meredith, and she had stood, arms around each other, in the circle they made for nightly prayers and sung the lullaby together the night before Fearndon. As Ine sang, Briana could hear her older brother's full baritone, her younger brother Meredith's voice cracking on the first note of the higher verse. She felt their sheltering arms around her again, as for the last time, that cold December night between the death of Prince Llewelyn and the death of free Wales. *Ahr heed uh nochs* meant "all through the night," and her family had always used it as a bedtime prayer, for its imagery of guardian angels and God's loving care to carry them through the darkness.

It was the first song she had ever learned to sing, the first Ine had taught her to play on her little psaltery. It once had the power to banish childish terrors, to cast out nightmares.

No longer, Briana thought. *They went off into the dark and never returned.* She sternly ordered her eyes not to well up, and they obeyed her. She drew her concealed anger around her as a bulwark against sadness.

Ine finished singing.

I should not be here, she thought. Anger was her friend. After Fearndon, even as she wept, she battered at the floor with her fists, railing against what she had seen, what "the Lord's loving care" had created. Maud, despairing over the loss of her brother and nephews, but more worried about Briana than about herself, sent for Father Ciaran.

The tall, spare priest did his best to soothe the distraught child before she retreated into the private world of numbness from which King Edward shortly pried her and to which she was never able to return. Father Ciaran tried to convince her that mere humans could not begin to guess God's plan for the world, and then, perhaps sensing that he was not reaching her, he said one of the two things she had never forgotten from those last hours she spent in Wales. He said, "God did not create that horror, little one. Man did. God permits man to choose his own path."

By "man," Briana knew the priest meant King Edward and his chosen killers. She stored it away, and then hatred for the king set a fire inside her which kept her from weeping before him when he came to take her away from Flint the next day. Now, years later, she was so skilled at hiding her feelings from him that she would swear the king sometimes really did think that he had succeeded in securing her affection.

She realized that Eleanor had said her name. Hoping she had not been called more than once, Briana shook herself out of the memory. "Aye, Highness?"

Eleanor tunneled her needle back into the cloth. "I fear my ladies are likely to return shortly," she said. "Why do you not take Master Ine down to the west lawn and walk with him a little? I know you would be pleased to hear news of his travels."

Briana was not surprised that Eleanor had guessed she would want some time with the bard, and she was grateful that she did not have to resort to the fiction of a music lesson. "I would be honored to accept the duty of showing Ine the park," she said formally.

Ine rose, bowed to the princess, slid his harp into its satchel and slung it across his back. He accepted the small purse Eleanor held out to him and thanked her for the opportunity to entertain her.

"Doubtless I shall hear you again during your sojourn with us," Eleanor said.

He nodded to acknowledge the truth of that statement and slid the purse into his supertunic. He used the purses he received in noble houses to support his travels into the countryside, where he sang for the people he loved most dearly, who could not afford to pay him.

The princess's ladies bustled back into the queen's rooms, and Eleanor dismissed Ine and Briana. She did not have to warn Briana to be sure she stayed in plain view at all times in Ine's company. The man was in his early forties and had never touched a sword or dagger in his life, but he was still a man, and no one doubted that he carried the only weapon most men wielded against their women. Ine had no reputation for taking women's favors, as did some of the lesser minstrels, and he never spoke of his past. He deflected questions with ease. "Bards have no pasts," he said. "The past always writes the songs it wants us to sing. Bards pick up an instrument and write their own songs."

Briana curtsied to the beautiful woman who was the closest thing she had to a friend, but in whom she could never let herself confide, and led Ine from the queen's rooms to the gallery. They walked quickly to the stairs and out into the bailey, unspeaking. Once through the curtain wall and a good distance from the castle, their pace slowed, and they began to talk.

Chapter 12

Although he was an earl, although he was an accepted member of the royal family, albeit one whose lineage was spectacularly broken by a father he had never known, Rees chose not to stay in the apartments while at Windsor. Since he could not, by virtue of his title, stay in the knights' dorter, he had chosen to stay at the guesthouse at the friary of St. Anthony, two miles west along the Thames River. When he left the queen's rooms, more disturbed than he would have believed possible, he had no desire to remain in the castle. When Edward finally decided to speak with him, the king would need to send a messenger. Rees refused to be waiting conveniently to hand.

He had told the stablehands at Windsor not to unsaddle Basilisk, his big gray stallion. The horse was standing at a corner of the paddock, ears back, daring any of the grooms to come near him. When he saw Rees, his ears raised to points and he ambled toward his rider as if he could never possibly have caused anyone a moment's difficulty. Rees smiled, stroked the stallion's nose and then swung into his saddle. As he gathered the reins, he saw, out of the corner of his eye, a herald leaving the edge of the curtain wall and heading in his direction.

"Open the gate," he said to one of the grooms who had been hovering at a respectful distance from Basilisk's teeth and hooves. The boy ran to the paddock gate, unlatched it, and swung it wide. Rees clicked his tongue, and Basilisk leaped forward. Rees let him canter until they were most of the way across the park, and then he reined the horse down to a walk. He needed time to think.

Rees was a skilled fighter. He had proved in the Holy Land that he could kill, and he bore the scars of that experience both visibly and invisibly. At times he came near to wishing he had never gone on Crusade, and yet it was because of the Crusade that he had learned another skill, one in rare supply, rarer even than literacy. He had learned how to think. Most of his knights—men who admired his more workaday skills—never appeared to notice, but the two men he was closest to knew he did it and generally overlooked it because they loved him, though they would never have characterized their unwavering loyalty by that term.

They had accompanied him from Conway and remained at the friary when Rees went to Windsor. Sir Galen Knauter was thirty-two now and had left a wife and three children at Conway to accompany Rees to Windsor.

Sir Ralf FitzHugh was now twenty-six, seasoned, and recently widowed. He had become nearly as skillful a horseman as Rees. The three of them had shared danger, women, victories, defeats, everything, in fact, except Fearndon. Galen and Ralf had still never asked why Rees ordered them to stay away from the field at Fearndon, but they had never ceased wondering. Ralf was, by nature, more observant than Galen, and more inquisitive. He had seen that Rees was affected by certain things another man might simply have shaken off, and one of the things that most bothered Rees was meeting with his uncle, the king.

So Ralf had come out of the guesthouse and was sitting on the friary wall, watching the road that led to Windsor. Galen found him there and hitched himself up on the wall beside him. For a while they waited in silence. Then Galen leaned out, looked long and hard down the road, sat back again, and asked,

"No sign of him yet, huh?"

Ralf shook his head.

"Mayhap we should ride out and meet him," Galen suggested.

"He told us to wait for him here," said Ralf.

They sat for a while longer. Then Galen said, "He may take supper at Windsor."

Ralf nodded. "'Tis possible, but I deem it unlikely. He wishes not to break bread with the king. I'd wager he'll return sooner."

Galen leaned off the wall again. "You've the right of it," he said and nodded down the road.

Basilisk had come into sight. His rider was relaxed, the reins resting lightly on the horse's neck. As the horse and rider drew closer, Galen and Ralf could see that Rees's gaze was unfocused, faraway.

Galen nudged Ralf with his elbow, almost dislodging the smaller man from his perch on the wall. "Look at him," he said.

Ralf had been. Now he said softly, "Oh, Christ. He's thinking again."

Galen nodded as sagely as he could manage. Both of Rees's knights believed that most of Rees's discontent—and they knew he was indeed not a happy man—could be laid to the credit of the single trait that he shared with so few other people. In their opinion, Rees thought too much.

Men of action had no call to spend so much time in a pursuit better followed by scholars or clerics. It was generally accepted that men developed their muscles so that there was no need for them to develop their minds. And Rees was living proof that too much thinking was not the path to happiness for men like them. They could not deny that thought seemed in no way to limit Rees's prowess as a warrior. He was the best fighter they knew, and it was a joy to them to follow him. They had often, when not in his presence, talked about his skill.

"He always fights as if he knows he will not be killed,"

Galen said.

"Since he recovered from his wound, aye," Ralf amended. "But you've the right of that. Many's the time we'd've all fallen had he not been there."

Rees had led them into battle on Crusade, on the Borders, and in the Marches during the Welsh war. He did not like to attack, but he bore the brunt of any opposing assault with steadiness, determination, and mastery.

Ralf had analyzed Rees's tactics and said, "He doesn't think when he's fighting. He just reacts. Thinking can be such a dangerous thing. I know not why he chooses to engage in it." They would never ask him that, either. Not only was it impolite to question one's liege lord, but they sensed that Rees would not welcome the question. It was Rees's curse that *his* liege lord was the King of England.

Galen and Ralf jumped down from the wall as Basilisk drew up even with them, and Rees became aware that they were there. He dismounted and held onto Basilisk's reins. "There is likely to be a messenger from the king behind me some way," he said. "With luck, I'll not have to return to Windsor until the morrow."

"You've not seen the king yet," Ralf guessed.

Rees walked slowly in the direction of the friary outbuildings, where they had been able to stable their horses. "Why think you that?" he asked.

Ralf decided to be honest. "You've your temper well under control," he said.

Rees had once given signs of a legendary temper, though his knights had not seen evidence of it for some time. Ralf believed there might have been some correspondence between the absence of Rees's choler and the distance between Rees and King Edward.

"I've not yet seen him," Rees agreed, "but I know why he sent for me."

Galen and Ralf exchanged a glance, but did not ask. Rees

would tell them when he was ready.

Briana was careful never to touch Ine. She was not certain that they were being watched from the walls, but since she considered every servant and knight at Windsor a potential spy, she would certainly give no one a reason to reproach her in any way. As eager as she was for news, she would not show it by asking rude questions quickly. She would let Ine take the lead.

"How goes your playing?" he asked.

"It gives me great pleasure," she answered. "I cannot play daily, but I play each occasion afforded me."

Ine seemed to know that she was cautious and why, even though they had never openly spoken of her status in this place or Westminster, centers of English power, entirely dominated by the Plantagenet rulers. Even had she been willing to speak treason to the bard, she would not have done it in the palaces of Wales's conquerors.

When they were well away from the walls, out in open land removed from any trees, hedges or bushes where someone might lurk, they kept a distance of nearly two feet between them. Only then, when it could be clearly seen that no one was within earshot, did Briana say, "Tell me of home."

He had wondered what he would say to that question, for he had known it would be coming. "The Lady Maud does well," he said, "though the strain of holding the manor together wears her and has aged her unduly. She has not the hands needed, but she copes. The farming is tolerable."

"Has all struggle ceased, then?" she asked wistfully. "Is Prince Llewelyn's dream utterly abandoned?"

He did not say that many in Wales believed that Briana was now the hope of Prince Llewelyn's dream. Instead, he said, "There are still rebels on Snowdon. They are led by one familiar to you. Owen Glyn raids northwest to Bangor, north almost to Conway, though there was great risk there, for that manor is Connarc's, who is vigilant in its defense. Owen raids southeast almost as far as Bala. He goes not to the Marches. I know not how many men remain with him, but enough for the raids."

"But he is still well," Briana said gratefully. "That is good tiding indeed."

Ine turned to face her directly and stopped walking. "It grows less easy each year to find those still wishing to fight to see Wales free, though the memory of Prince Llewelyn is greatly treasured," he said flatly. "Wales wishes to live in peace, Lady Briana."

"'Twas the brutality of the conquest that broke our hearts." Briana's voice was soft and sad. "Too many of us died—good men and boys. And so many of our women given to the enemy to create babes of their bodies with English blood in them."

They resumed their walk across the park. Ine glanced up at the sky, assessing the possibility of rain from the gathering clouds. It always rained during Lent, and he had been drenched numerous times while travelling on the roads, but he doubted that Briana would welcome a soaking. "The treaties of men are often written on the bodies of women," he said. "'Tis well known that some of the matches, though forced, have been successful."

"'Tis possible you and I do not share the same idea of success," she said with dignity. "Despite your training, you are not Welsh, as you have on occasion said yourself."

"A Celt is a Celt." He said it with a smile. It had taken him years to come to the conclusion that he was, in his way, as good as Myrrdin had been in a different, older, way. "I have not the mysteries, but our roots are the roots of this land—before the Angles, the Saxons, the Norsemen, or these new Norman rulers. We were here together, your people and mine. And before Myrrdin died, he told me that the roots of the Celts had many branches."

"Is your family still in Ireland?" she asked. It was not the turn she wanted the conversation to take, but, stubbornly, she did not want to hear that Owen's fight was a small one, that her people were abandoning the battle. While she was not entirely aware of it, she expected more of Owen Glyn. She was to have been his wife, and would have been had the King of England not stolen her away. No one had ever repudiated the match made by her father, Bryn, and his father, Anian, those many years ago.

"My family is long gone, my lady," Ine said, "and I knew them not well before they went. I was only in Dubhain until I was six years old, and then Myrrdin took me. And he and Bertran were all my family from then. I inherited nothing but life from the folk who gave me birth. Everything else I received from the two old men who raised me."

"How sad," she said. "Not to have known your family. Not to know who you are."

Ine laughed, not unkindly, a full, boyish laugh that his trained voice made reverberate across the lawn. "I should not have expected such innocence of you, Lady Briana. Some innocence to be sure, but not to that degree. I am quite contented not to remember much of my family. I have seen in my travels that families are more the cause of misery, anger, or pain than aught else except possibly warfare." He glanced at her, read the disbelief on her face, and sobered.

"I have not found that to be true," she said carefully.

"I beg your pardon, my lady," said the bard. "Truly, I know your family—"

"God rest their souls," she murmured.

"—made you happy, and I believe you are thereby indeed one of the few fortunate in your blood connections."

She dropped her gaze to the ground beneath them, where the very first of the green grasses were poking their way up through last year's brown. "Ine," she said, "what more can you tell me of Flint?"

"The people miss you and speak always of their hopes for your return. The village would welcome good word of you."

She folded her arms beneath her cloak and rubbed them as they walked. "I'd send them further word if I but knew what to say. But I cannot know if the king will ever allow me to return."

"He fears the legend," the bard said.

"I am a person, not a legend," Briana said firmly, "and I much desire to go home."

The Celt in him rose to the surface, something which happened to him more often the few times he was near her than ever when he was distant from her. "Have a care what wishes you speak aloud, my lady," he advised. "God sometimes grants prayers, but seldom as we expect Him to."

The mention of God tempted her to say that she felt safe because God had never granted any of her prayers hitherto, so she had little cause to worry about it now, but instead she let his remark draw her thoughts to St. Maedoc's. "How does Father Ciaran fare? I trust he was still at Flint when last you visited?"

Ine nodded. "I swear he grows younger," he replied, "but since I know that to be impossible even for a Celtic cleric, I can assure you he fares quite well. Oh, and I near forgot. He has a new soul in his care. A recluse."

She was fascinated enough to let her preoccupation with the fate of Flint lessen. "Flint has a recluse living there?"

"Aye," said the bard. "I saw her not, but I did see her servant, who is a remarkable woman and has already befriended the women of the village. Father Ciaran told me he was asked to approve their residence in the hermitage in the yard of St. Maedoc's by no less a personage than the Archbishop of Canterbury. The recluse is, he said to me, a very holy woman."

"I should like to have met her," Briana said, "but I suppose 'tisn't possible. I'd like to know what makes a woman choose seclusion—" Her voice slid over the word.

"Think not on such a fate." Ine's voice was low. "Other paths await you."

She did not ask for his authority in making that statement; bards needed no authority. He looked at her, then past her, and she turned to see what he was looking at. The page was coming to call her back.

The herald from King Edward did not reach St. Anthony's Friary until after dark, so Rees, Galen, and Ralf took their evening repast in the guesthouse. Because the friars served guests the best they had, the meal was tolerable, the bread and ale neither old nor spoiled.

Galen, who never went anywhere without raw onions, which were his favorite food, produced one from the scrip he wore at his waist under his supertunic, peeled the skin off, and bit into it with his usual gusto, chewing somewhat noisily.

If Galen had not been one of his most trusted friends, Rees realized, he would probably not have brought the big knight along to court. There might be an occasion on which he, Rees, would need to present himself to the king and the nobles accompanied by his knights, and Galen had no court manners at all, nor would he make an effort to develop any. "I disdain the bowings, scrapings, false smiles and lies that go along with court manners," he had said hotly a number of years back and belched loudly to punctuate his words. Rees knew that it really was not manners Galen detested, it was pretense. He had no tolerance for it, and Rees valued him all the more for his preferences, even though they sometimes, as now, made him an abominable dinner companion.

Rees had been very quiet for most of the early evening as they waited for the herald to arrive. He had unsaddled and groomed Basilisk himself; the warhorse tolerated other hands on him, but not as well, as a succession of injured stablemen at Conway had proved. While he worked, Rees wondered at his own reaction to Briana of Flint. He had never before been so strongly, instantaneously, moved by a woman, not even by some of the prettiest and most skillful of the whores in Chester. *But then*, he reflected, *ere this, I've never known so surely that a woman will belong to me.*

He knew little about marriage in general. His mother's marriage to John, Duke de Bretagne, in which he had always felt somehow misplaced without understanding why, that marriage had been an unhappy one. He had come to wonder how much of that unhappiness should be laid at his own existence, a boy his mother's husband knew was not his own blood. The only other marriage he had cause to observe closely was Galen's; Ralf's wife had not lived a season after they wed. Rees thought that Galen had been very fortunate in his wife. Menty liked talking of issues with meaning, and Rees had had several good conversations with her before the babes started making their appearance.

Rees was careful, however, never to spend much time with Menty, for he suspected that she might have harbored a secret desire to lay with him, and Rees would not take what belonged to any other man, let alone a man he valued as highly as he did Galen.

The friary ale was almost gone when Galen decided they had waited long enough to see what Rees would say about his visit to court. So he set his tankard down on the table with a clack that startled Ralf and asked, "Did I tell Menty the truth when we left Conway? I said we'd be returning by Easter."

Rees considered what he was actually being asked for a moment, and then decided to answer both questions, the spoken and the tacit. "Aye, 'tis likely we can celebrate the Resurrection in our own chapel. Uncle Edward has brought me here to see me wed."

Ralf nearly choked on his ale. Rees did not look at him.

"At long last," said Galen, approving heartily. "Who's the fief he's picked out for you?"

It was well known in all of Europe that *people* did not marry, though they might or might not be fortunate enough to love. Only estates married, or, as in Rees's case, since he was only overlord of Conway in the king's name, an estate might marry a man strong enough to protect it.

"Flint," said Rees.

In the profound silence that followed that single word, the

far-off cloister bell at the friary proper rang softly. Then Ralf made a small whistling sound that prompted both other men to look at him. "The pair of you will have the fairest babes in England," the knight said. "I've seen the lady."

"When?" Rees asked.

"Remember after my—" Ralf paused, still feeling the loss of a wife he had more than a care for. "—marriage I escorted my mother back to Westminster. She was waiting on the queen for a season. I saw the Lady Briana then."

Galen looked from Rees's impassive face to the other man. "She's impressive, I warrant?"

"Make a man hard in an ice storm," the younger knight said before it occurred to him it might not be a wise thing to say about the woman his liege lord was going to marry. When he did realize, he let his breath go out in a hiss of self-deprecation that made Galen smother a laugh.

Rees did not appear to be offended. In fact, he thought as objectively as he could about Ralf's description. Coming as it did from a man who had had to be coaxed to enjoy a still-clean, still-pretty young whore just a few weeks earlier, it was truly a testimonial. "Aye, she likely could," Rees agreed thoughtfully, "but we'll not be living in an ice storm. We'll be living in Northeast Wales."

"Sweet Jesus," Ralf said softly, as Galen stared. Ralf understood something that had been clear to Rees from the moment Archbishop Peckham informed him of the bride's identity. "They will hate swearing fealty to you. They'll not do it. Not to you."

"If it comes to it, they'll have to," Rees said grimly, his mouth suddenly tight. "I think the reason the king is putting me there is to keep down any hint of rebellion. He will not allow me to be soft. He never has." Rees had to tamp down firmly on the rage he felt rising within him at the thought of his previous encounters with his uncle, and he could not risk being angry with King Edward now, not here in the center of his power.

Ralf recognized the incipient anger and sought to diffuse it. "I've no doubt you'll find a way," he said to Rees, but he was uncertain if Rees actually heard him.

Rees was already thinking hard. Ralf had successfully, almost offhandedly, made Rees even more conscious of his major problem, and Rees was angry with himself for allowing thoughts of the marriage to distract him from the complications of the suzerainty. Now he had to make himself think that his wife could not be nearly the problem for him that the people of Flint would be, because it was likely to be extremely difficult— even in light of Conway—for him to convince them quickly enough that he wanted what was in their best interests. It had been Flint which resisted longest in the Welsh war, and Flint which fell hardest at the very end of the fighting. He knew it well; he had been there when its blood was spilt onto the frozen field at Fearndon.

The rage began to lap at him again. He did not want to think about Fearndon. He would never forgive the King of England for what had happened at Fearndon, but at least Rees had thought it was behind him. Edward had just ensured that it might never be behind him again. *I could kill him just for that*, Rees thought treasonously. *But my mother needed me to swear fealty to him, and for her sake, I did.* He wondered whether she would have extracted the promise from him if she had known how the fealty would nearly destroy him, how it was still threatening to destroy him.

One of the brothers from the friary came to the guesthouse door and signalled to Rees. It seemed that the king's herald had finally arrived. Rees pushed himself away from the table to go and be summoned back to Windsor.

Chapter 13

The king was not at morning Mass. That would have been very common had he not been in residence at Windsor, but it was well known that he was here, and since the archbishop was the celebrant, Edward's absence was mysterious. The rest of the royal family was present, and no one seemed unduly worried by his being missing. Briana felt only relief. She was never easy in the king's presence.

She had not slept well. She had been able, while distracted by her conversation with Ine and later by Joanna's chatter at supper, to disregard the turmoil of feelings raised in her by the sudden, volatile appearance of the stranger in the queen's rooms. But once she was alone in her room after she had been scrubbed and brushed by Enlis and fussed over by Hulde, she had nothing else to think about. She climbed onto the feather tick, adjusted her body so the strings that supported the tick were comfortable, and then lay awake, reliving the moment when the man burst into the chamber and took her face in callused but surprisingly gentle fingers. He was not the first knight to have touched her, nor the first man. Owen Glyn had kissed her good-bye before he went off to war, and it had not awakened in her any of the disruption the unknown knight had caused simply by appearing. And—despite the fact that the stranger had been an English knight and her disdain for English knights had only increased since the rogue had tried to force his attentions upon her and nearly killed her outside Peterborough—she recognized that the stranger had stirred her. She shook her head at herself and told herself to go to sleep. She did not obey her own command.

As a result, she was still muzzy-eyed at Mass, stifling a yawn behind her hand, but she was not bleary enough to keep herself from looking around for the stranger. He was not present. She wondered if he had left Windsor and was surprised at the disappointment she felt at that notion. *I am very curious and nothing more*, she thought. *That is the total truth of that.*

She tried to enjoy the Mass, free from the gaze of the Plantagenet king.

Edward was, at that moment, in his receiving room, waiting impatiently for his nephew, a scroll in his hand. In later years, this chamber would be called a throne room, but the English were not yet as accustomed to the formal trappings of power as they would become. King Edward was more interested in successfully wielding his power than he was in decorating it. The king knew that some of his councillors referred to it as his "presence" chamber, and he did not discourage them. It was the room he used when he wanted to impress whoever he was meeting with—ambassadors sent by other rulers, quarreling subjects, churchmen thinking to give him advice, and in this case, a sworn vassal, his sister's son, whom he had confronted twice before, neither occasion a pleasant one. He expected this meeting to be no more cordial than the previous ones, even though this time he thought he would be presenting Rees with what could be considered a reward, rather than bad tidings. He did not have great confidence, however, in Rees's willingness to agree with any of his uncle's perceptions of matters.

The moment Rees was announced, Edward went to his large chair, which was set on a platform raised one step above the stones of the floor, as the high table was raised in the hall. Two tapestries from the Holy Land adorned the walls, and three large sconces with thick white candles kept the dark from this windowless room. The only other chair was a smaller one, set on the floor beside the platform. Ordinarily, Queen Eleanor would have used it, but she was at Mass, and besides, the king wanted his interview with his nephew to be conducted in private.

He seated himself on the large chair, laid the scroll across his knees, and nodded to the herald to send Rees in. He saw no reason to change his opinion that Rees had grown into a formidable man, and Queen Eleanor had once remarked that Princess Beatrice would have loved to see the proud knight her son had grown into. "She should not have died, then," Edward had said to her, offhandedly.

The king studied Rees's face as the younger man walked across the chamber, stopped in front of the platform, and made a graceful, exactly correct bow. Edward was unexpectedly reminded of the exactness of Briana's own carefuly proper obeisances. Neither of them would give an inch more than required, but neither would be caught giving an inch less. *They are a good match for one another*, the king thought suddenly. *He is as meticulous as she is in matters of court courtesy.*

Rees said blandly, "You sent for me, Sire?"

"Aye," said Edward. "I have made a choice to wed you to Flint." He waited to see if he would get any kind of reaction, but he truly expected none, and Rees, expressionless, did not disappoint him. Edward went on, "The Lady Briana has twenty years of age, but that should be small deterrent to children. My own queen, your aunt, did not quicken 'til near that age, and we have been blessed many times over. I would have children of my own blood ruling in Flint. You will have to make them on the Lady of Flint, for my brother's sons are mere babes, and I cannot legitimately touch her myself."

For all his control, Rees stirred minutely. Sharp-eyed, Edward saw it, but wisely refrained from remarking on it. Instead, he held out the scroll. "This conveys to you title as overlord of Flint, and though it is a Crown fief, I have chosen to make the suzerainty actual the moment the marriage is consummated. You will rule the castle, the manor, the village, and the parish of St. Maedoc, as well as the fief lands adjoining. 'Twill be your commission to guard the estuary of the Dee and to ensure there is no rebel activity. Should you find aught of rebellion, you will put it down as if I myself were in command of your knights." Before Rees could say anything in response, the king, still holding out the scroll for which Rees had not yet reached, continued, "As you are doubtless aware, Edmund Mortimer has occupied Flint castle this year past, for Flint lies within the Northern March, which became his purview at the death of his father. I do not give you the March with this. He will retain it, but I will order him to Harlech. He will be nearer Snowdonia there, and I believe 'twill please him to be placed in full Welsh territory." He saw Rees want to ask a question, but repress it, and he would not torment Rees to make him ask it. "I have chosen to have you retain the overlordship of Conway as well, but I seek that you turn your attention to Flint." He was still extending the scroll.

Rees slowly reached for it. He was not surprised that Edward had made no mention of peace. His gray-blue eyes revealed nothing as he asked tonelessly, "Will that be all, Sire?"

Edward clenched his jaw and rose so that he was taller than his nephew, but Rees was not cowed. Since the height had not achieved an effect, the king stepped down onto the floor and allowed Rees to look slightly down at him. "Rees," he said, "'tis un-Christian of you not to forgive me. I am your uncle, your own blood. I kept your mother from public calumny over her shame and your birth, got her wed away from condemnation, saw to it that you would be raised in the household of her husband, and I have honored you with an earldom, full as much honor as any knight who serves me, not barring even the Marcher Lords. I am also, not incidentally, your king and liege lord."

"'Tis something I never forget," Rees said, his voice steady.

"Have I ever failed in my duty to you?"

"Nay, you have not," the king admitted. "And I know for fact you've confessed Fearndon and been shriven. No stain lingers on your soul for that necessary act."

Rees went red as the blood rushed to his face. He fought strenuously not to permit rage to overcome him. His oath of fealty meant he could not physically attack his liege lord, though for many seconds he wanted nothing more. His fist unconsciously tightened on the scroll until its center crumpled in his hand. Slowly, he regained his equanimity, as Edward watched him, unmoving.

Rees did not even bother to think that the king's words meant betrayal of the sanctity of his confession to doddering old Father Michael, Conway's chaplain. He would deal with that later. He had always known that his uncle would set spies on him, and he had trusted few men. Now he would have one fewer to give his trust to, but that was no great matter. He no longer needed trust as he once had. As soon as he thought he could speak without losing control of himself, he asked, "Do you honestly believe there can be absolution for the carnage of Fearndon? Can you be that much of a fool?"

His tone was so harsh that Edward was grateful for Rees's honor. The king chose to ignore the insult, and his own voice gentled in response. "For you? Aye. I believe it with all my heart. The weapon is not to blame for the lives it takes, only the hand that wields that weapon. Absolution for Fearndon was never yours to seek. 'Tis mine. And kings have more grace in these matters than mere mortals. Relinquish not your hope of heaven because you were—and are—loyal to me."

Rees blinked. Until this moment, Edward had never taken responsibility for the battle that had crushed the men of Northeast Wales, had never come near to acknowledging that Rees thought it to have been a mistake, had never indicated that Rees was anything but a thickwit to feel it so deeply, just as he had never put right the spurious rumor that Connarc had lied to, trapped, and killed Prince Llewelyn at Orwein Bridge. Rees forced himself to calm, realized that he had crushed the scroll, and slowly made himself open his fist. He took the ends of the scroll and drew the parchment a little straighter, but he did not relent. "You cannot think that the people of Flint—or the lady herself, for that matter—will appreciate the idea that the man who commanded the troops was not responsible for the blood."

"'Twill be your challenge to make them appreciate it," the king said solemnly, and at that, Rees cracked a wry grin, the irony of it hardly lost on his uncle.

"As 'tis yours to make the Scots love you full as much as the Welsh do," Rees said.

Edward frowned and stepped back up onto the platform. "Have a care," he said after a long silence. "I accept only so many insults, even from my own family. And I will not have you lax with your villeins. Those who will not swear fealty to you— and to me, through you—are to be killed as an example to the others. I will have no more rebellion."

Rees bowed his head slightly to acknowledge the warning and the command, but not, the king thought, to acquiesce to them. He decided not to push Rees further and changed the subject. "You will join us at the midday meal, and also at our family supper this even. John Peckham will cry the banns for the marriage at Mass on the morrow —" He stopped midsentence as Rees held up a forestalling hand. He was not accustomed to interruptions, but something in the absent way Rees stopped him was intriguing. Rees was not looking at his uncle, he was thinking.

Rees stood very still, his mind racing. It was several minutes later when he asked, still not looking at the king, "Does the lady know of this match yet?"

Something in the intensity of his nephew's manner compelled the king to reply, and now he was also very curious. "I've not yet informed her."

Rees nodded. "Then she does not yet know who I am."

"I have not told her," Edward said. "'Tis possible that Eleanor may have."

Rees was silent again for a time, slowly lowering his raised hand to the scroll he still carried. His eyes were focused on something else, something Edward could not even imagine. A further minute or two passed, and then Rees looked at his uncle. "I shall need two days," he said. "Tell her not, and have the archbishop delay the banns."

The king had no idea what Rees was thinking. "I want to hold the wedding in the royal chapel on Sunday week. 'Twould be an aid to me to get you and your wife to Flint by Eastertide."

Still moving more slowly, more distractedly than Edward had seen him do before, Rees shook his head. "Nay," he said purposefully. "We must be wed in Flint. The people there are going to hate me mightily. I must be seen to be both able to defend myself and caring of their concerns *before* I wed their lady. Afterward, 'twill be a hundred times harder to begin to root out the hatred."

That way of thinking was so alien to Edward that it took him a long time to accept that there was some sense in what Rees was saying, despite his own inclination to dismiss outright the concerns of anyone he had the right to command. But what Rees wanted did not suit Edward's purposes. "I cannot let Lady Briana return to Flint without being entirely in your power. Marry her here and repeat the vows in Flint."

"Not good enough," Rees said promptly. His long fingers danced on the scroll, darting over the creases he had inflicted on it. "I would be as fair an overlord for Flint as I've tried to be for Conway, but the people of Flint will never see me as fair if we've vowed in the church before they have opportunity to speak their minds. I would see them given that opportunity."

"You know them not!" Edward burst out hotly, as if Rees had not spent the past seven years ruling Conway. "The Welsh are a stubborn, foolish, rebellious people."

"And you would give more of them to me." Rees could not

curb the edge of insolence that a returning irony washed over him. He was reminding the king about Conway, where there was neither rebellion nor unrest, where the taxes were collected without incident and paid into the royal treasury on time. Rees deliberately went on before the king had a chance to react to the effrontery. "It must be my way, uncle, if I am to rule Flint for you." He paused, then said, "I ask you to grant me this."

The words were heavy with significance. Both men knew that Rees had asked for only two things in the fifteen years since he'd sworn fealty to King Edward—the right to wed the Earl of Norwich's daughter Margaret, and the right not to command the battle at Fearndon. The king had refused both requests, and neither refusal was done gently. Edward's sense of it now was that if he refused this, too, Rees would never ask again. He had to be able to count on Rees's loyalty, especially now, when he needed to turn his back on Wales for the Scottish campaign. He had no notion of how close he was to the limit of the distance Rees's honor could be pushed.

"Very well," Edward said slowly. "You may have your two days. I'll speak to Peckham this afternoon. Delay the church vows for St. Maedoc's, but—" he added before Rees could thank him, "—I want a handfasting here, and the consummation. Do you agree?" It was a concession to Rees that he asked that question.

Rees was silent again for a time, thinking. An agreement was not a vow, but if he made an agreement, Rees could be counted upon to keep it. The silence stretched on, and at last Rees said only, "Agreed."

King Edward nodded and sat down again, indicating that Rees could leave. Rees bowed and turned away. The king watched his nephew leave with some regret that they were not closer, but with a strong conviction that Rees would serve him well in the future as he had in the past.

The large hall at Windsor was set for banqueting. The high table was on a dais at the head of the hall, where flagons of ale and wine already stood. Tall chairs in the center were for the king and queen, and lower-backed seats on either side of those for the honored guests, when there were any. Two long trestle tables stood along the long axis of the room from the high table to the huge fireplace at the foot of the hall, with backless benches on both their sides. The salt cellars on the side tables, two small silver dishes each with its heap of precious white crystals, stood in the middle of the table, neatly dividing the part nearer the high table from the part further away. The princesses and Briana sat above the salt, and a number of knights in residence sat below it or on either side. The archbishop did not join them at the meal, because his Lenten fasting was more severe than that the royal family observed.

Briana was pleased to see Ine at the high table, and she was smiling at him as she took her seat on the left side of the room between Princesses Eleanor and Joanna. Then, curious to see who else would be an honored guest today, she glanced at the doorway into the hall as the king and queen entered. Behind them she saw someone who looked like an ambassador, since he was too small to be a knight, dark and swarthy, though richly dressed; the king's younger brother, Edmund, who often visited Windsor without his wife or infant son; and then, appearing suddenly after the others were all seated, the tall stranger from the queen's rooms strode into the hall looking too big even for the loose, dark blue supertunic he wore. He walked past the princesses without glancing at them and sat down at the high table beside Ine. The other knights who would be sharing the meal crowded around the lower tables below the salt, and servingmen began bringing in trenchers of bread and platters of fish cooked with onions and cabbage. While they were showing these dishes to the king and queen, other servers brought the washbowls around so that everyone could wash their hands.

As Briana dipped her fingers in the herb-scented water,

Joanna leaned past her back and said to Eleanor, "I'd no notion Cousin Rees was such a giant."

Eleanor said only, "Hush, Joanna."

Briana thought to herself that telling Joanna to be quiet was as likely to be successful as telling the wind not to blow. She and Eleanor split the large bread trencher they had been given and waited while the page filled their cups with wine. The castle dogs were already roaming the room, ready to eat any scraps that fell their way and less particular than many of the knights about the absence of meat.

The knights were boisterous and loud, but that was normal. What was less normal was the quietness at the high table.

Briana stole a look at the guests, who had been served already. The little, dark man whom Princess Eleanor had informed her was from Italy, was plying his spoon with enthusiasm. Edmund Plantagenet, never a great eater, had taken little and did not seem particularly eager to consume it. Edward and Queen Eleanor spoke together, the queen smiling broadly and sometimes laughing aloud, a cheerful, clear sound.

Briana's eyes slid past Ine to the man Joanna had called Cousin Rees and found his level gaze fixed on her. Something fluttered inside her body at that, and she looked quickly at her trencher, picking up her spoon to scoop up a piece of the fish. Her hand trembled slightly, and she frowned at it. She wished he would stop staring at her.

Princess Eleanor said brightly, "Briana, the fabric woman is coming on the morrow with new cloths, and my mother has given us leave to purchase some lengths for a new season's gowns."

Briana murmured some interest at that information. She had not had a new gown in four years, since the queen last sent for the cloth merchant to come up from London. It was an occasion, and Briana tried to think about it, wondering why the idea of seeing the new fabrics was less interesting than it might have been.

Joanna leaned forward, stuffing a bit of bread in her mouth. "Something's on the path," she said to the other two women. "The little jewelry man is due on the morrow as well."

"I'd not been told that," said Eleanor. "I suppose Mother thought I'd want a new cloak brooch or necklace, though I think it more likely that you would be the person desiring gems. How is it she told you and not me?"

Joanna grinned and hid the vulpine expression behind her hand. "I said not that anyone told me. 'Twas something I overheard."

Eleanor's lips twitched as she winked knowingly at Briana, who managed a weak smile in return, still distracted.

Joanna went on chattering, between bites and sips, about the jewels she would one day possess, making them sound grander than those the queen wore, and Briana found it impossible to pay any attention to the childlike prattle about pearls as large as hen's eggs. When she risked a further glance at the high table, she saw that the man called Rees had moved his regard away from her and was deep in conversation with Ine. She felt a wash of relief and was startled to realize it was accompanied by an unexpected, powerful stab of disappointment. She was intrigued by Ine's obvious interest in Rees, and determined to find some further time alone with the bard to discover what the conversation might have been about.

"Briana."

She realized Eleanor was asking for her attention and looked at the princess.

"I asked what kind of fabrics you thought you'd be most interested in," said Eleanor patiently.

Briana resolutely kept her attention on her conversation with the princess, not looking at the high table again for as long as she could avoid it. And she avoided it until the meal was finished and the queen leaned past her husband and said something to Ine. The bard rose at once and reached behind him for the sack with his harp in it. Servingmen and pages began to clear the platters from the tables, refilling wine or ale cups as they moved through the hall.

Queen Eleanor asked the bard a question, and when he replied, she looked at Briana, smiling, and made some quick up and down motions with her closed hands. Briana knew she was being asked to accompany Ine.

Briana turned and beckoned to one of the pages. The boy came to her and waited respectfully. "Be so kind as to seek out my housekeeper, Hulde, and ask her to give you my dulcimer to bring to the hall," she said. He gave her a short bow and ran off. Briana had never tried to master the noble ability to give direct orders, because she knew how she felt when the king commanded something of her. In fact, growing up in Flint, she had taken care of herself as much as she had ever been cared for by servants, and it was several years before she grew accustomed to the attitude of nobles in England toward those who served them. While she now accepted it, she was still uncomfortable employing it.

Two of the servingmen brought a bench to the center of the room and set it down. A number of the knights with other duties left the hall as Ine sat on one end of the bench, facing the high table. He looked at the king. "Have you a choice, Sire?"

Edward waved a hand in as gracious a gesture as he ever used. "Whatever you prefer," he said.

Ine drew the harp up. Since the Plantagenets were Angevins, their roots in France, he began with a song by Guilhem of Poitou, composer of a series of love songs, then went on with a small pause to several of the songs of Bernart de Ventadorn, whose family of singers was as famous in its own realm as Bertran's had been. He sang one of Giraut de Bornelh's chansons and then stopped, waiting to see if his audience desired more, or if someone had a preference. By this time, Briana's dulcimer had arrived, and in the pause, she carried it to the other end of the bench, sat down, and slid the hammers out from under the strings. She and Ine tuned strings to one another for a few moments, and as they finished, Queen Eleanor leaned forward. "'Tis a joy to have you here among us again, Master Ine," she said. "I would much enjoy hearing you and Lady Briana render Cardenal's song to the Virgin, and 'twould be fitting for the season."

Briana pressed her lips together briefly, because the Latin was not as familiar to her as the French, English, or Welsh of many other songs were. Ine said softly, "Sing wordless beneath my verse lyric, and join in on the chorus." He struck the first chord and began. Briana followed his lead, letting her voice underlie his as he sang the stately prayer-song. The chorus, only six Latin words, was easier for her than the song would have been. She was relieved when it was over, however, for it was not among her favorite songs.

Ine looked at the high table. King Edward asked his Italian guest if there was a song he desired, but the little man, who was drinking copious amounts of the wine, declined. Edward leaned forward. "Have you a favorite selection, brother?" he asked Edmund.

Edmund Plantagenet was smaller than Edward and known to have no ambitions to rule England. He said, "I've not heard 'Le chanson de Roland' in many years. My own minstrel has never learnt it."

It was a long song, and both Ine and Briana knew it well. It allowed them to sing different melodic lines and different tempi as the heroic tale unfolded. Briana was delighted to be able to perform at a level comparable with Ine's, for he was a professional and very highly skilled. Her absorption in the music was enough to let her momentarily overlook the presence of Princess Eleanor's magnetic cousin, and when she realized it at the end of the epic song, she was grateful for the distraction. The notes of the song trailed away, and the audience showed its appreciation by tapping cups or fists on the table. Briana looked up at the high table and was surprised to see that Rees was no longer there. She searched the hall, but did not see him there.

Once again, her relief was mingled with disappointment.

Under cover of the banging, she whispered to Ine, "What were you and your meal partner speaking of?"

He bent his head as if to check a harpstring. "Music," he said, and that was all there was time for before King Edward rose and the hall quieted. The king and queen departed along with the Italian and the king's brother.

Briana slid the hammers under the dulcimer's strings and carried it to the table where she had been sitting. Joanna had run off as soon as her parents were out of the hall, and Eleanor was just rising, brushing off the front of her skirt. She looked up as Briana confronted her across the table. "Might I walk out with Ine again this day, Highness?" Briana asked the princess. "I'd welcome the opportunity to practice a few more songs."

Eleanor nodded. "I see no harm in it. Take care if it rains."

Smiling, Briana went back to Ine to tell him.

Chapter 14

The bales of hay by the deserted archery butts were still wet from yesterday's rain, but Ine spread his cloak over one to allow them to sit with their instruments, still at least a foot apart. They had spoken about possible repertoire as they walked, the conversation as professional as it could be. When they sat down, Briana asked at once, "Tell me, pray, why a knight—a Plantagenet knight—would want to know aught about music."

Ine smiled at her curiosity, as well as at the level of urgency he heard disguised in her voice. He had never before known Briana to show interest in any man other than Owen Glyn. "'Twas not so much a want of information," he said. "'Twas more a discussion of the major and minor notes of the chromatic scale."

Briana stared at him, open-mouthed. It went against every instinct she had to think that the Plantagenets might harbor finer sensibilities. She looked at him to question further, but something alerted her to look past his shoulder instead, and at the same moment, they heard measured hoofbeats.

There was something vaguely familiar, not to say haunting, about the image the horse and rider made, approaching them at a walk across the sward. The rider was the man Rees, and the big gray stallion he was seated upon struck a chord in Briana, but she could not have said why. Rees drew up beside the hay bales and dismounted with a fluid grace it was hard to credit to a man of his size. He was wearing a short battle tunic and hose, rather than a supertunic, which would have made riding more difficult.

He nodded once, his face neutral, to Briana, and then looked at Ine. "If you'd be able to break away, minstrel, I'd continue our conversation from the hall," he said, his voice low and vibrant with imprisoned energy.

Briana felt his physical presence like a blow. Something about his intensity, his obvious strength and beauty affected her in tangible ways, weakening her knees and churning her stomach. She realized she was staring at this Plantagenet cousin in open, if reluctant, fascination, and tore her eyes away, looking back at Ine, who was watching her with a half-smile at the corners of his mouth. She couldn't hold the focus. She had to look back at the giant again. Then she heard herself say, with a completely unexpected edge of belligerence, "He's a bard, sir, the Bard of Dubhain, not a minstrel. There *is* a difference."

The gray-blue eyes flashed to her face, the surprise in them giving way quickly to something which might have been admiration and might have been amusement. Yet when he spoke, his deep voice was both solemn and deliberate. "That being the case, I apologize most sincerely, bard, for any insult I may unintentionally have done you."

Ine was a little surprised and quite pleased by the apology, but Briana was no less than astounded. Never before in her life had she heard a knight or noble apologize to anyone, unless coerced to do so by greater strength. She was especially bewildered because he had begged pardon of an unarmed man.

Then Ine said easily, "'Tis not so great a matter as the Lady Briana would have you believe, my lord. When I sing my own songs, then aye, I am a bard. When I sing songs written by others, which I often do and which I did just now in the hall, why, then I may be called a minstrel."

Rees inclined his head, acknowledging the distinction, and

dropped the stallion's reins, allowing his destrier to nose at the bits of grass not altogether dead in the winter's chill.

Briana recalled with a start that he had expressed a wish to speak with Ine alone and made herself get to her feet and scoop up her dulcimer. "Forgive me," she said, her mouth dry. "I'll take leave of you now." She gathered her skirts with her free hand and ran lightly across the sward in the direction of the castle.

Rees opened his mouth to ask her to stay, despite the fact that it ran counter to his intentions, and he briefly wondered at himself, watching her go.

Ine rose and returned his harp to its satchel. "Your horse is a beautiful animal," he said, glancing at the destrier as he drew the drawstrings on the sack. "How old is he?"

Rees drew his attention back to the shorter, slender man beside him. "Basilisk? He's six years old," he answered.

"Ah, well, then," said Ine, "you could not have been riding him in the Northeast Wales campaign seven years past. Was it perhaps his sire who carried you then?" He set the harp down on his cloak and met Rees's gaze squarely as the taller man's steely eyes narrowed.

"You know who I am." It was not a question.

Ine sensed the muted menace held tightly under control. "There is only one man I can name whom Princess Eleanor would describe as a 'sort of a cousin' and who is a man grown. All the others are either much younger or are not actually cousins at all," he said calmly. "The 'sort of' makes you Earl Connarc." He read the instant question on Rees's face. "And nay," he added, "I did not tell Lady Briana. I am fair certain she knows it not."

Rees was unexpectedly tempted to laugh, but he did not. "Are you a magician as well as a bard?" he asked. "Is your name truly Merlin, and should I call you that?"

"You may, if you wish me to pay no heed," the bard said lightly, completely undeterred by the possibility of the earl's anger. "If you have expectation of my answering when you speak to me, then I suggest you call me Ine."

Rees found he truly liked the man's ease and wit, even more than he had liked their discussion of music an hour earlier. He smiled.

Ine was surprised at the way Rees's handsome face blossomed with his smile. He seemed, the bard reflected, to glow from within.

Rees's smile faded a little as he sobered. He sat down on Ine's cloak beside the harp, so that his head was lower than the bard's, and clasped his hands between his knees. He seemed to be debating what to say next.

Ine waited, uncertain why Rees was hesitating.

Rees looked up. "'Tis said you have recently traveled in North Wales."

"Aye." Ine was a little bewildered by that. "I did not reach as far west as Conway."

"Nor did I get to the Northeast," said Rees. "Tell me what I am like to find in Flint when I go there." The earl was entirely serious now.

Ine could not conceal the wariness that came over him at that question. "King Edward is sending you to Clwydd?" he asked.

Rees turned his gaze briefly toward the castle, then back again. "King Edward is making me overlord of Flint," he said softly, watching Ine's mobile face. "I need to know how to make life as easy as possible for my new fief."

"But Flint is—" Ine began, then stopped abruptly, moved the harp aside, and sat down next to Rees. Rees had sent Briana away before asking that question. The bard said, "You know who Lady Briana is." The earl nodded, his gaze neutral as he watched Ine reason it out. "The king seeks not to simply take the land from the lady," he said. Rees did not deny that statement. Ine was musing now. "The king knows that she would fade without connection to her home, and he too much appreciates a beautiful woman to cause such a thing could he avoid it." He tapped a finger on his lip. "The lady *is* Flint." He completed the reasoning. "King Edward has given her to you." The implications were conflicting, and Ine danced through them with lightning speed.

Rees half-smiled, saying, "You think a great deal of the Lady Briana, do you not?"

"I was present when she was born," Ine said, adding, in response to Rees's unspoken question, "I am forty-two. I knew her mother, her father, and her brothers. All are dead now. Do you wish me to tell you the circumstances of their deaths?"

Rees knew from the question that it mattered. "Aye," he said.

"Her mother, the Lady Nonne, died from milk fever after giving birth to Meredith, the younger boy," Ine said. "Lady Briana was just two, and the people of Flint thought of her in terms of the legend, though she did not. I believe she does not think of it still, unless reminded."

"What legend?"

Ine was surprised. "You've not heard the story of it? Even after all your time at Conway?"

Rees shook his head. "I've not been much interested in stories," he said, "but rather preoccupied with rebuilding the fief in my charge."

Ine debated the wisdom of what he was about to say and then decided to risk it. "If I may venture to give you a word of advice," he said tentatively.

Rees understood that the bard was asking for permission to say something, and the hesitation intrigued him. He looked over at Basilisk to be sure the stallion was still calm, saw the horse dozing, and returned his attention to Ine. "You may always speak your thoughts to me," he said sincerely. "I am not in the habit of punishing men for what they think."

Ine was pleased by that. He was beginning to form opinions about the man he was with now, and they were not the opinions he would have expected to entertain about Earl Connarc. "Stories are ever worth paying heed to," he said. "Even those we disagree with or choose to disregard can have truth for us in them."

Rees recognized something in those words. "I had a teacher once who might have told me just such a thing," he said. "He taught me much. I've not spoken of him before to any man."

Ine dipped his head in acknowledgment of the honor being paid him. "Perchance someday you will tell me of this teacher," he said.

"For now," said Rees, "tell me of the legend."

Ine fingered the drawstrings of his harp sack. "You've heard of Myrrdin, Bard of Bangor?"

Rees nodded.

"And mayhap," Ine went on, "you've heard also of Bertran, Bard of Poitou?"

Rees was so startled by that question that it showed openly on his face and he could not immediately reply.

Ine waited, wondering what Rees was thinking about.

At last Rees said, "Master Bertran also spoke to me of music."

"But he was not the teacher you spoke of," Ine said with a certainty he had not expected.

"Nay, that was another man."

"We have that in common," Ine said. "We both learned from two masters, and one of them was Bertran."

Rees half-smiled. "I've a notion 'twas the other teacher who most influenced each of us. Someday we must discuss it, but now I wish to speak of Flint. Tell me of the legend."

As the sun climbed sluggishly above the spring clouds, Ine related much of the story of Briana's birth to the earl, who listened with complete concentration. Ine was a storyteller; no one could be a bard and not understand how to spin a tale, whether set to music or not. He told Rees nearly everything— even about the presence of Prince Llewelyn—but he did not tell

Rees about the mystical connection he, Ine, had made with the newborn girl. He withheld that information in part because he did not understand it himself and in part because he was not certain it would be wise to tell the man King Edward had destined to be Briana's husband that the woman had a bond with another man as well. He finished the story by telling Rees how the legend was spoken of in the seven years since the King of England took Briana away. He did not use the words the people of Flint used: kidnapped, abducted, stolen from them.

When he was done, Rees stood up, nodding with satisfaction. "Ah," he said, "so they will be much pleased to have her returned to them."

"Of course," said Ine. "She is their hope, and the last of her family."

Rees remembered that the mention of the legend had distracted them both from the tale of Briana's family's fate. Now he said, "Her mother died in childbed. Her father and brothers?"

Ine rose as well, and did not spare him. "They all three fell at Fearndon," he said. "Griffith was sixteen, and Meredith was twelve."

Rees swore under his breath. "What possessed the father—"

"Bryn," supplied the bard.

"—Bryn to take a twelve-year-old to the field of battle?" Rees asked angrily. "Any sensible man would have known the cause was lost!"

"The Welsh are not always sensible," Ine said. "They are passionate about the land, about their freedom, and in their hatred for what was done to Prince Llewelyn and Prince David."

If Rees had not been as strong, as inured to horror, as secure in his dislike of his powerful uncle, he might have winced. Due to the false rumor, spread deliberately by Edward's men, the betrayal and murder of Llewelyn had been laid at Rees's door, and he was enjoined by the king not to deny it. All he could say was, "At least, 'tis not said I had aught to do with David's fate." Ine said nothing.

Prince David's end had horrified even the most battle-hardened veterans. When Edward invented his new method of execution for Prince David, a long dying now called "drawing and quartering," he had made a martyr of a mediocre man, and he had not bothered to notice any effect of the punishment except the death and dismemberment.

Rees made himself stop thinking about the unfortunate prince and drew his thoughts back to his present problem. "The people of Flint are most unlikely to welcome me, then," he said drily.

"But they will welcome Lady Briana," Ine said. "When do you leave? I'd accompany you. 'Tis time for me to return to Wales, and the purses I've gained here will be of use to the folk there."

Rees's lips twisted. "The banns will be announced at Mass day after the morrow, and the handfasting will be Sunday week. We leave the next day."

"Handfasting," Ine repeated. "A handfasting is most unusual in the presence of clergy." He did not make it sound like a question.

Rees understood that he was being asked why, nonetheless. He paused for a moment, as if making a decision, then said, "The king wished it otherwise."

Ine waited. The silence between them stretched on, but it was strangely companionable, unpressured.

Then Rees said, "'Tis my guess that neither the lady nor the people of Flint will feel her truly my wife unless she is wed to me on Welsh soil."

Ine nodded, accepting that and understanding more. He ventured, "Then the handfasting is to permit bedding."

"Not permit," said Rees. "'Tis to require it."

"You trust me with quite a deal of information." Ine watched the taller man's hard face when he said that, expecting it to close even more. To his surprise, it softened instead.

Rees said, "Aye, and I'm somewhat amazed by it, but if

I've heard aught of singers, 'tis that they carry a great many secrets they do not betray. Power and politics make betrayers. Music does not."

Ine suddenly wanted very badly to know what had happened to cause the dishonorable betrayal of Llewelyn and, even more, to cause Fearndon. He had seen and sung about most of the battles Llewelyn had fought against this man when Connarc commanded the Northeast Wales campaign, and he had never understood fully some of the decisions Connarc had made. At one time, Ine thought he was coming to understand it, but when he learned how Prince Llewelyn had been trapped by treachery and then learned of the unremitting brutality of Fearndon, he, like the rest of Clywdd, had thought Connarc nothing but an implacable, merciless enemy, whom they had called "the butcher baron." Now Ine began to suspect that Earl Connarc was in fact much, much more, and that carried a mystery all its own. "I would still ask to accompany you—and the lady of Flint—when you return to Wales," he said again, with more insistence.

"Come and welcome," Rees said. "You know the people, and they know you."

"Aye," agreed the bard. "And I know the Lady Briana."

Rees's gray-blue eyes were deeply thoughtful. "Now," he said, "talk to me of Flint."

Briana had taken her dulcimer back into the castle and directly up to her chamber. She sensed there would be no more music that afternoon. Once she had deposited the dulcimer on the chest at the foot of her bed, she turned and went back out into the bailey. She climbed to the top of the curtain wall and walked along it, pausing every few merlons to study the rolling hills of the park, the small, crowded roofs of the village some small distance from the wall, the river peeping out from its screen of trees in the distance, and, when she reached the appropriate portion of the wall, the archery butts. She thought that the two men would likely finish quickly and as soon as they were done, she would go back out to continue her conversation with Ine. But the bard and Princess Eleanor's powerful, hypnotic sort-of cousin went on talking far longer than she would have believed possible. She made another circuit of the curtain wall, but when she returned to the part of the wall that overlooked the archery butts, they were still deep in conversation with one another. She wondered if they had gone on discussing music, but Ine had bagged his harp. Whatever the subject of their discussion was, they were both absorbed in it. Her third circuit of the walls was interrupted by the arrival of a page to tell her that the queen was looking for her. The fabric woman had arrived, and Briana was wanted in the solar. She cast one last look at the two men, sighed, and followed the page down into the solar.

The center of the room was filled with princesses, the queen, the tall, thin woman who was purveying the fabrics, and lengths of cloth in profusion. Margaret had wrapped herself in a length of murrey russet and was demanding that her mother send her someone to make her a new cloak. Joanna held a length of white linen and was asking the purveyor to cut a particular amount for her. Elizabeth and Alice had been given small swatches of canvas in various colors and were playing with them. The two Eleanors, mother and daughter, were sitting on a bench, with bolts of richer fabrics—the velvets which only the royal family could wear, the silky fustians, and the fine wools.

The queen looked up as Briana came in. "Lady Briana," she called, gay as a girl, "come help us choose some cloth for our new gowns."

Briana joined them, pretending to be as interested in the fabrics as they were and frustrated because she did not dare ask questions about the strange knight.

Princess Eleanor selected a fine scarlet velvet and a light blue wool for herself and pressed lengths of pale green linen, dark green fustian, white samite, and slate and tawny wool on Briana, saying, "'Tis been too long a time since you had any new gowns or undertunics."

"And a new cloak as well," the queen said, ordering the fabric woman, "Bring that bolt of serge. Nay, the dark green one."

Briana was feeling overwhelmed, and she was also beginning to feel suspicious. Was all the fuss, to which she was entirely unaccustomed, in aid of something? She could not ask, and she dared not let herself think the king might have decided to send her home at last, because she knew he would not trust her to rule Flint. Its location was too strategic; the people had resisted too strongly. She struggled against homesickness.

"And some ribbons," said Princess Eleanor.

The fabric woman was just signalling some of the servingmen to begin gathering up all the bolts of fabric and spools of ribbon which would not be left at Windsor, when the goldsmith was announced. He was a portly man with a gray-white beard and plump fingers sporting numerous rings with different types and sizes of stones in them, an open testament to his art. Following him was an apprentice carrying a large box with his offerings in it.

Joanna immediately lost interest in the cloth and bounced over to the goldsmith, eager to see what he had brought.

Briana, who owned no jewels, was curious as well, wondering what the queen might choose.

Princess Eleanor asked casually, "What kinds of baubles do Welsh ladies wear most, Lady Briana?"

Briana thought about her Aunt Maud, who only ever wore a simple gold chain around her throat and had given it to Prince Llewelyn to buy food for his men. Bryn had owned a ring with his seal on it; he had been wearing it when he died at Fearndon, and she had never seen it again. If her mother had had any jewels, Briana never knew it. "Loop chains, one-on-one," she answered Eleanor. "Betimes the links were engraved, but not oft. And cloak brooches, of course."

"No earrings?" Joanna asked, sighing as the jeweler's

apprentice opened the box. Trays of beautiful pieces, as well as a tray with small bags of unset stones, appeared, the bright gold and polished gems catching every bit of candlelight.

The fabric woman had been taciturn, perhaps awed by the company, but the goldsmith was obviously accustomed to a noble clientele and was garrulous, holding up and extolling the qualities of rings, necklaces, pins, and earrings. As soon as he thought something was being particularly admired, he declaimed on its excellence, its artistry, and its uniqueness.

The three younger princesses, who had been taken to a corner of the solar by their nursemaid, since they were still too young to be permitted the luxury of a day without lessons, looked up from their teacher's instruction, interested in the torrent of words. Joanna was surprised, and Princess Eleanor and her mother were forebearant. Briana found the man highly amusing, but would never have considered saying anything impolite. When she noticed that Joanna was about to begin giggling, she stepped over beside the dark-haired princess and pretended to trip on the hem of her gown, so that Joanna's giggles would seem to be at Briana's expense. The goldsmith did not notice.

But as Briana straightened and shook out her full skirt as if to be sure it was not underfoot, she realized that Ine and the strange Plantagenet cousin had come into the solar, and both were looking at her with eyes which seemed to express comprehension of what she had just done. She felt heat in her cheeks as the blood rose to her face.

Queen Eleanor said, "Briana, how do you like this chain?" She held up a gold one-on-two loop chain, with each single link etched with a tiny Celtic cross.

Briana took it from her fingers as the goldsmith immediately began praising its delicacy and the exquisite taste of the queen in selecting it.

"Put it on," Princess Eleanor urged.

Briana lifted the chain and lowered it over her head. It

snagged in the net of her caul, and Princess Eleanor deftly freed it. The metal felt unfamiliarly cold. The chain hung down onto her breasts and made her conscious of them in a way she was not certain she had experienced before. It did not, somehow, occur to her that anything other than the necklace might have created that consciousness.

"New gowns, a new cloak, and jewelry," Joanna observed, as the queen put a cloak brooch with a small emerald on it on top of the neatly piled fabrics which would become Briana's new clothes. "Makes one wonder, does it not?"

"Joanna," Queen Eleanor said with unaccustomed sharpness.

Briana lifted the chain off over her head, suspicion blooming again inside her, but once again, she would not ask. She laid the chain beside the brooch. She was certain someone would tell her sooner or later what was going on.

"Mother, what of gloves?" Princess Eleanor was asking.

Ine and the tall knight went through the solar to the gallery, and Ine returned shortly, alone, took his harp from its satchel, and went to sit with the three youngest princesses and their nursemaid, showing them the strings of his harp and explaining notes and chords to them.

The queen waved her hand to some maids, one of them Briana's quiet Enlis, to gather up all the purchases and take them to the queen's rooms, where they would begin cutting and stitching, following the canvas patterns which had been created several years past.

Chapter 15

Briana spent dinner in the small hall that evening trying to avoid the gaze of the blond giant who sat directly across the lower table from Princess Eleanor, seated in her usual place at Briana's left. Ine played his harp throughout the meal, singing quietly. Briana longed to be alone with him to ask about the afternoon he had spent with the stranger, but she could not think of how to arrange it. She was trying to eat some of the cheese and bread when the stranger rose and went to the high table to speak to the king. At the same moment, Princess Eleanor turned to the high table as well, in response to a summons from her mother.

Momentarily unobserved, Princess Joanna took Briana's arm and squeezed it. Briana looked at her, startled. In a low voice, pitched to avoid any chance overhearing, Joanna said, "Well, I understand you're to be wed at last. 'Tis the reason for the new gowns and things. I heard Mother and Eleanor talking about it."

Briana felt utter shock and a sense of having known something was in the wind, but having wanted it not to be this.

"Guard your face," Joanna warned in a hiss. "Now that you know, you should be able to greet the formal announcement with better grace."

"Who?" Briana demanded. "Who has he matched me with?"

Joanna smiled.

For a moment, Briana thought that Joanna meant to torment her by refusing to tell her who her husband was to be. Then Joanna said, "Aunt Beatrice's son, Rees. 'Tis a great match for you, marrying into the dynasty." And she nodded toward the high table.

Briana did not absorb the entire message or follow its implications at once. The only thing that made an impact was the thought that she was to be wed to an Englishman, a member of King Edward's own family, a Plantagenet. It would not be good for her, and it could not be good for Flint.

She had never imagined marrying anyone but Owen Glyn, and she had never given over hoping for that, though she had neither seen nor spoken to him for seven years. Owen was everything her prospective husband could never be now that she belonged to the king—Welsh, a companion to and soldier for Prince Llewelyn, still committed to the freedom of Wales, a man who could be expected to share her dedication to the land. He had a Celtic sense of responsibility and outstanding loyalty, and he was the only man who had ever kissed her, when he bid her farewell and went to fight. She knew she loved him, because she felt about him exactly as she felt about her father and brothers, and to her, that was what love felt like.

Then the realization crashed in on her that Joanna's aunt's son would be Princess Eleanor's cousin; only one was presently at Windsor. She covered her eyes with her hand to keep from immediately looking over at the man to whom she now guessed she would be given. She sensed that someone was standing in front of her, on the other side of the trestle table and fought to compose herself, to wipe any distress from her face before she lowered her hand and raised her eyes. She fully expected to see the man called Rees towering over her.

To her shock, the man before her was King Edward.

She sprang to her feet, her composure hanging by the thinnest of tendrils. "Sire," she said. She was grateful her voice held firm.

"Lady Briana, I'd see you in my closet," the king said, adding with an immediacy she expected even less than she had expected the command, "Now." He spun on his heel, his supertunic swirling around him, and walked to the door of the small hall. She gathered her skirts in her hands and followed him, her eyes on the stone floor. She did not dare look up at anyone in the room, because she was afraid they would all see how shaken she was.

She had been in the king's closet only once before, five years past, when she had made her unsuccessful attempt to run away from Westminster. Then the king had threatened to destroy Flint and she, who had seen Fearndon and who believed this king capable of anything, had been subdued, cowed into submission, and forced to bury her hatred deep in her heart. She had no good memories, therefore, of the king's closet, no wish to return to it again, and no choice about following the king into that small room.

Edward paused at the door of the closet and allowed her to precede him into the room, then pushed the heavy door shut. The room was windowless, utterly bare of furniture or tapestries. A sconce of candles, previously kindled, illuminated the unrelieved stone. Briana spun to face the king, her head raised as if to meet a challenge. She had no idea why the closet had been emptied.

Edward sighed, and for the first time in all the years since he had taken her from Flint, he let his own guard down completely. "Be easy, Briana," he said. "I've no thought to jump upon you, nor will I pronounce any kind of sentence on you. What you say to me here will not leave here, on my honor as King of England."

She stared at him, allowing frank skepticism to show on her face. After a time during which she waited for him to speak again and he calmly waited her out—an attitude she found utterly unlike him, for he had never before evidenced any kind of patience—she asked, "Can you be trying to tell me that you believe I should trust you?"

"I have ever said that to you," the king said quietly. "From the day I brought you from Flint, I have ever sought trust from you."

She stared at him, able to remember nothing beyond his implacability in ripping her from her home before she had any chance to adjust to the deaths of her father and brothers, in threatening to destroy Flint to secure her obedience. She lost any vestige of her careful facade in astonishment. "And you sought to secure this trust you wish of me by destroying—" She stopped, started over. "Why me, so particularly? You seem not to have extended that courtesy to any other of my countrymen." She could not believe she actually said that, even after she heard it, and she expected him to be angry. To her astonishment, the king smiled at her, and she sensed the absolute sincerity of that smile.

"I'm proud of you," said Edward with unaccustomed gentleness. "I believe that to be the first time in five years, since your unwise flight from our benevolence, that you have allowed yourself to be completely honest with me." He leaned back against the stone wall beside the door and let his hands drop to his sides, as if he wanted her to perceive no threat from him. "I would have peace in my realm, Briana. I have been harsh with those who do not, and who will not, recognize my rule."

He waited again, watching her, to see if she would take the bait, but she did not. He counted in silence to ten, then went on, "I shall be completely honest with you in return. I had hoped, when I brought you here from Flint, that you would one day come to love me."

Briana had no control left over her expression, and the mask of amazement on her face tempted the king to laugh.

Having taken the first risk and emerged from it without penalty, Briana wondered how much more would be permitted her. Vaguely, she wished there were at least a stool in the room so that she could sit down, for her knees were trembling. "Surely," she said, trying to keep her voice from quivering as well, "you could not have believed that was possible."

He smiled again, not mockingly or unkindly. "Aye, I did," he said. "You were little more than a child when I brought you to court, and children often do come to feel affection for those who care for them. Had you not fled that time, had you not provoked my wrath —"

She heard the tones of regret. She had been bold, and still he had not condemned her. Briana glanced once around the room, small as it was, as if uncertain from what quarter the attack she was expecting might come, but she was not yet ready to yield up her new power. "I was never a child after Fearndon," she said. "My childhood died with my father and my brothers."

The king nodded once, acknowledging her words and astonishing her yet again. "This year past, I at last became convinced of the futility of waiting for you to prove affectionate," he said. "Had I realized it sooner, I should not have waited so long before arranging a match for you. I thought I could safely see Flint in the hands of a child of yours if you had come to trust me, but now I see I must have a blood tie to Flint, so you must wed a Plantagenet."

The unusual gentleness did not leave his voice, but Briana's trembling grew worse, and she clasped her hands together, gripping hard to still them, her chin raised defiantly. "You could take Flint from me," she said, her voice now the steadiest thing about her, "and give it utterly and irrevocably to anyone you chose."

Edward, watching closely, saw the deep flicker of pain that arced through her at the words, and he said evenly, "'Tis what I am doing, Briana. You are Flint. And there is no other Plantagenet of a good age to wed you to but Beatrice's son, Rees."

She fancied she heard the barest edge of an apology in his

voice. Was this Rees, of the intense gray-blue eyes and the long conversation with Ine, such a monster that even the bloody King Edward felt it necessary to apologize for him? She would not ask. She had no choice but to obey, and she would not beg to be released from her obligation. If she were to be a pawn to the king's schemes, at least she would still be a pawn for her beloved Flint. Just as she had complied these five years past for Flint's sake, now she would bend again.

He waited a few moments more, to see if she had anything else to say to him. He had, indeed, told her the truth, though he might not have scrupled at a lie had he thought it needful. He would have married her to his third son, had he and Eleanor been blessed with a multitude of sons, but Henry, John, and Alphonso were all dead, and now there was only the five-year-old Edward, the first English prince given the title Prince of Wales that once had been Llewelyn's, coopted to indicate the completeness of the victory King Edward intended to achieve at any cost. Rees was older than the king might have liked, but then, so was Briana.

She did not speak.

Edward straightened and reached beside him for the ring latch of the door, then said mildly, "Once we return to the small hall, you will no longer have my permission to speak your mind openly to me. When I open this door, I shall be fully the king again, not merely a man who has—whether you believe it or no—cared for you. If you have aught else to say to me, say it now."

Briana thought quickly and carefully about all her alternatives, at this one opportunity to speak freely. She could lash out at him, telling him at last of the anger and hatred she had borne inside her all these years, but even as it occurred to her, she recognized the uselessness of the gesture and discarded it. She could make some other gesture of defiance, some sort of statement about never bending to or accepting Plantagenet rule—either his or that of his sister's son—but her innate honesty cautioned her against that as well. In this closet or back out of it, Edward was the king, and she had spent her youth bending to his rule. Doubtless she would continue to do so, and she would have to bend as well to his proxy, his nephew, when the time came.

Yet, clearly, he expected her to say something. She realized that her trembling had ceased. The worst was over; he had told her she was to marry and to whom she would be given. Her choices—other than futile complaining or docile compliance— were nonexistent. She could live hating a Plantagenet husband as she had lived hating a Plantagenet guardian. And if she endured it, she would be returned to Flint. She raised her startlingly expressive eyes to his face and spoke so softly that the king had to strain to make out the words. "I cannot wish away the past," she said. "But could I do so, I would wish that you had decided you wanted all of Wales to care for you, not merely me, and that you had come to that recognition before you allowed the Baron Connarc to slaughter us at Fearndon."

Something changed in his face. Briana saw it without having the slightest notion of what had caused the muscles in his cheek to tense, his eyes to seem abruptly veiled.

Edward had realized that Briana did not know that his nephew Rees and the then-Baron Connarc were the same man. And he sensed that he should clarify that relationship here and now, but he chose not to, even though it burdened Rees unduly to have to tell a new wife that Edward himself had commanded the battle which destroyed her family. Rees had asked him for two days before the banns were announced, but for whatever reason, at the meal, he had told his uncle he could bring Briana the tidings of the match. Perhaps Rees wanted to know whether Briana was aware that she was to be wed to the butcher baron. Perhaps Rees had even wanted the king to be the one to tell her. Edward realized something else, as well. Briana thought Fearndon was Rees's enterprise and that he, Edward, had only approved the action. He knew quite well that he could lessen the impact of her inevitable discovery by taking the responsibility for Fearndon upon himself. But he did not speak. He told himself, with the tendency toward a noble excuse so many monarchs find for self-deception, that he thought Rees should be the one to tell her Fearndon was the doing of the Crown, that it would help him to mitigate the revelation of his identity. In fact, it was because Briana was a beautiful woman, and King Edward was vain enough to seek the admiration of beautiful women, so if he had been able to be honest with himself, he would have understood that he did not tell her the truth of Fearndon because he did not want to see the way her face would change toward him when she knew.

So, instead of telling her, he pulled the door open. Immediately, the tiny closet was filled with music. Ine's harp was being matched and enriched by the soaring dance of a recorder's high-pitched flight. The player was obviously gifted, if not extensively practiced, and there was such a merriment in the frolic of the two instruments around one another's melodies that it lifted Briana out of her tension and the resigned depression of the last few minutes.

The king waved her back into the small hall, unsurprised at the sounds. Briana slipped past him in the closet doorway, quickly seeking the source of the music. Ine still sat on his bench in the center of the hall, his fingers plucking his strings with a skill as developed as any musician's in Europe. Keeping pace with him, seeming to anticipate his rhythms, tone, and direction, was Rees, whose eyes found Briana as soon as she stepped into the small hall.

She faltered between one step and the next, caught her vanishing composure and forced it over her face, unable to look away from the golden giant making the recorder sing. It might have looked incongruous, had he not been so talented. He met her gaze as his fingers moved unerringly over the instrument's sound holes. His look was surprisingly gentle, not at all demanding or challenging, and Briana found herself drawn to it in a novel and unfamiliar way. She revealed it not at all. The king was watching her, and she was already regretting the little she had shown of herself in the closet. She walked back to her usual place at the lower table, between Princess Eleanor and Princess Joanna.

The song ended. The two players exchanged a glance. Rees nodded and laid the recorder flat on the table where he had been sitting for the meal. He waited for King Edward to return to the high table next to his queen. Then Rees asked his uncle a silent question which both of them understood.

Briana did not know what either the question or the answer was, but Rees seemed to absorb it thoughtfully.

After more than half a minute of silence, Rees leaned closer to the king and said in a low voice, "I'd walk out a little with the lady I'm to wed. I seek your permission, as she is your ward." Rees had not expected his uncle to have withheld his title from Briana when he told her of the match; he had hoped her seeing that he was a musician as well as a warrior would help to mitigate the revelation, but Edward had not done it, and now he would have to find another way.

Briana was not certain what Rees had said to King Edward, but then the king rose, smiling, and said, "Lady Briana, I have given my nephew Rees permission to walk out with you this even. Soon we will be hearing the banns read for your marriage, and I believe no harm can be done to your person or your honor by time you will spend with him this day or the next few."

The king turned his smile on Rees, his eyes narrowing.

Rees was carefully controlling his unavoidable anger at Edward's easy and offensive magnanimity. He objected to the great pleasure the king was taking in this, but he showed only the edges of it.

King Edward led Rees to Briana's seat on the side bench. As they approached, she stood up again, and Princess Eleanor, who had graciously risen to let her sit down, rose too, smiling, to let her out.

Briana stepped free of the bench and turned her face up toward Rees.

He let his anger flow away so he could concentrate on the problem at hand. He kept his steady gaze on the smooth shapes of her face and said, "Now I'd ask *your* permission, Lady Briana. Will you walk out with me?"

She was as surprised by the quiet question as she had been by his apology to Ine. Most of Edward's knights—especially the ones with royal connections—if promised her lands and body, would simply have taken her arm and propelled her from the room. This man asked her, as if she had some say in the matter. She was warmed by it, and, she realized, by more. She could not look away from him as she nodded, unwilling to speak yet. The top of her head nearly reached his shoulder, and before her face, his chest and arms seemed to exude a confident masculinity that, combined with his prowess on the recorder, made her knees weak again, in a much more pleasant way than they had in the king's closet. An unaccustomed nervous fluttering ran through her stomach.

He smiled and held out his hand to her. The smile lifted the even planes of his face to beauty, and Briana swallowed hard to keep from a sudden, explosive inhalation. She tried to recapture the relative detachment she had felt when she had not known who he was, and he had come out of the couvert in the queen's rooms and taken hold of her face.

But when she slid her hand into his, tiny and pale against his rough golden skin, a shock went up her arm, and she knew detachment would be impossible.

Princess Eleanor had once remarked to Briana, on a sunlit afternoon at the archery butts when they were working on their marksmanship, "'Tis a great gift to desire your husband. I have received my parents' promise that they will not wed me to a man I cannot desire."

Briana had paused in nocking her arrow and said, a little wistfully, "I fear I know naught of desire, nor do I believe I am ever likely to." She was thinking then that she would never again see Owen Glyn, and that he was the only man who was likely to stir her.

Now she knew how absolutely wrong she had been. She recognized this as desire, recognized that she had responded to Rees without ever speaking a meaningful word to him, without knowing anything about him except his beauty, his name, and the small evidences she had seen of his kindness. And one more thing. "Bring the recorder," she heard herself say. She was too nervous to phrase it as a request. She had a moment of apprehension that he would object to being given an order by a woman.

Rees seemed not to have noticed the nature of her words. He released her hand and walked around to his place at the other trestle table, taking the instrument from it. He and Ine exchanged one lightning glance, the bard nodding with a minuscule movement of his head. Rees tucked the recorder into his belt, returned to Briana, and led her from the small hall, across the gallery, where a page waited with their cloaks, and out through the bailey into the sweep of the park toward the river.

He dropped her hand when they were a considerable distance away from the curtain wall, asking, "How long have you been playing the dulcimer?" He had felt her trembling, knew it was not from cold, and did not want to push her too far too fast.

Briana was not certain she could hold a polite conversation, but she was willing to try. She looked over at the trees, revealing the river between newly budding branches, watched some birds rise into the air, and then said, "Ine taught me. I think I had five years of age when I began." She realized she was twisting her hands together and made herself stop.

"Need you a heavier cloak?" he asked. "We came away precipitate."

She shook her head. "'Tis often warmer out here than in the castle," she said. She looked at him, found the experience both satisfying and unsettling at the same time. "I had not thought any knight played music," she said. "I thought it was rather disdained."

"I am not," he said quietly, "any knight."

"Nay, you are a Plantagenet."

His eyes went darker as he looked steadily at her face, thinking her even lovelier on close inspection. "Do not confuse me with my uncle," he said. "We are very little alike."

"I am relieved to hear you say it," she said, her voice vibrating a bit. The very thought of a polite, nonmeaningful conversation had vanished. "I would be grateful to find reasons to trust you."

He admired her openness, and he spoke in measured tones. "I understand that. I would have you think that I want what is best for you and for the fief of Flint."

She looked away from him suddenly, biting her lip, and he took two steps following her head around. He saw the sparkle of unshed tears against the clear green of her eyes and the startling black contrast of her eyelashes before she could banish the dampness.

"What haps?" he asked.

She could not tell him that she had read between the lines of her Aunt Maud's letter; she could not bring herself to trust that much. "Flint," she said. "I fear they are hungry, that the occupation goes hard on them. We lost so many good men at Fearndon."

He heard the tones of hatred in her voice as she said the last word, and he wanted to get off that subject as soon as possible. "I have thirty knights, and the service of thirty more," he said, "and I will bring as many as I can with their retainers to Flint. I am also quite wealthy." There was no boast in the words; he was only stating a fact. "I will use every bit of that wealth to restore your lands."

"*Your* lands," she said.

"Our lands, then," he corrected. "Briana, I would not take

Flint from you. I'd share it with you."

She melted, and he saw the vestiges of resistance fade in the face of her absolute need to believe him. He was tempted to reach for her; he knew the power he could wield over women. With the face and body he had been gifted, he drew their eyes and sparked their interest. Galen had often said to Ralf, but in Rees's hearing, of their visits to any of the brothels in Chester, or London, or even in the Holy Land, "They see Rees and flock 'round. He brings them, and some of them then consent to spread for you or me."

Rees reached for his recorder instead of reaching for Briana. He raised it and, without hesitation, played the Welsh song he had overheard while secreted in the recess in the queen's rooms.

Briana recognized at once that he had seen what the new Welsh song meant to her, and he rendered it so well that she was threatened with tears which she had to fight strongly to hold back. It was absurd that a man of his size and obvious power could play with such a delicate, unerring touch. He was, she believed, a man of war, of arms, for knights fought, no matter how nobly, and the gray stallion was a warhorse. Yet this knight was showing her nothing but gentleness and kindness, when he need show her no consideration at all. She wondered why.

Rees would not have told her, had she asked him. He had made some very careful decisions about Flint, after long reflection, weighing a number of alternative strategies, using ways of thinking he had been taught by a strange Jewish physician as he recovered from his nearly fatal wound in the Holy Land. His conjecture on Flint had resulted in only one alternative that satisfied him, that spared the people of Flint from as much punishment as possible. The people of Flint would be, he believed, utterly loyal to the Lady Briana, not just because of the legend, but because they undoubtedly loved her. He would have to ensure that she, in turn, loved him. If she did, she might be kept safe from King Edward's anger, and so might her people.

When he had finished playing the song, she wiped her damp eyelashes quickly with a knuckle. "How is it that a knight is also a minstrel?" she asked him.

"I was encouraged in it by a man who played a viele," Rees said. "His name was Bertran of Poitou, and he came to the estate where I lived when I was but a lad."

She nodded. "Some young boys play, I've heard, but when they take their spurs, they give it over for the sword. How is it you did not?"

He fingered the sides of his recorder and replied honestly, "I was told never to abandon my playing, and I heeded my teacher's words." He did not add that Bertran had said his music would be as important to him as his ability with weapons, nor that he had felt a rightness in the command that he had never been able to explain.

"I've heard Ine speak of the Bard of Poitou," Briana said, "and I have always tried to heed the words of bards."

The sun had sunk toward the horizon, and twilight was coming on. Rees knew the rising evening mist would obscure them from the curtain wall. When he was certain their forms were indistinct in the fading light to anyone at a distance, he bent and laid the recorder on the grass. When he straightened again, he said, "Briana, I would touch you." He took a step that put his body very near hers, but he kept his hands at his sides, watching her. Her breathing grew more rapid, and he was conscious of the rise and fall of her breasts under the thick, smooth fabric of her bodice, revealed when her cloak parted below the clasp at her throat.

She realized he was asking for her permission, just as he had in the small hall, and she felt the thrill of being able to believe she had a say in her future once again. "You have the right," she said.

He reached up then and laid his hands on her shoulders, his thumbs stroking lightly along the line of her jaw where it met the cloth of the barbette. Her eyes widened until her long black eyelashes seemed to touch her eyebrows. His even regard kept increasing her inner weakness and causing heat within her body, and she did not understand why her reaction was so disconcertingly powerful. Then his hands tightened a little on her shoulders, and he drew her in against his body. Even through the layers of her clothes, his supertunic, and the shorter tunic he wore underneath, she could feel the hardened, battle-trained strength in his chest and arms. She had an unexpected flash of anger that there was so much cloth between their skins, because she wanted to touch him directly, unencumbered.

Rees read her ready response to him as easily as if she had painted it across her brow, mastered his urge to smile, and laid the callused fingertips of one hand against her cheek, stroking it lightly. He bent his face closer to hers, drinking in the perfection of her features.

Briana studied him back, finding him amazingly fair, his skin sun-colored, his golden blond hair curling down onto his forehead, almost no sign of stubble on his cheeks or lip despite the new court fashion, which was beginning to tend to beards. His lips seemed so firm that she wondered if he could use them gently, and then he covered her mouth with his, and she learned to her surprise how soft they were.

The kiss was intoxicating, nothing at all like Owen Glyn's had been. It made her believe she was webbed inside, as if her body had been built by a spider, and that Rees's mouth set vibrations running along the strings of the web, spreading sensation downward to suddenly tender nipples and loins. She had not believed she could grow weaker and still remain standing, but then she discovered she was clinging to him, uncertain if she was supposed to do anything except experience the feelings.

Rees was not surprised by the hints of passion that greeted his kiss, for he had seen her react to his presence at both the midday meal and the dinner in the small hall. He had not, however, expected to be moved by the sweet, open innocence of her lips under his, the trust and giving that accompanied her awakening passion. He had little experience of virgins, nor had he ever sought them out. He and Ralf had discussed Galen's boisterous techniques of lovemaking, and both of them had feared for Menty's well-being on their wedding night. They were somewhat relieved when she emerged from the bedding chamber a little sore and shaken, but at least in health.

Rees felt himself stir, remembering Ralf's description of Briana's beauty, and moved his mouth on hers, kindling a fire in his body from which he could not remain detached.

Briana gasped, caught in the flame as well, wondering about the conclusion of this growing tension, wanting to feel more of his hands and his arms than just his steadying grip on her shoulder and the tips of his fingers on her cheek. She felt abandoned when he broke the kiss and lifted his head, smiling down at her. She was as astonished as he when the tears which she had been holding at bay for two days now overcame her at last and began to spill from her eyes.

Rees's smile vanished, and he asked, concerned, "Did I hurt you?"

"Nay." She shook her head, raising a hand to wipe at her cheeks. Then, with uncharacteristic candor—but, she reflected, she had done nothing in character since Edward called her into his closet—she told him the absolute truth. "'Tis only that I have been able to trust no one for so very long, and I realized not how very unhappy that made me."

He could not resist saying, "Mistake not lust for trust," and was pleased when she smiled, even though the tears still glistened in her eyes.

"You are wooing where you have the right to plunder," she said, "and I am not so ignorant that I cannot tell the difference."

He mastered the throbbing in his groin enough so that he could bend and pick up the recorder again, but stopped, his fingers just gaining the instrument, when she asked seriously, "Is that all the wooing? A single kiss?" He laughed softly, scooped up the recorder, and took an end of it in each hand. He raised it over her head, lowered it behind her back to the waist, and used it to pull her against his body again. "I am your knight, Lady Briana," he said, his voice warm with both amusement and pleasure.

Without prompting, she raised her face to him, and he kissed the tip of her nose, her eyelids and her forehead before he took her mouth again, nibbling lightly on her full lower lip. She enjoyed the light-hearted playfulness, so different from her only previous physical encounter with a knight, the rogue brute who had battered and tried to rape her during her abortive escape attempt from Westminster. Only the timely—totally inexplicable—interference by several of King Edward's retainer knights had saved her. She had thought then that she would be repelled by any further advances from a man of violence.

Rees did not repel her.

She opened her mouth to speak to him and was abruptly in possession of his tongue as he deepened the kiss. It showed her the first real glimpse of his sexuality, the powerful drive he was courteously containing, the hint of realms of which she knew nothing.

He knew she might have become frightened, might have begun to struggle against him, and he would have released her instantly.

But she welcomed the invasion and the feelings it gave her. He had no way of knowing that these were her first utterly positive, welcome, unguarded emotions in seven years of concealed anger and apprehension, of half-truths she had to live with every moment, of limited affections and unspoken opinions. Her relief at being able to openly experience something genuine and wonderful, something she wanted to experience, was fully as intoxicating as the desire.

Even through the bulk of his supertunic and undertunic, and her gown and shift, she felt the growing hardness against her stomach, and that, more than any sensation of her own, made her cautious.

Rees sensed her hesitation at once and drew back, his shoulder-length hair dancing lightly in the freshening night breeze. "Enough for now," he said, his voice lower and thicker than it had been.

His tones sent more shivers coursing through her, as if her very flesh had become charged with energy.

He released her and slipped the recorder into his belt again. "We'd best walk back," he said. "Shortly they will be closing the gates and posting the guards."

Briana swallowed and cleared her throat. "I'd hoped we might speak a little about Flint."

"Have you a palfrey?" he asked, and when she nodded, he continued, "We'll meet in the stables after midday meal on the morrow and ride out together. I am not disposed toward serious thinking at the moment and neither, I'd wager, are you."

She nodded again, accepting his assessment of the situation.

He took her hand once more and led her back to the gates of the castle. In the shelter of the curtain wall, he bent and touched his mouth once, lightly, to hers. "In a week, we shall be bedded naked together. Think on that." He turned and was gone before she could speak.

Briana raised a hand to her lips, wondering if she dared to hope she might love a Plantagenet husband. Was it possible that God, not notable for His favors to her hitherto, would change His mind and be good to her at last? Would He, after so much loss, so much loneliness, so much near-despair, allow her to be happy? Did she dare to think she could hope for that? Later, in full darkness, bathed and abed, she hesitantly laid her palms on her own breasts, gently stroking until the nipples rose into them, trying to imagine how it would feel when her husband did this. She pressed her legs tightly together, trying vainly to ease the ache that had been awakened at the juncture of her thighs. She realized that she was already hoping.

Rees led Basilisk out through the gates just as they were closing and laid his supertunic over the cantle of his saddle. He swung up onto the destrier and rode slowly back to the friary. If he could keep her from learning his title for one day more, the last day of Edward's forbearance over the banns, then he might be in a position to counter any hostility which would arise in her. The first step had been promising, even pleasing, but he knew very well that things would become much more complicated, and very soon.

Chapter 16

It was not easy for a woman to seek seclusion; far less often than its being sought was seclusion granted by the church. Men could become hermits merely by going off someplace; monks often had no need even to seek permission. Women, on the other hand, were subjected to a lengthy examination by reputable church authorities before they were permitted to step aside from the world. In the case of Flint's recluse, the reputable church authority had been none other than John Peckham, the Archbishop of Canterbury, and no one in England would be in a position to question his approval, nor would they be inclined to look closely at a woman whose seclusion he sanctioned. Thus, when, in the coldest part of the winter, a wagon driven by a giantess and escorted by two guards wearing the badges of Canterbury on their cloaks drew up toward the church of St. Maedoc, in Flint, the soldiers from Flint castle let it pass without troubling it.

Riding on the wagon, dwarfed by the giantess, the recluse was wrapped in a heavy cloak, shielded against the world as she would be once she entered seclusion. The hood of the cloak was drawn far enough forward to restrict her view and to effectively cut off the sight of her face from the two guards and anyone else they might happen to meet on their journey.

The wagon arrived at the church before it reached the village proper, and the giantess drew in the reins to stop the horses.

St. Maedoc's was a small stone building with two even smaller buildings adjoined to it inside its low stone walls. Within the front wall was a cemetery containing several headstones, though the greater part of the burial ground was behind the walled compound and outside the churchyard. One of the two buildings was the priest's house, in need of some repair, but definitely in better condition than the other outbuilding, much more run-down and obviously neglected.

The guards dismounted, and one looked into the church, found it empty, and went to the priest's house. He banged on the door, but got no response. He came back to the wagon and said, "There's no one about, my lady."

The recluse did not move, her face still hidden. She murmured something to her companion. The giantess tied the reins off to one of the wagon posts and said, "The priest may be in the village, or at the manor. We will wait here while you seek him."

The guard remounted, and the two men rode off in the direction of the village.

The women on the wagon relaxed, glad to be out of the company of the guards, who had been taciturn companions, curious to see the face of the woman they had been escorting from Canterbury for the past weeks. For whatever reason, they fancied her as young and beautiful, mysterious by virtue of her inaccessibility. They had come to resent the noblewoman's companion, whose great strength and obvious protectiveness kept them from approaching too closely. Now the companion asked, "Would you like some water, my lady?"

The recluse opened her hood a little and took a deep breath of the cold air. "Nay, I've no thirst yet," she said. "I hope we can get to shelter soon. I'm unaccustomed to such prolonged travelling."

"The hermitage appears to be quite wretched," the companion observed, nodding in the direction of the derelict building.

The recluse smiled. "'Twill be good merely to have a roof," she said, "and I've complete confidence in your ability to rebuild it, Sabine." She produced a slender white hand from the folds of the voluminous cloak and laid it lightly on Sabine's powerful arm. "You rebuilt me, after all, so surely a small hermitage cannot be that great a challenge."

"The queen had some hand in the healing," said Sabine.

"My brother's wife made it possible for me to be in secret, so that I had time to find myself again," said Princess Beatrice, "but you were my guide."

Princess Beatrice of England was forty-seven years old and still showed traces of the beautiful woman she had been in her youth. That she was here in Wales, rather than in the tomb which bore her name in London, was indeed due to the auspices of Queen Eleanor, who was one of only three people living who knew that King Edward's sister still breathed air. The archbishop was the second, and Sabine was the third, unawed by her membership in that company.

The two women were a contrast to one another in many ways. Beatrice was tall, but fragile for a Plantagenet. Her sun-yellow hair, hidden beneath her cowl and wimple, as well as beneath the hood of her cloak, had faded nearly to white, and her blue eyes had paled. Her face was still delicately featured, but care had drawn a web of fine lines across her brow and around her eyes and mouth. Of the fourteen years since the world thought her dead, nine had been spent withdrawn in madness, during which Sabine had nursed and cared for her. In the last five years, Sabine had helped her find her way back to living again.

Sabine was twenty-one years younger than the princess and

would have overtopped the King of England by more than a head. Broad and muscular, she was hulking enough so that many people who encountered her thought her stupid. She ignored such judgments without concern. She was well accustomed to the world's opinions, and many of them she held in contempt.

"Would you step down, my lady?" Sabine asked. "My own bones would welcome freedom for a time from this wagon."

"We might walk a bit before the guards return," Beatrice agreed. Sabine immediately swung down off the wagon, much quicker and more graceful than anyone who did not know her would have credited. She walked around the front of the wagon, stroking the nose of each horse as she passed it, then held out her hand and helped Beatrice step down onto the earth of Flint.

The two women went into the churchyard to look at the ramshackle hermitage. The walls were fairly sound, though several stones had fallen from the sill and sides of the tiny window. The roof was in sorry shape, most of the thatch having fallen in or blown away and several of the rafters sagging. The fireplace was of a good size, but choked with ashes and leaves; the chimney was probably blocked. The room was comfortably large, though, and the door was hard against the wall of the yard, so the occupant of the hermitage could reach the church unseen by anyone simply passing on the road.

"I can get it into usable condition soon," Sabine said, looking around. "I hope you are not discouraged."

Beatrice laughed, a gentle, crystalline sound, like something brittle. "Sabine, think not overmuch on my sensibilities. If 'tisn't wet straw crawling with lice, 'tis a palace."

The sound of hooves made Beatrice draw the hood up around her face again, and the two women went back out to the road.

Father Ciaran had been at the manor with Lady Maud, who was more than curious about so prestigious a summons. He hurried through Flint village in the wake of the guards, and when he neared the church, he saw the women standing by a wagon whose bed was piled high with tools and household goods, covered with a large, tied-down canvas.

Sabine had already decided to use the canvas for shelter, as they had along the roads on their way to Flint, until she had gotten the roof rebuilt.

If Father Ciaran was awed by the sheer size of the woman with the uncovered face who came to meet him, reaching into the scrip at her waist, he did not show it as she asked, "Are you Father Ciaran?"

"Aye," he said.

She held out a letter she had carried from Canterbury. "I bring you this."

The spare priest took the paper, saw the seal of the archbishop on it, and wondered why the huge woman was carrying it, not the men in Peckham's livery. With a thin forefinger, he broke the seal and unfolded the letter.

"Ciaran, my son," the text began, startling the Celtic cleric with the revelation that he was known to so auspicious a prelate, "in the name of Christ, I commend to you this proper and holy widow and request that you allow her to be sequestered at St. Maedoc. My understanding is that the church at Flint stands in need of a source of income, and this she can, in a small way, provide. I ask you to accept that I have always wished for peace in Wales. To that end, I send her to you for seclusion. Pray you do not fail me in this. John." The familiarity implied by Peckham's signing his own Christian name and the quality of the appeal in the message were more of a surprise to the priest than the giantess, but even that was not nearly so surprising as the implication that a lone woman recluse was somehow related to the future peace in Wales. It had been hard enough for him to accept the legend that attended Briana, and that had come from Myrrdin, whom every Celt in the world honored. This was something very unusual.

He looked up from the letter at the two women, the servant and the shrouded, silent woman she served. "As you see, the hermitage is not fit for occupancy," he said. "It has been unoccupied in all my tenure here." He glanced behind him. "'Twould please me much should you choose to occupy my own quarters."

Sabine smiled just a little at his awkward gallantry. "'Tis quite generous of you to offer, Father," she said. "May we take it that you accept the charter?"

He had forgotten to say so; he was unaccustomed to any kind of noble manners, any kind of formality. "I beg your pardon," he said, not overly abashed by his gaffe. "I accept the charter and thank His Eminence for honoring our humble church at Flint."

The two guards nodded at the priest, then at one another, turned their horses, and without acknowledgment of the women or any further words of farewell, rode back along the road to start their journey out of Wales.

Father Ciaran looked after them, bewildered. Sabine gave a snort of disgust, but said nothing about their hasty departure. Instead, she said, "'Tis no matter, Father. We will do well without them. And we cannot avail ourselves of your most kindly offer. We have been travelling some weeks now, and the mere cessation of motion will be most welcome. The hermitage will be quite good enough."

"But 'tis likely to snow further," the priest protested. "The hermitage roof is unsound."

Sabine glanced up at the sky and said, "I believe the snow will delay long enough for me to sweep out the hermitage and get our canvas over the roof. Then we will be protected when the weather lours."

He protested again, but she overrode it, refusing as graciously as she could. The recluse had already slipped back into the churchyard. Then Father Ciaran tried to insist on helping. At last, Sabine welcomed his aid in carrying the contents of the wagon into the newly swept building.

Once the parcels, tools, bedframe, table and stools had been safely stored under the tied-down canvas roof, Sabine asked Father Ciaran if he could arrange to have the wagon horses stabled at the manor. He took the reins of the team awkwardly and drove the horses further along the road toward Flint manor.

Sabine went back into the hermitage. Beatrice had removed her cloak and hung it over the window, so the only illumination in the dimming afternoon was a set of candles in plain holders on the table.

Beatrice moved one of the stools near to the cold, still unventilated hearth, and sat down on it. "The priest is kind," she said. "He will, I believe, be less intrusive once the hermitage is repaired and the seclusion complete."

Sabine spread one pallet on the strings of the bedframe and put the other on the rough floor at its side. "I shall ask for fresh straw to renew the pallets after I meet with the village women on the morrow," she said, and when Father Ciaran returned to tell her Lady Maud was pleased to give her horses stabling and pasturage, Sabine went out into the yard to meet him and said, "While you are quite courteous, good Father, I know you are surprised by my appearance." Her tone was practical, and she allowed him no time to demur. "I can understand how people might have cause to wonder at my size. And as there must be no stain approaching my gentle lady, I would confirm my womanhood to every decent woman in Flint. I'd be most grateful for you to arrange it, perchance in the hall of the manor on the morrow, if the Lady Maud will indulge us."

Father Ciaran flushed, and said, "I am certain such an act will not be necessary."

Sabine shook her head and chuckled quietly. "Nay, Father, 'tis kind, but we know well the world we've turned from, my lady and me. The only way to stop the tongues is to ensure every woman of repute has proof enough to silence them. 'Twill be swift enough, if you'd be kind and arrange it for me."

The next morning, Maud, Annie, Med, Dechire, Fand, and the other mature women of Flint village and manor gathered in the hall. The day was cold and windy, with snow blowing down from heavy-bellied clouds that scudded in from the West. The women were grateful for an opportunity to leave off their work for an hour, and since they had lacked entertainment for some time, they were bemused and laughing together. They were struck dumb when the giantess came into the hall and shut the hall door behind her.

Sabine smiled at them. "My name is Sabine," she said calmly, and began taking off her clothes as she spoke. "My lady and I will be happy to greet each of you individually once I have rebuilt the hermitage and added the visiting bench outside the window. This should consume some weeks." Her voice was muffled for a moment as she pulled off her wimple and revealed a huge mane of sandy brown hair, thicker and shinier than they would have guessed. "We will become a part of your life in this place, and I am certain all of you and I will grow to be great friends."

At the word "great," she shrugged out of the top of her gown, revealing a pair of breasts that would have shamed the pagan Earth Mother. Fand gasped a little and covered her mouth to keep from giggling, which seemed a singularly inappropriate response in the face of Sabine's cheerful dignity. Maud was about to say that she thought it unnecessary for the woman to disrobe further when Sabine simply did so, then coolly began to dress again.

"Great friends," Sabine repeated confidently.

The village women exchanged glances, and Maud raised her clasped hands to her lips, thinking that an overwhelming force of nature had come to Flint and wondering what kind of person was the recluse it served.

Within a short time, Sabine had personally met with everyone in Flint except the people at the castle. There could be no doubt that Edmund Mortimer knew she and the recluse were there; the spies from the castle roved freely all over Northeast Wales and reported back with frequency. Because no one from the castle came to St. Maedoc's to inquire directly, Father Ciaran assumed that Mortimer had been told that the guards who accompanied the women's arrival took their orders from Canterbury and had decided it would be impolitic of him to ask questions or interfere.

Once Sabine had finished the roof and cleaned the chimney, the hermitage was a nicely cozy place to be. The recluse often sat on her stool by the window, behind a thin veil, sewing, for her needlework was excellent, and its sale would bring in further income for the area. True to her enclosure, however, she went out only to the church, but never when anyone else was around, or to the privy behind the priest's house. Sabine went to the village or the manor often, on many errands. Soon everyone grew accustomed to the huge woman, moving silently and with a peculiar massive grace around the village, helping with the tasks needed to pay Baron Wigmore his taxes: herding, shearing, farming, baking, brewing, taking nothing for herself or her lady which she had not more than earned.

When the snow fell heavily and drifted against the churchyard wall, the women worked at the table, Beatrice sewing, Sabine sharpening a knife or carefully crafting arrows, including cutting the fletches and honing the points. They did not often speak. There was little to say. Now there was only some peaceful time while they waited for the coming of spring.

About the time the Lady of Flint was discovering that she was to be wed and to whom, Beatrice watched Sabine stir a pot of soup hanging above the low fire in the hearth, and said, "'Tis strange that, despite my prayers every day, I cannot purge myself of my need for freedom from the past. I cannot find it in my heart to forgive either of the men for what they did."

Sabine went on slowly stirring the thick vegetable liquid. "You are not required to give over your hope of their downfall, my lady," she said. "Nor am I. We are neither of us religious."

Beatrice sighed. "I am religious enough to pray daily that Rees will have a more forgiving heart than I, else he will never forgive me."

"He is sure to be here before the summer," said Sabine. "Then we will know."

Chapter 17

Windsor—February 1289 A.D.

Because Rees was at neither Mass nor the midday meal, Briana was concerned that he would not be at the stables either. She was surprised at the strength of her desire to see him again, to be in his company. The thought of him was uppermost in her mind throughout the morning, as she stood still on a footstool in the queen's rooms and let the sewing women alter the patterns to fit her so that she would not have to endure endless gown fittings. She might have been impatient had she not known she was being given these gowns to take back with her to Flint. She was excited about going home, and she was honest enough to admit to herself that the excitement for Flint was colored by her excitement about Rees.

So despite the blustery nature of the day, she hurried back to her chamber after the meal to change out of her murrey woolen gown into a linen gown which would be thinner and less restrictive. She did it quite deliberately, though she was not as sure about her reasons for deciding to do it as she was about the absolute rightness of her choice. She felt fortunate that her older gowns went on over her undershift and laced at the neck in front. Her new gowns would follow the latest fashion and lace up the back, requiring the assistance of a maid, and Briana could not have explained to Enlis why she was doing this.

She pulled on her riding hose, stuffed her feet back into the pointed court shoes which were her only footwear, snatched up her cloak, and ran down the steps and out of the castle toward the stables.

He was already there, already waiting for her. He had left his supertunic at the friary, wearing under his cloak only the more revealing short battle tunic and hose he would normally have covered with chain mail.

Briana stopped abruptly as she entered the stableyard with her first clear view of his strongly muscled thighs and calves, speaking clearly of a trained strength of which she knew she had yet seen very little. She half-smiled in anticipation of the afternoon, but found her mouth strangely dry and her palms strangely damp.

Rees saw her after a moment or two and quickly absorbed everything there was to see—that she was flushed with more than normal hurrying might have produced, that she was wearing a thin summer gown and undertunic, leaving very little barrier between her body and the world at large. The message was clear to him, and he relished it. He had, he knew, less than a day remaining until the banns would be read. He had thought he was making her less reluctant to accept a Plantagenet match, but now he began to think he was evoking a stronger response in her than he had anticipated. He did not take the time to try and analyze why. He walked across the stableyard to greet her and was treated to a beautiful, barely hesitant smile. "Well met, my lady," he said.

"I trust you have not waited too long," she said politely. "I expected to see you before this, at Mass or in the hall."

"I shall attend Mass tomorrow," he said. "Which is your mount?"

Briana pointed to a fairly tall chestnut mare with a jagged white star on her brow, and Rees sent a hovering groom to saddle the palfrey. Briana said, "Ine played at the meal, and I missed the recorder."

Rees laughed lightly. "I would not play in the large hall. There are, as you spoke of yesterday, knights and townsmen who would disdain such a skill, and I do not wish to challenge their convictions."

The groom led the mare in their direction. His path took him past Basilisk, who was lightly tethered to a ring in the stableyard wall. The stallion snorted at the mare, who sidestepped a little, but bared her teeth at him.

Rees was impressed by the palfrey's courage when confronted with a warhorse, and he took the mare's reins from the groom and studied her confirmation briefly as the groom nested his hands to give Briana a leg up. "Does she belong to you?" he asked.

Briana settled in the saddle, realizing she had forgotten to bring her gloves, but not wanting to delay the ride to return for them. "Like all things I use here in England," she said, "Timbrel is mine at the sufferance of the king and queen." She gathered the mare's reins.

Rees swung up on Basilisk with fluid ease and let Briana set the pace as they rode through the curtain wall. "Is that also true of the dulcimer?" he asked.

She shook her head, her smile a little sheepish. "Nay, you've caught me out with that. The dulcimer is my very own." She gave Timbrel her head, and he let Basilisk keep pace. They rode toward the river.

He noticed that she rode very well.

When they reached the treeline and the river path, which was not overly far for Basilisk to maintain a quick pace, warhorses being bred for strength rather than for speed, they slowed to a walk. Since the town of Windsor lay to the east, they turned west without speaking about it.

For several minutes they rode side by side in companionable silence, enjoying the calls of the waterbirds and the crisp air. Then Briana looked over at Rees. He was even taller than she on horseback, because she carried a great deal of her height in her legs, and their horses were almost the same height at the shoulder. "How is it that Princess Eleanor calls you a 'sort of' a cousin?" she asked. "One would think that, as her father's sister's son, you would be a cousin pure and unquestionable."

He had thought how he would answer questions about his origins, and he decided that his wife should know the truth. "I am a bastard," he said flatly. "My father was not the man my mother married."

She was taken aback by that and was silent for long minutes as she tried to think of what she should say or ask now.

He waited until he thought she should have said something, and when she still had not spoken, he asked, "Feel you dishonored by being commanded to wed a bastard?"

She was visibly startled by the question. "Dishonored?" she repeated. "No more by this than by wedding a Plantagenet." She spoke honestly and quite unselfconsciously. "I care only that you wish to help restore my lands. My pride has been put to sleep in my years of captivity. And—" She stopped a moment, then continued, "—and I have long since given over any hope of wedding the man my father and Prince Llewelyn, may they rest in peace, chose for me. Bastardy is hardly a hindrance to power. Prince Llewelyn's father was a bastard, and we Welsh loved the prince greatly."

Rees was certain he did not want to address that issue. He had fought Prince Llewelyn at a number of battles during the Northeast Wales campaign, and he could not but think that Wales's love of the prince would inflame the hatred against Rees himself.

As if she had gathered the word from his unspoken reflections, Briana said, so softly that he had to strain to hear her over the fall of the horses' hooves and the creaking of the gear, "I had thought to hate any man that King Edward might want to gift me to. I have long believed that God turned His face away from me and from Wales."

Rees saw the pliability of her face, understood the hope that prompted her to tell him what she thought would not be true. He looked away from her to take control of his expression as he swore silently at the revelation which had to come and to which she could not possibly react well. When he turned to face her, leaning on his arm across the pommel of his saddle so that he was not towering over her any longer, "What man?" he asked. "What man were you promised to in Wales?"

She had wondered if he would think about that, and a small thrill went along her spine as she thought that he might be jealous. Knowing that she was so drawn to him, she welcomed evidence that he might be drawn to her as well. "He was the son of one of Prince Llewelyn's friends," she said, "and I was but five when we were pledged to each other. I saw him only a few times before the war came." She did not say that Owen was still fighting that war. The trust she wanted to bestow on him did not extend that far before the fragility of uncertainty set in.

Rees concluded that her intended husband must have met his death in the Northeast Wales campaign, along with so many others. It was impossible to speak of Flint without returning to the subject of the war, and that he did not wish to do. Nor did he want to ride far enough to reach the friary, because he did not want Briana subjected to Galen too soon. He had every intention of bringing his friends with him when he came to Mass the following day, and he thought that would be soon enough.

They had reached a spot along the river where the bank sloped shallowly down to the water's edge and where that land was sheltered from view by anyone not boating past. There were no fishermen in sight. Rees drew Basilisk to a halt, dismounted, and walked wordlessly to Timbrel, holding up his hands for Briana.

She looked down into the sudden heat in his eyes, let her reins lie on the mare's neck, and swung off her horse into his arms. He led her down the slight slope about halfway to the water and spread his cloak on the ground. She was never afterward certain how she arrived on it, lying beside him, her own cloak open, her body at his disposal. She was aware only of the burning touch of his lips and then of his hands, moving on her waist, her shoulders, her face and, finally, on her breasts through the thin cloth. She was unaware that the air was cold, for she was thoroughly warmed by the fever which seemed to radiate from him to her. She heard herself make small groaning noises as she traveled the unfamiliar path of increasing arousal at his urging, her hands tangling in his hair, her body shaking as he stroked the tender flesh that filled his palms.

He might have been tempted to unlace the gown and strip her to the waist, in part because he wanted to see her, and in part because of her reaction to him, but he dared not undress her in the open air in winter. He contented himself with unerringly building her sensations. In one way, he was astounded at the amount of passion he found in her, the hints of its depths still to be fathomed. Yet, in another way, he realized that her very abandon showed how deeply she had held her feelings under control for years, how much she was coming to trust him, how entirely she had wanted to trust someone during the time she had been kept far from home in Edward's court. He knew the moments he needed to pull back and let her find herself again. He took her into sensuality and brought her back out twice before he thought he might be pushing her too far, because he had no intention of frightening her by unleashing his own desire. When he realized how late the day had actually drawn, a few stray flakes of snow were falling, and the river sliding past had gone from green to deep slate. He leaned closer to Briana and caressed her lips once more with his tongue, then sat up, pulling her into a sitting position beside him. "Calm now, Briana," he said in a whisper. "We need to go back."

She barely heard him at first, swimming as she was in magnetic waters, recognizing that, unbelievably, there was something in the world she wanted as much as she wanted Flint.

He had to speak to her again before her eyes focused.

She recognized that they would have to stop. His expression was strangely tender after the passion of the minutes before, and she was conscious of a peculiar sadness beneath the warmth, as if their growing intimacy had given her a confidence about guessing his feelings. Her breathing began to slow to normal, but the tension in her body barely ebbed. She realized her hair had come loose from her caul and barbette, and she stuffed it back into the net with long fingers. "There will be more, will there not, Rees? More—excitement?" she asked wistfully.

He liked the way his name sounded when she said it so easily.

The affection in his face increased, his well-shaped features softening even as they moved not at all. "Much more, sweetness."

The endearment sounded natural to her, welcome.

He thought that he would treasure this moment no matter what happened in the future. He waited until she had finished recapturing her hair, and then he kissed her lightly on the forehead, glanced up into the leaden sky that was beginning to exhale more snow. "Come," he said, rose smoothly to his feet, and lifted her up.

When she stepped off his cloak, he swept it over his shoulders and hooked it at his throat, then helped her up onto the mare, who roused from a doze and shook her head to clear it of vagrant snowflakes. They rode slowly, as if unwilling to break the spell of the last few hours.

They reached Windsor just as the guards were preparing to close the gates, so he bid her farewell there and turned Basilisk back toward the friary.

That night, lying beneath her blankets but unable to sleep, Briana dared to think that it was possible she might actually be able to be happy again, after so long a time of forced cheerfulness. *Mayhap*, she thought, *God will smile on me once more*.

In the aftermath of Fearndon, when the king came to take her away and she said her good-byes to Maud—perchance, she had thought then, forever—Maud had taken her by the shoulders and said, "Child, swear to me that you'll not build a wall around your heart because of cruelty that may come to you."

"I know not what you mean," Briana had said, her mind still reeling from the deaths at Fearndon, the shock of a home without her family, and the command that she was to come to court before she had truly begun mourning her father and brothers, let alone be finished with her grief.

"Bitterness," Maud said firmly, overcoming her own sorrow in her fear for her niece's sake, her plain face glowing with the strength of the message she wanted to convey. "You are naught but a child still, and you deserve some measure of happiness. Should you grow bitter, you'll not ever have God's will for you."

"God's will?" Briana had repeated, incredulous. "God's turned His back on me!"

Maud's lips contracted into a straight line, and she drew back her hand and slapped Briana as hard as she could across the mouth. As the girl cried out, her shock at Maud's uncharacteristic gesture greater than the slight sting, the woman pulled the girl up against her, but Briana did not weep. She had cried herself out on the way back from the battlefield. "Child," Maud said fervently, "you can hate if you like. Hate the English king, hate the butcher baron, hate the English lords, hate *me*! But never, never turn your hatred upon God. Now swear to me."

Briana had not the presence of mind to rise out of her grief enough to keep track of what it was she was swearing to, so she simply swore, bewildered that her phlegmatic aunt had grown angry enough about something, in a time of mourning, to actually strike her.

Now, in the darkness of the tiny chamber at Windsor, a place which she had seen as both a prison and a refuge, sometimes simultaneously, Briana thought that she understood at last something of what Maud had been trying to tell her. If she had closed herself off behind solid hatred, she might never have been able to be open to what Rees was offering. And offering was what he was doing, not demanding, not commanding. It was intoxicating, just as he was. If she could trust him not to abuse her, she could trust him with Flint, and that idea made her even more hopeful than she had been before. She hugged herself under the blanket and thought, *Thank you, God, for remembering me at last.*

Hulde and Enlis both noticed how their lady seemed to float, distractedly, through the morning before Mass. She let Enlis brush her hair until it shone, put on her best caul, woven with silver threads, used her small polished silver mirror to be sure she looked the best she could. Mass today would be special, life-altering. She wanted to be ready for it.

She was not, could not have been, ready.

Usually at Mass she sat with the princesses, in a line behind the two cushioned chairs with the king and queen in them. The chapel was small, with two lines of ornately carved choir stalls on either side of the altar. An enamelled reredos behind the altar caught the light from the high windows and reflected it down onto the candlesticks and chalice. The third line of a single row of choir stalls, against the wall opposite the altar, was necessarily truncated, crammed in as an afterthought so that the chapel could accommodate more people as the castle grew. It was into the single short row that Rees, Ralf, and Galen had managed to fit themselves, even though, having got himself wedged into one of the unforgiving wooden seats, Galen feared he would never be able to pry himself out again.

When Briana came into the chapel, that small row of added stalls was the first thing she saw, and Rees filled her field of vision. He rose and handed her into the stall at the end nearest the door, sitting down only after she did. She barely noticed the men on his other side, nor anyone else in the other sets of choir stalls until the boy with the censer entered, and the smoky tang of the incense reminded her that she should be more conscious of her place and her obligation to pray. She demurely lowered her eyes to her folded hands. When she looked up as Archbishop Peckham, who was celebrating the Mass, entered the chapel, she was surprised to see Ine at the far end of the household choir stalls. He was wrapped in his cloak, and his face was strangely serious. She frowned, wondering what the bard was doing here.

Like most bards, Ine was a devout and spiritual man, but his loyalties lay with the Celtic church, driven underground when the Roman version of Catholicism flexed its muscles two centuries earlier. He had learned his faith from Myrrdin, who had never set foot in a Roman church. She could not imagine what had brought Ine to chapel this morning.

Archbishop Peckham reached the altar, but instead of beginning the Mass, he drew a folded paper out of the sleeve of his robe and turned to face the congregation, clearing his throat.

Briana toyed with a curl of hair that had come loose from her caul and twined itself across the barbette strip beside her cheek. She was thinking distractedly about her upcoming wedding. King Edward had, in a moment of magnanimous generosity prompted by the mistaken belief that Prince Llewelyn would be willing to become his loyal vassal, paid for an elaborate wedding between the prince and his lifelong love, the Demoiselle. Briana, as one of the bride's young attendants, had been in an excellent position to observe the richness of the feast and the opulence of the decorations. She wanted no repeat of the expense. If she could keep the king from spending too much on her wedding, he might be willing to dower her well. That way there would be even more funds to use for the revival of Flint. Thinking about King Edward, she could not help but look over at him. He was watching the archbishop and did not seem to feel her scrutiny. *How haps it*, she wondered, *that he has chosen for me a man I might enjoy wedding?*

Peckham lifted the paper and said, "We this morning announce the banns for the wedding today week of the Lady Briana ap Bryn, of Flint, in the shire west of Chester, the Northern March, and the Lord Rees, styled Plantagenet, nephew of the our gracious King Edward, Overlord of Conway, and in his own honors, Earl Connarc."

Briana had been thinking, with a hint of irritation, that the English had not even the grace to call the shire of Clwydd by its rightful name when her mind registered the words she had just heard, the utter stillness of the chapel now that the archbishop had stopped speaking, and the fact that a great many motionless people in the room—the royal family, the king's retainers attending this Mass, the members of the household staff, the bard, the men in the end choir stalls, and the archbishop himself—were all staring at her.

He had said Earl Connarc. *Earl Connarc*, the butcher baron.

She seemed to hear the fateful name echoing through the still chapel as ice entered her veins and held her unmoving, her perfect profile to Rees's steady gaze. She felt a great pressure hindering her breathing, as if a band of iron had been strapped across her chest and screwed tight. Through the haze of shock and the roaring in her ears, she was acutely conscious that everyone, from Peckham to Ine, from the king to the man she had thought to be her savior, was watching her, waiting for her to react.

Briana was frozen, her thoughts racing uncontrollably. First, that King Edward had just been as vicious to her as it was possible for him to be without tearing her limb from limb, as he had poor Prince David. Second, that her thanks to God had been wildly premature, even misplaced, for He had just betrayed her again, to show her that there could, after all, be something akin to real happiness and then to tear it away. Third, that the great gray stallion Rees rode had been familiar to her because she had seen him from a frosty, brush-choked knolltop on the day she learned what cruelty truly was, watching from above the field at

Fearndon as Wales fell. Fourth, that Flint was to be given to the man who had destroyed everything she loved. And then the horror of having let him touch her, of having responded to that touch, overwhelmed her.

She fought it. She fought it as she had fought her weakness when the king put his hands on her arms and took her away from Maud, as she had fought tears all the years she had been faced with living in the Plantagenet court. The band around her chest seemed to snap, and she gasped suddenly. King Edward's eyes glittered, challenging her across the space between them, demanding that she behave. Beside and behind the king, both Eleanors radiated compassion. Joanna, however, was having trouble repressing a vulpine excitement. Briana realized she was staring across at the royal family and looked away from them. Her hands tightened on the short arms of the choir stall as her body involuntarily arched forward, and she struggled to make herself sit back. It was an end to hope, an end to any kind of trust at all. Self-loathing at her stupidity in daring to hope, in trusting, in having enjoyed the touch of a monster, lanced through her body. In all, less than thirty seconds had passed before she successfully exerted over herself the most severe control that she had ever employed or needed.

Rees had not taken his level gaze from her face since they had sat down, and now he watched her struggle, with regret that it was necessary, as well as with apprehension lest she do something that would disgrace them both. He did not know her well enough, he realized, to guess whether she would turn on him in rage or disdain, whether she might weep or faint.

She did none of those things. She drew in a long, slow breath, using her lungs as she would if she were singing a fast song, with no time for inhaling during the long measures, then let it out just as slowly. Other than that, she did not move.

Ine, knowing the price she paid for that control, began to smile with pride at her. He quelled the smile, but nurtured the pride. For some reason, it was colored by apprehension, by a sense of wrongness he felt but could not place. He let the feeling linger, patient to wait until it explained itself. He knew the revelation was a serious blow to her, but he had spent enough time talking to Rees so that he had formed an opinion, and it was favorable. He hoped that she would recognize that Rees was not a complete monster, but he also knew that Briana had never recovered from Fearndon.

Briana understood all too well what defiance of the king would mean. He had the right to gift her to whomever he chose, and disobedience would be punished with more harm to Flint. She could not be responsible for that. She had at her disposal no means to retaliate, no weapons she could use against Edward. She acknowledged that. But she would have to strike somewhere.

Rees was surprised at the stillness in her, but he saw no signs of it breaking.

The archbishop, as if suddenly aware of the silence, continued reading the formal cautions and conditions of the banns. Then he handed the paper to one of his acolytes, who carried it to the door of the chapel and posted it there. The ritual was a meaningless one; no one would contravene the king's will in this. Peckham turned his back to the congregation to begin the Mass proper.

Briana did not participate in any of the responses. When everyone rose to kneel for the consecration of the Host, she moved as if the motions had no connection to her. She did not appear to notice the difficulty Galen had in extracting his body from the vise of his seat.

When they all rose, she trod on the hem of her gown, stumbling, and Rees instinctively took her elbow to steady her. It was, he knew instantly, unwise. The moment she felt his touch, as impersonal as it was, a low hiss escaped her, and she froze again. This time she turned her face up to him. It was as if he looked at a mask.

"Take your hand from me, my lord," she said clearly,

making no attempt to lower her voice, and causing the rhythm of the Mass to break as Peckham was readying the wafers and the wine. "You have not yet the right."

Much as he would have liked to spare her, he could not allow her to openly insult him. "Nay, lady," he said easily, taking a tighter hold on her arm, "I have the right, should I choose to exercise it. But because I'd treat you gently, and because the sacrament is more important than we are, I choose now to oblige you." He released her arm, expecting her to do or say something else, but she did not. Instead, she stood quietly, back rigid, chin raised, looking across the chapel at the reredos, her hands resting on the rail in front of the choir stalls. Rees risked one quick glance at Galen and Ralf and was gratified to find that they were neither amused nor angry, just sober in recognition of the struggle that had begun here. When he looked back at Briana, Rees saw tiny beads of sweat on her upper lip, although her breathing was even and seemingly calm. *What next?* he asked himself.

He did not guess.

Because it was a Sunday, because a royal wedding was being announced, John Peckham would be giving Communion to everyone present. That was at least one reason why the chapel was so crowded. The opportunity to receive the honor of the Eucharist on an occasion other than Easter was welcomed by almost everyone.

Had she been able to think logically, Briana might have been even more bewildered by Ine's presence. He valued only the Celtic forms, where Communion was prepared before any of the prayers, and the prayers themselves were ancient ones, with some Celtic melodies used for the collects, graduals, and hymns. Once during a music lesson, they had discussed the rituals of the old Celtic Mass and those of the new Roman Mass, and Ine had told her he would never choose deliberately to be honored by a Roman rite Communion. Briana had always thought of the sacrament of the Eucharist as a foretaste of the joys of Heaven, and she had shared that perception with the bard, who did not dispute it, but said only, "There are many different foretastes of Heaven, Lady Briana. We must each seek our own." And yet he was here. Something in his presence stirred in Briana, but she did not explore it.

John Peckham truly enjoyed giving Communion, seeing the contentment that came to the king when he was the only recipient, and to the congregation at times like this one, with the receiving of the Host, murmuring the Latin words of the Eucharist sacrament over and over for each receiver. Even the king was humbled at such a moment before the Power which was infinitely greater than his own, and Peckham believed that humility was responsible for the contentment. Communion was the archbishop's way of presiding at the union between God and His people on earth. It was the act which had made him become a priest.

He began, as always, with the king and queen, then continued to the others of the royal family, and then moved to the guests that day—Rees, his knights, and the Lady Briana.

Briana waited patiently enough as first Rees and then his two knights received the wine-dipped wafer, but as the archbishop approached her, Briana, acting purely on impulse, raised a hand to forestall him. "Nay," she said, "pass on by me. I am not fit."

Peckham, stunned, stumbled, struck momentarily speechless, his hand still extended with the offered Host in it.

King Edward was thunderstruck, and he leaped up from his knees before Rees could move or speak. "What mean you by that?" he demanded of Briana, his voice a growl and his eyes shooting out blue sparks.

Briana looked levelly at him, showing nothing to the man who had once foolishly hoped that she might come to love him. "I mean, Sire, that I am clearly cursed to be punished so. My body is no fit vessel to receive both my God and the lord to whom you have given me. Since I must in all obedience to you accept the latter, I can no longer accept the former."

Rees almost lost himself in rage at that moment, for her insult to him was worse than he could ever have imagined. Both his friends prepared to haul him back if wrath claimed him, but he won his own battle for control.

Princess Eleanor made a small sound of distress, quickly stifled.

Ine swore softly under his breath at Briana's recklessness.

King Edward was gathering himself to respond with the ferocity of which he was so capable.

But it was Archbishop Peckham who spoke then, before anyone else could, his wits restored to him, his usual serenity gone, his optimism shattered. His voice was unnaturally strident. "Child, endanger not your immortal soul through this foolhardy pride. Bend to the destiny you have been allotted, for your sake, and for the sake of the people of Flint."

He did not cow her. She said quietly, without even a hint of defiance in her tone, "I do bend to it, Your Eminence. I have no pride in this. Pride would keep me from bending. But I am not fit to receive my God, not in the face of the gifts He has seen fit so clearly to bestow upon me, and He will know that, even if you do not. I may be flawed in numberless ways, but I am not a hypocrite."

Princess Eleanor gasped again, and Queen Eleanor rose and took five steps across the chapel, pausing only to incline her head to the archbishop and the Host, clasped Briana by the arm, and propelled her from the chapel before anyone could hinder her.

The distressed archbishop, the furious king, and Rees, now rigidly controlled, watched them go. Ralf touched his arm and said softly, "She'll come 'round."

"She'll have to," Rees said grimly. "I am fair certain Edward will force me to destroy Flint if she does not." He took a deep breath and fought to calm himself as the archbishop finally recollected what he was doing and moved to the last set of choir stalls.

Ine had used the reaction to Briana's rashness to slip out of his seat and along the narrow passage behind the stalls. He did not so much fear for Briana's immortal soul as for more tangible, more worldly things such as her lands and her body.

Rees was thinking that, God willing, the worst was over, and now he would have time to make it better.

Even in her anger and her despair, Briana was surprised by the strength and clear distress of the customarily serene queen as Eleanor pulled her along to the small hall, now cleared of any vestiges of last night's meal, its fireplace cold and dark. Eleanor told the guards in the gallery to fetch candles for the torchieres, then stood, still grasping Briana's arm, until the room was lighted and the guards had left again, closing the doors behind them. The moment the doors were shut, the queen released Briana's arm and leaned back against the wooden panels of the door, her arms crossed. Briana waited for her to speak, a little apprehensive, but not overly so.

Eleanor studied her for a few moments. The queen had been the possessor of a remarkable Castillian beauty when she was younger, and she had aged well. There were few lines on her face, and those which edged her large, dark eyes could be said to have been caused by smiles, not by cares. She had once thought herself fated to be that most useless of creatures, a sonless queen, but her faith had never faltered, and now that God had chosen to reward her with a healthy boy, she could have found nothing to make her happier. Her natural compassion for the Welsh woman in front of her did not cause her to be less than stern. "In the nearly seven years since you came to live with us, Briana, I have thought you to be many things," she said, "but I never thought you a fool until this day."

Briana flushed, but she saw no need to guard her tongue with the unremitting vigilance she had been accustomed to using. She understood, now that the first shock was past and the reality began to truly sink in, why the king had seemed apologetic when he told her of the match. She thought that his wife could hardly be otherwise. She said only, "I have always been a fool, Your Grace. I am pleased that hitherto you noticed it not."

Eleanor shook her head. "Do not fence with me. You will marry my nephew Rees, who is one of the finest men I know, and you will cease humiliating him as if he were somehow unworthy of you."

"Aye, I will wed him," Briana agreed. "I full understand that. I full accept that I have been commanded in this. I do not believe I humiliate him. I believe, rather, that I am humiliated by being given to him."

Eleanor clasped her hands together and gripped herself powerfully. She was growing angry, something she normally did not do. "Have you no care for Flint? He will be Flint's overlord!"

Briana drew in a sudden breath that might have been a sob, had she allowed any tears to threaten her. Her voice trembled badly, and all her efforts to try and control it were futile. "He came near to destroying us at Fearndon. Now my lord of Connarc has an opportunity to finish the task."

"Do not put him in the position of having no choice," said the queen. "Briana, you must reconcile yourself to this. My husband will have it from you."

"Of course," said Briana, her voice suddenly weary and dull.

To the surprise of both of them, the door of the small hall opened, causing the queen to step aside, and Rees walked in, his chiseled face carefully taut. "Please leave us if you will, Aunt Eleanor."

Eleanor nearly refused, but something in his expression made her think better of it. And the queen knew some things about marriage. Just as she and Edward had had to find their meeting place, so Briana and Rees would have to find one that allowed them to continue with one another. "Bring her to table in the large hall as soon as you're able," she said to Rees and slipped out, shutting the door firmly again.

Briana looked down at the stones of the floor, her hands fisted at her sides but hidden in the full folds of her skirt.

Rees watched her for a moment, trying not to remember the feeling of her body pressed up against him as they lay upon his cloak, trying not to think of the beautiful smile he might never see again. "Briana, look at me," he said quietly.

She did not, asking, "Is that a command, my lord?"

He knew if he said nay, she would not do it, and he had to learn if he could count on her obedience. "Aye," he said.

She turned toward him and raised her eyes to his face, unprepared for the shiver that went through her as the unwanted memory of his touch rose in her. She was barely successful in keeping it from showing.

"We have to reach an understanding, you and I," he said then. "I want no more scenes like the one in the chapel."

"Aye, my lord," she said tonelessly, thinking, *I shall have to find some other ways to make my unwillingness known, then.*

"Do not give me reasons to treat you other than gently," he said.

"I understand," she said. "Having murdered my father, my brothers, and my prince, you are disposed to look kindly upon me."

He held himself still. "I have murdered no one," he said. "And I am disposed to look upon you with far more than kindness, Briana. I had thought you welcomed such attention. Or have you forgotten that you wore a summer gown yesterday so that you could better feel my hands on you?"

She colored, but she did not look away from him. "'Tis a mistake I shall not make again," she said, hoping her voice did not sound as weak as she felt at that moment.

He smiled. "But you shall," he said. "You and Flint will be very important to me." She opened her mouth, but he overrode her. "If you are about to say something to me with the word 'never' in it," he cautioned, "I strongly advise you to reconsider. Never is a very long time."

"Aye," she agreed. "Will that be all?"

He ignored the question. "We must needs have a few rules agreed to between us," he said. "I expect you to behave with dignity in my uncle's presence."

She looked down at the floor again. "Aye, my lord."

"I expect you not to cast insults at me when anyone else is in hearing."

That surprised her so much that she was glad her eyes were downcast. She had not expected him to as much as give her permission to insult him in private, but she resolved to take advantage of it. All she said was to repeat, "Aye, my lord."

"I expect you to continue to respond when I touch you."

Her eyes flashed upward at him, and her voice went lower. "Response is not needful."

"'Tis for me."

"Then *you* respond!" It was out, flung at him, before she realized she had said it, and she was disconcerted when he chuckled. "You shame me," she said.

"There is no shame between husband and wife," he said, serious again.

"Aye, my lord." The discouragement was back in her voice. "Will *that* be all?"

The flash of defiance had gone, and he found that he missed it. "Nay. I expect you to receive Communion."

She shook her head so hard that her hair sprang free of her caul and barbette, and her words were vehement. "That I will not do, my lord. There is too much anger in me to subject sweet Jesus to it. He deserves better. And God has abandoned me to hell where, I think, they do not offer Communion."

Her sudden refusal surprised him. There was a limit, then, to how far he could push her or compel her obedience, but it was not the limit he had thought to find. He would have to overcome the anger she held against him, and the tool he thought he would need to use was passion. "Come here to me," he said, his voice abruptly rough.

"You are not my husband yet," she said, looking down at the floor again. "And until you are, all I can see is the blood on your hands."

Because she was looking away from him, she did not see his face pale.

He had to stop himself from leaving the hall. He stood quite still, breathing deeply. When he thought he could speak without edging the words in helpless rage, he said, "We will go in and join everyone at the meal now."

"Aye, my lord," she said again.

He stepped aside and, without looking up at him, she walked past him and out into the gallery.

Chapter 18

Much as she had hoped to avoid him in the next week, it proved impossible. The royal family sat them at a shared trencher for every meal. Queen Eleanor seemed to have told the king that it would be best if he let the two of them find their own way with one another, and he seemed to have listened to her. For the first four days, they made their way largely in silence. Briana appeared to be allowing the time to pass without participating in any of the events transpiring around her. She submitted emotionlessly to the ministrations of Hulde and Enlis, both of whom were very excited about their lady's good fortune and bewildered by the fact that she seemed not to share their excitement. She went to Mass, accepted that she would be seated next to Rees and his two friends, to whom he had politely introduced her on the first day, and with whom she had exchanged only the most superficial of courtesies. When the Eucharist was offered, it was offered only to the king, and if she averted her eyes from watching the ceremony, no one commented on it. She did not know that the archbishop had spoken to Rees, asking if he should continue to offer Communion to the lady of Flint, and Rees had advised against it. She was grateful that she was not required to make the decision repeatedly, in the company of the Plantagenets. After Mass, at the meal, there were always a great many people in the large hall, and Ine usually played several songs to please the king and the other attendees. One day there were jugglers, despite it being Lent, but most days the solemnity of the season kept the entertainment to a minimum.

After the meal, Briana was usually taken to the queen's rooms to embroider on the linens she would be taking with her to Flint, and to be available should something need to be fitted. On the third day, some additional purveyors were brought to the solar to offer shoes, gloves, hose, a new caul, headdresses, and a new shift. She let the queen and the princesses choose her belongings and expressed only a detached gratitude for their generosity.

Her detachment was shaken, try to fight against it as she did, when she and Rees sat together at the main or lesser meals. He was aware of that and gratified by it, but at the beginning of the week he did nothing to try to increase it. If, in reaching for cheese or a bite of fish, their hands touched, it was entirely accidental, and while she jerked away as if scalded on the first occasion, after a time she seemed to accept that it was mere happenstance, not a deliberate effort to disconcert her further. He was unfailingly polite to her, but he did not try to feed her any provender or wine, as was the custom for lovers. He also did not use his recorder.

On the fifth day, having watched silently since the banns were announced, Princess Eleanor came to Briana as they were rising from the table in the large hall and asked, "Would you like to come to the archery butts with me? We've not practiced for some days, and today's sunshine would allow us a good session."

"Aye," said Briana. "I'd enjoy that."

They got their bows and quivers from the armory and walked through the curtain wall and out to the butts, whose target cloths had been replaced when Princess Eleanor made their intention known. They both donned the leather hand guards that helped protect them from the snap of the bowstring. As she nocked her first arrow, the princess said, "I shall miss you when you depart for home."

Briana realized that she could return the sentiment sincerely. "I shall miss you as well," she said. Then she honestly added, "But there are many things I cannot say I shall miss by leaving here."

Eleanor drew, sighted, and fired. "Will you grant me the right to ask you an impolite question?"

Briana was touched to be asked her permission, but wary. When Eleanor looked over at her, she nodded.

Eleanor stepped back to the hay bale in which she'd stuck a number of arrows. "Your shot," she said unnecessarily.

Briana drew one of her own arrows out of the hay and took her stance in front of the target.

Eleanor looked down at the targets. "If you could escape the marriage by staying here with us and not returning to Flint, but remain just as you have been these seven years past—but for your brief flight—would you do so?"

Briana had not made the shot yet, and her hands began to shake so much that she had to lower the bow, arrow still nocked. She had not considered any possibility that would give her a choice, and she was certain that Eleanor's impolite question was not based in any reality her father the king would accept. But the question had shaken her badly. It forced her to consider an issue she had avoided confronting. Was it better to stay or to go home, no matter what the conditions of going home were? Would it be better to stay in the half-life of Windsor and Westminster, never able to let herself be completely at ease, never feeling all of her feelings, always existing on the thin layer of obedience that overlay a pit of fear? Or to bend to a man who had destroyed the life she had been able to live for her childhood, in a place that she loved and needed?

Eleanor watched her friend struggle with the question.

Finally, Briana said honestly, "I would go back to Flint."

The princess nodded, accepting the answer. "Then why," she asked, "battle you so hard against the means that will take you there?"

Briana had never told the princess or the queen that she had been at Fearndon, that she had defied her father's orders to stay away and that she had thereby been witness to the slaughter. She did not speak of the Welsh war to the Plantagenets. Even now, with the departure to Wales only a few days away, she could not violate that particular rule of hers. She raised the bow, arrow still nocked, sighted, and fired. It struck the target almost at the center. She looked at Eleanor. "I have much enjoyed your company, Highness," she said.

Eleanor debated whether to continue to press the issue, or to ask any further questions, and then decided against it. "Your aim is as excellent as ever," she said.

Briana could not resist a small, wry smile. "As is yours," she told the princess.

They both knew that Briana was not referring to the archery.

They shot arrows and held a generally meaningless conversation for an hour, then gathered up the arrows and went back to the castle. As they passed through the curtain wall, a man with a lumpy sack on his shoulder detached himself from the shadow of the wall and stepped toward them. They both recognized Ine, and Princess Eleanor turned aside, leaving Briana to stand with the bard under the gaze of the guards who were too distant to overhear. The princess also stayed a few feet away, within earshot, but at enough of a discreet remove to permit the appearance of privacy.

Briana had not had an opportunity to meet with Ine since before the Mass in which the banns were read. She relaxed her face and let him see her despair, but kept her voice low. "They have given me to a monster!"

Ine let his harp satchel sink to the ground and contradicted her quietly. "Do not mistake monstrous deeds for a man."

To Briana, the words were little help, for she wasted no time thinking about them. "There is no way out for me."

He considered his response very carefully. At last, he said, "Lady Briana, we all build our own cages. If you choose to see no way out, then there will be none. Aye, you must wed him, for Flint's sake if no other. And you have the power to make yourself happy or unhappy in it."

"*I* do?" she repeated skeptically. "I should think that power would much more reside with Earl Connarc." Her voice dripped venom on those two words, making Eleanor wince.

Ine took the tone in stride. "He has spoken to me of you," he said steadily. "He cares very much that you will not be miserable in this marriage."

"Then let him withdraw his suit and let me return to Flint in peace." Briana was reluctant to say the words. Once spoken, they took on a life of their own.

Eleanor could not remain silent and took several steps back toward them. "Rees did not bring a suit for this match, Briana," she said. "'Tis the king's command. My cousin was much opposed to it until he saw you in the queen's rooms. I believe that my cousin is a good man, though I know him not as well as I might, for he heartily dislikes the court."

"Good!" Briana repeated incredulously. "He is the butcher baron. Everyone in Northeast Wales knows of his crimes."

"And yet," said Ine softly, "'tis a different kind of butcher who tenders an apology to a bard."

Eleanor stepped even closer to Briana and Ine. "I know not how any man of war could fail to kill," she said. "Some fall prey to it; some do not. My mother knows Cousin Rees better than I. Briana, speak with her."

"A worthy notion," Ine agreed. "'Twould help greatly if you sought ways to be easier with the fate you must accept."

Briana was, had always been, Ine knew, a child who understood the role of reason and fairness in dealing with other people. She had watched how her father had administered Flint, had seen how Prince Llewelyn ruled Wales. She could contrast those ways with the ways in which King Edward maintained power, without regard for anyone who was his subject. Indeed, it was her knowledge of and desire for fairness which had so outraged her spirit at the way Wales fell and the way she was snatched from her home.

"I shall ask for an audience with the queen," she said, her voice a little duller with resignation.

Eleanor, who was always pleased to see what she could cast as a happy circumstance, smiled broadly, showing usually hidden dimples. "I will undertake to tell her you will be approaching her," she said, turned, and ran across the bailey, leaving Ine and Briana alone, far enough from the surveillance of the guards to be able at last to speak entirely privately.

Ine said immediately, "Lady Briana, we have had no chance to speak alone since this match was confirmed. I'd tell you what things I know of Rees, styled Plantagenet, now Earl Connarc."

She sighed a little and fingered the bow she was still holding. "Tell me only if 'twill help me to hate him," she said. "I wish to hate him. He is my enemy, and already there is too much about him which fits not with the image I want to have of him."

Ine made a quick hissing sound. "Foolish," he said sharply. "Be not so foolish. He is to be your lord and husband, not your enemy."

"He is to be all three," she said with as much conviction as she could muster. "A bastard, a Plantagenet, and the man I myself saw in command of the bloody field at Fearndon. What else could he be but my enemy? Was the king's sister so very unwise that she toyed with some lover to get him?"

"Earl Connarc is not the son of a wanton," Ine said. "I've been on the roads enough to hear many stories, some I credit and some I do not. One of those I credit I was told in Dorset, about a noblewoman who was attacked and abused at the shrine of St. Candida in Whitchurch by a Norse ambassador to the court. 'Twas rumored in the town that she was royal, but the Norseman was protected by the king whose representative he was. The noblewoman near died, but the tale says St. Candida preserved her and the babe she bore."

"And think you that babe was Connarc?"

"Some years later, I travelled to London with some of the pilgrims from Dorset on the road to Canterbury, and one of them, in her cups, spoke of nursing a woman named Beatrice after a brutal assault which polluted the shrine and caused the church to need rededication."

Briana shifted uncomfortably, but nevertheless could not help feeling compassion for any woman assaulted by a stranger. She remembered all too well her own pain at the savage attack by the rogue knight, a probable potential rapist. She was blessed to have been rescued, but still, "Even if 'twere true," she said, "that is the mother, not the son."

"You have always been treated more kindly by the fates than have many others," the bard said to her firmly. "'Tis my belief Connarc will want to continue treating you kindly. To my own surprise, he seems to have neither the nature nor the reason to wish it otherwise."

"Why do you defend him?" Her voice rose, for she was angry that Ine spoke of the butcher baron as if he were any normal man.

Ine made a soothing gesture with his hand, warning her to speak more quietly so as not to draw the attention of the guards to them.

She reduced the volume of her words, but the vehemence increased. "You know what he did. He betrayed the prince. He destroyed Clwydd."

"He has been a fair overlord for Conway," the bard said stubbornly. "For near seven years he has handled the people well. He is hugely more well regarded than Baron Wigmore, the Marcher Lord for the North."

"That says little," Briana countered. "Edmund Mortimer is a beast."

"And Rees of Plantagenet is not," Ine finished. "You have yielded to the King of England for these past years—"

"—betraying my pride and my soul every moment of it—"

He wanted to shake her, but it was not his place to do so, and he sensed that, in any case, it would do no good. He took one step back to keep from grasping her shoulders. "Have a care, Lady Briana," he said. "The king will brook no defiance."

"I shall not defy the king," she said, "but what matter care if you are already condemned to hell?" She nodded her head to him in farewell and walked away.

He looked after her with deep regret. From childhood, she had been headstrong. That quality had often plunged her into difficulties, had caused her her greatest sorrow, but was so strongly ingrained in her character that it was part of her, like her love for Flint and her problems with diplomacy. In many ways, he loved her dearly. She had been a part of his own life since she was very young, and now that she was grown, no man who saw her could fail to be moved by her searing beauty. But he believed she was being extremely reckless. Despite everything the folk of Flint thought they knew about Earl Connarc, Ine had seen enough of knights to know that Rees was very unusual. He had thought that Briana was beginning to see it, too, but as long as she refused to accept it, her obstinacy would block out her ability to reason.

Briana did not want to be reasonable. She wanted the simplicity of hating a man who had turned out to be nothing like she had imagined him, a man who made her feel slack with longing just by turning to her. When she thought about that, she was very afraid.

Rees spent the five days watching Briana pass by him, usually in a flurry of skirts, or sitting passively beside him in chapel or at meals, unspeaking. He had not tried to draw her into conversation, but Ralf, seated on her other side and sharing a trencher with Galen, had tried to engage her several times.

Each time, she had made an effort to be polite in response, but she was distracted and made only monosyllabic replies. Galen might have pushed her further, but Rees ensured that he did not sit beside her.

When they were seated side by side, Rees sensed the tension in her, and the anger. She made an effort to mask it, but the effort was not entirely successful. He was trying to be sensitive to her feelings, and she was trying not to show him what those feelings were. He was marginally better at his task than she was at hers. Only once did he catch her in an unguarded moment, and then, before she could mask it, he had the impression that she would like nothing more than to poison the air around him.

On the night of the fifth day, when the handfasting was only two days away, Rees deliberately went to Briana's chamber after she had retired for the night. When Hulde opened the door, surprised to see him, he said, "I'd speak a few moments alone with your lady."

Over the years of Briana's captivity, Hulde had become fiercely loyal to her mistress. Her plump face, framed by the linen of her wimple, changed from a plain expression of surprise to one of dubious disapproval. Few servants were as opinionated as she had been permitted to become, because Briana had encouraged it in her. Not only was it the one area of her life among the royal family that she had been able to control, but it gave her the satisfaction of knowing that someone around her was free to express herself.

Briana had made the suggestion to Hulde a year after she was taken from Wales. The precipitating incident had occurred when a Welsh rebel—a fellow named Meluin ap Daffyd—was captured and executed at the White Tower. Ever since King Edward had created the penalty of drawing and quartering for Prince David—a penalty which sequentially subjected its victim to castration, hanging, disembowelling, and being ripped asunder, any one of which would have seemed more than adequate to meet the case—the enemies of the King of England died horribly. Briana had heard about Meluin's execution in the same way, and with almost the same words she had been told when Prince David died. Both descriptions had sickened her, and she had had to bite back everything she wanted to say until the effort gave her indigestion and cramps, for if she had spoken, it would have been treason, and it would have incurred Edward's wrath. Being Briana, she swore to herself that no one around her would ever have to do such a thing in fear of her own anger.

Hulde had been astonished and a little outraged at first. She was a servant in the court of the king, and she expected to have no opinions she could openly express. The Lady Briana was the king's ward and should be expected to treat her badly, or at the very least, thoughtlessly. Hulde stewed over Briana's request that they arrive at a way for her to speak her mind without her lady having to react to it, and, after a few days, she waited until Enlis finished Briana's hair and departed from the chamber, and then she said hesitantly, almost truculently, "I could mutter."

Briana stared at her housekeeper for a moment, thrown out of the context of her own thoughts by the belligerent, seemingly incongruous statement. Then memory clicked into place, and she hid a smile. Hulde was being very serious about this; Briana would not make light of it. "Mutter?" she repeated.

"Aye." Hulde's chin pushed out further. "I could mutter."

"Do so then," said Briana.

From the time the banns were announced, and word of the wedding had made its way around the castle, to the moment when Rees came to Briana's door, Hulde's muttering was constant when she and Briana were alone. The housekeeper thought that her lady was being blind to all the advantages of a match with a Plantagenet earl, and she was indignant that her lady was taking such obviously good news so badly. When Briana refused to acknowledge Hulde's opinions given in a normal volume, the housekeeper increased the speed and volume, until her muttering became a veritable torrent, still nonaccusatory, though occasionally a word like "ungrateful" would slip in, usually slightly more muffled.

But when she realized that Rees wanted to come into Briana's chamber, her natural protectiveness and propriety asserted themselves.

When Rees came to the door, Briana had been brushing her own hair, as Enlis had gone to her parents' cottage to bid them good-bye before she left for Wales with her mistress. Briana was wrapped only in the coverlet under which she would sleep, and she turned slowly toward the door, one hand raised to her hair, the other holding the coverlet closed over her breasts. She tried to keep her face expressionless, but the darkness that blossomed in his cool blue eyes when he saw her seemed to rebound in her own body, pressing at her skin from the inside. The sudden color that flamed in her cheeks made her angry. "He commands you to leave us, Hulde," she said, her voice thin and tight.

"My lady, 'tis not meet," Hulde protested directly. Briana reflected wryly that it was a great relief to hear her housekeeper express an opinion outright, for she was heartily sick of the muttering, but had no notion of how to stem it without stifling it.

"I'll not dishonor the Lady Briana," Rees said, stepping from the doorway to make room for the housekeeper to pass. He half-expected Briana to add something insulting, but she did not. She merely stood and watched him, wide-eyed, one hand still holding the brush to her hair, the other on the coverlet.

Hulde stood her ground, despite the fact that he towered over her, and looked at Briana.

Rees held his breath. If Briana told her housekeeper to stay, he would need to remove the woman bodily, which of course he could do quite easily and without hurting her. But he would prefer not to have to do that. He locked his gaze on Briana's face and waited.

At last she seemed to realize that he was waiting for her to make a choice, once again leaving to her a decision he could have compelled. She made herself look at Hulde. "'Tis all right," she said. "My lord will own me come Sunday. I believe I am safe this even. Go on. I shall call you when we finish our converse."

Hulde shot a look at Rees which nearly singed his eyebrows and stomped past him, waited for him to enter the tiny chamber, and then closed the door behind him more forcefully than strictly necessary.

"She is loyal to you," Rees observed, trying not to smile at the woman's obvious indignation.

Briana put the hairbrush on the trunk and took a step backwards in a room which suddenly seemed much too small. She took a firmer hold on the coverlet that nested in her armpits, extending downward to her bare feet. "No doubt you will seek to change that," she said, trying to sound calm.

He frowned, the expression shadowing his eyes. "I find it admirable that you would inspire loyalty," he said slowly. "Why should I seek to change it?"

She did not want him to be reasonable or kind. She wanted him to behave like the monster she thought him so that she could find it easier to hate him. "Why do you come here, my lord?" she asked, trying to make her words disdainful and failing as his unwavering gaze disconcerted her. "Why do you not merely wait for the wedding?"

"'Twill be a handfasting only," he said. "The wedding will be held at your own church, St. Maedoc's. The king has given permission for Flint to witness its lady's marriage." Neither of them mentioned the fact that the lack of a wedding also eliminated any need for her to confront the question of Communion again.

Briana felt a rush of relief that she was to be reprieved from the marriage, even in so small a way, and then was angry at herself for the stab of disappointment that wormed through her, undermining her relief. A handfasting might make the marriage inevitable, for it was as close to a guarantee as the law held, but without the solemnization of the Church, it could still be dissolved, should she be able to find a way to do so. "And you wish to tell me what?" she asked sharply, the anger seeping into her voice.

Rees said carefully, "At the conclusion of the handfasting, you will be asked to swear fealty to me." He saw her receive those tidings like a blow, her lips whitening suddenly as the blood left her face, but she did not immediately speak to deny him, as he had suspected she would. He went on, "The king, my uncle, as holder of your wardship, offered to overtop your response, thus removing your choice in the matter, but I have asked him not to do that and to allow you to speak for yourself."

She swayed and sat down on the feather tick, unaware that the coverlet parted slightly, exposing one long, slender leg and the firm roundness of a thigh. Rees felt his blood ignite and fought it back.

Briana's head was spinning. Even King Edward had not asked her to swear fealty to him, perhaps because she was a woman and perhaps because he had never felt any need for her pledge. Obviously, Rees did feel such a need. "Why?" It was barely a whisper, but he heard it.

"You must understand," Rees said, "that King Edward's disposition for Flint and its people is dependent upon your cooperation in this. I thought that you would like the opportunity to save them from any further cruelty."

Briana struggled against the tears that threatened her. "He has already given Flint to *you*, of all possible overlords," she burst out. "Surely he can do no worse."

"He can do far worse, Briana," he said grimly. "He can order the village razed, the people put to the sword, and the land sown with salt."

She had known that, had always understood that was the ultimate punishment Edward could inflict upon her. She had only refused to accept its reality in this matter. She said, "I should think that sort of thing much more your style, my lord."

Rees refused to allow her to provoke him. "Flint is to be my home," he said. "I want to see it prosper, not perish. I have already pledged my own wealth to make that happen. What more do you desire of me?"

It was out before she realized she was going to say it. "You might die, my lord." She refused to qualify it or retract it.

He bowed slowly to her, a courtly motion of infinite grace. "One day I shall no doubt oblige you, Briana, but not soon if I can manage it." He straightened, his face revealing nothing, his gaze once again steadily on her. "Will you swear fealty to me?"

She bit her lip and looked downward, realized the coverlet was open and drew its sides together, hiding her leg. She wished he would go away, knew that he would not.

After the silence had stretched between them for a lengthy time, he said reasonably, as if speaking to a child, "I know how hard it is to swear fealty when your whole heart is not behind it. I ask you to understand that I know what it is I am requiring of you."

She could not bring herself to look up at him. "How can you know?" she asked. "How can you have any notion?"

He would not tell her, because it might give her a weapon over him. He would not say that he had never wanted to swear fealty to King Edward. He would not say that he had hoped to swear it to the man he then thought his father, Duke John of Brittany, known as de Bretagne. He had thought himself the elder son, but John lavished all the affection of which he seemed capable on Arthur, three years younger. Rees had wanted his father's approbation more than anything else in the world. When he was eight, his father complimented the skills of a minstrel, and Rees began learning to play the recorder. By the time he discovered that musical prowess had no effect on his father's coldness, he had been playing enough to love it, and then Bertran, Bard of Poitou, had cautioned him never to put it aside. When John spoke warmly of a knight's skill at arms, Rees, then eleven, vowed to turn himself into the finest fighter possible, and just as he won his spurs, at fifteen, for the single purpose of becoming one of his father's knights, his mother sent him to England to swear fealty to her brother instead. Because he did not want to go, and because she was dying, she made him swear an oath to carry out her wishes, and he swore, and then was trapped into doing what he had sworn to do.

He hated kneeling to King Edward when it should have been his father. He found the king even colder toward him than John de Bretagne had been, and no sooner had he pledged than the king demanded he take the Cross and go to the Holy Land. His fealty had given him Galen and Ralf, for which he was grateful, but it had taken much else—his dream of being his father's man, his name, his honor, and, nearly, his life as well.

He understood very well what he was asking. But when she asked, "How can you have any notion?" all he said was, "You will have to believe that I do. Will you swear fealty to me?"

"It seems I must," she said at last, "for the sake of my home and my people."

He was not satisfied. "I must ask you to declare aye or nay," he said. "Briana, will you swear fealty to me?"

Her head shot up, and she glared in his direction. "Aye, damn you!" she hissed. "I will swear."

He nodded approvingly. "I want it to be possible for us to deal well with one another," he said. "We both want what is best for Flint and for Northern Wales."

"Had you truly wanted that, you might have refrained from slaughtering our best men." Her voice trembled, on the edge of a reckless insolence that made her keep remembering he had in effect told her she could insult him when they were alone. "But mayhap your definition of what is best for Flint is not quite identical to my own."

He fisted his hands, but controlled his temper. "Then we must needs spend some time bringing our definitions into harmony," he said. He let his gaze descend along the lightly concealed lines of her body, and she flushed, the heat rising into her face, but not remaining there. Instead, it coursed downward through her, following the path of his eyes.

He looked back at her face and knew that he had stirred her, knew, too, that she hated being stirred by him. It was unwise, he thought, to push her further at this point, but he could not resist it. "Drop the coverlet," he said, in abruptly thick and deep tones.

She almost challenged him to take it from her if he wanted it off, but she feared he would do just that, and the idea of him that close to her, of his hands on her skin, was far more unsettling than the command had been. He would, as she had told Hulde, own her on Sunday once the handfasting was completed and, she realized now, she would be less nervous in front of the witnesses if she had the courage to face his demands now. In two days, he would have the right to beat her for disobedience. She could defy him at this moment, but to what end?

He was actually astonished when she rose again and let the covering slide to the floor, where it pooled on the stones at her feet. She made no attempt to cover her breasts or the triangle of thick ebony curls that clustered at her body's root. Instead, she watched him study her.

She was fully as lovely as he had guessed, and her seeming boldness in openly revealing herself made his palms tingle and his loins ache. Her breasts were firm, heavier than he had thought, even when he had his hands on them, and under his gaze, her nipples hardened. Her waist was narrow, her hips flaring gently, her legs smoothly muscled, and her knees trembling ever so slightly at his scrutiny.

Briana felt even weaker inside as he continued to study her, and to keep from watching the desire that bloomed openly on his face, to keep from recognizing his uncompromising maleness, she fastened on the slow rise and fall of his chest under the cloth of his supertunic, which should have concealed more of his body than it appeared to.

He took two steps toward her, and her eyes flew back to his face, but she did not recoil. Rees bent and picked up the coverlet, draping it around her again. Where his fingers stroked against her skin, the touch seemed to burn her, and her shaking increased, but he was careful to avoid brushing against her sensitive breasts, knowing now that he could evoke a response in her without even touching her, and aroused by the knowledge. "I hope, Briana," he said in barely more than a whisper, "we will reach a time when you do not regret what King Edward has commanded for us."

She raised her head, squaring her shoulders and drawing the coverlet closed around her. "I have regretted all my life for these past seven years, my lord," she said, "but for several months in which I believed—I hoped—I belonged to myself, but I was disabused of that. 'Twould be a shock to have the situation altered now."

"Rees," he said. "My name is Rees. You used it once."

She was disturbed by his nearness, but not enough to rob her of a reply. "That was before I knew you were Connarc," she said. "England may make you my lord on Sunday, but it does not make you my friend."

"We shall see," he said.

As soon as he had left her, Hulde came bustling back in, muttering wishes that the earl would leave her lady alone until the wedding.

Chapter 19

Because of the queen's duties, Briana did not get her private audience with Queen Eleanor until after the evening meal the next day. By that time, Enlis had returned, and she and Hulde had packed the trunk with all of Briana's new gowns except the one she would wear on the journey back to Flint. All her other, rather meager possessions, including her dulcimer, were laid inside, though the dried lavender sprinkled among the folds of the clothing was not added to the hard items—her hairbrush, the bow and quiverful of arrows that Princess Eleanor had given her to take to Wales. "'Twill remind you of some of the happy times here," the princess had said.

Briana accepted the gift because the princess had always tried to be kind to her, so the Welsh woman did not say to the princess that she had not had any happy times in England, only days which were less sad than others. If the royal family was willing to accept her facade of cheerfulness as genuine emotion she was willing to let them believe it, especially now that she would be leaving.

At the Mass after she had stood naked in front of him and agreed she would swear fealty to him, Briana covertly watched Rees. She sat beside him, looking down at her hands, but tilted her head enough to be able to roll her eyes toward Rees and his two friends. She saw nothing new, but she watched with the knowledge that this man, who would become not only her lord but her liege lord as well, had once again let her make a decision he could have commanded. And because she was watching, for the first time she saw that Archbishop Peckham, who would administer the handfasting and then leave for Canterbury when Rees and Briana left for Wales, turned from the king after he had given him Communion and asked Rees a silent question. Out of the corner of her eye, she saw Rees minutely shake his head, and Peckham returned to the altar. She understood, with a sense of real astonishment, that he was protecting her from having to confront the most powerful prelate in the Isles by refusing Communion, an act which would also openly outrage the king, who did not react well to being outraged.

At the meal in the large hall, she ate very little, but she did turn to Ralf and ask softly, "How long have you been a vassal of the earl's?"

He was so surprised by the question—any question—from her that he looked past her at Rees before answering.

Briana did not know what expression Rees had. She toyed with the stem of her wine goblet and looked sideways at Ralf. Beyond him, Galen, never a master of tact, leaned forward and stared at her for actually initiating a conversation.

Ralf said, "Fifteen years now, my lady. I was Sir Galen's squire when the earl—then only Sir Rees—came to England."

"When did he become your liege lord?" she asked.

Ralf smiled at her. "When we all returned from the Holy Land, he was elevated to the barony. I won my spurs in the Holy Land, and Galen and I swore fealty to him on the spot."

Her face clouded, and her fingers tightened on the goblet. Mention of the barony was too close to mention of Baron Connarc, and that would draw her into the morass of the Northeast Wales campaign. She did not want to think about that. She could not think of it and go through with the handfasting. She would have to try and run away again, even though her past attempt had come to grief. And then, of course, she remembered that she could not run away because the king would take his revenge on her home. She felt, once again, entirely trapped, and she sighed.

Ralf realized that something he had said had saddened her, and he returned to his own meal.

Rees observed the exchange, which he could hear because Ine had finished the songs he would play that day and returned to his seat at the end of one of the lower tables. Nothing about it surprised him except the fact that Briana had asked the questions in the first place. He did not interfere or try to pursue any conversation with her after she turned back to the trencher before her. He thought he understood quite well what had made her retreat again into melancholy. And he thought he knew what had started to draw her from it. He was neither displeased nor dissatisfied.

During the evening meal, they did not speak at all, but he was not dissatisfied with that, either.

And then after the meal, Briana joined Queen Eleanor in the queen's rooms. Eleanor sat on a chair which was brought into the room whenever the queen was in residence there and removed to the gallery when she was not. When Briana came in and dropped a proper curtsy, the queen gestured her to sit on one of the benches, and waited until she was seated to ask, "Do you do well, Lady Briana?"

"As well as could be expected," Briana answered, with a touch of real irony in her voice. "Grateful that there is to be only a simple handfasting, not a full wedding. Grateful for more time to become accustomed to my fate."

Queen Eleanor had been embroidering an altarcloth, which she laid in her lap when Briana came in. Now she picked it up again and made a neat stitch with gold thread that sparkled in the candlelight. "I must remind you that 'twill not be a simple handfasting only," she said, watching the needle emerge from the linen. "The king will have you firmly bedded and the handfasting consummated before you leave Windsor." She did not look up. "My husband wishes to be assured that neither of you will break the handfasting or repudiate the match, so he requires the act of consummation not be delayed until after the church ceremony."

Briana trembled sharply, having to face what she had been trying to avoid facing, that it was really not to be a reprieve. She wanted not to believe it, and at the same time, shamefully, she wanted to see the golden giant naked and approaching her in a dimly lighted chamber. She tried to imagine it, then hastily tried not to imagine it. "I thank you for reminding me, Your Grace," she said as calmly as she could. "I shall be prepared."

The queen looked up from her embroidery and regarded Briana steadily with something approaching skepticism. "I much doubt if any woman is prepared for the actuality of her first time," she said, "but I have heard tell that Rees is a skilled and pleasing bedmate."

Despite her wish to remain disdainful of the subject, Briana lost the struggle to defeat her curiosity and surrendered to it instead. "Is it talked of overmuch?" she asked.

Eleanor laughed. "Women sometimes compare experiences, as men do." She looked at Briana more closely. "You know what happens, do you not?"

Briana nodded, unable to frame a spoken reply.

The queen leaned forward and laid a hand gently on Briana's arm. "Let him do as he wishes," she said.

"That is what I thought happened," the younger woman said, "that he does as he wishes." She suddenly sounded so bleak that Eleanor's natural compassion broke through the composure she wore like a garment.

"Child, child," she said, "there is so much tragedy in life— more than enough without making more where it need not exist."

Briana remembered, unavoidably, the tragedies of the Welsh war, fought not to follow that thought to Fearndon. She had spent so much time and energy in the grip of tragedy that one more seemed a normal happenstance. So she was utterly honest. "You think it not a tragedy to spread open and lie beneath a butcher?"

"Nay," said Eleanor simply. "I have done it these almost thirty years. That is often what 'tis to be wed to a powerful man."

Briana was taken aback by that and twisted her hands together against the dark gray fabric of her gown. "How can you—care for an unkind man?" she whispered. "A man who kills without feeling it?"

The queen said, "I have found that even an unkind man can be kind to the woman, or women, who bend to him. Bend to Rees."

"I believe I have no choice," said Briana.

Eleanor shook her head. "'Tis my notion that Rees will give you a choice," she said. "'Twould be very like him to do so."

The words shook Briana even more, for she heard the truth of them. But, stubbornly, she wanted to disbelieve them. "How can you know that?"

"I know Rees," said Eleanor. "I have seen how he deals with the world these many years. I know what he values."

"What?" Once again, it was whispered. She expected a quick answer, but Eleanor laid the embroidery in her lap again and folded her hands, conjecturing. At last, her eyes fixed on the distance, Eleanor said slowly, "He values the lands entrusted to his care. He values his friends. I believe he greatly values the music he plays. He values fairness. And I believe he will value you."

Briana turned her face away from the queen, thinking, unstoppably, of the blood on the cold ground at Fearndon, and the implacable figure of the knight on the gray stallion, directing the slaughter. "I do not want this marriage," she said in a low voice. "I gain Flint by it, but I lose everything else."

"Briana, you lose no more than any woman loses when given to a man in marriage," Eleanor said firmly. "I was but six years of age when I was sent from Spain to wed the king—he was not king then, of course. I lost my family, my country, and my ability to be independent. 'Tis the way of the world."

The last half-dozen words resonated in Briana so strongly that she fancied she heard her Aunt Maud's voice speaking them instead of the queen's. It had been when her father and older brother, Griffith, left to join Prince Llewelyn, just after the Welsh war began. The thirteen-year-old Briana had not wanted them to leave, fracturing her world and her happiness, and she had wept at their departure. Maud had said to her, in the flat, practical tones of an older woman, "'Tis the way of the world. Men make blood and women make tears."

Queen Eleanor saw that something had distracted Briana and spoke her name several times to recapture her attention.

Briana left the bit of memory behind her. "Your Grace, I am grateful for your advice, but I do not believe our cases are comparable. You were treasured. Your husband was not responsible for the deaths of all those you loved."

The queen set her embroidery aside and laid her arms on the arms of the chair. "We are not God," she said. "We cannot judge the responsibility for what has happened. I dismiss that. And, Briana, I believe that you, too, will be treasured."

Briana said nothing. She thought that she could not dismiss the deaths of Prince Llewelyn, her father, and her brothers with the same grace that the queen managed. And she could not let herself believe that the butcher baron would treasure her.

Queen Eleanor accepted that Briana was not going to speak. She sighed a little. "I stand in place of your absent mother here," she said. "Is there aught you would want to ask me?"

Briana shook her head, unable to thank the queen for her effort. All that was in her mind was that in two days' time she would be leaving Windsor for Wales. But she would not be leaving the Plantagenets; she would be accompanying one as he journeyed to rule her lands and her people.

The queen lifted a hand to dismiss her, but said, "All

women wonder much of the man they will marry until they are wed. Then they come to know him."

It was easier for Briana to let the queen see only the facade she had put up all these years of captivity. She rose, curtsied, and fled back to her room, where the new gown on her packed trunk shouted that she was standing at the edge of a precipice.

Galen and Ralf readied Rees for the handfasting, ordering the pages Edward had sent to the friary for that purpose back to Windsor. Rees's tunic was midnight blue velvet, ankle-length, but split to the waist at either side, revealing his stark black hose. He had refused headgear, and his long golden hair hung to his shoulders, a bright contrast to the darkness of his clothes.

"Menty would swoon to see you," Galen said with a laugh. "You bear the devil's own beauty."

"For the devil's own match," said Rees.

Ralf observed, "Surely you regret not the looks of the lady."

Rees did not smile, but his knights sensed, from long experience of his moods, that he was amused by that. "Nay, I regret those not at all," he said. "If the looks were not tied to the politics, the bedding would be uncomplicated."

"Bedding is always uncomplicated," Galen put in, and Rees silently agreed that, for Galen, it probably was. Galen went on, "If we could find them in bed and leave them in bed, 'twould be a happier world."

Ralf surprised Rees by saying, "I wonder if the women would find it so."

Galen roared with laughter. "God help us if we ever got hold of some who did," he said. "We'd be dead men!" Galen always performed with such great vigor that Rees and Ralf had often conjectured about Menty's ability to survive it.

Thinking of that drew Rees in another direction. Despite himself, his body warmed as he visualized Briana standing naked in front of him, her hands at her sides, her head high, her breasts rising and falling with her accelerated breathing. He made himself shake off the hot memory and reached for his sword.

Galen and Ralf exchanged a glance, and the big Saxon knight asked hesitantly, "Is a sword the usual attire for a handfasting?"

"For this one, 'tis required," Rees replied, fingering his swordbelt before slinging it around his hips to begin buckling it. The sword he had now he had obtained in the Holy Land when the one given him at his knighthood was lost in the battle which nearly took his life. It was the sword he had carried throughout the Welsh war, the sword he had been wearing when he met secretly with Prince Llewelyn and made the promise his oath of fealty to King Edward had forced him to throw away. It was the sword he depended on, which had saved his life on numberless occasions, and now it would have to stand between Briana and himself. He settled the belt more firmly on his narrow hips, wondering what Briana was thinking.

The lady in question was being dressed by the Princesses Eleanor and Joanna, assisted by Hulde and Enlis. The Plantagenet women had insisted on ministering to her themselves. She was, they told her, exquisite in the pale green linen, edged with silver and dark green threads. The greens brought out all the highlights of gold and black flecks in her eyes, and flattered her beige skin as few women were flattered by the color.

Her hair was let to hang loose, to denote her virginity, but Hulde had given her some small braids to accent the dark sheen. Joanna wound a silver ribbon across Briana's brow. "You outshine the stars in beauty," Eleanor said generously, smiling at the flushed Welsh woman. "I swear my sister eats herself up with envy."

Joanna made a face at her older sister and finished tying off the bow at the back of Briana's ebony head. "The only envy I feel," the princess said, "is that Briana gets to lie with Cousin Rees, and that I could never do anyway."

Briana flushed deeply as Eleanor stroked her oversleeve into a more flattering fold. "I believe we are ready," Eleanor said, throwing a quick scowl at her sister.

Briana did not speak, but thought, *I shall never be ready.*

It mattered, like all her concerns, not at all. She was led to the large hall, where the king and queen waited, seated, with many of the court standing around them. John Peckham stood, smiling, in the center of the room, with Rees beside him, hard-faced and tall. In less than a quarter-hour, she was handfasted to the blond giant who showed no emotion at all on his smooth, stern face. As soon as the legalities of the handfasting were done, the papers signed and witnessed, he turned to her and took her hands in his, riveting her eyes with his own, seeming distant and inflexible. He released her hands as soon as he was certain he had her full attention. Then he drew his sword and set it between them, point resting on the stone floor of the hall. The crowd in the hall quieted and stilled. The king clenched a fist that lay on the arm of his chair.

Rees said tonelessly, "I will have your pledge of fealty now, Lady Briana." He knew that, if she had chosen to humiliate him or insult him again, she could pick no better moment than this one. He tried to breathe normally, because he realized he was instinctively holding his breath.

But Briana had given her word that she would swear, and her honor was one of the only things still left to her. She took hold of both sides of the crosspiece, her hands nearly touching his as he held the sword's hilt. "I swear you are my liege lord," she said, vainly trying to control the trembling in her voice. "I promise you from this moment my loyalty and my service in all things before God and man." She bent her head to lay her lips against the sword hilt where it formed the cross with the guard, but he moved his right forefinger minutely, and her lips pressed against his warm flesh instead. The shock tingled through both of them, and she jerked her head up at once, but was unable to meet his gaze. With one fluid gesture, he resheathed the sword.

It was done. She could not know how vital that single moment had been to his plans, and she had not disappointed him. She had proved that she kept her bargains—and she had sworn to him. He tried to keep from showing what he was feeling, but he was not certain how successful he was. He felt nearly triumphant.

The king rose to lead the company around the great tables in the hall so that the servants could set up the feast. Briana and Rees were led to the high table and given the place of honor at the center. Ine, whom Briana had not seen in the hall for the ceremony, but who, she realized now, must have been there, took the bench the servingmen replaced the two royal chairs with. He played softly, but did not sing. The normal bawdy songs that preceded a bedding were inappropriate during Lent, so he refrained from any of the suggestive words, but snuck in some of the melodies. Knights who recognized the music smirked behind their hands.

Briana stared down at the trencher before her and her new handfast groom. She was so very nervous that her hands were visibly shaking, so she lowered them to her lap and held onto herself. Her mouth was very dry, and she longed for some of the wine with which a servant had filled the goblets, but she did not dare reach out for it in case her shaking should spill it.

Despite it still being Lent, they were served meats as well as cheeses, the servants piling the succulent slices of mutton and chicken onto the bread. Seeing the juices coloring the flatbread and smelling of pepper and garlic made Briana's stomach lurch. She knew in the abstract what happened at a bedding, but it had been considered improper for her to attend Prince Llewelyn's because she was too young, and none of the villagers in Flint availed themselves of the customs of the English nobility.

Rees drank some wine, set his goblet down, and took a morsel of chicken in his fingers. He was tempted to offer it to her—lovers were often expected to feed each other tidbits—but his instinct was that it would embarrass her. Still, when the meal had gone on for a while without her eating or drinking anything, he felt the need to ask, "Will you not take some food or wine?"

She glanced quickly at the wine goblet, but then looked back down at her untouched portion of the meal and shook her head.

King Edward, seated with his queen to Briana's left, overheard the interchange and leaned across the space between himself and the newly handfasted couple to say, "Best to eat heartily, as you both have a busy night ahead of you."

Briana tried not to recoil, but her face flamed.

Rees said nothing, only inclined his head toward his uncle in acknowledgment. To Briana he said, in a quiet voice, "Try to take a little wine at the very least."

She wanted wine. She wanted enough wine to dull her senses, to help her relax, but her hands still shook too much for her to risk using them.

Rees reached past her, across her part of the trencher, took hold of her goblet, and moved it to the very edge of the table in front of her, so that she did not have to stretch out her arm to grasp it.

She saw that he understood she was shaking, but would neither comment aloud on it nor use it to taunt her. She risked raising a hand to tip the goblet enough to take a large swallow of the honeyed wine. She took a second swallow, and he moved the goblet back so she did not spill any of it.

The wine warmed her and helped curb the shaking, but the supper seemed interminable. When Ine finished playing and slipped out of the hall, she felt as if she had just lost an ally. Everyone else at the meal was laughing, enjoying the sort of rich food that was in short supply during this season. She tried to keep thinking that this would be her last meal at Windsor or Westminster, under the gaze of the king, that in the morning she would at last start for home. But her thoughts kept returning to the fact that before she could leave in the morning, she had to get through the night.

At last, King Edward rose to indicate that the supper was over. Smiling with more mischief than Briana could comfortably accept, the princesses led her to a guest chamber whose draped bed was nearly as grand as that of the king and queen themselves. "You are being honored with the second-best chamber in the castle," Joanna informed her.

Once the three of them were alone in the chamber, the same hands that had dressed Briana in her finery efficiently stripped it from her. They placed her squarely in the center of the huge feather mattress that filled the bed, and tied back the drapes to allow a clear view of the bed's interior from the room. The chamber itself was not large enough for the bed to stand in the middle, so the drapes on the side against the wall stayed closed. There was also a thin table, on which several candlesticks held lighted tapers.

Joanna climbed up onto the bed to unbraid the accent plaits in Briana's hair, touching lightly on Briana's hot cheeks, ears, and neck until Briana almost screamed. When the hair was all loose at last, Joanna wickedly trailed her fingertips swiftly down Briana's front, brushing her nipples as she slid off the bed.

Briana bit her lip, fists clenched suddenly tight on the blanket that had to remain at her waist until the witnesses had all seen her. Her breasts had been sensitive, straining against their skin, before Joanna had teased at them. Now Briana was all too strongly aware of them. She frowned, wondering if there was anything she could do to lessen the sensitivity, but then hearty masculine laughter came through the door, and all reason fled from her.

The queen and king entered first, Eleanor smiling broadly, Edward looking guardedly pleased, his bright blue eyes sweeping once over Briana's body as soon as they were in the chamber. After them came some of the knights and ladies of the court, carrying wine. The princesses moved to the doorway to give the new arrivals more space near the bed. The knights were more interested in the bride's nudity than in any kind of ritual.

Then Galen and Ralf came in, drawing Rees, who overtopped everyone else by at least half a head. Rees had one small towel wrapped around his waist, but was otherwise naked and quite calm.

Briana stared at his chest, for it was carved by a pale scar that started near his shoulder and continued diagonally downward, disappearing into the towel. All she could think was that very few men survived a wound like that. It fascinated her enough to make her forget for a moment what was to follow. Then she became aware of the raillery in the room. The ribald jests paid no heed to the Lenten season, and they were echoed in comments now by Rees's two friends as they pulled Rees to the bed and urged him in.

Briana slid hastily wallward, pulling the blanket up over her breasts at last, her face bright red with embarrassment.

"Bedded for the night," King Edward pronounced with satisfaction. "Leave the wine on the table. My nephew has thirsty work to do." He ushered the others out, the two Eleanors smiling a farewell, Joanna waving with wiggling fingers as she darted from the room, Galen and Ralf looking slightly amused and slightly concerned. The king paused at the door when everyone else had left the chamber, his stare locked with Rees's for a few seconds. Then he went out and closed the door firmly behind him.

Rees swung his legs back off the bed, walked gracefully and unhurriedly to the door, shot the bolt home, and returned to the bed, but sat on its edge, only partially turned toward her, instead of lying down beside her.

Briana had stood before Rees naked, but until tonight had seen him only clothed. In the light from the candles, as well as a streak of pale moonlight that came in the chamber's slit window, she could see that his chest and shoulders were magnificent, broad and well-muscled, his chest covered with light golden hair that glistened when he moved. The scar made a pale line against the normal color of his flesh, but it magnified, rather than distracted from, his looks. His belly was flat, hard with muscle as well, and only the towel interrupted the muscles' descent to his powerful thighs, one of which sported another, much smaller scar.

He turned his intense, blue-gray gaze upon her, and she felt transfixed by it. "Briana, we need not do this if you choose," he said, unnerving her badly by fulfilling Queen Eleanor's prophecy that he would offer her a choice. She could not know how his blood heated at the thought of possessing her, and he was very careful not to show her.

She seemed unable to look away from the smooth planes of his brow and cheeks, the strong jut of his nose between those level, compelling eyes. When she tried, she found herself watching the firm line of his mouth and remembering the sensation of it on her own. She did not know if she was reacting or how, and she did not know if he could see it.

She said only, "The king says we must."

For the first time since she had met him, she heard vitriol in his voice. "My uncle can command a certain level of loyalty from me," he said angrily, "but this matter is my concern and yours, no more."

With a start of pure amazement, Briana knew absolutely something so unbelievable that she wanted to discount it, for she could in no easy way explain it. Rees hated King Edward fully as much as she did. He went on looking at her, steadily and warmly.

She knew her cheeks were still burning, and she managed to lower her gaze to her fists, clasping the blankets to her chest. "They will want—evidence on the morrow," she said haltingly.

"Look at me," he said.

She squirmed a little inwardly, wanting to tell him that she had just now succeeded in looking away from him. Then she felt the callused fingertips of his left hand under her chin, gently raising her face until she was confronted by his now surprisingly neutral gaze. As she watched, even the impersonal touch of his fingers on her chin sparking tiny fires under her skin, he reached up into the thick length of his hair and drew out a thin, needle-sharp poinard. She was astonished.

"I can pierce my own arm and leave a bloodstain on the sheets," he said, repeating, "We need not do this." His hand fell away from her face, and she sat quite still, listening to the suddenly overloud beat of her heart, her eyes again on the blanket.

Rees told himself that not taking her—much as the nearness and the tangy spice smell of her were working to enflame him—would show her as nothing else could that she had nothing to fear from him, despite the rights he held over her by law and custom. He realized that no women he had ever known stirred him as this one did, that he had been an unknowing fool to abhor the match when first he heard of it, and that he hungered for her so much now that he wanted to win back some of the trust she had needed so desperately to bestow on him. He fought, only partly successfully, against a reaction of arousal, exerting control over himself as strongly as he could.

Briana was in turmoil. He refused to behave as she expected him to, as it was necessary for him to behave if she was going to be able to successfully hate him. Even she could see the irony of her wishing he would brutalize her, make demands on her she would find it impossible to meet without unjust suffering. And she was too practical to feel she could goad him into that kind of behavior easily or without very serious consequences. He was, she recognized, an extremely intelligent man, which made it more difficult for her to reconcile him with the butchery of Fearndon. His extreme masculinity, his rugged beauty, and his mastery of the recorder combined to make him overwhelmingly attractive to her. Tricks she might have tried on lesser men—tricks, indeed, which she had observed in court but had never had opportunity to practice on anyone, even had she wanted to before this—such tricks would not succeed with this man.

And she had sworn him fealty.

He waited, studying her lowered lashes, the fine skin of her cheeks under the lashes, the brilliance of the highlights that danced on her dark hair. He was willing to be as patient as he needed to be, even though his body rebelled against the patience. He fingered the slender blade with both hands, to keep from reaching out and touching her again. He could not guess what was going on in her mind, but he was very surprised at the length of time that passed without a response from her. He had been certain that when he offered her an escape from his encroachment, she would take it instantly. He found the delay both puzzling and encouraging.

Briana realized she did not want to have to make this decision; she did not want the choice because he had made her desire him. She had thought to be made to yield to him by the king's command or by his own greater strength, not because she would have to admit that she had needs which drove her to it. She could certainly refuse him, but they were leaving in the morning for Wales, and she somehow felt herself less capable of coupling with him the first time outside Windsor than when she was inside it, where she was accustomed to submission. She sighed once, and her gaze drifted from her own lap to his. The towel hid a bulge that had, she was certain, not been there before.

If she said "aye" to him now, they would both know all their lives that she had done it, and she knew quite well that it put into his hands one more power over her. Yet, he was not using the power he had over her now. Did a bit more matter?

She cast about for something to delay the decision, fastened on the scar. "Where got you that?"

"In the Holy Land," answered Rees. "'Tis well-healed, and I scarce notice it now."

"Were you near death?"

He sighed a little, went on fingering the poinard without being aware he was doing it. "Death and I have been close for some years," he said. "I would prefer not to discuss it on this occasion."

She lowered her eyes, realized she was looking at the towel, looked quickly up from its intriguing shape, and encountered his long fingers on the poinard. "It should be my blood," she said. It was not at all what she had expected to say, and it surprised him as well.

He barely hesitated, reversing the blade and holding the small haft out to her, not certain he understood why she felt as she did, but knowing that he could not cut her himself.

Briana was startled by the gesture, not having anticipated it at all. The poinard was, true, not much of a weapon, but it was a weapon, and he offered it to her without seeming to wonder at all about her motives. He might be thinking that if she turned it against him, he could overpower her easily, but she saw nothing of calculation of his face. She reached out absently and took the blade from him, holding it gingerly, uncertain why she had actually taken it.

For the first time, he smiled, and the amused warmth of it, completely untainted by any hint of unkindness, made her entire body tingle. "Have a care," he said. "'Tis very sharp. You'll not want it in too deep."

He saw the bright color climb again into her face and knew instantly that she had interpreted the words in a very different way. He laughed softly, the sound stabbing at her nerves, and he took the blade back from her. "Or, if you prefer," he said, letting his voice linger sensuously on the words, "we could do some things." He leaned forward and captured her mouth with his, being careful to remain gentle and undemanding.

With a quick motion of his wrist, he tossed the blade aside and rested his hands lightly on her bare shoulders.

Briana was infinitely grateful that he had taken back the decision and infinitely relieved by the freedom of physical contact at last. Then he moved his mouth on hers, causing her lips to part for him and, when they did, sliding his tongue inside, slowly withdrawing it, inserting it again and again, to teach her the rhythm which was to follow later. When she showed no hesitation in accepting that teasing invasion, he deepened the thrust, strengthened the pressure, alert for any signs of repugnance or fear. There were none. She appeared to glory in the contact.

Despite his caution, Rees felt the fire swell within him. He made himself lift his mouth away, brushing her brow with it as he did so, and raised his hands to her face, his fingers buried in the hair below her ears, his thumbs stroking across her cheekbones. She blinked and opened her eyes, seeing his face floating just above hers. He read the unspoken question and answered, "Nay, we've no need to stop yet."

He put his hands back on her shoulders and applied enough pressure to bear her downward onto the feather tick. Then he drew the blanket out of her hands and down off her body, shifting himself off the bed long enough to slide the cover free. For the second time, she was naked to his scrutiny, and once again she made no effort to hide herself from him. He let his gaze travel to her breasts, followed the line of sight with his hands, cupping the firm globes in his palms, then using his thumbs to nudge at the straining, erectile flesh of her nipples.

She gasped, closing her eyes, surrendering to the sensation as she felt drawn taut as a bowstring. It started at the paired peaks of flesh he was caressing and plunged downward through her churning insides to the aching point at the juncture of her thighs. She forgot that she had been looking for reasons to hate him, forgot that she had wished he would die, thought only of the exquisite sensations he was evoking and building. It was the growth of the early promise he had kindled in her, bringing her nearer to some mysterious, unknown fulfillment whose existence she had never imagined and whose dimensions she could not conjure.

Rees enjoyed watching her reactions. He and Ralf had occasionally conjectured about the existence of such a woman, had wondered what forces would combine to create her. Briana was, he believed, utterly fearless and uncalculating when it came to her physicality, which made her unlike any other woman he had known. Most were sweetly compliant; one or two had enjoyed being used, but they were already well-experienced; several had tried to pretend that they liked an experience that they were in fact merely willing to endure. This woman, with almost no previous knowledge of what heated bodies could provide for one another, seemed willing to meet him wherever he decided to be. His mind leaped far ahead of where he was, and he wrenched it back, then lowered his head and suckled on one of the tender buds he had prepared with his fingers.

Briana found herself tangling her hands in his long hair, back arched to make her breasts more accessible to him, unable to form a coherent thought or utter a coherent sound. Her body had taken on a life of its own and had given that life over into the hands of this steel-muscled stranger who seemed to know it better than she did.

He lifted his head again, his tongue brushing at the hollow of her throat, holding himself steady until her eyes focused on his face.

He smiled, and the tenderness of it sank into her to add to the coil of tension that was heating her loins. "What?" she asked, her voice reedy and barely audible.

"I have only so much control," he said. "We can stop now, or we will not stop."

In one small corner of her mind, a single tiny voice cautioned her against giving too much too fast to someone who was, at the end, still Earl Connarc. That voice, sensible as it was, had no chance against her body's need to release the demanding pressure erupting in her flesh. He lay stretched out beside her, resting on his arm, his own tension as disguised as he could manage. She looked downward along the sweat-sheened muscles of his chest and belly to the now rather astonishing bulge in the towel, and she was unaware that a smile illuminated her face at that moment.

He had thought she might be done surprising him, but he was not correct. She reached out with innocently seductive slowness and slid her hand into the waist of the furled cloth, tugging at it. To her, it seemed only fair: she was naked, and so he ought to be naked as well. He covered her hand with his and used it to draw the towel away, wondering for a split second if she were not the untouched virgin everyone thought her.

But as she reacted to the sight of his rampant arousal with the first tremor of apprehension that she had experienced, he realized that she had never been with a man before, that the extraordinary passion he had unleashed was his, and only his. Hesitantly, looking down at his groin, she touched him, and then there could be no stopping at all. He closed his eyes for a moment, reveling in her boldness, then caught her wrist and lifted her hand away, twining his fingers in hers as he laid his weight on her for the first time.

When he had taken her hand from his body, Briana wondered if she had done something wrong, but the shocking strength of his body gliding onto hers, the roughness of his chest against her aching nipples, and then the pressure of his hips on her own drove doubt out of her. She tilted her hips upward to better accommodate the strain of bearing his weight, and her legs slid apart with the motion. He was instantly between them, his hard, flat belly rubbing against the curls of her woman's mound, finding her slickly moist and radiating heat at him.

He gave up any attempt at control, and when he took her mouth again, it was with a powerful demand he had never believed a virgin would be able to meet. Briana abandoned herself to it, caught in an overwhelming need for the release she could not yet conceive of, unconsciously biting at his tongue and his lips, writhing under him, lost.

He had wanted to be gentle entering her, but that option was no longer available to him. When he released one of her hands to guide himself into her body, her fingernails dug into the sleek muscles of his shoulder. She was nearly frantic with need, parting around him as if they had been formed for one another. He felt the blockage of her maidenhead stretch and vanish as he sheathed himself completely, and she cried out once and went still beneath him.

"'Tis nothing," he murmured softly in her ear. "'Twill pass." He sought out her face, expecting to see pain there. What he saw was amazement.

She forced herself to focus on him, panting, and said clearly, "Nay, 'tis everything." She had felt the pain, but it was engulfed by the incredible sensation of his filling her, fitting within her, the irresistible intimacy of the joining of two bodies that had always been separate. She was no longer an isolated being, cut off from everyone else in the world; she was part of something much more, something that banished loneliness. And then he moved within her, and the need flamed up and overwhelmed her again, destroying any capacity for thought.

Rees was absolutely unwilling to climax before she did, but he was very close to breaking. He put a hand between their bodies as he moved, to add pressure to the small pearl of feeling that controlled the heightening of her sensation, finding it larger, more prominent than he had expected, stroking it relentlessly.

For her, the tension grew momentarily unbearable, and then it suddenly blew apart into a release that drained her, carrying her along on throbbing energies that sang through her body in a crescendo of pure pleasure.

She was not aware when he gained his own release, but it nearly shattered him. He had not realized how extreme his arousal had become in the face of her lack of restraint. As he re-exerted control over himself, he drew her tightly against his chest, suddenly fearful that some other man might discover and be able to awaken the wildness he wanted for himself.

Rees had thought he was truly possessive of nothing since his mother died. He had never had the opportunity to be possessive of his father's legacy—title or lands—and then King

Edward had told him he was not a de Bretagne, but a bastard, so he had not even a name to be possessive of. Besides, extreme possessiveness was one of Edward's characteristics, and Rees had disdained it for that reason alone. He was possessive of Conway, but even that, he knew, the king could take away from him if he chose. Now he was violently possessive of Briana of Flint, his handfast bride. The rationality he had always been able to exercise in relationships with women vanished in the face of an indescribable passion for the slender, black-haired woman in his arms.

Briana lingered in the lethargy of repletion for almost a minute, eyes closed, a purring sound deep in her throat seeming to come from someone else entirely. She burrowed her head into the hollow of his shoulder and let herself begin to rise again to self-awareness and self-control. He kissed her hair, running a hand down the line of her back to cup the curve of her bottom and knead it gently.

She moved her head back a little and looked up at him. "Is it always to be like that?"

"'Twill be with us," he said confidently.

"Not with other people?" It was a casual, curious question, but it came so near to sparking his anger that his arms tightened around her convulsively.

"There are to be no other people," he commanded. "Understand me?"

"Aye," she said a little squeakily because he held her so tightly, pleased at the tone of his voice, "I understand."

She was asleep almost instantly, contented. She would not begin to hate herself until she saw Flint.

Chapter 20

The Roads—March 1289 A.D.

Before they departed from Windsor the next morning, the king, the queen, Ine, and Rees's two knights all reached the same conclusion: The consummation had gone well. Try as they would to conceal it, Rees and Briana behaved as if they had been a love match all along, touching each other's hands and arms covertly or as if accidentally, but nonetheless repeatedly. While the wagon was being loaded with Briana's belongings and the meager satchels of her servants' things, Briana seemed to catch herself smiling at nothing and would jerk her attention back from wherever it had drifted to.

Galen and Ralf had exchanged one long, knowing grin when they heard Rees singing under his breath as he checked over the final preparations for the journey. He possessed a fine baritone he used all too rarely.

The queen asked them to remain through the morning Mass, since it could not be ensured that they would be able to find a Mass every day of their journey, and Rees agreed, though he would rather have been on his way. Galen said in a low voice to him when the queen had gone back into the castle from the bailey, "We may chance upon a church now and then, but I don't fancy us seeking them out." Rees hushed him.

At Mass, he and Briana seemed distracted, missed the responses, and actually held hands. Archbishop Peckham had begun his return to his See in Canterbury at dawn, and Windsor's own priest was celebrating the Mass. He made no attempt to offer Communion to anyone but the king, so Briana was entirely unbothered by any attempt to present her with the Eucharist.

Ralf said to Galen out of the corner of his mouth, "That spells the end of it 'til Easter, at any rate."

Rees heard him, but did not respond.

Briana felt a rush of gratitude that the knights seemed to understand. She had originally refused Communion as a slap against Rees, but something had happened inside her once she had done it. There was a rightness to the choice that she had not investigated, but she did not question. It was as if she had stripped away a layer of hypocrisy she had never previously acknowledged, but which she now recognized only in its absence. She did not try to understand. She was just grateful that Rees had—for whatever reasons—taken her part and would not seek to make her perform this act which should have been faith-filled, but which she knew would be empty. She took his hand again as the priest continued the ritual.

Princess Eleanor smiled at the hand-holding; Princess Joanna looked fair likely to spit. Briana noticed neither of them. She was wondering how long the perfection of these moments could last, how the journey to Wales would affect it. She had been pleased to learn that Ine would be accompanying them to Flint, not only because she liked the man and loved his music, or even because he was so deeply a part of her beloved past, but because she had not recently had an opportunity to learn any new songs from him. The only time they had met for an ostensible music lesson, they had talked instead. Now she would have days and days to learn from him.

And in just over a fortnight—after all this time—she would be home. It would have been sooner, but they would not go directly to Flint. They would instead go first to Conway, so that Rees could gather the rest of his belongings and household furnishings, as well as some of his men.

Hulde and Enlis were in a state of complete excitement, for neither of them had been farther from Windsor than Westminster, and now it seemed to them that they were going to the end of the earth. Hulde's husband, Esrith, a fine herdsman with sheep or cattle, had been attached to the new household so that his wife could continue in service to her lady. Esrith would drive the wagon with Hulde and Enlis directly to Flint—"The manor, not the castle," Rees had ordered him—arriving there at least a week before the others. Though the servants would be slower than the mounted party, Rees planned to stop at Conway for several days.

"It seems overlong," Ralf observed when Rees told him and Galen the plans for the journey.

Rees just laughed. "'Twill take Menty that long to say farewell to everyone scattered about the keep," he said. "That and packing up the youngsters and her loom . . ." He let his voice trail away.

"Aye," said Ralf with a nod, "and there's no predicting what Flint will be for any of us."

Rees thought he had some idea.

Briana wrapped herself in her new cloak, fastened it with her new cloak brooch, pulled on her new gloves, and watched as one of the grooms brought Timbrel up to the mounting block. Ine was talking to Esrith, Rees was with Galen and Ralf on the other side of the wagon, all of them holding the reins of their horses, and Briana was just going to step up onto the mounting block when she sensed something behind her and turned. The king and queen had come into the bailey to see them away.

Briana dropped into a correct curtsy. *My last*, she thought with fierce relief. When she rose, Queen Eleanor held out her arms, and Briana suffered an embrace, hoping she was not too stiff to be courteous, but longing to be away. The queen drew back and said, "I hope, Lady Briana, that you are not unhappy at the fate we've chosen for you."

"Your Grace," Briana said softly, "I shall always be grateful for your kindness." She had to concentrate not to emphasize the word "your," because the king stood just behind his wife. She made herself look up at him. "Sire," she said.

Edward fixed upon her the same stare she had seen at some of the worst moments of her life—not just when he took her from her home or when he threatened to destroy Flint if she disobeyed him, but every time he looked at her and saw her as a problem or a menace. His eyes were a cold dark blue under the lowered brows. "'Tis important you understand that I will brook no rebellion in Wales," he said to her. "I send you back, but if the peace is broken, I shall be merciless."

She had no doubt about that. She felt a presence behind her, but it would have been a breach of manners to look away from the king. She was trying to compose a reply when Rees's deep voice came across her shoulder. "I will take responsibility for the peace in Northern Wales, uncle."

Briana wanted to look at him, but held herself still.

King Edward took that icy stare away from her, looking beyond her. "You choose to take on the rebels in Snowdonia?" he asked. "You choose to do from Flint what you refused to do from Conway in seven years?"

"I have kept the peace in Conway," Rees said, "and if I keep the peace in Flint as well, what matter if a ragtag band of outlaws roams here and there? You need not commit an army you need for conquest elsewhere." His voice was bland, but the king frowned.

"Have a care," said Edward. He was warning Rees, Briana knew, but Rees responded to it as if it had been a well-wish.

"My thanks," Rees said. He bowed, took Briana's arm and drew her toward the horses.

Ine mounted the docile gelding Rees had provided for him and hung his bagged harp on one of the saddlebags that held water and bread in case they did not find lodgings for the night. Ine was far more accustomed to walking than to riding, but he realized there was no way he could, afoot, keep up with the party.

Briana mounted Timbrel and turned her back on Windsor and her face toward Wales without a second of regret and without a glance over her shoulder. Ine rode beside her, glancing at her every so often and waiting for her to take her eyes off her graceful, attractive husband. Of them all, so pleased that the couple seemed to have found a measure of happiness in their night together, Ine was the only one who perceived there might be traps for her.

Not for the earl, though, thought the bard. Rees already knew what he would be facing at Flint. Briana, on the other hand, had been torn from them at the end of a punishing war, whose effects had not faded in the years since. The people there dreamed of her return, lived on it. And she would come back to them not merely as good as married to their enemy, but enraptured by him. Before the journey was over, Ine would have to find a way to convey his forebodings to Rees. His instinct was that Briana would not understand, but her handfast husband would see the danger.

Roskilde, Denmark—March 1289 A.D.

Bjorn Magnussen had been looking for his past for more than four years. When he started his search, his present was execrable, and that propelled him to leave his devastated home in Kaupang, Norway, and begin an armed assault on the rest of the world. All the luck he thought he had had as a young man had somehow run out through the massive fingers which grasped his sword or axe with equal measures of dexterity and brutality. He had had everything—a following, wealth, a beautiful wife, sons, his king's favor, and the ability to kill anyone who challenged him. In order to travel easily in Christian lands, he had ostensibly embraced Christianity, but he never believed any of its mythology, and when his luck changed, he blamed it on his lip service to a weak god from the south. The storm that blew in and destroyed his house, crushing his wife and sons under the rubble was, he concluded, the revenge of Odin for the loss of a worshipper. His rages at his fate plunged him into drink and viciousness, and his following deserted him. He spent months brooding on the triumphant days of his past, when women swooned—or could be made to do so—and when men fled from his skill with none of the contempt to which he was presently subjected. He decided to recapture his youth, and since capture in his arsenal invariably involved mayhem, he set out to create it wherever he could. It would be his reparation to Odin for daring to think that he needed to worship an alien god, instead of his own.

The Roads—March 1289 A.D.

The first night out of Windsor, the party heading for Wales reached the crossroads where the West Road divided to head either westward toward Salisbury or northward toward Oxford. There was a small manor outside the village of Knowl, where they could seek hospitality for the night. After they rode into the manor's front yard, Briana swung down from Timbrel before Rees came to help her, conscious of a slight ache between her legs from the afternoon's ride.

Galen said, "We have not made much distance."

"We shall do better on the morrow," said Rees. "If we leave at sunup, rather than delaying until after Mass, we cannot help but cover ground."

Galen was not to be mollified by reason. "We have not even caught up to the wagon," he said.

"They are not stopping for the night," Ralf said. "They will sleep on the wagon and drive on in turns, as swiftly as they can. Mayhap you should have ridden with them."

Galen glared at him.

Ralf grinned. "I'll speak to the steward about sheltering us if you see to my horse." He tossed Galen the reins.

Ine unslung the harp as he dismounted, smiling at the two knights, speaking to Ralf. "I will accompany you. If they see I can sing for our lodgings, they may find their ability to warmly welcome us increased notably." He and the young knight walked toward the manor proper as one of the house servingmen came out to meet them.

They had ridden into what would have been a tree-shaded courtyard had the trees been out of bud. Briana let Galen take Timbrel's reins and lead the horses toward the back of the manor, where the outbuildings peeped over a gentle hill. She walked to the edge of the yard and looked out over the greening fields and hedgerows.

Rees stroked Basilisk's nose and watched her. She had tossed back her cloak to reveal the gown in which they had been handfasted, since all her others were packed in the trunk. He watched her body moving under the gown and felt the tug of arousal he had held at bay all day long. He had not expected to be so hungry for her, but then he had not anticipated her ready acceptance of passion. *Nay*, he thought, *acceptance has not the sense of it*. He searched for another word, but to his vast amusement, he could not think of what it might be.

Galen trotted back into the front yard and took Basilisk's reins from Rees's hand, saying, "He'll let me groom him, or so help me, I'll tie his mouth shut." He followed Rees's gaze toward Briana and nudged him lightly in passing, grinning at him.

Ine came back and said to Rees, "Between my music and your earldom, my lord, they are properly overwhelmed. They are preparing to share their provender and their living space. I had to persuade them to allow you to enter in your own time, so I warn you, you are likely to be fawned upon."

Rees gave a short laugh and nodded. "I shall be prepared,"

he said. As Ine turned to go back to the manor, Rees added quietly, "Ine."

The bard stopped and looked at him quizzically.

Rees said, "My name is Rees. Make free to use it as you will."

Ine nodded once and went back into the house. All the work being done at the manor at this moment was being done by servants, retainers, or Galen behind the house, and the front yard was suddenly quiet in the gathering dusk. Rees walked across it to stand beside Briana, amused again as her nearness heated him. The breeze pulled at her hair, trying to pry it loose from her plain white barbette and incidentally carrying its fresh spice scent to him. He had reached up before he was aware of it and laid his forefinger against her cheek.

She had heard him approach. Ever since they left Windsor, as if freed to feel anything she wanted to whenever she wished, she was hyperconscious of his presence, unable to look enough at his incredible face or the powerful body barely restrained by his short riding tunic and hose. Now the clean, leathery, male smell touched at her briefly and then was gone as the wind carried it away. She felt the light caress on her face and inside her the pressure began to build again, seeming more insistent this time because now she knew where it would lead. She began to tingle.

"Briana," he said, his voice caressing her name just as his finger moved over her cheek, with tenderness and the warmth that lay as a thin veneer across the powerful, raw heat beneath it.

She finally looked up at him, her expression a mixture of the need and something else. It was the something else that made him pause, control his own heightening arousal even as her breasts swelled toward him with her breathing under the gown, the hard peaks of her nipples visible through both gown and undertunic. "What do you fear?" he asked gently.

Briana was startled that he had read her so accurately, but she shook her head in a denial that neither of them credited.

Because she did not gainsay him, he pursued it further. "Do you fear me?"

She realized he would not be satisfied until she said something, so she reached for one of the handy surface dissimulations she had used so effectively at King Edward's court all those years she had been a captive. "I fear what I'll find at Flint," she said, which was true as far as it went, but came nowhere near the core of the problem.

Rees's eyes narrowed suddenly, for in her perfectly normal voice, he had heard the falseness. He almost accused her of lying, then remembered which methods were related to persuasion and which to domination. He asked, "Why do you find it necessary to lie to me?"

She jumped. Had her surface diplomacy—so successful for such a long time—died because she had left the court? She fumbled for a moment and then said, "You cautioned me not to trust you."

He negated that with a gesture. "Nay, I did not," he said firmly. "I cautioned you not to confuse two very different things."

"How are they different?" she demanded, taking him by surprise with the vehemence of the question. "When shows a woman more trust for a man than when she opens her most—" Her voice faltered, and her head came up strongly as she forced the words out. "—personal parts and welcomes him in?"

She had said "welcomes," when there were so many other words she could have chosen, and it rang through him like a bell, making his body ache even more. His voice was lower, thicker than he realized when he answered; she heard the tones and tingled even more. "Lust is a reaction of the flesh, centered here." With the lightest of feather touches, his hand brushed her mound. "Trust is a reaction of the spirit, centered here and here." He lightly touched her breast, then raised his hand and touched her forehead. Each time he touched her, the tingling increased until it spilled over into trembling. "I can make you lust for me,

Briana," he said. His gaze followed his hand as it drifted back to
her lips, her throat, the valley between her breasts, the hot core
of her. "I can command it and control it." He drew his hand
back. "Your trust is a thing you can control absolutely. I can
only ask you for it."

Briana fought for reasoning ability as the waves of desire he
so unerringly built in her threatened to sweep her away.

"So I ask you again, why do you find it necessary to lie to
me?" She had no way of knowing the control he was exerting
was more powerful than her own could ever be. Even with it, he
still sounded huskier than he would have liked.

She shook her head.

"Tell me what you fear," he insisted.

She felt like a bird caught in a fowler's net, struggling
wildly and vainly for a way out, even though the net did not hurt
her. She struggled a moment longer, then sighed and
symbolically folded her wings, her eyes bright and fastened on
his. "I fear the way you make me forget—everything," she said.
"I fear losing myself."

Once again, her answer had gone far beyond his
expectations, and it stunned him with happiness. He would have
laughed aloud had he not seen from her face how very serious a
matter it was to her. "You cannot lose yourself by giving
yourself away, sweetness," he murmured, his words so dense
that she had to lean toward him to hear them well.

Before he could reach for her again, Galen trotted into the
yard from the stable area, indistinct in the twilight, and called, "I
fear our hosts may be growing eager, Rees. Put a bend in it and
bring it inside. I'm hungry."

As am I, Galen. Rees almost said it out loud. Instead, he
laughed.

Galen went up the steps into the manor house, and Rees
was reaching for Briana's arm when she understood the Saxon's
meaning and flushed a deep rose, her hands flying to her cheeks.

After the sound of the porter shutting the manor door with a snap to keep out the increasing evening cold, the hush in the courtyard was broken only by the sighing of the wind and the high call of a bird.

"Oh!" Briana said, suddenly embarrassed. "They all know what we did last night!" For some reason, it had never occurred to her that those private moments would be transparent to others, even after the blood-stained sheets were exhibited in the hall both as proof of her virginity and as evidence that the consummation had been accomplished and Earl Connarc was now overlord of Flint.

Rees pulled her into his arms, letting her hide her face against the front of his tunic. "They have no notion of what we did, sweetness," he said with real conviction. "And about that, I ask you to trust me." She trembled under his hands like the frond of a fern bending in the spray of a rill, and he sensed that there was no component of fear in it, not any longer.

She moved her thigh against his leg, feeling the hard muscles glide under his hose as he shifted position. And then against her hip she felt another hardness, throbbing at her through the cloth. Just above her head, his voice rumbled with amusement. "Nay, I've not been able to bend it yet."

Her voice shook as much as her body, but it was strangely buoyant. "I think not that I'm helping."

She had, he recognized, tried to make a jest. He put his head back and laughed openly and fully. The sound carried across the yard, and the porter popped the door open again, revealing Galen and Ralf hovering just behind it, waiting for them.

"We had best go in," Rees said.

Briana hoped her face was no longer flame red. She drew back from him, let him take her hand and lead her to the manor house. The porter kept holding the door until they had entered. As soon as they came in out of the wind, they heard the music of Ine's harp as he sang of Prince Pwyll and his lady love, Rhiannon.

Flint—March 1289 A.D.

Behind the veil that shaded the window of the hermitage at Flint, calmly stitching at the exquisite embroidery whose sale brought enough income from the noble families of France, Spain, and Italy to support her, Sabine, and the church at Flint, Princess Beatrice was content to watch the small world go by. She had never thought to be useful in this way, but now she was glad that she could be. John de Bretagne had married her to curry favor with her brother the king, and because he wanted an heir with Plantagenet blood. He had agreed to accept the boy Rees into his household, and he had not mistreated either of them, unless coldness could be considered mistreatment. But she always feared that, once she was gone or unable to stop him, John would kill Rees. She could not allow that to happen.

After the rape that had given her Rees and earned her the anger of the King of England, as if her single smile at a vigorous stranger had caused her own disgrace, no kind of lovemaking could be of much interest to her. She had endured John's attentions with stoicism because he had been promised an heir and she had proved both fertile and capable of surviving the birth of a child who lived. Once she quickened with the seed which would produce their son, Arthur, he left her bed with the speed of a man who has fulfilled an unpleasant duty he is relieved not to have to confront again. She was grateful for the cessation of attention, for his silent coldness while toiling over her body was distasteful at best. She might have regretted it when the duke took his heir away from her, but she had Rees's accomplishments to take pride in.

Sabine had asked her once—and only once—after Beatrice had left Brittany and Sabine had followed to companion her in England, in the last moments before the madness took her and held her more firmly than any man ever had, "How is it, my lady, that you were never angry at Rees for the way he was forced upon you?"

Beatrice had looked at her servant in real surprise. "The child was not at fault for the horror of the father," the princess said with as firm a conviction as she ever showed about anything. "I determined from the first that the sins of the father should never be visited upon my son."

They lived quietly enough at Flint now, but always in anticipation. When would he arrive? When would they be able to see for themselves what kind of man he had grown into?

Beatrice looked out the window at the mist and rain of springtime and sighed. What would he be like when he came to Flint? Queen Eleanor, her protector and savior all the years of her madness, had described Rees to his mother on many occasions, like a woman telling a familiar bedtime story to a frightened child. But how accurate were the descriptions? She wanted to see him and was afraid of his reaction to seeing her. She had lied to him about her death, sent him away from the only home he had ever known, and never told him any truths of his heritage. The man Eleanor had told her about might forgive her, but what if that man was the queen's perception and none of reality?

With a swirl of hooded cloak and a sprinkling of stray raindrops, Sabine came into the hermitage and set the basket she carried on the table in the center of the room.

"What tidings?" Beatrice asked.

Sabine took off her cloak and hung it on the peg by the door. "No tidings as yet," she said. "They may not even have left Westminster for Wales yet, but I know not with any certainty."

"'Tis difficult to wait," Beatrice said. "And yet, 'tis more comfortable than I thought, to hang in abeyance."

Sabine took a small, fire-blackened cauldron from the hearthstone and began moving vegetables from the basket into the pot. "The world is a place with many illusions," she said. "We know—you and I—which we should accept, and which we should endure, and which we should dismiss unheeded."

Beatrice smiled at her huge companion. "Friendship is not an illusion," she said warmly. "'Tis a blessing."

Sabine took a dipper and scooped water from a bucket under the table into the pot. "Aye," she said. "I wonder that there is not more praise of it in everyday discourse. But then," she added thoughtfully, "folk do not conjecture on such things while trying to survive."

Beatrice completed her last stitch on a tongue of flame edging the linen band which could be used to trim a neckline or a sleeve, moved her needle to a new tongue. "Thought is oft the first casualty of privation," she said. "At least, it was so in my case."

"Here, too." Sabine put the dipper back in the bucket and hung the cauldron on the pot hook over the fire. "The castle has taken much of what they have to sustain themselves."

Beatrice frowned. If she could still own to being royalty, she might be able to influence the Marcher Lord in his treatment of the manor and village, but she could not admit her identity, and a simple recluse—of no interest to the castle—could have no effect whatsoever. She concentrated on her stitching and asked casually, "Have we any remaining of the coin Queen Eleanor gifted us when we left Westminster?"

Sabine straightened. "I believe we have," she said.

Beatrice bent closer to a stitch. "Is it possible you might be able to give some of it to those most in need before next market day in Rhuddlan? In a way that will not obligate them to us?"

"It may be possible," Sabine said slowly. She was silent for a short while, then ventured, "You have chosen, then, to cast your lot with that of Flint?"

Beatrice looked up at her. "My dear sister Eleanor said that Flint was to become Rees's. I cast my lot with my son."

Sabine nodded and lifted a cloth-wrapped loaf of bread out of the basket.

Beatrice bent closer to her stitching, silently whispering his name to herself, as she had since his birth, as she did every time she prayed. There was much in her life she had determined to forget, but she would never forget Rees.

Chapter 21

The Roads—March 1289 A.D.

"Rees!" Briana cried it out with no awareness of having done so. It was a slightly muffled scream because her face, sheened with sweat, was buried against the hard muscles of his shoulder.

"Hold on, sweetness," he said, low and tight against her ear. He had tormented her with his hands and mouth far longer than he should have, holding her fulfillment at bay with a skill that left her half-mad with need, crawling up his body, twining her legs around him, trying to pull him inside her. Now he had to calm her just enough to help himself fit her. "Relax a bit and let me in," he whispered.

She arched her pelvis up to him in blind obedience, and he guided himself into the soft folds of her flesh, heated and wet and pulsing, braced his weight on his elbows and thrust with all his strength as deeply as he could. He caught her cry with his mouth, rising and falling, stoking the flames that consumed her until he felt her freeze, her body clenching around him with enough power to bring on his own climax.

Briana had not fully believed him when he said he could command and control her lust, but as she swam back through the vividly colored mists to awareness, she realized that he was absolutely right. He could reduce her to a frantic mass of hungry energy, begging for release. They were both covered with sweat, and she gasped for breath, trying to slow her heartbeat to match the torpor that followed unbearable pleasure.

"Are you well?" he asked, feeling drained and forcing himself to alertness for her sake. "I did not hurt you?"

"'Tis like madness," she said wonderingly, and then suddenly tried to sit up, though he still lay heavily upon her.

"What is it?" he asked, concerned.

"How could you wonder what I feared when you can turn me into—into—" She did not have anything in her frame of reference to use as a comparison.

"—into a passionate woman," he finished for her, shifting his hips slightly as if to withdraw. She moaned a little, involuntarily, following his hips with her own, and he relaxed, remaining within her.

"Are you certain this is decent?" she asked him doubtfully. "Am I to think on it as the work of the devil when we say the mea culpa at Mass?"

He wondered if her suspicion of evil in their coupling would prompt her to feel even more strongly that she should not receive Communion, but he knew very little of the motives for her continuing refusal, and he was not yet ready to broach the subject with her. Instead, he laughed softly, his eyes intent on her in the dimness of the curtained bed the manor owners had given them while they themselves vacated their solar and slept in the steward's rooms. Galen, Ralf and Ine had made beds on the solar floor near the hearth, where the body servants of the manor's lord and lady generally slept. The whole hierarchy of the manor was displaced downward, but it was a custom no one questioned.

Rees said, "'Tis not evil to feel pleasure, sweetness. We are handfasted and soon to be wed. We have the right to enjoy one another." He stifled a yawn and turned onto his side, drawing her with him.

She seemed deeply thoughtful, and then said slowly, "Enjoyment is not an adequate word, Rees."

"'Twill have to do," he said, pulling her head back onto his shoulder, but thinking that very shortly, if they did not stop this, a fairer description would be "obsession." He kissed her brow. "Next time 'twill be gentler," he said.

Still thoughtful, Briana said, "I think not." Her voice was drowsy, too.

They slept until daybreak, and when he awoke hard, it transpired that she had the right of it after all. She was sore enough that day that they never rode above a walk and made barely a dozen miles. Galen and Ralf might have teased the couple, but Rees gave them one warning look and changed their minds.

In truth, they were delighted to see Rees happy, for it was apparent he was reveling in his new handfast bride, and it had been a very long time—since before King Edward had ordered him not to seek the match with Margaret of Norwich—since they had seen him so carefree.

As they rode slowly along the road which would soon lead them to Oxford, Rees let his two knights range a little ahead. Briana lagged behind, unable to make herself urge the palfrey to any greater speed, and he wanted to stay near her.

Ine drew his own mount beside Basilisk and looked sideways at the tall, golden man in the shabby riding tunic. Rees felt his scrutiny and returned it, his look level. "You have aught to say to me?" he asked.

"Mayhap," said Ine. "And I thought I might be present should you wish to speak with one who is not your knight."

"You presume, Ine," Rees said, but there was no rancor in his voice, nor did he sound unduly highborn.

Ine smiled. "'Tis my thought that the faster the storm blows in, the faster 'tis likely to blow out again."

"I do not believe you discuss the weather," said Rees, still mildly, "but I cannot make myself think you would dare discuss aught else."

"Bards dare much." Ine played with his reins and glanced at Briana, riding behind them and half-asleep on her horse. "And I have known her from a babe. She will at some point recall that honor makes strange demands on her."

"I would hope by that time to have gained a measure of her affection, in addition to her vow of fealty," Rees said carefully, wondering at his ease at speaking so openly to this solemn, overwise musician with knowing eyes and an admirably agile mind. He realized with a start that there were things about Ine which reminded him of Abraham. He was fascinated by the notion. He put the thought aside as Ine spoke again.

Ine's voice went much, much quieter. "'Tis not her feelings for you I would question," he said. "I ask you to think on this if you please, my lo—Rees. When Briana gifts her loyalty to someone, she never withdraws it. She has gifted it to her family, to her nation, to the people of Flint. She has never gifted it to herself." Had Rees been any other kind of man, any other knight or nobleman in England, Ine would not have told him, but the bard had in the past days gained some real respect for Rees's ability to reason.

"Has she gifted it to you?" Rees's voice was soft, without any overt menace, but there was something in it that kept Ine from taking the question lightly.

"As far as we share music, aye," said the bard. "Music is a bridge from me to her, just as 'twas for you. The difference will always be that 'tis the only bridge I have to her, while you are building others." Even as he spoke the words, Ine knew them to be half-truth, but it was a necessary half-truth. He would not tell Rees about the mysterious bond he felt with Briana, at least not until he had some way of understanding it himself. He studied Rees closely. "Do you bear me any grudge for this?"

Rees slowly shook his head. "'Tis my belief you have, over the years, helped her to endure what might otherwise not have been endurable," he said, startling Ine with the accuracy and perception of that statement.

Rees tried to think about his handfast bride as objectively as he could. She had been a young girl, proud, probably carefree, doubtlessly pampered, perhaps even cherished as many girls were not, but she was a child of legend. And then her world had collapsed. She had been snatched from Wales and had spent seven years in the hands of her enemies, perhaps wondering why she had been allowed to survive, or even made to survive, when so much she loved was lost to her. He felt a moment's real regret that he had not known her before, when Ine had, when she probably laughed easily, when an honest opinion did not have to be swallowed in fear of the reaction it might provoke.

Ine watched him think. Unlike Galen and Ralf, to whom the process was somewhat alien and even unwelcome, Ine admired a fine mind bent on good. The bard had no doubts that Edward Plantagenet was an intelligent man, but he had turned that gift to domination, plots and schemes, suborned it in an appetite for absolute power. His nephew Rees must have taken a number of serious blows in his life—some of which Ine was certain the earl held tightly to himself—and still he cared about the well-being of others in ways the king would have disdained. Ine drew his conclusions as much from Rees's behavior as overlord of Conway, which was now the most prosperous place in all of Northern Wales, and that fact most accorded with what Ine had learned of Rees since their meeting at Windsor. What did not accord, but what he could not ask about, were the death of Llewelyn and the slaughter at Fearndon.

After a very long time, during which the steady clopping of the horses' hooves on the dirt surface of the road and the flutter of wings, as their presence disturbed some birds from nearby trees, were the only sounds, Rees said, "The intoxication will wane, and when it does, we can build a future on it." It was a baldly honest statement, and while it did not address Ine's concern about Briana's feelings toward herself, the bard knew that the seed had been planted.

Because he knew that Briana would be extremely tender from the vigor of their first nights of lovemaking, Rees determined to leave her alone the third night. They were being honored by having the entire guesthouse at St. Savior's Cluniac Priory to themselves. Rees thought that if he allowed her to rest enough not be overly sore, they could certainly get beyond Oxford the next day. When the monks welcomed them, Ine mentioned quietly that he would be happy to play something for them. Several of the younger monks looked hopeful, but one of the seniors demurred, citing the privations of Lent.

Ine then asked solemnly if the monks would have any objection to music being played in the guesthouse. The monks agreed that they would not be corrupted by music at one remove. Once the horses had been tied under a sheltering roof which covered a woodpile in the fall but whose wood was seriously depleted after the winter's cold, the five of them went into the small main room of the guesthouse, where a trestle table and benches consumed almost all the space.

Ine unpacked and tuned his harp as one of the younger monks brought in a bowl of some sort of vegetable broth and fresh bread, cast a quickly covetous eye on the harp, and went out to make room for one of his brothers who was carrying a large jug of ale, cups, spoons and bowls. A third monk appeared with the washing water and a cloth.

Ine drank a few swallows of the ale and then brought out his repertoire of sober church songs. He was a good enough musician so that anyone, overhearing, would never guess he performed Roman church songs with a strong undertone of irony.

Ralf and Galen rolled their eyes at one another during the third stately, reverential song, finished mopping up their broth with the bread, and discovered urgent business taking care of the horses.

Briana enjoyed the music, as she always enjoyed music, her fingers keeping time by tapping on the table, wishing her dulcimer had not gone on the wagon with Esrith and the women. Unexpectedly, his eyes twinkling, Rees produced his recorder and joined Ine for the last of the religious songs. Briana was gratified by the breadth of his knowledge of different kinds of music, for it showed her that music was as important to him as it was to her.

After the last notes of pious praise faded away under the low, beamed ceiling, Ine and Rees looked at one another, repressing identical grins. Briana watched the unspoken understanding that flowed between them and was a little envious. Then they both looked across at her, their expressions equally composed of mischief and purpose. She could not help smiling in response.

Ine struck a chord on his harp and began to sing the lewdest ballad he knew. Rees waited only a note or two before singing along, his full baritone blending well with the bard's tenor. Briana spent a moment being so shocked by the melodic lechery that she gasped and covered her hot cheeks with her hands. Then, as the description of lascivious acts grew more absurd, she began to laugh. She laughed even harder as Rees's two knights, overhearing the new song from the courtyard, burst in, singing along badly, but with great enthusiasm.

They did not know whether the monks could hear them until someone began ringing the priory tower bell so powerfully, and with such an uncontrolled rhythm, that they realized the monks could probably hear them perfectly well.

Briana covered her mouth with her hand, tears in her eyes from the open, unrestrained laughter that hurt her ribs. She had no idea how long it had been since she had laughed like this—or, indeed, laughed at all. The dull wariness of her entire adolescence seemed suddenly escapable, as if the years of captivity had no longer any power to harm her. The sudden tears were abruptly, unexpectedly, real, unstoppable, and she turned her face away so the men would not see them.

But Rees instantly saw her begin to weep, stopped singing, rose, took her by the shoulders, and led her into the tiny guest chamber they would be sharing. One of the benefits of a priory guesthouse that compensated for the uncomfortable beds and overly plain food was the ability to close a door between different parties of guests.

Ine watched them go, but did not stop singing, so Galen and Ralf were able to continue shouting the words the bell was trying to obliterate.

Briana tried to master her tears, as she had always been able to do at court, but when Rees drew her to the bed, sat them both down on it, and pulled her against his chest, she allowed his strength to hold her up and support her as she wept. When the first storm of tears passed, he asked quietly, "What happened, sweetness?"

Her answer stabbed him with its mournful simplicity. "I've forgotten how to laugh."

His arms tightened around her as a fiercely protective impulse swelled in him, coupled with anger. Edward had done this to her.

It was only their third night together. They had not yet reached anywhere near the point where his need to defend her or her need to be held could remain detached from the intense tide of sensuality that ran through their relationship and sparked in their touch of one another.

As her tears dried, her hands slid down his body, pressing against the tunic, then pulling at it as if to help him remove it. He took her shoulders and set her back from him, his eyes filled with that warm tenderness which always moved her so powerfully. "We should not couple this even," he said, his voice already husky with desire. "You are unused to being—" He hesitated. "—used so vigorously."

"I'll not become used to it if we do it not," she said, the protest sounding hoarse as her own voice roughened. The eyes she lifted to his face were both innocent and provocative, glowing like green embers.

He could not help laughing, but the deep sound was so kind that she knew there could be no mockery in it. "We have years, Briana."

She reached up and stroked his cheeks, feeling the slight stubble from his day's growth of beard. "Rees," she said quite seriously, "I want to feel—connected again. Not alone. I want to feel—" She stopped and, quite unexpectedly, blushed, but she did not turn her gaze away.

She heated him with her look, her restlessly roaming hands and her absolutely frank statement of desire. His looks and stature had made him the object of a number of attempted seductions, from Brittany onward. Some were successful, some fruitless, and they had ranged from the subtle to the blatantly obvious. None had ever been as arousing as this one, when he knew full well that Briana was utterly without guile. He stroked her face, unwound the barbette to free her hair, returned his thumbs to her cheekbones. He could feel her blush even through his calluses. He knew very well what she wanted to feel; the throbbing in his groin had informed him that he wanted to feel it, too.

She was still plucking at his tunic, and he gently put her hands aside and stripped himself. She watched him, eyes shining, then turned her back so he could unlace her gown. When they were both naked, he pushed her into the straw tick, careful to imply no urgency in his motions, touching her only lightly, without insistence.

For the first time, in bed with him, Briana could think coherently, even as he stroked her breasts, barely caressing the skin. There was no demand, no domination, she realized, and she did not understand why. It was a question she could never ask, for she would not have known the words to use. Rees was different from every other man she had ever met, including her father, her brothers, and Owen Glyn. But then, she thought, mayhap Rees was not so entirely different from Ine. *Why?* she asked herself. He was a man of arms, of blood, of the battlefield. She had seen his work herself, though she did not want to think about that. When would he revert? Would he? And why was he being so different now?

And then he drew her attention completely by laying his palm against the damp curls of her mound, saying, "For this night, we will not—connect, sweetness." When her surprise showed actively on her face, he smiled, with as much mischief as he had shown in the common room over the salacious song. "But fear not. You shall still feel—" He did not put a word to it, either, only bent, his eyes on her curious face, and kissed her belly, tracing its curve with his tongue.

When he raised his head, the mischief had been transformed into something she could only describe as wickedness. He slid his hands up her calves to the thighs, then used his forearms to lift and separate her knees, tipping her hips upward so he could reach the hot, aching core of her with his mouth.

Briana had not known such things were possible. She writhed in rainbows of brilliance as he did, indeed, make her feel—and then the bliss invaded every cell in her body and brain. Even mindless, she was aware that he watched her. He made her forget there was such a thing as shame.

When she swam back to full awareness after riding out the rhythm of the bliss, he was sitting above her, stroking her hair. She looked at his face, then down his chest along the huge diagonal of the scar to the muscled, slow-moving abdomen, and at last to the flesh-shielded blade that lay along his thigh, unsatisfied. "What of your own need?" she asked.

"'Twill pass," he said. "Try to sleep."

She raised herself onto an elbow, the lethargy of repletion swirling outward from her loins and making her more sluggish than she would have liked. Then she reached out and touched his rigid shaft.

With a sharp indrawn breath, he caught her wrist, but she

reflexively closed her grasp to avoid having her hand lifted free.

"Briana," he said, his voice tight, "you know not what you are doing. I have no wish to hurt you."

She smiled a little sadly, studying how the light of the single candle played on the regular, taut planes of his face, and she told him the truth. "'Tis possible that one day you may hurt me, Rees," she said, "but 'twill not be with this." She bent her head and touched her lips to his manhood without any hesitation, without any deeper sexual meaning.

The heat raging through him became more than even he could deny, and he was wise enough to know that if he waited much longer, he would lose control again. He lay back on the straw tick and murmured, "If you can bear it, lower yourself down onto me. If you cannot, use your hands. 'Twill be enough."

For a moment, trying to interpret what he meant, she did not move. When she understood, she rose above him and straddled him, wincing once, and then let herself slowly down along his hardness. "'Twill never be enough," she breathed.

He fought the urge to move as long as he could, and then he could fight it no longer.

When at last they lay twined around one another, when the capacity for intelligent thought could be extended beyond the dam their bodies had built around their rationality, he tucked her dark head under his chin and said, "The prior informed me when we arrived that the monks will honor us by offering the Eucharist in the morn. Will you receive it from the good fathers?"

He felt her shake a negation against his throat. "The monks will not understand," he cautioned.

Briana still did not understand it herself. She knew, rationally at least, that she did not now feel too degraded by the match or its wonderful aftermath to accept God's gift to His people on earth. But her continuing obstinate refusal had a reality completely separate from any instigating cause, from either him or her; it simply was.

"I cannot," she said against the hollow of his throat, "and especially not merely to please the monks."

After the first time he had tried to get her to agree, he had never tested her obedience by commanding her to do this. Instead, he had credited that she had reasons, and that they were reasons which appeared legitimate to her. He was not a superstitious man. He had never seen demons lurking in graveyards or under hollow trees. All the demons he knew of lived in other men.

"I will take good care of it," he said. "Now sleep."

She felt a wave of gratitude sweep over her with the power of the waves of desire he evoked in her. He had taken her part in this, from the outset, when it would have been so easy for him to fight her. She wriggled once in his arms, nestling closer, then slept. When her breathing evened and deepened, Rees stroked her hair gently and thought again how lucky he was. Not only was his handfast wife undeniably beautiful and astoundingly passionate, she was also that single thing he had thought never to find in a woman, let alone a wife—she was intriguingly complex. He had discovered the joy attendant on complexity of mind in himself in a bed in the Holy Land, stitched up against death by Abraham ben Zeniuta, who became his tutor. To rediscover it in a very different bed, in other circumstances here, was unanticipated, but marvelous. He thought then that not only was he unlikely to soon tire of her, she was very likely never to bore him. He wondered if he was, indeed, obsessed by her, for having her did not seem to relieve his need to have her. He wondered if she were obsessed by him as well.

Chapter 22

Flint—March 1282 A.D.

Despite one day being bogged down for several hours when one of the wagon wheels became jammed between two large rocks concealed by mud, the wagon driven by Esrith reached Flint in a week. Hulde and Enlis were glad the journey was ended, though sleeping on the ground beneath the wagon was not particularly more uncomfortable than sleeping on the stone floors of Windsor or on the dirt of the hut Esrith used when he needed to remain out in pasturage with the herds.

Heeding Rees's instructions, they gave the castle only a glance and drove directly to the kitchenyard of the manor, where Maud and the few remaining retainers met them. Hulde, conscious of propriety, climbed down off the wagon seat and dropped a stiff-legged curtsy to Lady Maud. "I am Hulde," she said, "and I have been useful as housekeeper to the Lady Briana these few years. I would be pleased to serve you as well, in any capacity for which you have need."

Maud had heard of Hulde and Enlis from Briana's rare letters, and she felt a wave of excitement that her niece was being returned to Flint at last. She signalled her own few retainers to help the newcomers unload the wagon. To Esrith, she said, "The stable here has a deal of space for your horse. We have few animals remaining now." She did not say that all but one of the horses belonged to the recluse, that the manor's other horses had gone to the castle for the taxes. She felt there was simply no need.

Esrith held the reins of the wagon horse as they unloaded, and with his free hand fumbled in his scrip for a folded piece of parchment. As he was pulling it out, one of the largest, most formidable women he had ever seen came out the kitchen door of the manor. He goggled.

Sabine said to Maud, "Is there any way in which I may render service, Lady Maud?"

Maud smiled at her, a genuine smile that lifted her plain, thin face nearly to prettiness, softening the sharp angles that poverty had created by lowering her surface flesh much closer to the bone. "We appear to have it nearly complete," she said.

Esrith recovered himself and pulled out the paper. "I have a letter for you, my lady." He held it out.

Maud took it from him, and he led the horse, still pulling the now empty wagon, in the direction of the stable. Maud looked at the letter in her hand, and then back up at Sabine again.

Sabine guessed that Maud had not been taught reading or writing. "I would be happy to read it for you if you would allow me to," she said.

Maud gave her the letter, because it would be faster than sending for Father Ciaran. They went back through the manor to the front steps, where Maud gathered her skirts and sat down. The front yard was not in good repair. One of the two sides of the gate had fallen into the yard and been left there, and the other was missing. Maud had sensibly decided some years ago that there was no sense trying to rehang the gate when Baron Wigmore would come in any time he pleased, and when he was the only one the gates would have been shut to keep away.

Sabine remained standing, showed Maud that she was

breaking the wax seal on the letter and unfolded it.

"Is it from Briana?" Maud asked.

Sabine looked down at the signature. "Nay," she said. "'Tis signed 'Ine, Bard of Dubhain.'"

Maud was surprised by that, and a little of her eagerness was blunted by caution. "Ine?" she repeated. "Ine has never sent us any kind of message before. What has he to say?"

Sabine had already scanned the contents of the letter, which was not long, but written in the neat hand of a man who knew how to make a precise rendering of music or lyric alike. She read out, "To my friends at Flint. You must be told that Lady Briana will return to you before the midpoint of Pentecost. She has no other way to return than as wife to Earl Connarc. I have come to know the man, and he is not what we thought him. He will take her heart. If we disown her for the match, she will die. I will come with her. Tell Ciaran to prepare to welcome her and the husband the king has gifted her to. Flint is his now. Ine, Bard of Dubhain."

Maud sat transfixed, motionless except for the play of emotions across her transparent face. Sabine could read them as if the older woman were speaking them out to her. Confusion, disbelief, anger, and real anguish battled with the joy of knowing Briana would be on her way home even at this moment. Sabine accepted that her role was to speak the words of the letter, not to comment on them, so she waited until Maud had fastened on some thought or other. When the Welsh woman rose, her face falling into lines of determination, Sabine held out the letter to her, breathing a hushed prayer under her breath, which Maud heard, but which did not register with her.

Maud said, "I must settle the new folk in the manor and the outbuildings we still have remaining. When you arrive at St. Maedoc's, would you ask Father Ciaran to come to me?"

"I will," Sabine said, knowing she had just been dismissed. She laid the letter on the step beside Maud and went out the open gate and along the road that led to the village, casting one glance at the towering bulk of the castle beside the estuary before she turned right. When she and Beatrice had first arrived at Flint, Sabine had wondered about the castle. Would Edmund Mortimer, who used it as the base in his ruling of the Northern March, be curious as to the nature of the recluse or the goings-on at the church? Would he try to discover anything about the new source of revenue, perhaps to levy taxes on it? But he had paid no heed to the new arrivals. The Marcher Lord concerned himself only with exacting tribute from the manor, not with anything having to do with St. Maedoc's. He never attended any of the Masses there, but used his own chaplain and kept to his own chapel. The presence of his wife with him did not seem to put any humanizing tenor upon his occupation of the castle, nor did it have a mitigating effect upon his or his soldiers' more rapacious activities.

Sabine wondered if he was aware that he was living in a fief of which he was no longer the overlord.

In fact, it would have occurred to no one in Flint to notify Baron Wigmore that the Earl Connarc and his wife, one of whom was a Plantagenet on the wrong side of the blanket, the other of whom was the lady of legend, would be journeying to take possession of the estuary of the Dee. King Edward had sent a messenger the morning of the handfasting, because the transfer of property in Eastern Wales was of material concern to the Marcher Lords even if they had not—as would be the case with Flint—direct involvement.

In giving Flint to Rees, the king was essentially telling Wigmore to move out. Edward had decided to place him in Harlech, in Gwynedd, even though that castle was far west of the normal boundary of the Northern March. It was a strategic decision, placing Rees's fief at Conway to the north of Snowdonia, and Wigmore to the south of the stronghold. The king hoped the dual pressure on the mountain fastness would rout the remaining rebels, whose very existence gnawed at the king as would a canker. And while Edward had for a time entertained the possibility of removing Rees from Conway, in the end he had to admit to himself that Rees had accomplished far too much to take the fief away from him. The king was well aware that Rees had kept the peace at Conway and that only poverty—not Mortimer—had kept the peace at Flint. On the other hand, Mortimer was a harsh taskmaster, and there was continuing rebel activity in the vicinity of Harlech. He did not expect Rees to eliminate the rebels, since in seven years Rees had not done so; therefore, the charter would go to Wigmore.

When Edmund Mortimer received the message, several days before the wagon with Briana's belongings on it arrived at Flint manor, he was not displeased by it. His knight, William de Blaisey, carried it to him in the northwest room of Flint's unusual, square castle.

Mortimer was not the brilliant strategist his father, Roger, had been as a Marcher, and he chose to serve him men who did not possess the intelligence to challenge him in any way. Wigmore was a rather mild-looking man of medium build, unfashionably dark-skinned and bearded in an era which favored fair coloring. He had been left rough-faced by a bout with smallpox when he was in his twenties, but then, as he had never tried to use looks as any part of his arsenal, it mattered little. Though Mortimer often affected to be mild-mannered, to the point of diffidence, he shared certain salient characteristics with the King of England: He demanded absolute obedience, and he had no compunctions about being ruthless to achieve it.

William de Blaisey, on the other hand, was a typical knight of the sort that Wigmore hired. He was hulking, bloodthirsty, unlettered, and loyal to the coin that paid him and the man who gave him the opportunity to engage in occasional butchery. He had not had any such opportunity for a while. Flint was a relatively docile fief, because the people were poor and downtrodden. They paid their tribute to the castle without overt complaint, and there were few young men to harass or press into any kind of service to the knights. So by the time he was given the message from the king to take to his employer, he was hopeful it could mean action.

de Blaisey gave the scroll to Mortimer, who broke the royal seal and read the message and the charter.

"Sit down, William," the baron said.

Over his ten years of service to Wigmore, de Blaisey had developed a real sensitivity to only one thing—the moods of his employer. He had heard the barely audible hiss Wigmore made as he read the king's words, and the knight immediately examined a split thumbnail to indicate that he had no connection to whatever it was that had made the baron angry.

Mortimer smiled humorlessly and set the scroll down on the table at which he sat. "We are going to be moving to Harlech, William," he said in his rather high voice. "The king has hopes of cleaning out the abcess in Snowdonia."

de Blaisey looked up. "Leave Flint, milord?" he asked for clarification.

"Oh, aye," said Mortimer, well accustomed to the lack of speed with which de Blaisey processed information. "Flint is to be Earl Connarc's."

"Which one would he be, milord?" the knight asked, his brow wrinkled with the effort to place the name among Edward's more than one hundred noblemen.

"The Plantagenet bastard sown on the king's sister." Mortimer was searching his memory for all the intelligence his spies had discovered about the earl who would be coming to take the fief of Flint away from him. "He served with Gilbert de Clare's company in the Holy Land, and I heard de Clare say he was the strongest swordsman he had ever seen. de Clare said the Mamelukes as good as fled before him. I never did understand why King Edward chose not to claim Connarc as his own." Mortimer stroked his beard, brow wrinkled. "Of course, his service in the Welsh war was much in doubt, and I know for fact that he claimed more honors than were due him. Especially in the matter of the dispatch of Llewelyn."

de Blaisey nodded as if he had placed Earl Connarc, but he had not, and Baron Wigmore knew it and cared not at all.

"I believe," the Marcher Lord said, secure in the honest purity of his own line and the prominence of his illustrious father, "we should prepare a welcome for the earl. I believe I shall send you to tell the Lady Maud I'll require a bull to slaughter. This occasion should permit feasting, whether it occurs during the Lenten abstinence or after Easter." He knew very well that the manor and the village were low on both livestock and provender after the privations of the winter, but if he was to turn the fief over to Connarc, he thought that he might as well bankrupt it first. "'Twill hardly be my concern any longer," he said with satisfaction, looking at the scroll again.

He would also issue an order that each of his knights and any borrowed workers he conscripted should begin polishing mail and sharpening weapons, but he would not issue it now because William would not remember it long enough to convey it to anyone. The knight was only good for one order at a time. The baron picked up the scroll to reroll it. He had some time yet, and he understood patience. He smiled again, this time an expression with a genuine edge to it. This promised to be amusing, and there had been so little amusement lately.

Father Ciaran threw his cloak over his shoulders and hurried to the manor as soon as he heard from Sabine that Lady Maud wanted to see him. He hurried because he wanted to respond at once. He and Maud had formed an alliance of deprivation in the years of occupation; of the Marcher Lords under whose sway Flint had fallen since the end of the Welsh war and the abduction of Briana, Edmund Mortimer was by far the worst. However, the priest knew it would impossible for him to pass through the village without speaking to everyone he encountered. He made slow but steady progress through the cluster of buildings, greeting all those whom he passed, pausing to comment on the sporadic repairs to thatching or wattle, noting that the smithy fire was out, petting a thin cat who crouched under a bench at the abandoned mill. Then, past the village, he walked faster on the uneven road surface, but slowed again, inevitably, climbing the slight rise to the manor gate. He was, he reflected dispassionately, an old man. Once inside the manor itself, he turned to the left and entered the hall, the most likely place to find Maud.

Indeed, she sat on a bench at one of the three tables set in a horseshoe configuration opposite the fireplace, a folded piece of paper in her hands. When she had heard him come in, she looked up and lost custody of her face again. Such a mixture of conflicting emotions played over it that the priest was taken aback. Maud was a simple woman, but from her rapidly altering expressions, Father Ciaran guessed that she was now wrestling with a difficult problem.

"What haps?" he asked.

"She is coming home," Maud said, blinking rapidly at tears that sprang into her lashless brown eyes. "The king is sending Briana back to us, at last." She paused, but before he could speak, added, "At least."

"At least?" He heard some joy and relief in her voice, but heard as well that something else colored it, and her words stirred some foreboding in his soul. "Surely her homecoming is wonderful tidings," he said carefully. "Is that a letter from her?"

"Nay, 'tis from the bard. He returns with her."

"From Ine?" That was indeed unexpected, and the foreboding grew. "How comes it that the message is his to give?"

Maud's lips trembled, and she shoved the paper across the table at him. He did not think to ask how she knew what it contained. "Her English servants brought this, and Sabine said 'twas from Ine. Connarc," she said. "King Edward has given her—and us—into the hands of Connarc."

"Sweet Jesus," Father Ciaran said softly, "is he still so vindictive? Or has he finally decided to destroy us?"

"It grows darker," Maud said, though the priest's caring heart had a difficult time conceiving how it might. "Read Ine's letter. Tell me if Sabine had the right of it."

He unfolded the document and glanced at it, then sat down on the bench opposite her and read it slowly, word for word. When he had finished it, he understood what it had to say, and Maud's distress made sense. "He will take her heart," he read again. "Not merely her body, then."

"Briana could never love Connarc!" Maud said hotly.

Father Ciaran pushed the paper away from him. "Ine is rarely wrong about what people feel, and I have never known him to be wrong about Briana. He makes it plain that, if she does love him, we must needs support her in it."

Maud looked at him, unblinking. "But, Connarc!" she cried, angry.

"'Twill be her name, too."

Maud tried to hold her head up, but it fell into her hands as her shoulders slumped. "Poor child," she said. "How can Ine believe she would love him? He is evil!"

"Mayhap not," said Father Ciaran, reciting, "'He is not what we thought.' Mayhap God has found a way to reach him."

Maud lifted her head slowly. "I have remembered something. After Sabine read the letter, she said something I barely heard. Strange."

"What did she say?" Father Ciaran asked.

Maud's brow wrinkled as she made herself recall. "She said, 'God be praised,'" she answered. "As if Ine's letter had aught to do with her."

"We may ask her later," said the priest dismissively. "Ine has taken care to ensure we have sufficient warning. People here must be brought ere Easter to accept the idea that when she returns, Briana of Flint will belong to Connarc as well as to us."

"And we must prepare in other ways as well," Maud said, her thoughts now racing ahead. "Father, I must ask you to write a letter for me, but not to judge me for it. Will you do that?"

There might have been people he would have refused such a request from, but he and Maud had shared too much for him to disappoint her, no matter what the letter she wished to write might contain, or to whom she would direct it. "Bring me the writing materials," he said.

Maud rose and hurried across the narrow corridor to the tiny room that had once served as the manor office, back in the days when it was necessary to administer things.

The priest waited for her to return and used prayer for a peaceful outcome of Connarc's coming to Flint so as not to dwell on what it was that Maud wanted to accomplish. When she returned and laid the paper, ink, and quill on the table, he took a small knife from his scrip and trimmed the point of the quill, then carefully returned the knife to his scrip, praying all the while. He opened the precious bottle of ink, dipped the quill, and waited, trying to make himself a simple scribe.

Maud had been gathering her thoughts. Now she folded her hands, ran her tongue over her lips, and said, "The letter is to be directed to Owen Glyn."

Snowdonia—March 1289 A.D.

In a hollow in one of the great shoulders of Snowdon, Owen Glyn ate some of the meat and bread he and his men had taken in their most recent raid. For seven years, since the end of the Welsh war, Owen and the forty men who still followed him had hidden in and around the wilds of the mountain, striking throughout Gwynedd and further south. They killed soldiers of the king when they could and stole the food, ale and fodder they and their horses needed to live. Sometimes they stole horses, as well. At twenty-seven, Owen Glyn was not overly tall, but he was as well-muscled and battle-hardened as any man who served the English king. He had not lived a week in years without a sword, dagger, or bow in use in his hands, and he was beginning to be very weary of the fact that there was a price on his head and that he risked his life with dependable regularity.

There was no boyishness left about him, no sentimentality, no illusions, and no softness. He had known for the past three years or more that he was fighting a losing battle and that it would eventually kill him. While he did not particularly want to die, he knew nothing else now, and he saw no way out. His only real determination was that he would not die horribly, as had Prince David, but cleanly, as had his hero, Prince Llewelyn. He recruited no more men to fight with him; the ones who were left now remained from the hundred or so who had sought refuge in Snowdonia when the charnel house of Fearndon spelled the end of any possible Welsh army.

Since he had no illusions, Owen knew he accomplished very little in the great scheme of things, but he did not yet have to yield, and every so often—as recently, when he and his men had been able to steal some supplies the English needed for Beaumarais—he scored a small victory. The rebels lived a nomadic existence on the slopes and in the wooded valleys of the mountain fastness, just as the early Welsh had done for centuries in partnership with the land, and the peak towered over them like a guardian spirit. His men ranged in age from just under twenty to just over sixty, and all of them wanted Wales to be free, even though all silently doubted it would happen. Most of them had one specific man or men they wished to revenge themselves on for something that had happened in the war; some had achieved their individual goals and gone on fighting; others had simply forgotten what had brought them here, but had nowhere else to go.

Because they moved their camp so often, and because their years of familiarity with the wilds had made them almost part of the scenery, it took Maud's messenger days longer than he had thought it would to find them, and he was very weary by the time he was seen.

Maud had chosen Annie's husband, Havgan, to carry the message. He was a thin, hard-working farmer, tanner, or woodworker, depending on what needed his efforts, and he had been spared Fearndon by virtue of having been wounded at Dinas Bran and unable to go to the field when the call to Fearndon went out. He had a strong sense of loyalty to his family, his village, and his nation. He had, in the past, taken several messages back and forth between Flint and the men on Snowdon, because Maud was concerned about Owen, so he knew generally what area to begin in, but the wilds of Snowdonia were huge, and if he did not run into any of Owen's outlying guards, he would not find the camp. Doggedly, he kept searching.

He was tired enough so that when a bowman finally challenged him, Havgan snapped, "'Tis past time and more that you found me! I'm out of Flint. Take me to Owen now!"

It was still light enough for the bowman to see the lines of toil and poverty on Havgan's simple yeoman's face, and he ordered, "Dismount and follow me."

Havgan swung down off the tired brown mare he had ridden uncomfortably for far too long. She was the only horse Flint village could boast now, and she, like he, was too thin. He tied her to a tree and scrambled along after the bowman. They passed through a narrow defile to the small vale which had for the past two days sheltered the rebel camp.

Always alert to the sounds of approach, Owen emerged from his small tent, his hand on his sword, his brown eyes searching out the source of the disturbance. Havgan waved a hand in greeting, and Owen recognized him in the fading light and let go of his sword hilt.

The bowman vanished back in the direction of his post.

Owen gestured to Havgan to come join him on a fallen log near the small campfire. "You're welcome back," he said. "Is Lady Maud well?"

"Aye." Havgan took out the letter he had carried under his shirt and gave it to Owen.

Owen unfolded it, there being no seal on it, and held it

closer to the fire to silently read Father Ciaran's neat script. "King Edward has decreed that the Lady Briana wed Earl Connarc and has added Flint to Conway. They will be at Flint manor during Pentecost, perhaps early, since Easter comes next week and they have set out from England. We have a debt to collect from the earl. Will you aid in this? Maud ap Emrys."

Owen had not heard Briana's name for quite some while, but he had often thought of the angular, pretty girl he had kissed good-bye and promised to return to marry. He did not react to the news about Connarc immediately. Owen had had only one direct experience of the earl, because he was absent from the north when Wales fell. He had been far south gathering supplies for Llewelyn's starving army, and by the time he returned, Fearndon had spilled the blood of the army of Northern Wales onto its frozen ground.

Owen's sole encounter with Earl Connarc had come only a year and a half before now, during the single raid he had ever tried to make on the area controlled by Conway castle. Connarc was a vigilant overlord, and his information systems were obviously superior, for Owen and his men had barely arrived at what appeared to be an unguarded storage building when Connarc and a huge party of his men swooped down upon them. The battle had been fierce, but, amazingly, Owen had gotten away with every one of his men and only minor injuries. It was his least effective raid as pertained to spoils, but he still did not understand how he had managed to lose no men despite having been seriously outnumbered. He had mused on it for some time without reaching any conclusion other than that he should forbear to raid Conway's lands again if he wanted to be successful at obtaining food or horses.

Now Briana was at last being returned to her people at Flint, but in Connarc's power. Owen allowed himself to feel anger. As was the general knowledge, he believed Connarc responsible for the deaths of Llewelyn and of the Lord of Flint, Bryn ap Emrys. And now the man had taken Bryn's daughter, who had been promised to Owen himself. For any one of those things, the earl probably deserved to suffer and die. Yet word of his overlordship of Conway had been strangely favorable, though very subdued when it reached Owen, as if the speakers were afraid they would insult him with a truth about the butcher of Fearndon that did not conform to Owen's desires. It had made Owen curious, though not curious enough to risk a second raid on Conway.

Owen's fingers played over the hilt of his sword. At best, he might rescue Briana from bondage—quite possibly the fetters of which the legend had spoken, through the legend implied she would break them herself—and avenge Bryn at the same time. And since Connarc was King Edward's chosen overlord for Flint and Conway, it could be an opportunity to strike a blow for the Princes Llewelyn and David, as well. It was, of course, why Maud had made certain he knew what was occurring. At worst, he might glimpse something of the future of Wales.

"Get yourself some food and rest," he said to Havgan. "On the morrow, we will make some plans."

"I'm not much of a planner," Havgan said doubtfully.

Truth be told, neither was Owen. His instinctive genius was in recognizing opportunities, not in creating them. It made him a survivor. "Leave it to me," he said, and showed Havgan where to take the mare so that she would have fodder.

It was not that he felt any desire for Briana. Their fathers had made the match when he and she were only children, and he had not seen her since she was still trembling on the verge of womanhood. He had known only her childish ways, though even then he could sense the early promise of her beauty. If he took her, it would be because she had been promised to him by men who had had the right to give her away. He turned and walked across the camp to a small knot of men sharpening daggers and fitting arrowheads. There was one in particular with whom he wanted to speak.

Folkstone, England—March 1289 A.D.

It was by sheer accident, during a momentary suspension of violence, that Bjorn Magnussen learned he had fathered another son. One of his more memorable, more satisfying rapes had occurred while he was on a mission from King Haakon to the court of England's King Henry III. He had behaved himself at the beginning of the mission, puffed up with the importance of being an ambassador. He had behaved well for such a long while that it strained his nature. Then the pious English king sent him on a tour of some of the religious shrines, and while he was at St. Candida, he encountered a beautiful woman with golden hair, exquisite features, and a dazzling smile. He followed her through the city until he knew where she was lodging, then drank a great deal, and waited for her to reappear. When she did, he followed her and her guard to a quiet square and dispatched the guard. Horrified, she fled into the shrine, but he was undeterred by the prospect of holy ground. He cornered her there, covered her mouth, and took his pleasure of her. He left her unconscious, but otherwise not, in his opinion, unduly inconvenienced.

He was surprised to learn shortly thereafter that his encounter had been with someone important—a daughter of King Henry—because women having any value other than as receptacles had never been part of his world. Henry was not a warlike king; indeed, his very weakness was his greatest vulnerability, and he could not bring himself to act against the duly authorized representative of another king. He sent his chamberlain to speak with the Norse delegation, asking them to respect his wishes and send Bjorn Magnussen home.

It was the chamberlain, dismissed from his post and stripped of his lands when Henry died and Edward took the throne, whom Magnussen encountered in a seafront alehouse in Folkstone. Magnussen was no longer an ambassador, but rather a raider when he had the opportunity, and England was one of the places he occasionally raided. He and the disgraced former chamberlain remembered each other, despite the years which had passed, and it was the embittered Englishman who told the Norseman he had sown seeds that took root and that the woman lay in a tomb in London. He had no knowledge of what had happened to the babe, but he thought they would know at Westminster.

In the ordinary course of events, Bjorn Magnussen might have been bemused and gratified by the information, but not overly disturbed. However, events were not ordinary, for his sons were dead. Therefore, he needed another son. He left that night to ride north to London, thanking Odin for giving him another chance at his posterity.

Chapter 23

The Roads—March 1289 A.D.

By the time they reached the Welsh border at Oswestry, Rees had led Briana through the first steps of sexual inventiveness at night, and they had begun to speak seriously by day about her concerns and fears for Flint, and his own.

It had rained intermittently for a few days, slowing their progress even more, but only Galen seemed to mind. He had tumbled one of the servingmaids at a tavern two days southeast of Oswestry, but he wanted Menty again, and he was eager to get back to her. He wanted to see his children, too. The slowness of the journey, made worse by muddy roads, tugged at him.

Ralf completely understood Galen's eagerness, for he had once felt the same need to return to his wife. He had not thought that Galen would fall prey to such an impulse, because Galen's fighting style had never been affected by his marriage, whereas that of some other knights was. Having a home to return to made some men cautious. Galen had not been one of them, though both knights knew men who were near ruined for battle because of other obligations.

Both of his knights now watched Rees with his new handfast bride and wondered whether his clear infatuation would have any effect on his fighting style.

There was a travelers' place at Oswestry which was not attached to a manor or a monastery. It had been built and opened by an enterprising English yeoman to take advantage of the heavy traffic which crossed the Welsh border here. He called his establishment an "inn" from the words the Knights Templar used for their property in London, and he charged a reasonable price for accommodation that provided both shelter and food. It allowed a traveler to be free of the demands of courtesy for hospitality, for the owner asked no questions about a traveler's destination or purpose. Rees had heard of it as far away as Conway; the party made for it as soon as they reached the town.

The inn was the largest and most comfortable place they had yet found on their journey. They reached it on Easter eve, which meant they should keep the vigil and attend morning Mass at St. Anne's, the English church that dominated the town which straddled Shropshire and Clwydd.

Ine had watched Briana grow more and more nervous as they neared both Wales and the most important Christian celebration. Rees and his knights were called to pay respects to John Welton, Baron Mulford, the Marcher Lord for the Middle March they were about to enter, a man who was less powerful than Wigmore and more powerful than de Erville, whose Southern March had been calmest since the early days of the Welsh war. Mulford had the care of and residency in Oswestry because it had often been a flashpoint, poised as it was between the two nations. Mulford was not a strategic fighter, and it was for that reason that Owen Glyn and his men had been successful at raiding the westernmost lands of the Middle March. When the Marcher Lord heard that Rees was at the inn, meeting with the earl had become his top priority, and it would have been an insult for Rees to refuse. The three men left as soon as they had refreshed themselves from the day's journey.

That left Ine and Briana at a corner table in the inn's common room, sipping a very fine ale. "It seems," Ine observed, "that when you sell ale and food for custom, rather than provide them for hospitality, you produce a superior kind." He watched her try to pay a distracted attention to his comment, and then he leaned forward and asked softly, "Is it Wales, is it Easter, or is it Rees?"

Briana thought wryly that he had just encapsulated the whole of her life's issues in one succinct question. "Aye," she said. "'Tis all that. And I know not how to resolve it."

"Why see you these as things which demand resolution?" the bard asked, watching as she furrowed her brow to think about his question. "These are conditions of life."

"I cannot take Communion," she said, fastening onto it as the single thing that would be easiest to dismiss. "I know not why, but this day that everyone else sees with such hope seems—" She paused for a very long time, choosing her word with great care, and he waited for it, his thin face very serious. "—painful," she finished at last. "'Tis not that I have no wish to believe. 'Tis more that belief—" She stumbled, slowed, the truth going deeper, hurting more. "—belongs to other people, different people, people that God has smiled upon. I made gestures of faith, but then I saw Fearn—" Her breath failed her, leaving her unable to say the word.

Ine's voice was suddenly strained, his look intense. "Have you asked him about Fearndon?"

She shook her head vehemently. "Nay, never! And I never shall. I was there, Ine. I know the truth."

"You know your truth," the bard said. "You know not his truth."

She raised a hand as if to keep his words away from her. "'Tis in the past," she said. "If we can leave it in the past, we may have a chance. And—and I want us to have a chance."

He expected her to say that she loved him, but she did not continue for quite some time, then burst out, "I understand it not, but when he reaches for me—" She covered her cheeks with her hands, but did not cover her eyes, forcing herself not to look away from his calm, non-judgmental gaze.

Ine said matter-of-factly, "He was raised in Brittany, you see, and the French put great value on the skills of the bedchamber. They have made an art of passion."

"So has he," she said frankly, challenging him to judge her.

Ine nodded, his gaze still neutral. "'Tis not a bad custom," he said. "A number of years past, I traveled the roads in Normandy, Gascony, and Brittany, and I was able to do some studying myself. 'Tis understandable, what you feel."

She wrung her hands, became aware she was doing it, and made herself stop. She seemed to have lost the facility she had used all those years in captivity for keeping her emotions under a veneer of numbness. Once she began to feel, she left herself vulnerable for feeling everything. She whispered, "They will hate me for it."

He knew immediately what she meant, and he could not deny it to her, as much as he wanted to. He had tried his best to soften the stony hatred of the people of Flint toward Connarc when he sent the letter to Maud, but he had no idea whether it had had an effect or not, and, if it had, he had no idea whether its effect would be the one he hoped for. Instead, he said, "I believe he will find ways to win them to his side at last, as he did at Conway. 'Twill just take time."

"Time," she repeated. "They will think I betrayed them."

"You will know you have not."

"Have I not?" The question was preoccupied, almost wistful.

"Nay!" His voice was, for him, powerfully insistent. "Your choices and your actions have not cost Flint. They may well save it!" And he knew even as he said it that she did not believe him. He tried another tack. "'Tis possible that they will recognize that you have room in your regard for them and for him both." He saw her face change for an instant and then reject the insight, telling him that she would not let herself believe he could be right. For the first time, he feared for her.

He reached down and took his harp out of the satchel he had lain beside him on the bench, checked its tune very quickly and softly played an old Irish lay, praying to his own gods that Flint, and most especially Father Ciaran, would understand and heed his hasty letter.

Rees saw them the moment he entered the common room, and he had to repress a stab of jealousy. He knew it was misguided, for he knew not only that he was appreciative of Ine's openness with him and coming to regard Ine as a friend—and Rees was not a man to make friends lightly—but also because he knew that Briana was, at least at this time, unable to see any man as a lover except himself. In time, that might change, but it had not changed yet. He knew it from the way her head came up and her entire body seemed to strain toward him the second she sensed his presence. With a feeling of detachment, he thought that he had set out to make her love him, with no notion at all of how completely, shamelessly, she would respond. And the response had ensnared him, as well. He told himself it was only a matter of time until his hunger for her would begin to lessen. He would keep telling it to himself until it started to be true.

Ine actually felt the energy flow between them as Rees swirled his damp cloak onto one of the benches and came across the room toward them.

Briana drew in a deep breath and painted a smile on her face as her handfast husband joined them at the table. His first words were entirely unexpected and addressed to the bard. "I've told Mulford that we must ride on at dawn and will therefore be unable to avail ourselves of the vigil or Mass at St. Anne's. I assume that you have no objection."

"You know I have none," Ine said, "but Sir Galen and Sir Ralf?"

Briana was looking at Rees with eyes that had abruptly gone soft and grateful. He had done this for her, she knew, without her asking him to.

"They believe that their immortal souls depend not upon a single Easter," Rees said drily, and added without thinking, "Mine, of course, is dark enough so 'tis no matter."

Ine froze, and Rees bit off a quick oath, looking quickly at Briana. Her expression changed, becoming slightly more withdrawn, slightly more wary. She was clearly apprehensive that he referred to things she would rather not know, and she was clearly determined not to ask him about.

Then Galen burst into the room, wet from the freshening rain, Ralf right behind him. "God's blood!" the big Saxon said gruffly, "but I am heartily sick of rain. I shall be wholly glad to get home!" He shouted for someone to bring more ale while Ralf, who came in behind him, brushed droplets of water from his hair.

Conway—March 1289 A.D.

Rees chose a longer route from Oswestry to Conway than they really needed to take, keeping the five of them south of a direct diagonal from Oswestry until they had passed Bala. It added another day to the journey, but it kept them well south of a place both Rees and Briana wanted very much to avoid: the field at Fearndon.

Briana was surprised at the size and seeming coldness of Conway castle. The massive structure surmounted a high rock ridge on the estuary of the River Conway, to the west of Flint and beyond the boundaries of the Northern March. Its eight huge towers guarded every possible approach to the long, comparatively narrow structure, and the approach from the estuary was entirely commanded by the east barbican.

Word had gone ahead that the overlord was coming home, and it seemed to Briana as they neared Conway town that every person in the neighborhood had turned out along the road. To her amazement, they cheered Rees with enthusiasm that seemed absolutely genuine. And these were people of North Wales.

True, it was Northwest Wales, which had not fallen under the blow of Fearndon the way the Northeast had, but nevertheless these people had loved Prince Llewelyn dearly, and she could not help but marvel that either they had forgiven Rees for the betrayal of their prince or they had found a way to ignore it and be happy, just as she was seeking a way to ignore it and be happy. She looked closely at the cheering people. They seemed fairly healthy and prosperous, as well as gladsome, as if the scars of war had somehow been washed away. They did not appear to be at all cowed by the overpowering hugeness of the castle.

She had seen none of King Edward's fortifications, except the castle at Flint, before she was taken to England, and the castle at Flint was tiny in comparison with this one. She had stayed one night at Rhuddlan in going from Flint to London, but she had been in shock and had no memory of the place, only of deep pain. Flint castle was relatively compact, not very prepossessing, for a conqueror's fortification. Conway was a blatant shout of the king's intention to maintain power over this land.

As they rode together up the approach from the estuary, Rees watched the uneasy awe on Briana's face at the strength of the place. He leaned toward her and said, "You are mistress here, as well as at Flint, you know."

It had not occurred to her. She raised her eyes to the heights of the castle walls they were nearing, noticing that people also lined the near battlements, more restrained than those who had cheered along the road, but waving nonetheless. "Mayhap they will like me here," she said softly, startling him.

"Of course they will like you." He frowned as he said it, uncertain what was behind her doubts. "They know you are my handfast wife."

They rode closer to the barbican gate through the curtain wall, and she looked ahead to the entrance at the top of the gentle slope their party was ascending. In its open picket stood two men and what looked like an immense wolf, though its presence did not seem to disturb the men. Briana was so riveted by the unexpected appearance of the animal that it was a few minutes before she could make herself look at the men. The beast's shoulder came to the waist of the taller man, who was sandy-haired, beardless, lean and smiling. The other man was a dark-robed priest, beginning to bend with age, his tonsured shock of pure white hair blowing around him in the breeze from the river.

Rees raised a hand in greeting, smiling back at the sandy-haired man in gray. "That man is Sir Thomas Newby, my seneschal here," he said to Briana.

She heard the warmth in his voice and was surprised and gratified that he could feel comfortable openly expressing his feeling for a servant.

Thomas Newby had gained a knighthood by honors of service rather than honors of arms, for he had provisioned Rees's army with admirable skill during the Welsh war. When Edward had knighted Newby and asked him what post he would most enjoy, Newby answered blandly that he wished to enter the service of then-Baron, soon to be Earl, Connarc, with whom he had worked during the war. And since Rees had never particularly wanted to spend any time administering a household, and at that point in his life, he expected never to be permitted to wed, he welcomed the offer. Because he would remain a bachelor, he would not have a wife to care for his property for him. He accepted Newby gladly and had never had cause to regret his choice.

Rees and the other riders were about twenty yards from the picket when the priest smiled and raised his hand in greeting. Rees pulled Basilisk up short, stopping their forward progress, swung down onto the causeway, and, ignoring the priest completely, whistled.

Rees had not given overmuch thought to Father Michael since he realized the old cleric had broken the seal of the confessional to report on Rees to the king. It was not so much

the suborning of the confession that angered Rees, it was the
evidence that the priest had suborned it to the king. Edward
might be Rees's liege lord and able to command his obedience,
but no man could prove to Rees that he served the king's
interests before Rees's own and escape unscathed by that. He
would have to decide how to deal with the priest.

At the sound of the whistle, to Briana's utter bewilderment,
the wolflike animal leaped forward, powerful muscles bunching
under a shaggy gray-black coat, and after some huge bounds,
launched itself at Rees, striking him at about the level of the
chest and knocking him flat. Briana's instantaneous reaction of
concern was overcome when the beast started to lick Rees's
face, wriggling and whining. She laughed at the sight of Rees
giving himself over to the ministrations of the animal. She
glanced at Ine and Ralf, Galen having fallen behind in Conway
town, where he wanted to buy some cloth to bring to Menty. She
found both men grinning boyishly at the spectacle of the
overlord of a good portion of Northern Wales rolling about on
the damp ground with an ecstatic mountain of fur.

Rees got the animal off him and rose, brushing at his tunic
and hose and laughing with the rest of them. "Briana, this is my
dog, Ulf," he said, more formally than seemed necessary. "Come
down here and let him get to know you."

The animal's size seemed intimidating, but Briana
unhesitatingly swung off Timbrel, who had stood her ground
despite being charged at by what might have been a ferocious
beast. Ulf regarded Briana with a singularly golden gaze.

Rees gestured Briana to come closer, and she walked to his
side. The "dog" barely had to raise his muzzle to sniff at her
face, his shiny black nose leather touching her chin in a cold,
wet caress.

Rees put one hand on the dog's head and with the other
stroked Briana's arm, sliding his fingers down to hers, bringing
them to the animal's cheek. He licked their joined hands,
wagged his great brush of a tail, and then trotted over to

Basilisk, touching his nose to the horse's muzzle.

"Is he a wolf?" Briana asked.

"A wolfhound," Rees answered, keeping hold of her hand. "Two years ago, in the winter, a lump of snow out by the causeway started howling. When the guards cleared the snow away, Ulf came out. He attached himself to me."

Briana felt her heart give a lurch. Wolfhounds had been part of Celtic nobility for a hundred years, though she had never seen one before. Ine had sung her—and taught her—a song of praise for the bravery of the wolfhound Gelert, owned by Prince Llewelyn's grandfather, and another, centuries old, of Finn's favorite hound, Conbec. She was awed by the fact that one of the gallant animals had given its loyalty to her husband.

Rees leaned closer to her and lowered his voice. "I should warn you that he's accustomed to sleeping with me."

She quickly measured the distance to the nearest people and said in a whisper, "Mayhap you should warn him that I am, as well."

He drew her a little closer, turned, and caught up the reins of the two horses. Ine and Ralf had also dismounted, though keeping a respectable distance from the dog. They all walked toward the picket.

Thomas Newby had a wide smile on his unprepossessing face. "Welcome home, my lord earl," he said. "We had no advance word of your coming, but of course your rooms are prepared." He glanced at Briana curiously, his gaze a quick one.

"Thomas, this is Lady Briana of Flint," Rees said, letting go of her hand. "We were handfasted at Windsor. Briana, I present you Sir Thomas Newby."

Newby's eyebrows rose in surprise, and it was a moment before he recovered his manners and bowed to her. "My lady, you are very welcome here at Conway."

"My thanks, Sir Thomas," Briana said. "I have heard good things of this fief, and I know you have a responsibility for that."

"We will speak the morrow even," Rees promised his

seneschal. "I will need your aid. Between now and then, gather all the intelligence you can on Flint and on Clwydd as a whole."

Newby nodded once and bowed again.

Briana turned with instinctive courtesy toward the old priest, but Rees's hand shot out, grasping her upper arm. "I will take you to our rooms now," he said, handing the two sets of reins to a boy who had darted up to the gate to meet them.

"My son," protested Father Michael, surprised at the gesture of disrespect.

Rees turned a face as cold as steel toward the dark-robed man as Ine and Ralf gave their reins to the boy and Ulf danced around the horses' legs.

Briana had never seen a look as filled with menace as the one Rees directed at Father Michael, not even on Edward at his worst. It chilled her.

"Father," said Rees, "you are from this moment discharged from my service. I detach you without prejudice unless you press me for reasons. I can spare no men to escort you from Gwynedd, but I will have you gone from Conway by nightfall. And go not to Clwydd, either." His voice rang with a metallic frost that left no doubts or alternatives.

The priest's mouth dropped open. "But—" he sputtered, "I have nowhere—"

Rees cut him off with a look which could have frozen blood. "I have never slain a priest," he said, each word dropping like a stone. "Do not give me cause to begin." Ine and Ralf exchanged one glance, then looked at Newby, who shrugged. Father Michael seemed to wilt a little, but knew better than to say anything else.

Still holding Briana's arm, Rees stalked through the picket under the curtain wall into the outer bailey of the castle. Ulf danced ahead of them toward the inner bailey, and once in the inner ward, trotted away to the right.

Briana realized that she feared this adamantine coldness in a man she had seen only as gentle. Rees discovered that he was striding, pulling Briana by the arm, and that she was running to keep up with him. He stopped abruptly as they entered the inner ward and muttered, "Sorry."

Though it frightened her a little, Briana asked, "What did the priest?"

Rees tried to gentle his voice, but the icy rage still came through. "He betrayed my confidence to an enemy," he said. "I have neither patience with, nor pity for, those who betray me."

She tried not to hear it as a warning, but it reverberated through her being and sank into her, stifling any kind of curiosity.

Ulf darted around their feet, impatient with their immobility, and disappeared into the ground-floor room of the tower that stood to the right of the inner bailey.

"Come," said Rees, but released his grip on her arm and led the way after the dog. He hoped his anger had not communicated itself through his hand, but feared that it had.

The ground-floor room of the tower was the private office with the fief account books in it, the office in which Rees had received—and long ignored—the charter granting him the title of earl. The office was walled with wooden pigeonholes, most of them holding rolled documents. The table on which writing was done was perfectly clear, attesting to Thomas Newby's efficiency. A curving stair led upward to the right, into the thick tower wall, and two narrowing slit windows looked toward the north over the moat.

"Follow me," Rees said and began to climb the steps. Ulf bounded past Briana and leaped up the stairs after his master.

Briana gathered a handful of skirt and climbed to the second floor, which held an exquisitely appointed private chapel. She glanced at it, seeing the gold candlesticks and the covered chalice as signs that this was indeed a rich fief. She realized Rees and the dog had climbed to the third level and continued up the steps.

The upper chamber was draped with tapestries. The

windows were slightly larger than those on the lower floors, and the room was dominated by a massive bed, curtains tied back. The bed now sported a wolfhound in its center. Chests stood at the foot of the bed and against the wall between the windows. There were no rushes on the floor; instead, a splendid carpet, obviously from the Holy Land, covered the stones.

Rees leaned negligently against one of the posts of the bed, his arms crossed, watching her as she climbed into the room. She stopped and let go of her skirts. "This is magnificent," she said sincerely. "We'll have naught like this to offer you in Flint."

His eyes darkened. "We'll be taking quite a lot of this with us," he said. "'Tis not the luxury that matters. 'Tis the show."

Having now, at last, seen his anger, Briana discovered that his size intimidated her, and she did not like that feeling. She made herself confront it. "Why have you always been so gentle with me?" she asked.

He grinned crookedly. "I recall not always being gentle. I get inside you and gentleness vanishes." He was surprised when she flushed, unused to her reacting with any kind of shame in private when it came to their coupling. His grin vanished. "What has changed?" he asked her seriously.

She bit her lip and looked down at the intricate pattern on the carpet. He waited for her to speak, and at last she realized he would go on waiting. She ventured, "We're in Wales, and I have—obligations here."

"Aye," he agreed at once, "first and most strongly, to your husband and liege lord."

She raised her chin, looking at him then, her eyes shooting sparks. "Are you in quest of a docile and obedient servant, my lord?"

He uncoiled like a rope pulled so taut that it snapped, took two steps, lifted her by the waist and tossed her onto the bed, causing Ulf to give a startled bark and leap out of the way. Before she could scramble upright, he had laid his weight across her body, pressing down at breasts and loins. "I seek not a docile wife," he whispered against her lips, "though obedience would not come amiss." He ground down on her mouth, as if the mention of Wales had triggered some suppressed violence in him. Her doubt and hesitation vanished instantly, swept away in the familiar timelessness of passion. He stripped her efficiently, then himself, drawing her up onto her knees and turning her so he could take her from behind, sheathing himself more easily into her softness now. She gave herself to it, not even aware that one of her hands was wrapped in Ulf's shaggy coat as she moved beneath Rees, answering his rhythm.

When she cried out, her head dropping onto the feather mattress, her hips still in his hands, he said with some satisfaction, "Wales or no Wales, this remains the same."

She felt him thrust several more times and freeze, and then he released her hips. She slid down flat onto her stomach, turning her head and sputtering as Ulf licked her nose.

Rees laughed once, splaying a hand across her buttocks and kneading lightly. It had been important to him to have her here in Conway, to confirm that no matter what happened elsewhere in the castle or elsewhere in the world, they could still meet naked and hungry for one another. It had been more than three weeks of daily lovemaking, and he so far sensed very little diminishing of the intoxication.

She lifted her heavy hair out of her eyes and turned to look over her shoulder at him. "Have you ever been this way with another woman?" she asked.

He shook his head.

"Then how did you learn—"

Her eyes, heavy-lidded even in her curiosity, stirred him again. He marvelled at it. "'Tis one thing to perform an act. 'Tis another to have it—" He chose the word with unexpected care. "—conquer you."

Her mouth made an "O" of surprise, and she rolled onto her side, then drew her legs under her and sat up. "Mean you that you think *I* have conquered *you*?"

Rees debated the ease or difficulty of discussing the obsession with her, the wisdom or foolishness of telling her that he had fallen into the trap of needing to bury himself inside her every time he could. "Our coupling has conquered me," he said at last, "as it has you."

There was no triumph in his voice, no threat. He was stating a fact, openly, expecting neither argument nor demurral. Briana thought with some real wonder that at times like this he seemed to be the most reasonable man she had ever known, that the control he exercised over her lust and his own in no way affected that reason. As if it were the most natural thing in the world, she opened her mouth to ask him about Fearndon, but just at that moment, Ulf's head came up and a ferocious growl started in his throat, teeth bared, his eyes flashing to the doorway.

Rees snatched a coverlet off the bed and wound it around his waist as Galen shouted up the stairs, "Rees, damn it, get off her 'til tonight. There's three messengers in the bailey, and Menty wants to give greeting."

Rees, grinning, said, "Ulf, guard." Briana gasped as the dog leaped over her, heading for the door and barking. Rees dropped the coverlet and pulled on his hose. "Get dressed, Briana. Three messengers is of some interest."

Flint—March 1289 A.D.

Sabine put one more set of branches on the fire in the hermitage and sat down in the oversized chair that she had had brought in from Chester. Its arrival had been quite an occasion in the village, because the actual purchase of something from Chester that was not earmarked for the castle was highly unusual.

The extra warmth from the fire was welcome. The nights were still cold and would probably remain so until the early summer. Easter had come early this year. Sabine had finished washing the wood trencher from which they had eaten their supper of cheese and bread, and two cups of wine still stood on the table. The new chair crowded the room a bit, but the two women did not mind. It was wonderful to have the large chair, as if it stood for their success at this much independence.

In her own, much smaller chair, using the firelight to see by since they had lighted no candles, Beatrice stitched unerringly on a border of flowers, herbs, and a Celtic pattern. "Think you that John de Bretagne still lives?" she asked conversationally. "I oft wonder if he has found any happiness. He certainly had none as my husband."

Sabine picked up one of the cups and sipped some wine. "You gave him Arthur," she said reasonably. "That, and the trade concessions from your brother, were his gain in the bargain. He should be satisfied."

"You are charitable," said the princess. "After I birthed his son, I believe he would rather have killed me than lived with me."

Sabine stared into the flames. "He openly desired it," she said softly. "He was such a fool to gamble that your brother would believe you dead."

Beatrice laughed, a light, tinkling sound. "But my brother *does* believe me dead," she said, "and a relief to him 'tis, I'm certain. I was always an embarrassment."

"But your son is not."

Beatrice bent closer to the stitching. "I thank God and St. Candida every day that I could see Rees and not hate him. Now I wonder if he will hate me for deceiving him."

Sabine said evenly, "There is little doubt he'll be exceeding angry at you for waiting so long to tell him the truth."

"I know it well," Beatrice whispered. "'Tis one of the things I depend on you to aid me with in any way you are able."

Sabine nodded, putting her cup back on the table. "I'd stand by you no matter what comes, but it may be that you will need more than me."

"I know that well, too." Beatrice smiled, the firelight

blurring the lines on her face to something of the beauty she had had in her youth. "If not for you and the queen—"

"Think not on that time," Sabine said firmly. "You will soon be past it all, and whether de Bretagne is well or not or happy or not is of no import at all."

"I wonder," said Beatrice thoughtfully, "what my son's wife is like."

"To hear talk of her in the village, she is a beautiful woman who is being forced to bend to a brutal conqueror."

Beatrice made a face. "Rees could not be brutal. I know that."

Sabine studied her carefully. "Suppose he has grown to become more like the man who fathered him."

"Never!" Beatrice's hiss was the closest she had come to losing her composure. "Bjorn Magnussen, may he burn eternally in the lowest part of hell, has given nothing to my son except the seed which sparked him. Of all the things I know, I know that best."

"I pray it may be so," said Sabine. "We shall know the truth ere long." She got to her feet, bent to the woodpile, and added a few more pieces of wood to the fire. "And then will you inform your brother that you live?"

Beatrice tunnelled her needle through the embroidery. "I have decided not," she said. "I will have need to think on it longer."

Sabine returned her large body to the chair, glancing at the window as the church bell began to ring, calling people to evensong. "Father Ciaran said this morn that he believes a storm is brewing. I cannot believe he means to speak of something unseen in the western sky. I believe he means the arrival of the overlord instead."

Beatrice rethreaded her needle with the second shade of green she needed for a floppy leaf. "I have ever lived between storms," she said quietly. "Some are worse than we thought, and some are better. 'Tis rare that we find a gentle harbor such as this one, and so very welcome."

"My lady," said Sabine, "Plantagenets were not made for gentle harbors."

Chapter 24

Conway—March 1289 A.D.

Briana followed Rees out of the northwest tower into the inner bailey. A group of people was gathered near the gateway from the outer bailey, and Thomas Newby was ordering torches lighted against the increasing darkness. Ralf was just emerging from the southwest hall that served as a dorter for the unwed knights, of whom there were presently about twenty in residence. Galen was standing with a small, brown-haired woman near the barbican. And the three messengers—of widely varying status—stood in the center of a ragged circle of other knights. It was clear that they were being guarded, but loosely.

One of the messengers wore the livery of the Plantagenets, a grand russet fustian tunic that spoke boldly of wealth and power. The second was a white-robed Cistercian monk of indeterminate age, tonsure freshly shaved, hands folded in his sleeves, and the third was a ragged youth with a grimy piece of paper clutched in his hand, as solemn as if he had been given a commission from God and was afraid to put the paper in his jerkin or his split-seamed scrip for fear he would lose it or forget it.

Rees looked over the three of them, then smiled at the boy,

who was probably about twelve, or perhaps a small thirteen, and asked, "What is your name, lad?"

The Plantagenet messenger looked deeply offended; the monk, highly amused. The knights knew their liege lord well and had clearly expected something of the sort.

From the corner of his eye, Rees noticed the angry, haughty flush on the face of the man wearing the livery and turned to him directly as he began to open his mouth. Rees cut him off before he could speak by asking, "Have you aught to say to me?"

The court messenger stuttered for one moment at the direct challenge, then recollected himself and said indignantly, "My commission is from the king!"

"All the more reason you can wait," Rees said coldly before the man could offer his name or his message. The sudden threat in the cool eyes, and the hand Rees casually dropped to his sword left the man in no doubt that Rees was royal as well as noble. The messenger's mouth shut with an audible click.

Rees looked back at the boy, who realized with a start that the conversation had come around to him again. He gulped and said, "Edwin, milord."

All the frost went out of Rees as he smiled. "Have you a message for me?"

Edwin's hand tightened on the paper. He looked around at all the people standing in the bailey, gathered his courage, and blurted, "If it please you, I will wait for the end."

Galen howled with laughter. Menty, who had been watching Briana with interest, nudged him sharply with her elbow.

Newby had finished getting the torches lighted and placed in sconces around the bailey, and now he returned to the group around the messengers. At the same moment, Ine came into the bailey from the guest accommodations in the outer ward, his harp in its satchel slung across his back.

Rees laughed softly, not unkindly, at the boy and clapped him on the shoulder as he turned to the Cistercian. "Brother?"

"Father Paul, from St. David's, Anglesey," said the monk calmly. "Lately I have served as chaplain to Flint castle."

Briana's head came up so suddenly that the abrupt gesture drew every eye in the bailey to her. Father Paul remained carefully expressionless.

Rees casually reached out and took hold of Briana's arm, asking the monk, "Did Mortimer send you?"

"Nay," said the monk evenly. "In truth, he would probably be displeased at word of my presence here."

Rees raised one eyebrow, intrigued and somewhat bemused. "Then perhaps you would care to tell me why you've come."

Father Paul shifted his arms in his sleeves, reaching for something, which he began to draw out.

Briana was stunned as Ralf's sword cleared its scabbard, instantly pointed at the monk's throat. Rees had not moved, but a muscle jumped in his cheek, and his hand on her arm tightened unbearably for a split second.

His calm unshaken, the monk said, "'Tis a paper, my lord earl, neither sharp nor edged."

Rees studied him for a moment, then nodded almost imperceptibly to Ralf. The sword vanished.

Briana was breathing harder. Violence was so close to the surface here, and Rees was absolutely accustomed to it. She had been able to forget that on the journey to Wales, bathed as it was in the misty haze of sensuality that surrounded her.

Now, it would be unforgettable.

Father Paul removed the paper from his sleeve. "Baron Wigmore has not held suzerainty with the same care you and your seneschal have shown Conway. Flint groans beneath him and of course can do nothing."

Rees's expression went so hard that Briana took an involuntary step backward. He released her arm, but did not even glance at her. "Mortimer would undoubtedly be touched by your loyalty," he said, the words dripping irony.

The monk's placid face did not change. "I have left his service. I should not have come here otherwise. If you are to help them, you should know what you will face when you arrive," he said. "I know not what he will tell you when you get there. I thought the true figures might help you to be—" He paused. "—enough of a savior to erase the entanglements of the name you bear."

Rees gestured once, and Thomas Newby took the paper from the monk, carrying it to the light from the nearest torch to scan it quickly. Rees glanced briefly at his seneschal, then looked back at the monk. "What gain you from bringing this to me?"

"For myself, nothing," Father Paul answered. "I am going back to Anglesey. For the people of Flint, I hope to gain peace and a measure of prosperity."

"I rarely credit men with unselfish motives," Rees said coolly.

Briana found herself staring at him as if she hardly knew him, realizing with a start that, in almost every way, she did not. She was growing to know his body, but his mind was still a complete mystery to her. Why did he think and react in the ways he did? Why was he so different from other men of violence with her and with Ine, and yet so like them with such ease at times like this?

Newby came back to Rees. "I can find someone to confirm the figures," he said. Rees silently asked him a question. Newby answered, "Grim."

Rees swore under his breath.

Father Paul said, "My motives are not entirely unselfish, my lord, if 'twill please you more. My grudge goes back to the war and is, I assure you, most unmonastic." He sighed a little and buried his hands in his sleeves again. "My first year in the religious life, I was hopeful that he might atone, but he has not, and I am not an idealist any longer."

Rees gauged the flat honesty in his voice and relaxed.

Father Paul then turned deliberately to Briana, watching the interchange silently, her heart still beating faster than it normally did. She was unused to this kind of intrigue, had been cushioned from it at court by her status as a nominal member of the royal family. She knew she would have to find her footing soon. Then she realized the monk was bowing to her. "Lady Briana, you are most welcome home," he said. "You will be a great reward to your people at Flint."

She felt as if he had accused her of something, but she held her face carefully neutral as she nodded to him in return, unable to speak.

The king's messenger snorted and shifted impatiently from foot to foot.

Rees turned to him with a suddenness that made the man snap to attention. "Very well," said Earl Connarc, "what message do you bear me from my loving uncle, the king?"

Recognized at last, the court messenger vacillated between outrage at the delay and the self-importance of his role in delivering a message from Plantagenet to Plantagenet. "I am commanded to say the following," he said stiffly. "We have received word that you have delayed your arrival at Flint by slowing your journey and by plans for a stay at Conway. We do not wish this. We need Wigmore at Harlech, and he must needs give you formal possession. I command you to make all haste to your newly granted fief, appointing a constable for stewardship of Conway in your absence. We await your precipitate reply."

Rees turned his head without taking his eyes off the messenger, and said, "Thomas."

"Aye, my lord?" The seneschal thrust the monk's paper into his scrip.

"You are hereby appointed constable of Conway." Rees's voice was very serious, but he was unable to keep the wickedness out of his expression.

"My thanks, my lord." Thomas Newby sounded appropriately honored, but Briana recognized that it was a complete sham. He and his liege lord were currently performing for the king's messenger, just as she had always performed for the household of the king at Windsor or Westminster. The difference, she reflected distractedly, was that she had been sincere about her falseness, whereas it was clear that Rees and Thomas Newby were steeped in irony about theirs.

Indeed, Rees smiled at the messenger with an artificiality that even the growing darkness could not fully disguise. "Here is my 'precipitate' reply to King Edward: As your obedient retainer and subject, I move with all possible haste to comply with your express command." He said no more.

"Is—is that the whole of it?" the messenger asked.

Rees nodded.

The messenger glanced around as if waiting for somebody else to contribute something. Ultimately, Thomas Newby did, stepping forward and saying, "'Tis past dark, and our hospitality is lacking. Sir Gregory will show you and the good father to guest accommodations and see to your comforts." He gestured to the group of knights.

One of the knights detached himself from the group, bowed shortly to the two men, and waved toward the outer bailey. There were a great many guest quarters at Conway. Ine had been installed in the one for most honored guests, and Thomas Newby would arrange for the others to be sheltered in an adequate but less commodious chamber. Father Paul moved after the designated knight at once, and after a delay during which he returned to bouncing from foot to foot in hesitation, the king's messenger had no real choice but to follow as well.

Rees watched him go, eyes slitted and glittering. When all three men had left the inner bailey, Rees turned back to Newby. "What kind of haste is all possible, think you, Thomas?"

"I believe your original estimate was five days, my lord. That seems quite accurate."

"So I thought," said Rees, the hardness fading from his features. He looked over at the ragged boy. "Now, Edwin," he said, "you are the last. What message have you for me?"

"None, milord," the boy said hastily, his thin throat bobbing in and out. He extended the grimy paper in Briana's direction. "My message is for the Lady of Flint."

Briana hesitated, wondering if she should defer to Rees, if he would expect her to let him see the message first. She was accustomed to having every bit of her correspondence screened, and she did not know if the process was to continue.

Rees said gently to Edwin, "Then give it to her, lad." The boy complied eagerly.

Briana took the dirty, wrinkled paper and unfolded it as she walked to the nearest torch. The scrawl was untutored and hasty, but readable. "Know you sojourn at Conway. Will await you at Flint. Owen." She felt ice run along her spine. Owen Glyn knew she was in North Wales and was coming to Flint. What would he think of her? What could she say to him?

Without pausing to contemplate her action, she thrust the paper into the flame of the torch and let it flare up, dropping it to the ground just as it might have burned her fingers.

Rees's jaw tightened, suspicion rising, not of her, but about the contents of the message. And then he realized that the boy, Edwin, had turned and darted out of the inner bailey. His instinct was to send some of his knights after the boy, but before he could even give the order, Ralf had disappeared.

Briana stamped on the last ember of the charred sheet and looked up at Rees, comprehending that her impulsive action might appear very questionable, but she could read nothing on his face in the darkness.

Nor did he ask her about it immediately. Instead, he called to Galen and Menty, presenting his knight's wife to his own.

The two women sized each other up in the torchlight. Menty saw an incredibly beautiful woman a little smaller than herself and almost too thin, but with full breasts and swelling hips, clearly of a level of Celtic nobility. Briana saw a wide-hipped Saxon woman, her long brown braids framing fairly pretty, even features, her complexion marvelously clear and touched with rose, her eyes bright.

"I am most pleased to make your acquaintance, Lady Briana," Menty said formally. "I have oft wished Rees good fortune in marriage, and Galen tells me he has indeed found it."

Briana let that statement pass, and said, "I hope you are not troubled overmuch by the need to uproot yourself and your family for the move to Flint."

"We go where goes Galen, and he goes where goes Rees," Menty said. "It has never proved to be a problem."

"Now that the messengers have gone," Rees said, "let's into the hall. I believe Thomas has arranged for our supper."

As they began moving toward the great hall, which was more than a hundred feet long and angled to follow the layout of Conway's walls, Ralf came back into the bailey and caught up with them. "He's gone," he said. "The boy could run, and he seems to know the area well." He glanced at Briana, but she was climbing the steps to the hall and did not show him anything more than her back.

Briana was conscious that her action had made everyone curious, and she was imagining the speculative scrutiny of the other people, especially of Rees, but in truth the only person really studying her was Ine. Once they reached the hall, where only the three tables closest to the high table itself were set with bread, salt, and tankards, the bard took his harp from its satchel, playing soft chords of no discernible melody.

Briana made light conversation with Menty, cautious, but glad of the company of another woman after so many days only of men. She asked Menty about her children, about the difficulty of moving from place to place when one actually had possessions to move, about how Menty spent her time.

Menty, it turned out, was a weaver. She wove linen and both rough and fine wools, and much of the clothing she and her family wore had originally come from her hands. "I have a bolt of pale green wool which would make you a lovely gown," she said to Briana. "I hope you will honor me by accepting it as a late wedding gift."

Briana flushed a little, but kept her head up, chin thrust out. "There has as yet been no wedding," she said firmly. "Rees and I are handfasted only."

Menty frowned and shot a look at Galen, who had obviously not told her, then looked indignantly at Rees. "Why have you not married her before God, Rees?" she demanded in tones more suited to admonishing a small boy than to addressing her husband's liege.

Briana wondered at the easy relationship among them all as she waited for Rees's reply.

"'Tis not to insult her in any way, Menty," Earl Connarc said easily. "'Twas thought that a marriage on the steps of the church in Flint might help the people there feel more a part of their own destiny."

"That sounds not at all like the king," Menty said frankly. "What wants he from them?"

"Fealty." Rees suddenly sounded very weary. "He will have it, or he will have them put to the sword."

Briana found herself staring at her hands. She twisted them against her skirt and tried to concentrate on them instead of what Rees had just said. If any of the others noticed her agitation, they were kind enough not to mention it. Ulf barked once as some of the castle servingmen began bringing in the ale and the supper.

She excused herself early, pleading weariness from the journey, went up to the chamber in the northwest tower, where a tub filled with hot water had been placed, and tried to relax. Briana was nervous. She still was not certain how to explain her burning the message before all of the watchers, for at the time it seemed only that she had to blot out the words. Owen Glyn was the most notorious rebel remaining in Wales, and he was willing to endanger himself for her. It was true danger; any knight vowed to the King of England would kill him if he could, even Rees. *No*, she corrected herself, *especially Rees*. She belonged to him now, but she had been promised to Owen, who undoubtedly remembered it.

She stripped out of her gown and undertunic, pulled off her shoes and let her hair out of the caul. For the entire journey since leaving Windsor, she had done this, usually with Rees's participation, without Enlis. She had not thought to miss the girl's presence or capable hands assisting her, and it had not seemed unusual to dress and undress without her maid. Yet here, in a castle again, surrounded by comforts, with her first hot bath in two weeks only moments away, she wished Enlis were there.

She stepped into the still-steaming water, gasping a little. Five days until they would leave Conway. Thirteen days until they would arrive in Flint. Six days in which it might still be possible to be utterly happy with Rees.

She gathered the washrag and cake of soap, which smelled of lavender, and began to wash, trying to picture what Owen might look like now. He would be a man full-grown, different from the young man who had kissed her good-bye before he went off to war. She had always thought that kiss had meaning, but now she realized it had been like being kissed by her brothers, that, though she loved Owen, it was a love of innocence, of childhood and family. It had nothing to do with passion.

Her lathered hands slid over her arms and her breasts, her stomach, her dark triangle of curls, her thighs. She could not keep thinking about Owen; her thoughts had to return to Rees. She had never been aware that bathing could be so sensual an experience, but then she had not been aware of sensuality at all until a blond giant had levered his shoulders out of the couvert in the corner of the queen's rooms and taken her face in his hand.

"Briana."

She froze, then looked across at the door, where Rees leaned his shoulder on the jamb. Ulf walked in around him and leaped up onto the bed, settling down quite comfortably. Rees's eyes were cloudy blue in the candlelight, but she saw no desire in them, and she had become very adept at reading his desire.

"What said the message?"

She had known the question was coming, had debated with herself how to answer it. She had not made any decisions, but now, confronted with the need to reply, she came as close to telling the truth as she could without actually telling it. "Before I was taken from Flint, I was betrothed by my father to a young man of Powys, the man I told you of before. He suffered much in the war, serving—" It was not easy for her to say the name, but she managed it with only a minuscule pause. "—Prince Llewelyn, but he lived. He sent me greetings and a welcome back to Wales."

His voice went even quieter, and he did not change his position, his arms crossed over his chest. "Why did you burn it?"

She stood up in the tub, the water sluicing off her body, the droplets sparkling in the curls at the apex of her thighs. "I belong to you now," she said, "and I have sworn you fealty. I had no wish to keep a memento of a match that could never be."

Her body shone, sleekly wet in the candlelight, and her answers sounded so very reasonable. His groin tightened before he realized it would, and even though he knew his arousal would lessen his ability to think clearly, he let it come over him.

She understood his feelings and reached for a towel, hiding a smile. Six days. She wanted to enjoy every moment of them.

The battlements at Conway were long, and a circuit of the walls could be made without ever having to descend to either of the baileys. Ine made one circuit, carrying his harp, until he reached the section of the curtain wall that overlooked the estuary. Despite the darkness of the night, the high clouds were moving quickly, and stray shafts of light from the waning moon broke through and turned the surface of the water a mottled silver before the clouds cut it off again.

Ine chose one of the merlons and sat in it, watching the intermittent silvering of the moving water and playing a melody on the strings. The notes drifted out over the estuary and vanished into the darkness.

He had been playing for about five minutes when he looked up and saw Ralf standing nearby, leaning against a crenellation and listening. Ine softened his volume.

Ralf said, "You mind not my overhearing?"

"Of course not," Ine replied. "A musician never disdains an audience." He played softly for a time longer, waiting, confident that Ralf wanted to say something and content to wait until he was comfortable enough to produce it.

At last Ralf said, "When first we came to Conway, at the end of the Welsh war, Rees would come up here with his recorder and play in the dark, just as you are."

"But he does not play for an audience," Ine said. "He plays for himself, which is the purest kind of music."

"I think," Ralf said slowly, "that he has to play for himself, because he fights for someone else."

Ine let his instincts guide him. "He seems an honest man," he said.

"He is the most honorable man I have known," said Ralf, "and I have been with him for fifteen years, since first he came to England and the court of his uncle."

Ine went on playing softly. "Were you with him at Orwein Bridge, when Prince Llewelyn fell?"

Ralf said simply, "We were none of us at Orwein Bridge."

Ine weighed the tenor of the other man's voice, felt that the knight would not balk or take offense at more questions, and asked, "Mean you that he went there without you?"

"We were *none* of us at Orwein Bridge," Ralf repeated. "None of us." He paused. Ine did not speak. Ralf's face was unreadable, since the clouds had covered the moon. At last, Ralf went on, "I know what is generally spoke of. Yet we had no knowledge of the death of Llewelyn until it became widely known."

Then Ine asked, "Why has the earl not denied the rumors,

then?"

Ralf sighed. "Galen and I know not, and there are many things we cannot ask. But I have seen him speak with you, and—"

"And bards dare much," Ine finished for him. "Aye, I see."

A stray beam of moonlight illuminated the knight's face for a moment, and Ine could see that he had smiled. Ralf nodded at him, and then turned and walked toward one of the towers.

Ine wondered if anyone trusted other bards with as many confidences as this group of people entrusted to him. He had always expected it of Briana. The inexplicable bond between them had existed since the day of her birth. The openness Rees showed had come as a surprise to him. Now the slowly expanding bubble seemed to have engulfed Ralf as well. Ine was as bemused as he was bewildered, but he accepted the truth when he recognized it. He continued playing a while longer, then went to find a staircase down to the baileys.

Chapter 25

The builders had chosen a strong position for Flint castle, though it was small compared with most of the others King Edward had built in Wales. It stood at the spot where the huge Dee estuary narrowed into the river, which flowed east and south, touching briefly at Chester, before winding back across the border into Wales. The long, flat sands of the western shore of the estuary were almost half a mile wide, leading to the restless waters and across them, to the huge peninsula between the Dee and the smaller estuary to the east, the Mersey. Seabirds wheeled overhead, their mournful cries echoing in the still air of springtime.

Briana urged Timbrel into a canter as the party cleared the last of the hills and entered the vast, dales-like valley that contained most of Flint, and certainly all of the fief's human habitations. The road led down past woodland and hedgerows, along the fields to the church, then beyond it to the village and the manor house. It was from this spot at the top of the last hill that Ine had first seen Flint, twenty years earlier. Then the land had been sleek with a prosperity that came with peace. Now—

Briana had not realized she had cried out at the sight of

home, but the sound drew Rees's eyes to her at once. Ralf, Galen, and Ine followed his gaze, and when she urged her mount forward, the knights started after her, but Rees called them back.

"Let her go," he said, waving them again into the long line of travelers and supplies. "She'll come to no harm here."

The moment Ine heard him say that, his head swivelled and he regarded Rees closely. Ine knew beyond doubt, without knowing how he knew, that Rees was wrong. It was not, the bard thought, that Briana might find harm here so much as that she carried the harm within her, and that Flint might be the trigger which would bring it out of her. Ine had not seen the figures the Cistercian monk gave to Thomas Newby, but even his nonjudgmental eye could see that Flint was not doing well. There were few cattle or sheep in the fields, and though some small areas had been plowed, the amount of land under cultivation was barely sufficient to sustain a household, let alone a village. But the caravan Rees and his knights were bringing was a very long one. The line of travelers, wagons, and livestock stretched behind them for more than two miles. Thomas Newby had been thorough. In addition to twenty-seven of Rees's knights, some with families, and their belongings, he had provided two hundred sheep, twelve dozen pigs, nearly three hundred chickens and geese, along with clutches of fertilized eggs, fifteen hives, and three wagonloads of seed. He was still buying cattle when they left for Flint, and the herd would be sent on later.

One sweep of the valley with his eyes told Rees they would need every bit of it, as well as the wagonloads of provender and supplies that followed. The few animals he saw were too thin and moved with the slowness of creatures conserving their strength. The plowed land was far too meager. The houses were in need of repair. The mill was not working.

Rees felt a hot wash of rage against Edmund Mortimer. This was not stewardship; it was uncaring subjugation. No wonder there was still rebellion.

Briana, too, had seen the poverty, even worse than she had feared, but she wanted to be home so much that she tried to put it from her, urging the palfrey from canter to gallop, her hood flying back and her hair springing loose from her barbette. As she crossed the wide bowl of the valley, she heard the church bell begin to ring, and soon from the village buildings came the remaining people of Flint, lining the road between the church and the cluster of small buildings, awaiting the return of their lady.

A tall, black-gowned man with a shock of white hair emerged from the churchyard, and Briana's breath caught in her throat. She drew Timbrel to a halt about ten feet from where the thin priest was standing and leaped to the ground, running into his outstretched arms. "Father Ciaran!"

She hugged him so fiercely that she could feel his ribs through the layers of cloth as he murmured, "My child, my child," in her ear. "Why, you've grown to a full woman now, and so beautiful." He smiled down at her. "You've your mother's eyes."

"I've come home," she said unnecessarily.

"Aye, we can see that." Father Ciaran laughed. "You have been much missed. And you look to be happy."

"At being here," she said.

"And with your fate, I warrant," said the priest, nodding in the direction of the rest of the party.

She wanted to shake her head, but said, "I have been given to Connarc."

"We have heard 'tis Connarc," said Father Ciaran. "We have heard he was kind to Conway. And if you love him, child, we will try to do the same, for your sake, if not for our own."

"Love!" The word hissed out of her with such venom that the priest was shocked. "Love! Oh, is that what they think of me? Is that what they are saying of me? God!" She tore free of his hands, stumbling once on her gown, and threw herself back in the direction of the motionless palfrey. Her whirling thoughts seemed to coalesce around a conviction that if the people here believed she loved the butcher baron, then they would hate her, and their acceptance, their respect, was what she had lived for for seven years.

Just as she reached Timbrel, she struck her foot against a stone and fell to the ground by the palfrey's feet. The pain had instantly brought tears to her eyes, and she caught her breath, wrenched into almost ungovernable emotion.

A shadow moved at the churchyard gate as Sabine stood, sheltered by the wall, watching.

In the column, Ine had seen Briana flee from the priest and fall before the palfrey. Rees had been studying the meager fields and the people gathering at the roadside. Ine called his name, and when Rees looked at him, the bard nodded in the direction of the church.

Rees's gaze snapped back in the direction Briana had gone, and for a moment, he could not find her. Then he saw her cloak at Timbrel's feet. He thought she had been hurt, had fallen off the horse, perhaps had even been trampled. He spoke to Basilisk, who leaped ahead of the others and thundered toward the crumpled figure on the ground, Ulf racing alongside him.

The people of the village had seen Briana fall to the ground, but before they could start in her direction, the wolfhound and the giant on the destrier were pounding up the road toward them, and they stopped where they stood.

Basilisk stiffened his legs and halted before he could spook the palfrey, and Ulf went on guard between Briana and the crowd of people nearby, further discouraging their approach. Rees jumped down and scooped her up, his face openly showing his fear for her.

She felt his hands lift her, and she knew his touch instantly. His hands burned her as her body responded of its own accord to him. Always before she had interpreted that burning as passion. Now she read her response to it as shameful.

"Briana, are you hurt?"

She heard the concern, saw the tenderness in his eyes, and it carved into her. Father Ciaran had come up behind the huge warrior and, as her eyes cleared, she saw the anxiety and bewilderment on his fine features. At this very moment, she found she could not abide kindness. She had seen the penury of Flint, and now she could not avoid the thought that they had suffered so much and would doubtless believe she had been, and would continue to be, happy at their expense.

"Let me go!" She pushed back at Rees, rejecting his compassion in her sudden, self-imposed unworthiness. When he did not release her, she doubled a fist and swung at him, missing as he jerked back with incredible speed, his hands tightening instinctively on her. She continued to struggle until he shook her once, very hard, and she stilled abruptly.

She had never fought him before, not even at the beginning when she had first learned his identity, and for her to do so now—for what reasons he could not fathom and did not have time to try and discern—at their first appearance in Flint, was worse than ill-timed and ill-advised, it was reckless. He needed the loyalty of these people, for their sake as well as his own.

"Get up," he said harshly, his concern that she had been harmed in some physical way vanishing in his recognition that this had to be some kind of performance, some kind of show put on for the people here. He felt betrayed by the histrionics, whose purpose he could not guess. He could comprehend this in no other way than as a deliberate choice to embarrass him at the most critical possible moment. He would not have believed it of her, but he had no time to investigate, and therefore could believe little else as he pulled her to her feet.

She gasped at the casual strength that lifted her upright.

"You and I will walk to the manor," he said tightly, "and I expect you to smile." He gathered the reins of the two horses, took her upper arm in one hand, and turned her to face the crowd.

Sabine moved back into the churchyard, quietly enough so

that no one in the long line of people noticed her. She was frowning a little at the interchange she had heard, but she would not openly seek to find out what was transpiring.

Briana scrubbed at her eyes with her free hand to clear the unshed tears out of them, as stunned at his behavior as he was at hers. She watched when Rees greeted Father Ciaran as if the scene on the road had not just taken place, aware that the priest was looking at her with some apprehension.

The people of Flint village dropped back to the edges of the road again.

The spare Irishman turned his attention to the new overlord of Flint. "On behalf of the church of St. Maedoc's, my lord, I welcome you," he said, hoping he sounded sincere. It would have been important to him to please a new overlord even had the man not been bringing Briana with him. They had not been pleasant to Mortimer, and they had paid the price for that.

The front edge of the column had pushed forward, Ralf, Galen, and Ine accelerating enough to leave the rest of the travelers behind. Ine was especially concerned about what would seem to others an attack of madness, but which he recognized as something he had feared for many days now.

Briana saw that Rees needed something from her here, and she had never been angry at him, only at his feelings for her. She wanted to do her best for him, even though all her people thought she had betrayed them. She stiffened her spine and raised her chin. Perhaps this was to be her punishment for daring to try to be happy with the man responsible for Fearndon and the deaths of her father and brothers, for forgetting that she was supposed to hate him. She looked up at her handfast husband, being so gracious to the priest, and comprehended that she could not possibly hate him, no matter what he had done.

"We have brought you a chalice and paten from the stock of ecclesiastical plate at Canterbury," Rees was saying smoothly as she forced herself to pay attention. "I mean not to supplant your own offerings, of course, but merely to add to them."

"I am most grateful, my lord," Father Ciaran said, and now there could be no doubt of the sincerity behind the words. "We have been using earthenware since —" He was unwilling to say openly that the previous castellan had taken more than he had given.

Rees nodded, understanding what had been unspoken, and said softly, "Father Ciaran, I ask you to believe that I want naught but good for this fief. Tell the others, if you will be so kind."

Father Ciaran agreed readily.

"And," Rees added, "we shall want a wedding here on the steps of the church in one week's time, should that prove to be convenient for you."

The priest looked at Briana, but she had turned her head aside and seemed not to be paying attention. "'Twould honor the church," he said.

"As 'twould us," said Rees, meaning it.

Briana's eyes had strayed to the churchyard, lingering on the window of the hermitage. There was no veil on it, but she had not seen it before to know that the veil was absent. Despite the dimness of the interior of the building, she sensed a presence there. Then her gaze drifted to the low-walled side of the churchyard, where her mother lay buried, and early hollyhocks crawled up the soft gray stone of the church wall near the spot. A simple headstone marked the grave itself; the flowers she used to sit among were in bud. Then she froze, making an involuntary noise that drew the attention of the two men.

There were four stones now. Her mother's, closest to the church, and three more. She had not expected to see them, had never anticipated this moment. Father Ciaran followed her gaze and said quickly, "They are only monuments, Lady Briana. We did not receive the—remains—back from the—battlefield." His glance strayed uneasily to Rees, who still held Briana firmly by the arm.

The earl did not notice the priest's uneasiness. He had seen what Briana was looking at, and he guessed what the graves meant. Now he was looking at Briana with compassion again, his earlier anger put aside. And as Ine and his two knights drew up to them, Rees murmured, "I know 'twill not be easy, sweetness. I need you to stand by me now." His appeal to her was more natural than his anger had been. Whatever had happened on the road when she lost control, he was willing to attribute to nervousness at her homecoming. He did not want to fight with her; there were too many other things to think about, too much else that had to be accomplished.

She looked up at him, dry-eyed. "I shall do my duty to you, my lord," she said as strongly as she could, startling him, because she had called him only "Rees" between the morning after their handfasting and the arrival at Flint.

Rees and Ine exchanged a glance as the bard and the two knights dismounted. The five of them, led by Ulf, who could not bear to follow even if he did not know the destination, began to walk slowly toward the files of villagefolk, which had grown larger as they played out their drama on the road in front of the church.

The people of Flint waited, eager to see Briana, nervous at the idea of Connarc—and for one other fear. Baron Wigmore was at the manor, waiting for the party to arrive, and everyone in Flint, acutely sensitive to whatever Mortimer did, was aware of it.

As Briana and the newcomers reached the first of the villagers, men began pulling off their brimmed farm hats, the kind farmers had worn since the Romans conquered Britain years earlier. The men did not quite know whether to bow or the women to curtsy, but then the first woman in line asked, "Do you remember me, Lady Briana? Dechire?"

Briana recalled the slender kitchenmaid eight years older than herself. "Aye," she said. "You used to sneak me extra porridge or bread when I was sent to bed without my supper."

Dechire grinned a little shyly. "You were too thin as a

child," she said, "and so often disobedient that you spent many nights without supper." It was a boldly familiar remark, but it made Briana smile.

You are too thin now, Briana thought, *and my guess is it comes not from disobedience.*

Dechire had set a pattern. As the incoming party walked through the knot of villagers to the village proper, the people of Flint gave their names to their lady, recalled some incident from the past if they remembered any, and fell into step behind the knights and the bard, glancing back over their shoulders with wide eyes at the length of the column behind them. They were very hopeful. They had, on market days at Rhuddlan, heard rumors of the prosperity of Conway, and they knew it to be a condition which originated when Connarc arrived, and had only increased since then.

Briana nodded and greeted people as they reminded her of their names, accepting that, unaccountably to her, they were pleased to see her. None of them spoke to Rees or his knights, though they were observed with a curiosity that seemed unhindered by outright hostility. Ine received frequent greetings.

The group passed slowly through the village and made its way along the road beyond it to the manor.

Maud had been alerted to the approach of the column and waited, tense, on the steps inside the front courtyard, the few remaining household retainers in a knot behind her. At ease in the yard, but concealed by the single high section of manor wall, built on the seaward side to provide a windbreak against the occasional storms that swept in from the estuary, were Edmund Mortimer and five of his knights, their swords and mail gleaming in the sunlight. Baron Wigmore, having received no formal message from Rees announcing his arrival, had concluded that Earl Connarc was unlikely to call at the castle until he was ready to take formal possession. And that did not suit Wigmore. Therefore, curious to see the legendary beauty of the Lady Briana, he had decided to tender a welcome of his own, and had come to the manor to do it. He glanced at Maud several times as the newcomers drew closer, noting her tension with pleasure. He enjoyed the fact that Maud feared him and could not conceal it. He found her entirely unattractive, being too hard, too thin, and too worn for his tastes, but that had not kept him from menacing her.

He was not her liege lord. Flint had not been required to swear fealty to its castellan as they would be to their overlord. Yet, he could have compelled her to his bed; he had sent his wife to Swansea when he knew he would be moving to Harlech. Having both his wife and mistress in other parts of Wales had left him restive, and he had taken one of the village women who served the castle.

Maud was thankful that Med had been the one to cross his path then, for Med had always been a bit of a loose-leg, and the few coins he gave her had helped them all.

Mortimer had watched the progress through the village with a growing sense of irritation. Rees had not ridden in with a show of force, establishing his rule as a conqueror, but was coming on foot, a pace behind his extremely lovely lady, who seemed uneasy but who was trying to be gracious to all the villagefolk. Baron Wigmore saw it as a sign of weakness, but was at the moment not so much of a fool as to mention that to Earl Connarc.

Rees sensed something as they neared the manor itself, and it had little to do with the fact that he could feel, through his hand on her arm, that Briana's entire body was shaking, infinitesimally, as if a deep-seated shuddering were being held under rigid control. When they crossed the open space between the end of the village houses and the gate of the manor, the trembling increased so much that it threatened to pull her free of his grasp.

He silently cursed himself. He had disregarded Ine's warnings because he had been certain that bringing her home to Flint, the thing she had seemed to want so much before the handfasting that she had agreed to become his possession, would make her happy. For reasons he could not yet understand, it was having precisely the opposite effect. He would have asked her why, but at that very moment, Edmund Mortimer stepped into the gateway, his hand raised in greeting, his dark beard parted by one of the most duplicitous smiles in England.

Rees started to thrust Briana behind him, then stopped himself and let go of her. "Edmund," he said with guarded politeness. Ulf, hearing the tones in his master's voice, went quietly on alert again, the hackles on his shoulders rising. Rees ignored him.

The earl and the baron had met twice before: once at Westminster years before Mortimer had actually become a baron, and once during the Welsh war on campaign in the south. In neither case had they cared for one another, but in neither case had any overt hostility broken through the overlay of courtly manners which members of Edward's nobility owed to one another.

"Well, Rees," the Marcher Lord drawled, his eyes shifting to admire the beauty of the woman beside the earl, then back again. "The king sent me word you'd arrive here full five days past. I've not known King Edward to be so far wrong ere this."

"'Tis a distance between Windsor and North Wales," Rees said evenly, his wariness barely noticeable, "and my uncle was hardly travelling it with us. We had to assemble the provisions we bring, and he may not have taken that into account in his calculating of time. I am fair certain my uncle did not intend to mislead you." He stressed the relationship each time a little more strongly than the rest of his words.

"Aye. Quite an effort you've made." Mortimer eyed the length of the column, the forward parts of which were passing through the village. The far end of the train had not yet entered the valley. "'Tis an age-old method of buying loyalty."

Galen growled softly, and Ulf lowered his head and overrode the sound with a rumble like rocks falling. Rees hushed them both with the same murmur, his right hand resting casually on his sword hilt. "And one you join the king in disdaining. I have not your preference for punishing."

"What a deal of pleasure you deny yourself," said Baron Wigmore. He stepped aside from the gateway and gestured them to come into the courtyard.

Rees did not move, so neither did anyone else. "I have no wish to intrude upon you, Edmund, as 'tis clear you reside here in the manor," he said smoothly. "I was badly misinformed when I was told you occupied the castle, else we would have gone there."

Everyone listening to the conversation knew quite well that Mortimer dwelled in the castle. Briana recognized the smooth tones of deception in Rees's voice and felt herself begin to taste again the old, familiar discomfort. She had never been easy with the currents of maneuvering that swirled through and around the court. She had grown up in a place where royalty resided in Prince Llewelyn, who was a friend, who encouraged openness and honesty about him. She had felt detached from this kind of fencing while she was in England. And while she had always covered her true feelings over, she was certain she had never deceived anyone about them. If they had misread her, it was surely their failure, not her own.

Mortimer experienced a flash of anger at Rees's clear mockery, but he swiftly masked it. "Your information is flawless," he said with acid courtesy in return. "I merely wished to greet you on your arrival."

Rees's smile did not reach his eyes. "How hospitable," he said. "We must reciprocate with a farewell feast in your honor on the morrow. You and, say, a dozen of your more trusted knights?" His inflection seemed to imply that Baron Wigmore would be hard-pressed to find one "trusted" knight, let alone a dozen.

Mortimer pursed his thin lips. "Mercenaries are always trustworthy," he said silkily, "as I know you discovered when you hired them."

For a second Rees nearly gave way to the impulse to draw his sword before Wigmore could add the fateful words "at Fearndon," but Edmund Mortimer knew better. Fearndon had been the only battle in the Welsh war in which Rees had not used his own knights, and Wigmore knew it. By and large, Rees hated mercenaries. He had the old-fashioned belief that a knight fought for honor, not for money, but he had seen that no honor would accrue at Fearndon, only shame, and while he was compelled to be there by his oath of fealty to King Edward, he would not use anyone else's oath of fealty to himself to stain their souls as he had stained his own. But if Mortimer mentioned Fearndon, here, now, it would increase Rees's troubles immensely. Mortimer did not say the words, and Rees forced his sword hand off his hilt and onto the belt that hung snugly on his lean hips. "Then you should have no difficulty in accepting my invitation," he said.

The column head was drawing closer, and some of Rees's other knights had broken free of it and were riding without due haste to be present at the confrontation.

Briana realized that Rees had no intention of entering Flint manor at Baron Wigmore's request, and she could objectively admire the tactic, as well as being grateful that it held her here, outside the manor she was somehow unwilling to sink into just yet.

Ine watched the confrontation with real interest and some deep appreciation for Rees's behavior. Rees had, Ine knew, been angry and apprehensive. Another knight might have been thoughtlessly drawn into the grip of those emotions; Rees had controlled himself. Ine told himself again that whatever else Rees might be, he was not thoughtless.

"We would be pleased to attend your farewell feast," Mortimer was saying, "and we of the castle will return the honor the next day. We have a fine spring bull to slaughter for the occasion."

Maud winced. It had been their last bull, and she had had to turn it over to the castle. And the description of it as "fine" cut her as well, because they had scrimped to get the bull enough fodder in hopes they could mate it with some cows from Rhuddlan and get themselves a heifer. That hope had died when Wigmore demanded it. She had been informed of the contents of the column and knew there were no cattle in it. She wondered if Earl Connarc would notice that Flint's herd was now nearly nonexistent, or if Esrith would have to tell him. Before Owen got around to slitting his throat, of course.

"Fine," Rees said to Mortimer. "I will take formal possession of the castle in two days' time."

"I will take," he had said, not "you will tender."

Mortimer opened his mouth to protest and suddenly Rees's eyes narrowed, shooting out sparks of warning. Mortimer thought better of speaking and instead signalled to his men, who still stood behind the wall. Only when they were all in plain view did the baron reach for Briana's hand, saying, "We will take leave of you until the morrow eve, lady."

She extended her hand to him, pleased that she had not yet removed her riding gloves.

The baron and his men left the courtyard, mounted their horses, which had been tethered out of sight behind the seaward, hence castleward, wall of the manor. The column began to halt, strung out across the road, and everyone watched as the baron and his men rode off across the rolling seagrass meadow between Flint proper and the castle on the estuary. It was only then, taking the first steps into the manor's front yard, that Briana saw Maud.

"Aunt Maud," she whispered.

The thin woman looked much older; Briana radiated beauty, despite her obvious uneasiness. Maud could not quite hold out her arms to the younger woman, and Briana could not quite move toward the steps.

Rees recognized that Briana was not going to rush to

embrace Lady Maud and walked forward to give her a slight bow. "Lady Maud, your stewardship of Flint has been remarkable," he said. "We hope to make it easier from this point forward."

She returned the bow, but said nothing, her look glancing over him once before it settled on her niece.

Briana looked away, her gaze traveling along the line of six women and five men who waited behind her aunt. Two of the women were well known to her. Hulde and Enlis were the only people on the steps who were smiling. Three of the women were aged and looked familiar, but she had forgotten their names. The last was a very young girl, perhaps barely nubile. Besides Esrith, two of the men were scarcely more than boys. The next was in his dotage. The last was in the prime of manhood, stony-faced, hauntingly familiar. His eyes locked with hers, hooded, brooding, and though changed from what she remembered, recognizable.

It was Owen Glyn.

Owen had been at Flint less than twelve hours. He had moved his camp several times before he felt secure enough in its location to depart with Havgan. He had no idea how long he would be gone, and he wanted to leave his men safe from attack by any of the guard patrols until he returned.

He had made his way to Trefriew, Prince Llewelyn's ancestral home, intending to strike northeast from there to Flint. But in Trefriew's small market square, he had heard rumors about the convoy Earl Connarc was assembling. There was talk of little else throughout the vale, for this was the earl's land and all his tenants, prosperous as they were now, had been asked to contribute, for Flint's sake. Only a few of them knew who Owen was; those who did not spoke freely about their overlord. Owen heard much unqualified praise.

Curious, he and Havgan, returning to Flint with him, turned north to Conway.

He had not been anywhere near Conway since the

unsuccessful raid several years earlier. Moving quietly and unobtrusively, as only a single man or a pair of men could, he encountered the middle of the column already on the move eastward toward Flint. He could not help being impressed, not by the show of wealth, but by the fact that it was meant for people who had nothing, least of all power.

Owen had great respect for power, because he wielded so little of it in the scheme of things. He was even more curious to see the man who gave so generously to people who could not return the generosity in any material way. But he judged the complement of knights a force he did not want to risk. He would see Rees of Plantagenet, Earl Connarc, at Flint.

There he would make decisions about what to do. Of one thing, however, he was certain. No matter what else happened, when he left Flint, he would take Briana with him. He and Havgan, still wide-eyed at the size of the convoy, rode on toward Flint without speaking and reached it in the night, ahead of Rees and Briana.

Chapter 26

Because Rees had to meet, pay attention to, and thus think about everyone he was meeting that first day at Flint, he could not direct any of his powers of analysis toward Briana. Instead, he talked to villagers, memorizing names, introducing to them some of the men he had borrowed from Conway to help. It quickly became apparent that Flint's small foundry was not enough, that along with near-starvation, there was insufficient economic activity to create any basis for prosperity. By the end of the day, as he finished his discussions, Rees had developed a long list of projects to be started—the mill would have to be repaired and land found and developed for a second mill; the foundry needed expansion; the fences all needed to be rebuilt to hold the flocks and herd. He let the people of Flint know what he was planning, assured them he would seek their counsel in all things, and felt satisfied with their hesitant responses to his overtures.

Briana spent the day taking care of accommodations at the manor, getting the dorter cleaned and swept, starting people on the repair of its roof before the rains came again; assigning chambers to Ine, Galen's family, and Ralf. She found that Hulde and Enlis had put fresh linens on all the beds, but that they had been unwilling to intrude on Maud's stewardship enough to get the sealed master chamber opened and aired out. Briana quailed at the thought, but she knew it had to be done. The chamber was Rees's right, but it had been her father's, and Rees had killed Bryn.

She could not bear that thought. With a shudder, she put it away from her and sought out Maud for the key to the master chamber. She had deliberately not asked Maud for the ring of chatelaine's keys, for she had seen and winced at the coldness of her aunt's eyes when she looked at Rees, as well as what she perceived as the contempt in Owen's. In Maud's case, there had been a distance toward Briana totally separate from her feelings toward the new overlord.

But when Owen had shifted his gaze from Rees to the woman who stood beside him, her dark head at the level of his shoulder, she had seen his hostility vanish in surprise, then in a kind of wonder, and finally, in warmth. She turned her eyes away, scalded by that look from the man she might have wed, the living man she had most entirely betrayed by being happy.

Rees saw Owen's expression without any more comprehension than that a man found Briana attractive, and he had become accustomed to, if not resigned to or complacent about, men lusting after her. He would deal with it later. Just now he was concerned with the delicacy of arranging to provide what Flint needed without seeming to patronize or antagonize anyone.

Ine had also seen the expression on Owen's face, but he observed it with a sense of real foreboding. He had, of course, recognized Owen instantly and had been momentarily stunned by the arrogance of the gesture that brought him here. He knew that Maud had had a hand in it. Ine bit his lip pensively and for the first time since the outset of the Welsh war, he wondered where his own loyalty lay. There had never been any question in his mind before. Myrrdin had made him the custodian of the Welsh dream, and Ine took that very seriously, but a healthy future for Wales now seemed to him to lie more with Rees than with Owen—and yet Owen was the holder of Llewelyn's legacy, and Rees had been Llewelyn's enemy.

Owen was introduced to the incoming overlord and his companions as "Owen ap Owein," and he then bowed shortly to the new overlord and vanished into the manor on the pretext of having work to do.

Briana was careful to keep Hulde with her as she went about her tasks, because she had no wish to confront Owen alone, and she had no idea from what corner of the manor he might suddenly appear. But when she went to find Maud for the key to the master chamber, she left Hulde gathering the fresh linen and cleaning supplies which would be needed in a room that had been shut up for seven years. It would be hard enough to confront her aunt without witnesses; it would be humiliating in their presence.

Maud was instructing the placement of provender in the previously sadly depleted larder. When she saw Briana, she excused herself from the men carrying bags of onions, beans, cabbages, flour, and herbs, and left the kitchen by way of the door to the kitchen court, gesturing to the younger woman to follow her.

Briana did so gratefully, pleased she had not needed to request privacy.

Activity in the kitchen court was at a minimum now, and the two women paused in the shade of the sloping roof that covered the somewhat scanty woodpile.

"Your husband seems much disposed to make generous reparations to Flint for his sins," Maud said drily, but without overmuch condemnation in her voice.

Briana forced herself to look directly at Maud's pinched face. "He reckons Flint his home now and wishes no hardship on her," she said. "Blame him not for caring, and refuse not his generosity."

"Oh, I have no intent to refuse aught," her aunt said, her expression as bland as her tone. "We are damn near starving.

Had you come a month later, we would have begun losing people from the village, either going elsewhere or staying loyally and dying."

"I beg you not to hate him for being generous." Briana was aware that she could have commanded, but she was unable to speak so to Maud, whose thin features were so familiar to her, and so like those she thought her father had had, features she could no longer bring to mind and could not recall when she had lost.

Maud shook her head. "I'd not hate him for the reparations," she said, "but for the destruction which made them necessary, for the slaughter which destroyed our family, our hopes, our prince, and so many of our fine young men. He must still be called to answer for that."

"How?" Briana hissed, suddenly afraid for Rees. "By Owen Glyn?"

Maud smiled unpleasantly. "Clearly, 'twill not be by you."

Briana's eyes shot away from the accusation, and she buried her hands in the folds of her skirt, twisting the material. "Blame him not for my flaws," she said in a husky whisper. "Only I accept blame for those."

Because she was looking away, she did not see Maud frown, for that was not at all the response the older woman had expected. Briana had not denied her attachment to the murdering conqueror. She had not accused him of seducing her, of stealing affections belonging by rights to others. Nor had she coldly, regally defended him. She had not asked for forgiveness for him. Any of those responses, Maud could have understood.

Briana raised her chin again. "I should like to have the key to the master chamber," she said. "'Twill need much cleaning to be useful."

Maud immediately unhooked the ring of keys from her oversmock belt and held them out. "I wonder that you did not ask for them at once."

"I need not take them from you now, should you wish to

retain your authority here," Briana said as firmly as she could. "I have been seven years gone, and I know not the way of things."

Maud's hand offering the keyring did not waver. "Nay, I'd prefer to give over the responsibility," she said. "'Tis not for me to be chatelaine to Earl Connarc."

Briana accepted that, reached out and took the ring of keys. Maud pointed to each of them in turn, telling her what it was for, and when she reached the larder key, Briana deliberately slipped it from the ring and made Maud take it back. "You have done so much caretaking in time of scarcity," she said, "that I believe you should continue to manage now there is a sufficiency." When she thought Maud was about to refuse, she spoke more quickly. "I have never had the opportunity to manage a household, having been imprisoned at Westminster when I should have been here, learning. I would take a few weeks to learn my duties before I take them all upon me."

Maud seemed to debate that for a moment, while Briana continued to hold out the larder key, then nodded and took it back.

"What does Owen want of me?" Briana asked quietly.

Maud's face went even more expressionless. "Best ask him that yourself," she said.

Just then one of the men from Conway came into the kitchen courtyard with two small kegs under his arms. "Salt, Lady Maud," he called to her. "Where shall I put these?"

Maud's surprise was palpable, for salt had a value almost as great as gold. She glanced at Briana. "Well," she said, "he understands the price is high, that I will readily admit." To the man, she added, "Follow me," and went back into the kitchen.

Briana hooked the keys onto her tunic and, instead of going back into the kitchen after the Conway men and her aunt, she walked out of the kitchen court past the as yet unplanted herb and vegetable gardens and around to the stables, where Basilisk now pranced in the near paddock, tossing his head and trumpeting at passers-by. Behind them were the orchards, with apple trees just coming into new blossom, the only part of Flint that Wigmore had been unable to vitiate, largely because he had made no concerted effort to do so. She rounded the wall of the orchard, noting where rocks had fallen and should be replaced, then reentered the manor at the garden entrance and ran up the stairs to the second floor. Hulde and Enlis were waiting at the door of the master chamber, holding a pile of linens and blankets and a brace of buckets and cleaning cloths.

Briana hesitated only a moment or two, clutching the key, then squared her shoulders and unlocked the room that had belonged to her father, the room in which she had been born.

Charing—April 1289 A.D.

Bjorn Magnussen had a talent for placing himself where the disgruntled retainers, those dismissed from service at the court, gathered to drink and complain. He could carouse with the worst of them, and he had the ability to ferret out bits of useful information from the dross of simple gossip and exaggerated injustices. In a week on the south coast of England, he had consumed great quantities of ale and enough talk to learn that the person who could tell him what he most wanted to know was to be found in the village of Charing. He set off there at once, in possession of a potential informant's name with the same monomania he had applied to everything in his life. The name was now his to do with as he would, just as women and property had become his as soon as he desired them. In Charing, he believed, he would find another clue he needed or perhaps a man who knew which bastard was his. He wanted a living son again, and he was pleased that he would not have to wait for one to grow up. That the son might have had other plans never entered his mind and, if it had, he would not have cared.

Flint—April 1289 A.D.

Father Ciaran rose from the altar rail in the tiny Lady Chapel off the main church and slid his string of counting beads into the pocket of his gown. The church was not, as he had thought, unoccupied. Two women knelt at the altar rail. By the size of one of them, he recognized Sabine and the recluse, started to quietly leave the church, but was stopped by the sound of a soft, cultured voice calling his name.

He turned, surprised. The recluse never spoke to anyone except through the veiled window of her hermitage. She gestured to him, asking him to approach them, and he did, curious and concerned.

It was his first look at her. She was a serenely beautiful woman, with the air of indefinable mystery that most women who sought seclusion carried with them. He had admired the skill of her embroidery on several occasions, especially when, at Easter, Sabine had presented St. Maedoc's with its first new altar cloth in a decade, decorated with a pair of Celtic crosses entwined with vines and flowers. The only other time he had seen the recluse without the veil between them, she had been wearing a fringe of cloth that fell from the headband of her wimple and shaded her face. She was not wearing it now, and the priest detachedly admired the size and shape of her clear blue eyes, the curve of eyebrows, the length of the golden brown lashes, the fineness of the bone structure. "'Tis a pleasure to speak with you, lady," he said. "How may I help you?"

"I understand there is to be a small banquet in the manor on the morrow," the recluse said in that low, refined voice. "I would be grateful if you could arrange to find a place there for Sabine."

The giantess also turned now, the dark brown marbles of her eyes expressionless as she waited for a response.

Father Ciaran was about to say that he had no control over the people at the manor, but he thought of all the things Sabine and this woman had done for the church and the village and hesitated. "I shall speak to them after Mass in the morning," he said.

"My thanks, Father," said the recluse with sincerity, rising from her knees, lightly touching Sabine's wrist, and leaving the church with no more than a sighing of robes.

Sabine remained on her knees, as if she were aware of how intimidating her height could be. "You wonder about my lady." It was not a question.

"'Tis the nature of people in the world to be curious about those who have sought seclusion," the priest said mildly. "'Tis generally thought they seek a level of holiness they have been unable to find in other ways."

"Generally," Sabine repeated, then added, "There is great evil in the world."

"Aye," agreed Father Ciaran. "We have seen much of it here."

"Rebellion often results in the application of responsive evil," Sabine said with practical calm. "But there is another evil, and that is the evil attracted to innocence, drawn to purity. That is an unbearable evil, you see, because an innocent is defenseless against it."

She sounded so matter-of-fact that the priest was shaken, both by the depth of the musing in a woman he had taken to be simple, even relatively ignorant, and by the nature of what she had said. "From where learned you these things?" he asked her.

She smiled, a sadly cynical expression. "I studied what I saw around me," she answered. "I would die for my lady, for she has endured."

"Is that why she came to Flint?" the Celt asked. "Because Flint has endured also?"

Sabine wet her lips, debating a number of possible replies. The silence stretched on for a while, and the priest waited. At last, the huge woman said, "Father, I ask you not to misunderstand this. Flint may have been punished harshly, but Flint provoked the punishment. The Lord Bryn ap Emrys defied the commands of the king. It helps to bear punishment if in your heart you know you merited some reprisal. But if you merited no punishment at all and were nearly destroyed, 'tis a different matter entirely." She rose as if to end the discussion, as if she were worried she had said too much. "My thanks again for seeing to my invitation, Father."

"I shall do what I can," the priest said, bewildered at the conversation. He watched her leave the church, her departure very different from the recluse's, a process of creaking boards and thudding footfalls.

Father Ciaran had thought Sabine a mystery before, but it had been a harmless, rather amusing mystery. Now it was something entirely different, and he felt inadequate to cope with it.

The master chamber had been crawling with workmen all day, for which Briana was very grateful. The few pieces of furniture which still remained from her father's time had been cleared away. Most were falling apart and no longer capable of being repaired. Once the chamber was cleaned, workmen assembled the large bed the convoy had brought from Conway, and the trunks, rugs, sconces, bed hangings, and tapestries were carried into the room. By the time the manor was readying the evening meal—somewhat more elaborate than most suppers not only because everyone had been working hard, but because many Flint folk had not seen a true meal in a long time—the chamber looked nothing like Briana remembered, and she was grateful for at least that favor. She could not have rested easily if her every moment was rich with memories of the room where she and her brothers had played together, where Bryn had slept until the day he and his sons left for Fearndon.

She looked the chamber over once before descending to join Rees in the hall and was satisfied that she could be here without having to dwell on the past. The present was treacherous enough.

Chapter 27

Briana was seated to Rees's right at the high table. She was nervous throughout the meal, while Rees seemed very much at ease. He had kept Maud at the high table, to his left, so that the wall of his chest and shoulders blocked her from her niece's view most of the time. The knights from Conway sat at the outsides of two of the trestle tables, while the insides hosted many of the men from the village. At the lower table were the village women and the other Conway men, along with Menty, who was deep in conversation with Annie and Med about fabrics, weaving, and Celtic design. The two Flint women had been fascinated by the size and complexity of Menty's loom when it was taken off one of the wagons; their own looms were much smaller and simpler.

Also at the high table were Ine and Thomas Newby's assistant seneschal, Adam of Southwell, who would direct the revival of Flint. Rees had been careful to make certain that people from the village understood Adam's responsibility would be temporary, that the ultimate goal was for a Flint man to become seneschal once the fief was self-supporting again.

Rees had also proved to be remarkable at remembering names, greeting each villager individually as they entered the hall, and this had as much effect on the villagers as had the abundance of supplies. At the high table, waiting for the meal service to begin, he smiled a little, let himself minutely relax, hopeful that this bloodless conquest would be as easy as he had dared to dream all along. He had to have Flint standing beside him for the next two days when he faced Wigmore. Only once Edmund Mortimer had departed for Harlech could he feel completely at ease and think about the wedding.

The recollection of the wedding made him aware of Briana's silent, unsmiling presence beside him, and he felt a belated stab of concern, wondering what was wrong. He lightly touched her arm and was stunned when she jumped and turned upon him a gaze so completely fearful and unhappy that he had to keep himself from frowning.

Her expression cleared instantly, becoming neutrally receptive, akin to the mask she had worn in the days before the handfasting. "How may I serve you, my lord?"

Rees wondered why, instead of being pleased with the slowly increasing warmth of the reception Flint was giving them, she was sinking deeper into a sorrow he seemed unable to fathom. He glanced at Ine, who immediately put down his cup of ale and retrieved his harp from its resting place in his satchel. He would eat later.

A ripple of appreciation ran around the room, shared even by Maud, who had always loved Ine's music.

The bard chose to sing of Coity as the plates of cabbage and carrots and bowls of beans were passed around. Coity was a Welsh castle which had found its way into legend almost two centuries earlier, in the wake of the Norman conquest, when Morgan, the castellan, was besieged by the soldiers of Payne de Turberville. The Welsh prince asked for a parley with the Norman warlord and appeared for it holding his sword with one hand and his lovely daughter with the other. "This be the choice I offer you," Ine sang as if he were Lord Morgan, "to fight to the last drop of blood, with death for our finest men, yours and mine all, or to wed with the beauteous Melusine and bring only life to the land."

The meaning of the metaphorical tale was lost on no one present except, Ine noted, the Lady Briana, who seemed not to hear it, eyes darting from one place in the hall to another, sliding past Owen as if fearful of lingering there.

Briana had gotten lost sometime between leaving the master chamber and sitting down at the high table. She did not know how or why, but she was certain that every moment Rees spent winning Flint drew it further and further away from her. The one thing that she did understand was that somehow it must have been proper, that she must deserve to be parted from Flint because she had betrayed it by her passion for Earl Connarc. There was no possible reparation for that crime; there could be no absolution. She did not know what could be done, if anything, to set matters to rights, and so her uneasiness grew greater.

When Ine's first song was done, Ralf rose, lifting his tankard, to propose a toast to the Lord and Lady of Flint. Rees's knights rose at once, the men of Flint more slowly.

Rees continued to smile, reaching for Briana's hand, gripping it tightly when he felt her muscles tense as if she were preparing to pull it away. "Smile," he commanded her under his breath, barely moving his lips, having no time for sweet reason.

Obedience penetrated in a way kindness never could have, and Briana painted an artificial smile on her face.

Rees discovered that he was very grateful for the obedience, because it gave him a vestige of immediate control, counterfeit as it might be, over a phenomenon he had not had time to analyze and therefore did not understand. He toyed with the idea of ordering her to relax, but thought better of it. He would not want to be put in the position of giving her a command she could disregard, because that would break her habit of obeying him. He stroked her hand and again felt the tremors coursing through her.

Then everyone was seated again, and Ine asked Maud what

she would like to hear him play.

For a long moment, Maud was silent. Then she leaned forward, looking directly at the bard and carefully ignoring Rees. She answered, "I should like to hear 'The Red Dragon.'"

The hall went completely still, and everyone at the trestle tables looked immediately at Rees.

Briana, beside him, her hand still in his, saw an apprehensiveness in most of the faces, a keen amusement, hastily masked, in Owen Glyn's. Her own self-involvement faded in recognition of the problem Rees had just been presented.

"The Red Dragon," the symbol and song of free Wales, had been sung lustily by the men who marched away to Fearndon to die, and it had not been heard since Wales fell. It was the song of Prince Llewelyn, never officially forbidden by King Edward, who did not see that music had a power of any kind, but it was understood to be at best misguided, at worst seditious.

Rees immediately understood the challenge and was utterly equal to it. "Hulde," he called.

The woman rose from her seat at the lower table, as uncertain as the rest of them, for of all the possible reactions the request for the song might have provoked, a summons to her seemed the least likely, even irrational. She bent toward Rees in an abortive curtsey.

Rees said clearly enough for the entire room to hear, "My recorder and the Lady Briana's dulcimer are on a table in the solar. Bring them here."

Hulde cast a quick look at Briana, whose eyes focused now on her husband's serious face and whose smile was slowly turning from painted to genuine as she guessed what he had decided to do. Without being aware of it, she stopped trembling.

Rees was more grateful in that moment that he could play the recorder than he was for his ability to wield a sword. Just as music had proved to be a bridge to Briana, it could also be a bridge to Flint. A flash of memory came to him, of Bertran, Bard of Poitou, telling him not to give over playing the recorder no matter what. At the time, when he was very much younger, he had thought it silly. Now he wondered how the old man could have guessed what the future had in store.

Ine's brown eyes glowed with admiration at the move, and his look at Maud, who had been waiting to be admonished, was nearly as triumphant as it was possible for a bard to be to a Celtic lady who outranked him.

Maud glanced at Owen, whose face had flushed with surprise at the unexpected gesture from the new overlord of Flint, and she bowed her head in acknowledgment of the fact that she had just been thoroughly outmaneuvered.

Hulde came back into the hall with the recorder tightly tucked under her arm and the dulcimer balanced on her palms. One of the wooden hammers teetered on the strings and fell to the rush-strewn floor with a small click. Before Hulde's step faltered, Ralf leaned easily off his bench, swept it up, and deposited it back on the instrument.

Rees took the recorder and gestured Ine to come closer as the housekeeper put the dulcimer down at Briana's place. For a minute they tuned, harp to recorder, dulcimer to harp, and then Rees said quietly to the room in general and to Maud in particular, "Brave men deserve brave music." He nodded to Ine, and the two men began to play the outlawed song. After the first few notes, Briana joined in, the speed of the dulcimer chiming along with the deeper harp and the soaring flute.

The song's marching beat throbbed through the room, compelling and welcoming at the same time, needing only a drum to be complete. As the people of Flint, Maud included, began to sway to this particular melody, which took their hearts back to happier times and seemed to promise such times ahead again, Owen began to strike the table with the flat of his hand in the beat the drum would carry.

Ralf shoved his goblet aside and took up the beat with the Welshman, and soon all the men in the hall were keeping time, while the music of the three instruments floated around them. It was a moment of pure unity, as if there were neither conqueror nor conquered, but only folk who loved the land and gloried in the courage of the land's sons.

Rees felt the peculiar grace the martial music had laid upon the company and, with a quick nod to Ine, who understood it as he seemed to understand most intentions, swung the lead into another verse. They played all four verses, and though no one sang, everyone heard the words, as if the ghosts of Wales's fallen had risen to sing them, to be honored by them once more.

Briana was aware that tears were stinging at her eyes, but that these were not tears of mourning or sadness, they were tears of joy. She was not the only woman shedding them.

When the song was done at last, the hall was silent. Then Maud said to Rees with a barely reluctant grace, "Very well done, my lord."

He nodded at her, acknowledging it, and added with a wry smile, "'Twould please me much, Lady Maud, if you could refrain from making a similar request in the presence of Baron Wigmore."

Her lips twitched a little. There had been no hint of an implied threat in those words, and the earl certainly seemed to be feeling an amused civility, but Maud understood well that he was reminding her of his power. It was the very gentleness of the reminder which undid her, just as it had undone her niece.

Briana had used the time of their short exchange to ache with the joy, but to distrust it. Now she allowed the spiritual bleakness she had been experiencing to creep back and overtake her again. She did not want to climb out of the pit yet. Though she was not aware of it, she felt that she had not been punished enough for the way she had been protected and fed while the people of Flint paid great prices and received great pain in return. She raised her head and said clearly, "I think you need have no fear of that, my lord, 'Tis our grace that my aunt hates Edmund Mortimer more than she hates—"

The expression he turned on her was so cold that his eyes seemed entirely gray with frost, and she silenced between one word and the next. Even Maud was astounded that the moment had been broken by Briana's rashness.

Rees was angrier with himself than he was with Briana, though no one could have known it to look at him. He had waited too long to try and discover what had been affecting her, and it had come out as an attack on him, at a moment when things had been looking promising. His grimness and suppressed rage angered him even more, because he had let himself be so hopeful about the evening's outcome.

Briana had been shaken far more by his reaction than she could reveal. He had turned upon her so suddenly that she had not been able to speak the last word of her declaration. It would have been "us." And now she felt she had no way of telling Rees what she had been about to say, for his face was so forbidding she could not try to say that he had mistaken her intention, that he was wrong in thinking that she had been about to say "you."

Ine played for the remainder of the meal instead of returning to his seat to eat supper, and between songs, Galen boldly told some humorously lewd stories of living with French-born Norman knights—nothing too salacious, but of an undeniably ribald spirit that soon restored the hesitant good humor that had been building before Briana spoke. Menty flushed and exaggerated her embarrassment at her husband's stories, because she quickly saw that the Celtic women enjoyed someone being obviously more discomfited than they were.

Rees waited with well-concealed impatience until he thought he could excuse himself without appearing to retreat, then he rose, took Briana firmly by the wrist, and bid everyone a fair night. Briana was subdued as she acquiesced to his tacit command, her gaze sliding past Owen's carefully expressionless face, pretending not to see how his gaze followed her.

Ulf had come into the hall with some of the manor's dogs, who were hoping for scraps, even though they had actually just enjoyed their first full meal in long days. Ulf never lowered himself to beg for scraps or handouts. Instead, he waited for people to rise and bid a fair night to their new lord and their returned lady. Then he rose up on his hind legs and removed a loaf of bread from a bowl on the lower table, with the aplomb of a nobleman who happened to be something of a thief. Bearing his prize, he trotted grandly after Rees and Briana, his head high and his thick tail like a proud flag behind him.

Rees had intended to wait until Briana was done with her bath before he joined her in the master chamber, but he finished speaking with Galen and Ralf about the deployment and watches of sentries much earlier than he expected. Once that was done, he wanted nothing more than to find out what had so unsettled his wife since they entered Flint, so he went to the master chamber without any further hesitation.

Briana soaked in the hot water longer than usual, wanting the heat to seep into her bones and relax her. She tried not to think about anything, but images kept creeping in on her— Rees's smoothness in beginning to win over everyone in Flint, including her aunt and probably Owen, the two people in the entire world whose opinion most mattered to her. She sensed Maud's coldness toward her, the contemptuous unspoken judgment that Briana had gone over to the enemy. She thought about Owen's recognition of her and his righteous condemnation.

She had changed the decoration and furnishings of this room enough so that it was possible, at moments, to forget that her parents had slept here, that she and Griffith and Meredith had been conceived here, and that the life journeys of everyone but her had taken them from this room and brought them in return, only to carved stones in the churchyard down the road.

She finally forced herself to soap up and rinse off, taking no pleasure in what could have been a sensual experience. She even felt some guilt that she had been able to feel so happy when they played "The Red Dragon." Without her realizing it, she had concluded that times of joy should be sharply divided from times of sorrow, blocks of her life that were either happy or sad, and that one should not intrude on the other. She had been happy at Flint, and then unhappy when Edward took her. She had been happy when she escaped from him, and then unhappy from the time the rogue knight attacked her until she had been handfasted. She had been happy on the journey to Flint, and then unhappy when she saw how it had suffered. That meant that she should presently have been unable to rejoice at anything. Had she actually thought about those divisions, she might have perceived their uselessness, their foolishness, but she had not begun trying to understand what she was feeling, only to experience it.

She stepped out of the tub and reached for a towel. Just then, Rees let himself in. Ulf, having devoured his bread, came with him. The dog leaped onto the bed with the pride of possession. Rees closed and bolted the door.

Briana stood still, the towel in her hands.

Rees pushed back his immediate reaction of desire at her beauty, hopeful that her physical openness was an indication that she would be able to be open to him in other ways.

She saw the desire flame up in his eyes, saw him put it aside, and sighed, trembling a little. He thought she might be chilled, for there was no paper over the windows. He reflected fleetingly that the windows had likely been uncovered all through the winter, then disregarded it so as not to be distracted from the problem at hand. "Is the water still hot?" he asked and began stripping off his tunic and hose.

Briana nodded and wrapped the towel around her body.

When Rees was naked, he walked to the tub and climbed in, sinking gratefully onto the stool. He had not realized how tense he had been all day, how vital it was to him to save as much of Flint as possible, the way he had been able to save Conway. He glanced at Briana and saw that she was still trembling. Not chilled, then. "Do you fear something?" he asked. He did not want to ask if there were any reason why she might fear *him*.

She made a barely perceptible nod, then shook her head, her heavy mass of dark hair shifting from side to side, and at last seemed to nod again, before saying as strongly as she could, "Not fear, my lord."

He shifted his body a little in the water, resting his arms on the sides of the tub, watching her carefully. "Does it have to do with the fact that you've ceased calling me Rees?"

She looked at him, startled, and he realized she had not even been aware that she was doing it. "Have I?" she asked wonderingly. "But I was thinking of you not at all."

He wavered between being relieved and being offended, even as a part of him wondered what was going on. He ventured a little farther into dangerous territory. "Briana, what happened to you at the church this morn? What made you throw yourself to the road?"

She did not hesitate or dissemble in her answer. Something compelling in his sun-browned face seemed to be seeking a kind of truth which might be described as obedience. "Father Ciaran accused me of loving you," she said, her voice and face utterly innocent of any suspicion that the words might evoke a reaction in him. "'Twas—unexpected."

Rees's calm exterior in no way reflected the turmoil he was feeling. His hope from the outset had been that he could make her love him as well as desire him. She and Flint would be safest if she did. He realized now, in a flash of belated insight, that she saw loving him as some sort of crime, outside the realm of what was acceptable. His mind began to sort alternatives, even as his body seemed to lounge perfectly at ease in the water. His heart clenched at the revelation that he wanted her to love him for more than the fief's sake, and that he had not been honest with himself about it until this moment. All he said was, "Love is not as unexpected as all that, even between husband and wife."

She made herself keep looking at him, seeing what Princess Eleanor had called his incredible fairness, feeling it strike her like a physical blow, and heard herself say, "Pain."

The single word gave him information, but nothing on which to fashion a question. He rose from the tub and took a towel to his body, rubbing roughly.

Briana tried to think coherently, even though she was soon wrapped in arousal as well as her own towel. His nakedness, the hard muscles bunching and relaxing under the bronze skin, the tightness of thighs and buttocks, the massive shoulders brushed by his golden hair, the pale slash of the scar she had never asked about across his chest and belly, all gave her a powerful sense memory of the things he had done to her body. She sighed again, her breath abruptly making a barely audible moan.

Warrior-alert, he heard it. His head came up, and he walked to unbolt the door and call for men to remove the tub. He had been delighted at first by her complexity, knowing how much he would have disliked a simple, docile wife, but now he realized that that very complexity was a trap as well as a challenge. She was experiencing reactions to being back in Flint which he could not have anticipated. He thought hard about it while the tub was being removed, the splashing of the water blending with Ulf's growls at having strangers in the room where his master clearly meant to sleep.

When the tub was gone, the door bolted again, and Ulf no longer in his "guard" stance, Rees walked to the bed and pulled back the tester, tossing his towel onto one of the chests that stood beneath the windows. He had made a decision. He sat on the feather tick and patted it beside him. "Briana, come here."

She could see that he was mastering his desire for her forcefully, for his arousal was evident, even as he sat seemingly at ease. His voice and face showed no sign of it, but his body had betrayed him to her. She kept her own towel around her as she obeyed him, her fingers nervously dancing over the spot above her breasts where one end of the soft cloth was tucked under the other. His steady gaze was already heating her.

"In this room." he said, "you and I have no connection to

the rest of the world. Whatever troubles me, I will not bring it here. I expect you to do the same."

She tried to digest what he had said, the fact that it had been a request, not a command. "How can I do that?"

"Easily," Rees said, running one large hand lightly down her arm. "The other world ends at that door. Inside here is our world, just yours and mine. There may be fear outside, or anger, or confusion, or, aye, pain, but it remains outside." His bright blue eyes riveted her, seeking, persuading, even seducing, but once again not demanding or insisting.

"Why do you never command these things of me?" she asked, bewildered, her hands drawing at her towel to keep it closed. "The law gives you the right. The king gave you the right."

He smiled then, the warmth and pure affection stoking her fires. "Listen to me, sweetness," he said, his voice as much a caress as the feathering touch of his fingers on her arm. "You will drown without a lifeline. I cannot—I will not—order you to catch it. I will only keep throwing it to you until my arms lose all their strength. Catch it, sweetness. Agree that in this room, we will have our own world."

It was seductive. She had thought of happiness and sadness as bound in time, not in place, but he was saying that there was a place in which she could be happy all the time, no matter what, and by now she was burning to touch him, to have him touch her. She had wanted a sanctuary for so long, for years on end, all the terrible tightrope years of swallowing her opinions because if they reached King Edward's ears, there would be penalties.

"What, should I make mistakes?" she challenged. "Say or do the wrong thing?"

Rees barely understood what prompted that particular question. "You mean as you did downstairs in the hall? Aye, I was angry. But there will be no penalties. There will only be you and I and what we—" He chose the word carefully. "—what we treasure about one another."

She was moving her hands in a more and more agitated fashion. He reached out, captured her hands, and held them in one of his, stilling their turbulent motion. "A safe haven," he said.

Briana spoke her mind. "We'll not ever be able to talk of aught."

Rees laughed. "We'll speak of the things we share. A hope for Flint's survival. A dislike for my uncle. The pleasure." With his other hand, he opened the towel she was wearing and let it slip away, leaving her as naked as he was. "Agree, Briana." He bent his head and covered her mouth with his, breathing into hers, tracing the edges of her lips with his tongue, whispering, "Agree."

"Aye," she breathed back against his gently moving mouth, trying to pull her hands free to touch him. "Aye."

"Say the words," he whispered, wanting to hear how she would describe it. He drew back a little from her quivering, parting lips so that she could speak, continuing to hold her hands.

Briana wanted nothing more now than to sink into the desire to forget everything else, but he had given her an order, and she welcomed the chance to be obedient. "I agree that this will be our sanctuary," she said, "no matter what happens outside."

He released her hands, which flew around his neck. She molded herself to him instantly, nibbling on his lips, and Rees was once again astounded by her passion. He did not know if he had solved the problem of whatever had begun to eat at her since they entered Flint, but at least he had succeeded in creating one safe place for her. It was his last coherent thought before he was so swept by hunger that he became, as she was at that moment, a purely physical being.

Ine saw Owen Glyn walking slowly across the kitchen courtyard toward the stables, quickly shouldered his harp and went after the rebel leader, unwilling to shout a name because he had not overheard Owen being introduced to Earl Connarc, and he did not know what Owen was calling himself.

Owen heard the footsteps behind him and spun, his hand going instinctively to his side for the sword he had left hidden at the edge of the manor lands. Seeing it was Ine, he relaxed, grimacing that he had allowed his wariness to expose his training as a swordsman. He swore soundlessly under his breath.

"I'd have a care about falling into a fighting crouch," Ine said mildly as he came up to the younger man. "If it had been someone other than me—"

"I know," Owen acknowledged ruefully. "Since he knows not my face, why call attention to myself?"

"What are you doing here?" Ine asked bluntly.

Owen debated any possible number of answers. "Maud sent for me."

Ine raised an eyebrow. "To what end?"

"You can ask that?" Owen actually sounded slightly amused.

"I do ask it," said Ine. "I have waited long years to see peace in this part of the world. 'Tis my belief Connarc means to have it."

Owen's amusement vanished and his eyes grew hooded. "'Twould be a fell thing if you went over to the enemy, Ine." He was testing, probing.

Ine carefully controlled any show of emotion. "Owen, there is no enemy any longer. The war is over, and we must needs make the best of what we have."

Owen's voice was no more than a hiss. "Never!"

Ine sighed. "Never is a time which does not match the length of our lives. But the longer the lives, the longer a time until we know that we will not see the arrival of never."

Owen turned away from Ine, squinting at the waning moon through some of the newly budding trees in the orchard. "She was promised to me," he said.

At that, Ine was alarmed. "The Lady Briana now belongs to Connarc in all eyes but those of the church, and that last will be remedied very soon."

Owen looked back at Ine and grinned, his teeth paler than the sun-leathered skin, no humor in his face at all. "Then I shall have to move swiftly."

"Do you mean to steal her?"

"If I do so intend, will you warn him?" The rebel's voice was suddenly very dangerous.

"Do you so intend?" Ine was insistent and not at all afraid.

Slowly, Owen shook his head. "She will come with me willingly," he said. "I'll not use force, not on her."

"How can you believe she will choose to accompany you anywhere?" Ine asked with disbelief. "She has tied herself to him."

Owen's eyes glittered. "I ask again, will you warn him?"

Ine knew he should, but a bard's loyalties were to his art and the hope of a peaceful time in which to spin his tales. He had made enough songs of war, had seen enough Welshmen die. And he had known Owen for many years and understood well why Owen was what he had become. Owen had just promised that he would not seek to take Briana by force to Snowdonia, and that meant to Ine that she would not choose to go. He searched his heart and arrived at a solution which sat easily with his honor. "Nay," he said, "I'll not warn him. But I shall warn her. Will you slay me for that?"

Owen understood the question very well. "I am not bloodthirsty, Ine," he said with sudden weariness. "Nor am I an idiot. I see what he will do for Flint, and I see that Maud will soon come to accept it as well. If Briana comes with me, then I'll not even seek his death. Wigmore was worse. The next overlord could be another Wigmore, and Flint would not survive it. I care for Flint, though 'twould never have been mine. He may keep it. But I will take Briana with me, and you may tell her I said so."

"What hap if she tells him who you are?"

"She will not betray me," Owen said with absolute confidence. "'Tis written on her soul. She will betray him long ere she betrays me." He turned to continue toward the stable, then turned back. "And you may tell her I said that, too. 'Twill make no difference."

Ine would not let him leave yet. "And how if she goes with you while loving him? Will you take the scraps? Will you shatter her chance to be happy?"

Owen froze, for he had never thought in those terms. He reflected that, honestly, he was not a happy man. Caring for Briana, he wanted at least her happiness. Someone in Bryn's family deserved joy of the world. Was he bitter enough to destroy that chance so all of them could suffer equally? For he never doubted Ine's word that she loved Connarc. He was not yet ready to try to answer those questions. "Ine, I shall not compel her to come with me. She will come anyway."

"He will follow," said Ine. "He also loves."

Because it was Ine speaking, Owen believed him about that, too. "Nevertheless," he said, "I have something she wants." He turned again and vanished into the night in the direction of the stable.

Ine stared after him, a feeling of foreboding growing in his heart. It was not a feeling that Briana was in danger; rather, it was that she was at risk. He did not know how exactly, and he did not know if it could be headed off, but he was determined to try.

Chapter 28

The preparations to host Baron Wigmore and his chosen knights consumed much of the next day, and Briana used them as an excuse not to attend Mass at St. Maedoc's, even though Communion was unlikely to be offered. Maud looked at her strangely when she said she would not be present at Mass, but did not insist.

Rees wanted to remain at Flint manor with her, but as the new overlord, he thought it was vital that he be seen to worship with his people, so he left her and accompanied the manor staff and the villagers to the church.

Ine did not. His absence from Mass would arouse no comment, even from Father Ciaran. Ine was well known to care deeply about Myrrdin's ways, the truths that had fallen to the Roman empire and then to the Roman church.

The priest noticed Briana's failure to attend, as did everyone else, but despite the curious glances at Rees, at the empty spot beside him where his handfast bride would have sat, no one asked any questions aloud. The residents of Flint castle never came to St. Maedoc's, as they had their own chaplain, the replacement for Father Paul. Thus, for the villagers, Mass was always a liberating experience, and now they saw that their experience would not be lessened by the presence of their new overlord, smiling and not at all remote.

He looked very handsome in a deep blue supertunic, and he greeted people by name. He allowed none of his knights to taunt them or behave in any way discourteously, even through the knights' very ease of manner, their laconic good nature, and their confident athleticism showed their confidence as fighting men.

After they had all gone to church, Briana walked slowly through the quiet manor, out to the kitchen courtyard, then back into the manor again. She wanted to feel it, to sense it as it had been when she was twelve years old and King Edward had not yet returned from his time on Crusade to claim Wales and destroy so many lives.

She no longer felt any urge to weep at the way things were now, though it was true that life had changed implacably and inevitably, and wishing would not change it back. She was not twelve years old any longer. Bryn was dead, his blood mingled with that of his sons and hundreds of others. And she had become the wife of the man who had slain them.

Be fair, she cautioned herself. *'Twas not his sword which slew them.*

And she knew even as she thought it that Maud and Owen would not have agreed with her. *I would not have agreed with myself as late as eight weeks ago*, she thought. *And then he apologized to Ine, played the recorder with such skill, offered me choices, and*—The last part of the progression did not bear thinking about. He had played her, too, and continued to play her, as skillfully as he played his flute. Was it all calculated or was he sincere? Did it really matter which?

She heard the sound of Ine's harp coming from the orchard as she walked into the kitchen, noting the baskets of carrots and turnips piled on the cutting table beside the mutton carcass which had been spiced and roasted. It would be heated and carved as soon as the servants returned from Mass. Once she knew the kitchen was in order, she turned and went out again into the kitchen court, following the sound of the music.

When Mass was over, Father Ciaran was successful at getting an invitation for Sabine to attend the banquet honoring Edmund Mortimer that evening. Rees was very gracious in agreeing, asking the priest to be certain and attend as well, though Father Ciaran demurred. Then Rees sent Galen and Menty back to the manor with everyone else except Ralf and went into the churchyard to look at the four stone markers. Ralf paused at the churchyard gate to watch both his friend's back and the road. He saw the small movement at the hermitage window, but he could not see past the veil to discover what was going on inside.

Rees was oblivious to it, studying the first of the markers. There was no effigy on the gravestone, only an exquisitely carved Celtic cross. These were not people who carved themselves into a rigid form to meet eternity, as did the English. The inscription, only a little weather-worn, read, "Nonne, Lady of Flint. A.D. 1241-1272. Receive, O earth, the body that you gave / 'Til God's life-giving power destroy the grave." She had died when Briana was about two. He wondered if she had been as exquisitely lovely as her daughter.

Rees was hardened to the idea that loved ones died, though in truth the only one he had ever lost to death was his mother; he had thought his father was lost to him, but by dislike and indifference, not by death. In spite of his detachment, he had to force himself to take the steps to the next marker. "Bryn ap Emrys, Lord of Flint. A.D. 1239-1282. Fell at Fearndon. He that endureth to the end shall be saved." The stone was carved with a sword whose blade and handguard served as the cross. Rees's eyes narrowed at the implied message of that.

The next marker read, "Griffith ap Bryn. A.D. 1261-1282. Fell at Fearndon. He putteth aside the fear of death." Rees's jaw tightened, and a muscle jumped in his cheek. The stone was carved with a simple cross and a small sunburst.

He turned to the last, smallest stone, tense beyond his

expectations. "Meredith ap Bryn. A.D. 1270-1282. All-guiding Trinity, guide my design / More bright than Heaven thy torches shine." There were no other carvings.

Rees felt again the helpless rage that a twelve-year-old boy had had to die. That he was Briana's younger brother made it all the worse. He could do nothing about it. Without his being aware of it, his large hands had fisted at his sides, and now he forced them open, spun on his heel, and left the churchyard, stalking on the hard-packed road. Ralf silently paced him.

At the window of the hermitage, behind the gauzy veil, Beatrice wept with the silent sobs she had learned in the long years when John de Bretagne had not wished to be troubled with any of her emotions or with her older son, the only son he would allow her to raise. Rees was so beautiful, tall and fine. He had grown into as magnificent a man as she could have imagined, quick, sure, more intelligent and certainly more sensitive to the concerns of others than his brutish sire could ever have been. Her son was everything she wished.

She heard Sabine moving around in the room behind her and turned, wiping away tears. "Did you see him?" she asked.

"Aye," Sabine answered. "He is less travel-weary now than he was yestermorn. And I think he has naught of the thoughtless about him. You can be proud."

Beatrice clasped her hands together and raised them to her lips as if to hold back the question she simply had to ask. "Think you that he will ever forgive me?"

Sabine nodded. "Aye, I think he will, though 'twill take some time. When do you wish to tell him?"

"After the wedding," Beatrice said. "'Til then he will have too much to see to for me to give him such a shock."

Briana stared open-mouthed at Ine. "Say that again."

He repeated what he had told her of his conversation with Owen Glyn, not mentioning his description of the bond he believed she and Rees had with one another. He watched the astonishment and the flow of contradictory emotions wash across her face. He had always been able to read what she was thinking, even when she was trying to disguise it, but now she was no longer dissembling. Her open face showed everything—the disbelief, the confusion, the sentimentality, even some fear and indignation.

"But—but—" Briana realized she was stuttering and tried to catch herself. Somehow it was ludicrous that Owen thought he could take her from Flint when she had spent a third of her life dreaming of nothing more than to return here. The paradox inherent in the thought never occurred to her—that she had tried so hard to return, and that being here at last was causing her such extreme turmoil. She was here, and here she would stay. "How can he think I would go with him? He's not even tried to seek me out."

"He seemed very certain of himself," Ine cautioned her, "but he swore he would not take you with coercion, that you would go willingly."

Briana shook her head. "I will speak with him," she said with conviction. "I will tell him 'tis impossible, but I want not to hurt him. He is very dear to me."

"Dearer than Rees?" He had no right to ask such a question, and they both knew it, yet he asked it, and she allowed it, flushing deeply.

The wind gently moved the branches of the orchard trees, and they clacked against one another. Ine had chosen to sit on a hillock at the western edge of the orchard, so sunlight danced in small patches over Briana's face and hair. As her cheeks colored, the spots of sun picked out the heightened rosiness and made it seem brighter. The bard studied Briana as she chose her words. She seemed to be exercising as much caution in speaking as she had when she was a prisoner of the English court, and he had not seen that since they left Windsor. At last she looked at him directly. "Differently dear," she said.

Ine could not resist saying, "Rees may find it difficult to

believe so."

"He must not know that Owen leads the rebel band in Snowdonia!" Briana was quickly adamant about that. "The king wants the rebels slain, here or in London matters not, and I want no more killing."

Ine nodded. "'Tis a good and noble goal, that, but it may not be possible, especially not if Owen takes you from Flint."

"He cannot," said Briana.

"I fear," Ine said carefully, testing her, "that he may believe he is in love with you."

Her face changed so swiftly to something he barely recognized that he was appalled. Briana hissed, "He must not! He must not love me! I am—loathsome!"

And then the sound of everyone returning from St. Maedoc's drifted through the orchard to where they were, and Briana gathered her skirts and ran back through the trees, across the kitchen court, and into the manor.

Ine scrambled to his feet and stood stunned in the dappled sunlight, trying to keep the earth from shifting under him at the suddenness of the danger, for even though he could read her well, even though he understood there were traps for her, he had not guessed at the depth of the self-hatred that had all at once sprung free from behind the beauty of her face. He immediately understood—or thought he understood—what had happened. Briana had needed to hate Earl Connarc, had spent years detesting the man who had trapped Prince Llewelyn, killed her family, ruined her life, and caused her to become King Edward's prisoner. The hatred was real, palpable, with a life of its own, and she had fed upon it to keep herself strong. She knew it better than she knew herself. Under the cool, wary exterior she had lived in for all the years since Edward had threatened to destroy Flint if she did not obey him, that hatred had kept her alive.

But Earl Connarc had turned out to be Rees, his physical magnetism equalled by his intelligence and his willingness to show caring. She could not direct the hatred at that man and slowly, over the weeks in which he had made her more and more completely his, the formless malevolence had turned inward.

"Oh, Christ," said Ine softly, a prayer, not an oath. Rees had to know, and quickly. Now that it had revealed itself, there was no predicting what the hatred would cause her to do.

But Rees did not immediately return with the first group from St. Maedoc's, for he had stayed to read the grave markers. As he neared the manor house, he slowed his driving steps, aware for the first time that Ralf had to trot to keep up with him. The earl murmured a soft apology, and Ralf grinned. "I've not trained as hard as I should recently," the knight said lightly. "Mayhap Galen and I ought to set up some formal training."

"Another few days will cause no harm," Rees said, making himself bring his thoughts back to the present from the useless rage at an unalterable past. "I'd wait 'til Mortimer has departed. I'd not have him note what level of prowess we have."

"Aye," Ralf agreed. "He seems a fouler man that I'd hoped for in a Marcher Lord."

"I knew him before he became a Marcher," said Rees. "My uncle the king favors strength and naked displays of power over the possible benevolence of rule." Rees glanced across the fields, past the copses, to the strange bulk of Flint castle, the square walls holding the hall, kitchen and apartments separate from the round keep, which stood on its own mound outside the walls.

"That being the truth, why has he let you retain Conway?" Ralf studied his liege lord curiously as Rees stopped walking and turned to face him.

"Why, Ralf," Rees said in a mockingly wondering tone, "that was a *thoughtful* question. Best not show Galen you are learning how to reason. He'll ask to be released from my service for fear it will infect him, too."

The two men were laughing together when Ine stepped out of the shadow at the manor gate, and Rees saw the expression on the bard's face. "Go before me into the house," the earl said to the younger knight. "I have a need to speak with the bard."

Instinct alone made him turn aside from the road onto a small track between the tall grasses that led to the rushes lining the estuary shore. The breeze was fresh and the day sunny, though wisps of cloud still scudded across the sky and spring stormclouds were massing low on the western horizon. Rees calculated offhandedly that there could well be thunderstorms before the night's banquet.

Once on the track, he waited for Ine. To his surprise, the bard was not carrying the harp. Ine almost never let his harp out of his hands, and its bulk on his back was so familiar a sight that he looked slightly misshapen without it.

"What's amiss?" Rees asked as the slender man came up to him.

Ine hesitated. "I know not how to begin."

Inarticulacy was so unlike him that Rees was surprised. "'Tis evidently of some import," he said warily.

Ine drew in a deep breath. "Recall you that on our journey here I said the Lady Briana had never gifted herself with her own loyalty?"

"Aye," Rees said, uncomfortable that the conversation was to be of his wife, not of Flint.

"She is so far from being loyal to herself that she has turned upon her very soul." Ine shook his head, aware that, while he understood what he was trying to say, Rees would not. "She has come to hate herself," the bard said bluntly. "She may well make some very bad decisions therefore. Damn it!"

Rees did not even think to doubt the statement. Ine was not only very intuitive, he was very certain. "Tell me how you know this."

Ine had anticipated this dilemma, and he would not betray Owen. "We were speaking of the people here, and I made the error of saying that they appeared to love her. She called herself 'loathsome.' She cannot bear to be loved."

Rees's ice blue eyes narrowed. "Have you a notion of why?" he asked, not doubting the information, thinking quickly that it could be part of the explanation of her obstinate refusal to receive Communion.

Ine struggled to find the right words, an unfamiliar situation that frustrated him by its absurdity. "She blames herself for a deal of woes," he said. "She blames herself for making things even harder for Flint. Until she fled from Westminster, King Edward had not given Flint a harsh overlord. After she ran away, he did."

"Ran away?" Rees repeated.

"'Twas two years after her removal from Wales, five years past," Ine said. "She was gone from the king's control, and she went for a minstrel, which is how I came to learn of it." In fact, Ine had somehow known that Briana had fled from Westminster, his inexplicable mystical connection to her strong even though he had been a hundred miles away from her. He felt it wiser not to tell Rees of that.

"You traveled with her?" Rees asked. There was, Ine was pleased to note, no tone of suspicion or jealousy in the question, though there might well have been.

"Nay," said Ine. "She was alone on the roads. Minstrels are rarely molested. Most people value the music too much."

Rees read something in his voice. "Most people?"

Ine looked away from him, speaking carefully. "I encountered her just north of Peterborough," he said, "and 'twas fortuitous. There were two other knights on the roads, decent men, as I am not a skilled warrior. She had been attacked by a rogue knight—whether his end was robbery or rape, I know not—but he had beat her and near killed her. The two knights killed him."

Rees was enraged thinking that his wife had been beaten badly enough to have had her life put in jeopardy, but he mastered it so that he could think clearly, and he did not interrupt.

Ine went on, "We rode as if the devil himself was pursuing us to bring her back to Westminster, where the physicians might save her. I bore her on my horse some of the way, and she babbled. In delirium, but I understood."

"Tell me," said Rees.

Ine told him, hesitating occasionally, trying to remember clearly words he had hoped he would be able to forget. Briana thought she should have been able to save the people she loved, her family, of course, but even Prince Llewelyn. Rationality had never intruded on that guilt; she disregarded it, and "She was not in any fit condition to be reasoned with," Ine said, "nor was it my place to try." It had been clear to Ine that the only thing for which she was grateful was that those people who remained at Flint were alive, even though so many others had died.

Rees was frowning, but once again, he did not interrupt.

"When she was recovered, King Edward told her that the fate of Flint was hers to decide, that if she rebelled against his rule again, he would destroy it, that because she had defied him, he would make the people pay for her defiance."

Rees swore an oath that blistered Ine's ears. "I saw only edges of this afore now," he said. "Think you that returning to Flint has brought it so strongly to the fore?"

"Only in part," Ine said slowly.

"What do you perceive the other part to be?" Rees asked.

"You," said the bard. "It must be you."

Rees's lips thinned into a taut line. All at once, a great deal was clear to him, and none of it was pleasant. Briana was still at war with the English; the English had made her helpless, had made it impossible for her to save the people she loved more than anyone or anything else; the English had, therefore, earned her undying enmity. By treating her well and by treating well everything she valued, he had made a part of her come over to the enemy, so now she was at war with herself. He closed his eyes, anger gone, and said, "Sweet Jesus" under his breath.

Ine saw that Rees comprehended what the problem was.

Then Rees opened his eyes again. "Sweet Jesus," he repeated, "if I cherish her, she will only continue to feel less and less worthy of being cherished. What in God's name am I to do? Abuse her so she can begin to care for herself again?"

"Nay," said Ine, for though the question had been asked in frustration, he took it seriously. "Abuse is not the way to win anything—not Flint, not its lady. Perchance domination? She has made only a single decision in seven years, and that choice, to run away from the king, placed her and Flint in real peril. Since then she has only had to tread carefully and be compliant to survive. She knows the way of that. And she was only a child when the king took her."

"What sort of child?"

Ine cast his memory back. "Happy," he said slowly, "a bit wild. She defied her father and older brother with some frequency, but always with humor and charm. Bright. Confident." He shook his head. "'Tis all gone now, or buried so deep—"

"Not all," said Rees. "The brightness remains. Even as she bent to the king's will, she never lost everything. But she has not been openly defiant latterly, except in the matter of Communion. And then I—" He halted. *And then I tapped into the ocean of her passion, and she decided she needed it.* He felt a wrenching pain in his gut at the idea of not touching her again, and he refused to consider it as an option. The implications of his need for her he had not fully grasped. The fire that burst out of her in lovemaking, the same fire he had seen in her chamber the night she told him she would be quite pleased if he died, that fire was real. Even if she held it in abeyance now everywhere but the bedchamber, it still existed. All he had to do was to help her see that her life was a blessing, not a curse, to her or to the people around her. Abraham would have known how to do it. But Abraham had also taught him each person was responsible for himself, before any other. "All I need do!" he said aloud, his voice suddenly cold. "God's blood, I cannot help her. Help is not what she wants. She needs to break it all loose herself." His hand fell heavily onto Ine's shoulder. "I will deal with this. My thanks for telling me."

Ine nodded once. "'Tis a challenge."

"Aye," said Rees, but his mind was already somewhere else. She had shown herself to be obedient to her given word. He would need to find a way to push her so that they arrived at a vow she was willing to give him.

Neither of them could know that the process which would save her was already in motion, that ultimately it would not be Rees's actions or words which would be most instrumental for helping Briana become whole again, but more the actions of three other people: a lean man with burning, tired brown eyes lately arrived at Flint from Snowdonia; a giantess who since puberty had not felt comfortable being part of the world in which she lived; and a Norseman currently on the roads to Charing searching for a son he had only lately learned he had.

When Rees went to look for Briana, at first he could not find her anywhere.

Briana had fled from Ine into the manor house, wildly unhappy at what she had revealed to the bard in an unguarded moment. The words which had sprung from her surprised her no less than they had him, but she was not nearly as appalled by them as Ine had been. For her, it was almost a relief to have uttered them. She had finally crystallized what had been building inside her since she had seen the condition of Flint and its people. She was indeed loathsome, had to be, to have turned her back on her people for so shallow a reason as ecstasy, to have not only allowed her family's killer to enter her body, but to have delighted in it and hungered for him.

Maud was a worthy successor to Bryn and Emrys. Maud had kept her integrity while holding Flint together, and the fine flame of her strength and righteousness continued to burn brightly. Briana welcomed her aunt's distance, the disapproval of, even contempt for, Briana's capitulation.

She found herself running to the stableyard for Timbrel, past Esrith's startled face. She did not wait for a saddle, just put

the bridle on the palfrey, snatched up the reins, flung herself
onto its bare back, and urged the sleek mare at the fence. She
had not jumped bareback in many years, since Bryn and Maud
had begun trying to make her behave like a lady, but Timbrel
responded well, and Briana kept her knees clamped tight to the
brown sides of the horse as they went over. She had no idea
where she was going until the palfrey's feet hit the pasture, and
then she remembered. As a child, she would go to Bally Bay, the
place to run when she was upset over anything. All those things
seemed smaller now; she had not been able to go there after
Fearndon. The king had not given her the time. Because the bay
was both tidal and sheltered, there were gentle waves, which
never crested, but moved rhythmically and restfully back and
forth, soothing, a source of solace.

She turned Timbrel's head up the coast in the direction
opposite from the castle and urged her into a gallop until the
track running parallel to the ocean narrowed. Then she slowed
her horse to a walk and let her pick her way down the trail
descending the escarpment to the shore itself.

Bally Bay's half-circle was cut into the cliffs like a giant's
bite. The rocks edging it gave way to a small crescent of smooth
pebbles which made tiny clinking noises as the little swells
washed over them. She had come here when her father and
Griffith first went off to war and been calmed by the quiet
sounds, punctuated occasionally by the raucous cries of seabirds
circling overhead or diving into the chill waters for fish. She had
come here, too, when word had come to them that Prince
Llewelyn was dead. This was a place that helped her reach a
kind of acceptance of things. She would not have described what
she did here as praying, perhaps even deeper prayer than she had
ever done in the closeness of a chapel, but she always found a
kind of serenity.

When Timbrel reached the edge of the pebbly beach, Briana
slid off her and left her on the last of the soil. Even in her own
distress, she would not risk the palfrey on the uneven pebbles,

where the footing was so uncertain. She walked out onto the shifting stones herself. At the edge of the restless waves, she dropped to her knees, oblivious to the fact that her plain brown linen gown was quickly sodden. *Mayhap*, she was thinking, *'twould have been better had that rogue knight killed me.*

She stared out to sea, wondering if there were reasons not to simply walk into the surf and keep walking until she breathed salt water long enough to forget everything. The fact that suicide meant she would go to hell in no way troubled her, for it was as if she had been in hell since Fearndon, and now, having been allowed a taste of what life could be out of hell, she had been drawn back in again. God had been punishing her for years, and she had not struck back at Him until she refused the Host. She believed He could do no worse to her now.

And despite the fact that the butcher baron, her husband, was the source of her pain, he was also the source of her joy, and that single paradox had to be God's doing as well, to add to her torment. She reflected, sitting down hard on the wet pebbles, that she could solve both issues—the pain and the paradox—by killing Rees, but even as the thought came to her, she knew beyond doubting that there was no way she would ever be able to do that. She did not think she was capable of killing any human being, not even the brute who had tried to despoil her in the meadow north of Peterborough. Besides, Rees was too valuable to Flint for her to even imagine his demise. So she asked herself as honestly and courageously as she could if she were capable of killing herself.

And, honestly, she recognized that she was not. She lowered her head into her hands, her body bent double, her lips very close to the glistening stones of the beach, and whispered, "Why did You not allow me to save them? Why could I only effect my own continuance?" She knew she could not end her own life, as unworthy as she thought herself for turning her back on the others by loving—Her breath caught in her throat, bringing in salt spray, and she began to cough. The villagers

were right. Father Ciaran had spoken truly. She loved Rees, and
there was no one alive to grant her absolution for it. She knew
that Maud could not, and Owen would not, and she thought they
were right.

She was suddenly infinitely weary, but she knew that she
was not going to die. If she could not live for Flint or for herself,
then she would have to live for Rees, because she had to live for
something. She stretched out on the pebbles just at the tide line,
ignoring the occasional slap of waves against her side, and tried
to think of nothing at all. She might have slept.

Rees found her two hours later, as the storm clouds were
crowding in with their heavy, rain-filled darknesses aimed at
North Wales. When he and Ine had returned and found her gone,
Rees felt both fear and rage. Ine went at once to find out if Owen
was still in the village, asking Rees only, "Will you be patient
for a few minutes to see what I can discover?" Reluctantly,
recognizing that Ine had known her longer, knew her well, and
had sources in Flint village, Rees agreed.

Ine eventually located the rebel leader in the village,
working side by side with some of the knights to keep the forge
going so Martin, the smith, could quickly improve the plows and
other farm implements, as well as add to the spearpoints and
arrowheads in the Flint armory, badly depleted.

When Owen saw the bard, he excused himself from the
bellows and, taking a cloth to wipe his gleaming face and naked
torso under the leather vest he wore to provide some protection
from stray sparks, came out of the smithy. "So," Owen said to
Ine, "who have you warned?"

Ine made a negating gesture with his hand. "I told Lady
Briana, who says she will go nowhere with you, but who appears
to have gone somewhere without you."

"She's run?"

"She's nowhere to be found, and young Colet says she took
her palfrey saddleless from the stable."

Owen remembered the childish Briana, who did as she liked

with no thought for the consequences. He did not know this new Briana, for whom consequences had become all-important, but he could not believe she had changed so completely. Once he had followed her to the estuary shore, and if she still retained some of her past self, it was the logical place for her. "Seek her along the seacoast," Owen said, unperturbed. "She went to the sea when she was angry or upset." He tossed the cloth aside and returned to the bellows.

Ine conveyed the message, sourceless, to Rees, who saddled Basilisk and rode west along the coastal track. He was not sure what he would say or do when he found her, but he knew he had to find her. When the ground began to rise, he saw her and the palfrey from the top of the escarpment. He did not realize she was asleep, and he was stabbed through with fear that she was dead. He did not want any more deaths on his soul, though he could have accepted them and ultimately moved through them, but this particular one would have come near to destroying him, and he knew it. He would not risk Basilisk on the extremely narrow cliff path, so he bolted off the warhorse and raced down the narrow track on foot, swearing and praying simultaneously.

Briana became aware of her surroundings when huge hands grasped her shoulders and lifted her from the beach. She realized Rees was calling her name. She brushed stray specks of wet dirt from her eyelashes. "Aye, my lord," she said groggily, as if he'd just roused her from bed.

Rees was relieved, then furious. He resisted twin urges— one, to crush her to his chest; the other, to throttle her. "You are never to ride off again without asking permission!" he growled instead, setting her back from him and making himself let go of her. "You could have been hurt or killed, and I'll not allow that!"

His words reminded her of something she had forgotten. When she had been brought back to Westminster, half-dead from the rogue knight's attack, King Edward had ordered the physician not to let her die. Both men had forbidden death to take her. Briana believed that Edward had said it because he believed she was his to punish, not death's. Why was Rees saying it? And she had been afraid of the king's anger, but she was not afraid of Rees's. "Have you a particular compact with death that you can make such a statement?" she asked.

Rees, for the first time in years, allowed some of his ongoing, agonized bitterness about Fearndon rise to the surface, as he sat down on the pebbles beside her. He cradled her body against his chest. "I have served death all I care to," he said with venom, "though I know he may call upon me again. Death owes me a debt, and I would collect it with your life."

She had never heard anyone speak with such reckless hubris, not even the king. Rees did not seek to save her merely to punish her. She felt safe in his arms, and she loved him for that. She reached up and caressed his smooth cheek lightly as she drew back to full awareness.

He shook her gently. "Swear to me you will never again go from me without asking for my permission," he ordered then, fear of having lost her still coursing through him. "Swear to me."

"You are my liege lord," Briana said. "If you require me to swear, then I do so."

"Aye," he said, aware that she had just provided him with a way of reaching her. "'Tis time I began to fill the role of overlord and ruler for the Lady of Flint as well as for the fief."

Thunder rolled in the distance.

Briana heard herself say, "Not in the sanctuary."

"What?" She had nonplussed him, and he frowned.

"You will not rule me in our safe haven." She was so strongly insistent that he thought there was a chance Ine had been wrong, but then Ine was so rarely wrong that he discounted that. Instead, he decided that Briana of Flint was even more intriguing than he had guessed.

"Will I not, then?" he asked.

"Nay. You are my liege lord outside in the world. Inside, we are equals."

Rees had to admit that "equals" was a fair description of their sexual behavior, that he would not be so enraptured by her were it otherwise. "Very well," he said. "Now come back to the manor. It grows late, and we have guests to prepare for." He got to his feet, lifting her along with him. "'Tis vital you look your best before Mortimer this even."

She clung to him, off-balanced by the weight of her wet skirts, and, as always, intoxicated by the nearness of his iron-hard body.

Then he said, "You will repeat your vow of fealty to me in the presence of Baron Wigmore and the people of Flint in the hall before the meal begins." He waited for her reaction, knowing that if the people of Flint saw her kneel to him, they might find it easier to do the same—and if they did not find it possible, he would have an alternative to offer them that could protect them from King Edward's wrath. He had planned it from the outset. Once she had openly sworn to him here, he could allow the people to swear fealty to *her*, sparing their pride.

Briana's eyes widened. At that moment, she would far rather he had knocked her to the ground than given her that particular command. It would humiliate her to swear the oath openly, even though she had done it before.

Rees recognized her turmoil. Under normal circumstances, he might have told her why he needed this gesture from her, that he had asked for it at the handfasting specifically to make it easier for her here. But he did not explain. "Briana?"

She could think only that Owen was the last man remaining from her childhood, since Father Ciaran did not count as a man. For some reason, she did not think of Ine as part of her past any longer; he had moved with her through the time of her growing up. She loved Owen, but she had no illusions now about loving him in any way but as a brother. Even Ine's rather unpleasant tidings that he might be in love with her had not changed that. Owen would see her swear to Rees, and it would shame her.

"Briana," Rees repeated more sharply. "You will do this

because I require it of you." His eyes seemed as dark as the storm clouds crowding closer and closer overhead. She remembered how warm they looked filled with desire. She asked herself honestly if she were willing to say something defiant to this man so as to try to avoid a look she did not want to see in the eyes of another. The answer came back wrapped in her feelings for Rees, and she bowed her head beneath its judgment.

"Aye," she whispered. "I will repeat the vow."

He masked his relief and held her arm as he walked her back to the palfrey, held the mare's head while Briana gathered a handful of mane and swung up on the horse, and then led Timbrel up the path to where Basilisk waited, delicately cropping the sharp-edged sea grasses as if he felt obliged to, but would really rather not.

Chapter 29

Neither Sabine nor Edmund Mortimer had laid eyes on each other before they arrived at the door of Flint manor simultaneously. Baron Wigmore came on horseback at the head of his selected knights, glittering with the chain of office that declared him a Marcher Lord and therefore superior to Earl Connarc, even though an earl was higher in the nobility than a baron. He had brought only eleven knights, and the distinction, though a subtle one, as not lost on Rees. Mortimer had been invited to bring a dozen men; by bringing one fewer, he declared that he did not need all twelve to ensure his protection, even in the home of a man who could be considered a rival, if not an enemy.

He had not expected to see anything like the elemental force that was Sabine. "Who in the name of Christ is that?" he asked Rees, dismounting and finding himself shorter than the woman, who bowed without any hint of servility to the two noblemen and crossed the manor courtyard to take Maud's hands. Mortimer had been prepared to be a head shorter than Rees; he had seen the day before that Rees was somewhat of a giant. He was dumbfounded to find himself more than half a head shorter than a confident woman of an age somewhere between twenty and thirty.

"I'm not certain," Rees answered, his own gaze following the woman's muscled bulk as it vanished into the hall. He beckoned Maud, and though she was clearly reluctant to leave her place at the door, she gathered her skirts and joined the two men.

The rain-battered flags in the courtyard had dried in the evening breeze, but in the torchlight the cracks between them still glistened damply with the remnants of the afternoon storm. The hooves of Wigmore's party made staccato sounds on the stones as his retinue dismounted, entering the house itself past a double row of Rees's knights, who stood at a casual sort of attention, one or two resting their hands on their sword hilts.

Maud identified Sabine to them as the recluse's companion, realizing as she answered that she was speaking directly and civilly to Rees and ignoring Mortimer completely. She was shocked to discover that she already felt much more positively disposed toward the infamous Earl Connarc than she would have believed possible.

"Please honor us with your presence at table," Rees said with counterfeit sincerity to Wigmore, gesturing the Marcher Lord in the wake of his men and glancing around to see if Briana had made an appearance. He had determined that he would not seek her out until the meal was about to begin.

Briana sat in the master chamber, on one of the two trunks, letting Hulde finish arranging her hair, since Enlis had been needed to serve at table and was down in the kitchen. Briana had dressed in one of the new gowns, a pure white samite edged in threads of gold, over a pale green undertunic. Hulde had combed and rubbed her thick hair until it shone brightly enough to rival the metallic threads in the gown.

"Seems to me," Hulde was muttering as she coiled the two balls of hair over her lady's ears, "that a lord as rich as this one could afford to gift his wife with a few baubles after they've been handfasted so many weeks."

Briana tried to study her own face objectively in the

polished metal mirror and not to hear Hulde's muttering. It was true that Rees had not given her anything tangible since the handfasting, but it was also true that he was providing everything for Flint, and that was all she cared about.

Hulde muttered a little more vehemently about a lady's beauty being completed with precious stones. "'Tis not like my lady is a serving wench."

Briana was suddenly fiercely glad that Rees had never given her any jewels. She would have hated wearing them in front of her people.

The housekeeper tied a metallic gold ribbon across her lady's creamy brow, and Briana accepted it as Hulde's need to decorate. "You are lovely, my lady," Hulde said admiringly.

"Even without baubles?" Briana could not resist asking.

Hulde flushed, the color unevenly blotching her plain, open face, and bustled to pick up the dress Briana had changed from and left lying on the carpet.

Briana made herself rise and go to the door that connected her sanctuary with the rest of the world, squared her shoulders, lifted her chin, took a handful of the soft white skirt, and went down the steps and into the hall.

At her entrance, all conversation trailed away, and the men of Flint rose to their feet as if the action had been agreed among them beforehand. The knights who had come with Rees from Conway were quick to follow their lead, without any kind of signal from Rees, who was now seated at the center of the high table, Baron Wigmore on his right.

Ralf and Galen, who had seen Briana every day for weeks, were taken aback by the image she presented. They had grown accustomed to her everyday loveliness; this beauty was breathtaking.

It certainly took Rees's breath away, but he did not rise. Instead, he leaned forward in his chair, one hand clenched around the stem of his goblet, the other resting on the hilt of his sword. He was keenly conscious that Mortimer was as amazed at her as everyone else was, and he felt a violent pride that she belonged to him.

Briana was barely aware of anyone else in the hall besides Rees. This oath, this open act which would shame her but was so crucial to the man she loved, was something between the two of them, something so intimate that she felt the observers for whom it was being enacted were in fact little more than voyeurs. She wanted it over. And at the same time, she wanted to make it memorable for him, a gift of her love.

She walked, with as much dignity as she could manage, around the trestle tables, passing people she knew without even a glance in their direction, her gown and hair shimmering in the light from the candles and the fireplace until she, herself, resembled a living flame.

It was as if no one had realized how magnificent she was, as if no one—not Owen, not Maud, not even Ine—had understood how completely gallantry had held her together all throughout the years she had walked a tightrope at Windsor or Westminster, how it had sunk into her spine and muscles.

As she reached the small dais on which the high table stood, Rees also rose to his feet, as did Wigmore. Briana lifted the hem of her skirt enough to step up onto the dais in front of the table.

Rees felt a strong glow of admiration for her. He had expected her to come up onto the platform behind the high table, so that no one at the trestle tables would have seen her when she knelt to say the oath. She might have chosen the concealment; Rees would have allowed her that choice. She had instead chosen to fulfill her promise to him in the most courageous possible way.

Briana nodded briefly to Baron Wigmore, but it was a superficially courteous gesture, and even as she did it, her eyes never left Rees's face.

He could read nothing at all in her carefully guarded expression. He did not doubt that she would pledge to him. She had given her word, and he had not yet known her to break her word. He did not expect it when she turned to face the hall, showing her back to him, Baron Wigmore, and Maud.

The serving people stopped in their tracks, platters of meat, cheese, bread and vegetables in their hands. At the end of the righthand table, by the fireplace, Sabine climbed to her feet and waited. Following her lead, the women of Flint rose for their lady, Maud last of all. Only the dogs kept moving—except, of course, for Ulf, who waited near the high table in what he clearly considered his place. The others prowled under the tables, waiting for scraps or bones.

Briana swallowed once, lifted her chin a little higher, and said clearly, "People of Flint, we have come through the cold and now 'tis springtime again. As your lady, I today speak to you of Rees, of Plantagenet, the Earl Connarc—" Her voice nearly faltered, but she held it. "—who rules over us all in the name of the king." She turned her upper body toward Rees, but kept her hips square to the hall, twisting gracefully into a semi-spiral. "My lord, these, my people, I give into your care, and I beg you to treat well with them." There was no tone of supplication in her words, and likewise, there was no sense of irony.

Rees watched her carefully, aware that, while she could do great harm to him here, he could do nothing to stop her now. A flash in her eyes warned him not to speak yet, and he accepted that, acknowledging it with a barely perceptible nod, proud of her for once again doing far more than he had asked of her, amazed at the strength that had brought her to this pinnacle from the depths of the beach at Bally Bay.

Briana turned back to the still room. "My Lord Rees, as your lady, I today commend to you the people of Flint, who will serve you wholeheartedly, as they served my father." Her voice softened unavoidably at that moment, and she strengthened it with a ruthlessness that took even her by surprise. "My people, this, my lord, I offer for your protection and prosperity. I beg you to treat as well with him as he will with you. And, to that end, to the coming of our springtime at last—" She sank smoothly to her knees, a flower bending in a gentle breeze, and waited.

As if they had rehearsed it, Rees walked past her empty chair and around to the front of the table, drawing his longsword as he did so, and setting it, point downward, on the dais in front of her serene face. He held lightly onto the crosspiece with the fingers of both hands.

There was no doubt in anyone's mind as she spoke the oath of fealty that it came from the depths of her soul, nor that she had been utterly wise to preface it with the small speech. Had she not done so, the depth of passion she invested in the words of the oath could have shocked her listeners.

Rees was moved nearly to tears. He sheathed his sword with one fluid motion, pulled her to her feet, and with an open tenderness that affected everyone, he kissed her lightly on the brow, each cheek, and then her lips, not permitting himself to lengthen the last kiss as he wished to.

For Briana, it was as if they were alone, as if he had taken the boundaries of the sanctuary and extended them to include the circle of his embrace, wherever they might be.

With a smile, he led her back around the high table to their seats, aware that Edmund Mortimer was staring at her as if he had never seen a woman before.

Ine leaned his harp against the stool he had risen from when Briana entered the room and strolled casually to the trestle table where Owen Glyn stood, expressionless.

"Can you still believe she'll come with you?" he asked Owen under his breath, his lips barely moving as the servingpeople began to approach.

Owen seemed more sad than triumphant as he whispered his answer. "Oh, aye. You see, Ine, what is between them matters not at all. She will come with me because she must."

Before the night had ended, Rees was nearly forced to kill a man.

Throughout the meal, Briana had been superficially gracious to Baron Wigmore. It was easy for her to do, because she had learned all the necessary skills at the court of the English king, and she used them without thinking about it.

Maud did not have as easy a time. She had to sit beside the man who had so degraded Flint and its people, while Briana had Rees's powerful chest and shoulders as a buffer between Wigmore and herself.

The first part of the meal was polite enough. But before the final offerings were served, Mortimer, having drunk substantial quantities of the excellent brandywine, began an increasingly less subtle campaign of comments to the effect that any man who showed public affection for his wife, of all people, must necessarily be a weakling. He did it by expansive storytelling—this particular knight had beaten his wife whenever he considered she needed it and had slain a hundred men in the battle for Acre. And then there was the poor fool of a knight who allowed his wife unprecedented freedom, instead of commanding her harshly, as he should. He soon could not lift his sword successfully, let alone ply it in battle.

The metaphor was so clear to everyone that Briana felt her cheeks burn with embarrassment. Wigmore's knights laughed heartily. Rees's gave frosty smiles, trying to be polite to their lord's guest, except for Galen, who glowered so much that Menty laid a lightly restraining hand on his arm and murmured softly over his growl that he should not create trouble.

Rees took Briana's hand and stroked her palm gently with his thumb, his face carefully expressionless. He looked over at Ine, a wordless request.

Ine immediately got to his feet with the harp and walked into the open space between the tables. Quite deliberately, he chose the song of Caedmon, the monk of Streanaesh-Alch, one of the finest hymns to emerge from seventh-century Christianity.

"Praise we the Fashioner," he began, and the beauty and solemnity of the song about the creation of heaven and earth quieted even the most raucous of the Marcher Lord's men. By the time Ine was finished with the wonders of the Lord of Glory everlasting, the hall was calmer and subdued. With one exception.

William de Blaisey had been grinding through the thought that his employer was interested in provoking Earl Connarc. The thought came not so much from the words he had heard Wigmore say, but because of the sound of Mortimer's voice, slipping greasily over those words. The tone reminded him of earlier times when goading was the baron's goal. Dense as he was, the massive knight knew better than to interrupt the bard. Once the song was done, however, he casually took one of the gauntlets from his belt and, before even Mortimer had an inkling of what the knight was going to do, tossed it past Ine onto the floor in front of the dais.

The clink of mail on the lightly rush-covered stone sounded sharply loud in a room still hushed after Ine's song. Then Galen bolted to his feet, crying, "What hellish trick is this?"

Maud hissed, "Hospitality!" under her breath.

Briana held herself quite still, feeling icy cold, as if the warmth had drained out of her with the metallic sound. She did not know if she could stand any more killing, and especially not if it involved Rees.

No one from Flint village moved at all. de Blaisey was known to be an entirely brutish man, but his skill with a sword was unquestioned. It seemed to be the only thing, other than breathing, that he had ever mastered.

Rees took one deep breath and looked over at de Blaisey. "You cared not for the meal?" he asked conversationally, but his eyes were beginning to burn.

William laughed, making a noise unrelated to humor. "Seems my master is not pleased," he said.

Edmund Mortimer had not sought this but he could see an

immediate advantage to de Blaisey's crude stupidity. He wanted to know if there had, indeed, been any weakening of Connarc by his obvious devotion to his handfast bride. Now he was subjected to, and uncomfortably riveted by, Rees's disconcerting gaze. "Is it true that we have displeased you, my lord baron?" Rees asked.

Briana studied her hands on the table, so aware that Rees radiated danger that she failed to see how Mortimer could be blind to it.

Ine recognized that something had to happen, quickly glanced over at Owen, and then realized that, while there was another danger spot in the room besides Rees, the rebel from Snowdonia was not it. He turned slowly past Rees's tense knights to find the source of this new peril.

It was Sabine. She had not moved, but every muscle in her huge body was so taut that Ine fancied she had become a weapon, rather than merely bearing one.

No one at the high table was aware of the sudden note of tension at the other end of the hall. Maud wanted to lay her hand on the arm of the Marcher Lord, who sat just beside her, wanted to charm him with skilled words to diffuse the situation, but she had not that much duplicity in her. She hated the man too much, and she was not practiced at hypocrisy.

Mortimer was. He smiled at his host. "I would be most pleased to see you and my William cross swords sometime, a pleasant little match of skilled warriors."

"To disprove—" Rees's voice was even and quiet. "—the myths about the opposing relationship between a man's two swords, the steel and the flesh." Briana's head turned abruptly toward him, but she did not color any more deeply. Rees did not allow himself to be distracted by her movement. He tapped his long fingers on the table, seeming to consider Mortimer's far-from-innocent suggestion.

"Hospitality," Maud whispered again.

Rees did not look at her, either. In the true fashion of the challenged, he now never took his eyes from William de Blaisey, who seemed neither aware of nor particularly interested in whatever verbal interplay was going on.

"Of course," Rees said calmly, "'sometime' must needs be fairly soon, since you and your entourage will be departing for Harlech the day after the morrow." He rose, a confident, if resigned motion. "Thus, I propose your champion and I go to the courtyard and settle the question now." He whistled once and pointed to the gauntlet on the floor. Ulf rose to his feet, trotted to the glove, scooped it up in his bared fangs, and leaped up onto the dais to present it to his master. Rees took the gauntlet from the dog and with a casual flick of his wrist, sailed it back at de Blaisey.

The knight was not expecting the gesture, but he got a hand up in time to stop the missile from striking him in the face. Rees assessed the speed of William's defensive movement and filed it away.

Briana wanted to ask them not to fight, for she had never been comfortable in the presence of swordplay, even if it was only practice. There was too much about drawn swords that reminded her powerfully of the carnage of Fearndon, She wanted to retreat up the steps to the refuge of the master chamber, and not watch anything which was to follow. But Rees would hardly come with her; he was now committed to a fight, and she would stand by him through it. She said nothing.

Rees had turned his back on Mortimer in order to keep watching William de Blaisey, who had risen, delighted at the prospect of a fight, and so obviously eager to begin that Rees wondered wrily if he would need to keep repeating the word "courtyard" until it penetrated the brain of his challenger.

But even the hulking de Blaisey knew better than to draw a sword at the table of his host. He made a happy, gargling sound and hastened out of the hall. The knights of both noblemen poured out after him, bearing many of the torches from the hall, and followed by the people of Flint. Rees, Briana, Wigmore and

Maud came last, except for Ine, who was not reluctant, but wary. He cared little for the brutish de Blaisey, but he did not want to see Rees harmed, not only because of Rees himself, but because he knew how Briana would react to it. She had only just learned to love someone again. If he, too, fell to the sword, that might create a pit for her from which she would find it impossible to escape. He moved close to her in the crowd of people. He had not actually laid hands on her since he had met her on the road outside Peterborough, drawn to her by the bond that drew him to her now. And Ine did not really know whose side Sabine was on. He was only certain that when currents of treachery swept by, they sometimes carried people away with them. He did not want Briana to be one of those people.

"A pleasant little match," the Marcher Lord stipulated blandly once they were all in the courtyard, with space cleared at the center for the combatants.

"As you wish," said Rees, aware that Briana drew a quick indrawn breath, but once again forced to ignore her. "After all, he is your knight." His quiet confidence pricked Wigmore at last, and the baron's face, already florid from the wine, colored more deeply.

Without regard to how it might look, Sabine shouldered herself to the front of the spectators, tautly alert.

Rees unbelted and unlaced his supertunic, flinging it to Ralf, and emerging hard-muscled and strong in his short undertunic and hose. He took his sword in his hand, tossing the scabbard aside.

William de Blaisey was already clad in warrior garb, though neither man wore mail. Thinking Rees still unready, he drew his sword and swung at the earl. Despite the speed of the blow, Rees caught it on his blade and deflected it so easily it might never have been struck.

In the silence that followed the demonstration of Rees's nearly superhuman speed and instinctive skill, even William de Blaisey recognized that he might have made a little error.

Edmund Mortimer grew very quiet, some of the ruddiness fading from his face. He had been told that Rees was so skilled with a sword that some of the denizens of the English court—most notably, Gilbert de Clare, commander of the company Rees served with on Crusade—called him an adept, but Mortimer had discounted a great deal of the praise as sheer exaggeration, another part of it as calculated to please King Edward. He believed it was puffery, too, because he knew for a fact that Rees had been credited with the betrayal of Prince Llewelyn which Mortimer himself had secretly engineered, at the king's request. He had believed Rees to be largely a fraud, and he had wanted to use William de Blaisey to disprove that reputation. He realized abruptly that it was quite possible the intelligence about Rees's prowess was that single thing he had not credited it with being— the truth. In seeking to disprove it, he might confirm it instead. And now he could do nothing to halt it.

Briana winced at the sound of metal striking metal, trying not to see, in her mind's eye, the battle she had witnessed at Fearndon, when Wales fell. But the memory rushed in unavoidably. She had defied her father's orders to stay away, and she had not realized that, by disregarding him, she would actually have to witness the fate of her family. When she reached a place where she could see the battle, she was sorry, but she could not look away. She recognized then the folly of watching those she loved putting themselves in peril. There must have been a thousand men on the field at Fearndon, most of them English, and yet she was able to find the men she loved among them.

Meredith fell first. Perhaps that was inevitable. He was so young and he had never actually been in battle before. His swordsmanship was all practice, his eagerness all bravado. His horse stumbled, pitching him forward over its head and then pitching forward itself. Boy and horse vanished in the ocean of seething movement.

Before Briana had time to think anything but his name—

"Meredith!"—she saw Griffith hauled from his horse. Her older brother fought off one attacker, but then was overcome by others. She felt the pain of his loss in her body before it reached her mind, and she cried out, "Oh, God!" as she searched for Bryn, the only one left to her.

Either God did not hear her, or He was too busy elsewhere. The moment her eyes settled on Bryn, he, too, was cut down by a dozen swords sent to the task by the devil, who was currently calling himself King Edward of England. She could not even close her eyes to shut out the sight of her father's roughly handsome darkness exploding in redness.

Now she was terrified that she would see Rees fall, too, and yet, once again, she could not look away.

It became very clear very quickly that Rees was in total control of the fight. He moved as if he were connected to his blade, centered, balanced, and deadly calm. He was also concentrating very hard, because he had no intention of killing the knight, only of disabling him and, as he had learned during the Welsh war, it was much easier to kill than it was to contain killing.

William de Blaisey sensed the restraint in his opponent and took it as an insult. He increased the violence and recklessness of his attack. Rees was largely unmoved by the change in tactics. He seemed barely to adjust his own response, but his speed increased, his face impervious to emotion.

Everyone was silent, watching.

To her amazement, now that it looked as if Rees would be unscathed, Briana was enchanted, and the feeling was totally alien to her. She had thought she would be sickened by the swordplay and instead she saw, and admitted to herself, the grace and beauty of it, at least in the variety practiced by her handfast husband.

William made another powerful swing, but instead of trying to block it, as he had all the others, Rees stepped into it, letting the blade pass him by a fraction of an inch, and swiped his own sword across the knight's thigh. It was a shallow cut and should have ended the pleasant little match, but Mortimer's knight seemed to feel he had been taunted or patronized. He redoubled his efforts.

For a moment or two, Rees merely deflected the blows, his own speed increasing yet again, waiting to see if Wigmore would call de Blaisey off. When he was certain that the Marcher Lord would do nothing, and that William would not cease fighting, Rees accepted the necessity of further damaging the knight.

Galen and Ralf saw Rees's face change and exchanged a glance. Rees had put on his killing mask, and the particular cold hardness seemed to strip away the humanity in his expression, leaving it resignedly grim and determined, a declaration of unfeeling power. It was the expression that had caused the Mamelukes to call him the angel of death when he was in the Holy Land.

Edmund Mortimer did not know enough to recognize the detachment it represented; William de Blaisey was too preoccupied with the movement of the silver steel in Rees's hand to notice its golden counterpart on the flesh of his face. But Briana was horrified by it. That face was utterly alien to her; it seemed to have nothing at all to do with the man she knew and with whom she was comfortably at ease.

Rees's lips tightened, and he ceased deflecting blows and began delivering them. de Blaisey fell back under the unexpected onslaught, his defensive moves far less coordinated than his attack had been.

Briana pressed the back of her hand against her mouth, heart pounding, uncertain how much of what she felt was fear and how much was an unexpected excitement she might well later find entirely shameful. She tried hard to control the turmoil that roiled within her, but it ignored her efforts at containing it. She thought, inescapably, *He must have looked like this at Fearndon. I could not have seen it.*

"Will he disarm him?" Galen murmured to Ralf.

"I think not," Ralf whispered. "Wigmore's pushed it too far."

Menty took Galen's arm to hush even the voiceless exchange in case it might distract Rees. She glanced from the fighting men to Briana, then back at the progress of the combat.

For, having decided to end it, Rees did not believe in taunting his opponent. He seemed to drop his guard, leaving his body tantalizingly unprotected, and de Blaisey had been provoked enough so that he could not let the opening pass. Incautiously, he turned his sword to lunge at Rees with it, but by the time he had cocked his wrist, it was too late. Rees swived in along the length of the blade now aimed at him and scored a long slash across William's chest, trying to keep it shallow enough not to kill, but still aware that his point had scraped ribs.

de Blaisey dropped forward as Rees stepped aside, the hard mask melting from his features but leaving them still grim. He turned his gaze on Edmund Mortimer with a look that firmly accused the Marcher Lord of responsibility for this.

Wigmore was in no way cowed, and said only, "Get him up and take him to the castle," to some of his own knights. Then he smiled at Rees. "I see the rumors of you exaggerated little. Your prowess, at least the prowess with this sword, is in no way lessened by your—" He had been about to say "weakness," but a sudden, anticipatory glitter in Rees's eyes forestalled him. "—softness in other ways," Mortimer amended smoothly, slightly mockingly.

Rees chose to ignore the mockery. "I trust," he said instead, taking a cloth that Ralf held out to him and wiping the blood from his blade, "we need have no pleasant little matches on the morrow."

"I see no need," Mortimer said mildly. "We will welcome you and your party to the castle at sundown, and I will tender you formal possession."

Rees nodded an acknowledgment and picked up his

swordbelt, sheathing the blade in his scabbard with one flinging motion that revealed the anger or disgust he had been careful to conceal until now. He watched the castle party leave with narrowed eyes, the slow smolder of rage lapping at him, even as he fought against it. He wanted to be out of Wigmore's company as soon as possible.

He looked over at Briana, saw Ine speak to her, saw her nod and gesture upstairs. Then she swallowed, laid her hands against her face for a moment and walked over to Galen, Menty and Ralf. He was distracted briefly by a familiar motion in the group of villagers, who were beginning to disperse. Sabine was putting a very respectably sized dagger into a sheath under her cloak. He wondered what she had intended to do with it, but did not have a chance to ask her before she joined the other people who were leaving the courtyard.

Briana did not think she could be alone with Rees so soon after seeing the mask. She wanted others around her, at least for a time. She looked at Rees, her face spotted with high color on her cheekbones, her eyes bright. She mouthed the word "solar," then spun and went back into the manor.

Rees had hoped they would go to the master chamber, but they still had guests. He sighed and tried to let all the rage slip away from him.

Chapter 30

Briana had always loved the solar at Flint manor. She had learned to play the dulcimer there; she had often knelt on the seat of the window overlooking the road and watched whoever was passing by for whatever reason. When the party from Conway arrived at Flint, the solar was empty. All the furnishings had been sold over the years to help buy food. Now it was filled with warmth. The stones of the floor were covered with carpets and the fireplace blazed merrily with piles of fragrant fruitwood which filled a trunk near the hearth. The window seat and a half-dozen chairs sported cushions in bright colors. A bench and several trunks completed the furnishings except for a new bed in the inside corner of the room, brought specifically for Maud, who had been sleeping on a pallet on the floor. Briana thought, watching Maud's face as the men set up the bed, that it did almost as much to win Maud over as the food had.

When they came into the solar after the banquet and the little match which left blood on the flags in the front courtyard, Ine took a seat on the bench, his harp resting beside him. Ralf, Galen and Menty sat in chairs close to the hearth, and Maud, who had sent Enlis to bring them cups of ale, sat on a cushioned trunk at the foot of her bed. Ulf trotted in and settled on one of the rugs in the center of the room with his singular air of ownership.

Briana came in before Rees did and went at once to the window seat, her favorite place, biting her lip a little, tapping lightly on the newly installed glass panes. No one spoke very much until Rees arrived, still carrying his swordbelt. "I've had a tub brought to the guest chambers as well as to the master chamber," he said. "Lady Maud, would you wish a tub brought here as well?"

Maud seemed to waver between possible responses, and finally she shook her head. "Nay, my lord. I do not feel as dirtied by the blood of a Wigmore man as I might have by others." It might have been provocative, but it seemed to contain more of weariness than of challenge about it and in the aftermath of the battle, Briana did not notice it, and Rees did not remark on it.

As Enlis came in with the cups and pitcher of ale on a tray, Rees sighed deeply and stood his scabbarded sword on its end, leaning it against the wall by the solar doorway.

"Are you well?" Ralf asked him.

"He touched me not with his blade," Rees said, walking to the chair nearest the hearth and sinking into it.

"They never do," said Galen to the other people in the room, especially Briana. "The first time I sparred with him, he kept disarming me—what age did you have then, Rees? Fifteen?—and I thought 'twas my skill lacking, but 'tis him. No one lays an edge on him in battle."

"Someone did once." Briana rose from the window seat, where the night chill was beginning to seep into the room, and walked back to the fireside. "Someone in the Holy Land."

Rees raised a hand unconsciously to his chest and touched the layers of cloth that covered the scar.

Galen sobered. "I'd forgotten that," he said.

"'Tis said," Ine put in, "that no man is fully formed except by war. I believe 'tis said most by warriors, but I find no surprise in that. Is it a saying with which you would agree, my lord earl?"

Rees grew thoughtful and for a time sat still, his only motion the flexing and unflexing of his sword hand. "I think," he said at last, "that war is only one of the experiences which forms men. Some it completes; some it splits apart."

"Aye, the blow you took would have rent a lesser man in twain," Ralf said. "And yet you survived it."

"'Twas that crazy wizard," said Galen. "He did it."

Enlis left the tray on one of the trunks and let herself out of the solar, closing the door firmly behind her.

"I never afore this heard you call him a wizard," Rees said with a grin at Galen. "'Tis an odd name for him, and yet—" He paused, deep in thought, then looked at Ine. "Would you like to hear a tale, bard?"

Ine smiled. "That's asking me if I would breathe," he said. "Is it a thing I can make a song from?"

"Perchance," said Rees. "We took the Cross and sailed for the Holy Land with Gilbert de Clare. I think 'twas in 1275."

They had arrived in November and were able to occupy a fortress at the very edge of Antioch. It was a large fortress, in good repair, the kind of place King Edward tried to imitate in building his Welsh castles, and it should have been fairly impregnable. Their relative ease in taking it was likely more due to negligence on the part of the defenders, rather than any particular tactical genius of de Clare's. "I think if someone believes a place cannot possibly fall, they give less energy to keeping it guarded," Rees said. "In any case, we took it handily. I believe it made de Clare confident, and the confidence was shaken not by our first battle."

They had fought that first battle in the streets of Antioch, and Rees had found it intoxicating. Up to that point, all his knowledge of warfare had been theory, and now he could take the entirety of his training, all the philosophy of keen edges, sharp points, and human flesh, and see how they worked in reality. The first time his sword cleaved a man, he felt a shock of recognition jar him, travel up his arms into his body, and settle upon him like a cloak.

"'Twas what I'd trained for," said Rees. "'Twas what I knew how to do more than I knew anything else. 'Twas riding and arms and a mission—I've no memory of it now. I think that even then I knew not how many men I dispatched." The absence of awareness was a new experience for him.

And then, after the battle was over and the other knights were all laughing at their victory, Rees felt his awareness return, and unexpectedly, overwhelmingly, he was sickened by the carnage.

Briana drew her knees up, resting her heels on the seat of the chair on which she sat, wide-eyed at what she was hearing. She hugged her legs to her, her heart beating faster, absently expecting Maud to reprimand her.

Maud seemed oblivious and stared into her cup of ale, frowning.

Menty laid a hand on Galen's arm to keep him from interrupting, an impulse which did not seem to have struck Ralf at all. And Ine listened intently, his eyes narrowed as if memorizing every word.

Rees described the slaughterhouse he had recognized with a voice which neither glorified nor lessened the horror of pieces of what had been whole men falling to the ground through a curtain of ever-changing crimson splashes. He had thought the skill of fighting was a dance, that there would be a relation between the rhythms of the physical activity and the rhythms of the music he made with his recorder, but he realized that he had been entirely wrong. Music was a generative activity. Battle was its polar opposite, destructive, polluting, the diminishment of its practitioners, rather than the glorification he had always believed it to be. He discovered that he was disgusted by it.

And he knew he was very good at it. He could share none of those thoughts with the other knights in de Clare's company, and perhaps because of that, his realizations ate at him.

In the second battle, which took place in Antioch's only

market square, Rees found he could not extinguish his awareness a second time, not now that he had seen through it. He could not recapture the unthinking rhythm of destruction that had sustained him so completely throughout the first battle. He became clumsy, fumbled, lost his balance on a stone surface slick with gore, and took the sword blow that might have killed him. "Whoever it was I was fighting had a clear road to kill me," Rees said, "and would have, but for—" He nodded at Galen.

The big Saxon grinned at him. "After the constant thumping you gave me in practice, it seemed the only way I could prove my worth, saving your life," he said.

Rees did not remember much of the immediate aftermath of the battle, but Ralf did, and took over the telling for a time. Of the injured knights who had not been killed outright in the marketplace, Rees was the most seriously wounded. "de Clare fair split himself from worry," said Ralf. "You were our strongest fighter—he'd seen that in the first battle, and of course you were nephew to the king. We tried to keep you from losing your life's blood, and he went screaming for a physician, saying he'd pay in gold."

In three minutes or less, as if he had been waiting for the call, the "wizard" arrived and had Rees carried from the steaming, stinking square into the fortress. The physician was dressed in Saracen robes, but he was bearded much more thickly than any Saracen or Mameluke, and under the robes he wore clothing that was strange to the knights, a garment of stars, crescent moons, and geometric shapes of no real definition. He could have been any age, for though his beard was black, his face was wrinkled in ways suggesting many years of life past.

Galen and Ralf refused to leave Rees once they got him to the dorter in the fortress. They were both leaning so heavily on him to stanch the bleeding that the physician, who appeared not to speak or understand French or English, had to push their arms to get them to give the fallen knight enough room to breathe.

The man unrolled a bundle he had carried into the fortress

with him, laying it on the dorter bed next to Rees's. He made motions to the two knights and the hovering de Clare, indicating that they needed to cut away Rees's clothing, mail and all. When no one moved quickly enough to suit him, he made a kind of growling sound deep in his throat, and suddenly everyone accelerated. Even de Clare followed the old man's wordless directions, taking a pair of shears to cut the links of Rees's mail, first the tunic, then the leggings.

"I never saw anyone move as fast as the physician did then," Ralf said to Rees, "not even you when you're fighting." He frowned a little. "I know not why we've never spoken of this hitherto."

Rees shook his head. "Worry not on that. Speak of it now."

"He had some sort of crystal eyepiece," said Ralf, "and he studied the wound close. I thought he could do nothing. I'd never seen a worse wound that hadn't killed at once."

But the physician did not seem distressed. He said something in a language no one understood, and then he stitched some things within the wound itself, moving quickly but seeming to take enough time to assure himself that things were as he wished them to be. Then he began to sew the great wound itself, taking care to match the tissues on either side of the slice, packing the flesh with oils he took from a multitude of sacks and vials he carried in his bundle. He put in nearly two hundred stitches before he was done and covered the scar with herbs from his bundle. Rees had sustained a smaller wound in the thigh, which the physician rightly ignored at first, but when he turned to it at last, Rees was beginning to stir.

de Clare tried asking questions, but the physician's responses were in no known language, and at last de Clare ceased asking.

When Rees began to struggle to consciousness, the physician mixed a potion in an earthenware cup and bent close to Rees, holding the cup to his lips with one hand and stroking the knight's throat gently with the other. Rees swallowed and almost immediately slept again, this time breathing more easily.

The physician finished stitching and wiped sweat from Rees's forehead and chest, then covered his wounds with a clean white cloth and covered Rees's lower body with a blanket. He glanced around, found a chair in the corner of the dorter, dusted it off, pulled it over to the bed, and sat down. Ignoring de Clare and Rees's two friends, he reached into his robes, drew out a bound sheaf of papers with markings on them which were as incomprehensible as his speech had been, and began to read.

de Clare shrugged, nodded to Ralf to stay, and said, "Leave him not until he wakes or dies." He beckoned to Galen, and they left.

"You slept for three days," Ralf said. "I dozed betimes, but I swear the old physician never slept at all."

And then Rees awakened, in pain, but with clean wounds and only slight fever. And after de Clare assured himself that Rees would not give him cause to have to apologize to the king, he organized another foray and took his remaining knights back out into the city to fight.

"I was glad to see you go," Rees said. "I was glad not to go with you."

More than the pain, Rees was taken by a fear of never being able to fight again. He could share these fears with none of the other knights, for he did not know if he would ever be of use to them again. He lay on the bed of fresh linens and wondered what he would do if he were incapable of fighting any longer. "My only other skill was playing the recorder," Rees said, "and I knew I was not skilled enough to make a minstrel."

Ine smiled at that, but did not interrupt.

"After a day of that kind of doubt, I wanted to think about anything else," Rees said. "When the physician came in with food, I ate it. And after he gave me some sort of nostrum and replaced my bandages, I thanked him for his care of me." Rees looked at Ralf and Galen. "He said, ''Tis my singular pleasure.'"

Galen swore and Ralf jumped. Both tried to speak at the

same time.

Briana remembered that Ralf had implied Rees had never told them this before, wondered why he was telling the story now, wondered how he could still fight as he did.

Rees's expression was slightly amused, and slightly distant. Part of him was back in Antioch, staring at the physician and saying, "My friends told me you could not speak to them."

"I chose to let them believe that," said the old man. "It allows me more freedom in my work. You are healing well."

Rees felt a rush of relief at that. He might not have known what he could do with the rest of his life, but he wanted to live it. And he had not yet known of his bastardy, so when he named himself to the physician, he said, "I am Rees de Bretagne." He held out his arm gingerly.

The physician clasped wrist to wrist. "My name is Abraham ben Zeniuta," he said, "and if 'twere known I was a Jew, either side in this war might well slay me without a qualm. So I keep it and my counsel to myself."

"A Jew!" Galen said it explosively. "The king hates them!"

Briana drew in a breath. "Then they are in company with the Celts," she said. "Surely anyone the king hates must be blessed in other ways."

"Surely," Rees repeated. "I asked him why he was talking to me."

Abraham made a humming sound, high-pitched, not so much singing as chanting. Then he said, "I was called to be here, and 'tis a blessing to save a life." It was not an answer, though he acted as if it were.

Rees said softly, "I do not save lives. I take them."

"But not with pleasure," said Abraham.

"How came you to know that?" Rees asked. He did not trouble to deny the truth of it.

The physician reached over and tapped one of the bags from his bundle. "The drugs I gave you for pain also opened your lips. You spoke much to me. 'Tis only fair I speak to you in return."

Ralf started. "'Tis untrue," he said. "You made sounds, but you were not coherent. I was there."

"Mayhap," said Rees, "I was speaking his language."

Ralf did not know whether to regard that as a serious response or not.

"I told him I believed I had not ever met a Jew before," said Rees.

Abraham said drily, "You will doubtless be able to survive the experience."

"But only because you saved my life," Rees said. "Else I might not have survived aught. I give you my thanks."

"That," pronounced Abraham, "is fine thinking. Let us discuss this business of war, you and I."

"Discuss?" Rees repeated. "Mean you planning battle strategies?"

"Nay, I'd know naught of the ways of fighting. I'd speak with you of the *idea* of war."

Rees frowned. "I'd not considered war an idea. 'Tis a thing." He struggled to find ways to express what was to him a new and entirely alien concept—that something as solid and perilous as war, something so real that it consumed the health and lives of hundreds of thousands of men, could be merely an idea.

"We have a word for 'thing,'" Abraham said, watching Rees struggle with abstract thought instead of rejecting it. "As it happens, the same word means 'idea.' Interesting, is it not?"

Rees nodded slowly.

For the next six weeks, until the physician allowed him to get up and begin relearning how to use his muscles again, Rees and Abraham spoke, hour after hour, though not when anyone else was in earshot. They talked not just about war, but about life and death, and ultimately about talking itself, about critical thinking, about protest and acceptance, about reasons for living.

Because he had never met a Jew before, Rees had no way

of knowing whether Abraham was typical or unusual. He merely enjoyed the conversations, the arguments, the unaccustomed pleasure of mind meeting mind.

"And in the very last conversation we had," Rees said to the people in the solar, "we talked of what makes men whole."

"Was it war?" Ine asked.

Rees shook his head. "Abraham told me the way he believed the world works."

The physician said, "We are each of us born incomplete. But in addition to some of the parts of our own lives, we are born with little pieces of other people's lives in us as well. When such people meet one another, as when we met, there is a recognition. When we meet those people, we give them the bits of their lives we have been carrying within us, and they give us the pieces of our lives they have been carrying within them."

Rees looked at Ine. "'Tis not war which makes men whole. 'Tis other people."

After the physician took de Clare's gold and departed, Rees came to terms with how he could be who he was, how he could continue to be the man he had been, how he could reconcile that with the man he was discovering inside himself. By the time he was well enough to join the last months of battle before de Clare finally made the decison to sail for home, Rees had found a way to keep himself from falling again into the kind of doubt which had resulted in his nearly dying. He did it by becoming two people—the one who fought, and the one who did not.

"And you never met the Jew again?" Ralf asked.

Rees's eyes suddenly grew hooded. "I met him once again," he said slowly. "I'll not speak of that. Not now. Mayhap never."

For a very long moment, no one moved or spoke. Then Rees shook himself, as if casting off a spell, and said, "I'm sure the bath water grows cold." He rose, and so did Ulf.

Ine took his harp and watched Briana uncurl herself from the chair in which she had been sitting. He knew how conflicted the story had made her, and he thought he understood why Rees had had to tell it. Rees had been upset that Briana had seen him fight, because watching the cold mastery Rees had with weapons could only remind her of the subject they both wanted desperately to avoid—Fearndon. Rees had, Ine believed, needed to diffuse any condemnation. It had been an elaborate tactic, but Ine would not have traded the opportunity to hear the story for anything simpler. It made Fearndon even more difficult to comprehend.

And Ine was correct that Briana was conflicted. It had begun as she watched Rees battle de Blaisey, and hearing the story had contributed to it even more. Her mind whirling, she bid her aunt and the others a fair night and, as Rees retrieved his sword, she fled to the master chamber. Hulde and Enlis were within, waiting by the still empty tub. The buckets of water stood crowded by the hearth, whose fire Hulde was keeping high so that the water would stay warm.

Briana tried to control the agitation showing on her face as she stopped her headlong rush in the open area between the tub and the bed, panting, hoping her heartbeat would return to normal.

"Lady, do you wish me to undress you?" Enlis asked.

"Nay," said Briana. "Go to bed."

"I shall fill the tub," said Hulde.

"No need," Rees said from the doorway as Ulf trotted past him and leaped up onto the bed. "I shall tend to the water." He laid his sword on one of the trunks and stood still just inside the room until the two servingwomen had gone out. Then he leaned over and pulled the door closed. He watched her, waiting, but he neither moved nor spoke.

Briana did not know what to say. She realized she was wringing her hands and pressed them against her skirts to keep them still, wishing she could press her mind against something to keep it still, too. She looked at the sword and immediately moved her gaze from it to the buckets of water in front of the fire. That gave her something else to think about, and she went to get one to start filling the tub. She bent to lift a bucket, took hold of the handle, and failed to budge the container of water.

Rees hid a smile, crossed to the fire, lifted the first bucket and emptied it into the tub. Six buckets later, the tub was full enough, and he set down the last bucket and accepted that she was not going to speak first. "What is it, sweetness?"

She jumped a little. "I know not if I can say it."

Rees sighed. "In this room, you know you can say anything."

Her clear green eyes rose upward to meet his calm, infinitesimally wary gaze. "I have never seen—individual swordplay before. I've seen men practice, but 'twas always—only practice." She stopped.

"And?" he prompted.

She was afraid to say what she was thinking. He saw the fear and shook his head, discounting it.

"Your face." It was halting, just above a whisper.

He nodded, his voice low and under aching pressure. "'Tis my way of fighting. It allows me not to feel. Briana, I am not a predator. But I refuse to become prey."

She understood that he hated killing as much as she hated the thought of killing. It was, she admitted to herself, something else they shared, a thing she had not anticipated. He yielded to his role as a warrior the way she had yielded to hers as prisoner and hostage.

She lifted her chin in that slightly challenging gesture that he had come to learn meant she was about to take a risk. "I felt," she said.

He braced himself for condemnation, but he knew he would have to confront it, if not now, then later. "Felt what?" He waited for her to say she had felt disgust, revulsion, even hatred, though now he knew the hatred would be of his actions, perhaps of the dead mask his face had become, but not of his self. He no longer doubted that she loved him. How would she reconcile that emotion with the other? Could he help her once she actually said it, soothe her, bring her around to accepting it as a part of him? He had not wanted to fight, but Wigmore had left him no choice.

Once again, Briana astonished him. "I felt—" she began, then stopped. "There was something beautiful about it, about you. The grace of it. The skill." Her voice dropped. "The power. So unlike aught I expected to feel. It made me—want you." She covered her face with her hands. "'Tis shameful."

For a moment he was too surprised to move, and then he felt again that stab of happiness when she gave more than he had ever expected. He took two steps and drew her into his arms. "'Tis not shameful," he said strongly. "'Tis not shameful to respond physically to something like swordplay. Why do you feel 'tis?"

She drew in a deep breath, feeling the warmth of his arms and body against her. "It must be evil," she said, not certain herself of the explanation.

"You confuse wickedness with evil," Rees said, suddenly aware, because he had just been reminded of the Jew, that this was the kind of conversation he could have had with Abraham ben Zenuita. He had no doubt that Briana understood what he meant. "Killing is not always evil, sweetness. And sometimes 'tis even necessary."

She shook her head, thinking of her family and the princes and wanting to deny it, but she understood what he was saying. She admitted, "I've asked myself countless times if I could kill, should I need to. I think I have hated with sufficient power to drive me to it, were I capable, so I've come to think I have not the capacity."

"I know naught of the depth of your hatred," Rees said into her hair, "but I know much of the strength of your passion. I believe you could kill if you felt strongly enough that you needed to."

Her gaze flew up to the smooth planes of his face. She chose not to address the fact that she had tried to hate him and yet he could blithely dismiss that as if it mattered not at all. She fastened instead on his quiet belief that she might be able to kill someone. "You condemn me not for that?" Her voice cracked with surprise. "Women's task is to bring life, not to take it. Men make blood, and women make tears."

"When heard you that?" He was gentle, probing but soothing at the same time, his voice holding her just as securely as his arms did.

She tried to remember. "Aunt Maud said it to me sometime or other," she said, blessedly forgetting that it had been just before Fearndon. "I've no memory of when."

"Do you believe 'twould be better were the tasks shared? Or worse?"

Briana considered what he was asking, for it was an intriguing notion, something that had never occurred to her before. "Nay," she said at last, "not entirely. 'Twould be no bad thing for men to learn to weep, I think. But—" She hesitated, and he waited her out, his lips on her hair. "—taking a life is so very selfish."

Rees was surprised by the word, chewed on it for a time, then bent to regard her directly, eye to eye. "We must defend ourselves, sweetness. We must obey what we've pledged to obey."

"I am pledged to obey you, my lord," she said evenly. "I know not if I could do so should you command me to kill someone."

"I would never do that," he told her. "Life and death issues require individual choices." And he heard echoes in his head of King Edward taking any choice away from him before Fearndon. "Should require individual choices," he amended.

She heard the reverberations of hidden pain in his voice, but she would not ask about it. He had drawn enough out of himself today, and she was not certain she wanted to hear any more. She said simply, "My deepest thanks for my safe haven."

He decided that one more risk was bearable. "Briana, do you trust me?"

Once again, she considered the question without exploring the possible motives behind it. She gauged her own feelings and responded with the boldest possible truth. "I know not yet," she said at last. "My body trusts yours absolutely. But I know not whether my heart does the same." She looked up at him apprehensively, as if saying it would somehow anger or disappoint him, and then asked, "Do you trust me?"

Rees was surprised to find that he could not simply say aye. "I am learning to," he answered. "Keep encouraging me."

Briana smiled. "I shall try, my lord."

"Rees," he said, a whisper of emotion.

"I shall try, Rees."

Chapter 31

Bjorn Magnussen found his man in Charing and plied him with enough drink to loosen his tongue. Had the drink not accomplished its purpose, he was perfectly prepared to resort to mayhem. Fortunately, a full night of drunkenness—his own and that of his informant—gave him exactly what he sought. His son bore the name Rees, of Plantagenet, but had been granted honors and lands in his own right. The lands were in Wales. The informant drew a shaky, distorted map with one finger in the grime on the tabletop. Magnussen was extremely annoyed that he could not immediately set upon the son he intended to claim, for while he could be dogged in pursuit of an end, he was not a patient man. He decided to sleep a little, then ride west to recapture his lost future. He was determined that it would not elude him, and he would certainly not lose it by praying to any Christian gods this time.

In the hermitage, Sabine told Beatrice everything that had happened at the banquet, from Briana's unforeseen rendering of the oath, to Rees's power and control during the unwanted match with de Blaisey.

Beatrice kept her hands occupied with embroidery while she listened, her feelings flowing openly across her handsome face. Only when Sabine was done did she stop the rhythmic motion of her stitching and let her breath out in a soft sigh. "He has made himself proof against the world," she said. "How glad I am he has the strength."

"He has not, I think," Sabine said, "made himself proof against his bride. This appears to be a true love match, my lady."

The smile crept out, lifting the recluse's face to a haunting beauty. "Oh, God, be praised. I am so very joyful!" She had always wanted a love match of her own, but after she was despoiled, it had become impossible for her. She was pierced with delight that her son had found a happiness she herself had been denied. Beatrice thought it was almost worth the suffering she had endured. "Mayhap," she said wistfully, "'twill make it easier for him to accept me—accept my sending him away and letting him believe me dead."

She refused to think about what might happen if he disdained her. The things she had heard of him, the little she had seen, made her believe he would not turn away from her once he knew. She briskly lifted the embroidery again. "Sabine, you must protect her as you do him," she said. "He values her, and she must come to no harm."

Sabine nodded, agreeing.

Although she was weary, after everyone left the solar, Maud shook off the remnants of the strain she always felt around Edmund Mortimer and returned to the hall to confirm that it had been cleared, the fire put out, the hearth swept, and the old rushes gathered from the floor and discarded. It might have been Briana's task, but Maud had done it for so long that habit was too strong to simply put aside. She raised her candle to look around, saw a figure at one of the trestle tables, and came into the hall, pulling the door shut behind her.

Owen Glyn had been sitting in the darkness, toying lightly with a dagger, but it was preoccupation, not menace. He glanced up at her, then looked down at the dagger again.

Maud set her candle into one of the wall sconces and sat across the angle of the table from him, clasping her hands on the rough wood in front of her. "Well," she said quietly.

Owen looked back at her. "'Tis an interesting turn of events, this," he said. "It seems he no longer wishes to destroy us. Now when suppose you that happened?"

Maud shook her head. "Mayhap I was precipitate in sending for you."

"Nay, I'm glad to have seen it for myself. It gives me hope for you." He twirled the dagger between his thumb and forefinger.

"And for you?" she asked.

He was silent for a very long time, so long that Maud thought he had not heard her and was about to repeat the question when he sighed and tucked the dagger into his belt. "There's a thing I must do," he said. "And then we shall see."

She wondered if she should tell him what Rees had said in the solar earlier, but decided she should not, reached out and laid her hand on his arm. "She called it springtime," she said. "Think you she could have the right of it?"

He repeated, "We shall see." He rose and pulled the door open, walking through the corridor and down the front steps of the manor. He saw someone at the courtyard gate and recognized the harp before the man.

"Owen," said Ine.

"He's a powerful swordsman," Owen said by way of greeting. "I find I am quite grateful not to have challenged him openly."

"Believe you still that you can take her away?" the bard asked seriously, barely able to pick out the shapes of the other man's face in the dim light.

"I'll not be taking her. She will come willingly."

Ine was not passionate about anything but his music. He had not been really angry in more years than he could remember. He was beginning to feel angry now.

"Owen, I have thought many things of you over the years I've known you, including thinking you a fool for failing to give up a fight lost many years hence, but I never thought you an idiot 'til now."

Owen did not take offense. "'Twill happen as it must happen," he said.

It was by a sheer fluke that Menty overheard the conversation and saw them leave Flint on the day before the wedding. Because there were so many people in residence at the manor, and Wigmore had left the castle in no fit condition for immediate occupancy, there was no room inside any building for Menty's huge loom. So the men had set it up in one of the long sheds that held wood or peat or hay, and the area was rarely frequented. Some days Menty brought her daughter, Eaglyn, to watch her work or to learn something of the care of a loom, but on this day the little girl had a slight chill, and her mother came alone.

Menty was finishing a supple, Celtic-patterned blanket to give to Rees and his lady for their imminent marriage. She wanted it to be a special gift, so despite her fully Saxon background, despite Rees's Norman forebears, she had chosen the Celtic symbols as appropriate, for they were the ones which would be most meaningful to Flint in general and to Briana in particular.

Galen's wife was trying hard to overcome a weakness and was not certain how well she was succeeding. Menty had admitted to herself at Conway that she was envious of Briana. In all the years she had known Rees, Menty had hungered for a closer relationship with him than had ever been possible. The few times they had been able to sit and speak alone, their discussion had been much more enjoyable to her than the conversations she had with her much less intelligent, much more prosaic husband. She had nurtured a secret hope that, so long as Rees remained uncommitted to any single woman, she could have at least as much of him as anyone else did.

She harbored no illusions about who she was in life, despite her Merton College childhood. Galen was the father of the three children she had borne live, as well as the two babes she had lost. She was a good, devout Saxon matron, keeping what she did of her looks as much by accident as by design. And she had known the moment she saw them that Rees had made his commitment to the exquisite-looking Celtic lady who seemed slightly removed from full emotions. Menty wondered about the particular containment that surrounded Briana. It felt not at all like detachment; Menty believed that Briana experienced deep and powerful emotions. It was as if she was unable or unwilling to access them through a screen of restraint. But Rees cared deeply for her, and Menty knew he would not care deeply for anyone who was shallow, stupid, or overly simple. His caring spoke volumes to Menty about Briana. Thus, she was putting an extra effort into making the blanket lovely, and that consumed additional time. So very early on the day before the wedding, when there was just enough light to see by and the cock had not yet crowed, Menty left the room she shared with her family and went out into the kitchen court to work at her loom.

The morning was still dewy and cool, its silence broken only by the occasional animal noises that drifted over the wall from the pasturage and the chicken pens. Menty crossed the yard, soft-footed, and slipped into the shed, leaving the door ajar to allow the gray-yellow dawn light to fall upon the cloth she was weaving. She had not yet started the loom moving when she heard the voices and held still, listening, recognizing one of the speakers as Briana.

Owen had finally been able to exchange a few words with Briana in the hall the night before. "We need some time to meet and speak alone."

She looked at the face which had once been infinitely dear to her. "I am pleased to see you well, Owen," she said, "but meeting you alone would be unwise."

He smiled gently at her. "I have information for which you will be more than grateful. Meet me in the kitchen court at dawn. And, Briana, wear a cloak."

People had approached them then, before Briana had an opportunity to reply or decline, and Owen bowed to her and moved away.

She had not mentioned the encounter to Rees, even after their discussion of trusting. Owen's life was at risk if Rees discovered his identity, and she was unwilling to be the cause of his being found out. She had, instead, thought of Ine's warning that Owen was here for more than a simple greeting. He wanted to take her back to Snowdonia with him. No doubt he would argue that it was what Prince Llewelyn would have wanted, what her father, Bryn, would have wanted. He would tell her that her legend meant she would have to be part of Snowdon, not part of the English occupation. She could hear the reasons in her head, and she swore to herself that there was no way she would be swayed by them. She would not go with him, and she would meet him at dawn and tell him so in a way that left no doubt.

If Rees thought she was a little distracted, he put it down to the upcoming wedding ceremony. Though they had not discussed it, he knew she would be nervous about the nuptial Mass which would follow the marriage on the steps of St. Maedoc's. It would be the first time she would be unavoidably confronted by the Eucharist since they had left Windsor. Father Ciaran had not pressed her to come to daily Mass, but everyone knew that the two principals at a church marriage would be expected to celebrate God's blessing on their union in the specific, tangible way that Briana found untenable.

He knew she was restless, so when she rose in the dark, dressed hurriedly, and left the master chamber, Rees, awake and alert, let her go without a word. He would seek her out later.

Briana deliberately did not take a cloak with her, not merely because Owen had ordered her to bring one, but because she was confident that nothing Owen could say would be able to sway her. She reached the kitchen court just as the cock crowed, and Owen was already there, waiting.

"I've saddled the horses," he said as she arrived. "We can be in the mountains in three days."

Briana braced herself against the courtyard wall, hands behind her, fingers spread flat on the gray stones. "Seven years, Owen," she said as kindly as she could. "Everything has changed. I cannot simply go riding off with you."

"Are you pleased to be home?" The question was unexpected. "In the power of a Plantagenet?"

She heard curiosity in his voice, not challenge or condemnation. "'Tis not the prison I'd feared 'twould be when first I heard of it. 'Tis not the wondrous freedom my legend promised."

"But you love the butcher of Fearndon." There was still no accusation in Owen's voice. "'Tis why you failed to bring a cloak with you."

Briana did not want to see pain on his face, but she thought it was likely unavoidable. She had made a choice when she agreed to the public oath of fealty. And no one could deny that Rees would be a fine overlord for Flint. Even Maud was warming, not only because she had been much taken by the story of Rees's experience in the Holy Land and because of his contrast with the now departed Baron Wigmore, but because, the day before, the herd of cattle arrived, to everyone's delight.

"Whether I love him or not is hardly relevant," Briana said. "He is my liege lord, and I am his vassal as well as his wife."

Owen watched her smooth face in the increasing light as the sun crept closer to the open air. "What of your duty to your family?"

Briana twisted a little inside, though she had thought she was fully braced for his argument. "Oh, Owen, you know you and Aunt Maud are the only family I have left to me now."

"And yet you will not consider coming with me, as I request?"

She shook her head. "I cannot. Surely you see that."

"I see nothing of the kind." His brown eyes caressed her face.

She realized that she had been fearful he would try to embrace her, would confess to her that he loved and needed her, but he did neither of those things. He only said, "You should come with me now, before the manor awakens. We can speak more on the way."

She was astonished. "Owen, how can you continue on? I will not come with you."

"I think you will," he said calmly. "You see, I know a thing which changes everything."

She could not help being curious, for there was no quality of triumph about the statement, no teasing, no persuasion, only a strange, quiet confidence. She said, as firmly as she could, "I cannot imagine anything you could say which would convince me to leave Flint today or any other day."

Watching her face, his gaze soft and entirely neutral, Owen Glyn spoke two words.

For a moment, Briana could not move, could scarcely breathe. Active shock flowed over her face as she tried to adjust to the inconceivable revelation that echoed again and again through her mind. She wanted to believe him and yet sought disbelief. Wordlessly, she asked him for confirmation. He nodded, his face perfectly serious, open, honest.

Owen had said, "Meredith lives."

"Where is he?" she whispered.

"Our camp in Snowdonia," he said.

"Why did he not come with you to Flint?" she demanded, suspicion springing up in her at the unlikelihood of something she had wanted so much but for which she had never dared to hope. "Why did Maud never tell me he was still alive?"

"She knows it not," said Owen. "As for the rest, I think your brother had best tell you himself." He glanced around as if to assure himself that no one was stirring. "The horses are in the orchard."

Briana cast one near-despairing glance at the manor house, under no misapprehension that she should ask Rees's permission to go, but afraid of the consequences should she tell him about Snowdonia, about Owen. Yet she knew she had to go. She bowed her head to acknowledge that Owen had won, then squared her shoulders and raised her chin.

"I needn't a cloak," she said. "Let's be off."

Menty waited until they were out of the kitchen court before she emerged from the shed. She was not certain what to do. If she went to Rees now and woke him, which would be presumptuous, but probably correct, she knew he would take Basilisk and ride after them at once. He would catch them before they went a mile. And then Rees would be reunited with his handfast bride and the next day's wedding would seal it all.

As good as Menty wanted to be, she could not be that unselfish. She went back into the shed to work on the blanket and wait for the manor to fully awaken.

Chapter 32

She had left him. For the first moment or two, Rees could barely think for the killing rage that swept over him. *She had left him.* She had ridden off after she had given him her word not to leave without permission. The expression on his face grew so feral that Menty took several steps backward to escape it, crashing into Galen's solid chest, for she had forgotten that he was standing behind her. She would have fallen if he had not caught her arm.

Rees fought for control, unwilling to discard his fury completely because he sensed its absence would leave him desolate. He was not aware of when she had become vital to him, when her softness and unsparing honesty, her habit of giving more than was asked, her strange complexity, had entered his heart and settled there. He was not aware of when he had begun to love her.

He gained enough control to unlock his tense jaw. "Where did she go with him?" he asked Menty, barely seeing her.

"He said Snowdonia," she answered, regretting in the face of his sweeping anger that she had told him anything at all. "He said something about a camp there."

Ralf and Galen exchanged a fast look. They had been startled when Menty found them in the hall with Rees, poring over a map of the Flint lands, but they had not understood the seriousness of her message until the men realized they were dealing with the rebels. When that fact sank in, Ralf swallowed an oath and said, "I'll get the horses saddled."

Without looking at him, Rees nodded and said to Galen, "Have someone bring our mail to the stableyard. I've a need to speak with Lady Maud." To Menty, he added, "Come with me."

She followed him out of the hall as Galen and Ralf went in two separate directions, leaving the map abandoned on the table.

Maud was in the herbary, whose wall of pigeonholes had lately been mostly empty, but now were being refilled as the manor found its way back from the edge of penury. She sat at the minuscule table with Fand and Sabine, who bulked almost from wall to wall, picking over fresh flowers, berries, and mushrooms that Sabine had just dumped onto the tabletop from a basket. They all looked up when Rees appeared in the doorway, pushing Menty in front of him so that she was visible to the women in the room. No one could move anywhere comfortably. Maud and Fand were startled by the grimness of their overlord's face. Sabine's eyes narrowed speculatively.

Before Maud could ask him what he wanted, Rees said to Menty, "Tell the Lady Maud what you overheard."

Maud, Fand and Sabine all looked at Menty, whose composure was momentarily shaken by the expression on Sabine's face, but she was not easily cowed, and she was well aware that the only way in which she herself was culpable was in not telling Rees until she actually encountered him in the hall as she was preparing to go get the children ready for Mass.

She said obediently, "My Lady Briana met with one of the household staff, a man named Owen, in the kitchen court at dawn, and he asked her to come with him to a camp in Snowdonia." Menty was fair. From the outset she could have said that Briana had simply agreed to go, but she told the truth, not wanting to hurt Rees any more than necessary. "She was reluctant 'til he told her that Meredith was alive, and then—"

She broke off, for Maud had turned a pasty white, grasped the neckline of her gown, and staggered up from the table, crashing into Fand, who caught hold of her to keep her from falling onto the tabletop or into a wall.

Rees was also startled by the reaction. Sabine, closest to the door into the kitchen, shot up, gently moved Menty out of the way, and shouldered past Rees to grab up a dipperful of water and pass it to Fand. Fand cupped Maud's head in her hand and forced water between the older woman's lips. No one spoke until Maud had recovered enough to gasp out, "Meredith is alive? It cannot be! Owen would have told me!"

Rees felt a calm settle over him not unlike the calm that took him in battle. His voice was quiet, but hard as iron, edged with menace. "Lady Maud, have you oft dealings with the rebels in Snowdonia?"

Fand set the dipper down and tried to squeeze herself into a corner of the herbary, wanting to be entirely out of the way, but having nowhere to go. Menty, though shaken by the change in Rees, stood her ground. Sabine did not move either, but her gaze shifted from Menty to Maud to Rees and back again.

Maud recognized there was danger, but she was still shocked enough to be incautious. "My lord, I swear to you that I deal with no one save Owen Glyn," she said, "and he is like a son to me."

"How came he to be part of the staff here?" Rees's question was contained, but intense. "And by a different name?"

Maud could have lied, but she decided to be open, even in the face of her overlord's anger, bewildered by the realization that Owen had not told her about Meredith, and because Rees had shown himself to care for Flint. "I sent for him," she said flatly. "We had word from Ine that Briana was besotted with you, and as she had been promised to Owen in youth, I thought—" She stopped abruptly as he reacted with a jolt of perception. Owen had been Briana's betrothed and was therefore the man who had sent her the message she received at Conway.

"You thought what?" he asked, his tone even harder and lower. "That he would take her and save her from me?"

"Nay," Maud said with naked honesty. "I thought he might kill you."

He believed that, and he was less offended by it than he would have been by either a denial or a hope that the man might indeed win Briana back. He knew that Maud was testing him. Some of the deadly calm left him. "Do you understand that he is taking her out of my domain and into Wigmore's?" The question was quiet, but Maud paled again. She had not thought it, and she was suddenly conscious that Wigmore was a palpable danger to Briana, not only because he would desire any woman of Briana's beauty, but because she belonged to Rees. Maud's breath caught in her throat.

"You have earned a penalty, Lady Maud," Rees said, calm now without the edge of deadliness. "Its severity will be dictated by my wife's condition when I bring her back."

"My lord." Maud's voice was sharp, urgent, ignoring the threat of punishment as if it was the least frightening thing that had happened. "If her brother Meredith lives, and you do not let her reach him, she will never forgive you."

Ralf, wearing mail, appeared in the kitchen.

Rees looked at him, then back at Maud. "I must impose upon you to keep stewardship of the fief until we return with Lady Briana. Do not fail it or me."

She stared at him, unable to respond.

Sabine said, "I shall accompany you, my lord. 'Twill be only a moment for me to secure a mount." She spun and left the kitchen, her actions graceful despite her bulk, forcing Ralf to take a step backward to make way for her. She turned briefly in the doorway of the kitchen. "If you choose to depart before I am ready, I shall follow you. Fand, come with me, if you please."

Fand was grateful for the chance to escape. Everything that had just happened was beyond her. The two women hurried off.

Rees signalled to Ralf to wait outside, then gestured to

Menty to leave as well. Only once he was alone with Maud did he speak. "Lady Maud, if you sent for Owen Glyn, you know how to reach him. Do me the service of telling me how to get to his camp. I prefer to bring my wife home sooner, rather than later, before harm befalls her, rather than after." His voice went softer. "I think you would prefer it, too."

Maud was silent for a time, understanding what he was asking of her, understanding what Briana might need, remembering that either Owen was lying about Meredith or had known all along that her nephew lived, and he had not told her. "Find Havgan," she said at last, "Annie's husband, and take him with you. He can find them."

Rees turned on his heel and left the kitchen at a run. Maud sank back down on the stool from which she had risen and buried her face in her hands, her elbows pushing flowers and berries off the table onto the herbary floor.

The Roads—April 1289 A.D.

Briana worried about leaving Flint for the first mile or two, and then realized that she had not felt so completely free since her days being a minstrel on the roads between London and Peterborough. She knew it was madness to feel that way when she had just left her handfast husband the day before their church wedding, but nevertheless, inevitably, it brought back the time of her brief independence from Plantagenet rule. She had nearly paid for it with her life, but before the rogue knight attacked her, she had been happy, and she remembered that now. Owen rode a fair distance ahead of her until they reached a small, but clear trace, and then he let her ride ahead, giving her the illusion that she was once again alone, but this time she was in Wales, not in England. She reveled in that, just as she reveled in the knowledge that her younger brother was not dead, that he had somehow come through the bloody crucible of Fearndon. His life removed some of that battle's power to harm her. If she felt remorse for breaking her word to Rees never to ride out without his permission, the emotion was so subdued under the irresistible lure of liberty and of seeing Meredith that it had no effect on her. Owen had saddled a black gelding for her rather than Timbrel, for he had not known which horse was hers, and the gelding was a high-spirited animal. She had no idea which knight actually owned him. She urged him into a gallop four times the first morning, causing Owen to speed his own horse to catch up with her.

Occasionally she would remember she was here because of Owen, and she unthinkingly flashed him a radiant smile each time. By afternoon, he was wondering if she had any idea what she had done by coming with him. By evening, stopping in a copse clustered on the side of a deep valley near Swallow Falls, he began to wonder if he had had any notion of the changes that would come over her by the simple act of leaving Flint.

He built only a small, sheltered fire beside which they shared bread, cheese, and ale. They spoke very little until she asked, "How did Meredith survive?"

Owen answered her carefully. "He took a blow to the head which made the English think him dead. When we heard of the battle and came out of the hills to see if any lived, we found him. Only him. We took him back to Snowdonia with us."

She rolled a crumb between her thumb and forefinger. "Why did he not return to Flint? Why did he choose to let us all think him dead?"

He found he could not meet her gaze, even in the shadow-strewn circle of firelight, and he busied himself with extinguishing the fire and scattering its traces, making certain the embers were all out. "You will have to ask him that," he said.

Briana could not imagine why her brother would do such a thing, but he clearly had decided not to come home. She took another swallow of ale from the flask Owen had given her and tucked her skirts more firmly around her legs. She could barely see any of his face in the darkness, and she wondered what he was thinking. The night air began to chill. She was sorry, after all, that she had not brought a cloak.

"Are you cold?" His voice was cautiously neutral.

"A little," she admitted.

"My cloak is big enough for two to lie beneath."

She felt a stirring of alarm and chose her words with deliberate care. "Owen, I love you as if you were my brother, but I cannot lie with you."

He was silent for a long time, weighing any number of thoughts, and she waited, holding her breath. There was no doubt in her mind that he was physically strong enough to overpower her, should he choose. And she could not fight him as she remembered having fought the rogue knight. This was Owen. She knew she had taken that risk when she rode out with him.

Owen wondered if she thought so little of him as to think he might be capable of raping her. And, if so, why she had simply come with him, without even thinking of going to Earl Connarc and telling him. He had known that she would not betray him, but he had not known whether she would betray her husband. Not until now. He said in a whisper, "I am not a rapist."

Briana felt her face heat. "Oh, Owen," she said sadly, "what happened to us?"

"War happened," he answered. "Imprisonment. Loss. I went to Flint to see if I would need to kill Connarc for Llewelyn and Bryn, and then I saw he was willing to resurrect what he and his English owners killed, and I could not do it."

Tears stung her eyes as the chill of the night air seeped more deeply into her body. "He might have killed you instead," she said. "You saw him fight de Blaisey."

She heard Owen's humorless smile through the darkness. "'Twould not have been a fair fight. I may not be a rapist, but I am a murderer."

He heard her gasp at that, and then she was weeping softly.

As much as he would have liked to take her into his arms and comfort her, he did not reach for her. After a time, she quieted a little, and having nothing but her sleeve to use as a handkerchief, she scrubbed it across her face.

Only after she seemed in control of herself again did he say, "It appears you have come to love him."

"Aye," she said, her voice surprising him with its sudden uncertainty. "He is a good man, and he and I—" She hesitated.

"—do well together," he finished for her. "Aye, we all saw that."

"Do you hate me for it?" The question was spoken in such a tiny voice that she sounded very young and vulnerable.

"Hate you?" He was astonished. "I care for you, Briana, but I have no life to offer you. Too much of what I am grew out of hatred." He had relaxed into the dark, sitting with his back braced against a tree. "After first I saw you with him, I thought you would be telling me to give it all over."

"Nay," she said easily. "One of us must do it, and 'twill not be me."

Maud had said almost the same thing to her before the people of Flint encountered the reality of Earl Connarc.

Now Owen said, "You think not? What will he do when he finds you gone?"

Briana's quick indrawn breath told him plainly that she had not thought about that. "He will—I know not what he will do."

"Then you are blind," he said. "He is already in pursuit."

She shivered uncontrollably.

Owen lifted his cloak from the earth beside him and held it out to her. "Roll yourself in it," he said. "Then I can sleep against you without feeling your body."

She hesitated a long time before she took the cloak, despite the fact that her hands were trembling with cold. She had not slept away from Rees since the night of the handfasting. "When he finds us," she whispered, "will you fight each other?"

"Roll yourself in the cloak," the rebel leader repeated. Once he had been certain that a battle would be the inevitable result of his taking Briana, but now that he had had a week to observe Earl Connarc, he had begun to hope for something unimaginable instead. He pulled her shielded body against his chest, his arm across her, warming her.

She had not slept on the ground in five years, and even then she had barely thought about the inconvenience. Now she was thinking about Rees.

It was, Rees reflected, the strangest party with which he had ever traveled. It consisted not only of himself and his two knights, but also of a woman almost his own size, bearing a bow and quiver on her saddle, and a villager who came unarmed and a little uncertain, to show them the way. Also riding with them was the bard, who had heard what was happening and, fearing the violence which could easily result, insisted on joining them. Rees saw no reason to exclude him, since he had, for causes that escaped him, accepted Sabine. Ulf raced along ahead of the horses, beside the horses, or behind the horses, running three miles for their every one.

Rees had calmed, though he was still upset at the dangers Briana might be exposed to and the fact that her traveling companion was not only one of the holdout insurrectionists, but had been her father's choice as her husband. They moved quickly on the roads toward Gwynedd, Ralf or Galen riding scout to try to anticipate any patrols which might be loyal to Wigmore.

They reached Blychau at sundown and found that, while the monastery did not have a guesthouse, it did have a common room for travelers. They sat up late around the table in the common room, as the fire in the hearth burned low, drinking the plentiful outpouring of strong ale and reluctant to retire to the straw pallets on the floor far from the warmth. Sabine proved that she could match the men tankard for tankard, much to the knights' bemusement. Havgan, unused to strong drink, threatened to slip under the table after his third tankard, and Galen snorted, hoisted the man up over his shoulder, and carried him to the corner of the room, lowering him to a pallet and dropping a blanket over him before he returned to the table.

Ine drank very little, so he was still nursing his second tankard when Rees, Ralf, and Sabine had downed their fourth. Galen was rapidly catching up, because he had come in late, having stabled and rubbed down the horses.

Rees had drunk enough to cushion his anxiety and the inevitable nibbles of doubt about Briana's loyalty which had originally sparked his rage. Now he determined to distract himself from the thoughts which could easily drag him back, for at the bottom of the wrath and doubt was a very specific fear which he was as yet unwilling to face directly.

Briana was an endlessly passionate woman, with a confident physicality that had led her to be openly curious about sexual experiences—so much so that he had been able to lead her to one of the sophisticated acts he had learned in Brittany but had not practiced since he encountered the reticence of the English. That very sensual curiosity of hers now gnawed away below the level of his conscious reflection, for he feared it could lead her to want to try other men—and who better than a childhood sweetheart?

On another level, he thought that she would never be unfaithful to him, but the doubts remained, undermining the confidence. He repressed them and asked, "Where do you come from, Sabine?"

A smile curled the corners of her mouth. Without any hostility, she asked, "Do you intend to ask where I was born, or how?"

Ine choked on a swallow of ale as Ralf and Galen dared one another to laugh. Rees had not moved his mild enough gaze from Sabine's face. Now he said gently, "The question was geographical. I'm not nearly drunk enough for theology."

Sabine gave a short laugh. "I was born in Bristol," she

answered. "My father was a trader with Europe and the countries around the Inner Sea."

"You obviously have attained an education." Rees meant the statement as a compliment, and the giantess seemed to recognize it as such.

"Aye," she agreed. "It became clear early that I was unlikely to win a place in life through feminine beauty. An education might have suited me for the church. Though I did not begin to grow unusually 'til my flux began. Earlier, I was merely homely."

At the notion of the colossus in a modest habit, Galen could not contain a snort, and then had to wipe ale from his mustache.

Ralf, intrigued by the conversation, commented, "You did not find the church to your liking?"

"I never tasted it to find out," Sabine said easily. "I believe a convent would be a retreat, would clearly state that I am too grotesque to live in the world. That I would not accept."

Rees acknowledged the spirit of that declaration and took another swallow from his tankard. "Yet you've chosen a life partially removed from the world," he said. "Recluses' companions mix not with much nobility."

"We define 'nobility' differently, my lord." Sabine drained her ale and signalled Ralf to pour her another tankardful, which he did with a grin. She went on, "And I have seen my share of danger and adventure."

Ine remembered the undisguised menace radiating from her in the manor hall and had to speak then. "Have any of those adventures the making of a song?"

Sabine turned burning brown eyes on him. "Not for a hundred years yet, bard."

"Are you willing to tell any of them if Ine swears not to put them to music?" Rees asked.

Under other circumstances, she would have refused without a second thought, but it was Rees asking, and Sabine knew well the revelation which awaited him at St. Maedoc's. "When I was ten, I was sent by my father to a family in France. I was to companion and protect a young bride. As my own appearance would be unlikely to attract unwelcome attention, I chose to learn the ways of a guard, rather than simply those of a handmaid. Over time, I discovered a power in wielding edged weapons."

"One does," Rees murmured.

"Her husband did not value her then, did not wish her to have a friend. And because I was then small, he believed not I could protect her, so he cared not if I were her companion."

"What happened to her, do you know? The young bride?" It was Ralf asking, but softly, unwilling to intrude.

"She was nearly destroyed by circumstances she could not avoid," Sabine said. "I stayed with her. She minded not my increasing grotesquerie. And then she had not the mind to disdain what I had become."

Galen refilled his own tankard. "You bear not a sword," he noted a little blearily.

"I never had need," said Sabine. "The dagger, the bow, and my strong arm have been enough."

For some reason, probably inebriation, Galen took that as a challenge, set down his tankard, and rested his elbow on the table, hand open. Ralf groaned. Rees watched, amused. Sabine raised an eyebrow, put her own tankard aside, braced her arm, took his hand, and flipped him backward off the bench and a good two yards across the room.

The three men still at the table discovered they did not want to laugh, but the strain of keeping straight faces was telling in the tautness of jaws and the quivering of lips.

Galen hauled himself to his feet, brushed the rushes from his shoulders and backside, and growled at Sabine, "Still a virgin, huh?"

The men at the table lost control and roared with laughter, causing Ulf to raise his head from the exhausted slumber into which he had fallen and stare at them curiously. Sabine grunted and returned to her ale.

Ine, Rees, and Sabine outlasted Rees's two knights, who soon collapsed onto pallets near the snoring Havgan.

Rees studied Sabine. "Did she ever find happiness, your mistress?" he asked.

Sabine glanced once at Ine, who excused himself to visit the privy. Then she addressed her tankard as much as Rees. "She sought it in madness, my lord."

Rees nodded slowly.

She waited to see if he would comment further or ask a question, but he did not.

Rees remembered what unhappiness looked like. He had seen it often enough on his mother's face and that of the Demoiselle. He understood the retreat to madness, as well.

Ine returned, and Sabine excused herself to go to the privy.

Ine sat down at the table again and asked quietly, "May I speak about Briana, Rees?"

Rees sighed and wondered how drunk he really was. "Aye," he said after a short pause. "Say what you will."

Ine steepled his fingers and stared at them as if he would find words scribbled on them. At last he said, "I believe in her. I believe she will not betray you."

"She swore fealty to me twice," Rees acknowledged, "but she has run away with him."

"Only, I feel certain, because he told her her brother was there."

Rees accepted that; Menty had been open about the conversation she had heard, and it had not tied Briana's leaving Flint to the man, but to the boy. "But 'tis, after all, a question of honor. Both mine and her own."

"Hers I am not certain of," Ine admitted, "but she will die to protect yours. And that means she will not betray what she values so highly with you. She will not share her body with him or with any other man."

Rees discovered he was not quite drunk enough. "How

pretend you to that kind of certainty?"

Ine ignored the steel that had crept into Rees's voice. "When I studied my craft with Myrrdin, Bard of Bangor—the last great bard—I wondered often why he chose me for his student. I thought myself a poor candidate. I had none of the old ways, none of his power at the old mysteries. He told me that the old ways were dying, that there would be new ways, new mysteries, and that I would be master of those."

Rees waited, listening, some of his intoxication waning.

Ine took another drink of his own, marvelling a little at his boldness and at the trust he felt for the man across the table from him. "The old mysteries allowed a bard to understand the gods. 'Tis my belief the new mysteries allow a bard to understand other people."

"Say you that you think to understand my wife?" Rees asked.

And you, Ine thought, but did not say. "More than I do anyone else," Ine said. "I began the learning of her the day she came into the world. She has been captured by the overwhelming nature of your joining. Nothing in her life prepared her for you."

Rees was undeniably warmed by that, but said stubbornly, "And yet she left me."

Ine shook his head. "She went to find her brother."

"With another man."

Ine smiled ruefully and shook his head. "There is no other man for her," he said with conviction. "If you believe that not, you insult yourself and the lady."

Sabine let herself back into the common room.

Rees rose from the table. "We shall see when we catch them," he said.

Chapter 33

Briana woke suddenly, listening to the startlingly nearby song of a bird. Her shoulders and hips ached from the hardness of the ground. She did not recall aching so much or so quickly when she ran from King Edward, and she wondered why she seemed so tender this time, but she would not complain of it.

Owen was no longer beside her as she unrolled herself from the cloak and smoothed her wrinkled skirt. He stepped out from a copse and said, "There's a stream downslope you can visit. Then we need journey on." His gaze slid over her quickly as she folded his cloak and set it on one of the bushes. "You'll want to tie back your hair," he advised, suddenly smiling at her. "You really do look a mess."

She lifted her chin with some attempt at dignity, but it was ruined by a giggle she could not control. "'Tis a relief," she said. "I've been too many years having to look well and behave better." She turned and descended the hill to the cold running water.

Washing her face and hands made her shiver, but she had no hesitation about it. She had been fastidious among the English for years, but her body had not forgotten the wild childhood of tree- and rock-climbing and building mud forts and castles in the fields or on the sands of the estuary. Performing personal ablutions for herself in the open air did not disturb her at all. Meredith was alive! Barely noticeable sacrifices made in reaching him were clearly not to be heeded, including not having Rees to make love with the night before.

Briana pulled a hazel twig from a nearby bush and bent over the stream to scrub her teeth. It was strange. Since she had been handfasted to Rees almost six weeks earlier, there had not been a night, no mattered what happened during the day—

She stilled suddenly and straightened, her spine rigid, the hazel twig in her open mouth, her eyes wide. For almost six weeks, they had coupled every night. She had not had to cease because she was bleeding. She tossed the twig away and crossed her arms protectively across her stomach, as if to guard the tiny spark of life which must be within her.

"Briana! We must needs keep going," Owen called from above her on the wooded slope.

"I come," she yelled back. She could not believe the lightness of her voice. It was absurd to feel so overjoyed, but she did, as if there could be no possible trouble in the world at this moment because after so long a time of being alone, she had the multiple promises of a brother to be returned to her, a child starting within her, and an almost-husband who might actually forgive her for fleeing his company with his Uncle Edward's most hated enemy in Wales. She put aside any fears she might have had, at least for the moment, regretting only that she could not immediately tell Rees they were to have a child.

Baron Wigmore had set out men to patrol the easiest, known approaches to Snowdonia, for he was zealous to begin digging the rebels out of their nest on the mountain's slopes. But Owen knew the wild fastness better than any other man alive, and he and Briana were able to slip easily past the baron's guards, unnoted and unseen.

The pursuing party would not have similar fortune.

Briana had become more at ease in Owen's company since the first night of the journey, for it was clear to her that Owen had no intention of trying to exert any kind of ownership rights over her. He had wanted to bring her out of Flint to Meredith, had gotten her away, and now seemed quite content to let her think and feel and even act as she chose. That, combined with her growing certainty that she carried a baby within her, gave her a fierce joy the like of which she had not believed she would ever feel again. She found herself singing softly as they rode, unworried about being overheard as long as Owen did not caution her to silence. She began playing a game with herself, beginning unspoken sentences with the words, "My child." *My child will never know the sadness of captivity. My child will be able to laugh and sing any time it wishes. My child will not have to endure the privations of want. My child will not know the blood men make or the tears women make. My child*—The game went on and on, with Briana thinking her dreams were all for the unknown spark of new life within her, not realizing they were all the dreams she had always wanted for herself.

Owen hushed her unconscious chanting before they neared the Marcher Lord's guard patrols, and she heeded him with a smile of such brilliance that it made him feel old and tired. Not even near thirty, Owen was beginning to think that he had wasted his life. King Edward's people came on, like an inexorable tide, unbeatable and undeniable. Owen was realizing that he could not fight Connarc's kindness any more than he could fight Briana's love for the man. "The Red Dragon" had been a revelation to him, seeming as it did to herald the change of rulership in Wales more thoroughly and eloquently than bloodshed ever had.

Some foreboding, some part of his Celtic soul, told him that, one way or another, this would be his last trip to Snowdonia.

Briana had seemed to take easily to the outdoor travel and occasional stealth needed to cross Northern Wales, which surprised him. He had never learned of her days on the roads in England, so her cheerfulness seemed unusual, especially in a

place which Owen had thought of as entirely grim for a very
long time.

It was only at the end of the second day, in the wilderness
of Snowdonia itself, its powerful beauty surrounding and
welcoming her, that she realized with a start that she had made
an irrevocable step in leaving Flint. She had sworn to Rees that
she would not go without asking, and she had gone anyway. The
insight caused a thrill to run along her spine, but it was not a
thrill of fear at what Rees would do to her; it was a thrill of
delight, a familiar reminder of childhood, not felt since she had
been taken from Wales. She had, in reality, defied him. And she
had not thought twice about it.

"Owen," she said quietly, turning toward where he sat
across from her, unseen in the darkness of the hollow in which
they had stopped.

"Aye?"

"Owen, I trust Rees." She heard the laughter and wonder in
her own voice. "It never for a moment occurred to me that he
would hurt me or punish me for going to Meredith with you, so I
defied him without hesitation, just as I used to defy my father.
Not as if he were a Plantagenet at all. Owen, I only defy people
that I believe love me, people that I love and trust."

He thought to himself that he had never heard a finer
declaration of love. Of course, he reflected fairly, for the past
seven years he had lived in Snowdonia out of the company of
women. He had not thought it had hurt him until this moment.
Now, he recognized, like the perception of a pit opening at his
feet, that it had hurt him very much indeed.

"Briana," he said, and she was stunned to hear his voice
suddenly break, "I want to hold you right now."

She sensed that he had not moved, despite the words, but
she heard in the raw tones much of pain and nothing of desire.
From somewhere within her the first stirrings of wisdom rose up,
perhaps because for the first time in her adult life, she was happy
enough to let them in.

"You need to be held, Owen," she said, got to her feet, found him in the darkness, and put her arms around him. "And I'm the one who's here." After a few moments, as if he were the child she hoped to birth live and raise to adulthood, she began to croon lightly to him. He wept against her shoulder, shielded by the dark.

Harlech—April 1289 A.D.

Harlech castle was a more formidable structure than Flint castle had been, with more garrison space and an entirely new area surrounding it for Baron Wigmore to despoil. He set out with a single-minded desire to fulfill the king's command to clear out the abcess on the mountain, and that involved a large number of guards and pickets, as well as some infiltrators among the Welsh themselves, acting as spies.

It was one of these spies, a vassal knight of Wigmore's, who had seen de Blaisey defeated at Flint, who happened to see the party passing into the wilderness of Snowdon. The man rode at once to Harlech to report.

Edmund Mortimer tried not to seem overly eager at the tidings. "The Earl Connarc is entering Snowdonia? You are certain of this?"

The vassal repeated his message word for word. "The Earl Connarc, with two knights and three others, has crossed the guardlines around Snowdonia."

"So small a party," Wigmore said. "Such arrogance." And why? For what reason was the overlord of Conway and Flint journeying into the territory King Edward had specifically given into the baron's charge? He could not be making any kind of formal call, nor was he likely to do so, for in order to enter the fastness, Rees had passed by the road that led to Harlech. And Rees could not possibly be mounting any kind of raid on the rebels, because a party composed of six people, of whom only three were knights, would make such a foray tantamount to suicide.

Edmund Mortimer wanted to know what Rees was up to. He might be able to find ways to take advantage of this, from driving a wedge between Connarc and the king to perhaps ridding himself of a rival for power in Northern Wales. He rose from the large chair he had always fancied as a throne-surrogate and went to find a singularly useful, if oddly snakelike, servant to send on an errand. At the same time, he assessed the number of his mercenary knights to alert. With six people in the target party, only three of them trained to fight, he calculated about thirty mercenaries to be adequate. He was smiling grimly as he sought out the man who called himself Eald.

Eald was thin, with ropelike muscles and slick, colorless hair. He seemed to bear a natural camouflage unaffected by the clothes he wore or the surroundings he frequented. The eye slid past him as though it had no desire to linger, and as a result he had more freedom to come and go unremarked than the commonplace. He listened without speaking to Wigmore's request, then nodded once and was gone.

Mortimer was thankful he had such skilled people in his service. It was, if he'd ever stopped to think about it, the only time he wasted any effort in acknowledging the gifts of a higher power.

Snowdonia—April 1289 A.D.

Briana eagerly scanned the faces of the men who approached her and Owen as they rode out of the narrow defile and into the secluded glade that currently sheltered the rebel camp. These were hard men, every extraneous ounce of life burnt away from their bones and leathery, tanned skin. Above their beards, their eyes were hooded, brooding, and strangely empty, the way Owen's had been when she first saw him. None of the faces looked dearly familiar to her. Several of them touched hands to brows in her direction.

She looked at Owen with sudden accusation.

He dismounted and held up his hand to help her from the gelding, but she swung off quickly, ignoring his proffered hand. "If you lied to me—" she began, her anger as free as the rest of her emotions for the first time since she was thirteen.

"Follow me," Owen said shortly. He turned, gestured for one of his men to take the horses, and strode through the camp.

Briana glanced around once more, seeing bowmen slipping out to guard their trail, then gathered her skirts and hurried after him. He led her toward another narrow rock defile, clearly a possible escape route in case of any kind of surprise attack. She barely noticed the meanness of the camp as she passed through it, was barely aware of the desolation these men—and Owen— had made of their lives. She was aware only that there were no lustful glances in her direction, as if years of futile fighting had burned their manliness away with the bulk of their humanity, leaving shells.

Owen had seen the man huddled in the shadow of the rocks, knew who it was, understood the emotion that prompted him to hide. The rebel leader paused, waiting for Briana to catch up with him, and then took her arm. "I had to argue a long while to convince him to let you see him," he said softly. "Hide your reaction, or I swear, 'twill kill him."

She stared at Owen, open-mouthed, and then her voice dropped into a low hiss. "What have you not told me?"

"He paid a price for his life at Fearndon. Meredith, your sister is come to greet you!" He stepped back and nodded Briana forward, his face expressionless.

Briana looked at that unrevealing face for a moment, then turned toward the young man who had risen from his crouch and was standing now in shadow, his shoulders hunched as if to ward off a blow. She felt a reluctant fear, then told herself that this was her younger brother, with whom she had played as a child, whom she loved, had missed and mourned for.

"Meredith?" she asked hesitantly, hopefully.

The thin shoulders squared, a gesture much like her own, and he turned.

She recognized him by the half of his face which was only marginally scarred. The other half was buried in scar tissue that made his head more resemble a tree trunk than skin, the eye gone, the nose flattened, the side of the mouth seemingly melted down and lost. Holding her instant revulsion and horror in check was the hardest thing she had ever done, but she managed it, grateful for the years of training in the English court, which now came to her like faithful companions. Instantly she knew that if she showed him any ounce of the pity she felt for him, he would turn from her with self-loathing as great as any she herself had ever known. His remaining eye challenged her for a reaction, and behind her, to one side, Owen waited, watching them.

Blessing the fact that the left side of his face was relatively normal, Briana walked up to him—he was taller than she—raised her right hand, and slapped his cheek with all her strength. "How dare you be so selfish!" she raged at him. "How dare you let me think you dead these many years! Know you how many weeks I wept for you? Beg my pardon before I'll embrace you!"

Owen had jumped, startled, at the blow, which staggered the young man. He watched as Briana finished her angry tirade and stood, hands fisted on her hips, waiting for a response.

Meredith ap Bryn was not much used to talking, for his speech was badly slurred now by the distortion of his mouth. Briana was nothing at all like the scrawny near-child he remembered; she was magnificent, and he had not seen any women at all for years. He spoke very slowly, a habit developed painfully to make himself understood. "Didn't want you or Maud to see me like this." It was explanatory, not defiant, nor apologetic. He had to suck in air around the words.

Briana battled the urge to put her arms around him. "Think you for one minute you looked wonderful before that happened?" she demanded. "You have been thoughtless and unfair, and I await your request for forgiveness."

The left side of Meredith's face had reddened from the impact of her hand, and now that side of his mouth stretched a little. "Sorry, Brinna," he said, using his baby name for her. "Gladsome seeing you."

The rage drained out of her in an instant, and she gave a cry and launched herself at him. Owen smiled as the two of them embraced hard enough to leave marks on the skin under their clothes. Then his name was called, and he glanced back at the man who had summoned him. The man shifted his bow from his right hand to his left and made a series of rapid gestures. Owen signalled him to go back to his post and turned toward the brother and sister. "Briana, I think your husband's caught us up."

"Husband?" Meredith lisped.

Briana smiled. "I'll explain in a bit," she promised, letting go of him and running back toward the camp proper, in Owen's wake, noticing uneasily that his hand now rested on his dagger.

His men had dispersed to positions that afforded some shelter in the rocks and trees, bows out, arrows nocked, but not at the ready. Briana saw that, too, and caught Owen's arm. "You will not fire on him!" she said sharply.

"Not unless he draws on me," Owen said, responding to the power in her voice. He shook her hand off and planted himself firmly in the center of the small clearing.

Briana took one step away from him, but did nothing more to leave his side, her eyes on the place everyone else was watching, seemingly a wall of trees, most just beginning to bud, for sunlight was scarcer here than on more rolling hillsides. The high slopes of the mountain reared up beside and behind them. Every sense she had was warily on alert, but she felt no fear, only a growing sense of excitement over the encounter to come, and great joy at the nearness of seeing Rees again.

Ulf burst into sight first, peering around, seeing her, growling generally at the men, barking at Briana, and then standing still and waiting for the riders to catch up with him. His barks echoed back off the stone precipices.

As soon as he was certain they had reached their destination, Rees told Havgan, who had been guiding the party, to get behind him. He did not draw his sword, though his hand itched for it. He did not want any more killing, and at the moment, he did not know whether anything that had happened between Briana and Owen might have changed anything between Briana and himself. Once through the outer defile, Ralf drew up on one side of him and Galen on the other, and they guided their horses through the trees and into the clearing.

He saw her the moment his destrier cleared the trees, and he knew something had changed. She was unkempt, her clothes wrinkled, her face smudged, her hair half-wild around it, but that was not the sum of the difference. Her eyes were alive with green fire, her face with a vibrancy he had never seen in her before. And for a few seconds, he felt a stab of fear that it had been Owen who created the alteration in her. Then she looked at him and smiled with unbridled joy.

Briana glanced once at Owen, then walked forward to stand at Basilisk's gray muzzle, not even conscious of the other riders, her gaze now fixed only on Rees. He swung down from the stallion, his face unreadable, the ice-blue of his eyes raking over her as if her appearance alone could tell him what he wanted to know.

Briana understood that he was not going to speak first. "I beg your pardon, Rees, for leaving Flint without asking your permission," she said, her smile not diminishing in any way. "Should you seek to punish me for it, I will understand."

"Will you?" His voice was deliberately neutral, and one deep golden eyebrow rose as if he were coolly skeptical. Yet he was aware that she had called him by his name without hesitating or thinking twice about it, and that meant she felt entirely at ease in his company.

Briana nearly laughed at the control he was exerting and let all the warmth and tenderness she was feeling toward him show clearly. "Aye, for if you think I've earned it, then I have. I've learned a deal in three days, Rees. I've learned that I can remember how to be free, and I've learned that sometimes men do make tears as well as blood. And I've learned that I trust you with my whole heart." Her smile wavered a little, and for the first time he sensed an edge of uncertainty in her. "I believe," she continued, "I am about to learn whether you trust me as well."

He knew very well what she was saying, and it was clear she would now wait for a response from him. He was very aware of Owen's taut figure thirty feet behind her, and of everyone else in the clearing, both the people who had accompanied him here and Owen's men, spread out on the higher ground around them, bows in their hands. He discounted those men; if Owen wanted him shot, he would be a pincushion now.

He kept his voice level. "I am curious as to how you discovered this sudden trust," he said. "By running off with someone else?"

Her smile returned fully, and this time it was so wide it was accompanied by a pair of dimples he had not known she had. "Rees, the whole of the time I bowed to King Edward's will, 'twas because I feared and hated him. The one time I tried to defy him, he threatened to destroy everything I loved. After that, I would never have dared defy him again, for fear of what he would do to me or my people. I have no fear of your retaliation. If you choose to punish me, 'twill be fair, and I know that. I trust it." Her voice softened. "And 'twill be worth the cost. I have found my brother Meredith did not die at Fearndon." She said the word offhandedly, as if it bore no pain, as if it had no connection to either of them at all, and that fact shocked him more than perhaps anything else could, nearly costing him his composure.

Her smile wavered again when he did not respond.

He cleared his throat. "Briana, you are handfasted to me. You would have been my wife by church rites two days past, had you not fled." There was still no emotion in his voice. "You cannot expect me to be delighted. You would not expect me to be completely free of anger." For the first time, there was an audible strain in his voice, and the listeners realized he was exerting a powerful control over himself, though to keep from doing or saying what, no one could have guessed.

She forgot that anyone other than Rees could hear what she was saying, for it was important to her to make him understand. "But anger would mean you thought I would—and I'd never let anyone else touch me as you have. Nor would I touch anyone else in the ways you've taught me. I'd be too ashamed!"

Ralf stifled a whoop of laughter before it reached full volume, but the sound reminded her that there were other people listening, and her hands flew up to cover a face suddenly burning.

Rees had had no expectation of such a statement from her, but its very indiscretion went a long way to confirming its validity. He tore his eyes from Briana and fastened his gaze on Owen.

The rebel leader shifted a little and took his hand off his dagger. "She did not betray you with me, my lord earl," he said calmly, "though had she been willing, I would have been most cooperative."

"I should think you would not scruple at taking what was not yours," Rees said. "I seem to recall a raid on Conway some months back which I believe can be laid at your door."

"A raid in which none of my men were killed, even though it seemed 'twould've been simple for all the armed knights around us to have ended us with fair ease." Owen relaxed. He thought he could judge the earl's character, and he knew, strange as it seemed, that there was presently no danger in the man.

Rees, always a sublimely reasonable man, responded to the relaxation more than he had to Briana's sudden, unexpected joy. "You've reached that conclusion, have you? When?"

"Only recently," Owen admitted. "Only after I saw what you gave to Flint. Only after I heard Briana speak of your methods and your hopes."

"'Tis possible we may have some things to discuss," Rees said. "But first—" He turned to Briana, who still held her hands against her face. "I should like to meet your brother now." He saw the embarrassment flow out of her, replaced by a hesitation unlike her.

"I am her brother, my lord earl." The voice was slurred, but understandable, and a young man, too thin, but otherwise well-built, came slowly up to stand beside Owen Glyn.

With his single eye, brushed but not distorted by scar, he looked at the faces of the newcomers for signs of horror or disgust; only Havgan made any sign, for he had known the young lord well. Ine was good at concealing his emotions; Ralf and Galen had seen the wounds of battle often before; and Sabine's eyes burned like coals, but there was no judgment in them.

Rees walked past Briana, dropping Basilisk's reins. He ran a finger lightly down her arm as he passed her, but did not look at her as he did it. Instead, he walked directly to Meredith, who made himself hold still in the face of the formidable size of the older man. Rees bowed his head briefly to the startled young lord. "I thank you for living," Rees said firmly. "You are one less stain I carry on my soul." He pulled the other man into a rough embrace, then set him back and tipped Meredith's head to study the disfigurement in the fading, early evening light. "You were trampled," he said.

"Aye." Meredith was soothed by the clinical manner in which Rees examined him. "I was told I am actually quite fortunate." He secmed to be speaking a bit more clearly, as if tension had inhibited his facility with speech. "Hands and feet make me useful."

A bowman ran into the clearing, gesturing to Owen, who quickly joined him, then beckoned several of the other men after him and returned to Rees. "It seems you were followed," the rebel said grimly.

Rees let go of Meredith, swearing under his breath. "How many?"

"Only one, but he escaped before the pickets could stop him." Owen shook his head. "Who would put a track on you?"

"Wigmore," said Rees, Ine, and Sabine simultaneously.

Rees told Owen, "Edward has commanded Baron Wigmore to eliminate you."

Owen sighed. "We shall pack up camp and move in the morning." Something in the tenor of his voice alerted Rees to unimagined possibilities as Ine asked, "Move where, Owen?"

Owen glanced at him, then looked squarely at Rees and took a deep breath. "This time I was hoping—perhaps to Conway?"

Briana turned toward Owen in surprise, and Ine's eyes glittered with sudden pleasure. Rees made no attempt to hide his own astonishment, but in the silence which followed, a slow expression of satisfaction spread over his face. So many circumstances had come together to create this moment that he could not sort them out quickly enough, but he knew beyond doubt that the world had just changed, and it pleased him, not least because it could discomfit Wigmore, but most because, like Meredith's being alive, it had about it a quality of redemption.

"We have much to discuss," he said to Owen.

Owen signalled the remaining bowmen on the slopes to come back into camp. "You are welcome to share what little we have this even," he said.

Rees thanked him and gestured at last for the rest of his party to dismount. He looked at Briana, who had been watching them with narrowed eyes. He could not guess what she was thinking. He took her hand and said, "As, indeed, you and I have some things to discuss as well, preferably private."

Owen nodded toward a small grove near the edge of the camp. "That copse is most private," he said.

Briana was grateful for the unexpected harmony, though a little bewildered because Rees seemed to be more willing to be amicable to her brother and to Owen than to Briana herself. Then Rees said, "Excuse us betime," and took her arm, yanking her along into the copse. Once they were within the trees, he pulled her tightly against him, knocking the air out of her lungs.

"I should thrash you for defying me," he said against her hair.

She caught her breath, warmed by the direct contact, but she did not relax against him yet. "Such a mild penalty, my lord. May I assume you think not that I lay with my old friend Owen?"

"Once I saw you here, I doubted you did," he said. "And your indiscreet words convinced me of it. Nay, the punishment would be for leaving me without permission, and you might even enjoy it. I believe I should take pleasure in it."

She realized she was being teased and pushed at him, though her pushing had no more effect than it would have had he been a tree.

"I missed you," he breathed at her. The stubble of three days' growth of beard rubbed against her forehead, then her cheek.

She needed to maintain a little distance—if not physically, then at least emotionally—because his nearness, smelling of leather, Basilisk, and the spicy sharpness that seemed to be his alone, affected her instantly and powerfully. She asked, "Mind you about my brother?"

He raised his head and looked down at her. "Mind? Why should I mind? Rather, I rejoice. He belongs at Flint full as much as you."

"Welsh law makes Flint his," she said. "Therefore, there is doubt 'twas mine to bestow through marriage." The words were a little hesitant. She knew he had been commanded to wed her because of Flint, and she feared Edward might find a way to dissolve the marriage should Flint not actually accompany it.

Rees simply shook his head. To her frankly inquiring look, he said with great gentleness, "Welsh law no longer governs

Wales. My uncle set it aside with the conquest. By English law, and the charters are archived in Westminster. Wales is in the king's gift now, and Flint is a royal fief. It transferred to me by the will of the crown, not by the marriage." If possible, his voice went even gentler. "If you had not become my wife, you might have lost Flint forever."

She realized that she had misunderstood entirely. She had thought he married her to take Flint from her, when actually he had married her to ensure she kept it. A truth rose inside her, and she had to acknowledge it. Her words came out as no more than a whisper. "I would have lost far more than Flint." He bent close to hear her, and she was unable to look at him when his face was so near, so startlingly handsome in the now fast-fading daylight. She put her hands over her stomach. "I carry your child." She had, she knew at once, no notion of how he would react, and she waited, holding her breath.

For the first time in years, Rees felt stupid. "Are you certain?" was all that would come out of him.

She nodded. "I've not bled since first you bedded me," she said, "and I was always one with the moon."

Rees absorbed the news and felt weak at the knees. He was bemused with himself. "Uncle Edward will be delighted," he said without thinking.

Briana stared at him, beginning to feel angry, biting her lip against anything she might say in response to that.

Rees knew he was doing this badly. "I am sorry, Briana." He kissed her forehead. "'Twas wrong of me to say that. I am very pleased at this child." He kissed her lips, not with the urgent passion of the first weeks of their handfasting, but with a tenderness that communicated itself to her nerves by heating them in a completely different way.

When he released her, her eyes sparkled, and she said softly, "They were right, the people of Flint, to think that I love you." She laid a hand on his arm. "Rees, you will consider letting Owen and his men come to Conway?"

"Of a certainty," he said instantly. "The opportunity to do so is a gift to me."

"What mean you by that?" Briana asked.

Rees drew in a deep breath. "I gave a pledge to Prince Llewelyn to try to preserve his army," he said, "and I was not permitted to keep my word."

Chapter 34

"Prince Llewelyn?" Briana repeated, her voice scaling upward in astonishment.

And then Owen's voice cut into the grove. "And what mean you by *that*, my lord earl?"

Rees instinctively tensed. "It appears," he said, "that this copse is not particularly private after all."

"'Tis better when the leaves are out," Owen said. "Now that we've heard, will you explain it?" When Rees said nothing, Owen added, "I believe those of us here have a right to ask. We are what remains of that army you say you pledged for."

Rees debated that with himself, then took Briana's hand and walked back out of the trees.

Someone had built a fire in the shelter of the rocks near the copse, and most of the camp was gathered into the area around it. The horses had been tied near the mounts the band had managed to steal recently, and Ulf had lain down by Basilisk, his head on his paws. The party which had come with Rees sat near the fire, except for Havgan, who had joined Owen's men at a greater distance from the small blaze. The expression on their faces was one of uniform surprise, which told Rees instantly that everyone had overheard the conversation in the copse.

Ine was fascinated by the idea that the man everyone believed responsible for Llewelyn's death had a secret involving the prince, and he knew Rees well enough by now to know he would have to be telling the truth. In addition, he could tell just by looking at Ralf and Galen that they knew nothing about this, that it would have surprised them less had Rees declared himself a heretic.

Only Sabine looked as if nothing would actually surprise her.

Briana glanced around and found Meredith crouched with the other rebels, and she beckoned him to join them at the fire. He hesitated, obviously feeling that he was making a larger choice than simply where to sit.

Owen had hunkered down near the fire, and he waved an arm as well. Meredith rose and came forward to join the party from Flint. Briana settled on the ground next to him, and after a moment, Rees sat down, too. They passed some bread and cheese Owen's men had; the Flint people contributed the wine they had brought with them, and no one spoke. Somehow it was understood that Rees would decide whether to tell them or not.

Rees was in some turmoil. He had thought he was speaking just to Briana in the copse, and now that that had turned out not to be the case, he was uncertain what to do. Finally he concluded that Owen was right. This was the remnant of the Welsh army, and perhaps it did indeed deserve not only to ask about his pledge, but to be answered. He took a long drink of the wine and said, "After the battle of Dinas Bran, I sent a private messenger to Prince Llewelyn, asking him to meet with me alone."

Rees knew that Llewelyn would accept the invitation without fear of treachery, because they had faced each other on the field in the recent battle, and had fought with one another until the battle boiled up and separated them. They identified each other at the very beginning of the battle: Rees was known never to wear a helm, a habit he had adopted in the Holy Land when the fearsomeness of his killing mask, the face that allowed him to fight without feeling, proved more of a deterrent to attack than a helmet would have. For his part, Llewelyn was the only soldier in the Welsh army who carried the red dragon on his shield.

Llewelyn came at Rees on foot, as his men engaged the English knights, and Rees, aware that while being mounted gave him an advantage, thought it likely that the prince's first sword slash would be at the horse. So before the prince reached him, Rees reined in the destrier and leaped to the ground, putting himself at Llewelyn's level. He held his sword ready to meet the prince's charge, but did not rush to press any attack of his own.

Llewelyn slowed when Rees dismounted, obviously not expecting his opponent to dismount. The noise of the battle sounded very loud around them in their momentary stillness— the clash of steel, the shouts and screams, the enraged bellowing of angry or hurt horses. Then Llewelyn lunged forward.

Rees met him stroke for stroke, catching some blows on his sword, some on his shield, waiting to see how soon the prince would tire, when his greater age would begin to slow him. Llewelyn did not tire. He was a strong fighter, whom years had not burdened overmuch, and he did not let anger affect his technique. Rees sensed a second attack to his right, flung up his shield to deflect Llewelyn's next blow, used his sword to hack downward at a spearman on his righthand side, and then stepped backwards to get both adversaries into view without having to turn from one to confront the other.

The spearman stumbled back. "I think he was unnerved by the fact that I noticed he meant to kill me," Rees said to his listeners. Now that he had decided to tell it, the words came easily, without hesitation. "I pushed Llewelyn back with my shield—I was bigger than he was, and heavier." But before he could turn his full attention to the spearman, the warhorse charged this second attacker, his huge haunches brushing Rees and knocking him slightly off balance.

Llewelyn kept his footing well despite the shove by Rees's

shield, and he sprang at Rees again. Rees let the destrier handle the spearman and used his shield to deflect Llewelyn's blow, but the shield began to split. The blade of Llewelyn's sword slid into the slit and became, momentarily, trapped there.

Both men, highly skilled fighters, knew that for those seconds, the prince was vulnerable, despite his own shield. Too much of his weight had been behind the swing.

Rees had, indeed, begun a stroke which would have overtopped his splintering shield and swived in against Llewelyn's sword, but that sword could not now parry it. The result seemed inevitable, and the slash would have caught the Welsh prince in the neck. Without his sword to stop it, Llewelyn must have seen—as did Rees—that death had to be the outcome.

"But," said Owen, "Prince Llewelyn did not die at Dinas Bran. He died some days later, at Orwein Bridge."

"Aye," Rees said. "When I knew he was helpless, I stayed the blow."

All the men, including Ine, knew the impossible speed it would have taken to stay a killing blow already begun. And yet no one doubted that Rees was capable of it.

Rees and Llewelyn looked directly into one another's faces, breathing hard, their eyes less than a foot apart, though Rees's were inches higher than Llewelyn's. Then Llewelyn wrenched his sword free and took a step back from the confrontation.

That was the moment when the battle separated them. That was the moment that made Rees certain the prince would parley with him when he sent the messenger under a flag of truce. "And," said Rees, "I told him to set any place he chose. He picked an old tower somewhere south of Dinas Bran—I remember not exactly where."

"I know where," said Owen.

"Truly, it matters not," said Rees. "Not now."

The tower was actually mostly a ruin, a pile of stones that had been a base and rubble from the upper part of the structure lying about the heap. In the thin silver moonlight that illuminated their night meeting, the stones also looked faintly silver. Rees rode up to it, dismounted, let his reins drop, and walked into the ruin. He was not afraid of ambush. Llewelyn had agreed to the meeting and would come alone. Indeed, a few minutes after Rees arrived, a small Welsh pony came at a walk down a nearby knoll, and Prince Llewelyn dismounted from it and left it near the warhorse. He walked into the rubble and to within two feet of Rees without speaking.

Rees said politely, "My thanks for agreeing to this meeting, Prince."

The prince said, "I saw no reason to refuse. You might have slain me on the fields at Dinas Bran, and yet you did not. I'd know why."

It was a direct question, and Rees thought it called for candor. "I want not your blood on my hands," he said. "Mistake me not for my uncle." He glanced at the horse and pony, then looked back at Llewelyn. "I seek not the blood of those who follow you either, but I shall be forced to take it unless—" He broke off.

"Unless?" Llewelyn prompted.

"Unless you choose to surrender," Rees said evenly. "I offer you that opportunity."

"I cannot escape by surrendering," said Llewelyn, seeming unoffended.

"Nay, *you* cannot," Rees agreed, "but the men who follow you may. Wales will lose much by the continuation of this war. Must she lose all her men as well?"

"Do I understand you to say you have a care for the troops you are presently attempting to destroy?" Llewelyn asked, his voice making clear how incongruous he thought the question was.

Rees ignored it. "You cannot win this war," he said.

"We very nearly won at Dinas Bran," said the prince.

Rees acknowledged that the Welsh had fought well, but said, "A single battle is only that. You can hold Snowdonia, but if you want to retake the Marches, you will fail. My uncle is determined on it, and he holds more than twenty thousand men in reserve at Chester and Shrewsbury."

Llewelyn frowned. "I wonder that he has not thrown them at me ere now."

Rees shook his head. "He wants them for Scotland, but if it appears you are gaining ground, he will send them to the Marcher Lords, and they will use them mercilessly. He has determined to destroy you. If you would surrender, he may let your army live."

Llewelyn was quiet for some minutes, and Rees did not interrupt any of his thoughts. At last the prince sighed. "I am embarked upon the sole path I can take," he said. "I cannot surrender."

Rees inclined his head once, accepting that. "In that event," he said, "I will do what is in my power to save as many of your men as I am able to."

"Once again," said Llewelyn, "I'd know why."

"Wales may have need of them later," Rees said.

They parted without bidding each other good-bye.

It was Ine who asked, "Did you bring the prince to his death in order to save his men, then?"

Briana looked from the bard to her husband, startled.

Rees said, "I had naught to do with Orwein Bridge."

"But the message to Prince Llewelyn that took him to Builth and Orwein came in your name," said Owen.

Rees repeated, "I had naught to do with Orwein Bridge."

Then Sabine said, "The earl did not send the message. The king sent it, by way of Baron Wigmore."

Into the silence that followed that, Rees asked, "How is it that you know this, Mistress? 'Twas to be kept close. I did not learn of it 'til 'twas done, and I was sworn not to speak of it."

"Such a charge was not laid on me," said Sabine. "Let me just say that I was in close contact with the queen at Westminster, and in a position to learn it."

"Westminster can be a sieve," Rees said, "but that particular secret was one I did not think leaked through the meshes."

"'Twas not widely known," said Sabine. "But the queen knew it."

Owen had been thinking hard about what Rees had said, and now he said, "That goes some way to explain Aber."

Aber was the only battle fought between Dinas Bran and Orwein Bridge, and it had been the battle in which the Welsh were sorely outnumbered, and yet almost none had been killed. No one had understood how it happened that so many lived, when Baron Connarc had so many men to deploy.

"Aye," said Ralf to Rees. "You asked us to try to fight to contain and turn aside, not to destroy. Not to let ourselves be killed, but not to kill if we could avoid it. 'Twas a difficult battle."

"'Tis the one of which I am most proud," said Rees.

"Pray," Briana burst out, "tell me then what caused Fearndon!"

There was another silence, longer than the first, and it stretched until Ine said strongly, "'Tis long past time to speak of Fearndon!"

Rees sighed, looked down at his big hands in the firelight. Briana laid a hand lightly on his arm. He turned his face in her direction, but she knew he did not see her. He was still a long way back.

"I was not at Orwein Bridge," he said at last. "I knew not that Llewelyn was dead until my uncle sent for me."

He hated going to Westminster or Windsor, but this time it was not necessary. King Edward had come to Rhuddlan, one of the Welsh castles in the Northern March, wanting to be on the soil of Wales when that nation fell to his men. When Rees arrived, he was immediately conveyed to a room containing a table, a single chair, several braziers lighted against December's bitter cold, and the King of England.

Rees bowed to his liege lord and before he had straightened again, Edward snapped, "Even despite your efforts, the traitor Llewelyn has been subject to my justice."

Rees held his face expressionless. "To what justice has he been subjected, Sire?"

Edward ground a fist into his palm.

Rees knew then that Llewelyn was dead. He thought that perhaps the war was over. He said nothing, a reaction which appeared to provoke the king.

"Do you not wish to know the details?" Edward asked.

Rees started to bite back his reply, but something in the king's expression made him incautious, and incaution led him to think that, on balance, he would mourn more for the prince's passing than he ever would for his uncle's. This was the man who had thrown his bastardy in his face, had forbid him his desired marriage to Margaret of Norwich, and who saw him less as a nephew than as a tool. That thought moved his incautiousness into pure recklessness. "Not so much as you wish to tell them to me," he said.

Edward's face went bright red, then darkened.

Rees braced himself for a blow. It would not be the first time the king had struck him—quite a blow had accompanied the news of his ignoble origins—and he was honor-bound not to strike his liege lord in return.

But this time Edward did not lose control of himself, and his attack on Rees was not physical. Instead, he said with satisfaction, "'Tis said you betrayed the Prince of Wales and led him into the ambush that has sent his head to London to rot on the bridge."

Rees fought his own surge of anger somewhat less successfully than Edward had. He could not help the low and dangerous note that crept into his voice. "Who says it? And how is it that you have permitted such a lie to be noised about?"

"Permitted? I have encouraged it! Do you believe I will let it be said that a member of my own family—no matter the circumstances of his birth—is incapable of winning a victory for his liege lord?" His own voice deepened. "Or unwilling to win one?"

Rees honestly did not know how to respond to that, for it was too close to a truth that he knew Edward would find at best dishonorable and at worst treasonable. He kept silent and held still.

Edward waited long enough to see if Rees would deny it, and when he did not, a cold calm settled over the king. He glanced behind him to confirm the position of the chair, stepped back and sat down, resting his arms on the chair's high sides. "You will say nothing now or ever to contradict the general impression that the betrayal and death of Llewelyn are your doing. That will satisfy those of my nobles who wonder why I favor you, other than that you are my sister's son. And you will now do something to satisfy me of your loyalty."

Rees waited, apprehension seeping in and washing away the anger.

Edward's eyes narrowed. "You will take an army to the center of the Northern March—I will tell Wigmore to stay out of your way. You will go to the field at Fearndon, which is open and visible, and you will challenge the men of the North to avenge the death of their prince. Since they believe you responsible, they will doubtless choose to come to the field." He leaned forward, his fists clenched. "You will achieve a decisive victory of your own, and—" He seemed to measure his words with deliberation. "—you will leave no Welshman alive who fights against you. Leave no wounded; take no prisoners. I want them all dead. Then we will have peace in the North."

Briana pressed her hands to her mouth. Owen stared into the fire. Ine watched Rees closely, seeing nothing there but naked honesty and naked pain.

Rees shifted his seat and looked at his hands. "I realized then how completely I had trapped myself," he said.

He was caught between his pledge to Llewelyn, a promise

he believed in, and his oath of fealty to his uncle, who had the power to destroy all his hopes for the man he wished to be and the life he wished to lead. He swayed, took control of himself, debated briefly with himself over his hatred of the king, and then swallowed his pride. He went down on one knee. "I ask you most humbly," he began, then started again. "I beg you not to require this of me."

Edward shook his head, his eyes glittering. "I do require it," he said, "and you will render it to me."

Rees heard the inevitability in Edward's voice, knew there would be no reprieve. He made his mind work rationally. He would not use his own knights for this; he would spare them. "I would have the service of your mercenaries," he said harshly, getting to his feet.

The king did not hesitate. "They're yours, as many as you have need for. Add them to your own troops as you wish. But finish this business before the year's end."

Ralf and Galen were nodding. "'Tis the reason you did not take us to Fearndon, then," Galen said. "We always wondered."

"You asked not," said Rees.

"'Twas not our place," Ralf said.

Rees was unable to sit still any longer. He rose and paced for a time, then stopped behind Briana. "I ask you to believe that I never drew sword that day," he said to the back of her head. "I knew 'twould be a slaughter, and I have no taste for slaughter, whatever the world chooses to think of me."

Meredith raised his head. "Everyone knew 'twould be a slaughter, my lord. Or at least, my father knew."

Rees froze in place. Briana rose without thinking about it to stand beside him, and slowly, all the other people at the fire stood up.

Meredith went on, "Griffith told me the night before the battle that Father said we would all likely die on the field."

"Then why—" It was all Rees could get out before his throat closed.

"Griffith said Father told him we would be greatly outnumbered, and Baron Connarc was not commanding his own knights, but the king's mercenaries, and they were as bloodthirsty as their master."

Rees fought his throat open. "Your father knew all that?"

"Aye." Meredith nodded decisively.

Rees sounded so anguished that Briana made a small sound and took one of his hands in both of hers. "Then why, in the name of Christ, did he come to the field?" he demanded.

"Because of Prince Llewelyn," answered Meredith.

"But he knew he would not be able to avenge his prince," said Ralf, when Rees seemed incapable of pursuing the question.

It was Ine who said, "He was not seeking vengeance, was he, Meredith?" Meredith did not respond. Ine continued, "Lord Bryn ap Emrys wanted not to fail Llewelyn by living when the prince had died for Wales's sake, did he?"

Meredith sighed. "I've come to believe he thought 'twould be loyal. I think many of the men who went with us to Fearndon felt the same."

Ine's voice was hard. "'Tis difficult to think that a man would destroy his family because he hated himself for being alive when his prince was not."

Briana felt a wave of nausea sweep over her. It was as if someone had shined a light on her self-hatred and showed her clearly that she had learned it from the father she loved. It was not a reaction she had come to in isolation; she had absorbed it in her blood.

Rees's face was turned away from the firelight and his voice in the darkness was thick with emotion. "All these years, I thought I'd presided over a senseless murder."

Ine said, "And now it appears you were used for a senseless suicide. Owen!"

"I heard," Owen said. "Meredith had hinted as much to me some years past, but I put it aside. 'Twasn't something I recalled until I saw how the earl was doing everything he could to save

Flint."

Briana swayed, and Rees sensed the motion through her hands on his. He swept his other arm around her and pulled her against him to hold her up.

Galen cleared his throat. "Why was it," he asked, "that you did not return to Conway after the battle at Fearndon? We feared you had been hurt or—" Ralf punched his arm.

Rees looked at them. "I returned some days after," he said.

"We know that," said Ralf. "We were relieved to see you." He did not say, "You were different."

Briana raised her head and looked at Rees. He was, she recognized, suffering, and she forgot her own feelings in a desire to comfort him. She knew better than to be overly solicitous in front of his and Owen's men, but she wanted to put her arms around him and draw him into the sanctuary that was so far away from them now.

Ine said, "Some days? Where went you, Rees?"

Rees looked at the bard, tempted to tell him to leave off asking questions, but, as if he read the reaction, Ine said in a low voice, "Tell it all. You'll never be free of it unless you tell it all."

In the silence, a whistle sounded, and light flickered into existence at several other fires, kindled nearer to where Owen's men were. The general darkness of the little valley grayed, allowing more vision.

Rees looked at Ine. "I felt unfit for the company of other human beings," he said. "I was disgusted at the carnage. I was disgusted with myself. I rode for the borders, but south of the Northern March. I wanted not to encounter anyone I knew. I hoped I could go mad."

Sabine stirred, but said nothing.

The snow began as he crossed the border near Oswestry, having ridden hard for more than a day. He was so weary that he knew he would have to stop, and he found a monastery.

Mendicants seeking shelter were never turned away. The monks received him in welcome silence and took his exhausted horse away to be groomed and fed. One of the brothers led Rees to the guesthouse, which was thankfully empty of other guests. Rees flung his saddlebags onto the bench that, along with a bed, was the only furniture in the room. Then he began to pace, two strides from one side of the room to the other. After fewer than a score of paces, he had to leave the small chamber and, despite the bitterness of the cold, pace in the cloister, where he could take huge, fast strides. He needed to dissipate the energy that kept building up inside him, even though he had not slept in days. By midnight, as the sounds of the monks singing joyfully in the church mocked him with the reminder that it was Christmas eve, he was cold and physically used up. It helped him not at all, but he was finally too drained to keep on driving his body. He returned to the little room, wrapped himself in his cloak, ignoring its dampness, and fell into a fitful sleep.

"And," Rees said in a low voice, "I was back in the Holy Land."

It did not seem strange to him, for his mind had lost its ability to reason. He accepted that he was beneath the hot yellow sun that had beat down on Gilbert de Clare's company in Antioch. He could see the dunes and wadis, feel the rough earth and dun-colored stones beneath his feet. He had always thought the land untamed and alien in a way that even the treeless stretches of moor never attained in England. He wandered it, soundlessly moving across rocky sand from the sea to Antioch. He could see in the distance the dust and turmoil of a battle, but he did not know where it was exactly, and he did not want to seek it out. He was fearful that if he did not find it soon, he could not guard against it; it might sweep over him from the side or from behind, and he would be powerless to stop it.

He turned toward it, but there were mud-brick walls in the way, and he walked through an archway into a courtyard tiled in polished, multicolored designs. Green plants, some with bright blooms, grew in raised beds and hung from eaves in pots. In the center of the courtyard a fountain played. A man in pale blue robes, seated on the lip of the fountain, looked up as Rees came in, and Rees saw that it was the Jewish physician, Abraham ben Zeniuta.

Rees was surprised to see him.

"Come, sit beside me," said the Jew, and Rees walked across the courtyard and sat on the lip of the fountain.

They talked, he thought, for hours, as they had when he was recovering from his wound, and it did not seem strange to Rees that the sun did not move in the sky. A breeze played gently with the greenery and scattered droplets of water from the fountain's spray. At the end of the conversation, Rees could not remember anything they had said. He remembered only that he said then, "I understand not why you've come to me."

The physician smiled. "You have come to me," he said, "and you are most welcome."

"But why?" Rees asked.

Abraham asked in return, "Did you previously think me a healer only of men's bodies?" He laid a hand on Rees's shoulder. "I think you knew better from the first moment we spoke with one another."

Rees awoke in the freezing cold of the monastery guesthouse, his eyes crusted with rheum, but somehow he was calmer. The rage and disgust had drained out of him, and he felt his flight from Wales had been unnecessary.

The ringing of bells filled his tiny room. For a moment, he could not imagine why. Then he remembered that he was at a monastery. He did not even know what day it was, and it was not until later that he learned he had slept well beyond Christmas. The monks must have thought he was deep in contemplation, and had not tried to disturb him. He sighed, rubbed his eyes and got to his feet to find his horse and return to Conway.

The Rees who had been formed by the English king and the Jewish physician looked up from the hard earth of Snowdonia at the people around him, waiting to see if they would judge him. The rebel camp was completely silent, but for the sounds of the horses.

Briana was still within the circle of Rees's arms, and she burrowed nearer to him, holding him very close.

Had any of the people within earshot of the story been seriously Christian, there might have been questions or skepticism, or even condemnation. But even Sabine, who lived in a churchyard, had made her peace with the mysteries of the world years before. Rees waited to see who would speak first, but he was surprised when it was Meredith, saying quietly, "Enough prices have been paid." He touched the side of his face. "Mine is only one of them."

Owen moved as if he were returning to motion after a long time of stillness. "We all," he said, "want to go home. The war is over."

Briana drew in a deep, shuddering breath, her eyes closed.

Ine thought that he had just witnessed some actual magic, and he wondered which gods were responsible for it.

Chapter 35

They sat around one of the campfires late into the night, more easy with one another now, talking of practical things and things previously untouched. Even the painful subjects did not, somehow, cause anyone pain.

Owen spoke of finding Meredith on the field at Fearndon, when the earth was frozen too solidly to bury anyone. "We wanted to honor them with burial," he said, "but the ground was like iron."

Meredith raised the hood of his tunic in an unconscious gesture of hiding, then took his hand away from it and let it fall back again. "I wanted not to leave my father and brother, but I could not stay. I was barely conscious, but I knew we wanted not to leave them for the badgers. We covered them with limbs and leaves. At least no one took their heads."

Owen stared at him. "You've not spoken that much in all the years since you came here."

"I've not had so much to say," Meredith said.

Briana touched his arm, smiling at him, unable to believe that he was really here.

Ine sat quietly, composing a song. Sabine, for some reason of premonition, or just to give her hands something to occupy them, sharpened her dagger against a whetstone with a slow, even movement. Galen and Ralf helped Havgan and Owen's men pack their meager belongings into traveling bundles.

Rees and Owen sat together, near Briana and her brother, and once they had finished speaking of Fearndon, the forbidden topic having no power over them any longer, they spoke of the future.

"Some of the men will be needed for Flint," Rees said, "but I would prefer you to be part of Conway."

Owen nodded. Neither of them spoke of Briana, but both were aware of her, leaning against Rees's side, half-dozing, still smiling.

"Will you swear fealty to me?" Rees asked quietly.

Owen gave a short, explosive laugh. "Of all the outcomes I might have seen," he said, "that is the least likely I could have imagined." He sobered as Briana stirred and sat straighter. Clearly, the question did not come as a surprise to him. "I will allow those of my men who wish to take the oath to do so, but I will compel none. Draw your sword, my lord earl." He rose from his sitting position and dropped onto his knees.

Ine lifted his eyes from the small tableau to the huge bulk of the mountain that towered, unseen in the darkness, above them. Snowdon was witness to the changing of the world, and Ine was struck by the notion that he was here to witness it, too.

Briana felt both relieved and exultant when Owen kissed Rees's sword, and even happier when Meredith asked to follow suit.

The men of Owen's band had been homeless for years now, and over the course of the next half-hour, every one of them not guarding the approaches to the camp came, one by one, not speaking to one another about it, to kneel before Rees and say the oath.

Only Havgan did not, and no one questioned him about it or tried to get him to join them.

When they were done, Rees resheathed the sword, and Briana looked at Meredith and said, "I'd sing the lullaby with you. I've not sung it since we all did, the night before Fearndon, but I'd sing it now."

Half Meredith's face stretched in a smile. "I'd forgot the lullaby," he said.

"'Twill return to you when you seek it," said Ine.

Briana began to sing the beloved Welsh words. Meredith and Ine joined in almost at once, and after a few notes, Rees, who did not know the lyric, but had heard the melody at Conway, hummed beneath the verse. Briana's voice broke. She imagined Rees and herself and their child, making a circle in each other's arms, and singing for the peace of the night. The joy of the moment was completely fulfilling.

At the end of the song, Owen fed sticks to the fire, which had been near guttering out. It blazed up again, and Ralf and Galen sat down on either side of Meredith. Sabine joined them on the other side of the fire, once again running a whetstone over the blade of her dagger. Ine sat down beside her, and with a gesture drew Briana into the circle as well, leaving Rees and Owen to settle the details of the journey away from Snowdonia.

Briana, smiling at Meredith, saw him glance nervously at the three strangers. He seemed fascinated by Sabine. "Who are you?" he asked her.

"A friend of your Aunt Maud's," she answered. "I live in the hermitage at St. Maedoc's."

"You're no hermit," Meredith pronounced carefully, earning a laugh from everyone in the circle, and Galen's muttered, "No saint, either," which made Ralf laugh harder.

Sabine said mildly, "You felt a need to hide here in this wilderness all these years. You cannot disdain a need I might have felt to hide in another way." She tested the edge of her dagger by running it lightly over her thumbnail. "I admit 'tis more difficult to hide a grotesque of my size than one of yours."

Everyone looked at Meredith, who seemed to be fighting for words. The two knights were hiding smiles, because it was clear that the young man had never openly been called a grotesque before.

Briana held her breath, fighting the urge to reach out and put her arms around her brother. Ine, as if sensing her impulse, touched her on the shoulder and, when she looked up at him, shook his head. She understood immediately that he was telling her there was a certain ritual required here. Meredith had chosen to be ashamed of what had befallen him at Fearndon, just as he had chosen to hide away from any possible responsibilities he could have undertaken at Flint. If they let it pass now, it would be because of pity, and no one—least of all Sabine—wanted to pity him.

"I was but twelve years old," he burst out at Sabine.

"You are no longer twelve years old," she said placidly. "If I have the right of it, you've not been twelve years old for some time now. What plan you to do with your life now?" Before Meredith could reply, she added, "You are, after all, a young lord. Surely, marriage and children."

"What woman would have this?" It was one of the questions which had kept Meredith in Snowdonia for seven years.

Galen laughed shortly. "Any woman commanded to have it," he said. "Such is a lord's privilege."

Meredith swore.

"Oh, aye," said Ralf lightly. "Once the torches are out, a woman's not concerned with the face. I would assume the horse that trampled you touched not the part she *would* be concerned with."

Sabine concentrated on her dagger, watching the whetstone slide slowly along the blade edge. "I'd wager that'd not be a problem for this young man," she observed as if to herself. "For unless he pads his hose, there seem no reasons to doubt his endowments."

As Meredith's smooth left cheek reddened, Galen and Ralf began a genial argument about the size of the endowments versus the liveliness of their use, which soon had Briana gasping in an effort not to laugh.

"Beauty," Ralf summed up, "hasn't a bit of the attraction of skill. And skill can be learned." He glanced at Briana, twinkling, as she blushed darker than her brother.

"There's a lady at Flint named Med," Sabine remarked, "who'd be delighted to help the young lord learn, if I mistake her not."

Meredith was fascinated.

Ine smiled and lowered his head so that the smile did not show. Meredith would be all right now. All they had to do was get back to Flint.

Briana hugged her brother and planted a kiss, quite unexpectedly, on Sabine's cheek when Rees came to claim her at last. He and Owen had decided how they would leave Snowdonia, a process made more complicated by the spy who had followed Rees's party in and escaped.

"If it comes to it," Owen asked Rees, "will King Edward take your word for events?"

"I believe so," Rees answered. "He has in the past, and I've not given him reason to doubt what I say. Let us hope it comes not to a question."

Briana had not realized how much she had missed Rees until he rolled her into his cloak with him and lifted her onto his chest to keep her off the ground. "You are as hard as the ground is," she complained wearily, squirming a little in an effort to move beside him.

Rees clamped his hands on her shoulders, then slid them across her back. "Keep still," he commanded in a low growl, "or hard will not be the half of it. We need some sleep, and we'll not get any if you do that."

She held still, her hands climbing from his chest to the sides of his face, where a beard was beginning to sprout, as were the other men's, except for Ine, who seemed somehow immune to facial hair, even in the absence of shaving. "I love you, Rees," she said very seriously.

"I always intended that you should," he said, curling her head down under his chin. He stroked her tangled hair as she fell asleep, and for some time afterward.

Despite the war having ended, they were attacked as they neared the edge of Snowdonia the next day. Wigmore sent thirty-five knights and Eald. That size force should have been more than sufficient had the party actually consisted of the six or seven people they thought it would when they swung out to block the road, swords drawn.

Rees, at the head of the small column, battled the instant surge of rage at the overwhelmingly unfair odds. He noted the drawn swords, decided talking would be a waste of time, and drew his own sword from its scabbard. At his shoulders, Galen and Ralf did the same. Ulf, already uneasy at the hostile feelings, was alerted by the sound of sliding steel. His head went down and he began to growl.

One of the Wigmore knights laughed, and the laughter turned into a gurgle as he took an arrow through the throat. He toppled forward off his horse, his sword striking a rock with a clang as it fell from his hands. The sound was very loud in the brief silence.

Rees dropped his reins and urged Basilisk forward, Ulf leaping at his side, and the rest of the people in the small group drew swords as well. Except for Rees's two knights, they were Owen's men, and in the trees and rocks along the narrow track, Owen and the rest of his men fired arrows into the semi-circle of knights until the seven men in the obvious party engaged them. By then, the odds were a little less uneven.

On a hillside somewhat removed from Owen, Meredith stood, holding a dagger, with Sabine, who had fired the arrow that dispatched the first of the Marcher Lord's soldiers; Ine, who bore no weapons; and Briana, who held a bow and lightly nocked arrow, but who had no intention of actually firing it. All the practice she had had with Princess Eleanor had not prepared her for the reality of being near a battle, let alone fighting in one. She had told herself that if it looked as if they needed her, then she would shoot. But they did not appear to need her, and she simply trembled as the sounds and movement brought back the images she had tried for years to forget. She wanted to cry out against it. She wanted to look away. She could do neither, because she could not take her eyes from Rees and Basilisk, who made a glorious dance of death.

He, Galen and Ralf fought like a single entity, dispatching the lesser-trained, lesser-motivated enemy with a grim grace that made a mockery of the beautiful day. Even when Galen took a slash on the arm, he did not falter or stop. He would not notice the bleeding until later; now, committed to battle, he had no time.

Sabine spied the weasel-like Eald trying to slip away, calmly nocked another arrow, drew her bowstring taut, and estimated when he would clear the thickest boles between them. Briana was aware of her composed, relentless presence, even as the shouts of the battle held the major part of her attention. As soon as Sabine sensed the motion of Eald in the space she had marked, she fired. The arrow caught him square between the shoulderblades, and he pitched forward and lay still.

When only a few of the attackers remained, the rest having been eliminated by arrows or swords at a small cost to what should have been the outnumbered defenders, Mortimer's remaining knights turned to run and were cut down. Sometimes arrows struck them; sometimes their horses were hit, leaving them afoot or even partially trapped under their fallen mounts for Rees and his men to deal with. The knights and the remaining two of the four rebels who had ridden with them, eliminated them.

Rees dismounted and wiped his sword on the grass, glancing around to assess casualties and to make certain that Ulf was all right. The dog was bloodstained, having ripped out a throat without regard to neatness, but none of the blood appeared to be his own. Rees's practiced eye gauged that Galen's wound was acceptable, and he smiled at his friend as he passed, continuing to check the people who fought with him. He glanced up at Owen's position, received a short wave, and shouted, "Any escape?"

From behind him, Sabine called, "None, but be certain everyone has passed on, my lord."

Meredith scrambled around several of the large rocks, heading down to the knights, and Ine followed more slowly. Briana let her bow drop from nerveless fingers, watching Sabine pull up arrows she had stuck into the earth at her feet to increase her speed in firing. Wiping dirt from the arrowheads, she eyed the younger woman. "I see battle is not to your liking."

"I never thought 'twould be to any woman's taste." Briana had to clear her throat twice before she could continue. "I see that just as men can make tears, women can make blood."

"Can?" Sabine put the arrows back in her quiver. "Women must, my lady. If they do not, men will conspire to destroy them, and they will fall without a fight." She glanced at Ine's retreating back. "Most men," she amended. Her gaze wandered to Rees. "Some men."

Briana frowned. "'Tis war that destroys," she said slowly, "and 'tis true that men make war, but—" She stopped, unable to carry the thought to completion, but finding herself uncomfortable with the big woman's assertion.

"My lady discovered that war is not necessary," Sabine said, slinging the quiver over her shoulder. "War is the excuse that men give to put a noble face on their brutality. But they need it not to be brutal."

She studied the activities of the men below her as they stripped weapons from the bodies and prepared to dig a large grave. They would be some time on the task. Sabine realized that Briana was not going to pick up her own bow and the arrows she had not used, and packed them away for her. "Tears are not the only things women make because of evil done to them, my lady.

They also make babes."

Briana's arms went across her belly before she thought about it.

Sabine saw the gesture. "Ah," she said. "Not all babes are conceived in love. The lady I serve had one such."

Briana could not imagine what it might have been like had the rogue knight succeeded in raping her on the road outside Peterborough and left in her womb the result of his attack. She whispered, "How did she survive it?"

Sabine said, "She had a level of honor which was not permitted to be stained. She had faith that St. Candida would give her the grace to love the child, and she loved him mightily 'til her son was grown enough to stand on his own." She cast a look at where all the various men were, found them far enough away, and said, "And she had a father who was King of England as, indeed, she has now a brother who rules in his place."

She watched Briana absorb the words, her eyes wide, her mouth dropping open.

Sabine said firmly, "I choose to tell you this because my lady will need allies when she tells him, and I wish you to be one of them."

Briana had to say it aloud. "Your lady, the recluse, is—"

Sabine said, "Princess Beatrice Plantagenet, sister to King Edward of England, and thought to be these fifteen years dead. And, in a way, she was dead. I was but a girl then, but I got her to England, to Queen Eleanor. Her mind could no longer remain strong, and it fled. The queen sheltered her, I nursed her, and God saved her. She wants to be with her son again."

"—his mother," Briana finished. "Dear God—How is it that he knows you not? You lived with him in Brittany."

"I was but a child, then, not yet nubile," said Sabine calmly. "I did not bear the body that now contains me. It grew after he left us for his own destiny." She studied Briana. "Will you help her when she tells the earl she lives? He may well be exceedingly angry." Sabine held out to Briana the quiverful of arrows.

"Briana!" It was Rees, calling her.

Sabine glanced at the man and the mass grave, then shouted, "My lord, there is one more over that way with an arrow in his back." She pointed at where Eald had fallen.

Rees looked up at the two women, then sent some men to find the body.

"And now that you know," Sabine said, "you'll not tell him before she's ready."

Briana shook her head slowly. "Nay, 'tis not my place, but—"

Sabine waited, expecting more.

Briana found she could neither move nor speak. This was a different kind of tragedy, and it made her own melancholy seem petty. In fact, it showed her beyond all doubt how fortunate she had been, and how ungratefully she had responded to it. Taken by the king, she had been made part of his family. Attacked on the roads, she had been saved from the very kind of degradation Princess Beatrice had fallen prey to. Forced into marriage, she had been given to a husband she loved, whose physical prowess and greatness of mind and spirit she could recognize and cherish. And now she carried a child who would be born into a safer world than her own and would rule her beloved Flint. Even more, she had been given back a brother, whom she had thought gone forever. The list of blessings made her dizzy.

She thought, *These gifts are so great. Mayhap there will be no further need to save anyone from aught else. Ever.*

Rees came to her rather than calling again, and Sabine found it prudent to go down the hill to where the rest of the party was gathering, nursing the wounds that needed attending, packing the captured weapons. He put his arms around her and held her tightly.

Briana remembered how much he had hoped to avoid any further killing, and how, because it was Wigmore, who must not be given any evidence of Rees's collusion with the rebels, all the men he sent had to die. She could not think of anything she might say to make it easier for him, except "I love you."

He held her more tightly, said nothing for a time, and then said, "God, I hope that is the last killing I shall ever have to do. I want only to heal now."

She did not know if he meant healing himself or healing others or both. "What will Mortimer do when his friends do not return?" she asked.

"Buy others," Rees said shortly, "but he'll have no proof to send my uncle. Come. We want to camp at Swallow Falls tonight, and we're a large party. We need to move quickly."

She refused to let him go, and he was concerned, stopped trying to move toward the rest of the people in the party, and cupped the back of her head, his long fingers entwined in her tangled, twig-matted hair. "What haps?" he asked. "Tell me."

It came out in a way neither of them expected. "When we marry at St. Maedoc's, I want to receive Communion."

He wondered what had changed, but he did not ask. There was no time before they needed to be back at the horses. He turned her so that they could walk side by side down the slope.

Flint—April 1289 A.D.

Owen Glyn and thirteen of his remaining thirty-two men— the others had fallen to Wigmore's knights—remained in Conway when the rest of the party went on to Flint. As constable of the manor, Sir Thomas Newby was told where the men came from, but Rees swore him to secrecy. Newby had no reason to betray Owen's origins or recent occupation, and the two men talked warily, but at some length, with one another, at first in Rees's presence and then alone. Emerging from the latter meeting, Newby nodded once in Rees's direction, expressing satisfaction.

Havgan, Ralf, and Galen had not stopped at Conway, but had gone immediately onward with those of Owen's men who would be relocating to Flint. Meredith did not want to go to Flint without Briana, so he stayed at Conway, because Rees had decided to stay a little longer and allow Newby to guide Briana through the estate account books. She would need to administer Flint, and he thought she could only benefit from Newby's experience. Rees had also asked Ine to stay and provide some entertainment for the people of Conway town. Sabine simply announced that she would stay as well, and return to Flint when they did.

They passed a very pleasant night, and planned an early departure for Flint the following morning.

At Flint, the time was not so congenial for the recluse. Bjorn Magnussen had arrived.

He went to the castle asking for Earl Connarc and was told to seek at the manor, since the castle—gates wide and the walls only very lightly patrolled—was being readied to serve as a barracks for the knights and their families, as well as for sheltering any pregnant animals. Magnussen went immediately to the manor, introduced himself to Maud as the ambassador of King Haakon and asked again for Earl Connarc. By the time he appeared, Maud knew from Ralf and Galen that Rees had stopped at Conway. She asked the Norseman if he would honor the manor by enjoying Flint's hospitality for the night and join them at Mass in the morning, while waiting for the overlord to return.

It pleased Maud to be able to offer hospitality to someone again, after so long a time in which there was nothing to share, though she was a little bewildered as to the reasons why the King of Norway would be sending an ambassador to North Wales.

Magnussen had ridden hard and was tired, so food and drink he did not have to steal were welcome. And much as he would have liked to refuse the invitation to Mass, he would have to accept it to maintain his facade as an ambassador, and for once in his life, he chose to be consistent.

Word went swiftly through the village, carried by the people who served the manor, that the ambassador from Norway had come to honor Earl Connarc. The people of Flint had already learned, from Havgan's excited story, that the earl had brought Owen and his men out of Snowdonia, fought alongside them against Wigmore's troops during the ambush, and that Owen had sworn fealty to him. They were preparing themselves to do the same. And, as he told everyone, Lord Meredith was coming home, injured, but alive.

Fand decided to be certain that Father Ciaran knew, too.

Beatrice was kneeling in the tiny Lady Chapel when Fand came into the church looking for Father Ciaran, who was at the altar rail. He had discovered that he enjoyed praying when the silent presence of the recluse contributed to the atmosphere of companionable reverence. He never spoke to her at such times, having no desire to intrude, and she rarely spoke to him. They simply knelt together, sharing neither the same space nor the same prayers, but somehow with one another.

As soon as Fand saw the priest, she hurried to the altar rail and waited with some impatience, bouncing from foot to foot, not particularly quietly or subtly, until he looked up.

"Fand, is there some trouble?" the priest asked, climbing to his feet.

"Nay, Father," she said, bursting to tell him. "The King of Norway's sent an embassy here to Flint, to us. Can you imagine?"

In the Lady Chapel, Beatrice turned toward the sound, not unduly alarmed, but concerned at the fateful word "Norway."

"An embassy?" Father Ciaran repeated. "Here? Why?"

"He asked for Earl Connarc, they say," said Fand. "It must be because the earl's the king's relation. Else why would the man come here?"

"I must put out the earl's gifts for the Mass on the morrow," Father Ciaran said, "as if 'twere a Sunday. Will the earl be back, I wonder?" He was already hurrying toward the tiny closet that served as a sacristy.

Fand, pleased to have passed along her excitement, turned to go see who else she could take the tidings to, and Beatrice rose to her feet. She had spoken with all the village women through the hermitage window over a period of months. They would ask for her prayers, as if seclusion in and of itself conferred holiness upon her, and they curtsied to her window when they passed it, the brief, bobbing curtsies of greeting, not the deeper ones of reverence. So when Beatrice called softly to Fand from the Lady Chapel, Fand dropped a quick curtsey in her direction and was delighted to have someone else to tell. "Have you heard, Lady?" she asked.

"I have," said Beatrice. "Happen you to know how many people are in this embassy?"

"Why, I believe only the one man. I heard of no others."

"Happen you to know the name he bears?" Beatrice asked.

Fand shook her head.

Beatrice stepped from the Lady Chapel, showing more of her face to Fand than she had done before, but keeping her head down to minimize the exposure. "Do me the favor to learn it for me and return. I shall be at the hermitage window."

She waited for Fand to leave the church before she slipped out and back into the hermitage. She was more curious than disturbed, though even the hint of the past resurfacing, which might not have made her uneasy had Sabine been with her, now had the power to unsettle her. She added branches to the fire and sat by the window, trying to remember nothing of that moment in her past.

The fire was burning brightly when Fand came back and delivered the horrifying information. Bjorn Magnussen was in Flint.

Beatrice could not even thank her. How had he found her? Where could she hide? The church was not safe, for she doubted St. Maedoc, who had no shrine here, but only a name, would guard her any more than St. Candida had. Her throat closed, and her hands flew uselessly to her sides, her face, her hair beneath the wimple, her sides again.

Fand could see none of it through the veil, but she knew the recluse had heard her; faintly, she recognized sounds of distress. "Lady, is there a way I may be of further service?" she asked.

Beatrice got out a single word. "Wait." She was fighting for control of herself, fighting to make her mind, which had deserted her once before, though not for a long while after her victimization, stay calm. Sabine had taught her to reason again, and she had to reason now. She made herself slow her accelerated breathing. Panic had not helped her then, and Sabine had been careful to teach her that if it had not helped before, it would not help now. And she needed help. She needed Sabine.

She could not leave her enclosure without a dispensation to do so, and she would not imperil her soul by leaving. Someone had to find Sabine, and someone had to be with Beatrice when he came to get her. She had no doubt that he would come for her. What else could possibly have brought him to Flint?

Fand was waiting.

Despite her pounding heart, she made herself sound at least partially calm. "Fand, ask Father Ciaran to come to me." She realized it sounded abrupt, added, "If you please." Then she sat quietly, her hands still moving independently of her volition, but now the sole expression of her agitation.

Father Ciaran came at once, fearing that she was ill. She had never sent for him before. He hurried to the window, with Fand behind him, but at a discreet distance; such a distance, to Fand, meant far enough for courtesy but near enough to overhear the conversation. "What haps, Lady?" the priest asked as soon as he reached the window.

Beatrice sounded more composed than she was. "Father, I need your help and that of the people of Flint who can aid me," she said. "I am abjured from speaking of my past, as you know, so I cannot tell you why I ask. Someone must find Sabine and say to her, 'Bjorn Magnussen is in Flint,' and it must be done in the greatest haste possible. Until she returns here, I must not be left alone. I beg you, Father, help me in this."

He was bewildered, but willing, and he asked no questions, for it was not his way. He turned to Fand and said, "Seek out some of Earl Connarc's knights, if you would, and ask them to see me."

"Havgan's only just returned," Fand said. "He'll know where they are. I saw him arrive not two hours since."

Thus it was that Havgan bore a message back to Conway, and Med came to sit outside the hermitage window, while Father Ciaran stayed in the church and prayed, alert for who knew what, aware only that something was wrong, and that Flint owed much to the recluse.

Chapter 36

When it came, the encounter occurred on the road between Conway and Flint, nearly at the spot from which Ine had first seen the valley and manor twenty years earlier.

Rees, Briana, Sabine, Meredith and Ine had been riding from Conway in the morning when Havgan found them, having ridden all night, and delivered his message to Sabine. The transformation of the big woman into a predator happened in a matter of seconds, and everyone else was taken aback by it.

Rees asked, "What haps?"

Sabine started to urge her horse forward, but Rees leaned out, took firm hold of her reins, and used his own sheer force to keep the animal's head steadied. Sabine's horse slewed about and stood stiff-legged as she said to Rees, "Let go, my lord! I must go to her."

"Tell me the danger," Rees commanded.

Sabine would not stop to make explanations, made an immediate choice, looked directly at Briana, and said, "'Twas Magnussen at St. Candida's. *Tell* him!" She wrenched her reins free of Rees's hand, spun the reluctant horse and kicked him into a gallop. Rees made another grab for her, but missed.

Ine recognized the reference to St. Candida's, but could not place it in any kind of context. Havgan had no more expected Sabine's reaction than had any of the others, but under Rees's scrutiny, he said, "My message came from Father Ciaran, and he said it was from the recluse."

Briana saw Ine's face cloud for a moment, then clear.

Rees looked at his wife. "Tell me what?" he asked.

She was suddenly in a position she had not wanted to be. Things too unexpected and too unlikely had conspired to place her here, and she had no time to try and figure out what the best words would be, but that did not stop her from hesitating while she tried.

Sabine's figure was disappearing down the road.

Ine saw Briana's bewilderment, saw Rees's growing impatience, and asked the question directly. "Briana, what is it that you know?"

Briana unconsciously chose the very words of Owen's revelation to her. "The princess Beatrice lives."

Rees turned stunned eyes on her, and Briana stumbled on, "Aye, and at Flint."

"What said you?" Rees demanded.

Briana took a deep breath. "The recluse is your mother," she said.

The expression on his face did not change, but his face went deadly pale. "'Tis impossible."

"I know not the whole of the tale," Briana said, "but Sabine told me that she is the sister of your uncle, the king, and that she was about to tell you that she lived."

Ine was putting together Havgan's message of a Norseman named Magnussen with the story he had known of the noblewoman at St. Candida's. He said, "Rees, if the man in Flint is the man from St. Candida, she needs must be protected from him."

"Why?" Rees asked, frowning.

Ine said softly, "Rees, I am so sorry. He would be your father."

Rees clutched his reins, his hands closing so convulsively that pain shot up his arms. He remembered clearly the words

King Edward had thrown at him in refusing him with match with Margaret of Norwich. "—raped by a brute of a man, whom I hoped you would grow to be like."

He felt lightheaded, as if he might pass out, but he swallowed hard and fought for control of himself. Then his face hardened, the color returned, and he swung down off Basilisk, ordering Meredith, "Change horses with me now!"

Meredith swung down at once and took Basilisk's reins, and the big stallion shied away from him but did not try to bite him.

Rees vaulted onto Meredith's horse and galloped him in Sabine's wake. Ulf hesitated a moment, uncertain whether to follow the man or stay with the destrier.

"Go after him, Briana," Ine urged. "Ride hard!"

She did not question the rightness of his order. As she clapped her heels to the gelding's sides, Ine gestured Meredith up behind him and said, "Give Havgan the reins. Havgan, go slowly with the warhorse. He's no runner." As soon as Havgan had a firm hold on Basilisk's reins, Ine kicked his own horse and, with Meredith clinging to his waist, began to canter in Briana's wake. Ulf leaped out in front of them, heading after his master and new mistress.

While the people heading toward Flint were increasing their speed at different points along the road, Bjorn Magnussen, entirely oblivious to the presence of the woman upon whom he had sown the child he wanted, was suffering through Mass in St. Maedoc's. He had been aware that the graciousness of Maud's welcome had become somewhat muted, but he had not paid it much heed. He often wore out his welcome and never questioned why, as no one's opinions would have accorded with his.

Galen and his family and Ralf were among the attendees at Mass, and while they were dispersing after the Mass was over, the knights talked about leaving Rees at Conway, and the Norseman overheard, asked where Conway was, received directions, got his horse, and summarily left Flint without ever going near Beatrice.

The realization that he had not come for her after all was a startling one to her. Weak with relief, she told Med, who had nodded the night away wrapped in blankets beneath the hermitage window and thought the exercise an entirely futile one, that she could leave, thanking her for her attendance.

Beatrice wiped perspiration from her brow, thanking God and St. Candida not merely for protecting her, but for helping her find the strength to endure.

So close to his goal, Bjorn Magnussen was ebullient. He rode toward Conway at an easy lope, unaware of the approaching storm.

Had Rees been thinking clearly, he would have taken Briana's mount, rather than Meredith's, for the gelding from Flint was in far better condition than the horse from Snowdonia. But he had not been thinking clearly, other than to realize that he could not gallop Basilisk all the way back to Flint. Briana caught up with him before they had gone two miles, but did not try to speak with him, only rode beside him, glancing every so often at his grim, unreasoning expression. He was likely aware of her presence, but had too much else whirling in his mind to acknowledge her. How could his mother be alive? How could she have deceived him for half his life? How could she have left him in the hands of his uncle? What was happening?

Sabine expected to find Bjorn Magnussen in Flint, menacing—or worse—Princess Beatrice, and she had never seen the man before, so she rode past him outside the valley, barely noticing the large stranger riding toward Conway. He might have come from Chester and been on the road to Bangor, for all she knew. By the time she reached Flint, learned that Beatrice was unharmed, and realized her mistake, it was too late to do anything but tell her lady that Rees now knew everything, and why.

Beatrice fled to the Lady Chapel, dropped to her knees, and

tried to lose herself in prayer.

Briana saw the resemblance between the two men before the horses they rode were nearer each other than thirty yards. It was, in fact, the very distance which made it easier for her. Seen closely, the similarity would have been less, for the thoughtless evil of Magnussen's features was in no way reflected in Rees's face, where the beauty of the Plantagenets held sway.

Fifty feet away, the men recognized the likeness in each other's faces, Magnussen with delight, Rees with wariness. He had gotten control of his racing thoughts halfway through the ride, and distrust of his uncle made him wonder if Edward's words had been true or simply chosen to provide the maximum pain.

Rees drew his horse to a halt, and Briana pulled up beside him, looking at the hulk of a man on the approaching horse.

"Rees Bjornson!" the Norseman shouted as his animal barreled down at them. "I am your father!" He plainly expected Rees to be as completely happy about this as he was.

"Halt your advance!" Rees commanded, his own voice a roar of absolute undeniability. Even the Norseman recognized the sound of a man accustomed to being obeyed and reined his horse down to a walk, but kept moving forward.

"I have sought you for many months," Magnussen said, "since when I first learned I sired you. My two sons with my wife are dead, and I have need of another." He looked at Briana once, then a second time, more closely, appreciating her beauty in an open and not particularly wholesome way before he looked at Rees again.

Briana felt her skin crawl. Even with Rees beside her, something in her was revolted at the thought that this man might want to touch her. Her body seemed to remember the violent touch of the rogue knight, and she knew that she would not fall to another such man undefended. Rees would protect her, but—
Before she was even aware of it, she had jerked her bow free of her saddle, pulled an arrow from its quiver and nocked it,

holding the weapon at her side. If need be, she was prepared to defend herself.

Rees leaned forward on his horse's neck. "I have had no true father since my birth," he said. "My mother never spoke of you."

Magnussen laughed, more of a crow of pleasure. "Mayhap she did not speak of me, but I warrant she recalled the fuck," he said.

Briana gasped at the crudeness. The Norseman expected, she thought, to find a son just like himself, a man he could take his own kind of pride in, a man formed in the values he himself had in abundance.

Rees was not such a man. He exerted a powerful control over himself and said, "And they call *me* bastard." He remembered he was not riding Basilisk, who would have known how to behave under him if it came to a fight, swung a leg over the animal's neck, and dropped to the ground.

Magnussen, frowning, did likewise. "I had not thought to have an English nobleman for son," he said.

"Nor have you," said Rees, iron creeping back into his voice. "Think you that seed alone makes a father? I tell you it does not!"

Magnussen's face clouded. He had never before been balked by anyone or anything in which he placed value, but only by people or situations through which he could rage his way. "I have need of a son," he blustered, "and you are mine. I had thought to take you with me, but you are landed, so here will I stay!"

Rees did not grow angrier, nor did he soften. "You may wander where you like, but on my lands you may not linger."

Ine and Meredith caught up with them then, and Rees caught sight of Basilisk out of the corner of his eye. For some reason, the presence of the warhorse calmed him.

Magnussen's cloud became thunderous. "By the gods, I permit not my sons to speak to me thus!"

"I am not your son," Rees said in steel tones. And without thinking about it, he spoke a truth. "If I am son to any man, I am the son of a Jew from Antioch!"

Magnussen could not have conceived a greater insult. To be denied, after so long a search, and for a Jew at that. "Then you'll die!" he shouted and drew his sword.

Ulf let out a snarl which made the nearest horses shy, and Rees ordered him back.

Rees blinked at the absurdity of a man of fifty years or more, hulking and red-faced, drawing sword upon him, then gave a short laugh, which seemed to incense the Norseman even more.

Magnussen leaped forward, thinking Rees unable to draw in time, and was shaken by the clang as his sword encountered a sword which had been scabbarded a second before.

Briana was horrified. Ulf began barking, but did not move.

Once again, Rees did not fight to attack, but only to defend himself, and just as his restraint had infuriated William de Blaisey, it enraged Bjorn Magnussen. He had small grasp of reason at the best of times, and his angry frustration made him more and more frantic. Rees continued to fend him off, and that continued to add to the Norseman's choler. Clearly, Rees wanted simply to wear him down, to let him exhaust himself, but after five or six minutes, it began to become apparent that even if he tired, Magnussen would not stop. Rees tried to step back from him several times to give him the opportunity to withdraw, but each time the Norseman used the slight retreat to press his own attack.

"Break off," Rees ordered, "else I must harm you."

"Harm me?" Magnussen rasped out between gulping breaths of air. "Either you kill me, or I will kill you!"

Briana had been shaking with a mixture of awe, fear, anger, and pain since the two men began fighting. Rees had not known or cared for a father his entire life, and then to finally be confronted by this was horrific. Rees wanted no more killing,

and to be put in the position of killing the man who sired him
was abhorrent, a mortal sin, a soul-stain he could never wash
away.

I want to save him from this, she thought. *How?*

Rees disarmed the Norseman twice, but could not stop him
from picking up his sword again, because the first time
Magnussen ran at Rees's blade to impale himself upon it, and
when Rees turned the blade aside the second time, Magnussen
crashed into him, trying to flatten him. Only Rees's size kept
him from falling. He tried to club the Norseman with his sword
hilt, but Magnussen scarcely seemed to notice the blow and tried
to wrench the sword away from Rees. Thereafter, Rees let him
keep his sword, as it made the fight more controllable though, it
seemed, no more winnable.

After another nearly ten minutes of fighting, Rees accepted
that he would at least have to wound the man, and he scored
three hits, two on Magnussen's arm and one on his thigh. That
only seemed to stir the Norseman to greater effort.

Ine had concluded some time before that this was a fight to
the death, and he wondered whether Rees would bow to the
inevitable and slay the other man before too much longer.

Rees held off for several minutes more, and then, suddenly,
they all saw the killing mask come over his face.

Bjorn Magnussen fell back before that face, just as the
Mamelukes had so long before. Meredith, who had not seen it
closely before, cringed at the sight of it. Ine glanced away, for it
made his friend unrecognizable. Ulf's barking ceased, as if he,
too, could only respond to the mask by drawing back from it.

Briana felt her heart split at the sight of it, drew a deep
breath, compensated for the wind just as she had always done at
the archery butts, laughing with Princess Eleanor, raised the
bow, and shot the arrow true, almost as if the Norseman had a
target painted over his heart. The arrow might have hit Rees, had
Magnussen not fallen back, but as it was, the shaft skimmed past
Rees's shoulder and buried itself nearly fletch deep in

Magnussen's chest.

With a look of complete bewilderment on his face, Magnussen stumbled backward again, looking upward at the beautiful woman still holding the bow and staring at him with an expression of fierce determination on her face.

Rees spun, amazed, the mask fading away, then swivelled back to the other swordsman, whose hand still gripped his weapon, but who could not raise it.

Magnussen tried to draw in a breath, but got only half a lungful and gasped, "I should not—gone into—church. Odin!" Then he dropped to his knees and pitched forward, lying still.

Meredith said, "Good shot," and slid down off Ine's horse to reclaim his own.

Ine stared at Briana, understanding and approving her action entirely.

Rees sheathed his still bloodied sword and walked to Briana's horse, but before he could speak, she said, "You must not be a patricide."

He had no words to speak to her. Nothing came to mind. He reached up, lifted her from the horse and held her, his face against her hair.

Briana half-expected to begin weeping at what she had done and half-expected to feel some kind of exaltation, but she felt neither. She had done only what needed to be done to protect the man she loved, and it gave her a sense of satisfaction which made her feel weak.

Rees was battling the overwhelming emotion, struggling to hold onto reason long enough to get one word out and, finally, into her hair, he asked, "Why?"

As she had understood the need to comfort Owen, Briana understood the need to give Rees a reason other than the one that spoke to the church. "You have been used for sufficient suicides," she said. "You needed not another. I am your wife, and 'tis my duty to help guard you from harm." His arms tightened around her so much that she could breathe only shallowly.

Ine leaned across the saddle, watching them.

Sabine arrived at that moment. After she had spoken with Beatrice, Father Ciaran told her where Magnussen had gone, and she realized the rider she had thoughtlessly passed on the road was the one she wanted to encounter. Swearing as foully as any seaman, she had run back to her horse and caught the party up just as Rees was finally finding the strength to let go of Briana. She vaulted to the ground and bent over the body, seeing the arrow point and a bit of the shaft protruding redly from the man's back. She knew whose arrow it was.

Rees exerted control over his thoughts and turned to the huge woman. "How haps it," he asked, "that you serve a woman who claims to be the sister of the king?"

"You are less than an hour from asking her that question yourself," Sabine said, unintimidated. "I suggest that you do so." She looked at Briana. "So you, too, have learned to make blood, my lady."

Briana reached without looking for Rees's hand, grasped it, and said, "What I have learned is that sometimes tears are joyful as well as sorrowful, and that sometimes blood is necessary as well as horrible."

Rees was coming back to himself now, just as he had come back to himself after Fearndon, this time with the help only of what his past years had built inside him. He whistled to Ulf, who finally broke out of the immobility in which Rees had placed him, yelping and running to his master with wriggles of delight.

"To the horses," Rees said and helped Briana onto the gelding. They turned and rode toward Flint, Sabine leading the way, Ine bringing up the rear, already composing his song about this meeting and its meaning for the people involved in it.

As they reached the edge of Flint village, Sabine urged her horse into a canter, to reach the churchyard first, and though Rees could have ordered her back, he let her go.

Briana rode the gelding closer to Basilisk than might

actually have been wise, but she wanted to lay a hand on Rees's arm, and the warhorse suffered it.

Rees looked at her.

"My brother returned from the dead," she said, "and I thank God for it. Now it seems that your mother has returned from the dead as well, and I pray you may be grateful for it."

"We shall see," he said.

They reached the churchyard and dismounted. Meredith rode on to the manor house, courageous enough now to want to see Maud, but Ine stayed, and neither Rees nor Briana gainsaid him. Rees remained seated on Basilisk when Sabine came out of the hermitage door and stepped to one side of it.

Briana dismounted and tossed the gelding's reins to Ine. She waited by the churchyard wall, her face turned upward toward Rees.

After a moment longer, Rees swung down off Basilisk, let his reins drop, and walked past his wife into the churchyard. Sabine took one wordless step out of his way.

Rees went past her into the hermitage and looked at the woman who stood, hands clasped before her, so tightly gripping each other that her knuckles were white. He saw the Plantagenet lines of her exposed face under her wimple and veil and recognized that they were softened by suffering, not hardened by power. "Rees," she whispered.

He saw the fifteen additional years of age on her face, but he knew her. He had thought her on her deathbed when last he saw her, and while the face was infinitely precious to him, he could not simply hold out his arms to her. "You sent me to Edward," he said, "and you let me believe you dead. Why?"

"Forgive me," she said, her voice still hushed. "John de Bretagne would have killed you once you won your spurs. My brother was your sole protection. You could be safe as his vassal, and I needed you safe."

"de Bretagne would have killed me?" he repeated, not understanding.

"You were a threat to Arthur," she said, "and Arthur was everything to him. You were only a boy, despite your knighthood."

Rees absorbed that. "And the rest?"

She lowered her head. "I pray you forgive my weakness." She could not speak further.

Sabine said, "She fell prey to madness, my lord. She wanted you not to see it, and to see her only when God brought her safely through it, as you see her now."

Beatrice caught a sob in her throat and said, "I beg you to forgive me." She dropped to her knees before him.

Rees heard many things in his mother's plea, but besides the helpless love which he knew underlay her words, he heard the tones of absolute contrition. It lapped against the stone of his resistance and melted it. He took a deep breath, stepped across the hermitage floor, took her by the shoulders, raised her to her feet and folded her into his arms. She clung to him.

Maud made Meredith tell her the story twice after she finished weeping over his homecoming. Everyone in Flint rejoiced over him and those of Owen's men who had come out of Snowdonia to dwell with them. Havgan's tale of Rees's saving the rebels from Wigmore and from continued isolation cemented Rees's hold on Flint as little else might have done.

With a fine sense of irony that even Father Ciaran appreciated, they retrieved Bjorn Magnussen's body and buried it beneath Meredith's headstone in the churchyard, in case he really had been an ambassador of the King of Norway. A hundred years later, people would wonder why the churchyard at St. Maedoc's held two grave markers for the same man, one showing that he had fallen at Fearndon, the other that he lived to the age of sixty-eight and died in his bed. And the years proved that no one came to Flint asking questions about an ambassador who had vanished.

In the darkness of the master chamber the night of their

return to the manor, with Ulf asleep in the middle of the bed, Briana lay curled against Rees's chest as he stroked her hair, her shoulder, her hip. She clung to him, her fingers twined in his long hair. She felt his lips brush her head, his thumb stroke her cheek. Then she heard him ask, "What made you decide to receive the Host at our wedding?"

She thought about it, and at last she said, "I think I understand God a little better now. And I think I understand us, as well. We women are not better than you men. We only judge ourselves differently. God had no need to give me back Meredith, nor you, your mother. Those were gifts, so—" She stopped.

Rees said, "So you forgave Him for past transgressions. Or was it neglect?"

She smiled in the darkness.

He felt the motion of her mouth against the skin of his chest, beside the scar. "'Tis arrogant of me, I suppose," she said. "Think you I'll burn in hell for it?"

"No more than shall I, for owning to a Jew for a father. And God cherishes forgiveness. Even the priests say so."

He felt her smile slowly fade. "Then please forgive me, Rees."

He was startled. "For what?"

"For the time I hated you and wished you dead and failed to trust you."

He pulled her closer against him. "Sweetness, that time is behind us forever." She raised her face to his and he found her mouth. Ulf rose with a snort and moved to the side of the bed as they rolled on top of him.

Windsor—January 1290 A.D.

Though it was icy cold outside, the queen's rooms were warm enough so that cloaks were not necessary near the fire. Queen Eleanor sat in her chair near the flames and opened the letter the messenger had just brought her from Flint. She read it carefully, smiled, and tossed it into the flames before King Edward came in to join her.

He strode into the room tossing his own cloak over one of the chests and walked to the fireside to warm his hands. "The noise is good," he said without preamble. "I've had a message from Mortimer."

She smiled at him and lifted the embroidery she'd put down when her own message had arrived. "What says he?" she asked.

"The rebels have been rooted out." The king's voice was triumphant. "Mortimer has accomplished his purpose, and now I can turn to Scotland."

"Your nephew Rees has accomplished his purpose as well," Eleanor said. "Briana of Flint has been brought to bed of a son."

"So much," said Edward, "for the legend."

Flint

In later years, the song the minstrels sang about the peace that came to Northeast Wales, called "Ine's Song," mentioned the legend of the Lady of Flint, who, it was prophesied at her birth, would rise from fetters and bring freedom with her. Ine's song allowed that the prophecy had been heard wrongly, that it had been thought to mean that the lady would somehow free Wales from English rule, but that politics had no part in its truth. The fetters were of her own forging, went the song, traps of the old gods' interfering in the lives of men. The freedom was of her own choosing, taking her from a worship made up of fear and blind obedience to a worship made up of love and trust, a change in the world epitomized by this single woman—and any man, anywhere, could follow her lead.

He, Ine, had seen it with the eyes Myrrdin used to see the old mysteries and Ine had understood it all. He wondered how Myrrdin had known that it would come to pass, and that he was to be its witness.

About the Author

Roby James has been writing since she was nine years old, with a ten-year hiatus to ensure that her marriage would succeed (it has). She is the author of five novels and of heaps of nonfiction. She has spoken before audiences as large as 1,000 without being pelted by tomatoes or cabbages. At one time, she wrote for television (where assault by vegetables is one of the *nicest* things that happens to you), and her plays have been presented in Los Angeles, Ohio, and Pennsylvania. She is also the editor of the science fiction anthology series *Warrior Wisewoman*.

Her other titles include: *Commencement* (Hawk Books, 2000); *Commitment* (Hawk Books, 2000); *The Soldier's Daughter* (Wildside Press, 2001) and *Beyond the Hedge* (Juno Books, 2007).

Visit her website at *http://sff.net/people/robyj/*

CPSIA information can be obtained at www.ICGtesting.com
Printed in the USA
LVOW071947201011

251352LV00001B/391/P